Praise for

The City of Dusk

"Tara Sim's adult debut is a glorious tapestry of magic and murderous gods and a perfect entry for anyone looking for a new series starter."

—*BuzzFeed News*

"Lovers of epic, dark fantasies, rejoice! There's literally a lot here to love...including immersive writing that excellently builds this magical world, badass queer characters, and an interesting plot. Fans of *A Darker Shade of Magic* and *All of Us Villains* will want to pick this up sooner rather than later."

—*BookRiot*

"Through its generous number of perspectives and gorgeous prose, Tara Sim proves herself again to be a talented worldbuilder and detailed storyteller."

—*Locus*

"A delightful, complex, intimate yet explosive debut adult fantasy novel."

—*Strange Horizons*

"Recommended for fans of large scale fantasy sagas with diverse, frequently queer protagonists."

—*Booklist*

"Fantasy readers will appreciate Sim's attempt to create an expansive world in the vein of *A Darker Shade of Magic* or *Gideon the Ninth*.... There's a lot to love here."

—*Kirkus*

"A good fantasy, with a cracking ensemble cast and a wonderful world."

—*Grimdark Magazine*

By Tara Sim

THE DARK GODS

The City of Dusk
The Midnight Kingdom

TIMEKEEPER

Timekeeper
Chainbreaker
Firestarter

SCAVENGE THE STARS

Scavenge the Stars
Ravage the Dark

THE MIDNIGHT KINGDOM

BOOK TWO OF
THE DARK GODS

TARA SIM

orbitbooks.net

Copyright © 2023 by Tara Sim
Excerpt from *A Dowry of Blood* copyright © 2021 by Sarah Gibson

Cover design by Lisa Marie Pompilio
Cover illustrations by Shutterstock
Cover copyright © 2023 by Hachette Book Group, Inc.
Map by Tim Paul
Author photograph by Tara Sim

Orbit
Hachette Book Group
1290 Avenue of the Americas
New York, NY 10104
orbitbooks.net

First Edition: August 2023

Orbit is an imprint of Hachette Book Group.
The Orbit name and logo are trademarks of Little, Brown Book Group Limited.

The Hachette Speakers Bureau provides a wide range of authors for speaking events. To find out more, go to hachettespeakersbureau.com or email HachetteSpeakers@hbgusa.com.

Orbit books may be purchased in bulk for business, educational, or promotional use. For information, please contact your local bookseller or the Hachette Book Group Special Markets Department at special.markets@hbgusa.com.

Library of Congress Cataloging-in-Publication Data
Names: Sim, Tara, author.
Title: The midnight kingdom / Tara Sim.
Description: First edition. | New York, NY : Orbit, 2023. | Series: The Dark Gods ; book 2
Identifiers: LCCN 2023000629 | ISBN 9780316458931 (trade paperback) | ISBN 9780316458900 (ebook)
Subjects: LCGFT: Fantasy fiction. | Novels.
Classification: LCC PS3619.I5563 M54 2023 | DDC 813/.6—dc23/eng/20230113
LC record available at https://lccn.loc.gov/2023000629

ISBNs: 9780316458931 (trade paperback), 9780316458900 (ebook)

Printed in the United States of America

LSC-C

Printing 1, 2023

To all the video game soundtracks that got me through countless hours of realm hopping. I'm looking at you, Bloodborne.

And of course, to my parents. Thank you for indulging my skull obsession.

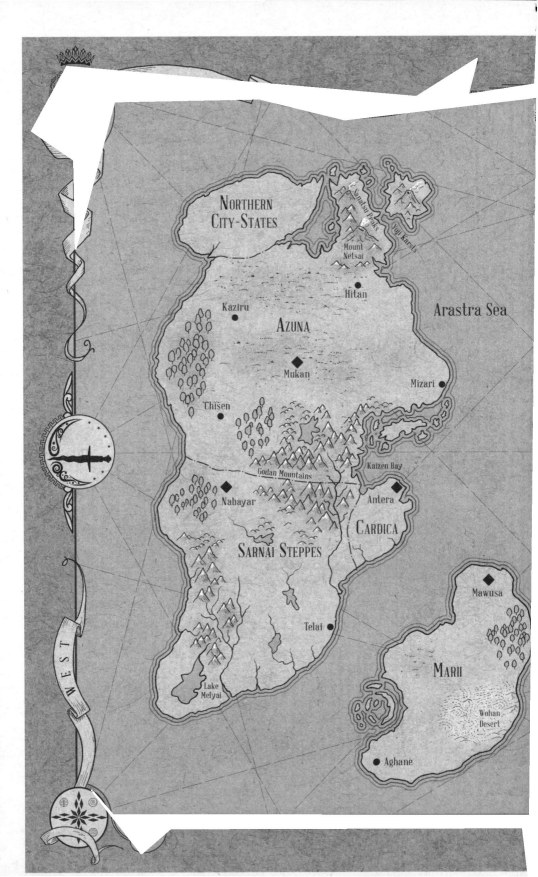

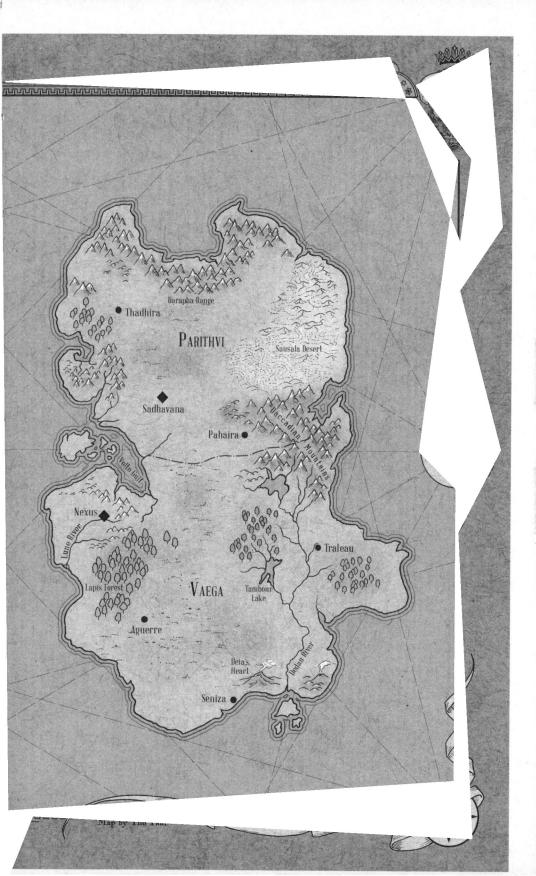

Barapha Range

● Thadhira

PARITHVI

Sausala Desert

◆
Sadhavana

Pahaira ●

Daccadian Mountains

Volto Gulf

Nexus ◆

Lune River

Traleau ●

Lapis Forest

VAEGA

Tambour
Lake

● Aguerre

Deia's
Heart

Dolan River

Seniza ●

THE FOUR NOBLE HOUSES OF NEXUS

House Mardova

Heads of House: Adela and August,* Miko
Heirs: Angelica, Kikou,† Eiko†
Realms: Vitae
Power: Elementalist
God: Deia

House Cyr

Heads of House: Waren* and Madeia
Heirs: Nikolas, Rian
Realms: Vitae / Solara
Power: Lumin
God: Phos

House Lastrider

Heads of House: Elena and Cormin
Heirs: Dante, Taesia, Brailee
Realms: Vitae / Noctus
Power: Shade
God: Nyx

House Vakara

Heads of House: Rath and Darsha
Heirs: Risha, Saya
Realms: Vitae / Mortri
Power: Necromancy
God: Thana

* deceased
† adopted

When the moon wept the stars fell,
And when the stars fell the sky opened,
And when the sky opened we emerged from its sanctum,
For Nyx is the pale moon's light and we
the celestial shadows beyond,
Given to the night,
Given shelter of the dark,
Here in our midnight kingdom.

—Noctan prayer

CAN YOU
HEAR ME?

There is much you do not know of the universe or how it came to be. But I am here now, and I will tell you.

To describe the pandemonium of Beginning would be inadequate. No word exists for it; not even *storm* can conjure that heat and rage and lust, that cycle of pensive violence. A cycle of things born and killed and born again.

But then there was this: a thread of quintessence, shimmering, eager, stubbornly riding out the storm. So stubborn it took some of that storm into itself, *themself*, holding it close to where the heart would beat, would that we had any.

(We had the freedom to choose, once, across a spectrum—which parts, which appendages, which forms. We became beasts to savor in savagery, and we became humans only to find they were beasts of a different nature. After the division, we could change no longer. The others might begrudge me this.)

The thread grew and learned from its stark surroundings in the battering storm. It desired to be crafted, and shaped, and realized. The thread became a sphere, or what some would more romantically call a star.

Are you paying attention? This is the important part.

The star of quintessence devoured the storm. As much as it could stomach.

We call that star and what came from it ███████

No—Orsus. The first, the Beginning, the maker of the doorways.

(I still remember the turbulent heat of it, the flashes of cognizance like emerging from deep water, with small sustaining gasps. But most of that time is now lost.)

Orsus allowed quintessence to do as it pleased, lending a hand when they wished to, delighting in the process of conception and fabrication.

Can you see where this is going?

The sphere, the star, gradually became a world. So many of you emerge into the light screaming and struggling, which is to say there was a great deal of pain involved. For with life comes death, withering, and loss.

Perhaps that is why Orsus set their sights on Mortri first. Then came Vitae, for the elements were unruly strands that required a loom.

Between Nyx and I, it is hard to say who emerged first. As Orsus was fond of saying, there is no dark without light.

(No, I will not speak of it now.)

I simply want you to understand: Ostium was built of a violent, longing storm, and Orsus gave to us what they could have easily kept for themself. Their realm became the commonway, the material from which to *build*.

You must realize why I whispered in Deia's ear, why I gave away my body to those who did not deserve it, why I grasped at the flesh Orsus had gifted themself and swallowed. Why Deia, upon finding out, took their remains and fled before the doorways shut.

We do not have hearts. But this was Orsus's: the spinning sphere of a storm, violet and crimson, with the power to make and shatter worlds.

And now a thread grows within me.

As it will grow within you.

PART I

The Dead and the Dark

I

Taesia Lastrider dreamed of color and woke to darkness.

The waking was against her will, and she struggled. A grunt of pain sounded beside her.

"It's all right," a low voice said. "You were having a nightmare."

Taesia stared at the ceiling above her, slanted stone washed in shadow, and evened out her breathing. Her back ached, and twin flares of pain lit up her wrists when she lifted her arms. They were shackled with a heavy, dark material, bitterly cold against her skin.

She reached for Umbra, for the shadows around her. Nothing happened. It was as if a pit had grown in her core, swallowing what made her a Shade, a Lastrider, a being forged from godsblood. It left her dizzy and weak. Panicked.

Flashes of memory like the winking facets of a gem: the unraveled cosmos of sky, the distant screams, the hands forcing her away and down, down into the underbelly of the Bone Palace. The lightsbane shoved over her hands.

And the person next to her—

Taesia clumsily pushed Julian away and sat up. "Fuck. *Fuck*. Why did you wake me up?"

Julian was mostly an outline in the dark, though she sensed his heat and smelled the dried sweat on his skin. Yet his eyes found hers unerringly, the flecks of green in his hazel irises like glowing embers in a banked fire.

"You were thrashing," he said. "I didn't want you to hurt yourself."

Taesia scooted back until she could lean against the cold wall. Behind her eyelids hid an afterimage of a cyclone of color, and in her ears echoed the faraway cry of a voice so familiar it made her chest ache.

"Brailee," she rasped. "She's a dream walker. She was trying to find me."

"I'm sorry."

She wanted to hold on to that flare of anger, but there was no point in it. No way to tell how long they had been down here, or what was happening above. No way to contact anyone in Vitae unless Brailee was able to locate her.

The last she had seen of Vitae was the chaos of Godsnight. In the aftermath—if there had been an aftermath—had Risha and Angelica shed their gods' possession? Had Dante been able to escape?

Were they even alive?

"Why am *I* alive?" she murmured. "Why hasn't he killed us by now?"

Julian settled down beside her. "I'm still not entirely sure who he is."

She tried to swallow, but her throat was too dry. She vaguely recalled Julian coaxing her to eat something that had been thrown into their cell, but it might as well have been air for how it filled her stomach.

"Rian Cyr," she said. "Nik's younger brother. He... We all thought he died years ago. I don't know how he got here, how Phos possessed him." She shuddered at recalling Nyx's presence within her, using his power to close the portal her aunt had unleashed over Nexus. "I don't know. I don't... I don't know."

When Julian pressed his shoulder to hers it was warm. Unconsciously she leaned into it, the lightsbane weighing down her wrists.

Julian reached for her hands. Gently, so carefully he could have been handling a just-hatched fledgling, he adjusted the shackles and brushed a thumb over the welts they'd made on her skin.

"Why aren't *you* tied up?" she muttered.

"Maybe he doesn't think I'm a threat."

But she had seen Julian in the Bone Palace's courtyard, eyes blazing green, pupils thinned to slits, black veins crawling over his skin. The bone-aching presence of him as she'd held him up.

Phos was an idiot to not consider him a threat.

"Your mother," she whispered. "Is she...?"

"When I left, she was alive and in the care of the Hunters."

Some of the built-up pressure in her chest released. "I didn't know what my aunt was planning. If I did, I would have done everything I could to stop it."

He hummed vaguely. He was still inspecting her wounds, and her fingers twitched under his attention.

"Nik said you were the fifth heir." At her cautious words, Julian paused. "What does that mean?"

What are you?

She heard the click in his throat when he swallowed. "I'm not sure. My beastspeaking, it..." He sighed, stirring the small hairs on her forehead. "It's derived from a demonic ability."

"You're a demon?"

He winced. "*No.*"

"Then—"

"I don't know how I got it." His voice turned brittle, and his fingertips pressed harder into her skin. "All this stuff about Ostium and demons, I...I don't understand it. And I might never get answers."

Because we'll die here, Taesia thought. Far from their home, and the people who loved them.

She didn't know how many hours passed in a daze by the time someone came down the steps. Julian shifted to stand in front of her, muscles tensing. A small sound left his throat, not quite a growl, that raised the hairs along her arms.

The person heading for their cell carried a faint nimbus around them, edging away the darkness as if refusing to be touched by it. The light illuminated a tall, lithe form, caressing the planes of a familiar face that looked at her with unfamiliar eyes, burning sun-bright gold.

Taesia staggered toward the bars. "Nik," she croaked. "*Nik.*"

Under Phos's thrall, his expression was as rigid as the stone around them. Gone was the way he'd raise his pale eyebrows, or smile shyly with just the corner of his mouth, or squint his crystalline eyes when she'd said something particularly crass.

"Nikolas," Julian tried. "Lord Cyr, please." Again no reaction, not even a minute twitch.

Silently Nikolas inserted a key into the heavy lock and pried the cell door open. Julian tensed again, but Taesia brushed her fingers against his lower back.

"Don't," she whispered. "I don't want to hurt him. Even if we restrain him, Phos will retaliate."

So they allowed Nikolas to pull Julian forward and roughly bind his wrists together—not with lightsbane but common rope. Then he took each of them by the arm, his grip bruising, and hauled them toward the stairs.

Taesia was used to calluses and blades, but Nikolas had always touched her like dew rolling off a leaf or a melody hummed under one's breath, unbearably soft. He had never handled her so roughly, not even in their most fervent moments.

It's not him, she thought. *Not really.*

The doors to the throne room had been thrown open. Onyx columns soared toward the ceiling above the throne's grand canopy, where hundreds of bones interlocked into vaults constructed of vertebrae and coving made of cleverly placed femurs, clavicles, and breastbones. Underneath the canopy of black velvet was the throne itself, gilded and padded, bearing heavy armrests and twisting branches that sprouted from the cresting rail, much like the tree at Deia's basilica.

Lounging on that throne was Rian. One leg was hooked insouciantly over an armrest while he twirled the Sunbringer Spear in his hands. He watched as they were brought forward with a small, unfeeling smile on his lips.

Taesia had grown up with Rian, had joked with him at galas and ganged up on Nikolas at his side, had mourned him when the ash fever claimed his life.

This young man was a stranger. He had grown taller, his face leaner, his shoulders broader.

He looked like Nikolas.

Or at least, he would have if he weren't so malnourished, so gaunt. Although his eyes had burned gold during Phos's possession, they were now the pale blue shade she remembered. As if the longer Phos inhabited him, the more his influence was etched into Rian's bones.

"One would think being in Noctus would make you stronger," Phos said through Rian's voice, which had deepened in the years since Taesia last heard it. "That bit of stone must be potent." He dropped his gaze to Taesia's shackles.

She smirked. "If you want a fair fight, you should take them off and give me back my sword. Then we'll see who's stronger."

"I'm humble enough to recognize a bad idea when it's presented." Phos snapped Rian's fingers, and Taesia startled as a figure scurried forward from the shadow of the columns. She'd been so focused on the throne that she hadn't noticed the handful of servants cowering along the walls, on their knees with their heads down.

They must have been trapped in the Bone Palace when it was transported through the Conjuration circle. Phos had made quick work killing off King Ferdinand and his advisors, but he had left enough servants to wait on him.

Had he left anyone else alive? Taesia craned her neck to try and find her erstwhile cousin—*crown prince*, she couldn't help but snarl to herself—when Julian's intake of breath made her turn back.

Phos had sat up and leaned the Sunbringer Spear against the throne. The weapon was radiant, the feathers encased within the metal reacting to the god's presence. The servant he'd summoned placed a bundle at his feet and scurried away. Phos leaned down and flung off the coverings.

Starfell's black blade glittered in the wan light. Taesia longed to tear out of Nikolas's hold and dive toward it, curl her hands around its cool grip.

"Quite an interesting weapon you've designed," Phos murmured, studying the spinous ridges along the blade's sides. "Made from astralam bones, if I'm not mistaken. Curious beasts. The power that resides within their bodies is...familiar."

He reached down but paused before touching it, frowning slightly. "How much do you know of your ancestry, little Lastrider?"

Taesia shared a glance with Julian across Nikolas's back. He shook his head a fraction.

"Enough," she answered. "You going to give me a lesson, old man?"

Phos let out a huff. "Then surely you've heard that the late Lunari royal family possessed an heirloom of great power, also forged from an astralam. A crown."

She had heard of it. A crown made of an astralam's fangs, passed from monarch to monarch, giving them the power to erect a protective barrier around the capital city of Astrum.

In the earliest days of Noctus, the Lunaris had learned how to harvest the dust from fallen stars. After generations of exposure to this stardust, their Shade magic was the strongest in the realm. Which meant that in their hands, an astralam's power was immense.

Now all that remained of the Lunaris lay crushed under the Bone Palace.

Phos noted the shift in her expression. "You understand, then, what the destruction of the Lunari family means."

He wrapped a hand around Starfell's hilt, but hardly a moment passed before he dropped it with a hiss. His hand was burned, the golden brown of his skin angrily flushed. Phos narrowed his eyes and signaled for the servant to take the sword away. Taesia again fought the urge to lunge toward it.

Phos stood, leaving the Sunbringer Spear to approach them. "Without the Lunaris' enhanced magic or their crown, no one can shield Astrum."

"What are you going to do?" Taesia demanded.

Phos turned toward one of the tall, narrow windows. Though they were largely comprised of stained glass, casting jewel-toned shapes across the floor, the bottom halves were clear enough to reveal a view of Nexus—that is, if the Bone Palace had been in its proper place.

Now, as Phos strolled to the window and Nikolas dragged them behind, Taesia was greeted with an entirely new sight. The palace's courtyard was washed in nighttime gloom, a small valley of destruction left over from Godsnight. If she squinted she could just make out the misshapen forms of bodies, the corpses of the king and his advisors left to rot.

And there, at the edge of the courtyard, stood a wall of golden light. A barrier, cutting off the Bone Palace from the rest of Astrum. She couldn't perceive the city beyond other than the vague, blurry forms of buildings in the distance, and darker figures moving along the perimeter.

But who was powering it? Taesia looked up at Nikolas's impassive face.

"Nik," she whispered, unable to stop herself from trying again, to keep trying until the cold light left his eyes and he regarded her the way he used to, with warmth and patience.

Even if she'd squandered that warmth, that patience. Even if she was no longer worthy of it.

"It's no use." Phos leaned beside the window, crossing his arms. "He can hear you, perhaps know who you are to some extent, but he won't comprehend."

"What are you going to do with him?"

"Other than haul you around?" He flapped a hand at the window. "You're already looking at it."

So he is *channeling Nik's power.*

"This will give us some privacy with which to work," Phos went on, seeming smug. "Dear Rian already helped considerably by making those circles around the city, and we have Ostium's remains implanted within the palace. It's only a matter of refining the spells."

"To do *what*?"

"It's not obvious?" He shrugged one bony shoulder. "You'll see soon enough."

Julian opened his mouth as if to speak, then thought better of it.

It didn't escape Phos's notice. "The heir of Ostium will play a part, naturally. I do need an offering."

"He's not an offering," Taesia growled. "If you touch him, you're dead."

Phos lifted an eyebrow and walked over to Julian. He roughly grabbed the Hunter by the jaw and dug his fingers in, Julian's tawny skin paling under the pressure. A dagger of blazing-hot light appeared in his other hand. He held it close to Julian's neck, watching Taesia coolly.

"Well?" Phos said.

She wouldn't rise to the taunt—she couldn't. Julian's eyes were shut tight, sweat beading at his temple and rolling down his cheek. A drop hit the dagger and sizzled into steam.

"Thought not." The dagger disappeared and Phos let Julian go. "Maybe I *should* take those shackles off. I worry I'll get bored otherwise."

Taesia swallowed her fury, though it scorched her throat like she'd consumed that dagger. The helpless fear that had engulfed her in the dungeons now burned away with renewed purpose.

She would snap Nikolas out of Phos's possession, at least long enough that they could escape the barrier. Rian—Phos—wouldn't dare kill him.

She met Julian's solemn gaze. He gave a slight dip of his chin, jaw already mottled with bruises in the shape of Rian's fingertips.

We won't die here.

Not if I can help it.

II

R isha Vakara walked hand in hand with a ghost.

She made sure to stand between him and the wide river they followed, keeping him as far from the water as she could while not losing sight of it. From here she heard the rushing of its grayish-green current, the faint humming calls of the spirits, the constant *drip, drip, drip* from the stalactites above. All around them rose arches and columns of black opal that glimmered with hints of red and green and silver.

The river was the Praeteriens, sometimes referred to as the Forgetting Waters. It was where spirits accumulated once their souls made the journey to this realm, borne to different recesses of Mortri and whatever fate awaited them in the afterlife.

"Where does this lead?" Jas asked, nodding toward the river.

Risha's chest clenched when she looked at him. He was no longer substantial, the whole of him washed in gray. Yet his smile was unchanged, the warmth of it easing her heart a little.

But she couldn't forget that he was dead. Dead because he had tried to help.

Dead because of her.

"It branches out in four ways," Risha said eventually. The ground was rocky and uneven under her boots. "Each leads to one of the four cities."

Though they weren't cities in the way Risha and Jas understood them, as they were inhabited by the dead. Jas nodded with a thoughtful expression.

"And each of those cities is ruled by one of the four kings of Mortri."

"That's right."

"The founder of your House fought a war against those kings. Leshya Vakara." Risha quirked an eyebrow at him, and he laughed softly. It had, after all, been Leshya's finger bones Jas had stolen to fuel his Conjuration efforts.

"Yes. The kings wanted to march on Vitae and claim more souls in order to overthrow Thana, but Leshya subdued them. The decisive battle happened here in Mortri. We don't know much about it other than it wasn't an easy victory, and she had to abandon her weapons to make it back to Vitae in time."

"In time for what?"

Risha drew a deep breath, taking in scents both familiar and not, of rich minerals and dust and the faint underlying sweetness of rot. Though she stood in Mortri, her body was alive, her heart pumping and her organs working to keep her that way. There were things dwelling in this realm that would catch one whiff of her fresh blood and know a feast was near.

"No living being can stay in Mortri," she said at last. "Leshya was here for about a month before the realm attempted to claim her. That's why she had to hurry at the end."

Jas's hand was cold and whisper soft, but it still tightened around hers. "*Risha.*"

"We'll find a way out." She nodded to give the words more weight. "Both of us."

Jas was silent, but his gaze rested like a touch against her cheek, reproachful and mourning.

Truth be told, she didn't have a plan. Didn't even know how long they had been here. All she had to go by was how her feet ached with fatigue, how her stomach cramped with hunger, and how her throat stung with thirst. She had no rations—she had been fully prepared to die at Godsnight along with the other heirs.

Every second spent thinking about the other heirs—their unknown fates, or the one they would have suffered at her hand—twisted her stomach tighter. She'd thought at the time it would be a mercy to cut the threads of their lives, too steeped in fear to see any other alternative.

The plan had been foolish, and so was she. But she had to be better than foolish now.

They weren't going to survive otherwise.

Far ahead she spotted an opening in the labyrinth of caves, emanating viridescent light. The river had now split, snaking left and right, deeper into caverns so dark she instinctually knew to avoid them at all costs. There was no way to cross.

Jas stared at the river, the churning current reflected in his eyes. He took a step toward it.

Risha placed herself before him. "Jas, look at me."

His gaze was vacant. Risha remembered standing with him in Thana's basilica and sounding the bone whistle. The spirits who had arrived at its call had stares every bit as empty as his was now.

He blinked once, twice, and focused on her face.

"Risha," he murmured. "Maybe you should—"

"*No.*" It was practically a snarl. She reined in the sudden lash of fury, unsure where it had come from. "No, Jas. You didn't deserve to die, and you don't deserve..." She glanced at the river, the pale limbs and faces floating by. She swallowed. "You don't deserve *that*. I'm not letting it take you."

Something like resignation settled on his face. "You said you only had a finite time before Mortri claims you. The same is likely true of me. Instead of wasting your energy—"

"I need your help," she blurted. "You wouldn't leave me alone, would you?"

That made him pause. Slowly a smile touched his pallid lips, fondness creeping through the resignation.

"All right," he whispered. "But I don't know how long I can stay."

For as long as I allow it, Risha thought.

She was a Vakara, a descendant of the god of death. She would find a way to bend the rules of this realm in her favor.

But first: They had to find a way to cross the river.

Risha approached the bank. The air grew colder with each step she took, the ground laced with frost. She shivered as the whispering spirits went by.

"—*could have done so much more—*"

"—*be remembered? I can't think—*"

"—*her name, what was her name—*"

The Forgetting Waters would gradually wash away their memories, their lives, until they were stripped of earthly desires and submitted fully to Thana's judgment. If Jas were to forget himself, forget *her*...

Risha was shaken out of her thoughts when Jas pulled her back. The bodies had begun to churn violently, the turbulence creating white water. A large shadow stirred in the depths.

"What are they doing?" Jas demanded.

Spirits rose from the river, water lapping against their gray, naked bodies. There were at least a dozen, all with their heads bowed and hands lifted. Across their shoulders rested a platform made of the same black opal as the columns around them.

A bridge.

The spirits didn't move, only holding the bridge aloft as water dripped off its edges. Uncertain, Risha moved forward and stopped right before her foot made contact with the bridge. There was a nervy feeling inside her, a kind of warning or premonition, stitched deep into her muscle.

"I have to hold my breath," she whispered to Jas. She didn't know *how* she knew, just as she didn't know why the bridge had appeared, other than perhaps the spirits had recognized something of Thana in her. "Don't startle me."

"I'll keep my shouting to a minimum," he said dryly.

Risha filled her lungs with that dusty, mineral-rich air and pinched her nose before finally stepping onto the platform. She expected it to dip with her weight, but the spirits held it steady.

With her lungs still and her chest tight, Risha carefully made her way across. The Praeteriens was twice as wide as the Lune River that cut through Nexus, so she quickened her pace once she was confident the bridge wouldn't suddenly give way under her. Jas was close at her heels.

Halfway across came the burn of deprivation. It didn't help that her heart was beating wildly, fluttering at the base of her throat, urging her to go faster. Jas matched her pace, reaching out to hold her hand again, either to make her slow down or to avoid being seduced by the Forgetting Waters.

Puddles of water lingered on the platform, and her boot slipped in one near the end. A gasp ripped out of her as she stumbled, Jas's grip preventing her from tumbling into the river below.

But the damage had been done. With her indrawn breath the spirits writhed and howled, their wails like storm sirens. The bridge tilted and Jas pitched them forward, the two of them rolling onto the far bank as the water frothed and roiled.

"Run!" Risha yelled.

They made for the green light in the distance. The wails built behind them, a foreboding chorus that rang in her ears. Like the spirits were crying for something—or someone.

Risha fell to her knees panting once they stumbled out of the caves, even as the adrenaline coursing through her begged her to keep going. Jas knelt beside her.

"We should get as far as we can in case something comes looking for us," Jas said. Briefly she envied his phantom body's lack of exhaustion. "Although I think that's going to happen regardless."

Risha sat back on her heels and wiped her mouth. "They know we're here," she agreed hoarsely.

Then she looked up and let out a quiet sound of disbelief.

There had been sketches of Mortrian landscapes in the books her father made her read, but nothing could prepare her for the real thing, the realm of her birthright spread out before her. The sky was a swirling mass of black and cadmium green, giving off a vaporous, otherworldly light. Underneath those clouds were valleys and fields that dipped and rose into sharp peaks, as well as the dark spine of a mountain range to the east and what looked to be a city carved into its side. Behind them, the Praeteriens emerged from the caves and split into four tributaries; one of them snaked its way toward the mountain city, the other three leading elsewhere.

Risha got to her feet. Beside her, Jas laughed mirthlessly.

"All this time," he murmured. "All this time I longed to reach Mortri, and now I'm here."

Risha blinked away the stinging in her eyes. They stood in a field of flowers, blossoms bending in a cold breeze. Their heads were made of compact, frilled petals, and though they were a dark green rather than orange, Risha would recognize them anywhere. Marigolds. She carefully touched one and marveled at its softness.

"'A realm both beautiful and terrifying,'" Jas said. "I read that in a book. Or maybe it was a poem. Either way, it's not wrong."

Risha plucked the marigold and handed it to Jas. Surprised, he took it in both hands, cupped together like he was accepting an offering from a Parithvian priest.

Under the light, he looked even more like a ghost. But the flower stayed nestled on his palms, refusing to pass through him. Risha's conviction hardened. So long as they stayed together, she could keep him whole until they found a way out.

Provided nothing found them first.

III

Nikolas Cyr was not.

He used to be, perhaps.

But now he was not.

He walked where he was told to. He stood where he was told to. He did as he was told to.

He followed the glowing one, the god, the brother, gold and somber and dead and not, too confusing a concept to hold any one shape in his mind, so he let it go.

He was told to open a door. He opened it.

Beyond, a large room. A floor giving way softly under his boots. *Rug,* came a word from the dregs, a bubble rising to the surface, popping and then gone.

He followed god brother to a person in the room. A name gradually unearthed: *Fin.*

Something in his chest kicked and beat.

The god smiled coldly. A glowing spear was slung across his back. Nikolas's gaze kept straying toward it.

Fin was chained, sitting in a padded chair. The set of his eyebrows, the downturn of his full mouth, indicated fear and concern. His chains rattled as he tried and failed to move forward.

"Nik," Fin rasped. His eyes were blue, bright, big. "Nik, please—"

The same words as the woman. She was called…Lastrider. *Taesia.* The same tightness in his chest and the same nothingness in his mind. He stared at Fin. Fin stared back at him. Fin's face scrunched, eyes filmed with water.

"Nik…"

"Don't bother with him," the god said. "He's gone. I should be your main concern."

Fin's jaw clenched. "What have you done to him?"

"You're not in a position to be asking me questions, princeling. How long have you been secreted away? How exactly was your father planning to explain you?" The god scoffed. "Deia's constructs are unbelievably stupid."

Again Fin looked to Nikolas. Nikolas blinked and there were two images at once, overlapping in his vision. One image: Fin in a chair. Another image: a corridor, a heated exchange, a vague idea of threat, assassination. It made no sense, so he discarded it.

Fin swallowed. "What are you planning to do with *me*?"

"Finally, a good question." The god walked around Fin's chair, pulling on a chain. It yanked on the circles of dark stone at his wrists. "Are you wondering why I haven't killed you like I killed your father?"

Fin paled. The chains rattled, but this time because he was trembling.

"It's very simple. You have magic. He does not. You have *Deia's* magic, and the Mardova was removed from the circle before the spell took effect. I need a replacement."

"You wanted Angelica Mardova? Why?"

"Offerings. The more magic used, the more *diverse* the magic, the better the outcome." The god tilted his head. "From what I saw earlier, your element is earth, is it not? Any secondary element? Tertiary?"

Fin did not answer. He was still ashen. He was still trembling.

The god waited. The god sighed.

"Being quiet now won't help. I can be merciful. I *have* been merciful. I could have thrown you into the dungeon with the others, to rot in the dark." A stretch of his mouth, the shine of teeth. "Did you know that without light, Vitaeans will die?"

Fin closed his eyes. He trembled harder.

A moment of silence. Another sigh.

Soft footfalls. Nikolas stared into a face that seemed to crush him without force. It was a contrasting mask of gentleness and cruelty, of familiarity and foreignness, wrong, wrong, *wrong wrong wrong wrong*—

"Nikolas," the god crooned, and the spinning in his mind abruptly stopped. "Would you please hold out your arm?" Nikolas held out his left arm.

"What are you doing?" Fin demanded.

"I said I could be merciful," the god explained as he lovingly rolled Nikolas's sleeve up to his elbow. "You didn't want that. So this is me, not being merciful."

A steel blade in his hand. Nikolas watched impassively as its tip sliced his flesh, splitting skin, parting like a fruit rind broken with his thumb on summer days, juice rolling down his hand, a brilliant laugh at his side, the sun—

"Stop!" Fin fought against his chains, chair legs scraping against the rug. "*Stop!*"

The god paused. "Secondary element?"

Fin panted harshly. The liquid in his eyes had fallen to his cheeks. He stared at Nikolas's arm and whispered, "Water. Not...not as strong as earth."

"Good to know." The god wiped the blade off on Fin's shirt, crimson staining the light fabric. "This will help when adjusting the circle."

Nikolas stared down at his arm, which he still held up, because he had not yet been told to put it down. Red seeped out and over, dribbling onto the rug. Some part of his body told him it was painful, stinging, aching. His blood was very bright. It dampened a piece of tangled string on his wrist, dripped off a small charm in the shape of a tree.

"Come, Nikolas," the god ordered. "And lock the door behind you."

For some reason his eyes met Fin's. They were wide and wet, in the shape of a plea.

Nikolas closed and locked the door behind him.

IV

Angelica Mardova stood at the edge of a massive hole in the center of Nexus and thought about doors.

The hole was really more of a crater, a hollow cavity, as if a giant had dug a spoon deep into the city's foundation and scooped out a chunk of earth along with the Bone Palace.

But this wasn't the work of a giant. It was the result of a Conjuration circle that had engulfed the city, drenching the square and nearby buildings in otherworldly light until everything within its center—every*one* within its center—had disappeared.

It had taken Angelica two days to wake up after Godsnight. Once her mother and Miko had made certain she was fine, they'd answered her questions.

The Bone Palace? Gone.

The king? Also gone, along with all his staff.

The other heirs?

Her mother and Miko had exchanged a look.

"Taesia Lastrider, Nikolas Cyr, and Risha Vakara are also missing. They've likely gone wherever the palace went." Adela had swallowed, reaching up to touch her injured shoulder. "Dante Lastrider escaped the Gravespire."

"*How?*"

"No one knows. The Lastriders are in hiding, but I've been in communication with Elena. She insists she doesn't know where her son is." The slight twist of Adela's mouth showed what she thought of that.

"What kind of communication?"

"His Majesty is *gone*. Waren Cyr is dead. Someone needs to keep the city and this country stable."

Which was how she'd come to learn that her mother and Rath Vakara were openly working together to sort out the aftermath of Godsnight. The Lastriders had all but dissolved, their public image ruined, so Elena could only assist them from the shadows. Often quite literally.

Angelica had asked her mother why she bothered working with the other Houses at all. The time was ripe for the Mardovas to step forward and claim Vaega as theirs.

"It's not so simple." Her mother had sighed. "The Cyrs and Lastriders may be done, but Elena knows the most about Vaega's commerce and resources. We need her, whether we like it or not. And the Vakaras are still a strong and necessary presence in our kingdom. Not to mention they have the backing of Parithvi."

"We're descended from the god of *this realm*."

"A god who's been ignoring us."

Angelica now curled her hands into fists and stared into the empty crater. Everything the Mardovas had worked for was nothing but an empty pit. She remembered standing on a stage and being filled with Deia's might, the doors to her powers banging open with the god's presence. Doors that Deia herself had constructed and then barred.

She had made Angelica her puppet, and she would do so again at the first opportunity.

Unless Angelica learned how to open the doors herself. Unless she learned how to better wield her powers, to maintain control in the face of its intensity.

But her violin was shattered—the instrument a gift from her father, who'd known how much the music meant to her. The one she'd attuned to fire in order to calm the elemental addiction that plagued her. She kept telling herself the sacrifice had been necessary, that Deia would have engulfed Risha in an inferno. Instead, Angelica had sung, the notes reaching for that intangible element just beyond her grasp. She had *created* something, a hazy portal, had been able to push Risha through it to...

She didn't know. Maybe she'd ended up killing her after all.

Angelica pulled the hood of her fur-lined cloak down farther. Autumn was creeping toward winter, and the chapped skin of her hands stung in the cold. Somewhere nearby came the sound of muffled sobbing. The crater tended to draw citizens who were curious or mourning, and all along its rim were dozens of small offerings for the souls of those who had been taken: candles that quickly guttered out in the breeze, incense, fruits and small delicate cakes, prayers written on paper that ranged from creamy ivory to coarse ochre. As Angelica watched, a couple of urchins quickly ran toward a pile of fruit and grabbed as many as they could before someone noticed and chased them off.

Who are you even doing this for? she wanted to demand of the mourners. *A king who didn't care about you or your safety? The high commissioner's killer?*

But then she thought of Nikolas Cyr, who in his persistent kindness had always been a bright spot among the gentry, despite being the weakest heir. And when Angelica looked closer, it wasn't just sorrow she saw in the citizens' eyes, but terror.

Their ruler was gone. Half the Houses were gone. Something unspeakable had happened to their city.

What were they supposed to do now?

To her right, someone approached the lip. They were also shrouded in a cloak, head bent over the small offering they laid upon the broken, pitted cobblestone: a single bun dusted with cinnamon and sugar. The wind stirred the trim of their deep hood as they stared down at the crater.

"Angelica."

For a wild moment she thought she heard Taesia's voice.

Don't you dare fucking haunt me.

The person raised their head, and Angelica's panic washed away. Brailee Lastrider looked solemnly up at her with those unnerving Lastrider eyes, a shade of brown so dark they seemed black.

Angelica glanced around to make sure no one was watching them. "What do you want?"

"We want to talk." Brailee stood. Though her brother and sister were too tall for their own good, Brailee was petite, much nearer to Angelica's height.

"*We?*"

"Don't pretend the Mardovas have completely shunned House Lastrider. Our mothers are working together."

"If this is about reallocating resources—"

"It's about Deia's fulcrum." Seeing the shock flit across Angelica's face, Brailee dipped her chin. "Will you come or not?"

★   ★   ★

"I don't like being manipulated, Lastrider," Angelica groused, wrapping her cloak tight around her body as she followed Brailee down a narrow alleyway.

"This concerns you, too." Brailee's voice was similar to Taesia's in pitch, but the tone was far softer, giving Angelica a feeling of wrongness. "I wouldn't call that manipulating."

Angelica took stock of their surroundings. They were in one of the outer districts, not the river quarter but close enough she could hear its faint murmuring. The Lastrider villa was currently being held by the city guard—now under a new high commissioner chosen by her mother and Rath—and Angelica had to admit she was curious about where the family had gone into hiding.

Brailee ended up leading her to a small two-story house sitting on a quiet, damp street. It was stained white with lime mortar, its wooden shutters closed against the chill. Or perhaps to prevent anyone outside from looking in.

"Did you kick out a family to squat here?" Angelica asked.

"A friend of my father's is in the housing trade. This one was empty, and he's allowing us to use it."

"Isn't that risky? He might give you up for a reward."

Brailee shrugged and unlocked the door. "Nothing we do now is without risk."

The inside of the house smelled like dust and something bitter, like tea that had been steeped too long. Everything was wooden in design, from the old floors to the timbers above their heads. The central floor revealed a small kitchen space and a scarred table. An open doorway led to a room in the back.

Brailee hung up her cloak and made for the back room. Angelica followed slowly, hand drifting to the thin knife tucked up her sleeve. The always-present urge within her made her fingertips flare hot, just on the brink of bursting into flame.

As soon as she crossed the threshold behind Brailee, they did just that.

Standing next to a threadbare armchair was someone the kingdom had labeled *traitor*, a man who should have been hanged, who had somehow managed to escape an unescapable prison.

The erstwhile Lastrider heir turned and locked eyes with Angelica. There was an ashen hue to his brown skin, his handsome face gaunter, leaner, making the sharp angles of his jaw all the more prominent. His black hair, which had always been well styled, had grown shaggy and unkempt during his imprisonment.

But the smile he directed at her was exactly as she remembered it. That charming, deceptive grin, setting off the dimples in his cheeks and the spark of cunning in his gaze.

"Angelica," Dante greeted. "It's been too long."

The flames alighting her fingers spread down her hand. "Not long enough." Angelica started forward only to have Brailee step between them.

"*Stop.* Please, Angelica, just listen. Dante didn't kill Prelate Lezzaro. He was falsely accused."

Taesia had told her as much, but it had been without evidence. And now that she knew Taesia had murdered Don Soler and Don Damari, she was even more convinced the older Lastrider siblings had been working toward something sinister.

"Fuck this," she snarled, ready to turn back to the door. "I'm not going to talk to a—"

"Do not leave."

Angelica froze. The words were in Dante's low voice, but they had a strange, chiming quality that drove out all thought or incentive. Her mouth hung slack as Dante's fathomless black irises flashed green.

She wasn't sure where she was. What she had been doing.

"You will not tell anyone that you've seen me," Dante said in that ringing, chiming voice.

Angelica's body floated without motivation. For the first time in a long time, she was . . . calm. She nodded slowly, uncertain what she was agreeing to but peaceable enough that she didn't care.

Brailee moved toward her brother, brow furrowed. "Dante. You said you wouldn't."

He sighed and raked a hand through his hair. "I'm sorry. I panicked."

His voice and eyes were back to normal. Angelica blinked rapidly. "What was I . . . ?"

"You were about to hear us out," Dante said. "To learn the truth about Prelate Lezzaro and my aunt."

"Your . . . aunt?" Angelica frowned. "Camilla Lorenzo? What about her?"

"You might as well sit down," Brailee said. "I'll make tea."

"Let me get this straight," Angelica said once Dante and Brailee were finished. They sat on the pitiful couch across from hers, Brailee's hands held tightly in her lap. "Phos has taken control over Rian Cyr—who's supposed to be *dead*—and he was the one who took the Bone Palace."

Brailee nodded. "He summoned it to Noctus. We think that's where Taesia and Nik have gone."

Angelica turned to Dante. "And *you're* saying that Camilla read Lezzaro's grimoire, found out about Ostium and the fulcrums, and decided to summon a demon that would help her bring the Ostium fulcrum *here*."

"That's the heart of it."

Angelica had read that very same grimoire, had learned about the missing fifth realm and how each god needed to be tethered to their world, and so had hidden the cores of themselves.

I would have taken of their flesh, but all I have left are remains, Deia had told her in the basilica, confirmation that the Bone Palace was constructed with the fifth god's bones. And Phos, if he really had possessed Rian, knew it, too.

She touched the spot on her arm where Deia's burning handprint had scarred her. Her mother had been trying to get her to return to the basilica, but Angelica refused.

Her god was no longer fit for her worship.

"I still don't understand why Aunt Camilla wanted it so badly," Dante murmured as he gazed into his mug of swampy-looking tea. "She'd never struck me as power hungry, but..."

"But with a god's fulcrum, she would likely receive that god's powers," Brailee finished softly.

Angelica finally took a sip of tea to help the dryness of her mouth. She made a face, and Dante huffed.

"It's not exactly what we're used to either," he said. "I miss my peach rooibos. And coffee." He sighed, long-suffering, as if it weren't his own fault he didn't have access to such luxury anymore. Then again, after hearing what he'd been through—witnessing his aunt's demon breaking Lezzaro's neck, then the betrayal of Camilla incriminating him—perhaps it wasn't. Fully.

Angelica glanced around the room, a far cry from the stately blacks and silvers of the Lastrider villa. "Where are your parents?"

"Helping yours." Dante arched an eyebrow. "At least it's easier getting around the city when you have control over the shadows."

"Why even stay in the city if there's a price on your head?"

"I don't plan on staying." Dante placed his mug on the low table between them. "That's why we wanted to talk to you. We have no idea where our aunt is, but I'm sure she's left Nexus."

"You want to go after her?" According to him, Camilla Lorenzo still had possession of the grimoire. There was no telling what the woman could do with the perilous secrets it held.

"Partly. But also..." Dante exchanged another look with Brailee. "I have a feeling she's going to go after the Vitae fulcrum next."

Angelica set her mug down hard, splashing bitter tea over her knuckles. "*What?*"

"Her chance to get the Ostium fulcrum was only possible during Godsnight. What else can she do now but turn to what's available?"

"Deia won't allow it," Angelica said flatly. "She still has plenty of control in this realm. She wouldn't let a mortal get near enough to claim it."

"But my aunt knows how to summon demons," Dante countered. "And there could be other rituals in the grimoire we don't know anything about."

"We figured you would want to put a stop to it," Brailee added. "Or at least help locate the fulcrum before she does."

Angelica studied Dante. Everyone had always fawned over him, wanted to impress him, wanted to *be* him. Sometimes she thought she was the only one who could see that behind all his charm was someone overflowing with ambition and desperate to use it.

"You want the fulcrum for yourself," she deduced.

Brailee opened her mouth to deny it, but Dante put a hand on her shoulder. "Not for the reason you think," he said.

Brailee's eyes widened. "Dante—"

"No, listen. Phos made the most of Godsnight by taking the Bone Palace. We can't create those conditions again...unless we had access to a god's full power."

Angelica leaned back. "You—you want to use Deia's fulcrum to open a rift in the barriers?"

"If possible." His somber expression was just as unsettling as his smile. "We have to save Taesia."

"I should have guessed." Angelica stood and brushed out her skirts. "The other heirs are finally out of my way. Why should I save them?"

"It isn't just about them," Dante countered. "Vitae is withering. We're heading toward extinction. We *need* to get the barriers open."

That stilled her. She'd rather chop off her hand than agree with him, but...

"Where would it even be?" she demanded, her voice harsh. "The fulcrum."

Dante's soft laugh wasn't quite mocking, but it made her bristle. "One would think you'd be the best person to answer that."

"It could be in Deia's Heart," Brailee supplied.

Deia's Heart was a volcano in southern Vaega, one of the largest in Vitae. Deia did seem to have a fondness for fire, and there were plenty of legends that had her forging things out of flame and heat.

"It's too obvious," Angelica muttered.

"Almost as if it was named Deia's Heart on purpose, to mislead," Dante agreed. "But there's another volcanic land in Vitae."

"In *Azuna*. Halfway across the damn realm."

"And you know what lives among those volcanoes? The sorankun. Cousins to our wyverns. Think about it, Angelica."

For a dizzying moment she was a young girl again, sitting beside her father as he read her myths about the gods. The one she remembered with the most clarity was the story of Deia and her wyvern.

"He was a large, winged creature with a fearsome roar that could make the earth tremble," August had whispered dramatically while Angelica clutched his arm. "Deia crafted him within the heart of a boiling volcano, fashioning his scales from fire and ash. He was named Yvri for the eternal flame that birthed him, and his bond with Deia was so strong that she could ride him across our lands swifter than any bird."

Angelica had tugged on his sleeve. "Is Yvri real? Or is this another made-up one?"

August had smiled down at her. "I'm not sure. No one knows for certain if he actually existed, and if so, what happened to him. But I like to believe he did."

Seeing her waver, Dante smirked. "This is where we become useful. Brailee and I will go to Deia's Heart. If my aunt is there, or heads in that direction, we'll stop her."

"And I'm supposed to drop everything and go on a vacation to Azuna?" She moved to the door, ready to be done with the conversation.

Brailee stood. "Angelica, we need your help. You're the one best equipped to find the fulcrum."

Angelica's fingertips began to heat again. Her god's mocking words rang through her mind.

You think this is a power you can wield? You cannot even wield that which you currently have.

I closed you off from what you most desire so one day I would have my perfect vessel.

If she really could find the fulcrum, would she even be able to use it? Would its power transfer into hers? Would she be able to break away from Deia for good?

Slowly she reached into her pocket, where she'd been carrying the sketch of a Conjuration circle—the one she had taken from Nikolas's task force.

Wondering if she was making a mistake, she balled it up and tossed it onto the table.

"You like mysteries, don't you?" she said. "Maybe that'll help you find out where the others have gone."

"Angelica."

She felt a jolt in her heart. Dante remained sitting on the couch, but for a split second something was perched behind him, a warped black shadow with a grinning mouth. It rested its hands on Dante's shoulders, and his eyes flickered green.

Then he blinked, and his eyes were their normal dark shade. The shadow was gone.

"Just think about it," he said.

Although she didn't want to give them the satisfaction, she did think about it. So much so that she couldn't sleep that night, tossing and turning for hours.

She longed for her violin. It had been the best conduit for her magic, the shovel that broke the earth's crust for water to seep through, filling up the well of her desire. The only other way was channeling her anger. She lifted her hand and concentrated on her irritation at the Lastriders, her chest tightening painfully until a flicker of fire licked against her palm.

It didn't satisfy her. Angelica shut her eyes tight and let the flame gutter out. After a few minutes she slipped out of bed, pulled on a robe, and headed for her mother's room.

Halfway there, she noticed the door to Adela's office was open a crack. Firelight spilled through into the hallway, a flickering warmth that danced with shadow. Angelica was about to reach for the doorknob when voices stopped her.

"I don't know." That was Miko, her Azunese accent softening consonants. "I don't want to leave you right now. It feels too precarious."

A sigh from Adela. "It *is* precarious. The king is gone, and Vaega could very well slip into a civil war if we're not careful. That's why I need to keep by Rath's side for now, and why I need you to go to Azuna. The Vakaras have connections to Parithvi. We need the empire's backing."

The tectonic plates within her shifted and suddenly snapped into place. Before she knew what she was doing, Angelica pushed into the office.

Her mother and Miko were sitting in the winged armchairs before the fireplace, both dressed in robes, similarly cursed with a restless night. Brandy glasses sat empty on the small round table. They were holding hands, Adela running her thumb over Miko's knuckles with an intimacy she would never show in public.

At Angelica's appearance, Miko started and dropped Adela's hand.

"What's wrong?" her mother demanded.

"I need to speak with you."

Miko made as if to leave, but Angelica stopped her. "Both of you."

Surprise flitted across Miko's face before she slowly sat back down. Adela's lazy intimacy was gone, replaced with a stern vigilance more befitting the head of House Mardova.

Angelica took a deep breath. "Miko is from one of the royal families. That should be enough to gain an audience with the empress so we can bid for Azuna's support to rule Vaega."

Although it would be even better to gain an audience with the four great warlords, who governed each of the empire's four states. The empress was more of a cultural figure, residing in the imperial seat in the middle of Azuna where the four states met. She was surrounded by staff, servants, and gentry, the latter made up of distant relatives. Miko's family—the Uedas—was one such branch.

Angelica pressed her thumb against her warm fingertips. The fire state of Azuna was home to the Sanatsu Peaks, a range of mountains and volcanoes, the largest of which was Mount Netsai. If Deia really had hidden her fulcrum within a volcano... If Deia's Heart was named to fool anyone who knew about the fulcrums...

As much as she didn't want to entertain the Lastriders, her desire to be free of Deia's control weighed greater than her pride.

"I'll go to Azuna," she said. "As a representative of House Mardova."

Her mother and stepmother stared at her in shocked silence. It was Miko who stirred first.

"I ... I am not so sure about this, Angelica," she said in the cautionary tone she employed when her daughters were fighting.

"I know the language. Mother ensured that. And I have a passing knowledge of Azunese customs."

"A passing knowledge won't be sufficient," Miko stressed. "Not when it comes to the politics, the tensions, the history. It would be better if I went, but ..."

Adela took Miko's hand again. "Do you want to return? Be honest."

Miko dwelled on it, staring at Adela's left shoulder. The one bandaged and healing under her robe, where an arrow had struck during Ferdinand's attempt to assassinate the Houses.

"No," Miko answered. "I want to stay here with you. With the girls." Her gaze swung back to Angelica with a sigh. "But this will be more dangerous than you think. There is much you have to study in preparation."

"I'll accept whatever help you see fit to give me," Angelica said. Once she would have rather chewed stone than say the words, but she would be a fool to reject Miko's aid.

Adela studied her, as if to seek out any chinks in her armor. But Angelica knew what she was really thinking: Some had seen Angelica Mardova possessed on Godsnight, a terror of rage and flame. It could strengthen their House's position if Angelica were to avoid notice for the time being, at least until Adela could soothe the masses.

"Are you sure?" Adela asked.

Angelica rolled her shoulders back, ignoring the way the flames in the fireplace leaned toward her, as if also anticipating her answer.

"I'm sure."

V

Julian Luca knew the minds of monsters because he was one.

Lying on his back, he stared at the faint green veins at his wrist, remembering when they had flooded black. How his blood had so quickly turned once he'd acknowledged what swam within it. The prick of sharp teeth against his lip, the hunger for something to destroy or else conquer—the furious intention all around him lit up gold, and him at its heart, a being both foul and favored.

Julian slowly curled his hand into a fist. His knuckles protruded, one bearing the white line of a scar he couldn't remember getting. There was a new one on his palm, scabbed over and itching. As he squeezed his fist tighter, a drop of blood welled there.

Red, bright, winking in the candlelight like a ruby. Not black.

Not yet.

He could sense it, now—a distant presence crouched inside him, like a bird of prey surveying a field, ready to swoop down. It felt like fingertips against his skin, the lightest touch that nevertheless threatened to dig into muscle and rip apart the man who called himself Julian Luca, son of Marjorie and Benjamín, a Hunter of Vaega. A beastspeaker.

A demon.

Azideh. When he closed his eyes he could hazily remember the events of Godsnight, remember a man—Dante Lastrider—and a dark shadow at his back, its eyes bright green, its mind a jumble of confusion and surprise and delight.

Azideh.

He saw the name embedded on aged paper in fading ink, written

within a grimoire, followed by the words *control the mind of living beings...*
and every manner of beast.

Julian rubbed at his eyes. They were hot and itchy from lack of sleep.
His head and body ached.

But he couldn't relax, couldn't surrender to exhaustion. He kept
thinking about the flash of those green eyes, the words scrawled in the
grimoire. Wondering why his power only seemed to work on beasts and
nothing else.

Wondering if he could make them work on a human.

Julian hissed through his teeth. After Godsnight, the thought of using
that power again made his skin crawl. It was a power that had snuffed out
the lives of other demons, turning them to dust. It was a power that had
given Taesia alarm.

He opened his eyes and stared at the ceiling. The room he'd been left
in had no windows, and the door was locked from the outside. Taesia had
been sent elsewhere; Phos likely didn't want them scheming together.
But they already understood they had to find a way through the barrier
surrounding the Bone Palace, and in order to do that, Phos had to be
distracted.

For a while he drifted. He couldn't tell if it was day or night—or at
least, what counted as day or night in a realm of perpetual darkness—and
he kept dozing off only to then jolt awake. This happened several times
until he fell into a state of numb existence, neither asleep nor awake,
barely clinging to lucidity.

It was in this state he heard a voice.

Can you hear me?

His eyelashes fluttered. *Hear you.*

A faint sigh, creaking and alive, the groaning of wood in a storm.

Join with me.

Why?

Do you have another option?

A deep, slow breath filled his lungs. *No.*

Images swept past, quick glimpses like the projection of a shadow
carousel lamp, spinning around and around. Looming white towers, a
cloaked figure prostrating, floating glyphs in the air, a crowded stepwell,
a vast and empty cosmos.

There was nothing, once, and also everything. Shaped not by hands
but by intention and desire. Just as rain falls and stars fall and light falls

across everything in its path—light breeding shadow, life encouraging death. All of it was sweet and all of it was possible.

Something brushed up against his mind and he flinched away.

You deny it now? came that soft whisper. *You cannot keep denying.*

He was in the belly of some unfathomable beast. This palace of bones was his prison and his god.

Ostium. A fifth realm, fashioned by a fifth, nameless god. A world where Conjuration had been born, had been a currency, had been wielded by those who had suffered when their realm crumbled—people who had tried to escape into the unmapped universe only to become ensnared in celestial matter. Julian tried to imagine it: their veins gradually running black, the raw, unfiltered energy of the Cosmic Scale claiming their bodies and their minds. Giving them powers remarkable and horrific.

Azideh had been one of them. Was one of them.

And he...

You carry the faint mark of our world, the echoing bones murmured. *You carry the gift of making and knowing. You must use it.*

Nothing to use it on, he thought blearily, still hovering on the edge of sleep. He was so tired. *Only beasts.*

But there had been a moment in his mother's apartment. A scarlet demon crouched above him, her thoughts and emotions flaying open under his suggestion. A demon who had once been human.

I am here. Through me, all is possible.

Azideh's power was to gain control over all minds. If he shared the ability...

"*No,*" he snarled, surging back awake. "I won't—"

The door's lock turned with a loud scrape before it swung open. "Talking to yourself, are you?"

Julian bolted upright. Framed in the doorway was Phos, wearing the face of Rian Cyr.

Boy or god, whenever Julian laid eyes on him all he could think of was a spear sinking into Paris's chest. That very spear was slung across the boy's back, glowing steadily over his shoulder.

A wave of heat passed through him, a foreign rage that made him bare his teeth. He could still smell Paris's blood, see the surprise in his partner's eyes before they'd dimmed forever.

He would never see Paris again. Maybe never see his mother again.

Rian—no, Phos—raised a pale eyebrow. "That's a fearsome expression you're wearing. Will you give me trouble today?"

He recalled the stinging warmth of Phos's blade at his neck and decided it didn't pose enough of a deterrent. But then Julian looked past Phos to the figure lurking behind him. Nikolas's eyes were shining gold, his face slack, beyond reach. Not even Taesia had been able to get through to him.

Julian would have happily avenged Paris's death on the boy before him if it weren't for the fact that Rian was Nikolas's brother, and for all he knew, an innocent party to his god's scheming. They needed a way to shed Phos's possession from them both.

Julian gritted his teeth and rose to stand. His hands were bound, his arms sore.

"Good boy," Phos murmured.

There was no point in running or hiding. No point in lashing out where there was nowhere to go. All he could do was follow Phos through the corridors of the palace. All around him was that unnerving awareness within the walls, the ceiling, the floor they trod. His bones itched at its unwavering attention.

I am not yours, he thought. *I am a man, my name is Julian, I live in Nexus, I am . . .*

He didn't bother finishing.

He was brought back to the throne room. Immediately he sensed a change, a sourness in the air that raised the fine hairs along the nape of his neck.

Taesia was kneeling on the carpet runner. But she didn't look in his direction; all her attention was on a young man who was also kneeling before the throne.

Julian vaguely remembered him from Godsnight. He had typical Vaegan features of light brown skin and dark, curling hair. Like Taesia, he was wearing lightsbane.

The young man was speaking in hushed, hurried tones with one of the surviving servants, the other man nodding as if receiving orders of some kind. When Phos walked in, they both froze.

Phos clicked his tongue and flicked his fingers. A shard of light flew from him and pierced the servant through his throat.

The young man screamed as the servant fell, lifeless eyes staring at the bone-cluttered ceiling. The other servants by the walls muffled their wails and ducked their heads. Even Taesia balked.

"So some of them *do* know of your existence." Phos pushed Julian roughly to his knees by Taesia and ascended the dais. He slipped off the Sunbringer Spear and leaned it against the side of the throne before sprawling into the seat. "Which means they'll remain loyal. Perhaps I should weed them out."

The young man glared at him, face shining with tears. "Do not hurt them."

Phos crossed his legs. "Are you giving *me* an order, Your Highness?"

Julian frowned. *Your Highness?* He examined the young man again. There was a subtle familiarity in his features, but other than Godsnight, he couldn't recall where he might have seen them before. His eyes bothered Julian the most—blue, bright, and brimming with loathing.

Where had he seen those eyes?

"These are my people," the young man rasped. "Not yours."

Phos lazily lifted his hand again. Multiple shards darted from his fingers and formed a perilous ring around the young man's neck, who only continued to face the god stubbornly.

"Ah, right." Phos wiggled his fingers, and the hazardous collar formed around Nikolas's neck instead. Though Nikolas was unfazed, the young man tensed. "I forgot about your lack of self-preservation."

"Fin," Taesia snapped. "Shut the fuck up."

Julian turned to her. She was more rumpled than she'd been the last time they'd seen each other, her hair messy and unwashed, her clothes disordered. Part of her sleeve had been burned away, revealing a large bruise like the ones twinging across his jaw.

His vision narrowed and his next breath scraped against his throat. It was only Taesia's steady dark eyes on his that held him in place.

"Are you all right?" she whispered.

He swallowed; he should have been the one to ask. All he could do was nod, wishing he could tell her about the voice in the walls, ask what he was supposed to do after catching the interest of a god.

Then again, he only had to look to Rian Cyr for the answer.

Taesia's gaze flickered past him. Following it, he spotted her strange black sword hanging haphazardly off the wall sconces, yet another decoration of bone within the already skeletal room. He'd expected Phos to lock it away somewhere, but judging by Taesia's grimace, it was being used as a trophy. Even if she were to grab it, she was shackled with lightsbane. It would be near useless.

"Enough theatrics," Taesia said. "Why did you bring us here this time? You need company while you take your tea?"

"I doubt you'd be a charming meal companion," Phos demurred. He snapped his fingers at the servants. "Position them the way I told you to."

A middle-aged man approached Julian, sweating and trembling under Phos's scrutiny. Julian's muscles strained against the urge to shake him off, but he glanced at the lifeless body and reluctantly allowed the man-handling, the servant whispering apologies the whole time.

He was brought to the center of the room, Taesia to his left nearest the throne, Fin at his front, and Nikolas positioned behind him. Once they were in place, Phos stood and walked around the dais, dragging something from behind it. The sour scent in the air grew stronger.

"Now, originally I was hoping for all the heirs," Phos said. "But no matter. I have workarounds."

Phos dumped what he was dragging to Julian's right, making his nostrils flare at the smell of decay.

"Father!"

Julian looked from Fin's stupefied face to that of the corpse. Ferdinand Accardi, the Holy King of Vaega. Their infamously heirless monarch.

Taesia noticed Julian's bewilderment. "Ferdinand was never going to choose an heir from one of the Houses. He wanted them gone."

"I didn't know," Fin breathed, his red-rimmed eyes fixed on his father's body. "He said—"

"It doesn't fucking matter what he said!" Taesia yelled. "He was a *liar*, and he raised you to be the same! You could have told any of us at any time. You could have told *Nik*—"

"I'm not in the mood for mortal politics," Phos said as he kicked Ferdinand's corpse over. "Be silent."

"Eat shit and die," Taesia countered. "What are you doing with us? Are you making another Conjuration circle?"

Julian noted their positioning and cursed silently. He was in the middle, like the Bone Palace had been—like Ostium had been.

"Something of the sort." Phos strode closer to Julian, though maintained a prudent distance. "We stand in a monument known throughout your realm. A palace fit for royal blood. The eye of the great portal city of Nexus, where doorways had been constructed between the realms."

Phos gave Julian a knowing look. Julian did his best to meet it even as that itch burrowed into him again, that eyeless gaze once more affixed to him.

"But this palace has always been a tomb," Phos went on, walking to the nearest wall and putting his hand against it. He took a deep breath and leaned his forehead against the marble. "Where Deia hid the last remains of Orsus."

Orsus. The name made Julian's head spin, his heart kicking into a new frantic rhythm.

"Orsus," Taesia repeated. "The fifth god. The one who made Ostium."

"Yes." Phos opened his eyes. "They were the one who siphoned quintessence from the cosmos, arranging it into the Cosmic Scale. Orsus and Ostium were at the Scale's very heart, steadily feeding quintessence to the realms."

Those hazy images assaulted Julian again, of glyphs being drawn in the air and beings of another realm ascending a stepwell.

"The portals were made by people from Ostium," Julian muttered. "And when their realm was destroyed, the portals were no longer fueled by its energy. Its . . . quintessence."

"Yes."

"Then the Sealing didn't happen because the gods made barriers," Taesia said. "It happened because of Ostium's destruction."

Phos said nothing at first. He walked back to the throne and picked up the Sunbringer Spear, resting its weight against his shoulder. The golden barrier surrounding the palace drenched the throne room in an imitation of midmorning light.

"All of the Cosmic Scale's energy was filtered through Ostium. Orsus had complete control. If we desired to make more worlds, we were stopped by their meddling. We grew tired of it. Or rather, I grew tired of it.

"Thana wanted more power, but she wouldn't listen to me. She's always been the coldest of us. Nyx . . ." He paused, face hardening, before going on. "Only Deia was receptive to my plan. Together we turned on Orsus. Eventually Thana and Nyx followed. In the resulting battle, Ostium was broken."

He faced them again. "There was not much left of Orsus in the aftermath, but Deia claimed what she could and fled back to her own realm just before the barriers snapped into place." A grin stretched across his face, slow and inhuman. "In her haste, she left a piece behind. I consumed it."

Taesia inhaled sharply. Fin, who'd been listening in confusion, swayed on his knees. Julian swallowed, the back of his throat tasting of copper.

"With this bit of Orsus inside me, I have some control over quintessence." Phos glanced at the bone-strewn ceiling. "Which allowed me to claim his remains. How lucky, too, that I've been able to collect an actual being from Ostium."

Julian scowled. "I'm from Vitae."

"Mm, your blood says differently." Phos planted the butt of the spear on the floor and regarded him. "With you both to amplify this power, I can break open the barriers between Noctus and Solara. Noctus will be flooded with my light." He laughed softly. "Orsus did not want us to create more worlds, so what other choice do I have than to redesign the worlds that already exist?"

With that, he lifted the spear and nicked the side of Julian's neck. Taesia gave a hoarse shout, but Julian only shut his eyes and fought not to flinch. Liquid warmth trickled down his neck toward his collarbone.

"Blood from Ostium, Vitae, Solara, and Noctus." Phos walked around the circle, nicking each of them in turn. "And the essence of death for Mortri." He gave Ferdinand's corpse another kick as he passed. Nikolas was the only one who remained standing, blood trailing down his throat as he stared ahead.

Instantly Julian sensed a change in pressure. His ears throbbed with it, his shoulders hunching in discomfort. His surroundings seemed to shudder and close in.

"That's it," Phos whispered, too close for Julian's comfort. "Open yourself up to their power. The more quintessence you absorb, the better the offering you'll make."

But the power around him shook in anger, in resentment, in sorrow. He gasped and doubled over, Taesia calling his name distantly as if they were separated by an entire universe.

There were only the bones, the last remnants of a world devoured by sharp teeth and sharper cunning.

You carry the gift of making and knowing.

No.

I am a man, my name is . . . I live in . . .

My name is . . .

Azideh.

I am here. Through me, all is possible.

Green eyes, black veins, the thundering thoughts of a beast turned rampant. The tangle of a human's mind—locks and traps, seeds planted too deep to ever take root, a man drowning under endless light, skin-close and pain-distant and breathing only because it was necessary—

Julian gasped again. *Nik.*

This time he didn't imagine the floor shaking under him. Someone was yelling—was it him? He was too far removed, too sunken into animal heat and a twisting maze of fear and longing, the sweet blood smell around him that turned into a cavernous hunger.

Fingers dug into his hair and wrenched his head up. The sharp pain along his skull brought him back to awareness long enough to see Rian's face twisted in bewilderment.

"What are you doing?" Phos demanded.

"*Nik!*"

Julian tried to turn his head, wincing when it made Phos's grip tighten. Nikolas reeled in his peripheral vision, clutching his head with a groan.

Both Taesia and Fin struggled to get to their feet. "Nik!" Taesia cried again.

Nikolas dropped his hands, staring at her like a person whose fever had just broken. "Tae...?"

Phos *tsk*ed as he shook Julian. "Focus on the quintessence. Forget him."

If Julian let go of this tentative connection, Nikolas's mind would be lost again. His lungs constricted with the need for air. The copper taste in his throat grew stronger.

Stay awake, he tried to say, shaping the words without sound. *Nik. Stay—*

Ignore him and accept what I am giving you, whispered the bones. *Accept it all. You must use it where I cannot.*

I won't.

You must. You must destroy Phos.

He wanted to. He longed to. But he wouldn't only be destroying Phos—he'd be destroying Rian Cyr.

I won't.

You—

I WON'T.

The power flooded out of him all at once, leaving him boneless and weak. Phos let go of him and Julian fell forward, coughing against the floor. He coughed until tears gathered in his eyes, until blood splattered against marble. He felt as if his body had been peeled open, his insides scraped raw.

A penalty for disobeying. But at least the bones were quiet now.

He opened watery eyes. Nikolas had fallen to his knees, hands covering his face. Taesia and Fin watched him warily. Their blood had already clotted, the uneasy magic of the circle dissipating.

Phos stepped behind Nikolas and laid a hand on his shoulder. Nikolas's hands fell and revealed a face that was blank once more, with eyes that burned gold.

"A solid attempt," Phos said with a glance at Julian. "I didn't account for your other . . . influence. No matter. I'll see that it doesn't happen next time."

There won't be a next time, Julian wanted to say, though his blood-flecked lips didn't move.

He would not accept Orsus's power no matter how much it cost him. He wouldn't give either god the satisfaction, nor feed the beast that slept inside him.

I am not yours, he thought again, and somewhere deep in the palace came a faint rumble of displeasure.

VI

"—aesia."

Her sister's voice rang through the darkness. Taesia hadn't wanted to fall asleep—had restlessly paced the room Phos had thrown her into after the failed Conjuration attempt—but exhaustion and discomfort had finally forced her onto the bed. And now she was here, in nothingness, being led around by ghostly voices.

"Tae? Tae!"

"I'm here," she breathed. She had no body, no control. All she could see were the faint tendrils of color at the edges of the dreamscape, the outer fringes of that universe where Brailee could travel. But Taesia was not a dream walker, and she was at its mercy.

"Bee!" she yelled into the swirling dark. "I'm here!"

"Taesia! Hold on!"

She needed answers, she needed *help*. In all her furious plotting she still didn't know how to evade Phos or get Nikolas out of his control. There had been a moment, one miraculous moment when Nikolas had looked at her and *seen* her.

How could they do it again?

"Please," Taesia whispered.

The colors stretched and bled into each other until they blended into the black all around her. There was a tingling in her fingertips—she was in her own body, wearing the clothes she'd worn at Godsnight—as purling, vaporous clouds stirred below her knees.

A hand fell upon her shoulder. Slowly she looked down at the long, knobby fingers, the black talons gently pricking her.

We have much to discuss, came a low, velvet voice.

Taesia spun around. She was no longer in the darkness, the edges of the universe of color. She stood now within a grand hall, the floor and walls made of gleaming silver marble, sculpted into embellishments and columns opulent enough to rival the Bone Palace. Before her rose a wide flight of stairs. A dark figure waited for her on the landing above.

Swallowing, she looked around. The rest of the hall was shrouded by those moving clouds. The only way was forward.

She ascended the stairs. Her footfalls made no sound; instead, there was a melodious chiming like a distant echo. Though the hall was cold she could barely sense it, letting it only pass through her like water sliding off skin.

Looming over her was a massive archway wreathed in carvings, open to a darkly purple expanse where more of those clouds were swirling, limned in silver. The light came from the eight moons in the sky, hanging in a perfect vertical line, in phases ranging from waning crescent to full. Far overhead was the glimmer of stars.

"THERE ARE NOT MANY WHO HAVE SEEN THIS PLACE," came Nyx's dulcet voice beside her.

"Wh…why am I here, then? Where *is* here?"

He remained quiet until she finally turned to him. The god was unnervingly tall, leaning over her like he wanted to merge her into his shadow, his cosmos eyes fixed unblinking on hers. Black hair hung in a silken, silver-speckled wave over his shoulders under his crown of moons and stars. The light of the moons reflected on pale marble turned his skin to alabaster.

"A PLACE THAT IS AND ISN'T," he answered. "WAS AND WILL BE. IT IS ME. IT IS YOU. IT IS SACRED."

"Stop talking in flowery nonsense. Is this a dreamscape?"

His pale mouth quirked ever so slightly. "IF THAT IS WHAT BRINGS YOU THE MOST COMFORT."

Nothing about this scenario brought her comfort. She had only seen Nyx once before in a vision in Nexus, when he had called her his general, claiming he had use for her. She supposed that was why he'd brought her here, away from Brailee.

Fuck. Brailee. She had been so close to reaching her sister, to hearing any scrap of news of Dante and her family and the state of Nexus. To warning them about what Phos was planning.

Thinking of Brailee almost invoked her sister's voice, a shapeless word of panic and desperation. Taesia turned around, but she and Nyx were the only ones here.

"YOU WENT AGAINST MY WISHES AT GODSNIGHT." She couldn't detect anger in his words, but nonetheless they made her skin prickle. "I TOLD YOU TO KILL THE BOY, AND PHOS WITH HIM. YOU USED MY POWER IN OTHER WAYS."

"The *boy* is named Rian Cyr." Taesia tried to focus on the moons, squinting at their luminosity. "And no matter what you say, I'm not going to kill him."

A moment of silence. She wasn't sure if her body in this dreamscape was real or not, but the way her heart thumped was too convincing to suspect anything else.

"THE BOY," Nyx sighed at last, "IS GONE. WHATEVER REGARD YOU HOLD FOR HIM IS POINTLESS, NOW."

"What do you mean?"

"PHOS'S HOLD ON HIM IS TOO ABSOLUTE. THE LONGER IT STAYS THAT WAY, THE MORE THE BOY'S MIND WILL DECAY, IF IT HAS NOT ALREADY. HE IS GONE."

She crossed her arms, as if that would keep the riot of emotions storming through her from spilling out. "You don't know that for sure."

Nyx walked to the archway, surveying that cloudy, amethyst gloaming. His broad shoulders were draped in a leather cowl that flared into sharp points, his robe a deep blue. From the back he could almost pass for human despite his size.

"SENTIMENTALITY," the god murmured. "A TRAIT THAT, AS I UNDERSTAND IT, CAN BE FOUND IN ALL BEINGS OF ALL REALMS. I WONDER HOW THAT CAME TO BE. IT HAS BEEN SUCH A LONG TIME SINCE I..." He looked down at one of his clawlike hands, curling and unfurling it. "NO. THERE IS NO USE FOR IT. NOT THEN, AND NOT NOW."

He turned back toward her, and any semblance of humanity was wiped away as she again met those unfathomable eyes.

"IF PHOS IS NOT KILLED, NOCTUS WILL BE DESTROYED," the god intoned. "LIGHT WILL SEAR THROUGH FLESH AND STONE AND NIGHT. IT WILL NOT STOP THERE. DEIA'S TERRITORY WILL BE NEXT, AND ALL OTHERS YOU HOLD SUCH SENTIMENTALITY TOWARD WILL BE REDUCED TO ASH."

Taesia shut her eyes, thinking of Brailee and her parents. Dante. Risha and Angelica, wherever they were.

"IT IS ONE LIFE TO SAVE MILLIONS," Nyx whispered. The small beads of pearl and silver on his robe clinked gently as he moved. "ALL YOU HAVE TO DO IS ACCEPT MY POWER. BE MY GENERAL." He stroked the tip of one talon down her cheek. "YOU ARE MY BLOOD. THERE IS NO OTHER THAT CAN DO THIS."

If I claim you, we will be linked, he had told her at Godsnight. If she hadn't accepted his power then, would he have been able to pull her here, to lay this ultimatum at her feet? Yet she couldn't find it in herself to regret the decision, not when it had stopped him from manipulating Brailee.

But that didn't mean she'd let him take control of her either. They may be linked, but she knew—in her gut, her bones, whatever starstuff swam in her marrow—that if she let him in again, the connection would become irrevocable.

And Taesia Lastrider had never wanted to belong to anyone or anything.

"When you say accept your power," she said slowly, "what does that mean? What do you intend to do?"

"WHAT I DO DOES NOT CONCERN YOU."

"It's my body, so yeah, it kind of does. Are you just planning to stab him through the heart while he's not looking? Suffocate him with shadows?"

Though Nyx's face barely showed emotion, this earned her a tiny twitch of one smooth, dark eyebrow.

"PHOS AND I HAVE A LONG HISTORY OF DUELING," Nyx said eventually. "I KNOW HIS WEAKNESSES, HIS STRENGTHS."

"Mind sharing, then?"

"HE IS PROUD. OVERCONFIDENT. PRONE TO UNDERESTIMATING OTHERS. IF HE IS GIVEN A REASON TO PREEN, HE DROPS HIS GUARD. HE ATTACKS WILDLY, CONTINUOUSLY, AND DOES NOT COMPENSATE WITH A STRONG DEFENSE. HE IS SLOW TO TIRE, BUT QUICK TO DISTRACT."

Taesia committed each word to memory. "So let's say someone doesn't have access to their powers. How would they go up against him?"

"MY POWER WILL BE ENOUGH TO OVERCOME SUCH AN OBSTACLE."

It had been worth a shot. Taesia regarded the new moon hanging in the sky like a dark disc. The stars above like watching eyes.

Her hands remembered the shape and weight of bone.

"You share something in common with him," she said. "You're both prone to underestimating others."

Nyx's cosmos eyes narrowed a fraction even as the corners of his lips ticked upward.

"YOU WILL COME TO SEE, IN TIME, THAT I AM RIGHT," Nyx promised as clouds obscured her vision. "I WILL BE WAITING, MY GENERAL."

When Phos fetched her again, she was foggy and exhausted from lack of true sleep, a residue of dread sitting in her chest. If her mother knew how she'd spoken to their god...

"Is this amusing to you?" Phos said. They were walking to the throne room, Nikolas once more steering her down the wide halls. After that too-fleeting moment of recognition, his placidity was even more heartbreaking.

Taesia's soft laugh died on her lips. "I find it amusing that you need multiple attempts to get this right. Haven't you been scheming for a thousand years?"

Phos regarded her coolly. "There are secrets buried in the Cosmic Scale that even I do not comprehend. I am willing to spill your blood as many times as possible to learn them."

Dramatic bastard.

They collected Julian along the way. He was withdrawn, his face wan. Whatever he had done last time had taken a toll on him, though Taesia couldn't begin to fathom what exactly had happened.

Nikolas had claimed Julian was the fifth heir. Phos said he was from Ostium. She herself had seen Julian destroy demons with no other weapon than what lay dormant within him.

"Are you all right?" Taesia whispered.

He turned dull eyes toward her, then Nikolas.

"Can you...?"

His thick eyebrows furrowed. "I don't know. I—"

"Enough," Phos snapped. They fell silent.

Fin sat chained and alone in the middle of the hall, watched by a ring of helpless servants. Judging from his expression, he'd likely ordered them not to come near, lest they also end up with a hole in their throats.

Taesia found herself back in her previous position by the throne's dais. Behind it, Starfell hung carelessly on the sconces. She sat back on her heels and tried to ignore the pain in her wrists and the trembling of her arms. The shackles on her wrists weighed heavy, intensely cold, harboring all her magic and leaving her empty.

Julian knelt in the middle of their makeshift circle, glaring at the floor as if it were to blame for everything.

"I won't tolerate your little demon tricks this time," Phos warned Julian, pointing the Sunbringer Spear at his chest. "Do you understand?"

When Julian didn't answer, a blazing white spike materialized before Taesia. She flinched back, unnerved by its heat. She could barely make out the flash of rage on Julian's face.

"The only reason I'm keeping her alive is in the hope of Nyx possessing her," Phos said. "But I don't *need* her alive. Do you understand?"

Julian gave a shallow nod.

"Good." Phos lifted the spear and made a fresh cut on Julian's neck, blood seeping into his already stained collar. He strode to Fin next and also nicked him open. Fin curled his hands into fists under his shackles.

Phos came to her last, stepping around the threatening spike of light that made sweat bead on her forehead. "I know that Nyx must be in communication with you," he murmured as the warm steel of the spear's blade touched her skin. "He wants a duel, doesn't he? You may as well let him have it."

Blood tickled her throat. "He chose my sister, remember?"

"For that particular battle. But he has multiple pawns to play." He glanced at Nikolas. "As do I."

Her anger soared, but she forcibly grounded it.

If he is given a reason to preen, he drops his guard.

"He must not be as smart as you, then," Taesia said. "This is his realm, after all. He could simply possess me with force if he wanted to."

Phos huffed and stared at the windows. "He is weaker, and foolish. Always has been. He was never one for plotting or deceit. Ironic, since he so loves to skulk."

Taesia dared a peek over her shoulder. Starfell's hilt jutted out behind the throne. Twenty, maybe twenty-five feet away.

Julian caught her eye and shook his head. *Don't*, he mouthed.

The faintest whisper in her mind, like the caress of wind against her face. *My power is here for the taking, my blood. Let me in, and I shall destroy him.*

Taesia exhaled shakily. The jagged spear of light hovered before her. She flexed the muscles in her legs.

"That is why my first target is Noctus," Phos went on. "It will be the easiest realm to conquer. Once my ritual is complete, he will have no choice but to come out and face me." She spied the edge of his grin. "For the last time."

Not if I end you here, whispered the velvet voice. *Now.*

Even with the lightsbane, her awareness of the shadows around her expanded. It was a cold sip of water on a particularly hot day, a relief both shocking and pleasant. She shuddered with the promise of those shadows swirling around her, doing her bidding.

That's it. Let me in.

Fin was watching her with confusion. She looked to Nikolas, gathered her resolve, and spared Julian a single nod of warning.

She sprang to her feet and sprinted to the back wall. Her head swam and she nearly tripped over the dais, her legs wobbly after days of disuse.

What are you doing? Nyx hissed.

Phos spun around. "You—!"

Taesia grabbed hold of Starfell and yanked it down. Despite the lightsbane, as soon as the sword was in her hands its power thrummed all around her, raising goosebumps on her body. An astralam's bones returned to the realm from which they'd been born.

She gasped like it was her first breath. Beyond the palace, beyond the barrier, beyond the city were thousands upon thousands of burning stars—a smaller universe nestled within a larger one, a creation of velvet darkness. Like the latest hour of night, smooth and crisp, quiet and humming, when everything and nothing existed.

I don't need you, Nyx.

Taesia lifted her arms and the velvet darkness worked through her, pouring into the astralam bones and focusing on a point between her wrists.

Phos's blazing spear of light shot straight at her, seeking to pierce her heart.

The place where her shackles connected was swallowed by a small, swirling vortex. It burned a chill into her hands, but she didn't dare let go of Starfell or let her concentration falter. She raised her arms higher just as the spear of light reached her.

It dove straight into the vortex and disappeared.

Come back, she pleaded, arms shaking. *Turn around.*

Phos advanced. Through heavy breaths, Taesia grinned at him.

"Wanna see a new trick?"

The spear of light shot back out of the vortex and pummeled Phos in the chest. He went flying across the throne room, wings rapidly unfurling before he crashed through the wall into the hall outside.

The vortex died. Her wrists were still bound, but now the shackles were broken in the middle, allowing her to move her arms freely. Nikolas staggered, and she ran to him.

"Julian, can you free him?" she yelled over the sudden rumbling of the walls and the shouting of the servants.

"I'm . . . trying," Julian said through gritted teeth. He was standing in the middle of the throne room, blood dripping from his nose. Fin scrambled to his feet as well, staring at the hole Phos had made.

Taesia grabbed Nikolas's shoulder and shook him. "Nik, I'm here! *Nik!*"

His eyes fluttered open and focused on her. They had returned to a pale shade, hazy but unmistakably his. "Tae . . ."

She choked down a sob and pulled him toward one of the windows. "Come on, we have to hurry."

Phos climbed back through the hole wearing a murderous expression. Blood trickled from his hairline, wings bracketing his body, clothes covered in mortar dust.

"Clever," he muttered as his eyes lit up gold and his voice deepened. "YOU ALL THINK YOU'RE VERY CLEVER, DON'T YOU?"

Julian faced him. His pupils were thin and vertical, his normally hazel irises washed acid green, black veins spreading across his body. Beyond the window, Taesia saw the golden wall flicker. Behind her, Nikolas shuddered.

"Julian!" Taesia cried. "Concentrate on Nik!"

His upper lip curled, revealing sharpened canines. But he did as she asked, moving toward them while Phos stalked closer.

"THERE IS NO ESCAPING THIS," Phos said. "ONLY—"

Fin rammed into his side, sending the both of them sprawling.

"*Go!*" Fin shouted.

Taesia didn't waste the opportunity. She smashed Starfell's pommel into the window, colorful glass spraying outward. Grabbing Nikolas's arm and trusting Julian to follow, she jumped.

The air was biting, the free fall making her stomach rise. She couldn't even scream, couldn't gather the shadows to break her fall, couldn't—

Light erupted overhead and she was soaring across the courtyard. She clutched onto Nikolas and gaped at him, at his *wings*, beating steadily like a heartbeat as he carried her down to the flickering wall.

But his breaths were strained and his shirt soaked with sweat. They landed haphazardly on the pitted cobblestone, Taesia scraping a knee.

"Tae," he gasped. "I can't. Fin—"

"Forget him," she snarled. "He deserves this!"

Julian landed in a crouch beside them, hard enough to crack the cobblestone. He was still wreathed in that unknown power, an uncanny resonance that made Taesia's teeth ache.

Above them, Phos was descending.

Taesia took Nikolas's arm. "We have to go. We'll come back and—"

"Taesia."

She stopped at the sound of her name. Remembered the way he used to sigh it, whisper it, evoke it like a spell. His eyes met hers and they were his own, his mind was his own, and she had to keep him like this, protect him no matter—

"I can't," he said again.

VII

He was Nikolas Cyr. A Lumin, an heir, a descendant of a god who wished them all dead.

He was also perhaps a coward.

Or simply unwise.

But the entity in his brain was painful and sharp, teeth gnawing at his memories, his reasoning, his very existence. He could remember the girl in front of him with her large, dark eyes and dreadful power, and he could remember the man behind her as something to be safeguarded yet feared.

And he remembered the young man up in the palace, a prisoner, always a prisoner, another coward yearning to make up for his mistakes.

But his wings—

He had *wings*. He could fly. And that was enough to make the withered vine of joy reach upward, out through his chest and to his shoulder blades, extending in beautiful arcs of feathered light.

The charm on his wrist trembled as he raised a hand and cradled Taesia's face. A tear fell from her wide eyes, reflecting the flickering light of his wings, the shielding wall beside them.

"Nik," she whispered.

He put a hand on Julian's shoulder, watched the unearthly color drain from his eyes and leave him disoriented.

"Protect her," Nikolas ordered.

Julian didn't get a chance to reply. Nikolas pushed them right as the wall stuttered again, their bodies stumbling out of the Bone Palace's courtyard and into the unknown.

It was all he had the strength for. Once they were gone, he sank to his knees and a blinding white light enveloped his mind, and he could have been screaming, or tearing at his own skin, or begging for the light to kill him—

And then there was blessed nothing.

He waited on his knees for Phos. His god looked from the barrier to him. He waited for an order.

A hand slapped him. He went down. Stayed there. Pain like a distant star.

"THIS IS NOT OVER," Phos promised.

He said nothing. Hadn't been told to say anything.

So he stayed on the ground, smelling blood and dirt, body reeling in the memory of what it was like to soar.

VIII

Time didn't mean much in a place like Mortri, where hours and minutes and seconds stretched and bent and folded in on themselves. Instead Risha measured the fall of her footsteps, the drag of her breaths, and the pinching of her stomach.

"My mother didn't want me reading Mortrian myths when I was a child," Jas said as they walked. They had made their way through the field of marigolds and onto a broader field surrounded by tall, naked trees, their spindly branches like pointing fingers. "Of course, that made me want to read them more. I learned about how adventurers snuck into Mortri and how the kings' Sentinels would find them. Torture them. Break apart their souls."

"That's putting it mildly." Risha had done her own reading of the perversions of the four kings and their long history of malice.

The ground squelched beneath her boots. It had the consistency of churned mud, but the green fog of the sky made it difficult to make out its color.

Something wet and cold hit the crown of her head. Above her, the branch of a tree was steadily dripping dark liquid. Another drop hit her forehead and rolled down the side of her nose.

She smelled it, then—blood. Thick and metallic and seemingly everywhere.

The trees around them were bleeding. It seeped through the ground and welled out between the bark, trickling over branches and staining roots.

She stepped away from the tree with a shudder. Jas moved closer to her side.

Then the whispers started.

"—*wanted it so badly, needed it*—"

"—*help them, please*—"

"—*it hurts it hurts it hurts IT HURTS*—"

Turn around.

Risha pressed the heels of her hands against her forehead and shut her eyes. The faint impression of Jas's fingertips alighted on her arm.

"Risha? What's happening?"

The steady *drip* of blood around them, the faint whistle of the wind, the distant lowing of some inhuman thing—all were magnified along with the sound of her own breaths, the creaking of the branches.

"—*would do anything for her to love me*—"

"—*didn't know it was a trap*—"

"—*what would even happen if I*—"

Turn around.

"Jas," she said so softly he had to lean in closer, his presence a chill against her body. "Don't turn around."

"What? Wh—"

He went rigid, eyes fixed on nothing. Not the same blankness as when he'd been called by the river, but something nearer to fear.

"I hear them," he murmured. "They . . . are they the dead?" He looked at the bleeding trees with dawning horror.

There were many creatures in Mortri, not all of which could be documented by Vitaeans. Risha knew the names of several—murmurs, who scented fear; bone snatchers, who were largely harmless unless you stole from their horde.

And there were those who could mimic or enthrall.

Turn around.

Look.

It wasn't a voice, but more a thought that bloomed frantic and vivid in her mind. She shook against the urge to follow through with it.

"What do we do?" Jas whispered.

Risha fumbled for his hand and held it as tight as she could. "Just keep walking."

The mud and blood oozed around her footfalls as they steadily made their way through the trees. Risha was already nauseated from hunger, her head pounding with a headache and encroaching dizziness, but she dare not let herself get distracted by her annoyingly human body. The presence she'd felt earlier seemed to loom right behind them, intangible yet taking up so much space it became harder to breathe.

"—can't do it, I just can't do it—"

"—IT HURTS IT HURTS IT HURTS—"

"—please, please, please, please—"

Turn around.

The thought raged bigger and brighter. Risha stumbled, but Jas pulled her onward, neither one of them even daring to look at each other.

The end of the tree line was in sight. They sped up, not quite running in case the thing behind them sought to give chase.

Turn around.

There's something you need to see.

You need to know what it is.

The curiosity will kill you if you don't.

You'll die weeping and in agony from not knowing.

Turn around.

Risha whimpered, her shirt soaked in sweat, the thoughts so loud her skull would surely crack open.

As soon as they crossed the boundary of the bleeding trees, the whispers died. Risha gasped in a breath before bending over and retching.

Jas cursed in Parithvian and did his best to rub her back. "Are you all right? Is that ... *thing* gone?"

Risha coughed and spat on the ground. Her throat stung and her mouth tasted foul, but the silence was a balm. "I think it's confined to the trees, or whatever spirits are trapped there."

"Then let's get away from it."

Her head spun when she straightened. They needed to find water soon.

"Stay with me," Jas whispered. They had reached a plain covered with dry, brittle grass, and the landscape dipped and fell with hillocks studded with stone doors. Barrows. Far in the distance Risha spotted the city carved into the mountains. "Tell me more about Leshya."

Risha could still smell blood. She tried wiping a sleeve over her face to clean it without much success. "Her time in Mortri, you mean?"

"Yes."

She took a breath to collect herself. "When the kings tried to invade Vitae, she held them at the threshold. She pushed them back into their own realm and fought them there."

Jas whistled. "How could she fend off four undead kings and their Sentinels on her own?"

"She wasn't alone. Not really."

As much as she honored her ancestors, many of them had chosen methods Risha could not understand or condone. She had a feeling it was why her father had always been so adamant about following the rules, to not let himself or his children fall back on immoral practices.

"I thought she was the only necromancer at the time?" Jas asked.

"Other than her children, yes, though they were much too young to fight. But she made a special weapon for herself."

They passed a barrow and Risha slowed. Beyond it was a building long gone to ruin. While it wasn't what she would consider large, it maintained an air of dignity in the rusticated stone walls and the flourishing pediment above. It looked like a mausoleum Risha would have found in the Nexus necropolis.

Jas took in the mausoleum's crumbling walls and partially caved-in roof. "You mentioned her weapon before, but I don't think I know about it. Obviously she wasn't using her finger bones then."

"No. This weapon she created solely to fight the kings. It was a pair of chain scythes. The blades were made of fused bone, from people and beasts alike. She called it Samhara."

A weapon built for destruction and control. A weapon that could not be used unless the wielder harbored knowledge of two things: necromancy and dance.

Tandshri was an ancient form of dance from Parithvi. It was traditionally used for theater, with grand gestures and positions for the head, hands, feet, and even eyes. The elaborate movements, when strung together in certain ways, always told a story.

Under her father's insistence, Risha had learned a version that focused more on the athleticism of her body rather than performance. How to better squat and extend her arms, how to use her core to turn and maintain balance. Her mother had argued that Risha should learn the correct way, the artful way.

"This is how Vakaras are taught the tandshri," Rath had lectured in his low voice. "It is a style developed by Leshya Vakara, who demanded on her deathbed that her children and their children's children learn it, too."

"But *why*?"

Rath's sigh had been small and soft. "I am sorry, but there are some secrets we must keep."

"I am your *wife*."

"And you are not a necromancer."

Darsha had been furious for days afterward, and Risha had felt guilty every time she practiced. But when her father met her eyes they shared a quiet, common knowledge, which buoyed her pride.

Leshya Vakara's greatest weapon was still hidden in Mortri. Only her bloodline, and those who were taught the tandshri, would be able to claim and wield it.

Risha explained this to Jas as they made their slow way through the barrows. "The tandshri's movements correlate to how Leshya used Samhara," she said. "She designed the weapon to react to those movements."

Jas shook his head in wonder. "She was truly amazing. Do you think if we find her long-lost weapon, it could help us get through Mortri?"

Risha hesitated, trying not to lick her already chapped and peeling lips. "I . . . I don't know."

For one thing, she wasn't sure if her power could fuel the weapon the way Leshya's once did. And for another . . .

"The blades act as a sort of conduit for nearby souls," Risha admitted at last. "They absorb spiritual energy, which is then unleashed against the attacker."

Jas grinned. "She really was a genius, huh?"

"What? *No.* Using the dead like that is . . ." She inhaled deeply, held the breath for a couple seconds before letting it out. "Jas, when a spirit is depleted of its energy, it dissipates. If that happens, they can't reincarnate. They can't move on, can't find peace or punishment. They simply vanish."

His face fell. "Oh."

They were passing the mausoleum, now. Embedded within an archway was a large stone door with a small chunk missing. It drew Jas's eye—or perhaps he simply didn't want to meet hers.

"If the alternative is death, then it's a viable method," he said. "Some spirits end up dissipating anyway. She used them to stop a war. I think it's justified."

"Of course you do."

Jas frowned. "Risha—"

"You and your *alternative* necromancy, your blatant disregard for the rules. You saw yourself how poorly that went during the Godsnight Gala."

He looked down, because she was right and they both knew it. Still, he countered, "Necromancy is dangerous. We both understand this. But your ancestor used a method that didn't threaten actual lives, only the souls of the departed."

"Don't the souls of the departed also deserve respect?"

"Yes, but—"

"But not to the same degree, you mean. Then should I say your life is less important than mine?"

His grayed-out eyes were now fixed on hers, stubborn and steady.

"Yes," he whispered.

Risha couldn't turn away from his face, all the lines and edges of him that had become foggy in this incorporeal form. Because he had already sacrificed himself once for her.

He reached for her hand. "Risha—"

A low, discordant cry shuddered over the ground and traveled up Risha's spine, followed by a hollow clicking. She clutched her chest, her heart suddenly pounding so hard she feared she would pass out.

Beyond the barrows where the shadows grew thicker stood the silhouette of a nightmarish figure. It was large, with four long, sharp-jointed limbs jutting out of its body, crawling over the ground as a spider would. She couldn't make out its features from this distance, but she didn't need to; the unsettling movements and echoing clicks were enough to tell her this was something to be avoided at all costs.

She grabbed Jas's wrist and pulled him toward the mausoleum. He followed without a sound, watching the creature stalk closer on those long, spindly legs.

Ignoring the tremors in her body, Risha scrabbled at the edge of the stone door. The creature's movements were disturbingly slow, like a predator who chose not to run because it savored the chase.

Mouth dry, Risha finally found the edge of the stone and pulled. The door didn't budge at first, and though Jas tried to help, his hands were only a breeze against the stone. Risha gathered herself and *heaved*. With grinding protest, the door scraped open one inch, two, digging a small trench in the ground.

The creature swung its head toward them.

Risha pulled with all her might. She stopped once the opening was large enough to squirm through, and she and Jas squeezed into the mausoleum before dragging the door closed.

She slapped a hand over her mouth and nose as her breathing quickened, as that unnerving, hollow rattling drew nearer. She knelt to peer through the hole in the door and saw bony feet right where she and Jas had been standing.

It was a being of skeleton and tissue, and tattered skin so tightly bound it had turned to leather. It rose to stand on two legs instead of four, its arms disproportionately long, its chest wide and hollow and flaring into stark ribs. The horned skull was large for its body, the rictus grin baring too-long tusks. On the creature's back rested a sword made out of the same black opal she'd seen in the caves.

It surveyed its surroundings, then stepped closer to the barrows. Its ribs made an undulating movement, the bones clacking together—the source of that eerie clicking. Another long, relentless pause, and the creature lowered itself back to all fours and scuttled over the barrows.

Her eyes stung with fear. Jas gripped her shoulder.

"What was that?" he whispered.

"I think," she said haltingly, "that was one of the kings' Sentinels."

She then surrendered to her body and collapsed to the stone below.

IX

Dante Lastrider lay down beside a demon and closed his eyes.

Brailee lay down on his other side, completely oblivious to the demon's presence. His sister claimed that another Shade's power helped amplify her own, and that his was needed if she was going to try to find Taesia again. No sooner had his eyes closed, their shadow familiars twining together, than Dante was hurtling past unconsciousness and into something deeper. Somewhere even the demon could not perceive him.

The maelstrom of colors and senses overwhelmed him. His mind was afloat in a cosmic jungle only Brailee could navigate; he was the hapless sailor who'd gotten swept out in a storm, and his little sister was the current steadily pushing him to shore.

It's all right, came Brailee's voice. *It takes some getting used to.*

He could only observe as they shuffled through the multicolored tendrils. They carried sounds and scents, the blast of a cannon and the chirping of birds, fresh rainfall and campfires and baked bread. Cloves and cold.

Brailee stopped. The tendrils around them spiraled and darkened, and Dante felt as if he were in free fall with no way to scream. There were only flashes as the dreamscape sped by—stars, black sand, an archway through which hung a line of moons in various phases.

Wait!

Brailee threw herself into the last image. But something resisted them, pushed them back. Dante saw two shadowed forms by the archway, one of them turning as if it had heard Brailee's thought—

Dante started awake with a gasp. A second later his view of the ceiling was obstructed by the demon's face appearing upside down before him.

Dante bit down a yelp. Azideh cocked his head to one side, an animal-istic gesture.

"Go *away*," Dante growled before sitting up.

Azideh smugly yanked on the thin black chain hanging between them. It made the collar around Dante's neck press into his skin. "You should have considered the need for privacy before you summoned me."

Brailee also sat up. "Are you talking to ... *him*?" Her bloodshot eyes searched the small, drafty room.

Azideh only made himself known to those he wanted to see him. Which was thankfully no one but Dante; he would have drawn no small amount of attention otherwise. The demon's skin was a deep blue, almost as dark as a Noctan's, and a crown of gnarly horns sprouted from his head amid a fall of black hair. His eyes were bright green with slitted pupils, glowing even in the daytime.

And he was constantly naked. *Constantly*.

"Don't worry about it." Dante sighed. "Do you think that was her, in the last one?"

"I don't know. Maybe." Brailee sat hunched over, biting her already abused thumbnail. "I think I'm getting closer, but it's like something is wedging a barrier between us."

Dante rose from the bed. "We'll keep trying. In the meantime, we need to get ready."

He was already packed, having shoved only the essentials into a bag. Judging by the outfits strewn around the tiny room, Brailee was having a harder time determining what to bring with her. "Functional clothes only," he reminded her. "There's going to be mud. Rain. *Bugs*."

Brailee made a face. "I know."

For a moment his mind fogged over, replaced with a wave of gray, sul-len despondency. Dante shook his head, dispelling the momentary lapse. If he wasn't careful, Brailee's emotions would take root in him and com-pletely change his mood.

A gift, of sorts, from the demon.

He went downstairs to the small kitchen. He wasn't used to this house, but he didn't need to be; he and his family had already decided he couldn't stay here, not when he was still considered guilty of murder and treason.

His parents were sitting at the small wooden table. Elena held a steam-ing mug between her hands while Cormin rested a hand on her arm.

Dante took the chair across from them, grateful when Azideh dissipated from view.

"How did the meeting go?" Dante asked.

His mother offered him her mug. He took a sip and refrained from making a face at coffee that was both burnt and watery. "Adela remains stubborn. Rath, at least, is easier to work with. He cares more about stability than public image. And right now, the city needs stability."

The remaining Houses—down to three due to the disappearance of Nikolas and the unexplained death of Waren Cyr—were trying to band together to form a united rule of Vaega as a temporary situation.

Dante could almost laugh at the irony of it all. From the start he'd been eager to get Ferdinand off the throne, to set up a parliament that served all people instead of just the wealthy. He could see now he'd been too ignorant and too hasty to enact real, lasting change. That, and he hadn't factored vengeful gods into his plans.

"Shouldn't you announce your collaboration with them?"

This time his father answered. "It might undermine Adela and Rath's current influence," Cormin said. "People are fleeing the city and panicking in the streets. We can't let anything upset them further."

Nexus was as fragile as spun sugar, and the slightest crack would make the whole structure crumble apart. He'd already heard the basilicas had been locked up to prevent people from rioting inside.

"I'm fine staying hidden," Elena said. "I just need Adela to stop arguing out every little thing." She reached over to grasp Dante's hand. For a moment the emotional channels opened between them, sending javelins of worry and despair into his chest.

Dante nearly grunted at their impact. Was this what his mother felt all the time? How could she shove all this down while continuing to get work done?

How long had she practiced hiding this for his sake?

His eyes prickled. Not wanting to make her worry even greater, he blinked hard and gave her a sympathetic smile. "Sounds like Adela."

"You'll be leaving tonight?" she asked, with no hint of what swam under the surface.

He held her hand tighter. "Are you sure you don't need me here? I can stay."

"Someone might discover you. It's too dangerous." The wrinkle between her eyebrows deepened. "And right now it's more important to find Camilla. Once you drag her back to Nexus, we can clear your name."

His father's expression turned pained. When Dante and Brailee had explained what Camilla had been doing, that Dante had been arrested for her crimes, Cormin had been loath to believe them at first. But his father had always been a sensible and honorable man, and in the end chose his children over his sister.

"Perhaps I should go with you," Cormin said. "Try to talk some sense into her."

"Have you forgotten how rarely she heeds your advice?" Elena countered.

"She rarely heeds anyone's advice," Dante said. "I'll do my best to make her feel as guilty as possible for your sake."

Cormin's faint smile was fleeting. "Are you certain she'll go to Seniza?"

"The guards at the southern gates reported seeing a woman matching her description leaving after Godsnight," Elena reminded him.

"But that doesn't necessarily mean she'll go south."

"She'll go south," Dante said. "There's a possibility something powerful is residing in Deia's Heart. Something of the god herself."

Elena tensed. "What would she need with something like that?"

I'll always put my family first, Camilla had told him, steel in her eyes and hidden meaning in her words.

"I don't know," he said. "But if she manages to create another portal, I can try to find Taesia."

His parents had been holding themselves so carefully. Their moods were fragile shifts, the vacillating temperature in the days between seasons. At Taesia's name they dropped to a cold, bleak autumn.

"Is that possible?" Elena whispered. Her touch gave off the tenderness of a new wound, the gray clouds of her despair broken by one solitary beam of hope.

"I'll do everything I can to make it possible."

His father swallowed. "You said Camilla summoned a—a demon." Elena squeezed her husband's arm. "Perhaps that'll make her easier to find."

Azideh's low, melodic voice rang through his head.

Strange, the demon murmured, *that you have told them of Shanizeh and not of me.*

Because they won't take the news that their son is infested with a demon very well.

Infested, Azideh repeated with a small laugh. *What an interesting choice of word.*

"—while you're down there," his mother was saying.

Dante blinked. "What?"

Elena gave him the piercing stare he'd been wary of since he was little, sharp with a mother's intuition. "Are you sure you're—?"

"Yes," he cut in. "You were saying something about Seniza?"

"I was telling you the less attention you bring to yourself, the better. We don't need Alma sending word back to Nexus that you've been spotted." Martín Alma was the baron of Seniza and its surrounding lands. Dante had once exchanged letters with the man over a limestone trade and found his usage of floral language off-putting.

"It's not like I'm going to loudly announce my presence," Dante said. "But I'll keep it in mind."

"Hopefully he'll be too busy anyway," Cormin added. "Considering all the noise being made about the tomb."

Dante had been about to stand, but at this he paused. "What tomb?"

"The tomb of Marcos Ricci." His mother scowled. "With all the chaos from Conjuration happening in Nexus, there have been people demanding Marcos Ricci's grave be exhumed and his body burned. Like setting fire to a dried-up husk will appease the gods."

Marcos Ricci, the brilliant yet possibly unstable man who had delved into the secrets of Conjuration and discovered the ability to summon demons. The author of illicit grimoires. Prelate Lezzaro's ancestor.

"I didn't know he was buried in Seniza," Dante said as the cogs in his mind whirred faster.

"Not for much longer. People are spooked. They want *some* sort of action." Elena clicked her tongue. "Just be sure to avoid all that."

"Of course."

When he went back upstairs, Brailee was debating between a long skirt and a pair of fleece-lined pants. Dante took the skirt and tossed it aside.

"Hey!"

"Pants are better. And there's a slight change in plans," he said. "I need you to send a message to the Vakara villa."

"Do you think she'll come?" Dante asked as he and Brailee unhitched two horses from the cart they'd hidden in to get through the southern city gates. The driver was a former House guard who retained loyalty to their family.

"I hope so," Brailee whispered, staring at the gates behind them.

The guard shook his head when Dante tried to press coins into his hand. "Don't mind me, my lord. It was enough to assist you."

"Don't be ridiculous," Dante said. He placed the money on the driver's bench. "You're out of a job now."

"The Lastriders will return," the guard proclaimed like prophecy. "And I'll be there when they do."

Dante *felt* the man's conviction. He swallowed the tightness in his throat and gripped the guard's forearm in solidarity before they turned the horses off the main road.

"I still don't understand," Brailee said after a moment. The night was settling around them, a song comprised of chirping crickets and rustling grass in the biting wind. He was glad Brailee had acquiesced on the pants. "You want to *resurrect* Marcos Ricci?"

"Sort of." Dante sensed Azideh solidifying behind him, turning man-shaped. The demon walked around the grass and looked about in curiosity. "He's the founder of Conjuration—or rather, the Conjuration we know today."

"Demons," Brailee muttered. "And . . . whatever took Taesia."

Azideh turned with a raised eyebrow. Dante was once again thrown by just how expressive the demon was, mimicking Dante's facial and vocal tics flawlessly. Almost as if he were training to better pass as human.

"Yes," Dante said. "We might not get our hands on Deia's fulcrum in Seniza, but we can get our hands on his corpse."

And get answers about the Conjuration circle that had taken the Bone Palace. He removed Angelica's sketch from his pocket, smoothing out the paper to study it in the moonlight: its double circle, its four quadrants. Was it something they could replicate? Go to wherever Taesia had gone?

Brailee straightened. "She's here."

A cloaked figure rode toward them on a black horse. Once close enough, the cloak's hood was pushed back to reveal Saya Vakara staring between them with round, disbelieving eyes.

"I, uh, heard you need a necromancer?"

Brailee stepped forward as Saya dismounted. The two girls hugged, and Azideh watched them with interest, his head tilted again.

"I'm sorry this is so sudden," Brailee said. "It's just . . ."

Saya nodded, looking almost as exhausted as Brailee. "Other than my father, I'm the only necromancer here." She glanced at Dante. "And he certainly wouldn't want to help you. No offense."

"None taken. I *am* still a fugitive." Dante shot a warning look at Azideh, who was attempting to come closer to sniff at Saya. As soon as Saya's attention began to turn to the demon, Azideh said, "*You do not perceive me.*" Saya blinked a few times, frowning.

"Saya, be honest," Dante said. "Are you all right with leaving Nexus, leaving your family, to come with us? To potentially resurrect the spirit of Marcos Ricci?"

Saya wasn't much older than Brailee, and he couldn't help but carry a bit of the same protective instinct for her that he carried for his sisters, especially when a wisp of her apprehension curled around him. But she drew herself to her full height and nodded.

"My sister is missing," Saya said. "As is yours. We should be working together to save them." She glanced over her shoulder at the dark, brooding skyline of Nexus. "My parents are where they're most needed. But I'm needed elsewhere."

"Good." Dante reached for his horse's reins. "We have enough moonlight to ride for about an hour. Should be far enough in case your parents decide to send guards for you come morning."

Saya winced. "How did you—?"

"Please, you think I don't know the face of someone sneaking out without permission? Who do you think taught Taesia?" Dante swung himself into the saddle. After weeks in a prison cell, using his body like this felt like the epitome of freedom. "Let's go."

The girls mounted and turned south. Azideh disappeared into his cloud form, but Dante sensed a pair of crossed arms resting across his shoulders, the whisper of a low voice in his ear.

"Do you like this?" the demon asked. "Commanding others? Being a leader? Did you summon me just to give me orders you know I must follow?"

"It's not like that," Dante muttered under his breath. "And you and I both know you won't follow every order I give you. Now shut up."

"I don't think that's true," the demon purred. Something cold and wet licked at the shell of his ear, and Dante shrugged him away. "I think you *like* control. Are starved for it."

"Shut *up*," Dante snapped.

Saya jumped. "I—I didn't say anything?"

Brailee seemed caught between a laugh and a scowl. "Don't mind him. He's...well...We'll explain later."

Azideh disappeared again with a chuckle. Dante focused on the open land before him, awash in darkness and starlight, and hoped Taesia could hold on a little longer.

X

Julian stared at the golden wall that shielded the palace until his eyes watered from the light.

"Nik," Taesia croaked. She held her sword in one hand, wrists still fettered with lightsbane. She stepped forward and touched the barrier, then yanked her hand back.

Julian clasped her shoulder. "We have to go. He gave us a chance to run. We have to take it."

"*No.*" She raised her sword against the barrier, but without her powers the bone blade bounced harmlessly off its surface. "Fuck! Nik! I can't let him—"

"Phos won't kill him, but he *will* kill us!" Julian spun her around to face him. "We'll come back for him."

Her eyes were so large, so terrified. Seeing her this way shook something deep within him that not even the god within the Bone Palace could touch.

He had done what he could to break Nikolas out of Phos's thrall, fighting against that voice demanding he kill Phos—kill Rian Cyr. Every second he'd disobeyed sent shooting pain through his skull.

But here, beyond the barrier, it was blessedly quiet. No more whispers or urgings. His blood finally settled, the itch in his bones gone, the pain receding to a phantom touch.

His fingers tightened on Taesia's shoulder. The Bone Palace had been a prison, if a somewhat familiar one. Now that they were outside its walls, it came crashing down on him: They were in a different realm.

The Bone Palace and its courtyard had demolished the royal palace, sitting high upon a hill overlooking Astrum, the capital city of Inlustrous. Above the sprawling city was a tapestry of stars and jewel-toned galaxies.

And nearby, a group of Noctans stood staring at them.

They were tall and dark, their faces displaying white tattoos in various designs, their hair falling in long strands of black, white, and silver. Some of their horns curved into S-shapes while others' were curled like a ram's. Their eyes, all fixed upon him and Taesia, ranged from black to emerald to amethyst, glowing with eyeshine the way a cat's would in the dark.

Julian had never had an opportunity to visit the Noctus Quarter in Nexus, though he had seen the occasional Noctan refugee—mostly mixed-race offspring. Now he understood how they must have felt, living in a place where they were forever seen as outsiders.

Taesia drew in a ragged gasp. It stirred the onlookers to life, many reaching for swords at their hips.

"*Vitaeans,*" one spat.

A couple others yelled out in a vowel-heavy language Julian had never heard before, but their angry tones were enough to get the gist.

Taesia must have understood some of it, since she jolted under his hand. "No, I'm not—I—"

A Noctan woman wearing the same black-and-silver uniform as the others let out a sound of disbelief when her eyes fell to Taesia's sword. She pointed at it and said something with an accusing lilt. A fierce, uneasy murmur stole through the rest of the crowd—soldiers, if those uniforms were anything to go by.

Julian took Taesia's elbow. They were in a strange city, a strange *realm*, with nowhere to go. The panicked instinct within him told him to move, hide, do whatever was necessary.

Protect her, Nikolas had ordered. So he did just that, and took off running.

Taesia faltered in his grip. "Wait, maybe we can—"

"You can't reason with them right now!"

They took advantage of the soldiers' shock and jumped off the lip of the courtyard and to the hill beneath the Bone Palace. They immediately lost their footing and rolled, Julian's shoulder hitting the ground hard before he scrambled back up and hauled Taesia to her feet.

The hill bore a wide pathway, on either side of which stood large sculptures of shimmering black stone intertwined with topiaries covered in pale white flowers. Julian and Taesia used them for cover when dark projectiles rained down on them. Some of the soldiers were Shades, then.

"Fuck," Taesia gasped. "If I didn't have these shackles on—"

A sheet of pitch blackness fell over them. Julian stumbled into a topiary, heart hammering. *This is it.* Nikolas's sacrifice had been in vain. Then Taesia grabbed him by the shirt and tugged him forward.

"You can see in the dark?"

He could hear her harsh breathing as she guided them through the shadows. "Not as well as they can, but they don't know I'm a Shade yet. If I just tell them who I am—"

"You can't prove it until we get those shackles off, and I doubt they'll want to do that. We need to lay low."

"We only look guiltier if we run."

Despite the frenzy and furor, he huffed. "I guess you'd know that pretty well by now."

Though he couldn't see her face, her fingers clenched harder around the fabric of his shirt.

Once they emerged from the shadows, Taesia darted behind a hedge. Not a moment later, soldiers ran by. Julian didn't dare breathe until Taesia signaled him, and he followed her at a crawl until they reached the base of the hill, stopped by a large fence.

Taesia looked to him, waiting. Julian swallowed past his dry throat and gripped the metal bars in his hands. He tapped into the beast within his blood, the same rush of adrenaline he'd felt that night in Haven Square when he'd punched through a hunk of debris.

Gritting his teeth, he pulled the bars apart. His arms strained at the pressure, veins bulging, until the metal creaked and parted, crumpling helplessly under his hands. He let go and leaned against the fence while his head swam.

"Good job." Taesia ran her fingers through the shorter hairs above his nape. He shivered. "Let's go."

They stole into the city proper. Julian wished they had time to stop and gape. As it was, he could only take in flashes of buildings made of dark stone, looming sharp spires and towers, and the arches of elaborately carved bridges overhead. Here and there came the glimmer of light refracted off jewels, the light itself coming from odd white-and-silver lanterns hanging high on wrought iron streetlamps. The ground seemed to be lined with something like cobblestone, though darker and streaked with cloudy, shimmering veins.

A ringing clamor resounded through the streets. Julian pushed Taesia around a corner as voices raised in confusion and fear joined the din.

"The whole city is going to be looking for us," Taesia breathed against his neck.

"It's either go up against them or go up against Phos." He took her hand and led her deeper into the dark.

The city of Astrum—or at least this part of it—rivaled the cleanest streets in Nexus. There was no vestige of piss or body odor; instead, every breath brought him the scent of rich, warm spice and the air on a late-winter night, cold and crisp. His teeth chattered as the sweat cooled on his skin, his shirt paltry protection against the deep chill.

"Where can we go?" Taesia murmured as they navigated narrow alleys between imposing stone buildings. Bioluminescent moss grew at their bases and crawled up the sides like ivy, casting a bluish glow.

"We leave the city. Phos said he made Conjuration circles. We find them and destroy them."

Running footsteps went past, and Taesia pushed him against the alley wall. Alarm bells were still clanging in the distance.

"I can't fight at full capacity with lightsbane on," Taesia said. "We need to get it off."

Julian wiggled his fingers underneath one of her shackles. He felt Taesia's suppressed wince as he brushed against chafed, raw skin and shot her an apologetic glance before he threaded that foreign strength through his body again. But no matter how much he tried, the stone would not budge.

"Let's get to a safe spot before trying again," Taesia whispered after more Noctans hurried by.

They left the alley, Julian squinting through the haze of silvery light shining in pockets of darkness. He couldn't tell what sort of district they were in, unable to determine which buildings were residential or commercial, the architecture too unfamiliar.

Where could they hide? If the alarm bells were telling citizens to bunker inside, was it better to stay on the streets?

A gasp sounded nearby. Julian turned and met the shining eyes of a young Noctan woman, her silver hair in three long braids.

Taesia stepped forward and said a word in their language, but the young woman screamed. A door banged open and shouts erupted around them.

Julian let Taesia take point when they took off running. He had no idea how big the city was, how long it might take them to reach the edge of it, if it would be easier to get caught in the surrounding lands without cover.

A door suddenly swung open on their left. Before they could react, a pair of hands yanked them into a dark room beyond.

Julian crashed to the floor. Someone wrestled the sword from Taesia's grip as another fought to get her arms behind her back.

Julian lunged at the latter and slammed them into the wall. He growled in their face while they struggled.

Something struck him in the side and he stumbled. The person he'd restrained broke his hold and kicked him back down.

"Enough," snapped a voice in accented Vaegan. "Let them see."

A rustle, and then a lamp was lit. Julian blinked against the sudden bright spot and quickly scanned the room.

It was small and sparse, barely large enough for the five people inside it. Their captors totaled three in number, all Noctans. They didn't wear the uniform of the soldiers; instead, they were dressed in nondescript surcoats and breeches, their tall boots well-worn and their faces dirt-smudged.

Two of them were men, both well over six feet. The one who'd kicked him wore a sour expression, his black hair tied in a queue and his green eyes narrowed at Julian. The tattooed stars on his face made a constellation across his forehead, the space under his eyes taken up by Noctan characters, and there was a choker around his neck that Julian suspected might be his familiar.

The other kept his pale silver hair in loose waves, his honey-colored eyes wide at the scene they'd made. His tattoos were less elaborate, the same simple lines as the Noctan soldiers, and he, too, carried a sword at his hip.

The one who had spoken stood at the fore, a young woman with long black hair and curved horns. She held a whip of shadow in one hand that trailed to the floor, curled like a fiddlehead. Above her eyebrows were small, intricate dots, and in the very center of her forehead rested a waxing crescent moon.

She looked between Taesia and Julian, her gaze lingering on Taesia's hand outstretched toward her fallen sword.

"Astralam bones," the woman whispered, still in Vaegan. Her accent was musical. She knelt beside the sword, fingers hovering above the glittering black blade.

"Don't," Taesia warned her.

"You're in no position to be making orders or threats," the young woman said. "The entire city is on the lookout for you."

Julian tensed, ready to fight their way out. The man with the sword noticed and shook his head in warning.

"We're not here to harm you," Julian said, the words slow and clumsy in his mouth.

"Oh?" The young woman rose to standing again, the movement fluid. A movement that belonged to someone who had trained physically for years. "A strange thing to say considering that everyone within the palace is now dead."

Taesia got to her feet, and Julian did the same. "We're not responsible for that," Taesia said. "You *are* in danger, but not from us. Look." She lifted her wrists, showing off the lightsbane. "We have information that can help you fight against the threat we escaped, but only if the hunt for us is called off. If we can meet with some sort of—I don't know, official, or—"

A snort came from one of the men behind them. The young woman moved forward, whip sliding across the floor like a snake.

"I don't know who you are, but we're not your enemy," Taesia said firmly.

The young woman stopped. The corner of her mouth ticked up.

"You want to speak to an official?" the young woman said, her tone lightly mocking. "Very well. I'm listening."

Julian frowned. "You?" He glanced around the shoddy room.

"Yes, me." Her hand tightened around the hilt of her shadow whip, lavender eyes flashing. "As I am the last surviving heir of the Lunari royal family."

XI

Nikolas was and wasn't and was again.

A spot of pain on his cheek, a whorl of pain in his chest. He focused on the former to stay in the moment, but was inevitably dragged to the latter. He picked and prodded like he would a scab, when he was a boy and had fallen, blood on his knee and tears in his eyes. Warm hands and soft linen. Stains in his sheets.

Nik, Nikolas, Lord Cyr, Nikshä.

His spear plunging into his father's neck.

Nikolas came back to himself with a shuddering gasp. He was kneeling on a carpet runner, red, red, *blood*, his? Looking wildly around, he realized he was in the throne room of the Bone Palace.

Taesia. Julian. The barrier had—and he had—

Run, he thought as he panted like a beast fleeing from its Hunter. *Run, leave this place, don't come back for me.*

A small ball of light sputtered into being before him. Nikolas choked down a sob and reached for his familiar. Lux nuzzled against his palms, pulsing the same uneasy rhythm as his heartbeat.

"I knew it," drawled a voice behind him. "The demonspawn did something to your mind."

Nikolas froze. The voice—familiar. The tone—not.

He slowly turned and laid eyes on his younger brother. Tears crawled down his cheeks as he took in the cold expression on Rian's face, the foreign cruelty in his eyes.

He'd barely had time to process it at Godsnight, or after. His brother, dead and alive. Gone and returned. The hole inside him that Rian's absence had made chipped open wider. He was drowning in it, suffocating, wanting so badly to die and be rid of it—

"Rian," he whispered. His lower lip, so dry from lack of water, split with a new flashpoint of pain.

"Don't try," Rian said. "I am not your brother, Nikolas. I am your creator. Your progenitor. Your god. Do not forget it."

"Rian," he tried again as the tears flowed faster. "Please, I know you're in there—"

Phos grabbed Nikolas's chin, forcing his neck to bend at an awkward angle.

"HE IS NOT HERE," the god snarled in his face, eyes glowing gold. "AND YOU HAVE COST ME MY CHANCE TO OPEN THE BARRIERS."

"Let him go!"

Nikolas tensed at Fin's cry. Images flashed through his mind, of Godsnight and the safe room and Fin chained to a chair. Fin stalling Phos to give them the chance to escape.

To give Nikolas the chance to let Taesia and Julian go.

Taesia had told him to leave Fin behind. A small part of him had been tempted.

He couldn't. He wouldn't. Fin had hidden his identity to the point of fatal repercussions, but like all the other heirs, he had been a pawn.

They both knew the desire of giving up, giving in. The call to not exist. To find freedom in nothingness.

Nikolas would not let him find it.

Phos looked over Nikolas's head to where Fin was standing. "AND YOU. A LITTLE PRINCELING ONLY JUST LEARNING WHAT BRAVERY MEANS." A hint of teeth. "SHALL WE TEST IT?"

His fingers began to burn against Nikolas's jaw. Nikolas fought, hurrying to escape into the pocket that had opened in his mind—ripped open by a voice that had sounded like Julian's, boring through his skull like an auger—but he wasn't fast enough.

The heat seared through his skin and into his teeth, into flesh and muscle and the ghost of a beating heart. His thoughts scattered away and he stood on brittle land that could not hold his weight and—

Nikolas's hands fell limply to his lap. His muscles loosened. The ball of light spinning in agitation beside him winked out.

He was buried under a mountain, hidden away from a painful world, and it was a mercy.

His god smiled as the light in his eyes leached away. "There," he whispered, gently stroking Nikolas's cheek. "Much better."

"Your plan won't work," came Fin's quavering voice. "There's no use controlling him, now."

"Isn't there? Nikolas, rise."

He followed the order and turned where his god directed him, facing Fin. He was standing, too, pale, shaking, sweating. The sweat on his own skin turned cold.

"I realize now that threats will not be enough," the god said. "I wonder, princeling, if you have been spoiled? Misdeeds and misdemeanors alike either ignored or given the barest punishment?"

Fin stared at the god, hands clenched beneath his shackles. He said nothing.

"Thought so." The god put a hand on Nikolas's shoulder. "I think it's about time that changes. How else will you learn that actions have consequences?"

The god leaned toward him. Whispered in his ear.

"Remove an eye. Only one. I'll let you choose which."

Nikolas took a step forward. Fin took one back.

"What are you doing?" Fin demanded of the god. His voice rose higher. "You sick fuck—"

"Struggling will make it worse. Remember, you put yourself in this position."

Fin tried to run. Nikolas was faster. Stark bones shifted under his hands, a warm body trembling like a fault line. A frantic, animal cry filled the throne room.

The back of his mind *howled*.

He was bigger than Fin. It was easy to wrestle him to the ground, on his back, face up. Eyes wide, terrified. So pale. Blue like the sky in autumn. Like the days he sat with his mother in the sun room, asking her if she needed—

He winced and held his head as a sharp whistle pierced through it.

"Nik, Nik, please—you can fight him, you can fight against this—"

"Nikolas," came the god's voice, and it was outside of him and also inside of him, rattling his rib cage and squeezing viselike on his lungs. "Do it."

He was a beast again, he was panting and he was afraid and he was running even while sitting still, he was on his knees and he was raising

a hand and he was looking into bright blue eyes defiant yet leaking tears
and he was

*Nikolas Cyr I am Nik Nikshä Lord I am not Nikolas Cyr I am an heir of Nik
please I can't he will I won't I*

I

I

I

A word and a voice and a thought and a being and *him*—

DO IT, thundered the voice of his god, and he was on his knees ready
for worship or retribution, or maybe they were one and the same.

Remove an eye.

I'll let you choose which.

Right—left—his to decide.

He raised his hand again. Fin drew in a breath.

And let it out as a scream as Nikolas dug his fingers into his own right
eye.

A firework, an explosion. Spilling and squelching as his fingers dug,
curling and pulling, rending, *snapping.*

The world caught fire. He was in the heart of it, burning alive, burning dead, some unholy state between the two. A whimper and a shout
and wetness trickling down his face onto Fin's chest. Beyond the watery
haze: guilt and fury and tears.

And against his palm—

His own crystalline eye looking back up at him.

His god had given the order, but Nikolas Cyr had chosen how to
interpret it. He laughed and tasted blood.

He wasn't gone. Not completely. Even buried under the mountain,
there was a source of light that was wholly his.

And if he remembered it was there, it would lead him through the
dark.

XII

The night before she was meant to leave, Angelica stood staring at the piles of clothes that had been laid out across her bed. They ranged in palettes of deep reds and oranges to breezy blues and greens, from heavy winter cloaks to thin summer fabric. Though Vaega was in the grip of late autumn, Azuna's weather was even more temperamental than theirs.

At least, that's what Miko had told her. She had been offering what advice she could ever since the decision had been made that Angelica would represent the Mardovas: terms of address for various members of the imperial family, manners pertaining to eating and drinking, what subjects were best avoided, how to give compliments without accidentally offending the receiver, and—most important—primers on the four warlords, if they happened across her path.

Angelica looked down at her fingertips. There was ash embedded under her fingernails, residue from today's practice of trying to form and maintain hold of her fire. But without her instruments, it was like trying to fish without tackle.

Her window was turning dark, the lamps around her bedroom casting flickering light against the walls. Angelica breathed in and felt the lure of their heat. She pursed her lips and whistled a song she made up on the spot, a simple melody peppered with minor notes.

The air around her seemed to condense, fitting in close to her body. The more she whistled and shaped the nameless song, the more heat the lamps gave off, their flames rising higher.

In the practice arenas at the university, the elements braided together in a way that felt so much like *life*, of something beating and breathing and born. When she passed the stepwell in the basilica it radiated from the closed-off portal. And when she sang...

A spark and pop, and a small ball of fire hovered above her palm. Angelica stopped whistling, eyeing it in wonder. Already it was beginning to gutter out.

A knock on her door made her start, and she smothered the fire by closing her hand into a fist. "Come in."

The door eased open to reveal Miko. She was dressed more casually for the evening, her long hair worn loose, her ornately embroidered dress replaced with a robe of mulberry silk lined with fur. The Mardova villa had turned noticeably drafty in the past month.

"I wanted to see how the packing was coming along," her stepmother said.

Angelica gestured at the mostly empty luggage on the floor in answer. Miko smiled fondly.

"Just like your mother in this regard," she murmured. "Would you like help?"

Despite the gradual ease between them during Miko's lessons, her first instinct was to refuse. For years Angelica had built a wall between herself and Miko, between herself and her stepsisters, furious at the implication that her father was being replaced. But now she was grown, and it was time to move past that childish thinking. It would take time to deconstruct the wall, but the first couple bricks had already been removed. She could manage a couple more tonight.

Angelica nodded to the piles of clothes on her bed. "Which would be best to bring with me?"

Miko hummed and walked around the bed, picking up certain garments and rubbing them between her fingers. "Pack more heavy layers than light."

"Anything in terms of...I don't know, design? I don't want to offend anyone."

Miko shook her head with another smile. "They're aware of Vaegan customs and clothing. Just don't wear anything too revealing."

"Because I do that all the time," Angelica muttered, and Miko laughed outright. Angelica picked up one of her favorite winter outfits and dumped it unceremoniously into her luggage.

Miko hesitated, fiddling with one of the simple rings she tended to wear. "Angelica...let us sit for a moment."

Though dread suddenly reared its head, Angelica obliged by sitting on the edge of her bed. Miko joined her.

"The letter I wrote to my family should arrive a few days before you do," Miko said. "The Uedas will take care of you. They'll be more than happy to provide whatever you may need. But please do not let that cloud your judgment. They are still members of the imperial gentry."

Angelica, who had grown up with her mother's tutelage in a city choked with politics, easily read between the lines. "You don't trust them."

"No, I do not. It has been many years since I last saw them, and in that time I don't know what alliances may have been made or broken. Who has grudges against whom, who is in favor or not. Especially where the warlords are concerned. It is . . . complicated."

"As if I don't know what that's like."

This time Miko didn't smile. "It's true that you and Adela have dealt with your own share of that. Much like the Houses wanted favor with your king, my family wants to be as close to the empress as possible—especially my eldest sister." Angelica nodded, remembering what Miko had had to say about Kazue Ueda. "But they also want protection and favor from the warlords, who gain more power over the states every day."

"Is a civil war possible, do you think?"

Miko made a regretful face. "We have had many of those in our past, and I don't doubt there will be more in the future so long as power keeps shifting. Right now the Uedas are closest to the empress thanks to my sister's scheming, which should help you gain an audience." Miko placed a hand on Angelica's wrist. "But be mindful, Angelica. *Please.* Of the warlords, should they happen to visit Mukan while you're there, but also of Kazue. There are . . . certain things that outsiders are not allowed to know. Things I am not allowed to tell you, or even your mother."

Angelica wasn't sure how to interpret the flutter this brought to her stomach. "I'll be careful."

After they'd made sufficient progress on packing, Miko excused herself for the night, and Angelica was left to wonder over which pieces of jewelry to bring. She was staring at a pair of garnet earrings, thinking of the fire she'd held in her palm with a song, when the window behind her opened.

Angelica spun around, the lamps flaring brighter in response to her panic. She scrabbled over her dresser for something sharp and grabbed a pair of small gilt-wreathed shears she used to snip loose threads off her clothes.

A figure lifted themselves through the window and dropped onto the seat below with a dramatic "*Brr!*" as they rubbed their arms for warmth.

"Damn, thought I'd turn into an icicle out there," Cosima said.

Angelica gawked at the thief. Realizing she was brandishing decorative shears at her, Angelica tossed them back onto the dresser with a scowl. "Were you never taught how to use a door?"

"Much as I'd love to see what'd happen if I knocked on the front door of your quaint little villa, I prefer a more direct route." The thief swung her legs over the window seat and grinned. "And it's more fun to see you spooked."

Angelica narrowed her eyes. She hadn't seen Cosima since before Godsnight, since the night she had...

She swallowed, the phantom taste of blood and offal in the back of her throat.

"What are you doing here?" she asked, more subdued than she would like.

Cosima's smile fell. "Couldn't help but notice the giant hole in the middle of the city. Folks're saying you were...involved." She shifted on the window seat. "Wanted to see if you were all right."

Much like Miko's offer of help, the statement unmoored her. Immediately she sought for an ulterior motive hiding underneath, but Cosima's face was earnest, her body language restrained.

"Being possessed by a god wasn't exactly fun," Angelica answered. "But here I am."

She could tell Cosima wanted to ask questions, but smartly cleared her throat and instead said, "I'm sorry. I don't know much about all that god business, but it seemed intense. Deia's tits, I could hear it all the way in the river district." She winced. "Sorry. Probably shouldn't bring up that name."

To her shock, Angelica's mouth twitched. "Did you really come all the way here to check on me? Why?"

Cosima didn't reply immediately, instead worrying her plush lower lip between her teeth. Then she stood up and began to take stock of Angelica's bedroom, keen eyes missing no detail. Embarrassment curled through Angelica while Cosima trod the same floor she did every day, lifting up and putting back her belongings as if to catalog them in her mind.

"That night…" Cosima stopped, her back to Angelica. "You were covered in blood. You were terrified. I haven't been able to get it out of my head."

Angelica shuffled backward, longing to disappear into the villa to escape this turn in the conversation.

"You don't have to explain it," Cosima assured her. "I just. I dunno. It's a lot."

An understatement, that.

"But I, uh." Cosima ruffled her own hair with a sheepish smile. "While I was waiting outside, I caught some of what you were talking about."

"Eavesdropped, you mean."

"Call it what you like. You're going to Azuna?"

"Yes. Tomorrow morning."

Cosima whistled and put her hands on her hips, surveying the open luggage around her. "That's quite a distance. For how long?"

"I don't know yet."

"And this is for…" She wiggled her fingers. "Politics, I'm guessing?"

"Yes." She hesitated, then added, "And no. I want to do some sight-seeing of the regional volcanoes."

"Volcanoes? Why?"

"God business," she said dryly.

Cosima laughed, then worried her lower lip again. Angelica found it rather rude that she kept drawing attention to it.

"So, I'm not good at the whole asking people for shit thing," Cosima said at last. She frowned at the wall as she spoke. "But I, uh. Well. It's not easy for someone like me to travel, and…"

Angelica's trepidation turned to disbelief. "You want to go to Azuna?"

"It's not like I *want* to go there *specifically*, but it might be good to head out of Nexus for a while. I promise I wouldn't get in your way."

"Why do you want to leave Nexus?"

"Are you kidding?" Cosima waved toward the window. "The city is in shambles. Can barely go anywhere without folks babbling about the end of the world."

She wavered before crossing the room. Angelica refused to back up any farther, even when Cosima was close enough that Angelica became surrounded by her scent. It wasn't unpleasant—in fact, it carried an undertone of mint.

"My brother's in Azuna," Cosima admitted.

You have a brother? Then again, why wouldn't Cosima have a brother? She barely knew anything about the thief in the first place.

"My parents were from Marii," Cosima explained, sensing Angelica's unspoken questions. "One of the Azunese colonies. After the occupation, we were poorer than dirt and sickness was spreading. My dad caught it. While he was dying he helped me and my mom get on a ship to Vaega."

Cosima's gaze drifted back to Angelica's luggage. "Probably no shock to learn things weren't much better here. Mom died when I was fourteen. Didn't really know how else to get by on my own, so I fell in with a group of other orphans."

"I'm sorry." She wanted to say *I've also lost a father*, but refrained. This was Cosima's story, not hers.

"Anyway. I was real young when we left Marii, and I don't remember a whole lot of what my life was like there. But I do remember the Azunese soldiers wanted my brother in their army. He's got magic, like you. Air and fire. And they said if he went with them, we'd be compensated. Some rule in Azuna about the military class. So he agreed, and we got some money. That's how we could afford passage to Vaega."

"And you haven't seen him since."

"Nope. Buuut…" Cosima leaned in, mouth quirked despite the air of solemnity about her. "I've been in contact with him. If you take me with you, he can meet us. He can be your guide."

Angelica crossed her arms, doing her best to show that Cosima's proximity didn't bother her in any way. "It would be easier for me to hire a guide when I'm in Azuna."

Cosima made a face. "But not one you can trust completely, I bet. C'mon, won't you be lonely? In need of a bosom friend?"

Angelica chose to ignore the word *bosom* entirely. "What's your brother's name? Is he still in the military?"

"Yeah, but he's high enough in rank to take time off, and he's done enough traveling that he knows the countryside well. His name's Koshi."

"He has a Mariian name. But you don't."

"Well." Cosima scratched at her cheek. "I do, but my mom changed it when we arrived here." At Angelica's pointed silence, she shrugged. "It's Veliane."

Angelica repeated it quietly to herself. Cosima's eyes fell to her lips before she quickly turned away.

"Really, I'd be no trouble at all." Cosima folded herself into one of the empty trunks, wiggling until she fit. "See? No problem."

"Get out of there," Angelica snapped.

"Right, right, I'll mess up your fancy things."

Angelica sighed and pinched the bridge of her nose. The truth was, she was more than a little nervous about traveling somewhere she'd never been, where she might wind up in the middle of a family feud.

If Cosima and her brother could help her get to Mount Netsai…

"There's no need to become a stowaway," Angelica said. "I'll convince my family to hire you. Maybe as a bodyguard."

Cosima stared at her a moment. Then she burst out laughing.

"So you've finally noticed my strength, princess?" Still sitting in the trunk, Cosima flexed.

"Stop it." Angelica refused to acknowledge the upsetting realization that the thief had muscles. Distracting muscles. "And don't call me that."

"What, 'princess'? You basically are one."

"I am not. *Get out of the trunk.*"

Cosima easily rolled to her feet. "But really, you'd do that?"

Hoping she wasn't making a mistake, Angelica nodded.

"All right, but we need to sell this," Cosima said. "You gotta lend me a sword."

Definitely a mistake.

In the frigid morning, Angelica made her way down the stairs to the antechamber, where her luggage was waiting to be stowed in the carriage outside. Her mother and Miko were there, as well as the twins.

At her side, Cosima was dressed in the red-and-blue uniform of a House guard they'd nicked from the laundry room in the middle of the night. Cosima had had to mix and match pants and jackets to find a uniform that best fit her frame while Angelica snatched a sword from the armory closet.

The sword now hung at Cosima's hip. It jostled against her thigh as they descended the stairs, and she slapped a hand against the sheath to still it.

"Do you even know how to use that?" Angelica muttered.

"No clue. But hey, I'm a quick learner. Pointy bit in the fleshy bit, yeah?"

Angelica sighed.

"S'all right, I got a couple knives, too."

"That doesn't make me feel better." They reached the bottom of the stairs, and Adela turned from Miko to approach her. Her mother did a small double take when she saw Cosima.

"I don't remember hiring you," Adela said with a furrowed brow.

Angelica saw Cosima stiffen and hurried to reply on her behalf. "I hired her."

Her mother blinked. "What?"

"She came to the villa a week ago, and I interviewed her. She has a brother who lives in Azuna, so I thought she would be useful for the trip."

Adela's frown deepened. "Why haven't I seen her around the villa?"

"I'm sneaky like that," Cosima said with a grin. "Staying out of folks' way and whatnot."

Angelica pressed her lips together and resisted the urge to tread on Cosima's foot. Adela looked between them before finally relenting and drawing Angelica closer to the door, leaving Cosima a few steps behind.

"We'll see you to the dock," she said. "Is there anything else you need from the villa?"

"I don't think so. I—"

"I don't *care*," came the voice of one of the twins. Both were crowding Miko, who wore a resigned expression. "I don't see why *she* gets to go and we can't!"

"Eiko, please," Miko said. "This isn't how I want you to return to Azuna. I promise one day we'll go together."

"I can barely remember anything," Eiko pleaded. "And if things continue to get worse, it might be too late by then. Maa, *please*."

Miko ran a hand down her daughter's hair. Kikou gazed at the floor, quieter and more willing to bend to their mother's orders.

"I'm sorry," Miko whispered in Azunese. "But this trip is dangerous enough for Angelica. I don't want you getting caught up in anything."

Over Eiko's and Kikou's heads, Miko met Angelica's eyes, and a rare moment of understanding passed between them. Of course Miko didn't want her daughters becoming pawns in a political dispute.

"Fuck this," Eiko spat, stepping away from Miko and glaring at Angelica. "Fuck *you*."

Miko and Adela called after her as she stormed outside. She would likely disappear into the gardens for a while, which she tended to do when she didn't get her way. Kikou hesitated, torn between going after her and saying goodbye to Angelica. In the end, one look at her mother's dismayed face swayed her to stay and take Miko's hand.

"I'm sorry," Miko said to Angelica. "She shouldn't have said that."

"It's fine. I'd be upset, too."

Adela rearranged Angelica's hair so that it rested over her shoulders, then dusted some lint from her cloak. "Are you absolutely certain you want to do this?"

"Yes. You and Miko are needed here." For a moment she wondered whether to tell her about Mount Netsai, and what she planned to do. But in the end, it would only add more fuel to her mother's worry. "It's better that I go."

Together they moved through the front door and toward the carriage that would carry Angelica to the port. She'd thought of going by river, but the boats that traveled the Lune to the coast were small merchant vessels and—as her mother had put it—unfit for someone of her status.

The handful of guards who would accompany her, all of whom she knew by face if not by name, were already mounted in the courtyard, their horses calm under the bright autumn sun. The carriage stood with its door open, waiting for her to climb inside.

Cosima nervously crowded in on her other side. "I don't know how to ride a horse."

Angelica figured as much. "She'll ride in the carriage with me," she told her mother.

Adela's concerned expression morphed into a suspicious one. "Why?"

"I'll...feel safer that way," Angelica forced out. "Besides, I'll need a partner for card games."

"The port's only ten miles away."

"Which means a couple hours' worth of boredom." Angelica nodded to Cosima, who took that as her cue to bow to Adela and Miko before scrambling into the carriage.

Miko hugged her, and Angelica stiffly returned it. "Remember what I told you," Miko whispered in her ear.

"I will." Angelica looked around, but it seemed Eiko wouldn't be returning. "Tell Eiko I said goodbye," she said to Kikou. "I'll, um...get you a new dress while I'm over there."

Kikou brightened a bit. "Really?"

Angelica shifted on her feet. "Sure."

"Can you..." Kikou flushed, clasping her hands together. "There's a snack I remember having when I was younger, a mix of rice crackers and peanuts. You should try some if you get the chance. And maybe... maybe bring some back?"

Miko's eyes watered, and Adela put a comforting hand on her shoulder.

"I'll see what I can do," Angelica said.

"Please write," Miko said as they walked her to the carriage. Inside, Cosima was struggling with how to sit without displacing her sword. "If anything strange happens, don't wait to tell us."

"I won't." Angelica paused. "Thank you."

Miko briefly squeezed her hand. Then she and Kikou stepped back, allowing Adela to hug her. Angelica embraced her mother with a feeling similar to drowning—something too big for her to swallow or spit out, that instead crowded her chest with everything she couldn't say.

Adela had raised her to be a Mardova, a royal heir, someone destined and worthy of greatness. But now she was simply a daughter being held by her mother, and she desperately wanted it to stay like this. To once again feel small and cherished. But eventually, she had to pull away.

Adela's lips thinned as she stared at Angelica's chest, like she could see through bone and tissue into the core of her magic, sealed behind Deia's doors.

"I'm not weak, whatever you believe," Angelica murmured.

"I do not think you're weak, Angel. But I also know that the world is not kind."

Adela handed her into the carriage. Angelica turned and met her mother's eyes for what she hoped wasn't the last time.

"Neither am I."

XIII

Risha's whole body was a fever of discomfort. There was a horrific pounding in her head, and her stomach was twisted into knots, the range of her abdomen feeling like an elephant's foot was crushing it. Wherever she was, it was dark and gloomy.

Her tongue sat leaden in her mouth. Only a faint sound escaped her throat.

"Risha," came Jas's voice as if from far away—but there was his body, or rather his spirit, glowing a dim gray. A cold hand touched her. "Are you all right?"

No. She was starving to death, and so dehydrated she couldn't remember what water felt like on her lips. She couldn't even cry anymore.

"*Shit*," Jas swore, and Risha nearly smiled at him using a Vaegan curse instead of a Parithvian one. "I don't know what to do. The Sentinel is still prowling around outside. I can...I can go out, see if I can find water for you?"

Risha weakly shook her head, then instantly regretted it when everything around her spun. She was sitting up against a wall of cold, rough stone, and it took a moment to remember the mausoleum. She could hear the Sentinel's lumbering footsteps beyond the cracked door, its discordant sounds, its rattling bones.

Other than the green light spilling through the crack, Jas's spirit was the only thing illuminating the inside of the mausoleum. The first thing she noticed were the engravings on the walls, which might have once been lovely but were now worn and faded. The second was a mound of pale, oval shapes against the far wall.

Jas followed her gaze. "They're skulls. All of them."

Risha saw it clearer, now. They weren't all human—some bore the curved horns of Noctans, and others had wider, longer jaws with sharper teeth.

There were niches within the far wall, most of them empty, some containing an eclectic assortment of dust-covered trinkets ranging from a candlestick to a tree branch to a broken mirror.

Typically the mausoleums in Nexus held coffins of stone or marble at their hearts. This one had a row of five columns, two of which were vacant, another two occupied by brass urns, and the final holding aloft a decapitated head.

Everything smelled like death in Mortri, but it was more concentrated in this enclosed space. Risha wrinkled her nose.

"I know," Jas murmured. "But I don't think we should leave until the Sentinel goes."

"It might not," she rasped.

"Then what do we do?"

She didn't know. It felt absurd, now, to think she and Jas could wander this perilous realm on their own. That she would have enough time to figure things out.

Risha realized she was staring at the head on the column. It sat there, with no obvious sign of decay, as if it had only just been severed from its body. Pointed ears poked out from black silken hair that fanned a pallid, gaunt face with full lips and a straight nose. The eyes were closed, serene in death. Soon, Risha thought, she might join it.

Jas suddenly perked up. "I have an idea. If you have enough energy for it, could you reanimate one of these?" He nodded toward the skulls.

She recalled standing across from Cristoban Damari over the dismembered body of Don Soler, the thick sutures reconnecting the don's head to his shoulders. "Why?"

"These...people?...have been here longer than us. They may have seen more of Mortri than we have. Maybe they know where to find food and water."

"That depends on whether their spirits are still around."

"Even if they're not, maybe you can lure another nearby spirit who'll have answers."

Risha flexed her fingers against her thighs, disturbed by their tingling numbness. "Even if they knew something, what then? Spirits are stronger in Mortri than they are in Vitae. It might refuse to leave."

"Then we contain it here and go."

Risha's headache seemed to encompass the entire world. "Jas," she managed through gritted teeth.

"What, are you going to say that it's irresponsible? Risha, come on. In this realm, the odds are stacked so far against us we need everything in our arsenal if we're going to last long enough to find Leshya's weapon and get out of here."

"I haven't even decided if I'm going to use it," she croaked. Her heartbeat was alarmingly slow, but it kicked in an effort to match her growing anger.

Jas ran his hands through his hair in frustration. They stayed like that for a silent moment, broken only by the Sentinel's low call, until Risha sighed.

"Use that one." She nodded to the head on the column. "I think it's been dead the shortest amount of time. That'll make it easier to find the spirit."

She was rewarded with Jas's smile. He carefully picked up the head and situated it between them. Risha reached for it, then shied away.

"Risha." There was pleading in Jas's voice. "If you're going to leave this realm before it claims you, you *need to use your power.* I don't care what your family insists, or what the rules are. In this place, *you* make the rules."

Though weakened, she sensed her power just under the surface of her skin. It flickered in response to their surroundings, like calling to like. Her breath rattled even as her rib cage sang. The stripe of green light on the ground could have been spilled tea, or blood, or poison—something intended for the living. Something forgotten by the dead.

Jas lightly touched her knee. "It's better to try and fail than not try at all."

"What if the spirit refuses to be banished? Or I can't find it?"

A new voice broke in, "That won't be a problem, seeing as I'm right here."

They both looked down at the head. Its eyes were now open, rolled upward to better meet Risha's gaze. The mouth split into a grin.

A startled wheeze left Risha's mouth at the same time Jas scrambled to get between Risha and the head. In response, the head laughed hard enough that it wobbled and fell over.

"For fuck's sake," it mumbled, one cheek squished against the ground. "Still, your faces were worth it."

"How," Risha demanded, unable to articulate beyond that.

The head moved on its own, rolling over until it faced the mausoleum's partly collapsed ceiling. Its eyes, a reddish brown, watched the two of them sidelong. "This is Mortri. Many things that should be dead do not stay dead, and things that should *not* be dead are... Well, you get it."

"Which one are you, then?" Jas demanded.

"Who's to say?" the head replied. The voice was that of a man's, a vibrant tenor.

"Are you... *from* Mortri?" Risha asked, ignoring the way her own voice cracked. With his pale skin and lack of horns, Risha doubted he was a Noctan, and he didn't have the characteristics of a Solarian.

"From one of the cities," he answered. "Can't remember which one, though."

That would make sense, as spirits usually took on a more physical form while they atoned or worked toward reincarnation. And it would explain how a disembodied head could move and speak on its own.

The head's eyes narrowed slightly. "Judging by the state of one of you, *you're* not from Mortri."

Jas looked at Risha. She nodded.

"We're from Vitae," Jas answered. "This is Risha Vakara, descendant of Thana. She's still alive and needs to return to her own realm."

We *need to return*, Risha wanted to correct him, but the head's eyes had widened comically.

"Did you say Vakara? As in descended from Leshya Vakara?"

This time Jas's look was uneasy. "You know about her?"

"Of course! She's a legend here. An infamous one, considering who she fought." The head snickered. "Now *that* was a showdown."

"You know of the fight between her and the kings?" Risha demanded.

"I *saw* that fight. Or at least, part of it, until..." He wiggled a bit, drawing attention back to his current state. "When the kings went to war, there were rumblings that Thana didn't approve. So when Leshya Vakara came, she was appointed spirits to help her. I was one of them."

Risha met Jas's gaze, seeing her own amazement reflected in his. "The spirits didn't have loyalty to the kings?"

"Depends on who you ask. Or what city you're in. Can't imagine being very loyal to a king once he's ordered your intestines pulled out your mouth."

Risha wondered if that was what had happened to this poor

soul—and if his assistance to Leshya had led to him being imprisoned in this mausoleum.

"A descendant of Leshya Vakara," the head murmured. "An honor, truly. Your ancestor was quite gifted."

After a moment's hesitation, Jas leaned forward and righted the head so that it balanced on the stump of its neck. "If you helped Leshya, then you must know about her weapon," Jas said. "Samhara."

"What about it?"

"Do you know where it is?"

The head scoffed. "Everyone knows where it is."

"Everyone?" Risha repeated. "Then why hasn't it been found? Claimed?"

"First off, no one can use it, so what's the point," the head said. "Second, it's in a bit of a . . . hard-to-reach place."

Risha closed her eyes and sank back against the wall. *Of course.*

Panic began to claw up her chest, into her throat. There was no solution she could see that would save both her and Jas. And even if there was a path that led only to her survival . . .

No. She refused to think like that.

Jas laughed bitterly. "We can't even get past one Sentinel," he muttered. "How are we supposed to get to Samhara?"

"Oh shit, there's a Sentinel?" The head glanced at the broken door. "I might be able to get you past it."

"You can? How?" Jas demanded.

"Well . . ." The head gazed at Risha, evaluating. "I could, if she wasn't dying. Then again, maybe dying would make things easier."

"She's not going to die for this," Jas growled.

"I didn't mean *literally*," the head said, rolling its eyes. "You have the same powers as Leshya Vakara, right?"

Wordlessly, Risha nodded.

"That means you can manipulate your own body."

Jas sat back, frowning. Maybe recalling the same thing she did: of feeling his heartbeat against hers, the roadways of his veins, the momentary control she'd had over his life.

The lives of six people in her hands, crowding her chest, waiting to be snuffed. Risha's fingers dug harder into her thigh.

"Leshya Vakara killed off certain parts of her own body to stay in Mortri longer," the head explained. "Why can't you do the same?"

Because she hadn't known that was something she could do.

"So she would be cutting off certain functions, but not truly killing *herself*?" Jas clarified.

"That'd be it."

Jas fidgeted with excitement. "Risha, will you try?"

What other choice did she have, at this point? Better to experiment on herself than on Jas or the spirits in this realm. Still, trepidation had perched on her chest, making breathing even more difficult.

Jas held her hand. "I'll be right here," he whispered.

Risha closed her eyes. Her body was riddled with pain and exhaustion, and the more she concentrated, the more she understood how little time she actually had left. But power floated within her—a sweet song, a clear, cold breeze.

Her blood was the murmuring of a funeral procession, her breath the last sigh of wind at the end of the world. Green seeped through her eyelids, and red, and black. She saw the taunting markers on the pathway within the void between Mortri and Vitae.

She delved deeper, deeper, until she burrowed into the space between her muscles, the fat and the tissue, the struggling organs. The protein and lean muscle within her was eroding, breaking down to provide her some semblance of vitality.

The mausoleum fell away and it became just her and her body. She traveled through her own lethargic blood, seeing for herself how everything necessary had been depleted from her liver and muscles, the fat stores drained, waste and toxins accumulating. Even her brain was affected, stifled and sluggish.

She needed energy. Water. The human body could not sustain itself without it.

But she could trick it into thinking it could.

Risha targeted her heart, lungs, liver. She threaded her power through her muscles and coiled it around the base of her brain where it met her spine. Slowly, carefully, she fed them the power singing at her core, dark and formidable. Her heartbeat pulsed in her fingertips as it grew stronger, nourished not with sustenance but with magic.

For a second she faltered, unsure if this would be enough. Then something cool and calming swept over her like shade on a hot summer day. She basked in it, lingered in order to collect her strength and continue.

Her headache gradually receded. Her dizziness diminished. She drew in a large breath and savored the expanding of her lungs, the moisture in her mouth. All the small miracles she hadn't properly been grateful for when she'd had them.

She opened her eyes and sat up straight. She felt as if she had woken from a long, deep sleep, her fatigue washed away.

"It worked." Her joints were no longer stiff and painful to move. "I really did it."

She turned to Jas and her smile dropped. Before, she'd noticed the edges of him had turned hazy. Now those edges had become even more transparent.

Risha fumbled the marigold out of her pocket and placed it in his hands. It held for a moment before falling through.

"Risha," Jas whispered.

"Don't," she snapped. "You— What did you do?"

His hand. He had been holding her hand, and when she had faltered, when that wave of energy had come to bolster her—

"It worked, didn't it?" Jas said. "Are you feeling better?"

Physically, yes. But to know he had siphoned off some of his spirit into hers—

She pressed a hand against her chest. "*Jas.*"

"I'm sorry." He dropped his gaze. "I didn't... I didn't know how else to help."

"Promise me you won't do that again." When his face tightened, she raised her voice. "*Promise me.*"

"I promise."

The Sentinel outside gave another cry that made the stone around them tremble. The head's eyes swiveled toward the door. "Well done, good job, but maybe let's get going now?"

Risha exhaled shakily before wiping her eyes and turning back to the head. "You want us to bring you along?"

His eyebrows rose. "Uh, yes? If you want to get past the Sentinel, that is. And if you want to find Leshya Vakara's weapon."

"What do you get out of it?"

"Well..." His mouth pursed a couple times while he thought. "All right, fine. My body is still somewhere out there. If I bring you to Leshya Vakara's weapon, you need to find it for me. It's the least you can do after my *heroic* sacrifice to aid your ancestor."

Risha didn't like the thought of traveling with a stranger, let alone one who was a decapitated head, but he'd been right about using her power to fix herself. He had been a guide for Leshya, which meant he knew enough about Mortri to be their guide, too.

"Deal. What do we call you?"

"Val will do," he said.

Risha gingerly got to her feet and picked him up, making sure he faced out to better see where they were going. The sensation of holding a live head in her hands was disconcerting, to say the least. "What do we do?"

"Usually squaring up against a Sentinel is impossible. They're incredibly strong, and those swords they carry aren't just for show. They can shred both spirits and flesh like they're parchment."

"In other words, we're all done for if one catches us," Jas said.

"Brains *and* beauty. You love to see it."

"What else can you tell us about them?" Risha asked as Jas blinked.

"Hold on a moment." They waited in tense silence until the clicking of bones sounded again. "Hear that? They can't really see, so they use that sound to guide them."

"Like a bat?"

"Precisely."

"So that's why it couldn't find us in here," Jas murmured. "But once we step outside . . ."

"It can only detect what's immediately in front of it," Val finished. "And is drawn to things that move."

"What direction is Samhara?" Risha asked.

"North."

Risha gathered her resolve and pressed her shoulder against the door. She carefully maneuvered it open wide enough to slip back out, which proved more of a challenge while holding a head.

The Sentinel stood to the north. It had become bipedal again, turning this way and that. It was much closer than she had hoped.

"It might be under orders to not return until it finds something," Val whispered as she shifted to hold him under one arm. The movement of his jaw when he spoke tickled her side. "We have to sneak past it."

"You said it's drawn to things that move," Jas hissed.

"It only senses what's in front of it," Risha reminded him. "We move when it turns away."

"If it rattles its bones at you, do your best impression of a statue," Val said.

With that last piece of advice, Risha moved away from the door. The Sentinel was at least a hundred yards away, facing south. The sky illuminated the creature's sword, creating a jade runnel down its length.

Risha slowed her breathing. The air around her felt thick enough to take a bite out of. Jas and Val didn't make a sound, but she couldn't help the way the grass whispered and bent under her footfalls.

The Sentinel turned. Risha froze, locking her limbs in place and accidentally squishing Val's head. The Sentinel's ribs undulated, clicking and clacking together, and it swung its skull-like head from side to side. After a long moment, it turned the opposite way and repeated the motion.

Risha covered her nose and mouth with her sleeve to better stifle her uneven breaths. Jas was slow and cautious beside her. They walked north for another couple minutes before Val bit her arm in warning and the Sentinel twisted back toward them.

She had to freeze midstep, swaying slightly. Jas was utterly still, his shoulders hunched, eyes fixed on the horizon. She hardly dared to breathe as the Sentinel took one step, two, its ribs clattering, searching.

Her foot trembled a few inches above the ground. She tensed her leg as tight as she could, silently pleading with herself to not fall over, to not move one inch. Her face grew damp with sweat.

The longest minute of her life passed until the Sentinel finally turned away. Risha held back a gasp of relief and set her leg down, ignoring the cramp in her calf.

They repeated this twice more, until they were far enough away that Val whispered they were in the clear. Risha ducked behind a barrow and sank to the ground, setting Val down.

"Are you all right?" Jas asked as he knelt beside her.

"I will be," she panted. "Just not used to everything wanting to kill me."

In stronger light, she noted Val's face was angular and handsome, some of his black hair falling in a wave of bangs over one eye. When he realized she was staring he grinned, revealing sharp teeth.

"If you want that weapon, you better get used to it," he said. "Because one Sentinel's going to be the least of your problems."

Risha wholeheartedly believed him.

XIV

Ah, fuck.

Taesia sometimes wondered if she had the best or the worst luck. At moments like these, it was a toss-up.

She should have remembered sooner. The Lunari royal family had a tradition of tattooing their foreheads with the phase of the moon under which they'd been born. But her mind was spinning, and her body was one cough away from falling over. Everything hurt, and Nikolas was still in the Bone Palace, being punished by his god—

"Bow," came a low, droll voice behind her. The Noctan man with the constellation on his forehead and the familiar around his neck lifted his nose at them. "You are meeting royalty. It doesn't matter from which realm you come—decorum must be followed."

Taesia glowered. But, seeing no alternative, she turned and made the appropriate genuflection while trying not to wobble. Julian copied her.

"Was that really necessary?" the princess asked of her aide. Then to Taesia and Julian, "You may rise. Or stay on the ground, if you prefer. I don't care so long as I get answers."

Taesia forced herself back up. Julian reached out to steady her. "Our story might be . . . hard to believe."

The princess regarded them with an unfathomable expression. "Two Vitaeans stand in Noctus," she said at last. "Do you know what happened to the Vitaeans and Solarians who were trapped here when the portals closed? They died. The Solarians went first, choked off from the light they need to survive. Then gradually the Vitaeans withered away, even with their homes surrounded by stardust lamps. We did the best we could to save them, but in the end, it was hopeless." Her gaze never left them, drinking in every detail she could. "No one has seen a Vitaean in Noctus in centuries. Which means you and that...that *building* came through a portal."

"Yes," Taesia said. "A portal created by Conjuration."

One of the aides asked, "What is that?"

"It's..." Taesia cast around for the Noctan equivalent of the word, but she'd either never learned it or hadn't cared to memorize it. "Isadril?" It meant summoning, but even that couldn't come close to describing the chaotic magic of Conjuration.

"Quintessence," Julian added softly. "Magic from a fifth realm that was used to create the portals between the others."

The princess narrowed her eyes in a silent order to explain. Taesia swayed on her feet.

"I think I'm gonna take up your offer to sit down," she muttered.

"You mean to tell me," the princess said when they were done explaining Godsnight to the best of their ability, "that Phos—the *god of Solara*—plans to destroy this realm? That he sits beyond that damnable barrier on the hill?"

"The god isn't here in the flesh." Taesia's fingers idly traced a whorl on the rickety table's surface. "He's probably in his own realm. He's using one of his descendants as a conduit and controlling the other entirely."

"How were you able to escape him?"

Her throat constricted, and Julian sent her a worried look. "Because we pulled one of them out of Phos's control long enough for him to free us. But he couldn't escape."

The princess and her aides communed together silently. Eventually the princess's whip retracted back into her shadow familiar, which looped around her wrist in a bangle.

"Four hundred and thirty-two," she whispered. "That's how many servants worked in the palace. There were at least three hundred guards. My three brothers and my two sisters. Their partners and children. My mother and father." Her voice hitched and she turned away. "Gone. *Crushed.*"

Taesia stared at the dark wood of the table. Julian touched her hand, but she barely felt it.

Hundreds and hundreds of deaths at Phos's hand, and more to come should he succeed with his plan. Innocents buried under the weight of a foreign monument, bones atop bones.

The aide with the sword—a soldier of some sort—approached the princess, but she raised a hand to stop him. When she faced Taesia and Julian again, she was composed.

She walked to Taesia and lifted her arm to inspect the lightsbane shackle. "What earthly magic do you possess, then, to make these necessary?"

Taesia bristled. The same inadequacy that filled her in the Noctus Quarter struck her now, of being among those with whom she shared ancestry but never quite belonging.

She had already proven herself a fraud by not immediately recognizing the status symbol on the princess's forehead, her lack of knowledge about Astrum, her paltry retention of their language.

In Vitae, her magic would have been a source of pride. Her lineage, her name, inspired awe. But here...

"I'm a Shade," she admitted at last.

The Noctans did not make a sound, and Taesia's molars ached from how hard she clenched her jaw. The princess released her arm.

"I don't understand your peoples' jokes," she said curtly. "Or perhaps my meaning alluded you?"

Taesia slid back her chair and stood. The soldier reached for his sword, and the Shade's familiar spilled down his arm in a shield of fluid darkness. Julian stayed seated, face pinched.

She and the princess were of similar height, but the princess carried herself like someone who understood that a mantle had been placed upon her shoulders; one that could not be removed. That she had not only inherited a title, but all the responsibility that came with it.

Taesia had tried to shove that mantle away. In the end, it had strangled her.

"I understood you," Taesia said. "My name is Taesia Lastrider, and I am a Shade from Vitae."

The princess frowned. "Lastrider..."

The aide with the familiar inhaled sharply. "Lilia," he hissed. "She is dalyr." The princess, Lilia, backed away from Taesia with wide eyes.

Julian stood at their reactions. "What does that mean?"

Taesia cleared her throat. "Dalyr is a word to describe the Houses," she explained. "Basically, the Noctan equivalent of godspawn."

The three Noctans stared at Taesia—not in awe or fright, but something between the two.

"And you?" Lilia directed at Julian. "Are you also dalyr?"

"No," Taesia cut in before he could respond. "He's a Hunter from our realm. He tracks beasts." Julian's throat bobbed.

"Phos wanted to use the descendants of the gods," the aide with the familiar murmured. "But you escaped. Which means Phos will be looking for you."

"And you, Highness," said the soldier. His voice was lighter, his accent more refined. "If he was targeting the Lunaris specifically..."

"Then as the sole survivor, I am a threat," Lilia finished for him. She flexed her fingers, long and tipped in black nails. "Nesch."

The curse brought a sudden memory to the surface. Dante, all of twelve years old, had learned the word in the Noctus Quarter and recited it proudly back at the villa. Their mother had overheard and pulled on his ear until he cried out an apology.

Taesia sank back onto the chair and closed her eyes. What would it be like, she wondered, to return to the Lastrider villa and find it crushed with her whole family still inside?

"Phos mentioned the Lunaris," Julian said. "And that getting rid of them was beneficial for his plan."

"We are one of the oldest clans of Inlustrous, so that is no surprise," the princess agreed. "We developed the practice of harvesting stardust." Taesia's mind supplied a drawing from one of the villa's books, of a Noctan sticking their long fingers into the pockets and holes of fallen stars and meteors to extract stardust. Inhaling it caused those with magic to become stronger, and created a drug-like effect on those without it. "The prolonged exposure enhanced our Shade abilities. The only ones who could rival us are Nyx himself, or..."

Or me, Taesia thought. She opened her eyes, vision hazy as she stared down at the shackles on her lap.

It would make the most sense for the princess to leave them on. When faced with multiple threats, it was best to leash the ones you could control.

"Why weren't you in the palace with the rest of your family?" Julian asked.

"You dare—" started the aide with the familiar, but the princess shook her head at him.

"Don't, Kalen. They deserve the truth." She turned back to the others. "We arrived in Astrum to celebrate Starfall. I was supposed to join my family for the festivities." She took a deep, shuddering breath. "I do not live in the palace. We came from one of the neighboring states."

"Why don't you live in the palace?"

"Julian," Taesia warned.

"No, it's fair," the princess said. "You answered my questions. I will answer yours." She touched the tattoo upon her forehead. "I was born Waning Crescent under the Malum Star."

To Julian this meant nothing, but Taesia understood. Noctans cared deeply about their star charts, especially the ones drawn at a person's time of birth. Most people were born under multiple stars, but a few emerged into the world under ones of great importance.

Not all of them made for positive omens. There were stars for greed, lust, and madness—and one that predicted great misfortune for anyone born under its light. The Malum Star.

"My family did not want an heir with such a chart," Lilia said, the words wooden, as if she was often plagued by them. "They did not want to be touched by my affliction. They tried to love me, but it was impossible in the shadow of their fear. So they sent me away."

"That's . . . that's not right," Julian croaked.

"Do not preach to us, Vitaean," the Shade, Kalen, spat. "We do not carry the same rules of your world."

The soldier laughed awkwardly and patted Kalen's shoulder, but Kalen jerked away from his touch. "What he means is that what you call . . . what is it, astromalagy? Astorolomy?"

"Astrology," Taesia supplied.

"Yes, thank you, what you call *astrology* is something far more tangible in our realm. There is magic and science alike in stars and planets." He nodded to Starfell in the corner. "As you likely know, dalyr."

"Just call me Taesia."

"Ah, so informal," the soldier murmured despairingly. "Kalen here is an astrologer, and they are revered in our society. He reads the past, the present, and the future in the stars."

"And those born under certain stars are handled appropriately," Kalen finished. "It is not a matter of hate or mistreatment."

"I shouldn't have come to Astrum," Lilia whispered. "If I hadn't come, maybe they—"

"This wasn't written in the stars," Taesia argued. "It was the will of a god."

The room fell silent, even the street outside eerily quiet after the commotion they'd created in their escape. The princess touched her shadow bangle, and her familiar wove gently through her fingers. Taesia's eyes stung, wanting so badly to feel Umbra squeeze her wrist in reassurance.

"Then, as a product of our god, you are beholden to help us stop Phos," Lilia told her.

"Sounds great," Taesia said. "Just one problem." She raised her shackles again.

"What happened to the lock?"

"Ah..." Taesia fought not to glance at Starfell. "Got smashed while fighting."

"There's only one substance that's able to cut through lightsbane," Kalen said. "You would call it diamond."

She perked up. "Is that all?" Diamonds were plentiful in Nexus, at least among the gentry.

Lilia shook her head. "Where you come from they might be common, but here in Noctus they are scarce. Our realm is degrading. Gems and minerals are becoming harder to find and safely mine, and diamond was already precious to begin with."

Taesia's flash of hope guttered out. "Then what do we do?"

Again the princess shared a silent conversation with her aides, which ended with a dip of her chin. "The last of our diamond is harbored within the Sanctuary of Nyx, which is guarded at all hours."

"You're a princess," Julian said. "Wouldn't it be easy to request access?"

Her face tightened. "Because of my star, I have never been allowed inside."

"And neither have Vitaeans," Kalen added pointedly.

Understanding dawned in Julian's gaze. "So we have to...steal it?"

Silence fell again. Then Taesia snorted.

"Same shit, different realm," she muttered.

XV

Although Angelica had never traveled to the western continent, she and her family had taken many trips along the coast. While visiting the eastern city of Traleau when she was younger, her parents had brought her onboard a ship for the purpose of spotting whales that lived in the cold, dark waters of the sea. Her father had held her up and pointed at the arc of a whale's belly as it breached the surface, its flipper easily three times her size.

"Amazing, isn't it?" August had whispered while the other passengers made awed sounds. "That we can share a world with creatures so vast."

Now, Angelica gripped another ship's railing and blamed the briny wind for the stinging in her eyes. Beside her, Cosima whistled.

"Biggest boat I've ever seen, that's for sure." She craned her neck to better study their surroundings. "Even the one that took me and my mom to Vaega was smaller than this."

"*That* is a boat." Angelica pointed to the delta where the Lune River met the Arastra Sea. One of the riverboats had just docked and was in the process of being unloaded; supplies, she guessed, as the crates were being transferred onto pallets and pulled by horses in their direction. "*This* is a ship."

It was a large galleon that had been refashioned to carry both passengers and cargo, but the canons mounted along the sides revealed its history as a warship. Useful if they were to run into pirates, she supposed.

When she'd stepped off the carriage, Angelica had been surprised by a small camp near the docks. When a shipmate had approached to get her luggage settled, she'd asked about it.

"Them? They've come from Nexus. Desperate to get transport out of Vaega, but most don't have the money, and ships're full up. Saw a couple young lads get recruited into being deckhands. Had to be split up from their parents."

He'd hesitated, then asked, "Is it true what they're saying, my lady? The palace is gone? The king's dead?"

Angelica had counted to five before answering. "Yes."

He'd stared at her a moment, and she wondered what else he may have heard—that the Mardova heir had become a ball of spitting flame, that she had killed the Vakara heir, that nothing but destruction followed in her wake. Eventually he'd muttered a quiet prayer to himself.

"In any case, welcome aboard the *Gladius*, my lady." He'd touched his forelock and disappeared into the busy churn of the crew preparing for voyage.

Cosima now hung over the railing, staring down at the water that lapped against the hull. "Boat, ship, s'all the same to me."

"Stand up straight," Angelica hissed. "You're not acting like a guard." She had excused the rest of the House retinue to get settled in their own quarters, which they had to share with the deckhands. Only high-paying passengers like Angelica were afforded their own cabins.

Cosima righted herself. "Yeah? How do they act, then?" She rolled her shoulders back and pulled her face into an exaggerated expression of grim attention, eyes narrowed and lips pursed. "My lady, I swear upon my life no dirty commoner shall touch you."

Angelica rubbed her forehead. The cold was giving her a headache. "Your brother better be as good of a guide as you make him out to be."

Cosima crossed her arms on the railing and studied the crew pulling supply crates up the gangplank. They were all stamped with a red merchant logo. "We'll get you to your volcano, princess."

She didn't bother bringing up the issue of the nickname. Besides, her headache was distracting; it sent sharp pangs into her shoulders, shooting down her arms and into her hands. Every so often a shiver wracked her body.

Cosima peered sidelong at her. "Old habits botherin' you?"

She knew Angelica dealt with some kind of addiction. She'd assumed it was opium, and Angelica hadn't yet corrected her, hadn't explained the cravings her body went through were for heat and flame, the thirst for both music and the need to burn.

The lapses came fewer and farther between after Godsnight, as if Deia's inferno had satisfied her for the time being. But it would come back. It always did.

Cosima wriggled something from her pocket and handed it to her. Angelica didn't need to look down to tell the small vial in her hand contained Hypericum. "Was gonna bring this to you the other night. Take it when you need to."

Angelica held the vial a moment, letting it grow warm from the heat of her skin, before tucking it away. "Thank you."

Cosima swiped at her nose with a thumb. "No need for thanks."

They continued to stand at the railing in silence as final preparations were made. Angelica contemplated the camp of evacuees, wondering if they had the right idea about getting out of Vaega or if they were simply too frightened to think clearly.

With a judder, the gangplank began to ascend. Cosima straightened as the anchor was raised and the sails unfurled.

"Here we go," Cosima muttered.

The ship lurched under their feet. Angelica would have to get used to the bobbing and rocking of the ship over the next several days. She wondered if Cosima was prone to seasickness.

But the thief-turned-guard didn't seem to mind the swaying movements as she stared at the stretch of land before them receding bit by bit, home soil stretching farther from their grasp.

"I haven't been so far from Nexus since I lived in Marii." Cosima's words were nearly eaten by the wind that made whips out of Angelica's hair. "Strange. I barely remember the journey, but at the same time, it's like reliving a dream."

Angelica didn't know what to say, so she only watched the fading coastline and thought of her mother, of Miko and the twins. Dante and Brailee heading south to Deia's Heart. Camilla Lorenzo and her cryptic plans. Taesia, and Nikolas, and Risha.

Somewhere within all this was a crown to be won, but Angelica now understood it had always been more than that. Just as Ferdinand had been a king unfit for rule, Deia was a tyrant who did not have Vitae's best interests at heart. If change were to happen—significant, widespread change—it would have to start at the source.

Listen to yourself, she mentally scoffed. *You sound like you want to replace Deia as a god.*

A foolish, odd thought. The need to find the fulcrum was born from desperation, from wanting to stop Deia from causing any more harm. But she hadn't fully considered what would happen if she actually found it.

Or what she might become.

Another shiver went up her spine, but this one felt different, like an icy finger touching her nape. She cast around with the sudden suspicion that she was being watched. Her gaze landed on a seagull perched farther down the railing. There had been plenty wheeling overhead at the docks, crying out for food, but apparently this one had decided to ride with them for a bit.

The longer she stared at the seagull, the more she realized how unnaturally still it was. It had affixed one blue eye on her—not the anxious stare of a creature yearning for food, but the steady scrutiny of a hunter.

As if it whatever resided inside it—controlled it?—wasn't a seagull at all.

Heart pounding, Angelica reached out and plucked at Cosima's sleeve. "We're going inside."

"Sure thing."

It wasn't until they were safely behind the locked door of Angelica's cabin that Cosima asked, "Something wrong? You seem...spooked."

Angelica swallowed the ashy taste that had risen in her mouth. "No, I...I saw one of the men looking at me, and it made me uncomfortable."

Cosima scowled and cracked her knuckles. "I'll take care of him."

"What? No, just...just stay here." She turned to the porthole, but thankfully there were no birds hovering outside. The cabin wasn't what she would consider large, but it was big enough for a bunk in the corner as well as a bench against the opposite wall. Most of the furniture had been bolted to the floor.

"All right, but I'll have to go find my hammock at some point," Cosima said.

"Hammock?"

"Where all the other guards're sleeping."

Maybe it was nerves, or the lingering uneasiness of what had just happened, but the thought of Cosima being somewhere else—of Angelica being *alone*—was deeply unpleasant.

"I'd like you to sleep here instead," she said without thinking. She only realized the mistake when Cosima rocked back on her heels.

"Oh," Cosima said. "You. Huh." Her eyes darted to the small, singular bunk.

"*No*, gods, no, I meant the—the bench? Or we can ask for a cot, or... or something," she finished in a near-rasp.

Cosima looked like she was battling between amusement and offense. "Didn't know the thought of sharing a bed with me was so horrible. Do I smell?" She made a show of lifting her arm to take a whiff of her armpit.

"No," Angelica sighed. "I... don't want to be alone."

It was humiliating to say it out loud, especially when Cosima's face softened. "Oh, then yeah," the thief said. "I can do that."

Angelica was steadily becoming unmoored in more ways than one.

It was their second night at sea when Angelica was jolted awake by shouts. She sat up, pulse thundering as Cosima rolled off the bench into a defensive stance.

"Wahapun?" Cosima mumbled, swaying in the moonlight coming through the porthole.

Their travel had been uneventful until now. She hadn't seen the gull again, but when she stood at the railing it was as if the water was the pupil of some monstrous giant's eye, tracking her every movement. Angelica's imagination conjured shadows in the depths that kept pace with the ship.

Maybe it hadn't all been her imagination.

"I don't know." Angelica kicked the covers off and reached for her robe. "Come on."

She followed the commotion through the companionway and onto the deck. Moonlight slanted across the wood and metal studs while rigging creaked above their heads. Some of the deckhands were crouched around the entry to the lower decks, which was located midship. They started at her appearance, but none of them tried to prevent her from taking the stairs down to the cargo hold. Cosima kept right behind her.

The hold was packed with crates and barrels, the ground lined with straw and sawdust. Angelica wrinkled her nose and hoped the source of the musty scent in the air wasn't mouse urine.

A couple crewmates were standing near an open crate toward the back, yelling and gesturing at something hidden from her view. Even the captain, a weathered Azunese woman, had been roused from bed. She stood with her arms crossed and her cheek lined with an imprint from her pillow. When she spotted Angelica, she dropped her arms and sighed.

"Sorry for the disturbance, my lady, but it seems as if we've found a stowaway. Please don't worry, we'll handle this accordingly."

But Angelica had walked close enough to see the subject of the crew's outrage.

"What," she said lowly, "the *fuck* are you doing here?"

Eiko was shivering and hunched in on herself, brandishing a small knife at the crewmates and captain. But at Angelica's familiar disapproving tone she straightened up and lifted her chin, donning a stubborn mask.

"I'm going to Azuna whether Maa wants me to or not," Eiko said. Her voice was creaky, her hair lying lank and unwashed over her shoulders. She was wearing the same dress she'd worn the day Angelica had left the villa, when she had stormed off to the gardens in a fit of rage.

Only she hadn't gone to the gardens. Angelica looked at the open crate and saw piles of fabric, the wood stamped with the same logo she had seen on the crates coming from the riverboat. A barrel of water had been opened, and an apple core was rotting on the ground.

"You came by river, didn't you?" Angelica asked. "You hid yourself in a fucking *crate*?"

"If you saw me, you would have sent me back!"

"Of course I would have! Do you have any idea how dangerous—"

"Excuse me, my lady," the captain cut in, "but I'm going to need an explanation."

Angelica glanced at Cosima, who watched on avidly. "On behalf of the Mardovas, allow me to extend an apology to you and your crew, Captain. This is my younger stepsister, Eiko. She was not supposed to travel with me."

One of the crewmates swore so colorfully that Eiko flushed. The knife she held trembled in her hand. Her pale blue dress was woefully wrinkled and stained; Angelica had never seen her so disheveled.

"As soon as we dock in Azuna, I'm tying you up and sending you back to Nexus," Angelica said. "My mother and yours are going to be furious."

"I won't let you." Eiko extended the knife again, face hardened in resolve.

"Is any of this worth it?" Angelica demanded. "I understand you want to see your home country again, but think about the position we're in. Think about the state we've left Nexus in, and the politics that involve *both* your families. You really want to be in the middle of that?"

Eiko wavered, but the set of her jaw was obstinate. Angelica's palms grew hot.

Not now. They were surrounded by wood and flammable material; she couldn't entertain her ire.

To her surprise, Cosima stepped forward. Eiko blinked at her and the red House jacket she'd slung over her shoulders before rushing out of Angelica's cabin.

"Hey, so, you don't know me at all," Cosima started, "but I get it. I'm not from Vaega originally either. And I'd love to go back to Marii one day. But I also know that day's not now." She rubbed at her nose as if it was cold. "And I don't even have a mom to worry about me anymore."

Eiko stared at her a moment before lowering the knife. Her eyes shone wetly in the dim light of the lanterns.

"I just wanted to see it again," she whispered. "Angelica. Please."

Eiko had never been shy in voicing her dislike for Angelica. Likewise, Angelica hadn't been subtle in her antipathy. But instead of seeing a spoiled, angry girl, Angelica saw a young woman begging for autonomy and wanting honesty. One who hadn't asked to be a piece in a grand game, but was resigned to be one anyway.

Miko's warnings about her family were still fresh in her mind. She couldn't leave Eiko with the Uedas, nor could she bring her along on her journey to Mount Netsai. The best thing to do was send her back to Vaega the moment they docked.

The heat gradually left Angelica's palms. She was about to turn to the captain to arrange some sort of payment for Eiko's passage when the ship gave a sudden, violent lurch.

Eiko shrieked as they stumbled, water splashing out of the open barrel and spilling everywhere. The captain darted back up the stairs while Cosima helped Eiko up.

"Stay here," Angelica ordered the two of them before following the captain. The deck was a flurry of action.

"—swear I saw som'n!" one of the deckhands gathered at the railing was telling the captain.

Angelica joined them, staring down at the dark water. The moon cast sheets of pearl over the ocean's surface, mostly smooth except for the gentle waves around the ship's keel. Behind her the crew tried to soothe the handful of other passengers who'd emerged cranky and confused from their cabins, but other than that the night was still as an indrawn breath.

Angelica was about to turn back for the cargo hold when a large shape broke through the water.

A tentacle, writhing and dark, loomed over the *Gladius*. Before anyone could react, it surged forward and clamped around the deckhand who had spoken. He didn't even have time to shout before he was yanked over the railing and pulled into the icy water.

Angelica stumbled back as screams split the air. The captain bellowed for her crew to man the cannons.

"What in Thana's rotting grave was *that*?"

Angelica whirled around. Cosima had drawn her stolen sword, gaping at the spot where the man had been taken. Behind her, Eiko was pale and quaking.

"I told you to stay in the hold!"

"And let the screams lull us to sleep?" Cosima bit back.

"I–it's a kraken." Eiko stepped out from behind Cosima. "They dwell near the bottom of the sea and sometimes come up to sink ships. B–but they haven't been seen in a long time, I thought they were extinct!"

"Hate to break *that* streak," Cosima said faintly.

A second tentacle rose from the water, spraying them before it crashed down onto the ship's stern. The *Gladius* rocked violently and Angelica went sprawling, her wrist twinging in pain from trying to catch herself. Half a dozen more tentacles slithered up the hull, twining around the railing or else seeking more deckhands to drown.

At the bow, another figure emerged from the depths. It was large and bulbous, its hide a grayish green under the moonlight. The kraken's head. Below its gelatinous, dark eyes the flesh parted in a vertical mouth, ringed with prongs and spurs. Its low roar vibrated through the ship.

Eiko screamed. Angelica spun around just as her stepsister dodged a tentacle, the suckers along its underside pulsating. Eiko grabbed her small knife and jabbed it into the thick flesh. It thrashed backward.

"Get away from it!" Angelica shouted. Cosima shoved Eiko out of the way, holding up her sword.

A couple shipmates ran forward with hands extended. Water rose from the sides of the *Gladius* and hurtled into the roaming tentacles, pushing them across the deck. The water elementalists struggled under the onslaught.

The cannons fired below, their *booms* reverberating across the water and up through her soles. One of the cannonballs hit the monster, gouging a bloody hole in the side of its head. It writhed, its cry sharp and piercing. Great—now they'd angered it.

Angelica dove inward. She reached urgently for her power, for whatever crumbs Deia might have left behind.

Water wouldn't do much to a beast that lived in it. There was no earth nearby. Fire would threaten the ship.

Air, then.

Air comes from the part of an elementalist that rests below the breastbone and above the stomach, Eran Liolle had once told her. A university mage with sick desires, whose blood had ended up splashing across Angelica's tongue.

Angelica nearly lost her concentration, shuddering as bile singed her throat. Cannons blasted, and someone screamed.

Focus on your breathing, and let it guide your power.

In through her nose, a spiral of breath into her lungs, encircling her core, expanding her diaphragm. She sensed the air currents around her, ready to be plucked and woven. Opening her eyes, she reached for one of the stronger drafts and attempted to sharpen it like razor wire, the thinnest hairsbreadth of force that could split the kraken's head in two.

But just like in the university's practice arena, the current kept slipping away from her, a teasing chase between mage and element. Angelica concentrated on drowning out the chaos, on sending the current into the beast's flesh. It nicked its hide, black blood spurting in a fountain.

Again. Sweat dripped down her temples as Angelica picked another current to sharpen. Her skin grew feverish, the air around her warming.

Something compelled her to glance down. Embers had popped to life at her feet, eddies of fire swirling around her hands.

No—She couldn't let the fire take control, not now.

The crew were firing crossbows and harpoons at the tentacles with little luck. Blood pooled on the deck, a severed leg lying in a dark puddle.

It reminded her of a severed marble head in Haven Square.

The vortex that had formed behind Risha.

The song that had beckoned her violin.

Angelica shut her eyes and began to sing. Her voice came out croaky and breaking, but the more she pushed it out the more it stabilized, sinking into a familiar vibrato as she performed the aria from *The Gossamer Road*.

"Are you really performing at a time like this?" Cosima yelled.

She opened her eyes and focused on the kraken's head. It loomed over the ship, hugging it in its attempt to drag them down into the sea.

Angelica shifted to forte. Her voice resounded above the water, a song defying the night and the horror it had brought them.

The kraken focused on Angelica. One of its wounded tentacles struck at her with viperous speed. Angelica hit the crescendo and the swirling numbness in her core bloomed, her bones catching fire and the stars overhead winking out for just a moment.

The top half of the kraken's head vanished like mist. Its tentacles all collapsed, twitching and sliding off the ship, as what remained of its body swayed. Slowly it released the *Gladius* and sank pitifully back into the waters.

Angelica fell to her knees. She felt like a towel that had been wrung out one too many times. A tentative touch at her shoulder brought her attention to Eiko, who was staring at her as if she had never truly seen Angelica before.

On her other side, Cosima collapsed in a sweaty heap. "Please help me understand what just happened," she panted.

"*Kudei.*"

They looked up. The captain was standing over them, sword in one hand and blood streaked across her cheek. Her expression was difficult to read.

"What?" Angelica rasped.

Seeming to come out of some sort of reverie, the captain turned back to her crew, barking orders to assess the damage.

"Angelica." Eiko somehow still had hold of her little knife. "What happened? What did you just do?"

She flexed her fingers. The boards under her were singed. "This is why I need to go to Azuna on my own. It's not just about currying favor for the Mardovas. I need to learn more about my powers. *This* power."

Eiko looked between the boards and where the kraken had disappeared. "Maybe I can help."

"How can *you* help?"

"Vaega honors the four elements. But in Azuna, we were taught there are five."

"And?"

Eiko nodded to the captain's retreating back. "The fifth element is called aether in Vaega. In Azuna, it's called kudei."

The back of her neck prickled. Angelica thought of the grimoire, learning of Ostium and its fate, a fifth realm that had constructed the gateways between all the others. Portals crafted out of a substance named quintessence. Was that, then, the source of aether? Of kudei?

Angelica picked up a piece of wood broken off the railing. "This attack was planned, and I'm sure there'll be more."

"*Planned?*" Cosima echoed. "What do you mean?"

Angelica wondered if the thief had started to regret coming with her. "Deia knows what I'm doing," she answered. "And is trying to stop me."

She watched the realization dawn in Cosima's dark eyes, as dark as the spill of blood nearby.

"Oh," Cosima said weakly. "Well. That's not terrifying at all."

It was terrifying, but it also lit a wick of satisfaction inside her. Because with this attack, Deia had played her hand early.

If she was trying to stop Angelica, that meant Angelica was on the right track. Deia's fulcrum was hidden in Mount Netsai.

And she was going to find it.

LISTEN
CLOSELY

You are sad. You are anxious. I understand.

You may not think one such as I feels these things, but you would be wrong, as would so many other creatures who prostrate to statues and altars.

(Strange, isn't it, that they get on their knees and cry out words we usually cannot hear, gifting us bits of organic material we have no need for. Sometimes I smell blood and grow curious. Sometimes there is a symbol that gains my attention. Sometimes those who harbor my light require my blessing more urgently than those who do not. We all play favorites.)

My grief expands and fills up the parts of me I thought were long dead. Those dark, shadow-touched places I cannot bear to acknowledge.

(He was good to me, once. Between Solara and Noctus we met in a celestial belt, surrounded by raining stars and the tendrils of nebulas without names. His hands—dark, then, as dark as the distance between realms—encircling my waist and preening through my wings. I could have given myself wider hips or a different shape altogether, but he told me he liked me like this, all while tracing my jaw and testing how sensitive I could make my lips. Whatever form I had always responded so well to whatever form he had. I can feel, now, rough horns under my hands, a hot mouth on my stomach, the night itself enfolding and spoiling me until I had to cry *no more*.)

This is not a betrayal. Believe me, I recognize the concept when I see it. There is a time when this will end, and you will be happier for it. We will build new worlds together, where hunger is not a thing that exists.

Do you believe me? You will.

Look at this. Here is your arm, and here is your hand. Here are your fingers opening like petals to a new morning. Do you see this? This small, fragile thing, a piece of his body he willingly removed. Now it is ours. We won't waste it.

(I once thought we could create a world together. He said, w————? I said, y—. In that space between our realms, there was a promise that burned my skin the way only darkness could, the way his touch did, like I carried all of Solara's suns and he was trying to shutter the light before it consumed me.

I should have consumed him instead.)

The human body is so frail. You hold a part of him now, your own flesh and blood, and still the hunger stirs inside you. But I have already eaten of my own flesh and blood, and it was not so bad.

Listen closely: There are different forms of hunger. Mine nearly destroyed me.

I will not let yours destroy you.

PART II

Land of Ash and Steel

I

From a distance, Astrum had been lit up like a jewel, like the diamond they so desperately needed. Up close, Taesia realized the light came from tall streetlamps and from strands draped across buildings and bridges, a spectrum of silver, white, and pale yellow. It gave the illusion that everything was washed in moonlight, strengthened by the actual moon overhead, the curved scythe of a waning crescent.

The rooftops were steep and pointed, but Taesia and Lilia found a vantage spot against the iron railing of a turret. The wind was even harsher up here, knifing through the cloak Kalen had reluctantly handed to Taesia earlier. But at least they were able to get a good view of the Sanctuary of Nyx below.

It was massive, bigger than any of the basilicas back home. There was an ominous edge in its pointed arches, ornately carved buttresses, and pinnacles crowned with sculptures of the moon's phases. It was crafted out of dark stone that shone faintly under the eternal night sky, touched here and there with designs made of precious silver and gemstone. The massive doors had been flung open to accept a steady stream of worshippers, some of whom lingered in the courtyard where priests in black attire handed out food and fed peat into smoking bowls atop pedestals.

Taesia's nostrils flared at the scent of clove and anise. Sense memory dragged her back to the Nyx basilica, standing between Dante and Brailee and being forced to recite certain verses of lengthy prayers. Being anointed with lavender oil. Being confronted by the illusion of her god and shattering his statue into pieces.

A breeze swept by, and Taesia pulled her borrowed cloak tighter around her. It wasn't nearly thick enough, but then again, the Noctans didn't need fur-lined cloaks when their blood was attuned to the chill. Lilia wasn't even affected as the wind stirred her long hair and fluttered the hem of her dark blue surcoat.

"You mentioned circles outside the city," the princess said once they'd observed their fill. "Spells of...Conjuring?"

"Conjuration," Taesia corrected. "It's an old magic. Most knowledge of it is gone. But my sister is a dream walker, and saw Phos using it through a dreamscape." She paused. "He sacrificed Noctan lives for it."

Lilia flexed her fingers, as if longing to wrap them around Phos's neck. "A disconcerting number of travelers have gone missing in this area. There has been an increase in beast sightings, so we thought that was the reason. Most don't brave the wilderness without a guide for fear of them. But why would he need Noctan lives?"

"I don't know. Something about their magic, I think, helped fuel the circles so that he could...well, do that." Taesia nodded toward the barrier atop the hill. "He wants the remains of the god hidden in the palace."

The barrier reflected in Lilia's eyes was a golden spangle. "The remains of a god. A *fifth* god, you said? Then is there a fifth realm?"

"There was." She held Julian's name on her lips, but decided his secrets were his own to divulge. "The gods themselves admitted to it."

Lilia's shoulders stiffened. "Nyx," she whispered. "Has he ever spoken to you?"

Whether in Vitae or Noctus, what Taesia was—who she was—was considered auspicious. Begot of a god, someone who might have his ear.

She had it, all right. *He wants me to fight his battles for him. Surprise, your god is a coward.*

But there was no way of saying that to someone like Lilia, who had grown up with many of the same stories Taesia had, worshipping a being who had created everything she'd ever known.

"A bit," Taesia admitted. "But it wasn't very constructive."

Lilia deflated. "I see. Maybe when the lightsbane is off, we can try to commune with him."

Absolutely not. "You can't commune with him here in your own realm?"

Lilia gestured to the temple. "We try. I've done my fair share of praying, hoping for Nyx to help us with our water scarcity at the very least. Now I know why he's been distracted."

"Inter-realm wars tend to be distracting," Taesia agreed.

Lilia shook her head. "I've often wondered what it's like. Vitae, that is."

Taesia had no idea where to start. "The weather can be unpredictable. Imagine being hot one minute and freezing the next. We also have, um...wheat?" She was fairly sure Noctans used mushroom powder to make their breads.

"Is it true you have both night and day? You have a sun *and* a moon?"

"Last I checked."

"In the sky at the same time?"

"Nyx's piss, no. Well, technically, but it's more like they take turns."

"*What* did you just say?" the princess demanded. "Nyx's *piss*?"

Taesia fought not to laugh at Lilia's outraged expression. "It's a saying where I'm from."

"Disrespectful," Lilia muttered, but her mouth twitched with a suppressed smile. "What was it like to grow up in a House? I imagine your upbringing wasn't in line with a regular Vitaean."

"A lot of our duties were relegated after the Sealing, so other than our magic and our lineage, we were more on par with the other noble houses. I'm curious, though: Did Nyx ever interfere with your bloodline?" At Lilia's confused look, Taesia made a crude gesture.

"No!" Lilia slapped Taesia's hands apart. "Or at least, never to our knowledge. No one's ever come forward with the claim. The Lunaris' power comes from the merging of stardust in our blood when we learned to harvest it." Lilia opened her hand, her familiar spilling onto her palm. "We became stronger by evolution." She closed her hand, and her familiar turned into a long, wicked sword. "Now I'm all that's left."

The princess's gaze returned to the barrier, her short-lived levity sinking back into the depths. Taesia thought of Nikolas in the palace beyond and wished for him to be whole.

"I'm sorry," Taesia said softly.

Lilia let her familiar dissipate and rewrap itself around her wrist. "Being a Lunari has never been easy, let alone the youngest heir born under the Malum Star."

"How old were you when you left?"

Eyes on the temple below, Lilia answered, "Twelve."

"That young?"

"An astrologer made a prediction that the Malum Star would be the undoing of our people. Shortly after I turned twelve, my eldest brother's wife had a series of miscarriages. Once I was sent away, she delivered a healthy baby. An heir." Lilia's voice broke; that child had ended up dead anyway. "The prediction came to pass. This is the curse of the Malum Star."

"That's bullshit. I get why you value the stars and believe in their power, but—"

"Believe? Do you *believe* your Vitaean sun is warm, or do you simply say it is warm? So it is with the stars of our realm."

Taesia sighed. "Fine. I know you don't view it as a cruel practice, but it seems pretty cruel to me."

Lilia gave a rueful smile. "Maybe. Maybe not. In any case, they sent me to one of the southern states to continue my education. They assigned Mar as my personal guard." Marcellus, the soldier downstairs with the long silver hair. Taesia liked his genial attitude a lot more than the sullen astrologer's. "Kalen was also given to me as a minder. Their help has been beyond invaluable to me, especially when it came to fighting off assassins."

"*Assassins?* Did they want to ransom you back to your family?"

Lilia frowned as if Taesia was the one spouting nonsense. "No. My family sent them."

Taesia willed herself to say nothing. No matter her origins, this was not her world. But Lilia noticed the hardening of her expression.

"It's all right," the princess said. "It was expected, and fair. I hold no venom for it. They understood, too, that it was up to me to decide my fate. And Mar was a prodigy even at such a young age. He took the first two down singlehandedly."

Taesia ran her tongue over her teeth to dislodge the words she wanted to spit at the dead Lunaris. "Well, I know what it's like to have people after your life. Not fun, but it keeps things interesting."

"I suppose that's one way of looking at it." Lilia chewed on her lower lip before asking, "Are there any Noctans left? In Vitae?"

"Yes. A good couple thousand, at least. They all live in Nexus. My family checks in on them, makes sure they're taken care of." For a moment Taesia was standing in the Noctus Quarter, Starfell lifted toward a swirling vortex. "When I left, they were still safe." *I made sure of that.*

Gratitude flashed in Lilia's lavender eyes. "Thank you. I will not forget it."

Taesia coughed and turned back to the temple. "Yeah...anyway. Do you really think this will work?"

"If it doesn't, then at least I'll know I have done my duty to the best of my ability."

The princess didn't see Taesia's grimace when they turned to head back to the others. As far as she was concerned, duty had never gotten her or her family anywhere.

Julian had been left behind with the soldier—"Marcellus Rhydian, youngest son of the Rhydian dukedom. A pleasure, despite the circumstances!"—and the astrologer, the latter of whom had elected to sit at the table with his arms folded, watching Julian.

They sat like this in uneasy silence while Taesia and the princess were gone. Julian very much wished he'd left with them.

Finally Marcellus laughed and poked at Kalen. "Kal, you should introduce yourself properly."

"Do not call me that," the other man grumbled. He swatted Marcellus's hand away. "And stop touching me."

"But, Kal—"

"*Kalen*," the astrologer bit out. His gaze flitted back to Julian. "Kalen Braythe. If it matters."

Julian nodded, feeling too large within his own skin. "Julian Luca," he said hoarsely.

"Ah, there now," Marcellus said, all cheer. He tossed some of his lustrous silver hair over his shoulder. "We're all properly acquainted."

Kalen hummed noncommittally. Julian said nothing, and the silence became its own sort of beast. Marcellus fiddled with his sword, unsheathing an inch and then sliding it back in. Julian noted the blade was darker than steel, the hilt an ornate blend of onyx and silver with a twisting basket guard, the pommel set with a pearlescent jewel.

The soldier was definitely nobility. Yet both were travel-dirty and attired plainly, all the better to avoid attention.

After a few unbearable minutes, Kalen sighed and rummaged through a nearby pack. He slapped a piece of parchment onto the table.

"Where were you born?" he asked.

Julian looked to Marcellus, who only smiled. "I'm...sorry?"

"The place where you were birthed," Kalen drawled. "Somewhere in Vitae, yes?"

"Uh, yes, I . . . Nexus."

Kalen wrote something down. Julian couldn't read the looping foreign characters. "And the time?"

Another look to Marcellus, who nodded encouragingly. "My mother said I was born at night. After dusk, but before midnight."

Kalen muttered something to himself that sounded like "of course" before he made a note of it. "And the date?"

Julian told him, more and more bewildered as Kalen's pen scratched across the paper. "Your fifth calendar month would fall toward the end of our Full Moon cycle," the astrologer explained, drawing lines between symbols. "And in Vitae, that would mean . . ."

He quietly studied the paper. Marcellus kept smiling placidly beside him. Julian caught his eye and the soldier loudly whispered, "I love this part."

"You were born between the constellations Efuero and Bastion," Kalen said at last, crumpling the parchment in his hand before tossing it over his shoulder like it was trash. "Which means you'd have been born under the stars Belua and Praeses."

His tone implied this might not be a good thing. Julian waited for him to extrapolate. When he didn't, Julian prodded, "And those mean . . . ?"

Kalen narrowed his green eyes. "It means you're a contradiction, and I'll be watching your every move."

Marcellus chuckled. "He's always very dramatic about his readings," he told Julian with a wink. "Don't worry about it."

Julian, the holder of a very pressing, burning secret, worried.

It was a relief when the women returned. At first Julian thought Lilia was alone, but then the near-invisible shadows behind her parted to reveal Taesia.

"Oh, good, I'll put on some chori." Marcellus went to the small stove in the corner with a dented copper kettle and a large unmarked tin beside it.

"Tea," Taesia said at Julian's unspoken question. "Or their version of it. They don't grow the same types of leaves we do in Vitae."

Julian had wondered about what they could grow here, considering there was no sunlight. But this was a wholly different realm, with rules he wasn't familiar with. At this rate he wouldn't have been surprised to learn the moon was made of wax.

"How did the temple look?" he asked.

"Big," Taesia said.

"Helpful, thanks."

"Most of us haven't been inside before," Lilia added. "Which means we're at a disadvantage."

"Not to mention the dalyr does not have her magic," Kalen pointed out.

Taesia's mouth curved into something too sharp to be considered a smile. "Luckily I'm not completely reliant on my magic, like most Shades."

Kalen's familiar twitched around his neck. Before he could retort, Lilia walked to where Taesia's sword was leaning against the wall. Taesia visibly tensed as the princess wrapped her fingers around the grip and lifted the sword. Again Julian was awed by the violent shape of it, the glimmering specks within the bone—the same bone Taesia had killed a man to obtain.

He glanced at her and found her glancing back at him, both remembering the bone dealer's shop.

"There is much power in this weapon." Lilia held it with both hands, gentle in her reverence. "Have you named it?"

"Yes. Starfell."

"An unlikely name, but I suppose it fits. It has been many, many years since we have encountered an astralam. And yet you happened upon these bones in Vitae, of all places."

Kalen joined her and held a hand above the blade. "They feel old. Centuries, at least."

"Does it matter how I got them?" Taesia asked. "This sword might be the best tool to fight against Phos."

"Why should *you* be the one to wield it?" Kalen flung back at her. "Lilia has—"

"No," the princess cut in, setting the sword back down with great care. "This is not mine to wield."

Marcellus seemed a little disappointed. "Why not?"

"Because there is another tool we need to defeat one as strong as Phos. And it is also in the Sanctuary."

Kalen's breath hitched in understanding. "The coronal?"

"The coronal," Lilia agreed. "A sacred object of my family. It is made of an astralam's fangs."

"I know of it," Taesia said. "It can absorb a massive amount of starlight that can be turned on enemies."

"Yes, but it's also a defensive tool. In the Century of Eclipse, we suffered heavy blows from Solara. One of my ancestors used the bones of an astralam gifted by Nyx to make the coronal. With it she erected a barrier across all of Astrum to stop Solara's advances. Since then, it has been securely guarded in the Sanctuary of Nyx. But now, I... I am the only one capable of wielding it."

Marcellus rested a hand on the princess's shoulder. "We'll retrieve it, Your Highness." The kettle began to hiss and rattle on the stove, drawing him away.

"We should split into two groups, then," Kalen suggested. "One to get the diamond, the other to get the coronal."

"Is there any way to map the layout of the temple?" Taesia asked.

"There might be," Lilia said. "Kalen, help me with something."

The Noctans retreated to the table. Taesia turned back to Julian, who had long since decided his role was to be as quiet and helpful as possible. Now Taesia gestured for him to follow her into the corner Starfell occupied.

"We haven't had a chance to talk about what happened," Taesia said as they sat against the wall.

If Julian closed his eyes long enough, concentrated deep enough, he could feel the echoes of pain left in the wake of his refusal to accept what had been offered to him.

What even was it? A power, but not *his* power, not as he understood it. For most of his life he had been someone who could lock eyes on a beast and understand its intentions. For most of his life he had wrestled with the idea that this power made him a beast, too.

And now he knew for certain that he was. Not just a beast, but a *demon*, a remnant of a world long gone, and the only pawn left on a god's gameboard.

Orsus. Goosebumps rose along his arms.

A hand encircled his wrist. "Julian?"

He kept his head down, afraid to discover what emotion she was wearing. He was still looking down when a handleless clay cup was shoved under his nose.

"Sorry to interrupt," came a voice above them. "Just wanted to give you these."

Julian instinctively reached for the cup before he could think to deny it. Marcellus handed another to Taesia and bustled off to the table where Lilia and Kalen were scheming.

The tea was a deep blue color and smelled like jasmine. He took a small sip and almost burned his mouth, but it was worth it for the flavors that coated his tongue, a satiny blend of floral and spice he had never encountered before. It tasted of a night in autumn, enjoying a warm fire in the middle of a cold night, leaves blushing orange and red, crisp air scented with the last of the season's harvest.

His shoulders relaxed. He thought of his mother's apartment, sitting at the table with her and his father as they laughed over a card game. The wintry air on his face when he and his father practiced shooting outside. The way his mother had tucked a blanket around him when he'd fallen asleep in his chair.

A gentle touch on his face wiped away a stray tear.

"I know it's a lot," Taesia murmured. "Take your time."

Julian quietly drank his tea. Taesia sipped hers and waited, eyelids growing heavier.

Finally he said, "They spoke to me."

"Who?"

Julian held the clay cup closer to his chest, seeking its warmth. "Orsus."

She carefully set her own cup down. "The fifth god. Their...remains. Spoke to you."

"Yes."

"What did they say?"

He didn't know how long he had lain in the Bone Palace with that whisper in his skull, telling him to control, create, conquer. He didn't know what it meant, not even when he related it now to Taesia. What he'd been expected to do, other than destroy Phos with a power he did not comprehend nor want.

"I couldn't do it," he whispered, low enough not to carry to the princess and her aides. "I didn't know what was happening. I just wanted to save Nik."

"You snapped him out of Phos's control for a while," Taesia said. "That's something."

"But that wasn't Orsus's power, it was—" *Azideh's.* "It was mine."

"I thought it only worked on beasts?"

"I thought so, too. But I...I don't know. Being in that place..." He was trembling, he realized in a distant way. "It did something to me. I didn't like it."

"But you're not hearing the voice now?" He shook his head. "Good.

Don't give in to it." She spared a glance at the others. "Nyx wants me to accept his power, but I can't. If I let him have control over me, I might end up like Rian. Don't let Orsus take control of you."

He opened his mouth to say he wouldn't, but that wasn't a promise he could make. He was a simple man from a simple life—he was the least equipped person here to deal with something of this scale. And before him sat the daughter of a god, a daughter of kings, who had grown up steeped in magic and power. Who understood how to wield them.

What must she see when she looked at him? How much did she resent being here with him instead of Nikolas?

"I don't want their power," Julian whispered at last. "I've never even wanted my own."

He only wanted to return to Nexus, to his mother, to *home*. To preserve a life left in autumn.

There was a flicker in Taesia's dark eyes that may or may not have been confusion. Of course—she was one who sought strength, not rejected it.

But he had already seen what gods and demons could do. He would not allow them to destroy what little he had left.

II

Risha stood in the courtyard of the Bone Palace, in the eye of Thana's wintry torus. Tendrils of power grasped at beating, taunting hearts—hearts she needed to squeeze to pulp, hearts crowding her chest in a synchronized drumbeat, hearts she knew by feel and name. Ash and smoke drifted on the air. Deia raged in a tower of flame before her.

"—sha!"

The nightmare shifted, folded, and Jas became Brailee. She dove before Angelica's fire and held her hands up. The flames turned to rose petals.

"Where are you?" Brailee demanded.

Risha faltered. The petals were swept up within her torus, swirling around her in a fit. "How—?"

"Quickly! Where are you?"

"I'm—" *Vitae, Nexus, courtyard, portal*— "Mortri! I'm in Mortri!"

Another wall of fire, and Brailee disappeared into ash.

Risha woke with a choking gasp. Her pulse struggled, and for a moment she felt her body shutting down, a terrifying descent into dark waters.

See how easy it is to slip away? Thana whispered, grave-quiet. *You cannot go on much longer. You know this. You almost crave it—to let go and fall, and not have to get back up.*

Then Jas touched her shoulder and she could properly breathe. She shut her eyes again and focused on the blood traveling through her body, the rhythm of her heart, the electric response of her brain.

Risha rubbed her face before letting Jas help her up. "I'm all right. Just . . . nightmare."

Jas nodded, eyes pinched. She tried not to look too long at the outline of his body turning vaporous.

They'd found an outcrop to rest under. The vegetation around here was dense and strange, junglelike, with trailing vines and razor-edged ferns and purple silken flowers that Val had warned them not to get too close to.

Val was situated on top of a flat rock to keep an eye on their surroundings. But now his gaze was intent on her, as if trying to figure out the potential hazards of sleep on humans.

"I made this while you were out," Jas said. He handed her a bundle of vines that had been tightly bound together. "It's for the head."

"The *head*?" Val muttered. "I told you my name."

The tangle of vines felt smooth and durable, thickened in all the places they were woven together. Not woven—fused. "Did you use your magic?"

Jas smiled. "I wanted to see if I could access it in this form. I can, but it's not as strong as it was in Vitae."

"Jas," she sighed. "Thank you for making this, but you shouldn't be expending your spiritual energy this way."

"I'm all right. Honest."

She didn't feel like arguing. Instead, she stood and approached Val, who pursed his lips at the makeshift carrier. "Is this all right?"

"Better than being hauled around by the hair, I suppose."

She tried a couple different options before wrapping the vines under his chin. She tied the ends around her shoulders so that he could rest on her back.

"Hey, hey, I'm facing the wrong way!" he complained.

"You can be our lookout from behind," Risha said. "I'll turn around when you need me to." Val grumbled and fidgeted against her back. "It's not exactly pleasant for me either."

Val humphed. "All the more incentive to go find my body, huh?"

"Not until we have Leshya's weapon," Jas reminded him.

"Pfft, so impatient..."

He directed them to go north. When Risha and Jas only stood there, having gotten completely disoriented in their escape from the Sentinel, he clicked his tongue. "Over there! Over— For fuck's sake I can't *point* anymore. See where those plants get sparser? Go there."

"Where exactly are we going?" Jas asked as they began to walk.

"Toward the Vitae portal."

Jas made an intrigued sound. "I didn't know there were portals here. I thought the caves were the only way into the realm."

"Not quite." Risha readjusted the sling when it started to sag. "There *are* portals to the other realms here, but they're kept far away from the kings' cities. They used to be heavily guarded, too. Back in the day, people could cross over long enough to try and speak with their loved ones, but they had to be supervised by priests. And they couldn't leave the immediate area."

"I see. Then Leshya's weapon is near the Vitae portal because she abandoned it in her effort to return home."

"Yes." Risha ducked under a tree branch, her boots crunching against detritus. "I...don't know if I would be able to get it open. If our attempts at Godsnight didn't work, I doubt I can do anything on my own."

"But you said Angelica Mardova sent you here through a portal," Jas pointed out.

"I think so. I honestly don't remember it that well." *Nor do I want to.*

The foliage had become thicker again, and Risha had to concentrate on stepping over low, curving tree trunks and gnarled roots. Ferns and fronds rustled as she passed, and in the distance came a skin-prickling shriek.

A fern hit Val in the face and he sputtered. "Be careful! There are bugs in this area that can burrow into your skin, you know."

"Lovely," Jas muttered.

"You don't even have skin, what's your problem?"

"What can you tell us about Mortri?" Risha interjected. "Other than flesh-eating bugs, please."

"What about the kings?" Jas asked.

"Ahh, yes, the kings. Four undead bastards with lots of history. What do you want to know?"

"How they came to be, I suppose. Do they work directly under Thana?"

"As far as I know," Val answered. "When Mortri first existed, it was just the god and the souls that poured in from the other realms. She needed help managing it all, so she grabbed the strongest, meanest souls she could find and threw 'em all into a pit."

"What? Why?"

"So they could *fight*, obviously. She told them the ones who managed to escape the pit would become her generals, and wouldn't have to face the trauma of rebirth or eternal torture. Naturally, the souls fought like mad."

Val's words conjured images of the risen bodies in the necropolis tearing into one another. "That's horrible."

"That's Mortri. The weakest souls were devoured or dissipated. In the end, four of them crawled out, not quite alive or dead. Thana told them which souls they were in charge of and left it at that. Just fucked off somewhere and allowed them to build their cities and whatnot."

"I'm surprised they haven't tried to kill each other," Jas said.

"They have," Risha and Val said at the same time. Val snickered, and Risha continued, "There have been multiple skirmishes between them, but they're unkillable. The only one who has the power to fully unmake them is Thana."

"Not even Leshya could kill them?" Jas asked.

"She came close," Risha said. "According to her journals, she was able to injure them. That's how she was able to escape at all."

"Oh, and not just injure," Val said with a sly tone. "She took parts of their bodies."

Risha's gait faltered. "She did?"

"You should have *heard* the way they howled and cursed at her!" Val shook with raucous laughter. "And they've never gotten their parts back since!"

"But what would she need with them?" Risha demanded. "Where are they now?"

"What, you don't know?" There was a hint of smugness in the words. "I thought that's why you're so eager to get that weapon of hers."

She and Jas looked at one another in surprise. "Samhara is made of pieces of the four kings?" Risha deduced.

"Sure is. Leshya thought she could make a weapon powerful enough to take 'em out for good, but it didn't work."

"But she *did* weaken them." A thread of hope wove around her.

"And if Samhara is made up of the four kings, it has to be strong enough to get out of here," Jas added.

Risha turned to smile at him, and some of her hope dwindled. His outline had blurred, turning smoky and soft.

She touched her sternum and focused inward, attempting to locate whatever amount of strength he had transferred into her, but all she encountered were tangled threads of life and death—a contradiction of movement and stillness, vigor and inertia. A fruit frozen at perfect ripeness.

Even if they found the weapon and opened the portal, Jas would not return the same. His body had been burned to ash. It wouldn't stop her from trying everything she could to reverse it, impossible as it seemed.

"Tell me about life in Parithvi," she blurted, eager to escape her own thoughts.

"What's Parithvi?" Val asked.

"A country in Vitae. It's where our families are from. Leshya's, too." Risha fiddled with one of the buttons on her jerkin, made in the Vaegan fashion. "But I've only visited twice."

"Did you go to Sadhavana?" Jas guessed.

Risha nodded. During the two visits her family had made to the Parithvian capital, her father had busied himself with parliament meetings—King Ferdinand using him as a diplomatic envoy whenever possible—while her mother had brought her and Saya to various shops, tailors, and landmarks.

While Rath had been born and raised in Vaega, Darsha had come from a wealthy family in Sadhavana, influential and popular enough that Risha recalled never-ending visits to her mother's old friends and extended family. They'd all cooed and fussed over her while simultaneously complaining that she was *too Vaegan*, to which Darsha would force a small laugh and Risha would remain quiet.

Risha was many things: a daughter, a sister, a necromancer, Parithvian, Vaegan, a potential heir to the throne, a descendant of Thana. She had never put one of these things before the other. Instead they dwelled within her as harmoniously as they could, even if one became more prominent than the others depending on the day, the situation, the mood.

But she sometimes felt a pinch of something missing, the fear that she was too much of something and too little of another, a harmful imbalance. It made her jealous of those who belonged entirely to one place.

Jas was one of those people. She heard the accent dusting his words and remembered the bustling, broad streets of Sadhavana, the towering minarets and rows of sandstone haveli, the bazaars with their colorful awnings, the smell of smoke and spices in the air.

"The city is beautiful," Jas said. "As I'm sure you know. There's something about being surrounded by all that life, all that noise, that's comforting."

"I've never really thought about it. Although I find that a bit strange, considering your magic."

He grinned sheepishly. "Don't get me wrong, I adore nature. But too much time alone in the wide-open plains?" He pretended to shudder. "We had a large garden that kept me plenty occupied. And a greenhouse. I once tried to make karela grow faster, and it ended up turning them small and sour. My mother wasn't pleased."

Risha smiled. "So you've *always* been impatient."

He shrugged. "What can I say? I'm eager for results. Other than terrorizing the gardens, there was plenty to do in the city. I was in a kabaddi league with my friends for several years until I broke an arm. The sweets vendor near our home liked me enough to give me free laddoos and barfis when I passed by. I'd often read in the parks and play chaturanga with the old men."

Risha's chest had begun to ache at imagining a younger Jas running around causing trouble, but she laughed at this last part. "You played chaturanga with old men?"

"What's so strange about that?"

"I'm having a hard time picturing you being patient enough for a strategy game."

"The grandpas were always chewing on paan. They gave me a bit to try."

Risha rolled her eyes. "Now I can picture it."

"Paaja put a stop to that right quick when I came home with stained teeth." Jas's bright smile dimmed. "He doesn't know I'm dead."

Cold stole through Risha at the plummet from nostalgia into reality. No, Jas's father didn't know he was dead. Her own family probably thought *she* was dead.

"There's something ahead," Val said suddenly. "I can sense it."

They moved forward slowly. Risha had been so caught up in Jas's rumination she hadn't noticed the foliage around them growing stranger, the vines now covered in luminescent flowers. They gave off a scent she couldn't place, but had a similar effect as listening to Jas, a sweet and painful ache in her chest. Eventually they entered a wide clearing covered in soft loam.

Risha's gasp was soft. Anything louder seemed disrespectful to this place, and to the massive tree that took up the center. The trunk was thick and covered in silver bark, the pattern of which showed jewel-toned colors shining from within its knots. The branches were high and far-reaching, full of shimmering, dark leaves. Among the leaves were curious orbs of color, each no bigger than an apple.

For the first time since entering Mortri, peace washed over Risha. She knew from Leshya's journals that Mortri had once been a place that harbored both the terror and the beauty of death, yet so far all Risha had seen was the former. But this tree was emitting serenity the way trees in Vitae produced oxygen. She closed her eyes to better take it in, to ease the tightness of her chest and fill her lungs with fragrant air.

"What is this?" Jas asked as he stepped toward the tree.

Val shifted against her, straining to look up. "Those? They're souls."

Risha studied the colorful orbs. "How have they managed to take this form?"

"It happens, sometimes, if the soul is old enough. My guess is these are the spirits of those who didn't want to be reincarnated or dissipated."

"They're left in their simplest form," Risha murmured. Perhaps the feeling of peace was coming from these timeworn souls, those who had long come to terms with the fact that their lives had already served their purpose. There was no lingering sadness here, no regret, no anger. Just tranquility.

As her eyes scanned the branches, she noticed one was bare. It sat dark and empty amid the others, covered only in those wide leaves. Perhaps there weren't enough souls in Mortri due to the Sealing.

"We can rest here," Jas said, turning back to her. "It seems—"

He stopped and whipped his head around. Risha's fingers twitched for the shards of bone hidden in her pocket. Jas was so utterly still, so utterly silent, it raised the hairs along Risha's arms. As if he had taken another step from something recognizably human.

"Jas?" she whispered.

He finally moved, shifting toward the tree. "Amaa?"

Risha frowned. His voice had come out quiet, plaintive, almost like a confused child. "Jas, your mother isn't here. She's . . . she's in the void, remember? I tried to perform a séance with her."

Jumari Chadha had been in the middle of telling them something important about Ferdinand, the possible reason for her death. But they had been interrupted by the Conjuration circle in Haven Square, setting off the spirits the Revenants had been luring. Risha had *sensed* Jumari's spirit pulling away, fleeing toward the nebulous dark between Vitae and Mortri.

Even with the events at Godsnight, there was no way she could have entered Mortri as a spirit.

"Amaa," Jas said again, taking another step toward the tree. "Amaa?"

Then she heard it: a thin whine coming from the tree. A mournful cry that grew in volume the longer she focused on it.

Risha, came Saya's voice, sobbing and desperate. *Risha, help!*

The bone shards flew out of her pocket, fanning around her as if ready to dive into whatever was harming her sister.

Val swore. "You're hearing something, too, aren't you? It's not real, it's—"

"An imitori," she finished.

As soon as the revelation crashed down on her, Saya's voice cut off and was replaced with a low, rasping hum. Risha stumbled farther into the clearing, casting around for the creature it was coming from.

"There!" Val shouted.

Her eyes landed on it at the same time he spoke. The dark, barren branch hiding among the leaves, devoid of soothing souls.

"It's been luring in spirits to consume them," Val said.

The longer Jas stared up at it, the more transparent he became, revealing a sphere of glowing light in his diaphragm. His halting step turned into a run.

"Amaa! Amaa, I'm here!"

Risha let the bone shards fly. They embedded into the branch and it jerked violently, its shape contorting and extending, revealing an open, seeking mouth. The humming grew louder as the imitori detached from the tree and dove at Jas.

It was too fast. It wasn't a dead thing, and she didn't know how to stop it.

Then an idea sparked. An intuition, like holding her breath underwater.

Risha sought for that tangled ball of power where energies convened. Her godsblood sang and flowed, welled up to the surface as a cold wind kicked up around her.

She flung her hands out, flung *herself* out like an arrow and stabbed into the center of that glowing sphere at Jas's core.

For a heady moment she wasn't in Mortri, but on the streets of Sadhavana. Running down a broad avenue and stopping at the fringes of a small crowd. Looking toward a stage where large wooden puppets were being pulled and operated, from the joints at their arms to the turning of their turbaned heads, their blocky mouths opening and closing.

She was in the royal mausoleum under the Bone Palace. She was both her and Jas, watching her own self standing in opposition while simultaneously staring at Jas's mask, his heartbeat blooming across her palm.

She was in the courtyard under the raging skies of Godsnight, so many hearts within her, so many lives she had lived and watched and been a part of, all connected to her like the thread she used for larger spells.

Like marionette strings.

Her vision spun and danced sideways. She looked up and saw—her body. Standing with her hands outstretched, eyes pooled black, a torus whipping her hair out of its braid.

I'm controlling Jas.

She told him to move, and he did. It was not a body with joints and muscle and bone—it was fluid and fast, an essence made into something perceivable. He was on his feet and backing away from the imitori, which had crashed to the ground at the base of the tree. It had shifted and morphed into its true form, that of a bird with silvery feathers and a long, trailing plume of smoke.

"Jaswant," it spoke in Jumari Chadha's voice. It was much clearer than Saya's voice had been to Risha, so perfect in its inflection that Jas flinched. "Jaswant, please help me."

It's not her.

But Jas was wavering even under her control. Within this form she felt his loss, wide and gaping, a weight he had learned to grow around. The suddenness of hearing the news, the knowledge that she was gone, had created a storm of guilt and anxiety and doubt he carried with him always.

"Jaswant, I need you," his mother sobbed. "Help me. Please. Come here."

His wants rebelled against her iron will. Even as he took a step toward the creature she forced him to raise his arms, delving deep into the energy contained within his spirit, ringing with clarity when it recognized some of itself within her.

Magic swelled through him—not her magic, but his. She directed it toward the vines and roots, which stirred and slithered over the ground, reaching for the imitori.

"Jaswant!" his mother screamed, and for a moment the magic faltered and he fell to his knees, the storm inside him raging.

Risha forced the magic to flare stronger. Vines snatched the imitori before it could escape, and it gave off terrible, humanlike wails. Jas fought against her, but she overcame him, and the roots stabbed into the creature's body, cutting off its cries.

She blinked and found herself back within her own skin. The wind died down and she hurried forward, collapsing next to Jas as he stared blankly at the imitori in its death throes. Val cursed at being jostled, but Risha ignored him.

"Jas," she gasped. "I'm so sorry, I didn't mean . . . It was the only thing I could do, I . . ."

He was semi-opaque again, the sphere of light that was his soul once more hidden. He blinked and straightened slightly, coming out of the trance.

"She . . ." Jas continued to stare at the imitori, now motionless and quiet. "I see."

She put a hand on his shoulder. She had not yet lost a parent, but the echo of his grief remained within her, so deep and distinct it felt as if something had been carved out of her. Tears spilled down her face. "I'm sorry. I'm so sorry. For your loss, and for controlling you like that."

After a moment, he reached up and placed his hand over hers. "It's funny. Sometimes I'm so desperate to see her again, talk to her again, that even though part of me knew it wasn't her, I still wanted to fall into its trap. Isn't that ridiculous?"

She shook her head. "It's not ridiculous at all."

Jas looked up at the tree. Now that the creature was dead, the clearing had become peaceful again, all the branches laden with sleeping souls. "If we can get my mother's soul to Mortri, I'd want her to end up here. Somewhere she can rest and be at ease. Provided that sort of beast doesn't come back."

"With the way Mortri's declining, not even the most sacred areas are safe anymore," Val said behind her.

Jas turned to face her. "You forced me to use my magic."

She winced and pulled her hand away. He caught it between them. "I'm sorry, I—"

"No, Risha, listen. That was incredible. You weren't only able to control my body, but my magic as well. I can only imagine how much power that requires."

"Incredible?" She yanked her hand back. "It was invasive, and wrong. I *used* you."

"You saved me," he countered.

"I could feel you fighting me."

"In the moment, yes, but now that I'm not actively being tricked—"

"It won't happen again," she said sternly. Already the guilt she harbored was piling higher, threatening to topple. She had been the one pulling Jas's strings, forcing him to her will like a puppeteer before a demanding crowd.

Her father had raised her with strict rules for a reason. Necromancy, when unchecked, could do incalculable damage. A single necromancer in control of a hundred magic-wielding spirits could easily topple a city if they so wished.

It was why she had been so repulsed by the Revenants at first. Why Jas's vision and hers would never fully align.

She could tell he wanted to argue further, but he relented under her glare. "All right."

They sat in silence while the steady tranquility of the clearing washed back over them. It didn't take their lingering grief away but rather coexisted with it. Like the dual energies inside her, like the simple act of living with the knowledge that one day everything would end.

III

Brailee and Saya had wanted to make use of the long roads and way-stations heading south, but Dante had kept them to the open plains. They hadn't yet run into trouble, and Dante wanted it to stay that way.

He could tell they were close to Seniza when the weather shifted, making them shed their heavy cloaks. Stifling in his bedroll in the opalescent dawn, Dante moved away from their small fire and trekked up the hill that overlooked the distant city. It was far wider than Nexus, buildings and residences spread out over miles with a large fort to the north and a defensive sea wall to the south.

And of course, there was Deia's Heart. The volcano was massive, sitting at least fifteen miles northeast of the city, with plenty of farmland nearby to make use of its fertile soil. From here Dante could make out its dark silhouette, the brooding smoke that constantly rose from its mouth.

Was Deia's fulcrum inside? Dante was surprised to find that he didn't want it to be. Now that he knew Marcos Ricci's body was laid to rest in Seniza, all his thoughts turned toward the possibility of reanimation, to asking questions long burned out of time and memory. To figure out how to replicate the circle that had taken Taesia.

Not to mention that he had to find Camilla and drag her back to Nexus. Only then could his name—his *family's* name—be cleared.

"I'm bored," Azideh complained.

Dante hadn't noticed him shifting into view. He sat now beside Dante, leaning back on his hands as he lazily surveyed the landscape. In the sunlight, he really seemed like a myth come to life, all indigo skin and tangled horns and fearsome aura. Like one wrong move and he'd crush Dante's bones to powder.

Dante's cheek twitched. "Catching rabbits isn't fun anymore?"

"Hm. I do like it when they scream." Azideh slanted his bright green eyes at him, smirking.

Dante did his best to look unfazed. Truthfully, and perhaps concernedly, he was growing used to the demon's sense of humor. So instead of rising to the bait, he asked, "Can you at least put on some clothes? Even though my sister can't see you, it's...awkward."

"This form doesn't please you?"

"It's not about *pleasing* me. Fuck. Just...you know, clothes?" He plucked at his own shirt. "Modesty?"

Azideh leaned his head back, revealing the slope of his throat as his long, dark hair slipped over his broad shoulders. "*You perceive me wearing clothing.*"

Dante blinked a couple times to make sense of what he was looking at. There was Azideh, sure enough, but now he was wearing a pair of tan knee breeches and a loose white shirt untied at the collar with billowy sleeves that cinched at his wrists.

"What...are those," Dante said flatly.

"Clothes."

"It looks like something my grandfather would have worn."

Azideh's brow furrowed, as if genuinely insulted. Within another blink he had chosen something even more ridiculous: a peacock-blue coat with puffy shoulders and an outrageously narrow waistline. "Is this more to your liking?"

"Nyx's piss, *no.*"

"What about this?" Blink, and he was wearing an embroidered waistcoat with too-tight pantaloons.

Dante pinched the bridge of his nose. He supposed it made sense the demon's only knowledge of fashion was whatever people in Nexus had been wearing centuries ago.

"I suppose I could wear *this.*" He changed into an exact replica of Dante's outfit.

"Just go back to the first one," Dante grumbled.

When he looked up, Azideh had returned to the first, simple outfit. His smirk had grown, which Dante found distinctly unattractive.

"Wait, you said *perceive.* Are you actually wearing clothes?"

"No."

Dante sighed and turned back to the volcano. Even from here he caught a hint of its heat in the early morning breeze. Would Angelica be able to reach Mount Netsai in Azuna? If she found the fulcrum, would she use it for herself, or honor Dante's wishes?

He fell back onto the grass and stared up at the sky. Too many questions, and so few answers.

"During Godsnight," he said slowly, "there was a man in the courtyard. He saw you, and I could tell you were caught off guard. Who was he?"

Azideh was silent a long time, long enough that eventually Dante turned his head to make sure he was still there. The demon sat cross-legged now, staring at Seniza and the curling waves of the sea beyond.

"No one," the demon rumbled. "Only a figment of a memory."

Dante frowned, but Azideh's piercing, slit-pupiled glare prevented him from demanding more of an answer.

"When you summoned me, you offered me your life."

Dante's fingertips dug into the dirt below. He thought about dying here, in the middle of the countryside, with no one to look after his sister and Saya. Unable to prove the Lastriders were not guilty of treason.

"We did not conclude the pact," the demon finished. "I can only take your life once the parameters of your summoning come to fruition."

"What does that mean?"

"You summoned me because you needed strength and power. When will that purpose be served?" Azideh crooked a finger under Dante's collar. "Be warned: The longer you delay the pact's conclusion, the more severe the consequences. The longer we are bound together, the thinner the barrier between us becomes." He tugged the collar again. "I assure you, it will not be pleasant."

Dante's gaze slid back toward the sky, brightening beyond the dispersing clouds. He thought of how the sun didn't feel as warm as it once had, or how the stars didn't shine as bright. Of their realm withering and decaying on the vine of the Cosmic Scale.

"When the portals to the realms are reopened," Dante decided. "Permanently."

"Very well."

A shadow fell across his face. The demon loomed over him, one hand braced at the base of Dante's throat. Dante's breath caught, heart tipping between fear and surprise as he stared up at the demon's eyes, inhuman and intent. Azideh's fingers grasped hold of the collar around Dante's neck, invisible to all but them, and yanked him up.

Their mouths caught in a silent battle. Like the time Azideh had done this in his prison cell, Dante could sense the binding stitched between them, weaving out their pact. It sparked and strengthened as Azideh's tongue parted his lips, opening his mouth to receive more of the power that flowed in a spiral of energy. Dante made a noise in the back of this throat, struggling vainly against the demon, but Azideh only pinned his wrists to the ground and consumed.

When he finally pulled away, the demon licked his lips. Dante panted below him, dazed and lightheaded and more than a little mad.

Before he could say or do anything, a scream pierced the air. Azideh disappeared into his black cloud and Dante shot up, twisting to look back at their camp. Brailee was sitting up in her bedroll, frantically patting her body. Saya clumsily detangled herself from her own bedroll to reach her.

"What's wrong?" Dante called as he tore down the hill.

Brailee heaved for breath, her eyes watery with tears. Dante knelt beside her and grasped her hand.

"Sorry," she breathed, wiping the tears away. "The dream, I..." Saya handed her a waterskin and told her to drink. After Brailee swallowed, she said, "I found Risha."

Saya froze. "What? Where?"

"I was able to find her dreamscape, but I couldn't hold on to it. She...was having a nightmare." Brailee glanced at their doused fire and shuddered.

"Then she's not gone," Saya said. "She—she can't be dead if she's dreaming, right?"

"She's alive. But...she told me she's in Mortri."

Shit. How long could a human feasibly exist in the realm of death?

Saya rested her forehead on Brailee's shoulder. "How am I supposed to get to her, then?" Her voice wobbled, and gray despair clouded Dante's thoughts. "How am I supposed to bring her home?"

Dante laid one hand on Saya's forearm, the other on Brailee's unoccupied shoulder. "The same way we'll bring Taesia home." He gave them both a reassuring squeeze. "Then again, think about all the big sister pestering they'll do once they're back. Are you sure you want to go through with this?"

Saya sniffed and gave a breathy laugh, and Brailee offered him a smile. His job done, he turned to resaddle the horses and ignored his own frisson of unease.

They didn't ride long until they spotted the camp along the city's western perimeter. It was roughly an acre of tents and lean-tos with people milling between them. Guards in burgundy uniforms were stationed between the camp and the city.

"Refugees from Nexus," Dante said. They'd spotted some while on the road, keeping a safe enough distance so they wouldn't be recognized. "Not as many as I thought."

Saya shook her head. "The attack at Godsnight was frightening, but would that be enough reason to leave their homes?"

"They don't know what else might be coming." Brailee observed the camp with a soft, empathetic gaze. "I don't blame them. But why aren't they being allowed inside the city?"

"Because no one takes kindly to refugees," Dante muttered. "And if I were to bet money on it, I'd say Baron Alma gave the order to keep them out here."

Dante scanned the camp, but none of the people looked to be Noctan or Solarian. It was difficult enough for Other-Realm refugees to live in Nexus; he couldn't imagine how difficult it would be to travel someplace even less accepting. At least the Noctans had his parents; his mother would fight till her last breath to protect them.

Squaring his shoulders, Dante turned toward the camp.

"What are you doing?" Brailee demanded.

"Giving us cover."

His initial plan had been to compel the sentries at the border with the demon's power, but now the gears in his mind were turning. He thought he heard Azideh chuckle.

They smelled the camp before they reached it: unwashed bodies, campfires, spoiling food. Somewhere a baby was wailing, and a young woman in the priestly robes of Deia was handing out paper-wrapped buns as she wandered between the crooked aisles of tents.

They dismounted and walked the horses along the outside of the camp. They passed an old man wincing as he rubbed his legs, a group of children playing with an anthill, and a young couple curled up together with their eyes closed.

Dante flinched when a sea of hopelessness crashed into him. It came from everywhere at once, flooding his thoughts and making his heart stammer under the weight.

Brailee took his elbow. "Are you all right?"

"Fine." He knocked the palm of his hand against his head. *Stop it.*

It's not my doing, Azideh drawled. *You have this power now, remember? You must learn to use it.*

"New arrivals over here," called a bored-sounding voice. Dante followed it to a clerk who held a ledger in one hand and a feathered pen in the other. He looked up from whatever he was scratching onto the paper and blinked at the three of them. He frowned.

"You don't recognize us," Dante said, the words chiming.

The clerk shook his head and blinked again, eyes clearing of suspicion. "Are there only three of you?"

Dante ignored the disappointed glare Brailee was boring into his back. "Yes."

"Where are you coming from?"

"Nexus."

"Of course," the clerk sighed, making a note of it. "Names?"

"Rafael, Sofía, and Isabella Leon."

The clerk peered over his ledger to examine them again. "You're all from the same family?"

"I'm adopted," Saya spoke up, sounding far too cheerful about it.

"...Right." The clerk went back to writing.

"Why do you need this information, anyway?" Dante asked.

"For when we find proper shelter for you."

"I see." Dante smiled guilelessly. It was either that or scowl; contempt wafted off the clerk like rancid perfume. He suspected they were taking the refugees' information not to help them, but to keep track in order to hand out fines and penalties to anyone who caused trouble. Which would surely happen if they were forced to continue living in this encampment indefinitely.

Despite the warmer weather of the south, the breeze coming off the sea was brisk, and there were far too many people here without coats. His hand tightened on the reins, and his horse twitched its head nervously.

"Da—Rafael," Brailee said, a warning in her words. "We can—"

"Give me your ledger," Dante ordered the clerk.

The clerk's eyes glazed over, and he handed Dante the ledger without complaint. Dante grabbed it and strode to the nearest fire. A young woman sat beside it, mending clothes, and gasped when he flung the book into the flames. He watched the embers catch along its edges and felt something prideful stir in his chest.

There it is, Azideh whispered.

The clerk barked a question and Dante turned back to the guards, who were beginning to realize something was wrong. Dante planted himself before them as Azideh's hands clamped down on his shoulders, the demon grinning against his ear.

"Do it."

His fingers tingled, and Nox slid up his arm underneath his sleeve to escape the bristling power forming there. Dante held out his hand, eyes filling with a green, brackish light.

"*You will let these people inside the city and cause them no harm*," he ordered.

The guards who had been reaching for their weapons suddenly dropped their arms, eyes turned hazy and mouths hanging slack under the effect of compulsion. They turned to the gates and cranked them open.

"H-hey!" the clerk called after them, his sour panic setting Dante's teeth on edge. "What are you doing? You can't just—"

Behind them, the refugees who had been looking on were already gathering their meager possessions. The news spread across the camp, and suddenly tents were either being dismantled or abandoned as a crowd streamed through the gates.

Dante hauled Brailee and Saya along, using the commotion in their favor. Once they were through the gates he pulled the girls to one side to allow the rest of the refugees in. His chest was light, and a grin had settled on his face.

"You can't compel everyone we come across," his sister complained. "It's not *right*."

"Is it right to keep those people locked out, Bee?"

"Of course not, but—"

"I did what was best for them."

"Is this really what's best for them? Where will they go? How will they find shelter? What if guards you didn't compel come after them?"

His satisfaction subsided, but he couldn't find it in himself to regret what he'd done. He had given his life to a demon's powers, had opened himself up to receiving as much as he could carry—what was the point if he didn't *use* it? If he didn't take advantage to help those who couldn't help themselves?

I told you, the demon whispered. *You crave control. To have dominion over others, to bend them to your will.*

"That's not true," Dante muttered. "I only . . . I only want to help."

Brailee sighed. "I know, Dante. But we have to be careful."

Concern seeped from Saya while disappointment radiated off Brailee. All of it tasted acrid in his mouth.

He had to remember he was doing this for Taesia. For his family. The world needed fixing, but it had to wait.

He turned and ruffled Brailee's hair. "Sorry, Bee. I'll do my best to lie low, all right?"

She attempted a smile, but it didn't reach her eyes. He didn't blame her for doubting him, not after everything that had happened.

He doubted himself, too.

IV

They approached Mizari just past dawn on the sixth day at sea. Angelica stood at the railing and watched the port city grow closer, clutching a shawl around her shoulders as a northern wind blew past.

The crew was busy all around her, preparing to dock. Several of them had taken to avoiding her after the incident with the kraken, though she had caught some—including the captain—studying her with intrigue.

Angelica pretended not to notice, focusing instead on the flickering coral-crowned jellyfish swimming near the ocean's surface. Unlike normal jellyfish, these creatures had long arms covered in what looked to be coral shelves, which they used to lure in fish. The night before, they had risen and hovered over the water in a serene display of light, their bells glowing purple and red.

She ran her finger along the edge of a gouge in the railing. Kudei. Aether. Quintessence. It was something she only understood in concept and accidental practice, a forgotten piece of magic that had ended up saving not only Risha's life, but the fate of the *Gladius*.

But she couldn't understand how it worked. If she were to sing right now, what would happen?

She parted her lips. She drew in a deep breath.

"There it is."

Angelica flinched. Cosima had snuck up to her side, seeming more at home in her stolen guard's uniform now that she'd had days to get used to it.

"Never thought I'd actually get here," Cosima said. "Or that I'd see a port again."

"Enjoy it while you can. I'm sure there are plenty of things on land that can easily kill us."

"Always so cheerful." Cosima braced her hands on the scarred wood. Angelica immediately felt something was off when Cosima stared down at the jellyfish instead of the approaching docks.

"I, uh." Cosima cleared her throat. "I gotta admit something."

Angelica's stomach dropped. "Were you hired by my mother to spy on me?" The thought had crossed her mind more than once.

"The fuck? No."

She went over everything Cosima had told her this past week. "Your brother doesn't know we're coming, does he?"

"Getting closer." Cosima sighed. "What I said about me and him exchanging letters...might have been a lie."

"*Might* have been?"

"It was. The truth is, I have no idea where he is. I haven't seen or heard from Koshi since he was taken to Azuna."

Angelica's temple throbbed. "So you used me to get a free ticket to Azuna to find him."

"Well, when you put it like that—"

"You told me he could take us to Mount Netsai!"

Cosima rubbed the back of her neck. "Did I?"

Angelica scrubbed her fingers through her hair in an effort to not take the other woman by the lapels and shake her. "I should have known."

"Known what, princess?" There was a hint of frost in Cosima's words. "Known that a thief would lie to you? Have an ulterior motive?"

"You *did* lie to me."

"Only to the extent I needed to. Once I find my brother, we'll take you to your volcano."

"I don't have time for you to find your brother!" Angelica slapped her hand down hard on the railing. "What do you expect me to do now? I need a guide to take me there!"

"Look, what I said before doesn't have to be a lie. If you can help me find Koshi among the Gojarin-Kae, I'm sure he can help."

The military elite of Azuna—warriors who bore elemental magic— were called the Gojarin, specially trained and assigned to noble houses as well as hired to protect merchants. The lesser elemental division were the Gojarin-Kae, and they made up at least half of the armed forces.

"How am I supposed to find one person among thousands?" Angelica demanded.

"He'll be one of the only Mariian soldiers."

Which would significantly narrow the pool, but Angelica didn't care about that in the moment. She hissed out a breath that came out as smoke, her insides seething. Cosima swallowed and took a step away from her.

The process of docking was long and intensive, the crew far too busy to pay them any mind. At some point Eiko sidled up on her other side to take in the city's skyline, a ridge of peaked rooftops above the busy docks where fishermen in their smaller boats fought the larger ships in the harbor for space. The water reflected the streaks of red in the sky, rich veins of ruby against periwinkle.

Eiko was dressed in one of Angelica's spare dresses. It was too big on her, and she'd needed a belt to cinch it around her waist. Eiko hadn't thought to bring any essentials when running away, and as a result Angelica had to share her toilette for the first time in her life, a distinctly aggravating and awkward experience for them both.

Since Angelica was stewing in fury, the two sources of that fury wisely stayed silent as the *Gladius* safely pulled into harbor and dropped anchor. The House guards gravitated back to Angelica, Cosima half a step behind in getting into position.

Among the bustle of deboarding and retrieving her luggage, it took her a moment to realize someone was saying her name. A man appeared before her, tall and slim, swathed in a robe of dark blue embroidered with geometrical patterns of diamonds. Along his long, wide sleeves were Azunese characters that spelled out what Angelica thought might be a poem. His dark hair was done up in a bun secured with a polished wooden hairpin.

At having her attention, he bowed in greeting. "Esteemed Mardova. I am Noguchi Botan, chief scholar of the imperial family. I'm pleased to welcome you to the shores of Azuna."

She had been fully prepared to speak in Azunese, having been forced to learn the language at her mother's insistence for over a decade, but he'd addressed her in Vaegan. "Thank you, Scholar Noguchi. I'm eager to see as much of your beautiful lands as possible."

"You will see plenty on our way to Mukan."

Mukan, the Imperial City, where the empress and her familial off-shoots resided. It was located roughly in the middle of the empire, on the point where all four states met. Mount Netsai was to the northeast of that, right above Hitan, capital of the fire state.

Angelica felt a presence close behind her and shifted to reveal Eiko. "This is Ueda Eiko. She's come with me to reunite with her family. Will the traveling arrangements have room for her?"

Eiko seemed to want to retreat into herself. She was looking around with wide eyes, as if this wasn't a homecoming but a discovery.

Botan bowed to her as well. "We certainly have room. Welcome, Revered Ueda. I'm sure your family will be thrilled to see you." Eiko offered a tentative smile. "Our coach is waiting for us whenever you are ready to depart."

"Wait." The *Gladius*'s captain strode over, her face pinched as she spoke in clipped Azunese. "We had some deaths onboard."

Botan blanched. "What?" He looked to the ship, noting the broken railing on the starboard side. "What happened?"

"Kraken. Three of my crew are dead. The death procession is tonight, isn't it?"

"It is, but—"

"I don't want their spirits lingering on the ship. They need to be taken."

Botan hesitated, then exhaled with a nod. "I will make arrangements. Esteemed Mardova, the guards will escort you to the coach. I apologize for the delay."

"Not a problem." Angelica glanced at the captain, wondering if she should say something. After all, it had been because of Angelica's presence that they'd been attacked in the first place.

In the end, she decided it wouldn't matter. She made for the coach and found a handful of Gojarin-Kae in armor of lacquered iron plates, their sleeves patterned with the elements they bore and tapered at the wrists with bracers. They all wore thin swords with floral-patterned sheaths and helmets secured by chin straps.

"This way, Esteemed Mardova."

As they followed the Gojarin-Kae, she once again felt eyes on her back, the faintest whisper of "kudei" trailing after her.

The coach was wide and spacious, with enough room for four people. Angelica decided to observe the city from a distance as they waited for Botan to return. To the south was Kaizen Bay and its collection of small islands, with ferries going to and fro. To the north was a windy coastline that eventually fed into the low valleys of the fire state.

"I know only a handful of Azunese words," Cosima murmured, leaning against the coach. "But I heard them say something about death?"

"The death procession," Eiko said, the first words she'd spoken all day. "It's an old tradition. After the Sealing, the spirits of the dead were trapped here, even when bodies were cremated. Eventually so many spirits were prowling the wild that people kept getting hurt or killed on the roads. A merchant ship on its way to Vaega was hit by plague, and the spirits of the crew began to haunt the decks. Once they docked outside Nexus, the Vakaras were called to help with the situation.

"The Vakaras had them use what resources were available onboard to drive the spirits into the void, like incense and salt. When the story reached the empress, she asked the Vakaras to visit Azuna so they could work together to figure out the best method of restraining the spirits."

"The Vaegan queen at the time only allowed it because she wanted to garner favor for better trade routes," Angelica said as an aside to Cosima.

"Uh-huh," Cosima said. "So what was this method, exactly? This... death procession?"

"Exactly as it sounds," Eiko said. "The cremated ashes are stored boxes of cedar, since cedar is a natural spirit repellant. Four times a year, when the seasons change, the Kiyono bellwethers lead the dead from every city, town, and shrine where they've been contained and into the Godan Mountains."

"Lead them there to do what?"

"Contain them so they don't wander. There are markers and caches of salt all around the mountains to keep the spirits inside."

"Hold on." Cosima lifted a finger. "You're telling me that there's an entire mountain range full of ashes and creeping spirits?"

Angelica and Eiko nodded.

"That is. That is very creepy. I don't like that one bit."

"You live in a city with a necropolis," Angelica pointed out. "A very active one, at that."

"That's different."

"*How?*"

"My apologies," came Botan's voice. "Since the *Gladius* was the one that brought you here, I thought it my duty to offer them assistance in arranging cremations and finding someone who will join the procession tonight."

Angelica stood up straighter. "Should we be traveling during the procession?"

"It will be safe so long as we don't interfere. We'll also be stopping at an inn for the night, when most of it takes place." He paused, eyeing Angelica as if she were a particularly intriguing puzzle box. "It will take three days to reach Mukan, so let us make the most of the daylight."

She and Eiko climbed into the coach. When Cosima joined her, Botan cleared his throat in surprise but didn't comment before following them in and closing the door.

Angelica sat between Cosima and Eiko, wishing one of them would move to the opposite bench beside Botan. But they were both oblivious to her glares as they stared out the windows. Botan sat regally with his hands in his lap, amused at their intrigue.

Then his expression sobered. "Esteemed Mardova, I couldn't help but overhear some of the crew discussing the attack by the sea beast. They say you were the one to deal the death blow."

Angelica felt her companions stiffen on either side of her. In contrast, she kept herself loose and unbothered. "That's correct."

He considered his next words carefully. "They said this was done by using kudei."

Angelica pretended to pluck a piece of lint off her dress. "I'll admit I'm not very familiar with the definition of kudei, though I understand it's similar to the Vaegan concept of aether?"

"Yes, to a degree." He squared his shoulders, clearly now in his element at the prospect of educating someone. "As I'm sure you're aware, Azuna has advanced past godly worship."

She managed to school her expression at the wording. "Yes, I am aware."

"There are some who still pay respects to Deia, but we as a society have largely moved on from such archaic traditions. Ever since the Sealing, we decided it was more important to devote ourselves to the land, to nature and the elements that ensure our ways of life."

"Kiyonoism," Eiko said. "Didn't it begin as a cult?"

"I . . . would not use that word, exactly, but at the time it was perceived as heretical. Then a representative of the faction met with Empress Yua, and the two got along so well she adopted several of their practices. It wasn't long until she declared it should be acknowledged throughout the empire. Our shrines were converted even as the temples to the gods fell to ruins.

"Kiyonoism is the link between humans and nature, and the cyclical journeys between them. It is not a religion so much as it is a method of conservation. The gods have withdrawn, so it is up to us to preserve what is left."

"So where does this kudei come in?" Cosima asked. Angelica discreetly kicked Cosima's ankle under the cover of her skirts to remind her that *guards did not talk.*

"This is Cosima, my personal bodyguard," Angelica explained. "Curious to a fault." Cosima grinned, unrepentant.

"I do greatly value curiosity in others. The fundamentals of Kiyonoism are to acknowledge and give thanks to the elements. That is reflected in the landscapes of our four great states. Mukan, the Imperial City, sits on the point where all four meet to represent kudei, the fifth, invisible element."

Eiko raptly leaned forward. "Invisible?"

"It is an old concept, so old that scholars debate if kudei ever existed at all. But it must have, since we have the theory of aether in Vaega and akasha in Parithvi." Botan tilted his head toward Angelica. "And now we have witnesses believing they saw it with their own eyes. Is it true, Esteemed Mardova? Can you really channel kudei?"

Eiko nudged her, but she couldn't tell if it was in warning or encouragement. Angelica leaned away as much as she could, wondering if it was too late to turn the coach around and secure Eiko passage back to Vaega. This was what she got for being soft; her stepsister had no head for politics and was only going to get in her way.

Angelica had come here for two reasons: to find Deia's fulcrum, and to position her family for the crown. If she was perceived by the imperial family as a true Mardova heir, one who could wield *all* the elements— even one long fallen out of practice or understanding—that could only help their cause.

"I'm not entirely sure," Angelica said with apology in her voice. "It certainly *felt* different than the other elements. There have been times..." She sighed. "Although I know the concept of aether, I'm woefully uneducated in it, so it's hard to describe. But it was almost as if the elements had braided together."

Botan made a noise of fascination. Angelica knew she'd chosen well in letting *him* decide whether or not to believe in her power.

She caught Cosima's expression of wry amusement, one that seemed to say *Look who's a liar now.*

*   *   *

They were a few miles from the inn where they would spend the night when the coach came to a stop and the driver called out, "Parade passing."

"Oh," Botan said, unable to conceal his surprise. "Apologies, but it looks as if we've crossed paths with the procession after all. There seem to be more and more of them every year."

"We don't mind," Angelica said.

"May we observe it?" Eiko asked eagerly.

"I suppose—"

Eiko, shedding her newfound shyness, didn't wait for him to finish before all but flying out the door. Angelica apologized on her behalf and followed.

It was a chilly evening, the land swaddled in a deep purple gloaming. The Gojarin-Kae had lit lamps that hung from their saddles, casting them in a warm glow in the middle of the encroaching dark.

But there was a line of light emerging from the distant town. Torches and paper lanterns danced in the sway of the parade, listing from side to side in time with the eerie notes rising from reed flutes. The reeds were accompanied by hand drums that punctuated the air, as well as the swell of voices in a chanting song.

Botan joined them. "The parade masters are leading the collected spirits to the mountains." He indicated the massive ridges to the south, their peaks shadowed in an ombré of blue, purple, and black. "Many such parades will be occurring all over Azuna tonight. They will be accompanied by family members of the deceased who have asked to carry their loved ones' ashes, who must undergo a purifying ritual of bathing in salt before they can join."

They watched parade masters in voluminous robes sprinkle salt as they passed in their journey south. Some of the torches were nothing more than cypress branches, and Angelica remembered that just as cedar repelled spirits, cypress had been found to attract them. Any lost souls in the wilderness would be drawn to the haunting music and the smoke.

In the corner of her eye, figures stirred in the darkness. She started back, then felt Cosima's touch on her shoulder.

"I see them, too," she breathed in Angelica's ear.

The ghosts were all around them. Half-formed, hazy, hallowed. Slowly they drifted toward the procession, beckoned by smoke and song, until they fell into step with the parade masters and grieving families.

The sight was like something out of a dream not yet turned nightmare, captivating yet uncanny. Even Eiko shifted closer to Angelica, fingers pressed to her lips.

They observed the procession until it was a speck of wavering light in the distance. Then Botan took a deep breath and clapped his hands together, making them all jump.

"Now that we're safe from disturbing them, let's move on."

Angelica let the others climb back into the coach first. "You mentioned this is getting worse every year," she said to Botan, lowering her voice.

"Yes. We've had more widespread illnesses, more infections. Just last month the town of Hiiso reported a great number of deaths from poisoned crop." He shook his head. "Something is wrong, and we are not sure how to fix it."

The realm is dying. They were already aware of that, but not yet to the extent she was, having heard the horrific truth from Deia herself. This was not something that conservation or environmentalism could fix. This was the work of gods who no longer cared for their people, who had hidden the fate of Ostium despite what the fifth realm had done to create and maintain their universe.

That feeling of being watched pressed against her shoulder blades. Angelica glanced around, but all the stray ghosts had gone with the procession.

The handprint on her upper arm grew warm. She ignored it and climbed back into the coach.

V

Taesia found herself back in Nyx's dreamscape. She was sitting cross-legged before the archway, bathed in the light of the eight moons and the lilac phosphorescence of the clouds. It was both silent and not, like lying unbothered in the middle of a field with the tinkling of a far-off wind chime.

For a moment she was calm. She wondered how she'd nodded off at all when she'd been so uncomfortable curled up on the floor of the Noctans' safe house, her mind buzzing with dark thoughts.

But here, her shackles were gone. She rubbed her unharmed wrists and thought of the misery in Julian's eyes before the chori had put him to sleep. Without her magic she felt fangless; still capable, still strong, but missing an integral part of herself, her first line of defense.

They needed to get that diamond as soon as possible.

"Interesting," came a familiar velvet voice behind her. "You seek to enter my halls of worship, to remain undetected even while pilfering from my devotees, to restore yourself to your base level of power. All of this effort, when instead it would be simpler to accept my offer."

Taesia refrained from looking over her shoulder. "You're getting senile, old man. We've already had this discussion."

"I gave you an option you did not take. If you keep refusing to take it, you will end up dead."

"Then you'll lose one of your puppets."

"Without proper strength, your companions will also end up dead."

Taesia said nothing. The whisper of Nyx's robe echoed through the hall as he came to stand before her. The moonlight limned him in silver, an ivory corona.

"YOU SEEM TO THINK THIS IS ONLY BENEFICIAL FOR ME," he said, holding out a black-clawed hand. Shadows swirled above his palm. "YOU ARE NOT CONSIDERING THE ENORMITY OF POWER YOU WILL BE ABLE TO WIELD. POWER YOU ONCE SEEMED TO LONG FOR."

The shadows became shapes, and the shapes resolved into scenes. She instantly recognized her siblings and her parents being struck down by what looked like Solarian warriors with wings. The shadows shifted into Nikolas being skewered by his own spear. Risha torn apart by the dead. Julian's throat slit and his blood dripping into a Conjuration circle.

She watched and tried not to flinch, hands fisted on her knees. She seemed more stone than person when Nyx finally lowered his hand.

"THESE CAN AND WILL BECOME YOUR REALITY IF YOU KEEP REFUSING ME. UNDERSTAND THAT IT WILL BE YOU AND YOU ALONE RESPONSIBLE FOR YOUR KIND'S TRAGEDIES."

Taesia pried her jaw apart. "Fuck that. You can't *guilt-trip* me into becoming your puppet."

"YOU SEEM TO LIKE THAT WORD. *PAWN* AS WELL. YOU DO NOT SEE THIS AS A COLLABORATION?"

She snorted and got to her feet. He still loomed over her. "You didn't seem to want to collaborate when you took over my sister. I had to fight against you when I closed my aunt's portal. If I let you have full access, you'll use me in any way you want to. You'll make me kill Rian. That's not going to happen."

"I DO NOT KNOW WHETHER TO BE AMUSED OR ANNOYED," Nyx murmured as his cosmic eyes narrowed slightly. "HUMANS ALWAYS TEND TO THINK THERE IS ANOTHER WAY, DON'T THEY? IF THEY DO NOT LIKE SOMETHING, THEY WILL FIND SOME PATH AROUND IT. THEY WILL LIVE IN DENIAL UNTIL FATE CATCHES THEM BY THE THROAT."

"I don't live at fate's whim," Taesia said. "I live at mine."

Nyx's pale lips curved into a humorless smirk. Before he could reply, the ground rocked beneath Taesia's feet and she stumbled. The clouds drifting through the hall flickered with lightning.

"Taesia!"

A figure ran through the clouds, emerging only to fall into a heap at the bottom of the wide stairs.

"Brailee!" Taesia bounded down the stairs and gathered her younger sister into her arms. Brailee wore dark traveling clothes instead of a nightgown. Breathless, she held on tightly to Taesia.

"I finally found you," Brailee panted. The clouds around them continued to flicker ominously, pale purple deepening into a threatening crimson. "Where—?"

She looked up and balked at the sight of Nyx above them. Taesia took Brailee by the chin and turned her face away.

"Don't pay attention to him," she said firmly. "What's happening? Where are you right now?"

"Where are *you*?"

"I'm in Noctus. Phos summoned the Bone Palace to Astrum and took control over Nik. Julian and I were able to escape."

"Who's Julian?"

There wasn't time to explain, so Taesia just shook her head. "We're going to try to stop Phos and get back home."

"No!" Brailee clutched Taesia's wrist. "You can't be reckless, Tae. Dante and I are going to find you."

Her heart squeezed painfully. "Dante's safe? He's with you?"

"Yes. We've just arrived in Seniza. There's a—"

The clouds were thickening, eddying around the two of them. They muffled Brailee's words so that Taesia only heard half of what she was saying.

"—Aunt Camilla—fulcrum—get some answers—Conjuration—"

"You shouldn't be messing with Conjuration!" Taesia shouted through the thick fog. "If Dante's caught again—"

"—find you!" Only her sister's ghostly words remained. "Astrum— hold on!"

"As I SAID," whispered Nyx as Taesia's vision grew dark and her limbs heavy. "YOUR KIND LOVE TO LIVE IN DENIAL."

She woke with a start. It made one of her shackles scrape against the wooden floor, sending a jolt of pain up her arm. She lay completely still, dizzy even while lying down.

Nyx may have driven them apart, but at least Taesia knew Brailee and Dante were all right—for now. She had no idea what they were planning to do in Seniza, though Brailee had seemed confident they would be able to find her. But they couldn't do that unless they re-created the

Conjuration circle that had taken the Bone Palace, and that was the last thing she wanted them to do.

She turned her head. Starfell was leaning against the wall beside her, glittering ominously in the dark. She remembered how it had felt to hold it underneath the portal, the way it had magnified her power, channeled it through the bones of a celestial creature.

If she got these shackles off, would she be able to channel enough power to make not just a vortex into some unknown space, but a portal into Vitae?

The door opened and Taesia sat up. Marcellus and Kalen must have gotten up much earlier and gone for supplies, judging by the bags they carried into the cramped safe house.

"I told you, we don't need it," Kalen was telling Marcellus as they set the bags on the table. He was speaking Nysari, the northern Noctan dialect. Taesia wasn't talented at speaking it, but she understood enough when she heard it. "Just because it's a staple at your ridiculous manse doesn't mean it's a necessity."

"I'm not saying it's a *necessity*," Marcellus bit out; it was the most ruffled Taesia had seen him so far. "I'm just saying it would be *nice*, it might improve *morale*—"

"What morale needs to be improved? And by fruit, no less?"

"Lelith isn't just *fruit*, it's a cultural cornerstone. It would have been nice to share that with the others."

"You think Vitaeans are going to appreciate something like that? Besides, it's too expensive."

"I said I was willing to pay for it," Marcellus muttered.

"Stop squandering your money on trash. Although considering your family's taste in décor, maybe that's something you inherited."

The soldier took a step toward Kalen while shoving his sleeves up. A long-suffering sigh came from where Lilia sat braiding her hair.

"Can you two stop bickering for *one* day?" she pleaded. "One. That's all I ask."

Marcellus shifted on his feet, mouth pursed. Kalen raked a hand through his hair.

"Yes, Highness."

"Sorry, Highness."

Taesia quietly cleared her throat. Three sets of eyes—all glowing faintly in the gloom—turned to her.

"Great, the dalyr heard us." Kalen began rummaging through one of the bags. "As long as you're awake, you can get changed. Rhydian, prep the meal."

Marcellus grumbled something and grabbed the other bag before moving to the stove. Taesia turned to where Julian had curled up last night. They didn't have blankets or pillows, but the Noctans had given them their cloaks to ward off the worst of the cold. Julian was wrapped in Marcellus's, his brow furrowed in sleep.

Taesia gently touched his shoulder. He woke with a small gasp, fumbling for a weapon.

"It's just me," Taesia whispered. Their eyes locked, and he relaxed under her hand. "You all right?"

"Bold question," Julian rasped. He rubbed his face. "I will be."

"I find that water typically helps." Lilia had come over with a cup, which he took with a quiet thanks. "While Mar figures out breakfast, let's get you into some warmer clothes. We don't have a washbasin, but there's enough water to get the worst off."

Taesia felt a little better after splashing the cold water on her face. She would have killed to sit in a tub full of steaming water, using scented soaps on her hair and applying rose oil to her skin afterward. Instead she had to make peace with an itchy scalp and dried-out hands.

At least the Noctans had been thoughtful enough to get them clean clothes. Taesia had been wearing the same outfit for days now, if not weeks, torn and scratched and caked in dirt and blood. It was a miracle her scrapes hadn't gotten infected.

Kalen handed both her and Julian a pile of folded-up clothing. The room offered no privacy, but the Noctans didn't seem to care. Julian glanced her way, swallowed, and turned around.

Taesia wasn't exactly a modest person, but even she was compelled to face the opposite corner before peeling off her dirty garments. She sighed in relief, dipping the cleanest part of her old shirt into the water basin to scrub at a few spots where old blood had crusted over.

The new clothes were sturdy and thick, in shades of dark blues and blacks. The fabric was a mix of flax linen and wool, the trousers baggy, the undershirt formfitting, and the surcoat belted at the waist with a silver sash. There was also a fur-lined cloak for her, as well as socks and gloves. The sleeves were difficult to get over her shackles, and as she fought not to tear the fabric she caught sight of her silver ring, empty now that Umbra was suppressed.

Taesia took a fortifying breath and finished by tucking the trousers into her boots. When she turned around, her eyes were immediately drawn to the bare expanse of Julian's back.

Her gaze lit upon the wings of his shoulder blades, tracing down the length of his spine to the divots above his waistband. Faint scars were scattered in pale lines against his tawny skin. The strength he carried in his body was obvious from the way he held himself and the way he moved, lean muscle shifting as he reached for his shirt and slipped it over his head. Mouth dry, she headed for the table.

"—still in an uproar," Kalen was telling Lilia. "I saw at least a dozen of the Night Guard while we were out. They seem to have taken martial law until the higher lords can figure out how to handle things."

"That's what I expected." Lilia nodded to Taesia when she joined them. "Their vigilance isn't unwarranted. This is the first time we've seen Vitaeans in hundreds of years."

"They're considering them hostile," Kalen went on. "For good reason." He glanced at Taesia sidelong. "They also saw her holding that sword."

Julian stepped up beside her. He was dressed much like she was, but his surcoat was a deep green. "Could we leave the sword behind when we go to the temple?"

"Absolutely not," Taesia said. "I'm not leaving it lying around for anyone to find."

"It'll draw too much attention. It has an . . ." Julian gestured at Starfell. "Unconventional shape."

"I'll wrap it up like I did before."

"Shades will still be able to sense it," Kalen pointed out. "But I agree we shouldn't leave it behind. It's far too valuable."

Lilia rapped her sharp fingernails against the table. "There is another option to consider," she said as Marcellus returned carrying chipped plates. "Mar, the Rhydians are friends with the Verlith family, aren't they?"

Marcellus set the plates down. "That they are. Have them over every New Moon. Of course, it's been a while since I've attended those parties."

A flash of guilt crossed Lilia's face. "Do you think they might remember you? Be willing to help you?"

Marcellus blinked in confusion. "Help me with what?"

"You dunce," said Kalen. "The sword, obviously."

The soldier touched the hilt of his own sword. "Why, what's wrong with it?"

"*That* sword." Kalen pointed at Starfell. "The one made with *astralam bones* and carrying *very obvious power.*"

"Oh!" Marcellus nodded. "That makes more sense, yes."

"The Verlith family are the most renowned blacksmiths in Inlustrous," Lilia explained to Taesia and Julian. "In fact, I'm willing to bet a Verlith had a hand in forging that sword."

Taesia thought of Mirelle in the Noctus Quarter, who'd claimed to come from a prominent family of blacksmiths. Taesia had never inquired after her family name; now she wished she had.

"They can craft a sheath for the weapon to conceal it," Lilia continued. "That way we don't have to worry."

"They can make one that fast?"

Marcellus made an affronted noise. "This is the *Verlith* family. They can forge a pair of nightstone daggers in an hour."

"The point is that they're loyal to Mar's family and therefore might be willing to help us." Lilia stood up. "We should go as soon as possible."

"Not without eating." Marcellus pointed sternly at the food he'd laid out. Lilia obediently sat back down.

Taesia eyed the offered fare, a collection of odd-looking roots and vegetables, slices of pink fruit, and mushrooms in all shapes and sizes. Marcellus had cooked the latter in a buttery yellow sauce. Julian picked up a piece of fruit and chewed it with a blank face.

"And?" she murmured.

The faintest tightening of his eyes. "Not bad."

"You're a shit liar."

"I told you we should have sprung for lelith," Marcellus muttered at Kalen in Nysari. "Scintills are much too tart for this season."

"They were the cheapest. Get over it."

Taesia tried the roots, the taste of them not unlike beets, but whatever Marcellus had seasoned them with did wonders. The mushrooms were better. To Lilia she asked, "You said there's a water scarcity?"

"Yes. It was gradual at first, but it's become more severe within the past ten years." She nodded to the food. "That's why we tend to grow things that don't require much water."

"Or sunlight," Julian added.

The other three seemed to think this was an odd statement. "Yes?"

"It's just...in our realm...Never mind."

"Many crops *did* require moonlight to grow," Kalen supplied. "I'm not sure if you've noticed, but our moon is far dimmer than it used to be. It used to reflect Solara's sun, but after the portals were closed..." He shook his head. "Many of those crops have gone extinct."

"Are there signs of decay in Vitae?" Lilith asked.

A bit of mushroom nearly caught in Taesia's throat. "Yes."

Marcellus hopped up and returned to the bag of supplies. "I nearly forgot." He came back holding out small green spheres to Taesia and Julian. "Sun lichen."

Taesia reached for one. It was spongy and strange against her fingers. "Is this what the Vitaeans used to eat?"

"Just so. The longer Vitaeans stay in Noctus, the more their bodies fail due to lack of sunlight. But this lichen contains many nutrients to stave that off."

Julian braced himself before popping it in his mouth. This time he couldn't hide his grimace as he chewed and swallowed. Taesia did the same, doing her best to ignore the mossy taste and the way it scratched going down.

"I miss my mother's food," Julian murmured.

Taesia remembered Marjorie's almond cake and wondered if she'd ever have it again. "So do I."

The Verlith family had multiple forges throughout Astrum. The most popular of these were overlooked by the most experienced blacksmiths, and the smaller ones were given to the newly initiated to test their mettle and their craft.

"If I remember correctly, one of the lower forges is owned by Spar," Marcellus said. "Xe and I used to steal things from xir older brother and hide them in the manse's gardens."

"A bit base, even for you," Kalen muttered.

"Such is youth." Marcellus shrugged. "But xe would be under pressure now to perform well at xir family's forge."

They decided on Taesia, Lilia, and Marcellus going. Taesia fixed the wide hood of her cloak to fall just so over her face. Lilia had helped her put her hair into rolled-up braids to better pass as horns under the fall of fabric.

The streets were filled with the buzz and bustle of Noctans going about their day—or trying to, to the best of their ability. Taesia kept her head down and the sword hidden beneath her cloak, but couldn't help catching glimpses of worried faces and snippets of conversations in Nysari.

"—guards haven't caught them yet."

"Are we sure they're Vitaeans? The magic looks Lumin to me."

She was prickly with nerves by the time Marcellus held the door to the blacksmith's open and they hurried inside. A couple young apprentices were shoveling coal into the lit forge, which emitted a steady, inviting warmth. Another Noctan in a leather apron stood at the counter speaking to a customer. Marcellus indicated this was Spar.

"—all done," Spar was saying. "They should be able to cut through paper."

"Why would I need kitchen knives to cut through paper?" the customer asked with genuine confusion.

Spar gave a brittle laugh. "Are you sure you don't need a new set, Mistress Azur?"

"Oh no, these serve me just fine." She picked up a wrapped package from the counter. "Thank you, dear. And do be careful out there."

Once the customer left, Spar turned dreary, dark eyes on them. Xe was tall and well-muscled in the arms and chest, xir horns coiled tight against xir head. Long black hair had been tied into a high ponytail, and xir apron was stamped with a symbol of a hammer surrounded by stars like sparks. The white tattoos across xir face were the same as Mirelle's, with stars above the arches of the eyebrows.

"How can I help you?" xe asked. Marcellus lowered his hood, and Spar's posture straightened. "Mar? What are you doing here?"

Marcellus gestured at the apprentices. Spar frowned, but shooed them into the back room. It was only when they were gone and Marcellus had locked the front door that Lilia pushed back her own hood.

Spar's eyes grew round before xe fell into a kneeling bow. "Your Highness," xe gasped to the floorboards. "I—I thought—"

"That I had died with the rest of my family?"

Xe winced. "I am relieved to see you well and whole."

"We don't need you on the ground, Spar. We need you to make something for us. Something far more valuable than kitchen knives."

The blacksmith rose to xir feet. Xir expression was a blend of wariness and tentative excitement. "What were you thinking?"

Lilia nodded to Taesia. Taesia's pulse thundered and her stomach twisted, as if the lichen were suddenly disagreeing with her. She, too, pushed back her hood.

Spar immediately reached for the tongs on xir anvil.

"Vitaean," xe spat. "You—you brought one of them *here?*"

"She is not our enemy," Lilia said, her voice strong and sure. It brought up memories of Taesia's mother at council meetings. "She is here to help us defeat the one who murdered the Lunaris and razed our city. Phos."

There was silence save for the crackle of the furnace. No one moved a muscle as they watched Spar process the words.

"Phos," xir repeated. "Phos is in our city."

"You can believe me or not," Lilia said. "You can help us or not. But know that if you aid our cause, your contribution will be reported back to your family. To your grandfather."

There was a bitterness in Taesia's chest she couldn't identify at first. It hit her all at once: jealousy.

She was an heir who had grown up refusing to act like one, hoping Dante would take care of everything and she would be left to her own devices. But Lilia was an heir who had been abandoned by her family, practically exiled, and still found ways to present herself with surety.

The sudden insight made her feel pathetically juvenile. Something unripe and unformed, hanging sadly off its branch.

Spar looked to Marcellus, who nodded encouragement. Taesia could see thoughts churning behind the blacksmith's eyes, weighing the threat of harboring supposed fugitives versus the esteem of xir family.

"What exactly do you need?" xe asked at last.

Taesia didn't wait for Lilia's prompt this time. She parted her cloak and drew out the wrapped sword, uncovering it inch by inch until Starfell sat naked and heavy in her hands.

Spar hurried around the counter. "Is this real? Astralam bones—in a *sword?*"

"It was forged by a Noctan refugee in Nexus," Taesia said. "A young woman named Mirelle. I don't know her family name, but she claimed to be from a long line of famous blacksmiths."

Xir eyes, locked onto the sword, began to shimmer. "Oh," xe breathed as xe shakily touched one of the spinous processes along the edge. "I see it, now. It's...it's beautiful."

"And it needs a sheath," Lilia said. "One powerful enough to dampen it from a Shade's perception."

"Of course. The thing is, there's so little of it left."

"So little of what left?" Taesia asked.

"Nightstone. But my family has a store of it. I was saving my share in the event I got a wealthy Shade patron." Xe scoffed. "Instead it's all gardening and kitchen tools."

"I'm a Shade," Taesia said. "It won't be wasted."

Spar studied her, assessing if she truly was worthy of this Other-Realm material. She knew a little about nightstone; about how, like stardust, it could amplify a Shade's natural abilities. And, in the right hands, it could grant the carrier visions—or even re-create the power of a dream walker.

It could help her connect with Brailee again.

"I can't prove it to you." Taesia shifted her arm, showing off the dark shackle. "But I am a Lastrider, if that means anything to you. I carry Nyx's power."

The blacksmith exhaled shakily. "I don't have any diamond to cut those off," xe said eventually. "But I believe you. I think. When do you need this sheath?"

"Now," Lilia answered.

Spar grimaced. "Fine. I need my apprentices, though. Put your hoods back on. Also, I'll need the sword."

Taesia's hands tightened around it, nearly drawing blood. But a quiet, reassuring word from Lilia made Taesia offer Starfell to the blacksmith. Xe handled it with reverence, as if it were a newborn.

"Forged by a Verlith and sheathed by another," xe said quietly. "A star that's traveled between two realms. If this isn't enough to prove myself, I don't know what is."

A lifetime passed before Spar returned, but in actuality it had only been two hours. They'd only seen xir once in that time, when xe had come to the back room to cut a swath of dark leather from a bolt of hide.

"It's from an artican," Lilia had explained when Taesia asked about the leather's strange look.

"Fearsome things," Marcellus had murmured from his place on a wooden bench. "Big and fanged. Absolutely covered with hair. Though some people think they're *cute*."

Lilia had shifted on the bench beside him. "They are, when they're not hungry."

"So it's...a bear?" Taesia had asked.

"What's a bear?"

"Like what you just described, only with less fang and more claw."

"Honestly, they'd be cuter that way," Marcellus had said.

Spar now held out the new sheath. "I'm going to have blisters on my hands for weeks," xe complained. "But it's done. You'll stick to your word, Highness? You'll tell my grandfather about this?"

Lilia bowed her head. "Once it's safe to. I swear it."

Spar didn't seem particularly thrilled with the addendum, but xe still passed Starfell to Taesia. "Let me know if it needs any adjustments."

The weight of it was staggering and satisfying, a gentle pull on her muscles she'd have to build endurance for. The sheath was wide enough to hold the blade and its spines, covered in that black artican leather with silver fittings and studs, accented with a metal tip at its point. Spar had even gone so far as to etch a design down its length of swirling vines that ended in stars. A band sat snugly around the middle, smooth and glossy as liquid, not quite stone and not quite metal. It didn't even gather her fingerprints where she touched it.

"Nightstone," Spar said. "Be careful with it. It's almost as precious as the sword itself."

"It's beautiful, Spar," Marcellus said.

Spar scratched behind one of xir horns. "An astralam sword needs a good sheath. And it needs to be something my grandfather would be proud of."

"He will be," Lilia insisted. She dug into an inner pocket of her cloak, but Spar stopped her.

"No need," the blacksmith said.

"But—"

"Consider this my tribute to your family." Spar touched the center of xir forehead, then xir chest above the heart. "Long may they be sheltered in the dark."

The princess's face grew taut as her eyes brightened, furiously reining back whatever longed to claw out of her. Eventually she whispered, "Thank you."

Taesia's fingers curled around the sword. For the first time she had the niggling sensation that this was not supposed to be hers, that she had no right to wield it. Her blood ran with Nyx's shadows and starlight, but she was still a stranger. An outsider. A helpless observer of grief and destruction.

A hand settled on her shoulder. She met Lilia's somber lavender gaze.

"We have what we need," Lilia said. "Are you ready for the Sanctuary?"

Taesia cataloged the added weight to her body, from the pull of the sword to the drag of her shackles to the expectations placed upon her shoulders. They were not enough to pin her to the floor—not yet.

"I'm ready," she said.

VI

Sleep was heavy and honey-thick, a red dark blurred at the edges with gold. There was emptiness like a maw, poised to swallow whatever fell inside it. Below, the blue ash of earth where bones were buried; above, the trace of pyre smoke. Somewhere between the liquid of starlight and the open gash of sunshine.

He traced the gash until it spilled out crimson, bubbling and steaming over his hands. A blade caught on a neck, slicing open artery, lifeblood, godsblood, and his father's eyes open as he left the world the way he'd entered it: without wings.

Nikolas woke and was immediately enveloped with pain. He bit back a whimper and dug his fingers into something soft below him, his fingernails grown long enough to scratch at fabric. He wanted to rake them down his own face if only that would get rid of the throbbing, burning pressure in his skull.

It was a sickening tension that started at his right eye and radiated outward, prying into every corner and cranny it could reach. He wondered if his father had given him a particularly nasty hit. Nausea gripped his stomach, and for a while he floated in feverish warmth, lamentably tethered to his body despite his best efforts to dissociate from it.

Something cold touched his forehead and he jerked. His movements were sluggish and uncoordinated, but he did his best to knock away whoever was leaning over him.

"Now, now," came a breezy voice. "You've done quite enough harm to yourself already."

Nikolas was finally aware enough to take in the image before him:

Rian standing over the bed, a cloth in one slender hand. His younger brother's face was unusually gaunt, his expression one of cool observation.

"Rian," he croaked, lifting his hand again. His brother ignored it.

"Again with this." Rian tossed the cloth away. "I wonder if the heir of Ostium permanently muddled your head."

The phrase *heir of Ostium* finally cleared some of the haze. The feverish warmth drained away as he remembered, remembered, remembered.

The young man before him was not his brother. It was his god, his protector, his destroyer.

Something else was wrong, beyond Phos wearing Rian's face. There was an unevenness to the world around him, a strange lack of depth that didn't come from vertigo.

Nikolas clumsily reached for his face, for the apex of the pain. He found bandages and followed them up to his eye. He gently pressed, and an explosion of throbbing heat made him choke on a scream.

Remembered, remembered, remembered.

He covered the empty socket with his hand, the bandages wet against his skin. There was a low sound he realized was coming from his own mouth, something primal and wrecked.

"I told you," Phos said softly, "that you only have yourself to blame for this. I gave you an order. It could have been *his* eye instead of yours." A slow, heavy sigh. "I suppose the message still got through."

The price of disobedience, impiety. Of sparing Fin this empty, resounding agony.

It was a while until he caught his breath, until the shock turned to tremors across his body. Eventually he asked, voice small, "Where is he?"

Phos scoffed. "That's what you care about right now? You should hate him for putting you in this position."

You put me in this position. Despite the pain and discomfort, there was a respite in this moment of clarity, the fog in his head burning off. He didn't know how long it would last.

"Your sacrifices were worthless, in the end," Phos went on. "I know where the others will go. They will attempt to find the astralam crown hidden in the bowels of Nyx's unsightly temple. Only a Lunari may wield it, though I'm guessing that won't stop Nyx's heir from trying."

Nikolas turned his head until he could make out Phos again. Rian—Rian's body, the one he'd raced and grappled with, that leapt and tumbled and wielded weapons like a true soldier.

Remembered, remembered, remembered.

Their father running them through drills and maneuvers, his voice a sharp drumbeat on the wind.

The heat of Rian's side against his, his brother's arm around his shoulders, soft words after a hard day.

Blood on his hands and falling, falling, over the edge of a roof as the sky rent apart.

His left eye watered and spilled over. The bandages over his right eye seeped with blood.

He wanted to tell Rian, wanted to confess and be done with it, throw himself at someone's mercy. What was the cost for ending a cruel man's life? What was the punishment for the son overcoming the father?

There were many pieces of him missing; perhaps he deserved this particular hollowness.

"They will try to stop me," Phos went on, "but it won't be enough. One of the advantages of this body is that it is largely Vitaean. The shadows do not harm me as much as they could."

"What happened to it?" Nikolas whispered. "My eye."

Phos was quiet a long time. The empty socket throbbed.

"He's always so hungry, your brother," Phos murmured. "My mind has absorbed his, but I can *feel* it. A grip in my belly for something to complete me. Comfort me. Nourish me."

Phos laid his hand gently over the bandages. Nikolas lay utterly still.

"The piece of Orsus I consumed filled me the way nothing else ever had before. I've found myself yearning for it now and then, knowing nothing else will satiate the craving."

A tingling warmth traveled from his palm and into Nikolas, the feeling of stepping into sunshine after hours shivering in the dark.

"I feel it now—he wants the hunger to *end*. It is an incessant madness. A plea."

Phos stared down at Nikolas with irises the same pale ice as his, and just as cold.

"Let it not be said I am not merciful," his god whispered.

VII

L oath as Risha was to leave the calming presence of the soul tree, they needed to move on.

The landscape changed again, from verdant jungle to high cliffs and stone runs streaked with veins of gold. Flowers grew from the cliffs in dark, spidery shapes, giving off the fragrance of rainfall, sweet and cold.

Every so often Risha paused to strain her ears for the sound of rattling bones. But so far they hadn't come across another Sentinel, which she took to mean they were either very lucky or running out of time until their next encounter.

Jas was quiet at her side. He'd been reserved since the incident with the imitori, and Risha worried it was because of what she'd done. Or maybe he was simply remembering his mother, carefully tending to the wound of his grief.

In the shadows of the cliffs, she longingly recalled early summer nights at the villa, sitting outside with her family in the pink gloaming while lanterns were lit and food was laid out. The way her wine glass was always full, and the tea that came with dessert had just the right amount of milk. How it felt to lie in her bed afterward, warm and relaxed and safe.

She imagined Jas there as well. Someone who was welcome and at home with her, who knew how to charm her mother and how to graciously lose at cards to Saya. Who would discuss politics with her father in a way that wouldn't ruffle his feathers but at the same time provide a unique point of view.

When this is over, she wanted to say, but the words wouldn't come.

There was nothing she could promise him, and he wouldn't believe it anyway.

"You're a cheery duo," Val drawled from his place on her back. "Know any songs or stories to pass the time? Getting a little tired of the bleak, introspective silence."

"Forgive us for being introspective," Jas said.

"Can you tell us more about Leshya or her weapon?" Risha asked.

Jas perked up at this. "Is it true that Samhara can only be wielded by using tandshri?"

"What, that little dance of hers? That's what she said, but don't ask me how it works."

Risha recalled the tandshri lessons she'd been given as a child. Rath had instructed her on how to breathe, how to hold her arms and legs, how to flick her wrists just so. There was a movement they had practiced often where she had to spin with her fingers held in mudras. She'd kept falling out of position.

"A strong performance is only possible if the person giving it is strong to begin with," her father had told her, nudging her foot until it settled in the right placement. "That means treating your body with respect and listening to what it has to say. Do you know what this movement is called?" She'd shaken her head. "It is Sada—an invitation to dance. A request to meet strength with strength, judged not with muscle but integrity and power."

Val yawned loudly and excessively. "All I know is it was strong enough to chop off Tenamar's arm." He giggled. "Idiot."

"Tenamar?" Jas repeated. "Is that the name of one of the kings?"

"Yup, and Leshya went and stole his arm. Fused the bones into the weapon's handles. He was so *mad*," Val whispered in delight. "Leshya wasn't a boastful sort, so I did the heckling for her. Nearly got beheaded early for my trouble."

"Bet she appreciated that." Jas sounded lighter than he had before. "Hopefully the kings don't come running to reclaim their bones once we get Samhara. Didn't you say you came from one of the cities? Which king ruled it?"

"I don't remember. The whole decapitation misadventure shaved off quite a bit of my memory. Oh! I do remember a song, though. It's coming back to me. There was this gnarled old fellow who was always sent to the rack, and afterward he'd have to be carted back with his limbs in a pile for someone to reattach 'em. Was a good sport about it, though. Every time he trundled past he'd sing,

"They tie the ropes around and 'round
They love to hear my wailing sounds
My wrist goes crack
My foot goes snap
The spikes tear up my ugly back!"

"That's, uh, lovely," Jas said.

"It sounds like you came from Cruciamen," Risha said. Of the four Mortrian cities, one was filled with spirits who were waiting to reincarnate, one was inhabited by those who didn't wish to move on yet, the third was for those who needed to atone, and the fourth was more or less a torturing ground for souls that would eventually dissipate. The latter was Cruciamen.

"Hmm, that does ring a bell. Good thing I don't recall much from my time there. Though I do remember my face being *quite* handsome."

Risha was surprised by the urge to smile. There was something about him and the way he spoke that reminded her of Taesia.

Or at least, the Taesia she had once known. The Taesia she had known leading up to Godsnight had been more stranger than friend. And now she had no idea what had happened to her. The last she'd sensed of her was the moment when...

Risha shuddered and pushed it away.

"What's wrong?" Jas asked.

"Nothing." Risha didn't enjoy lying, so she followed it up with, "I was thinking about the people back home. My family. The other heirs."

He drifted a little closer, ghostly fingers brushing hers. "I don't know that much about the other Houses."

"Where to even start." Risha noticed a piece of frayed string on her sleeve. She gently pulled it out and began to weave it around her fingers, like she was conducting a spell. The familiar sensation grounded her. "Nik is the easiest to get along with. He's always been a little awkward, a little rigid, but he's genuinely kind. Angelica, on the other hand..."

She faltered over the phantom heat of fire, the smell of ash on the wind. Jas only frowned and nodded for her to go on.

"She...well, she's Angelica," Risha mumbled to the string she tightened around her fingers. "Abrasive. Cunning. The best mind for politics out of all of us, I think. In contrast, Dante—" No, Dante was no longer heir. "That is, his younger sister Taesia is impulsive. Confident to a fault. But the Lastriders have a certain charm to them. She always..." The words nearly got stuck in her throat. "She always knew how to make me laugh."

"You miss them."

She pulled on the string until her fingers paled. "Yes."

Around them the cliffs rose higher and the shadows deepened. But there was a faint light up ahead—not the flickering warmth of a fire or the green tinge of the sky, but something muted and blue. It put her instantly on guard, but it wasn't like they could turn back.

Soon, the source of the light revealed itself to be a series of pools, all of them glowing the same luminous cobalt. Small, dark shapes were crouched at the edges of the pools or scurrying between them. At Risha's gasp, they froze.

There were about a dozen bone snatchers watching her, their eyes large and black. The small creatures had pale, scaly skin and wore brown, threadbare robes. Each of them carried a tiny lantern with a white-hot light encased inside—their life forces. They must have caves nearby where they lived amid their carefully organized bone hoards.

Risha slowly spread out her hands. "We mean you no harm."

In response, they all drew sharpened bone knives from their robes.

"Give them something," Val hissed.

"Like what?" Risha asked.

"I don't know, something to appease them!"

Risha checked her pockets and the pouches at her belt. Other than plenty of string and a few sachets of herbs, she only had her bone shards. Rattling them in her hand, she knelt and arranged them on the ground.

"For you," she said. "If you'll let us pass."

The bone snatchers regarded the bone shards, heads tilting one way and then the other. They exchanged chattering sounds before they hurried forward and grabbed the pieces. Risha and Jas were suitably ignored as the bone snatchers tucked away their knives and returned to the pools.

Risha exhaled. "For once, nothing's trying to kill us."

"Well, they *did* try, technically," Jas said. "Are you sure you don't need those?"

"I'll get by."

They had been wandering for what felt like hours. Her body was sore in places she hadn't expected, and the soles of her feet were throbbing.

"Will they mind if we hunker down with them for a while?" Jas asked, likely sensing her need for rest. The nearest bone snatcher, who'd been moving its arm around the shallow end of one of the pools, pulled out a yellowed bone with a happy chirp.

"They seem busy. As long as we don't get in their way it should be fine."

Risha gratefully settled down against the cliffside after taking Val out of his sling. She pulled off her boots and socks, trying to rub feeling back into the toes that had become numb. One of the bone snatchers cautiously approached Val, holding up its little lantern to get a better look at him. Val snarled and the creature skittered away.

"Damn things'll run off with me if you don't pay attention," he warned them. "They *love* skulls."

Jas knelt at the edge of the nearest pool and peered within its depths. "I've seen water like this in Vitae. There was a whole stretch of beach with bioluminescent algae. It was beautiful."

"No algae here," Val said. "These are acid pools. You'll always find bone snatcher caves nearby 'cause they use 'em to strip the flesh off the bones they collect."

Jas, despite no longer having flesh, jerked away from the water. Even Risha, who had been debating soaking her feet in the nearest pool, inched farther away.

"They don't seem to be affected, though." Jas pointed at the bone snatcher fishing its arm around the glowing water.

"I don't know how bone snatcher physiology works!" Val huffed, blowing black bangs away from his eye. "Just make sure they don't chuck me in there."

Risha leaned against the stone and closed her eyes. Eventually she managed to doze off, lulled by the darkness and the gentle sloshing of water and a soft humming. When she woke, the humming was still there. It took a moment to figure out it was coming from Val. The song wasn't the one he'd sung before—thankfully—but something slower and deeper. Mournful. Oddly familiar.

"What song is that?" Risha asked him.

He stopped. He was currently facing outward, so she could only see him in profile. His usually smirking mouth was flat, his gaze distant.

"Something Leshya used to sing to herself," Val answered. "Said it made her less homesick."

"I thought it sounded Parithvian," Jas said.

Another bone snatcher approached them. Val bared his teeth, revealing sharp canines, and the bone snatcher chittered anxiously while skirting around him. It held something between its hands, its lantern swinging as it placed its offering next to Risha. A pile of small teeth.

"Oh." Risha sat up straighter. "Thank you."

It ran back to the others, as if embarrassed. Risha smiled and Jas laughed. The teeth were mostly human, an odd assortment of molars and incisors. Some of them were stained black, likely having come from the mouth of a tobacco chewer.

Remembering what Jas had said about the old Parithvian men and their paan, Risha picked up the teeth and began to arrange them in neat lines.

Jas watched her curiously. "Is this some sort of necromancy trick?"

"No. It's a game of chaturanga."

He raised his eyebrows in obvious delight. He helped her by drawing a grid in the dirt, mimicking the game board. They only had six teeth each, so Risha grabbed a few pebbles to add to the lot.

"What's this?" Val asked.

Jas repositioned him so he could better see. "A strategy game. My mother taught me how to play. She said all the best generals and warlords learned it. Not that she thought I'd be a general or a warlord, but politics are their own sort of battle. It helps with decision-making. Choosing between what you can afford to sacrifice or concede, or what the other person's weakness is."

"You learned a far stricter version of it than I did," Risha admitted. "In Vaega we play it for fun."

"Trust me, those grandpas I played with? Tons of fun. I'm pretty sure they cheated, but they were so sneaky about it I could never catch them." He gestured at their makeshift board. "Do you want to be white raja or black raja?"

"Black."

Since they didn't have enough pieces for the infantry, Jas's first turn was to bring out one of his horse pieces. Risha chose to move one of the blackened molars on her side in the place of an elephant. A memory flickered of her playing against Saya in the villa, holding a beautifully carved elephant made of jet and placing it on the board as sunlight flooded the room. She wondered what her sister would say if she could see Risha using teeth and dirt instead of stone and glass.

"Interesting," Jas murmured, then later made a questioning sound as Risha moved out her general. "Seems early, but all right."

"Are you trying to get in my head?" she asked. "Or simply annoy me into making mistakes?"

Jas grinned. "I wouldn't dare." He then took one of her horses with his chariot. "Just making observations."

"Make them *quietly*."

"That's no fun."

"Yeah, it's boring otherwise," Val agreed. "Actually, this is boring no matter what. I have no idea what's going on."

Risha focused on evading Jas's pieces while he made aggressive moves toward her raja. She let him chase her across the board, waiting until some of his pieces were vulnerable before snatching them up.

"That's your second elephant gone," she said, setting the tooth down beside her.

He shrugged. "I can afford to lose some pieces. You're so busy running around trying not to get snatched that you've left your raja wide open."

His general *was* worryingly close, she just noticed. He would likely win the game in two moves. Risha studied the board as he made the first of them, most of her pieces too far away to offer aid. But her remaining chariot, which she'd primed to get close to Jas's raja, was positioned in such a way that moving it could block Jas's general.

Sighing, Risha made the move. He immediately claimed the chariot, and she claimed his general with her raja in turn. He laughed.

"See? Sometimes losses lead to gains."

Risha wanted to be grumpy about it, but the urge melted away at the sight of his smile. It was nice to see him having fun.

In the end, she lost despite having more pieces than him on the board. Risha leaned back against the cliff and rolled her eyes while Jas crowed in victory.

"If I'd known this would inflate your head, I wouldn't have—"

The air around her seemed to shiver and bend. Risha straightened as a cold wind stung her face, bringing with it a wave of gloom that leached color from her surroundings. Even the glowing pools dimmed to a dull gray. Jas was frozen in the middle of his triumph, one arm raised.

Risha stood. A crushing dread filled her chest.

"I ALMOST PITY YOU."

Before her was a cloud of swirling darkness that carried the scent of sweetly cloying rot. The god revealed herself in increments: the silhouette of four arms, a fluttering veil, a wreath of bones. Thana's presence was large and oppressive, making her want to drop to her knees and press her forehead to the ground.

"YOU BELIEVE YOU CAN SAVE HIM," her god said, glancing at Jas with a slight curl to her upper lip. "STOP LIVING IN A DELUSION, CHILD. YOU MAKE A MOCKERY OF MY BLOOD'S GIFTS."

Risha curled her shaking hands into fists. "I didn't ask for these gifts, but I'm using them as best I can. And I'll use them to bring him back with me. I'll use them to..."

To reopen the portal. The words felt sticky in her mouth, bitter and impossible.

Thana took a step toward her. Where her bare foot trod, the ground decayed and blackened. "THERE IS NOTHING YOU CAN DO WITHOUT MY HELP. SOON HE WILL FADE, AND FACE MY JUDGMENT. THEN YOU WILL BE ALONE. ABANDONED. WITH NO ONE BUT ME TO TURN TO."

Risha almost gave in to the childish impulse to cover her ears. But she forced herself to stare up at her god's ashen face, the gray light playing with the shadows across it, turning it from flesh to bone and back.

"You abandoned us first," Risha whispered. "You and the other gods."

"STOP BEING OBSTINATE. WHEN YOUR ANCESTOR CAME TO THIS REALM, I WAS THE ONE TO HELP HER PUT A STOP TO MY UNRULY SERVANTS. SHE WAS GRATEFUL FOR IT."

Risha glanced at Val, wondering if it had been Thana who'd appointed him to Leshya. "The help you offered her is nothing like what you want from me now. And besides, I am not my ancestor."

"THAT I CAN SEE. LISTEN WELL, CHILD: YOU CAN SERVE ME, OR YOU CAN SUFFER ALL THE TORTURES MY REALM HAS DESIGNED," Thana said, matter-of-fact. "ONCE YOU ARE ALONE AND MISERABLE, YOU WILL SUCCUMB."

"I refuse to be a part of this pointless war. I'm going to leave you in this realm where you belong."

The wind picked up, lashing Thana's veil as her eyes darkened to pure black.

"YOU WILL TRY," she whispered, "AND I WILL DELIGHT IN YOUR SORROW WHEN YOU FAIL."

The grayness lifted, and the god was gone. Jas broke off his laugh and looked up at her, blinking.

"Risha? What's wrong?"

"Nothing. We should get going." She turned to pick up Val. "How much longer until we reach the weapon?"

"It's not far. Remember how I said it was difficult to get to, though? I'm assuming you have a plan?"

"We'll figure it out once we get there," Risha insisted as she stuffed him back into his sling.

"Perfect. Spontaneity never got anyone killed. Love this for us."

Once Risha put her boots back on, Jas wrapped a hand around her arm, or tried to.

"Are you all right?" he asked softly. "Are you sure you're up for this?"

She couldn't feel his hand—not even a whisper of touch. She nodded, forcing Thana's warning out of her mind.

"Yes. It's time."

VIII

The Imperial City of Mukan was walled and gated, the streets beyond laid out in a checkerboard design. It made for easy navigation as the coach made a beeline for the imperial palace at the city's heart.

"Mukan harbors four walls," Botan said as they rattled through bustling streets. "We just entered the earth gate, and next is water, then air, and finally, fire. The palace rests in the middle to accommodate all elements and represent none." He glanced at Angelica. "Or, some would say, to represent kudei."

She nodded, taking in the tall, narrow residential buildings and townhouses built on stone plinths, the uppermost stories used for homes and the bottom stories used for shops and restaurants. The roofs were peaked and tiled with pointed eaves, some with exposed timbers and others plastered over in case of a fire. They went over bridges that spanned narrow canals, where small boats carried people to other districts.

The farther in they went, the more sophisticated the architecture and clothing became. There were villas here among gardens and public parks, and maple trees still clinging to their crimson leaves. Women strolled together under sun umbrellas, and a group of teenagers eagerly crowded around a meat skewer vendor. The smell of sizzling chicken made Angelica's mouth water.

Surprisingly, she also saw remnants of Deia worship. The other gods were not as prominent in Azuna as they were in Vaega, and so much of Azunese culture revolved around Deia's elements and nature, a precursor to the practice of Kiyonoism. But here and there she spotted braziers of ambergris and cedar, common offerings to the god of Vitae, as well as

Deia's symbol carved into the keystone of buildings, which looked like an upside-down horseshoe.

Botan spoke up again when they reached the innermost district. "Here you'll find museums, theaters, archives, storerooms, and administrative offices. This is where many of the state officials live—including myself— as well as the residences reserved for the bushan and their families." The bushan were the Azunese warlords.

They entered the final gate, a massive thing of iron and steel crafted into the likeness of two serpentine beasts. They were long and lean, with scales etched along their bodies that winked with gold, and each bore two arms with the claws interlocked.

Just as Vaega had wyverns that dwelled in the eastern mountains, Azuna had their own serpentlike creatures called sorankun. They were found in large bodies of water, deep forests, the high peaks of the Godan Mountains, and even the volcanoes of the Sanatsu Peaks. The fact that the sorankun lived in every conceivable habitat made them sacred here, to the point they'd become the imperial family's crest.

For a moment she was back in the Mardova villa, studying the fresco of the four elements. The golden wyvern that wrapped around them, cousin to the sorankun that carried the same balance between it and nature, a natural reminder that all elements were tied together.

The gates shut behind them, and they were in the shadow of the imperial palace. The red ceramic tile of its massive roof shone invitingly in the sunlight. Sharp gables arched out into long, gently curved eaves over verandas and railed walkways. Surrounding the main building were much smaller estates as well as colorful five-tiered pagodas amid elegantly maintained gardens.

The coach went over a flat stone bridge spanning a manmade river to arrive at the foot of the palace. A handful of nobility and their retainers had already assembled before the open doors of the audience hall.

When Angelica and Eiko approached with Botan, an older woman stepped out of the group with a pleased smile. She was willowy and carried herself with grace, the long hem and sleeves of her dark blue dress gently swaying as she moved. Her mouth was touched with red safflower, her graying hair done up in an intricate chignon decorated with a gilded owl feather.

"Esteemed Angelica Mardova, it is a privilege to receive you," she said in Vaegan, her accent heavier than Botan's. "I am Ueda Kazue."

"She has the most influence over the empress, and communicates with the warlords regularly," Miko had said of her eldest sister. "Everyone knows to obey her orders or else risk exile from the palace." Miko had paused, retreating to some internal wound. "She's always been talented at manipulating others. Do not mistake her kindness for compassion."

Angelica bowed and responded in Azunese. "It is a privilege to be received by you, Revered Ueda."

Kazue's eyebrows arched subtly at Angelica's delivery, and one of the cousins hid a giggle behind their sleeve.

"No need to be so formal," Kazue replied, still in Vaegan. Angelica's face heated. "We are family now, aren't we? First Aunt will do." She looked to Eiko and her brown eyes sparkled. "And speaking of, here's darling Eiko! You've grown so much since I last saw you."

Eiko made a move as if to hug her, then noted Kazue didn't mirror it, so she restrained herself at Angelica's side and bowed instead. "Aunt Kazue. No, sorry...First Aunt Kazue." A flush bloomed over her cheeks.

The woman laughed good-naturedly and switched to Azunese. "How much have you forgotten across the sea?"

"I haven't forgotten," Eiko murmured.

"I'm glad. But where is Kikou?"

Eiko shot Angelica a brief warning glare. "She felt more comfortable staying ho—staying with our mother. Things have been difficult in Nexus."

Kazue nodded. "Yes, so I've heard. We will speak about it shortly. For now, you'll be shown to your quarters to rest and refresh yourselves before our welcoming ceremony."

There were some polite, if stiff, introductions among the rest of the Ueda clan—Angelica counted three older cousins, another aunt, and an uncle—before servants shepherded them away.

Eiko was shown to her chambers first. Before they left, Angelica took her aside.

"Be careful," she whispered. "They will listen to everything you say, and try to get information out of you. We don't need to give them any ammunition against my family. Do you understand?"

Eiko's face hardened. She refused to look at Angelica as she said, "You really know how to pick your words."

"Do you understand?"

Her stepsister lifted her chin, that telltale stubbornness returning. Oddly, it gave Angelica some relief.

"Only if you understand that you're a stranger here, and I'm not," Eiko said.

That, Angelica knew very well.

Angelica's rooms were spacious and simply furnished. The decoration largely came from the natural building materials and winter-themed scrolls hanging on the walls with motifs of snow flowers and oranges. There were mats of woven rushes along the parquet flooring, and when she took her shoes off at the door she felt how soft they were against her feet.

The servants brought in her luggage and put her things away in the built-in drawers and cupboards along the walls with practiced ease. She wanted to ask them to stop, but unwilling to appear rude a mere five minutes into her stay, she made herself walk to Cosima. The thief was inspecting the smaller bedroom that would be hers. Angelica had requested she sleep there rather than in the soldiers' outbuilding with the rest of the guards.

"There's no bed?" Cosima waved at the room, empty save for a narrow, wooden couch and a set of drawers.

Recalling Miko's lessons, Angelica opened a nearby cupboard, revealing a thick pallet.

"Hmm." Cosima shifted on her bare feet. She'd been quiet and on edge since they'd passed the first of the city's walls.

"Is it strange? Being here, I mean."

"You have no idea. The colony I grew up in had some Azunese customs, but we mostly kept our own." Cosima rubbed at her arm as if she were cold despite the hearth radiating warmth from the central room. "It feels...different. Weird."

Angelica could only imagine the experience of visiting a land that had once tried to subjugate your own. There was a reason why those from Cardica didn't enjoy traveling to Vaega, who had long held the small country in a vise grip for their prized trade routes. But Cosima had been so keen on coming here she'd gone to the trouble of deceiving Angelica for passage.

Angelica was about to point this out when she realized Cosima's hands were trembling.

She stood rooted to the spot, unsure how to proceed. Angelica was not someone who consoled others—her hands were made for destruction, not comfort.

"I . . ." Angelica's sudden panic scrabbled at her chest with sharp little claws. "That must be . . . hard." She tried not to grimace.

Cosima studied her. Her lashes were naturally thick, and this close, Angelica noticed a freckle in the space between her nose and left eye.

"Ah, yeah," Cosima mumbled. "It's all right. I mean, you know. It will be." She cursed. "Look, I didn't tell you the truth from the start because I knew you wouldn't have brought me otherwise. And frankly, there wasn't any other way I could get to Azuna on my own. So I used you. And I'm sorry about it."

Angelica huffed. "No you're not. You got what you wanted."

Cosima looked like she didn't know whether to laugh or frown. "Maybe I'm not sorry about that bit, but I *am* sorry 'bout lying to you. I imagine you get a lot of that when it comes to politicking."

"You have no idea." Angelica flexed her hand, not sure what to do with it. In the end, it remained at her side. "Apology halfway accepted."

"Halfway?"

"Once we get to Mount Netsai, I'll accept the other half."

"You'll still help me find my brother?"

"Yes. I promise."

Some of the shakiness left Cosima as the corner of her mouth quirked. "Huh. An actual, god-sanctioned promise from a Mardova? How lucky."

Angelica turned with a scoff. "You stay here and rest. I'll ask them to bring you dinner."

"As you say, princess."

Angelica chose an appropriately understated dress with just enough embroidery to be respectful. She could tell she'd chosen correctly when Kazue dipped her chin in approval.

They were in the tea hall, members of the imperial family seated at low wooden tables arranged around the sunken hearth at the center of the room. Their backs were arrow straight, and their eyes kept sliding toward her.

Kazue was directly to her right, Eiko to her left. On Eiko's other side were her cousins, who eagerly drowned her with questions about Vaega. Eiko seemed both overwhelmed and happy for the attention, though her smile stiffened when the topic turned to Godsnight. Angelica was about to cut in with a diplomatic—if curt—response when Kazue tapped her finger against the side of Angelica's lacquered table.

"Let them talk freely," the woman murmured. "It has been a long time since they have seen each other."

"I understand," Angelica said. "But I'm not sure it's appropriate to discuss international affairs in this setting."

"Isn't it?" Kazue gazed at Angelica from under the fan of her lashes, lifting her hand so that she spoke behind the fall of her long sleeve. "We use tea ceremonies to welcome guests, but it is also an invitation to speak and negotiate. To learn and listen."

Angelica sensed Kazue's desire to ask about Godsnight herself, to have Angelica relive the horror of her god's possession, the unspeakable damage to her city. Yet nothing would make her speak a word about that day to anyone who wasn't Adela.

Even then, there was a lot she hadn't said to her mother.

The conversations around the hall quieted when the doors opened and two attendants stepped through. Unlike the palace servants, they wore fine silks of lavender and lilac, and silver combs sparkled against their hair.

They bowed in unison and said, "The Imperial Empress of the Reign of Fire, She Who Touches the Soil and Waves, She Who Tastes the Wind and Flame, Satake Asami."

A young woman walked through the open doorway. She wore heavy robes of silk dyed gromwell purple, and silver bells hanging from her embroidered belt chimed with every measured step she took to her place at the widest table at the circle's apex.

So this was Azuna's empress. She was barely older than Eiko, her pale face still childishly round. Despite this she moved as a grown woman would, allowing the two attendants to rearrange her hems before easing her to the floor. Her sleeves were wider than Kazue's, her hair styled into a perfect bun and crowned with a golden wreath in the shape of dancing flames. On her extravagantly embroidered dress was a motif of wisteria flowers, the crest of the Satake clan.

Everyone had stood to bow and only sat once the empress was situated. The young woman turned her face toward Angelica and Eiko.

"Esteemed Angelica Mardova, Esteemed Eiko Mardova, allow me to officially welcome you to Mukan." Her voice was high and sweet. "A visit from one of the Nexus Houses is an honor."

Beside her, Eiko drew in a breath as if to correct her, then caught herself and bowed her head. Angelica copied the motion. "The honor to visit your exalted city is ours, Your Imperial Majesty," she said.

Kazue gave a short, practiced laugh. "Asami, address her properly as your cousin."

The empress turned her gaze down with a light flush. "I apologize, Fourth Cousin Eiko. Allow me to welcome you home."

Eiko swallowed hard and nodded.

Angelica had known Kazue was the matriarch of the imperial family, but not that she had the power to publicly chastise the empress. Some of the older family members wore smirks, as if this were a regular occurrence.

A musician carrying a long stringed instrument entered the room, followed by a woman holding a tray. The latter went to the sunken hearth while the musician sat on a rug by the wall and quietly tuned their instrument.

At the faint vibration of a string, Angelica bit back a gasp. Something in her core *ached*, painful as a punch and pleasurable as a night in the Garden, her calloused fingertips twitching for something that had been reduced to cinders.

A murmur swelled through the room. The teamaker had flinched back from the hearth as stray embers spiraled upward.

"Angelica, are you all right?"

She drove her fingernails into her skin and focused on the sharp, bright pain. She forced herself to take a deep breath before turning to Kazue. It didn't go unnoticed that the woman had spoken her name without a title.

"Yes, thank you. I'm afraid all that traveling has worn me out."

Servants entered in a quiet procession and placed dishes on the tables, light and simple fare ranging from fried fish, pickled vegetables, and rice to soups in lidded porcelain bowls. Each portion was small and artistically arranged, and as soon as Angelica finished one, there was another set down before her.

While they ate, the teamaker meticulously cleaned each of her utensils, every movement precise with the routine of one who had done this hundreds of times. She then scooped tea into a deep ceramic bowl and picked up a large ladle. The imperial family made appreciative noises as the teamaker—a water elementalist—ladled boiling water up into the air over her head, letting it spiral and aerate before she directed it over the tea leaves. It was exactly the sort of food theater the dons and doñas in Nexus would have swooned over.

"So, Esteemed Mardova," said one of the elder male relatives in

Azunese. He sat on Kazue's other side and rudely leaned into her space. "There is a rumor that your ship was attacked at sea."

Angelica curled a hand around the small cup of sweet wine that had been served with the last course. She was tempted to glance at Eiko, but even if she saw trepidation on her stepsister's face, she'd already made up her mind on how to handle this.

"Yes, we were beset by a..." She didn't know the word in Azunese, so she used the Vaegan one instead. "By a kraken. Through the combined efforts of everyone onboard, we were able to defeat it."

The uncle's cheeks were ruddy; he'd already waved over a servant to refill his wine cup twice. "But it was you who delivered the final blow, was it not? The rumors suggest you used kudei."

There was a small sound, like paper tearing. Angelica looked to Kazue, wondering if she had made the noise, but the woman's face was only set in a concerned, if curious, expression.

"I could not tell you definitively," Angelica said.

Kazue chuckled throatily. "This is a topic that's been heavily debated among scholars and philosophers. Truthfully, no one quite understands what kudei is, but isn't that the point? There should be some elements of our world that remain a mystery. Some things that should best be left alone." The last seemed to be aimed at Angelica.

The uncle wanted to continue his line of questioning, but whatever look Kazue threw his way made him settle back with a grumble. Angelica busied herself with her own wine, pretending she hadn't found the interaction troubling.

The teamaker carried the first bowl to the empress, bowing low and offering it with both hands. Only after the empress had raised the bowl to her painted lips were the rest handed out to each family member. Confectionaries were brought out, delicate squares of steamed cake and sticky rice dumplings in a fruit-based sauce. Eiko's eyes lit up at the sight of them. Even Angelica, who had never been partial to sweets, found the cakes quite good paired with the earthiness of the tea.

It was at this point the empress took her leave, everyone once again standing to wish her a good night and holding up their tea in a sort of toast.

"Asami must get plenty of rest while she can," Kazue told Angelica when they'd resettled. "The end of harvest season is here, and the winter welcoming festival will take place shortly."

"I'm sorry we're intruding on such an important occasion."

"Hardly intruding. We are glad you and Eiko will be here to enjoy it." Kazue spared a glance at her niece, who was sipping her tea sleepily. "In fact, this will be good timing for you."

Angelica pressed her fingertips to her bowl, taking comfort in the biting heat and the music behind her. "How so?"

"The bushan from each state will be arriving in Mukan to celebrate. It will be easy enough to corral them to speak with you."

Kazue smiled good-naturedly. Once again Angelica fought to keep her face clear of emotion.

"That will be fortunate," Angelica murmured. "As I'm sure you're aware, my family has a unique position in Vaega. After the tragedy we experienced at Godsnight, it is imperative that our country be led by those who understand how to wield power, how to unite the people."

"And the Mardovas are that," Kazue agreed. Whether or not she actually believed it, Angelica couldn't be sure. "You must understand that Asami, while having the people's ear, does not actually *control* the people."

"The warlords do," Angelica said lightly.

"Yes. They may take some convincing, but I will be there to help." Kazue lifted her bowl in a shallow salute. "And in return, I hope you may be of help to me as well, Angelica."

That night, she dreamed of fire and light. Of soft-winged creatures and the rumbling of the earth beneath her. Of Kazue's intelligent eyes becoming pools of tar she could not escape. Her hand grasped the slender, smooth neck of a violin as she sank.

No one will save you, Deia whispered. *Not when they know they will burn for it.*

Angelica wrenched herself awake. The thick pallet underneath her was soaked with her sweat. She sat up, shaken and disoriented, and had to fight the urge to be sick. Her skin was prickling, flashes of heat radiating up the back of her skull. She may have groaned, may have gagged. She may have possibly died.

It took a while for the worst of it to subside. Once she could move, she crawled to her toilette case. She'd stored the vial of Hypericum inside, the one Cosima had gifted her while leaving Vaega.

She reached for the clasp and paused. On the ship she'd been able to whistle while standing at the railing, alone and unobserved, with her hands over the water. That had been enough in the moment, but the withdrawal might get worse the longer she stayed in Azuna. She had to save the vial for when she really needed it.

Angelica slumped against the wall and closed her eyes, breathing deep. Sweat rolled down her temples. Only a faint warmth was coming from the hearth in the next room, but she inhaled it greedily, her senses narrowed on the smoldering coals.

She began to hum softly.

It was a lullaby her father had sung to her on nights when Angelica had missed her mother, Adela kept up late by paperwork and stress. August had held her and soothed her tears, his warmth and the vibrations of his chest lulling her to sleep.

Her humming faltered.

"Mardova?"

The door slid open and the yellow light from the hearth spilled through. Cosima stood on the threshold wearing a night shirt.

"Shit." Cosima knelt beside her. "Thought I heard something. Maybe, uh, don't do that so close to walls made of paper?"

Sparks popped along her fingers. Angelica shook out her hands as Cosima reached for the water ewer. It wasn't until Angelica drank the whole thing that she spoke again.

"Why don't you take the Hypericum?"

"It'll get worse," Angelica whispered. "I'll need it then. Go back to bed. I'm fine."

"Very convincing, but no. What can I do?"

Angelica closed her eyes. She remembered sitting beside a cold river, her hands tacky, her mouth tasting of copper. Questions being asked of her she refused to answer. Being cared for in a way she did not deserve.

"Nothing," she muttered. "Leave me alone."

Cosima was silent a moment. "Y'know, I once had a run-in with a dog who was injured. The mutt was so scared and so in pain it bit anyone who tried to help it."

Angelica snorted. "You're comparing me to a dog? Let me guess, it eventually realized no one meant it harm and it was treated?"

"No," Cosima said quietly. "It died."

Angelica said nothing. Her head ached. Even her veins were itching, and though she desperately wanted to scratch at her arm, claw them out of her musculature if she had to, she didn't dare do it in front of Cosima.

Cosima reached out, and Angelica forced herself not to shrink away. Her fingertips landed on Angelica's forearm, soft as dragonflies.

"What usually helps?" Cosima asked.

Her instruments. Hypericum. The Garden. All things she no longer had access to.

Her gaze fell to Cosima's lap. To the hem of the nightshirt and the length of thigh it exposed, smooth and dark, a midnight horizon.

Cosima's fingertips wrote a song against her arm, stirring the fine hairs there. Somehow soothing the itch while waking starved nerves. They traveled down to the underside of her wrist, to her pulse.

"Oh," came a murmur from Cosima's throat; or maybe it was "ah." Angelica's thoughts had turned to velvet, concerned only with the pinch in her abdomen and the craving of her mouth.

Cosima straddled her in one fluid movement. A hand on her shoulder and her chest, the glimmer of teeth, the scent of wild mint. Cosima's hair was a corona, as if she were god-touched.

Angelica's hands climbed the slopes of her warm thighs, dragging up the hem of her shirt until she could fit her thumbs into the hot, silken plush of Cosima's hips. She pressed hard, feeding off Cosima's hitched breath, the frisson of her body at the touch of Angelica's lips to her collarbone.

The hand at her chest roamed upward, tried to caress the side of her face. Angelica shoved it back down to cup her breast. She responded like a plucked string to the sweep of Cosima's thumb.

"You should've told me before," Cosima breathed as Angelica discovered the heated valley of her, pliant to her questing fingers. "We could've—"

She swore when Angelica bit down on her collarbone and entered her at once. Cosima rolled against her hand and squeezed her shoulder hard enough to bruise, hard enough to make her body her own again. To rebuild herself out of mortal pieces: the lushness of a parted horizon, the brackish smell of desire, the weight of words unsaid bearing down.

If the light of the hearth grew brighter, neither of them noticed.

The next few days were a whirlwind of activity. A cousin showed her the imperial gardens, and an aunt brought her to a teahouse. Kazue and her children invited her and Eiko to a play with music and dancing, Angelica hypnotized by the musicians and the way they focused on single, pure notes rather than chords, sometimes pausing to allow silence to become part of the song. Another cousin, perhaps intending to scandalize Angelica, brought her to the entertainment district. Angelica showed only mild interest, to the cousin's disappointment.

Cosima accompanied her everywhere to keep the appearance of being Angelica's bodyguard. There were times when she looked around with avid curiosity and times when she withdrew into herself. The latter happened after the entertainment district, where Angelica had spotted several Mariian entertainers.

"*They* were the ones to try and take control of my country," Cosima muttered one evening. She shoved her boots off and left them lying haphazardly on the floor. "So why do some of them flat-out stare at me? Are they so surprised to see a Mariian wandering around?"

"They're probably fascinated by your outfit." Angelica had noticed quite a few stares in her direction as well.

Cosima plucked the front of her guard uniform. "Maybe. I still don't like it."

They settled into the new, strained silence that had become their third, unwanted companion. Somehow they had come to a wordless agreement to not bring up the night of Angelica's relapse—nor to repeat it.

For Angelica, it wasn't a matter of regret or embarrassment. In fact, she'd felt considerably better the morning after, waking alone in her own bed. But this was not the time for distractions; and besides, she rarely visited the same girl twice at the Garden.

"When are we going to start looking for Koshi?" Cosima asked suddenly.

Angelica hid her relief by rummaging through the shopping bags she had accumulated that day, souvenirs to send back to her family. Among the bolts of fabric and slim boxes of incense were packaged snacks. She grabbed one and made for the door.

"Tomorrow, after the meeting with the warlords. I've asked Noguchi Botan to escort us to the archives."

Cosima blinked, as if surprised Angelica was already making good on her promise. "Sounds good."

Angelica hummed in acknowledgment and walked down the corridor to Eiko's rooms. Eiko had been flourishing here, spending her days with her cousins and speaking more Azunese than Vaegan. But when she answered Angelica's knock, the smile she was wearing instantly fell.

"What is it?"

Angelica refrained from rolling her eyes and held out the package.

"I bought the snacks Kikou wanted. This one's for you."

Eiko gazed down at the offering as if it contained something poisonous. Slowly she accepted it with both hands.

"Thank you," Eiko said quietly.

"Do you want to stay here?" Angelica asked.

Eiko's head snapped back up. "What?"

"I need to go north for... well, I don't know for how long. You can stay in Mukan with your family while I go."

"Why do you need to go north?" At Angelica's raised eyebrow, Eiko huffed. "Fine, don't tell me. If we stay much longer, we might end up having to spend the winter here. The ships will refuse to make the crossing when the weather gets bad."

"We'll play it by ear."

Eiko rattled the box in her hands, the rice crackers and peanuts jostling inside. "I want to go to the meeting with you tomorrow."

"No."

"Why? I'm also a representative of House Mardova."

"You're *sixteen*. Your mother didn't even want you coming here."

A storm brewed across Eiko's face. "You're not the only one who was born into this. If you're going to use my family, you may as well accept my help."

"Did I say anything about using your family? We're only getting their support—"

"For a *crown*."

"I was sent by both of our mothers, in case you've forgotten. This is what your family wants, too. If we have power, *they* have power."

Eiko's eyes grew alarmingly damp. "What's the use of power if bad things still happen? If people I—if others get hurt?"

Angelica wondered if Eiko was thinking of Godsnight, of the giant crater left behind by that brutal battle and the wound in Adela's shoulder. Something seemed to skitter up her spine, like she was back in Deia's basilica, on her knees before the might of her god. Insignificant.

She reached out, hand hovering over Eiko's shoulder. Eiko stared at her, expression unreadable save for a pinch of yearning at the corners of her eyes. Angelica hesitated too long, and ended up dropping her arm.

"Bad things happen regardless." Angelica turned to leave, but her voice softened somewhat. "Our role is to pick up the pieces."

★   ★   ★

Kazue and her maids helped Angelica prepare for their meeting with the warlords. She was presented with a finely tailored Azunese dress of soft red silk, and to her surprise, the Mardova crest had been embroidered near the collar.

"It will help them see you as an ally if you are dressed to their liking," Kazue said while the maids folded the robes just so around Angelica and tied a belt around her middle. "A couple of them are not fond of Vaegans."

Understandable, considering the numerous skirmishes the two countries had been involved in over the years. "I don't mind. In fact, I was told to make sure I had some dresses made while I was here. I see the tales of Azunese tailoring are true."

Kazue gave a closed-mouth smile as the maids fussed over Angelica's hair. The woman's presence was like standing on a ship staring out at an approaching storm. Angelica wasn't sure what would happen if she reached it.

By the time Angelica stood in the Camellia Chamber, the traditional receiving room for meetings between the imperial family and the warlords, her hair was already pulling at her scalp from the heavy elemental ornaments affixed to her chignon. Cosima had whistled at the sight, and Angelica was certain it had the desired effect, but did the ornaments have to *weigh* so much?

The chamber contained a large round table of red pine. There were no chairs, as everyone was required to stand while discussions ensued, no matter how long they lasted. The blush-pink walls were crafted with geometrical motifs of camellia petals. There were no windows, but the ceiling let in natural light due to slats made from bamboo.

In addition to Angelica and Kazue, a few older relatives were in attendance, such as the uncle who had asked her about kudei. Even Botan was here, a hefty ledger placed before him.

They didn't have to wait long for two of the warlords to arrive. One was a middle-aged woman of average height and muscular build, her long hair tied into a simple braid with little adornment. Her robes were similarly understated, cinched at the forearms with bracers much like the two Gojarin warriors who accompanied her.

The other was a man at least a decade her junior, his long hair pulled into an elaborate crown and his belt flashing with bits of silver. He'd also brought two Gojarin with him. Angelica remembered suddenly that the warlords themselves were required to be Gojarin, or else they couldn't inherit the title. Although they weren't allowed to wear their swords in the Camellia Chamber, Angelica traced the colorful embroidery on their robes that spiraled into the shapes of air currents and water.

"Bushan Takenaka, Bushan Wakiya, welcome," Kazue said. "We hope the journey to Mukan was uneventful."

"Unless you call getting shit on by a bird eventful," the younger warlord said in a bright tenor. His open, round face was cleanshaven, his skin bronzed by the sun. The crest of water lilies on his breast told Angelica this was Wakiya, warlord of the water state.

"We passed a death procession, but beyond that, nothing," said Takenaka, warlord of the earth state, her crest one of a cedar branch. She had deep lines bracketing her mouth and a ragged scar decorating one side of her jaw. She assessed Angelica without giving anything of her internal thoughts away. Wakiya, however, tilted his head to one side as he addressed her.

"Angelica Mardova, is it?" he asked in Azunese. "All the way from Nexus, the Holy Kingdom! Surely *your* travels have been eventful?"

"We were also briefly held up by a death procession," Angelica replied in the same language, dipping her chin to Takenaka. "And there was an incident on the ship that brought us here." Then, in Vaegan: "To be honest, I would have preferred the bird shit."

Wakiya laughed. Takenaka studied Angelica over the rim of her teacup, unimpressed—with her Azunese or her word choice, she couldn't tell. She wished Cosima were here, awkwardness notwithstanding, but Kazue had insisted Angelica leave all her House guards out of the chamber.

Angelica smelled the third warlord before she saw them, the doors opening to a waft of cinnamon that heralded a tall figure. They wore fanciful robes shortened and cut into slits over wide trousers, their dark hair worn defiantly loose. Their eyelids were dusted with dark blue powder, and a hint of blush had been swept over their angular cheeks.

"You haven't started without me, have you?" they complained. A sachet attached to their belt swung as they made their way to their spot at the table, the source of that cinnamon bark smell. "My tea better not be cold."

"Of course not, Bushan Sugi," Kazue said with a bow. The warlord of the air state bore a crest of a maple pod, as well as embroidery symbolizing both air and flame. "But if you would prefer your water even hotter, let us know."

"I like it *scalding*." Sugi waved away a servant and poured the tea themself. "Blame it on my secondary element. Ah, but there's a Mardova here." They grinned at Angelica across the table. "Surely you understand."

Angelica, who had been avoiding reaching for her cup for this very reason, nodded stiffly.

"It is not like Daiji to be last," Takenaka mumbled.

Sugi made an amused sound. "Are you mad because you don't want to make small talk with me, Chikao?"

The warlord of the earth state scowled, revealing how the crags had been chiseled onto her face.

Wakiya set down his tea. "It's likely due to that new pet of his," he drawled. Sugi snickered.

"I did hear that Bushan Nanbu has recently become soul-bonded with a creature," Kazue said. "A very high honor."

Botan nodded in agreement. "The edicts of Kiyonoism state that all creatures are to be respected. If you win the respect of one in turn, you are considered soul-bonded," he explained to Angelica. "It's quite a beautiful thing."

"Unless you're soul-bonded to a *snake*," Wakiya muttered with an exaggerated shudder.

Angelica was about to ask more about these edicts when the handprint on her arm suddenly pulsed with heat. She couldn't quite cover a gasp.

Kazue leaned in. "Is something wrong, Angelica?"

She shook her head even as the handprint on her arm burned, the pain like jagged glass carving into her skin, making her eyes water. "I . . . do not like snakes."

Angelica finally lifted her cup and took a few sips of tea, a lighter blend than the one from the ceremony. It helped steady her while the pain faded, retreating to an uneasy stinging.

The doors slid open and two heavily armored Gojarin entered. Their iron plates were lacquered black, their shoulder guards linked to metal scales that stopped at heavy bracers and gauntlets. Their black helmets bore small curved horns, and though the other Gojarin had opted for half masks, these two chose to wear masks that covered the entire face, styled in the exaggerated likeness of snarling animals. One was of a tiger, the other a bear.

They swiftly parted to make way for a man with silvering hair pulled into a severe topknot, his face handsome yet hardened by both age and duty. He had chosen an unpretentious outfit of dark fabric with the symbols of fire and air crawling over the sleeves. The crest near his lapel was that of amaranth.

But what drew Angelica's attention was the large serpent draped around the warlord's shoulders. It was easily five feet long, with the markings of a pit viper, its sleek green scales crossed with black stripes. It scented the air with its tongue, head dancing curiously beside the warlord's.

Wakiya gave a true shudder before everyone bowed to the last warlord.

"Bushan Nanbu, thank you for your attendance," Kazue said. "We are honored to receive you and your new companion."

Nanbu nodded in acknowledgment before his dark eyes settled on Angelica. Like Takenaka, his expression was difficult to read, but she thought she caught a flash of interest.

The air in the room was stifling. Underneath her silks her skin dampened with sweat, her throat tickling like she had to cough. Sugi's sachet of cinnamon was overwhelmed by the odor of smoke, acrid and bitter, and even if she were to take another sip of tea she knew it would taste of ash. Her fingers pressed against the table until they turned bloodless, until they became as numb as the rest of her.

Kazue spoke, but the words were muted, underwater, meaningless. The doors opened again to admit the empress, only a hint of purple in the corner of Angelica's narrowing vision.

She kept her focus on Nanbu Daiji, who all but ignored her while he paid his respects to the empress. The snake around his shoulders shifted, flexing its lithe body as it slithered across his chest toward Angelica.

Staring at her with eyes so bright and blue they could rival the base of a flame.

IX

Seniza was a beautiful coastal city built on the ruins of ancient dolmens, the tombs of those who had lived in the walled villages on top of the nearby hills. The remains of those villages were still there, but reportedly haunted and infested with beasts, and—much like Deia's Heart—best avoided.

The buildings here were made largely of lime mortar mixed with volcanic ash, the architecture positively drowning in multifoil arches and lattice windows. One surface out of ten was covered in colorful frescoes and murals. And, to Brailee's delight, small parrots liked to nest in niches in the walls, flying overhead in streaks of yellow and green.

Dante watched her break apart some bread and scatter the crumbs for the two birds perched on the food vendor's awning. Bright morning sun slanted across the street, warming the small table where the three of them sat to enjoy a cheap breakfast. The food was likely much better in the market districts, but Dante wanted to keep to the less-inhabited areas, so they had to settle for too-hard tomato bread and too-strong coffee.

Saya was sitting next to Brailee with her lips pursed in discomfort. She fiddled with the silver bangle on her wrist, twisting it around as her gaze focused on nothing. When the parrots swooped down to pick up Brailee's offering, she started.

"Something wrong?" Dante asked.

Saya scratched at her hair. The boardinghouse they had stayed in last night hadn't been able to accommodate them with baths, and Dante felt itchy, too. He wondered if the bedding had lice.

"It's the city," Saya answered. "It feels...off? Not in a bad way, just a weird way."

Brailee turned from watching the parrots. "Weird how?"

"In Nexus I can sense the distant spirits in the necropolis. They're just sort of...there? In the background? But here, that feeling is constantly under my feet. I can't escape it."

Dante nodded. "Seniza was built on old tombs. I doubt they moved all the bodies to the necropolis."

Saya made a face. "After all this is over, maybe my father should come down and do a calming ceremony."

All this, as though catching his traitorous aunt, saving their sisters, and reopening the portals was a mildly irksome chore.

Saya fidgeted with her mostly untouched coffee cup. "Are we actually going to the volcano?"

"We might have to, if Aunt Camilla came to find a fulcrum." Dante stood. "But not yet. Can you lead us to the necropolis?"

"Sure." Saya bounced up, clearly relieved to have avoided volcanic exploration. "I don't think it's far."

Dante kept an eye out as they followed Saya through the cobblestone streets. His hood was up and Nox was hidden in its ring, but he feared someone recognizing him despite only having come to Seniza once or twice in his life when he was younger.

Brailee had been too young to remember much, so she now made sure to take everything in, from the coffee vendors on street corners to the decorative palm motifs along buildings. While she and Saya exclaimed over interesting sights, Dante listened to snippets of conversations they passed. The southern accent shortened vowels and made the words clipped, precise.

"—ran straight in, like rats."

"Where are they now?"

"No idea, but they better not cause trouble."

"What in Thana's grave were the guards doing?"

"Scratching their asses, probably."

Dante didn't regret letting in the refugees, but after a night of restless tossing and turning, he'd decided Brailee was right: He had to be more careful. If his actions ended up causing more harm than good, it would be his fault and no one else's.

That's no fun, murmured the demon. The pinpricks of his fingernails scraped through Dante's hair, making him jerk. *What's the use of having my power if you don't use it?*

"I'll use it when I need to."

Brailee looked over her shoulder at the sound of his voice. He shook his head, conveying he was fine, but sensed a weary concern that had become common in their interactions.

"Did you see Risha in your dreams last night?" Saya asked suddenly.

Brailee's attention turned back to her friend. "No, I'm sorry. I tried looking for her and Taesia, and Ri..." Her voice faltered. "It's been difficult. Like they're being shrouded."

Dante frowned. Brailee had told him about her dreams of Rian Cyr. From what he understood, Rian had been bitten by ash flies at the base of Deia's Heart, leading to the fever that had put him in a coma and then, eventually, taken his life. Or so they had thought. How had this led to Phos getting a hold of him? And more troublingly: How had Brailee gotten mixed in with him?

The wrought iron gates of Seniza's necropolis had been left open, and the three of them traded uneasy looks before venturing inside. It wasn't as large as the one in Nexus, but it was somewhat similar in design. On either side of the gravel road were crumbling ruins of navetas, chamber tombs made of limestone. Among these were newer, showier tombs of marble and dark granite, some with statues of either the gods or of the deceased person's likeness, and one—Dante's personal favorite—with statues of the departed's various pets.

Saya gasped. Dante and Brailee followed her gaze to a tomb that had been smashed up, its doors fallen to rubble. Claw marks gouged the ground around it, as if something had wanted to get in. Or get out.

The farther in they walked, the more they heard voices raised in agitation, until they came upon a crowd amassed in front of a mausoleum. Its four columns were topped with a low dome, underneath which sat a sealed door carved with motifs ranging from moon phases to symbols of the elements.

But it was the design in the pediment that Dante focused on. A Conjuration circle filled with familiar glyphs and sigils, a five-pointed star in its center.

Marcos Ricci's tomb.

"How long can we be expected to live with this?"

"Soon enough we'll end up like Nexus—"

Guards in burgundy uniforms barred the yelling crowd from the building. Their frustration created bright sparks of red behind Dante's eyes. He drifted as close as he dared while Saya stuck close to Brailee, the girls holding hands.

"I don't like this," Saya whispered behind him. "The feeling of this place..."

The noise of the crowd swelled as a figure walked toward the mausoleum. It was a man of average height, glossy black hair slicked back with pomade, his clothes stylish and embellished with gold. Even his boots had been polished to a high shine, gleaming in the morning light. He ascended the three small steps and turned to face the crowd with a benevolent smile.

"Friends, I understand your concerns," the man said, his words slow and carefully enunciated. "Believe me, I share in them."

"Is that the baron?" Brailee whispered to Dante.

He nodded. Baron Martín Alma, inheritor of his family's monarch-appointed legacy as governors of southern Vaega. Martín Alma was only in his forties, but he had proven himself by winning the people's loyalty through various displays of charm. Dante had to admit there was something vaguely pleasant about the man as he studied him in detail, from the streak of gray in his hair to the laugh lines bracketing his mouth.

"What happened to Nexus was ghastly, no doubt a backfire of magic produced during Godsnight. I have sent inquisitors to investigate the incident, and I'm sure they will report back that it was some working of the Houses."

Dante sneered. Beside him, Brailee and Saya stiffened. However, most of the crowd noticeably settled down, the man's words some sort of balm to their agitation.

One of the unaffected aggressors shouted, "That doesn't explain why the dead've been walking!"

"You're very right, it does not. But that, too, is a phenomenon in Nexus, one that House Vakara tends to most diligently. Once the chaos up north has settled, I will call on one of their family to assist us."

Saya let out a tiny squeak.

"Is it because the gods are angry?" someone else cried. "They've left us for good, I'm telling you—"

"It's 'cause that *abomination* is still here!" A woman nudged a couple people out of her way to point at the mausoleum. "Wasn't he the fool who brought demons to our world? What if this is the work of *demons*, and not the gods?"

An uncomfortable murmur ran through the crowd. Azideh laughed softly in Dante's head.

Martín Alma gave her a patient smile. "I'm not certain that it's possible for a man to summon demons from beyond the grave. However, the concerns of the public have been heard, and I am here to address them. In a few days' time, we will officially exhume the body of Marcos Ricci and cremate whatever remains of him. His tomb will be dismantled and replaced with a memorial to honor those who lost their lives on Godsnight."

This was met with more agreeable mutters, and the crowd's remaining aggression fizzled. Dante clenched his teeth, sensing the clock looming overhead. They only had a few days to steal Marcos Ricci's remains and have Saya reanimate him. To get long-awaited answers.

"But even though this will assuage many, it will not be a proper solution to the new trials we face," the baron went on. "Even now, we—"

The doors to one of the nearby tombs banged open. The crowd screamed and scurried back as another set of stone doors smashed apart, then another. From the empty mouths of the doorways came shuffling, lumbering corpses, their skin pressed tight as leather against their bones, their eye sockets hollow above mouths in rictus grins.

The crowd scattered. Martín Alma gaped at the newly risen dead, all confidence wiped from his features. The guards stepped forward, weapons drawn.

Then the doors behind the baron exploded outward. He fell under a rain of stone dust before a guard helped him up and away. Through the mausoleum's opening Dante spotted a shadowed figure, which slowly floated out into the light.

Marcos Ricci was shrouded in too-loose garments of black. Although he had lived centuries ago, most of his features were still intact due to a special embalming procedure of the Vakaras. His brown skin had paled to gray, his dark hair brittle and falling to his shoulders.

Saya frantically searched through her pockets until she found a ball of string. She cut off a segment with her teeth and wrapped it around her fingers, staring at one of the crawling corpses as she wove a spell and then—*snap*. The body kept moving.

"They're not being controlled by spirits!" she said over the din. "It's like—like something else is making them move!"

Dante watched the corpse of Marcos Ricci float down the mausoleum stairs. The baron ordered his guards to stop it, but their arrows and blades only met with a barrier around the body that flashed red whenever it was hit.

Four people rushed forward. Their heads were covered in hoods, their faces hidden under masks in the likeness of skulls.

Conjurers. The group Dante had been accused of leading, earning him a spot in the Gravespire.

They wrapped the body up in sheets while the guards were knocked back by some unseen force. One of the Conjurers threw the body over their shoulder.

"Where did they come from?"

"Help—!"

Brailee pulled on the back of Dante's jacket. "We need to get out of here before someone sees you with them! Use the crowd as cover!"

Reluctantly he turned toward the southern gates along with a handful of spooked petitioners. Others—including the Conjurers—were running in the opposite direction, toward the western gates. Dante made sure to keep Brailee and Saya from getting trampled.

A shiver stole across his shoulders and the demon growled.

She is here.

Dante turned his head, guided by Azideh's instinct. Time seemed to slow as he took in the fleeing crowd, the terror on their faces, their wide eyes, their open mouths.

One of them was not afraid. She turned and met his gaze, eyes of brilliant, bright blue flashing in recognition and surprise.

A flicker of red, and he was pushed off the path by an invisible hand. He went stumbling against the nearest grave, the stone digging into his side. He hissed in pain while Azideh writhed in his black cloud.

"Dante!" Brailee helped him up. "What happened?"

He looked around in vain; she'd disappeared. The demon rumbled his displeasure.

"Those corpses weren't raised by necromancy," he said. "Or Conjuration. They were being manipulated by a demon."

His sister's fingers tightened around his arm. "Then that means..."

"Aunt Camilla is here, and she's leading the Conjurers."

And she had gotten to Marcos Ricci's corpse first.

X

Angelica walked as quickly as she could back to her rooms without outright running. Her legs were weak, her heart palpitating so hard she was at risk of going under any second.

In the end, she didn't make it in time. Close to her rooms, she hurtled herself off the exterior walkway and into the nearest bushes before throwing up everything in her system.

She was one enormous, contained scream, her lungs filled with the agony of salt rubbed into wounds, of bone that broke badly and never reset. She was on her knees in the way she prayed to her god, the way she had learned to plead, to beg, with nothing to show for it other than teeth cracked on pride.

She keened and pressed her feverish forehead to the cold ground, about to burst into a flame that even she would be forced to feel with its full might. Her ashes gathered and swept into a cedar box, then paraded to the mountains.

"—elica!"

She jerked when something hard pinched her outer thigh. Panting, she pushed herself up and stared at the figure beside her, thrown into the palace's shadow.

Kazue's face had lost all pleasantness. It now sat in sharp lines as she hauled Angelica to her feet, forced her to turn in the direction of her rooms. Angelica barely had the presence of mind to clumsily toe off her shoes before Kazue all but pushed her inside.

Cosima was reclining on the floor, an open book before her. At the sight of Angelica, she leapt to her feet.

"Fuck, what happened?"

The details were both sharp and blurred. Standing in the Camellia Chamber with the warlords and the empress, niceties and formalities, introductions, bows, and a stumbling, disjointed speech from her own mouth about the importance of trade, truce, and thrones.

All while Deia stared at her from the body of an Azunese pit viper.

"What's happening?" Kazue demanded. Angelica wasn't sure what she meant until there was the sound of running footsteps, a screen sliding open, and then something cool and hard was being thrust into her hands.

Her hands, which were crawling with sputtering flames. Cosima yanked her own hands away, the glass vial beggining to warp. Angelica fumbled to pop it open and downed it all.

"Elemental addiction," Kazue murmured when Angelica dropped the vial and folded to the floor. "That's what you have, isn't it? Sometimes Gojarin are afflicted with it."

Angelica swallowed and hung her head. The ornaments in her hair were so damn heavy.

"Maybe you should leave?" Cosima suggested to Kazue.

Kazue scoffed. "Make yourself useful and get some water," she said, moving to kneel beside Angelica. Cosima shifted on her feet, hands curled into fists, before she reluctantly turned to the ewer in the corner. "And as for *you*, calm down and look at me."

Angelica wanted to bare her teeth against the words *calm down*, against the urge to curse the older woman out. She looked up and feared to see a single, unblinking blue eye staring down at her, but Kazue's irises remained brown.

"Something upset you in the Camellia Chamber," Kazue said. "Was it Nanbu Daiji?"

As the flames receded she turned cold, her teeth chattering. Cosima returned with a cup of water, but when Angelica tried to take it, it slipped from her grasp and spilled across the floor. "Shit."

"S'all right, I got it." Cosima poured another cup and held it to Angelica's lips. Humiliation ran rampant through her, especially with Kazue watching her so closely.

"Was it the snake?" Kazue continued in that steel-toned voice. "I could sense something was off about it."

"It's..." Angelica managed to hold on to the cup and took a bigger gulp, washing away the Hypericum's herbal flavor. She heard her mother's voice in the back of her mind.

Do not tell them anything they don't need to know. This is Mardova business.

The same words Adela had spoken to her throughout her life. Always warning Angelica away from the other heirs, fostering contempt instead of cooperation.

Angelica stayed silent. Kazue took a breath and let it out slowly.

"It would be a shame," Kazue said quietly, "if Eiko was not able to return home to her mother."

Angelica stilled. The parts of her body that were free-floating reassembled, and the headache that had been building under the weight of the hair ornaments throbbed.

She had come to Azuna for power both political and magical. She'd thought she was well on her way to obtaining the first, but it seemed there were more games to play.

Kazue waited patiently, sitting on her knees with utmost poise. The eldest, like Angelica, born to be a wielder and weaver of influence.

Angelica set the cup down. "The snake Nanbu Daiji carries is not a natural animal," she whispered. "It is a form of Deia."

Kazue took a moment to digest the words before cursing violently in Azunese.

"So that is his plan," the woman growled, poise forgotten as she regained her feet.

"What?"

Kazue covered her mouth with a hand, glaring at the wall. When she lowered it, her lip paint was unsmudged. She gave Cosima a pointed look.

"She stays," Angelica said firmly.

"Very well. In this land, there are some who believe Kiyonoism is a weaker substitution of our worship of Deia. That even though we care for nature, we forget this realm and its elements were her gifts to us, and our lack of offerings and prayer offends her. Never mind that she—and all the gods—abandoned us first. I have eyes and ears stationed at Daiji's estate that tell me he has welcomed some of these malcontents into his home."

Kazue flicked her sleeves. "The god must have whispered in his ear. She wants revenge on us for forsaking her."

Cosima's mouth hung open, but at this she shook her head. "If she wanted revenge on Azuna, why not...I don't know, make a hurricane or an earthquake or something?"

"You think we haven't been struck by natural disasters?" Kazue snapped. "We know full well Vaega has felt them, too. Just look at what has befallen Nexus."

"That's because the entire realm is dying," Angelica said. "It's not Deia. At least, it's not directly Deia." Shakily she reached up to pull the ornaments out of her chignon. Cosima saw her struggling and knelt behind her to help. "But she's manipulating Nanbu for a reason."

Kazue thought this over. Angelica sighed in relief as the last ornament slid free, wondering how she'd once again come to have Cosima's clever hands in her hair—and tried not to think of them in other places.

"He wants the empress's sway over the people," Kazue said slowly, coming to a revelation. "He and the other bushan have their laws and taxation and control of military forces, but the people find solace in the empress. It was why Kiyonoism was adopted at all. If he can prove that Deia is still here, that we were wrong to cease our worship—"

"The empress loses what little power she has left," Angelica finished.

Kazue rolled her shoulders back and looked down at Angelica. "There is something I need to show you."

Angelica refused to go anywhere without Cosima, so Kazue begrudgingly let her tag along. Despite Cosima not knowing how to use the sword at her hip, Angelica didn't want to be alone if this ended up being a trap.

"She talks to me like that again, I'm sticking her hairpin somewhere uncomfortable," Cosima muttered as they followed the woman down increasingly dim and deserted corridors. "Hey, you doing all right?"

Now that the Hypericum was making its way through her system, Angelica realized how insensible and defenseless she had become in front of Kazue. Heat bristled along her face and palms as she touched her mouth and hair, wondering how rumpled she appeared.

"You look fine," Cosima murmured. "A little gray, but fine."

The heat flared higher and Angelica dropped her hand. "If you say so. And you have my permission to stick her anywhere you please."

Cosima muffled a snort, then brushed her arm against Angelica's. "Really, though, was it . . . her?"

Angelica's hands refused to stop trembling. She pressed them to her stomach and whispered, "Yes."

There was no mistaking those eyes. The laughter and cruelty dancing in them even in the form of such a creature.

They were deep within a distant recess of the palace when Kazue stopped before a set of doors flanked by two imperial guards. Their blank, wary faces turned to Angelica and Cosima.

"They are allowed inside only with me as an escort," Kazue told them. They bowed in acknowledgment before sliding the doors open.

Beyond was a wide room, the space largely empty save for the hanging hearth in the center and a beautifully painted privacy screen in the corner. The walls were of rich pine and bamboo, and somewhere an incense burner was giving off the fragrance of agarwood.

Along the far wall was another set of doors, opened to let in wintry light. Beyond was a carefully cultivated garden with a small, trickling waterfall. Sitting on the wooden porch overlooking it was a child.

Angelica's misgivings rose higher as Kazue stepped into the room and the doors shut behind them. Even Cosima shuffled closer to her, one hand on her sword hilt.

"It's too cold to be out here," Kazue said to the child. Her tone had not honeyed or softened at all. "Come inside. I've brought you visitors."

The child—a girl, judging by the adornment of wisteria hanging from her updo—shifted on her knees. She was enveloped in a heavy winter robe embroidered with plum blossoms.

She turned her head, and Angelica inhaled sharply. Fastened around the girl's mouth, chin, and jaw was a muzzle like a half mask, constructed of bamboo, fabric, and metal. While someone had taken pains to carve a design of primroses onto it, it did nothing to soften the shock.

"What is this?" Angelica demanded, stepping forward.

Kazue held up a staying hand. "Would you like to continue this alliance? If so, you will let me explain."

"Explain why a kid's in a gods-damned muzzle?" Cosima shot back.

Kazue narrowed her eyes. "You'll do well to keep your guard in check."

"She speaks as she wills," Angelica said. "And trust me, I share her sentiment."

The girl had shrunk into herself as the adults above her argued. Angelica guessed she was around fourteen years old, her skin pale and her eyes the brown warmth of mahogany. She'd hidden her hands within her long sleeves, her thin shoulders hunched.

Angelica sank to one knee beside her and reached for her muzzle.

"Esteemed Mardova." The title was a whipcrack from Kazue's mouth.

"Do I come into your house and touch things that don't belong to me? You Vaegans might think you wield control beyond your borders, or that you have special privilege due to your heritage, but we no longer recognize the gods here. This is not how a future queen behaves."

Blood stung Angelica's skin in a flush. She and the girl stared at one another, both confused, both chastened, both children under Kazue's supervision.

Slowly Angelica retracted her hand. Kazue made a gesture to the girl, who stood and walked back into the main room with a rustle of her hems. Angelica followed.

Kazue slid the doors closed before settling her hands on the girl's shoulders. "Esteemed Mardova, I would like you to meet the Imperial Empress of the Reign of Fire, She Who Touches the Soil and Waves, She Who Tastes the Wind and Flame, Satake Asami."

Angelica stared at the girl, who kept her head lowered. "This... is not the same girl I saw at the tea ceremony, or the Camellia Chamber."

"That is her half sister, Akane," Kazue said. "She was born from a union that the family did not authorize, and therefore her right as heir was forfeit from the start. However..." Her fingers tightened on Asami's shoulders. "This was around the time the bushan began making subtle bids for more control over the states. Do you know how the Satakes came into power, Esteemed Mardova?"

Angelica glanced at Cosima, the thief looking just as lost as she felt. "They created the Gojarin."

"Yes." Kazue let go of the girl—Asami, the *real* Asami—to stoke the hearth. "Their leader was a woman named Satake Akari. She wielded three elements: water, earth, and fire. She was one of the most powerful elementalists in not just Azuna's history but Vitae's as a whole. It is even said she once leapt into the cauldron of Mount Netsai and survived."

Angelica twitched. Kazue spared Angelica a sidelong look.

"Due to her relentlessness and strength, she subdued the other clans. She became the first sitting empress of Azuna, admired and feared by the people. They thanked her for the protection of the Gojarin even as they spat at the idea of the clans being consolidated under one banner. There were attempted coups, and infighting. All were snuffed.

"The remnants of the clans were allowed their own noble houses and bodyguards, a class of warrior called the kaikushine. They specialized in secrets and assassinations, in keeping to the shadows. After many years had passed, the spurned noble houses finally struck back. The kaikushine assassinated the then-sitting empress, and turmoil followed."

"The War of the Great Families," Angelica said.

"Yes. The Satakes went into hiding for seven long years while the Gojarin slaughtered or disbanded the noble houses and thinned the kaikushine's numbers. Only then was it possible for the Satakes to reclaim what was theirs. But Azuna was never the same. We split into four states, and the nobles who had survived the war—those who had smartly surrendered and vowed themselves to the service of the imperial family— were each given a state under the empress's rule."

"Those families became the warlords," Angelica picked up. "The bushan. I know all this already." Or at least, she'd known most of it.

"Then you should also know how that turned out." Kazue's lips thinned. "Through years of political pandering and scheming and forced marriages, the bushan's influence grew. Only the strongest heirs with Gojarin training could inherit the title. *They* were seen as the military might of the empire, not the Satakes. Eventually the imperial army was split between the states, leaving the empress as nothing more than a cultural symbol. A reminder that something that scratches can be declawed."

Kazue turned back to Angelica, eyes smoldering like the hearth's coals. "If Nanbu Daiji truly is collaborating with...with *her*, that's more than enough to tell me they are growing tired of how things stand. They don't merely want the people to follow their orders—they want their devotion."

"The same devotion they give to the empress."

"Just so. But we have always anticipated it would come to this. That's why we parade Akane as the true heir." Kazue put her hand on Asami's shoulder. "Their mother died giving birth to Asami. Since she was in seclusion during the later stages of pregnancy, the public was told she passed from a grave illness. They don't know of Asami's existence."

Cosima clicked her tongue at how impassively Kazue spoke of the past empress's death in front of her daughter. But Asami's expression didn't waver.

"How many *do* know?" Angelica asked. She suddenly recalled Miko's warning that there were things she was not allowed to tell anyone, not even Adela.

"Only the eldest members of the imperial family. The girls look enough alike that once Asami is fully grown and we deem it safe enough, she will switch places with Akane."

"And if it's not safe?" Angelica demanded, not a little incensed at the idea of using some poor girl as a decoy, having her pretend to be the very thing her family had denied her in name.

"Then Asami will rule from behind the palace's walls. Though," Kazue sighed, glancing at the top of Asami's head, "that might end up being the case regardless."

"What do you mean?"

Kazue brushed her knuckles against the skin of Asami's temple. Asami's eyebrows twitched.

"No matter how powerful the bushan become, no one will soon forget that this empire was founded on the strength of the Satakes," Kazue said softly. "That strength has been passed down from empress to empress. Even Akane shows proficiency with fire. But..."

Kazue lightly touched the strap of the muzzle.

"While Akane knows how to spark flames, there is a larger beast within Asami," Kazue murmured. "Something beyond even the greatest Gojarin. The elders call it a curse."

"A curse?" Angelica repeated skeptically.

"Whenever Asami speaks, something breaks." Seeing the confusion on Angelica's face, Kazue told Asami to get one of the tea bowls.

"That's not necessary," Angelica said as the girl moved to follow the order.

"For you to properly understand, it is." Kazue grimly accepted the bowl that Asami put into her hands. "Go ahead."

Asami hesitated. She looked up at Angelica and Cosima, swallowed, and reached for the straps of her muzzle. Angelica nearly tried to stop her, to argue with Kazue—but it wasn't her place. This wasn't Nexus. Kazue was right: She had no authority here.

Kazue had also been correct in that the half sisters looked incredibly similar. There was a same roundness to Asami's cheeks, tinged pink under all the attention. Her mouth was small and pinched with trepidation.

"Greet your guests," Kazue instructed. Asami set down the muzzle and signed something with her hands. "No. The correct way."

Asami opened her mouth, then closed it again. There were faint red marks on her face left behind by the muzzle. She breathed in, breathed out, gaze fixed on the ceramic bowl in Kazue's hands.

"Greetings to our honored guests," Asami whispered, the sighing of wind through barren branches.

Angelica sensed a compression between the girl and the bowl. It sparked against her skin and in her core, taunting in its familiarity.

A crack ran down the side of the bowl before it split into two pieces. Each piece fell into the safety of Kazue's palms, the edges cut cleanly as if by an expertly sharpened sword. Cosima swore in surprise.

Angelica stepped closer to better study the break. The feeling in the air was gone as quickly as it had come, but there was no mistaking it.

"Angelica," Kazue said quietly, "is this kudei?"

Angelica couldn't speak. She had only been able to touch this elusive new magic recently, had thought perhaps it was due to her being a Mardova, a wielder of every element.

And yet here was a young girl who spoke it into existence, just as Angelica breathed a song to sever and amplify. As if aether really had been one of the original elements, and there were a few in this realm who could still touch it.

Kazue must have seen the realization cross Angelica's face, for she smiled slightly. It was clean and sharp like the edges of the broken bowl.

"If you can channel kudei, you can teach Asami how to better wield it," Kazue said.

Angelica stepped back. "I . . ."

She was about to say *I barely know how to wield it myself.* But then her mother's voice was there to restrain her, redirect her.

Do not let them see you as anything other than powerful.

Asami held her muzzle to her chest, reluctant to put it back on, and stared at Angelica with widened eyes. Wide with fear, perhaps, or curiosity; certainly not hope. The girl would be a fool to put any hope in her.

"I can try," Angelica said at last.

Kazue's smile broadened. "I am pleased to hear it. The stronger the imperial family becomes, the better we can suppress the bushan's plotting. There will be a hallowed alliance between the Satakes and the Mardovas—rulers of half the realm."

"There's no point ruling half the damn realm if that realm's gonna die soon," Cosima reminded her once they were back in their rooms. "Look around, princess. What's the point?"

"You think I don't know that?" Angelica paced the floor, holding a

clammy hand to her burning forehead. "I wanted to head to Mount Netsai after the festival, but—"

"But now you have to teach a little girl how to do magic good or
whatever just happened," Cosima said impatiently. "On top of your
promise to help me find Koshi."

"I'm—"

There was a quiet tapping on the door. They fell silent as it opened to
reveal a servant.

"Apologies for intruding, Esteemed Mardova, but I have a summons
for you. Bushan Nanbu has asked for your company as he takes a walk
around the east gardens."

Angelica, already perturbed by the day's events, felt herself wobble.
"I . . . yes. Of course. Allow me to freshen up, and I'll be out shortly."

"Thana's bloody rotting grave," Cosima muttered once the door shut. "It
never ends. That's the warlord, isn't it? The one with the . . . divine noodle?"

"Div—? For fuck's sake." Angelica attempted to fix her hair. "I did *not*
want to speak to him so soon, but there's no choice."

"I'll come along. Make sure he doesn't try anything."

"No." Angelica took a deep breath, inhaling the vestiges of lingering
incense. She missed the smell of the Mardova villa. "Kazue was right to
keep my guards out of the Camellia Chamber. If he sees me with them
now, it'll send the same message of distrust."

"But—"

"I can handle myself," Angelica snapped.

Cosima's mouth twisted. "Of course you can." She turned and
flounced into her room, shutting the door a little too hard.

Angelica ignored the flare of annoyance this provoked and finished
straightening her robe before allowing the servant to escort her to the
entrance of the east gardens. It was chilly outside, so she'd added a wrap
of heavy fabric over her Azunese dress, embellished with tiny scarlet
peonies. Although it wasn't yet cold enough to snow, the air carried the
scent of it, the promise of a long and arduous winter ahead.

Nanbu Daiji waited under a vermillion archway, flanked by the same
two Gojarin who had accompanied him in the Camellia Chamber. A
maid—one of Kazue's—stood with her hands clasped and head down, no
doubt having been instructed to act as an escort. Angelica, who hadn't
expected such a display for a simple walk, ground her molars together;
she should have brought Cosima after all.

But it was too late now. And if Angelica could handle a kraken, she could handle one man.

Thankfully, Deia was nowhere in sight. Without the snake, Nanbu Daiji seemed smaller, though he was built with a sturdy chest and long legs, his muscles testament to a life spent training with steel.

He bowed when she approached. "Esteemed Mardova," he said, his voice carrying the faintest hint of a rasp. Although his Vaegan was fluent, he spoke somewhat haltingly. "I apologize for asking you to step out into the cold."

"I don't mind," she responded in Azunese, which was just as halting. "I was growing overheated indoors. My speech in the Camellia Chamber may have been affected by it."

A faint glimmer of—surprise? amusement?—reached his eyes before he switched back to his native language. "They tend to stoke the hearths too vigorously, in my opinion. But come, let us walk."

She fell into step beside him as they passed under the archway and into the gardens. The white gravel paths spiraled into a wide circle that surrounded a lake. In the early weeks of winter, most of the color came from the greenery: the shrubs and ferns, the evergreens, the black pines. Yet there were still touches of pink and red from the blooming camellias and winter peonies, like specks of blood on snow.

"You did seem distracted in the Camellia Chamber," Nanbu said. He walked at a steady, stately pace, arms held behind his back, while his Gojarin and Angelica's borrowed maid kept a respectful distance behind. He had the carriage of not only a soldier, but a commander. "I was worried, considering you have traveled such a long way to deliver it."

You know why I was distracted. "I'll admit, I was a touch embarrassed afterward. Perhaps all the travel, all the..." Her Azunese was slower than her thoughts, giving her a glaring pause. "All the shock of the last few weeks may have affected me."

He dipped his chin in understanding. He had an appearance her mother would call *ruggedly good-looking*, from his chiseled cheekbones to the wide square of his jaw.

"We heard stories of what happened in Nexus, each more unbelievable than the last," he said. "Perhaps you can enlighten me with the truth? If it does not cause too much pain, that is."

Angelica pretended to waver. "It *was* a painful day, but I believe it's important for everyone to know what truly happened."

She gave him the most stripped-down, undetailed recounting she could manage, eventually admitting defeat and switching back to Vaegan. She said nothing of Deia or her possession, and focused largely on the Conjuration circle.

"This is most peculiar," Nanbu murmured. He stopped to appreciate a rock formation. Some were covered with moss, others looking to have been eroded by sea wind, others still bearing lines of strata.

"I agree," she said. "Not to mention devastating. With the disappearance of the palace, our monarch is gone. Two of our Houses have practically been disbanded."

Nanbu hummed in thought before he continued walking. She kept pace with him.

"You have an auspicious tie with the imperial family," Nanbu said as the pathway led them through a small bamboo forest. "Ueda Miko married your lady mother several years ago."

"Yes, it is a...fortunate union," she said. "In that I have gained another mother and two sisters."

"Lucky for the Ueda house as well, to have such an extended family with godly ties."

They came to a water fixture that trickled down dark stone and into a small pond. She stopped in the pretense of admiring the colorful carp while sorting her thoughts. The fish came up to the edge of the pond as if expecting her to feed them.

"I realize that Azuna has a complicated relationship with the gods," she said at last. "Please know that I find no offense by it. I respect the ideals of Kiyonoism."

A small quirk of his mouth. "Indeed, it is meaningful to many. Protecting our natural world grows more important with every passing year. However, I am one of the admittedly few who remember who to thank for such gifts."

The pond warped in her vision into the circle of offering bowls at Deia's basilica. Each stood for an element, even the one that had always sat empty, a symbol of nothingness, void, abyss.

"Your esteemed family was founded on Deia's bloodline," Nanbu went on. "I feel that many here would no longer find that significant, but I do."

"I appreciate you saying so."

What has Deia told you? What has she manipulated you into doing?

Angelica glanced over her shoulder at the maid, who stood quietly to one side of the pathway—no doubt prepared to give a full report to Kazue later—and the two Gojarin. The warriors stood with arms at their sides, swords hanging from their hips, neither at ease nor at attention. Their animal masks were even more unnerving out here in the gardens, a stark contrast to the scenery around them.

One of the Gojarin turned their head. It was difficult to tell because of the distance and the mask, but Angelica thought they were staring directly at her.

"In Vaega, House Mardova is still prominent, still respected," she said, resuming their walk. "Which is why, with His Holy Majesty regrettably having been caught up in the attack on Godsnight, we should be the ones to assume his position."

"I agree."

It couldn't possibly be this easy. "Oh?"

"The Vakaras carry the blood of Thana. To put such a family in charge of Vaega..." He *tsk*ed. "That would be begging for disaster. You do not want the seat of a country symbolizing *death*."

Angelica had never thought of that. "A wise observation. They are also missing their firstborn heir. She was..." *Swallowed into a portal.* "She was caught up in the attack as well."

Another *tsk*. "That is a shame. But all the more reason for the Mardovas to prevail."

They came across a stretch of maple trees. Most of them were barren, their burning leaves having been swept away by cold winds. But one tree still bore branches wreathed in bright orange and reds, defiantly rejecting winter's approach. All along the pathway were stone lanterns, their flames dancing merrily.

Angelica allowed him to lead her toward an arched wooden bridge. It led to the small island of white sand in the center of the lake. "Forgive me for being forward, Bushan Nanbu, but does this mean you and the fire state will support the Mardovas' claim to the throne?"

He stopped in the middle of the bridge. She had no choice but to stop as well, shivering as the wind off the water blew icy fingers into her wide sleeves. The maid and the Gojarin remained on the shore behind them.

"No one but the empress is allowed on that island," Nanbu said, eyes half-lidded as he stared at its shore. "During certain ceremonies, like the seasonal welcoming festivals, she stands upon it and lights a lantern.

Formerly, offerings for Deia were given here." He pointed out the path they had taken to get here. "It is surrounded by the elements. Earth, air, water, and fire." His finger stopped at the maples and stone lanterns before falling back to his side. "Here in the very center represents kudei. The element that connects them all."

Angelica's pulse throbbed in her wrists, at her throat, each a deadly point that only needed the lightest cut to bleed her out.

"From what I have heard, you have managed to channel kudei." Nanbu finally looked at her, and there was something of the snake in him as well, patient and intent. "Truly, you are Deia's child. A wielder of all five elements."

She thought of the actual child hidden away in the palace, the bowl that had cracked from her voice. Her fingertips began to heat, and she quickly hid her shaking hands within her sleeves.

"It is because of this you must understand that Kiyonoism is not enough to save us," Nanbu whispered. "It is a departure from proper worship. Our world fades a little more every day, and the imperial family believes the answer is only to tend to nature. They have forgotten Deia's might. Her influence. Her *power*."

Angelica's neck was stiff from how still she held herself. Nanbu reached out to touch the railing of the bridge. The wooden surface looked to have been carefully charred and then coated with oil.

"We prefer to use natural materials in our gardens," he continued. "We desire for them to become worn and aged, to better blend into the landscape we've created. But it is also a reminder that time moves on regardless of what happens. That all things, eventually, erode."

He turned fully toward her, and she was forced to look up at him. "I urge you to consider the effect of time on Vitae and its people, as well as the manner of your homecoming."

To return to Vaega with the backing of a warlord and his army of Gojarin. To make some sort of truce with Deia that would ensure Angelica continued to be her vessel.

And with a god inhabiting her, forcing out her powers to their full, terrible capacity, could anyone truly stop her?

"Thank you for accompanying me, Esteemed Mardova." Nanbu bowed. "I'm sure I will see you at the winter welcoming festival, if not before."

Angelica stayed in the middle of the bridge as he left, his Gojarin falling into formation behind him. She gripped the railing until her fingers ached.

A strong gust of wind rippled the surface of the lake and raced toward the maple trees. The last of the vivid leaves were plucked off, spiraling up into the air like a cyclone of embers.

XI

The Sanctuary of Nyx was even more daunting at ground level. The courtyard was a massive space flanked by colonnades and filled with worshippers, as well as the overwhelming scent of anise and clove.

"Keep quiet," Lilia murmured out of the corner of her mouth when Taesia coughed.

To anyone nearby, she was essentially invisible. It was the same trick Lilia had performed when they'd scouted the terrain of the temple, using her shadows in a way that redirected any light source and made people's gazes skip right over her.

"And other Shades can't detect me?" Taesia had asked.

"No one but me. A benefit to having Lunari blood."

But the trick could only work on one person at a time, and it didn't prevent others from hearing her. Taesia suppressed another cough.

The princess was pretending to be a common devotee, her hood pulled low. The moon tattoo on her forehead was covered with a dangling brass ornament she'd tied to her hair. It reminded Taesia of the gold maang tikkas Risha had worn to important functions.

An image of Risha flashed through her mind, eyes deepened to black, surrounded by a torus of power as Thana took control.

Focus, she snapped at herself before the claws of her thoughts dug in. *Get the shackles off and find Brailee again. You can ask her what happened.*

The solid weight of Starfell on her back helped ground her. Although the nightstone band was working to dampen its presence to nearby Shades, her close contact enabled her to feel its steady power, a gentle thrum against her spine.

"I've never seen it this crowded before," Lilia whispered.

Taesia scanned the courtyard full of anxious worshippers. In Nexus she was considered tall, but the people of this realm held an average of six feet. There were murmurings in Nysari all around the courtyard, many of the words unknown to her. But some things were staggeringly similar: the songs of prayer, the dried flatbreads that priests handed out to the poor, the bowl of lavender oil that Lilia stopped to anoint herself with. After a slight hesitation, she touched the oil again and peered through her shadows to press her finger to the spot between Taesia's eyebrows.

The nave stretched at least half a mile to the ambulatory, hugged on either side by columned aisles with open archways that led to side rooms, the span of it so wide it functioned as a prayer hall. The floor's polished blue marble was dark and cloudy like swirled paint, the walls covered with glazed black tiles and gemstones that glittered brilliantly in the stardust-fueled lamplight. The ceiling was a field of dizzying geometric tilework that opened up into high windows. Taesia couldn't help but marvel at the sight.

"I've only ever seen it from the entrance," Lilia said softly. "I've never actually set foot inside before."

Because of the star of misfortune. "Well, it's still standing," Taesia said.

"How does it compare to your Nyx temple?"

Taesia tried and failed to find the right words. In the end all that came out was: "This one's bigger."

Lilia hummed and they continued on. They reached a transept that extended east and west, the center of which held an orrery.

Taesia immediately recognized the shape of the Cosmic Scale. It had been built in brass and silver, with orbs of multicolored gems used for each realm, all affixed to a turning mechanism. Right now all the realms were just slipping out of alignment—Godsnight come and gone.

In the middle was an empty dome. Taesia stared at it, thinking about Julian and the voice he'd heard in the Bone Palace.

"Ostium," Lilia whispered. "It seems like something out of a story. Something to fascinate children."

A memory came to her, unbidden: of being seven and behaving badly, and her mother retaliating by threatening her with the knowledge of demons. She'd had trouble sleeping for a week afterward, convinced one was hiding under her bed.

She hoped Noctus wouldn't face any such infestations.

"Which way are we going?"

Lilia looked around. "I know the basic layout of the Sanctuary. The wings on either side of us lead to the closed-off portals. There's also a wing for astrologers that houses the planetarium where the others have gone."

"That's a lot of ground to cover."

"Which is why we split."

Julian had made a face at the suggestion that he go with Marcellus and Kalen to find the diamond while Taesia and Lilia set their sights on the crown. Even Taesia had had misgivings, but Marcellus seemed more than ready to defend Julian and Kalen should they encounter any trouble.

"The crown will be in the coronal chamber," Lilia went on, lowering her voice as a priest in dark robes walked past.

"And where is that?"

"We're standing on top of it."

"It's *underground*?"

"Yes. The only access to it is from the royal prayer chamber." Lilia swallowed. "Mar told me how to get there."

"Fantastic," Taesia muttered. "Lead the way."

She followed close behind Lilia, careful to stay within her shadows, through an aisle and into a side hall that eventually merged into the eastern wing of the temple. There was a lingering bitterness on her tongue she couldn't seem to swallow, an incessant nudge in her mind like a gnat flying about her head.

As if Nyx were trying to get her attention. She aggressively ignored it.

The walls on either side of them were filled with colorful mosaics. "The lore corridors," Lilia explained when Taesia's step slowed. She gestured up at one as they passed, featuring a young Noctan woman with ornamental chains hanging from her horns, sitting with a set of tools across her lap.

"It's the story of Noria Lunari. The eldest princess who was born near the end of the Century of Eclipse. Many of her siblings took part in that war, but she wasn't trained to fight. Instead, she valued invention and craft."

In the next mosaic, Noria was in the middle of weaving something on a loom with a shocked look on her face, gazing up at the unmistakable figure of Nyx, who had favored the form of a woman back then. "Eventually her diligent prayers for the war to cease culminated in an audience with Nyx. The god told her a large battalion was coming from Solara, and could very well be the thing that destroyed the seat of Noctan civilization for good."

The next mosaic depicted Noria sitting with her parents on either side of her, both leaning their foreheads against their daughter's knees as they wept. Noria's hands were placed upon their heads in a benevolent gesture, though tears of chalcedony lined her face. In the background, someone carried the corpse of a wolflike beast.

"Nyx told her there was a way to stop the battalion from defeating them," Lilia went on. "But it would require sacrifice. Nyx told her that if Noria were to acquire enough pieces of an astralam, she could fashion them into a powerful tool."

The coronal.

"Her siblings hunted down an astralam and managed to bring back most of its fangs to her. She fixed them into a crown that could make an impenetrable barrier around Astrum, that could leach the light from the stars and unleash it as something hotter and stronger than fire. But to destroy a battalion of that size . . ."

In the last mosaic, Noria had her arms outspread, eyes closed, as starfire burst from her fanged crown and winged warriors fell around her.

"It required her life," Lilia whispered. "But it marked the end of the war." She stared up at the mosaic, lingering. "I've never imagined death looking this peaceful."

"Because it probably wasn't. It probably *hurt*." Taesia glared at the tiled likeness of Nyx. "Nyx asked too much of her."

Lilia drew herself up, and if Taesia didn't know any better, she'd say the princess seemed proud. "She was my ancestor, a Lunari who understood her place in this world and her duty to those who inhabit it. She sacrificed her life so that others could be saved. To me, there's nothing nobler."

For an instant Taesia's skin prickled white-hot. "There's nothing noble about following a god's orders to *die*."

"She wasn't merely following Nyx's plans. She prayed for a solution, and she received one she was willing to follow through with. Every Lunari is taught that their kingdom comes first."

Taesia thought of Ferdinand Accardi, a greedy, cowardly man who would have never put his kingdom before himself.

But the opposite was just as terrible. To lose your autonomy to duty, to throw your life away because it was *expected* of you.

There was no happy in-between. That was partly why she'd become enamored of Dante's idea to get rid of the system altogether, to instead focus on building a leadership of those who willingly chose that responsibility and all it entailed.

Her thoughts were a chaotic jumble of resentment and confusion. The blood that others had fawned over in Nexus felt like ichor in her veins, thick and black as tar and just as toxic.

"Taesia?"

Taesia turned away from the mosaics. "Let's keep going."

The corridors widened gradually. The design shifted into oranges and reds and greens, forming panels of fire and ferns, the tile curving into sinuous waves of water and swirling air.

"This leads to the Vitae portal," Lilia whispered so that her voice wouldn't echo. "Farther down is the royal prayer chamber."

"Won't there be guards?"

"They're not a problem."

She was about to ask why when Lilia signaled her to step behind a niche at a bend in the corridor. Taesia did so, careful not to let Starfell knock against the wall. Lilia peered out.

"Only two guards. Neither are Shades."

Before Taesia could react, Lilia expertly wove the shadows away from Taesia and instead flung a thin sheet of darkness before the two of them. Her familiar then shot down the hall in the opposite direction, banging against a wall.

"What was that?"

The guards rushed past, following the careening familiar. Lilia and Taesia slipped out of the niche.

"It's up ahead." Lilia hurried down the hall.

Taesia had every intention of following her, but a grand trefoil archway snagged her attention. It was tall and wide, its voussoirs imprinted with symbols of the elements. The chamber within was dimly lit, but from here she could make out the edge of a familiar shape.

A stepwell.

Although she knew the portal was dormant, although she held no elemental magic, she still felt a frisson of something pass through her— something like the scent of grass on a warm day, or sunshine on a lake. The humidity of summer and the chill rainfall of winter. Animal hide and campfire.

Home.

She descended the stepwell. It was a wide basin of a gleaming, dark material like obsidian. Instead of water at the bottom there was a mirror-smooth basin where Noctans and Vitaeans alike had once stood to be transported to another realm.

"Taesia!" Lilia hissed behind her. "The portal is closed. We don't have time for this. And even if you could get it open now, would you abandon us?"

No—she couldn't leave Noctus, especially not with Nikolas still under Phos's thrall. But she couldn't bring herself to turn, the pull toward home so strong she ached. Starfell thrummed gently against her back.

She drew the sword from its sheath. Staring at it, she wondered if it were trying to tell her something.

Lilia had come to stand beside her. Taesia held Starfell in both hands, touching its tip to the floor. The scent of grass and smoke grew stronger. Closing her eyes, she imagined ripping open a vortex, taking the residue of the stepwell and feeding it into a new portal.

Her wrists throbbed with a fresh wave of pain, and she nearly dropped the sword.

"As I said. We need to move," Lilia said. "You don't understand the disadvantage we have because of the Malum Star. If we linger, I guarantee we'll be caught."

"We won't be." Taesia held out the sword. "Try it."

Lilia stared at her as if she had turned into Nyx himself. "What?"

"I need to see—I don't know if we'll be able to try, later—"

The princess's face was twisted in exasperation. But there was also a hesitant desire in her eyes.

Slowly Lilia reached out and wrapped her hand around the hilt. She inhaled between her teeth.

"There is...something," she agreed softly.

"What does it feel like?"

"Whatever it is, I do not think it's Vitae. But I recognize it." She held the sword before her. "I felt it before, at the safe house, but it's stronger now. I don't know how to explain it, but—"

Footsteps echoed beyond the archway. The guards were coming back.

"—swear I'm hearing voices." Two shadows darkened the entrance. "Hey! Is someone in there?"

Taesia froze like a rabbit at the snap of a twig. She considered herself proficient in running away, but in this situation, there was nowhere to go. Lilia reached for her shadows as the guards moved to the lip of the stepwell.

Somewhere in the distance came a deep *boom*. The walls shivered, dust raining from the ceiling. The guards took off running again.

Taesia let out her held breath. "That...wasn't your familiar, was it?"

Lilia shook her head and handed Starfell back. "We need to get going."

This time, Taesia didn't argue.

XII

Julian could only just see the top of the golden barrier from behind the outer wall of the Sanctuary of Nyx. He stared at it, huddled within his cloak, and waited.

There—a faint tremor ran through the barrier. Julian exhaled, his breath turning to fog.

In being so close to Orsus, Julian had been able to turn his beastspeaking ability on Nikolas long enough to escape, but he'd hoped his infiltration of Nikolas's mind would be long-lasting. If the barrier was showing weakness, that meant he'd succeeded to some extent.

Could he replicate the maneuver with Rian? Could he absorb enough of Orsus's power to drive Phos out while simultaneously keeping Orsus's influence at bay?

Don't let Orsus take control of you, Taesia had told him. Whether a suggestion or an order, he planned to follow it to the best of his ability.

Soft footsteps on stone made him slip his fingers into his waist sash, where he'd tucked away the knife Marcellus had given him. He relaxed somewhat at the approach of Kalen and Marcellus. Kalen was carrying a bulky piece of fabric in his arms, which he shoved at Julian.

"Quickly," the astrologer said.

Julian fumbled to shed his cloak and handed it to Marcellus before he slipped into the new garment. It was far too large for him, and thick with silver embroidery along the sleeves and hem. It smelled like dying leaves and spice-laden smoke.

"How did you get this?" Julian asked.

"Don't worry about that," Kalen said. "No priests were hurt, if that's where your concern lies."

"It wasn't until you said that." Julian raised the hood. "Are you sure this is going to work?"

"Absolutely!" Marcellus said at the same time Kalen said, "No."

Julian sighed. "What happens if someone tries to speak to me?"

"Sometimes the priests enter vows of denial for a period up to a full lunar cycle," Kalen explained. He held up two fingers together. "This gesture means you are currently unable to talk. But we'll stick close in case someone bothers you."

Julian pulled the hood down lower until he could only see the ground immediately before him and held the skirt of the robe so that the hem didn't drag. "Let's go, then."

Kalen had insisted the easiest way to get inside was through the front entrance. Julian regretted this now as they walked through the court-yard of solemn, worried Noctans. The back of his neck turned hot at the notion that they could perceive him through the robe and raise an alarm.

They were halfway across the courtyard when a real priest holding a tray full of thin, crumbly flatbreads approached. He said something in Nysari while lifting the tray higher.

Gripped by mind-wiping dread, it took a moment for Julian to raise two fingers the way Kalen had told him to. The priest said something else, a question threaded in the tone.

Julian, hoping his face was sufficiently covered in the hood's shadow, shot a panicked look at Kalen. The astrologer mimed picking something up. Julian slowly reached out and took the tray of flatbreads, hands hid-den within his sleeves. The priest said something Julian guessed equated to *thank you* and walked off.

"Uh," Julian said.

"Just set it down somewhere," Kalen said.

"Hold on." Marcellus took the tray from Julian and trotted up to a nearby Noctan dressed in roughspun wool, a woman whose figure was stooped with age. He said something to her and her filmy eyes widened. She nodded creakily and accepted the tray from him.

Julian watched Kalen. The astrologer's face was carefully blank. Julian got the sense it wasn't from disapproval.

"You didn't have to do that," Kalen muttered when the soldier returned. "The supplicants would have found it easily enough."

"She looked hungry." Marcellus gestured Julian on.

Julian stopped beside a wide silver bowl that held a pale liquid. Following Kalen's quiet instructions, he touched the oil—careful not to let anyone see his distinctly un-Noctan hands—and pressed it to the aides' foreheads. The gentle fragrance of lavender rose around them.

Turning, he allowed himself a moment to gape at the opulence of the temple's interior. He'd never been particularly religious—ironic, all things considered—but his mother had dragged him to the Deia basilica several times while growing up. She'd told him it was important to make sure the god didn't feel forgotten or unloved, and that small offerings based on what they could afford—usually a loaf of fresh-baked bread or a stick of incense—would help Deia remember there was a realm to take care of.

A god shouldn't need to be reminded, he'd thought then. The sentiment welled back up as the initial awe of the temple waned. Instead of taking care of his realm and his people, Nyx was busy attempting to seduce Taesia to do his bidding. Even Orsus, a god truly forgotten and unloved, only desired Julian for his ability to become a vessel.

The gods had long ago ceased to care about anything or anyone outside of themselves. This temple, these prayers, were in vain.

Julian followed Kalen and Marcellus through an archway, head down and hands clasped within the wide spill of his sleeves. With his peripheral vision limited he could only focus on the aides' feet, stepping where they stepped.

"The Sanctuary is full of twisting hallways," Kalen had told them earlier. "Take care that you don't get lost. We'll be taking a circuitous route to the planetarium so that we don't arouse suspicion."

"Will they recognize you?" Julian had asked.

"I've only been to this planetarium once, and it was in my youth." The other man had paused a beat too long. "It should be fine."

Julian was already sweating with every possible consequence of getting caught. Did Noctans hold trials, or did they simply execute criminals? Would it matter, considering he was Vitaean and the possible source of the attack on the city?

They were in an echoing hallway lined with paintings in gilt-wreathed frames when Kalen and Marcellus suddenly stopped. They doubled back and pulled Julian into an alcove with a door.

"Others up ahead," Kalen whispered.

"Is that...?" Marcellus leaned out a bit more, squinting. "Nesch. I think that's one of the royal astrologers. Caelith Pyrin—I remember her and my father getting drunk at a well-blessing ceremony."

Julian lifted the edge of his hood to better see. A group of five people were clustered before a set of wide, dark doors etched with designs of the moon's phases and inlaid with a material that shimmered like quartz. Three of them were guards, by the look of their uniforms; the other two bore the same tattoos as Kalen, except the constellations upon their brows were different.

The woman who was currently talking was tall and silver-haired, dressed in fine silks with tinkling silver bells hanging from her horns. She would have looked ethereal had it not been for the terror creasing her face and the way her voice wavered as she spoke. Julian, unable to decipher the words, knew they couldn't be good by the way Kalen clenched his jaw.

"What does she mean by *calamity*?" Marcellus whispered.

Kalen shook his head. "She must have charted something. A prediction. Or maybe she's referring to the attack on Astrum."

At that moment, the group turned and began making their way down the hall—right toward them. Kalen reached for the doorknob, not bothering to look inside the room before he shoved the other two in.

As soon as Julian tripped forward he was consumed by darkness. He raised his arms to feel around.

"Where did you go?" he whispered. His voice only echoed back, the range rising and falling and distorting. "Kalen? Marcellus?"

He wandered farther into the room—or what he thought was a room. The pitch-black felt like an entity around him. Like he was in the bowels of a beast, if the beast was pure shadow.

The longer he stood, the more his mind began to unravel, spinning away and away until his arms numbly lowered back to his sides. He didn't know if his eyes were open or shut.

There was breathing in the dark. From his own chest, from the vaulted ribs along the beast's sides, from nothingness itself. He wanted to turn but found his body unwilling.

Eventually a tableau grew out of the nothing, a gray wash of images that brightened and sharpened the longer he stared at them. A scene from a memory, a dream, a reality filtered in contentment. A table littered with steaming dishes, and two chairs occupied across from his, a man and a woman beaming first at each other and then at him.

"Da?" he whispered.

Benjamín Luca smiled at his son, one hand holding his mother's. In a voice Julian hadn't heard in years he asked, "What is it, Jules?"

"*Da!*"

It was all Julian could do not to fling himself across the table before his father could disappear. But he was solid and real in Julian's desperate embrace, and he could taste his own tears, and hear his mother bemoaning the food he'd knocked to the floor. Relief as strong and violent as a tidal wave crashed through him, and he let himself be swept away by it.

Shift, and there were calloused hands rearranging his arms from behind, showing him the best way to hold a bow.

"You want to pull back until you feel it in your shoulder," Benjamín instructed. "It'll get easier with practice."

The wood was solid under his hands, the bowstring biting into the soft pads of his fingers. As he pulled it back he found no resistance, found himself growing taller, older, while his father's hair grayed and the fine lines at the corners of his eyes deepened.

This is how it should have been.

Running through a field, tracking down beasts, Paris swearing and laughing at his side. The medals above the fireplace grew in number, some now bearing his name. The apartment fell away and instead there was a house, well insulated against the biting winters, with a bigger kitchen for his mother—Marjorie laughing with ease, with no coughing to disrupt her joy. Benjamín took her by the waist and kissed her cheek.

But this isn't how it goes.

The warmth in his chest waned. He looked around at this unknown place, this unknown version of his father whom he'd never met.

"Jules?" His mother turned to him, worry in her eyes. "Is everything all right?"

"Do you want to go out back and practice?" his father asked, because of course he knew the best way to calm him. Julian started to nod, started to slip back into the current.

No, his mind yelled, to assert this wasn't reality, wasn't possible.

But what if it was? What if everything up until now had been a nightmare, and he was finally opening his eyes to a different morning, a different life?

He took a step forward. Stopped. Stood in his indecision until fingers brushed his back.

"He didn't sleep well last night," came a midnight voice behind him. "Nothing a strong cup of coffee won't fix."

His scalp prickled. He didn't want to turn around, even though every part of him screamed to do just that. A warm hand on his arm, a body leaning into his. The scent of cloves.

Julian turned his head.

Taesia smiled at him, sweet from sleep but still sharp at the edges, a cold yet brilliant dawn. Her hand trailed upward, cupping the back of his neck. They swayed together, inching into closer orbit.

"What do you think?" she whispered against his mouth. "Cake for breakfast?"

Pain blossomed along his palm. He yanked himself back.

"Jules, your hand!" His mother rushed to get a cloth as his blood dripped onto the freshly swept kitchen floor.

Taesia came closer and Julian fisted his hand tighter, driving his nails in deeper, lusting after the pain even as he attempted to writhe away from it.

Something curled up tight in his chest kicked awake. Whether it was god or beast, or merely the urge to let the outer world and its problems fall away into oblivion, he couldn't tell.

This could be yours.

He groaned. It wasn't his—it never would be.

But here, maybe...

Here, he could forget what he could lose, forget what he had to fear. There would be nothing to mourn.

I need to mourn, he thought fiercely as tears burned tracks down his face. *I need to remember.*

Remember his father's guiding hand, his mother's cooking, the simple serenity of waking up to a rainy morning and lounging in bed. Sleepless nights and labored breaths and bandaged wounds. The things that made him human and fragile and troubled and *real*.

He ripped himself free from Taesia and pushed her away. He only caught a glimpse of her aggrieved expression before hands grabbed him from behind. Julian fought them, twisting and snarling.

A yelp of pain preceded a blinding light. He gasped and fell to his knees, throwing up a protective arm.

"Kir, I think he dislocated my shoulder."

Someone forced his arm away from his face. "Get a hold of yourself, Vitaean."

Julian struggled to open his eyes, vision blurred by tears and silvery light. They were back in the hallway with the paintings. Kalen knelt before him, his face difficult to read. Marcellus stood rubbing his own shoulder.

Kalen grimly studied the wrist he was holding. Julian blinked until he could make out the bloody pinpricks on his palm, the black spindle of his veins. As they watched, the black faded back to green.

"Let me see your eyes." The astrologer gripped Julian's chin. Julian jerked his head away.

"I'm fine," he rasped. "What—what happened?"

Marcellus crouched down. "Exteri sulumn. It would translate to, ah . . . dream room? Vision chamber?"

"A chamber fortified with malachite," Kalen clarified. "With the right properties, the stones draw out traumas, wishes, and fears from those who enter. It's used in certain therapies, as well as priest training."

Julian noted the strain in Kalen's eyes and the pale, thin line of Marcellus's mouth. Marcellus glanced at Kalen and away, uncharacteristically reticent. Whatever these two had seen had also shaken them.

"How is *that* supposed to help people?" Julian demanded.

Kalen huffed. "You typically have a guide to assist you. To lead you through processing what you experience. Then healing begins." He shook his head. "But we don't have time for this. The guards are gone—we can enter the planetarium."

As if Julian could simply move on from the crushing blow of remembering which reality was his, bereft of the newfound joy at thinking his father was alive, his mother healthy, and that Taesia was . . .

He shivered and clutched the front of his robes, allowing the horror to sweep through him for only a moment before shoving it down, along with everything else he was too afraid to touch. Everything that room had wanted to expose.

Marcellus helped him to his feet. Kalen regarded him, gaze flitting between Julian's eyes and his wrist.

"Belua," Kalen murmured to himself before turning away.

XIII

Shale and pebbles rained down as Risha climbed the last slope leading to an overlook Val had directed them to. Together, she and Jas made their way past shelves of tourmaline and crouched behind a boulder of gray hematite to survey the land below.

The field was flat, surrounded by huge standing stones like sarsens. It had obviously been the sight of a battle. The ground was a patchwork of brittle grass and pockets of mud, littered with fallen weapons that had long since been devoured by rust and moss. There were tracks belonging to animals or beasts or both, freshly stamped into the dirt and mud, though there was no sign of what had made them.

But what was most alarming was the massive skeletal arm that seemed to have punched its way through the ground, exposing half an ulna and radius along with a puzzle of carpals and phalanges. The bone was weathered and yellow, the hand curled inward.

Risha slipped Val off her back and turned him around. "Is this the place?"

"The one and only. That's where the weapon's hidden."

"What...is it?" Jas asked.

"It's an *arm*, what else does it look like?" Val snapped.

"But where did it come from?"

"Leshya," Risha guessed. "If she was pressed to abandon Samhara, she would have kept it somewhere safe. She would have made sure no one other than a necromancer could reclaim it."

"Not even the kings? Seems like they'd be desperate to get their bones back."

"The kings have power over spirits, but I don't think they can manip- ulate bone." She reached into her pocket before realizing she'd given away her bone shards. Instead, her hand settled on the hilt of her small knife. "Val, didn't you say this area was dangerous?"

"Well, yeah," he muttered. "Lots of things are drawn to a battlefield, no matter how old it is. But this is weird. I've never heard of a battlefield without—" He stopped suddenly, then hissed, "*Shit.*"

Risha heard it, too: the rattling chime of a rib cage.

She lurched forward to peer around the boulder. There, making its gradual way toward them, was a Sentinel.

"That's why there's no beasts," Val growled. "This ugly bastard drove them off."

Jas stared anxiously at the approaching Sentinel. "We could wait here until it leaves?"

"That'll take too long," Risha said. "And I can't get the hand open without alerting it."

"Do you *really* need this weapon?" Val wheedled. "It'd probably be a lot safer to fuck off out of here and find my body instead."

Risha was almost tempted to do just that. The Sentinel turned and gave her a good view of the massive sword of black opal on its back—the one that could easily erase spirits from existence.

She glanced at Jas's ghostly edges. The longer it took to get home, the more energy he would expend. She could lose him entirely.

"No," she decided. "We do this now. We're just going to have to go slow, and once the hand opens, I'll grab Samhara and..."

And what? She didn't know how to use the weapon yet. Didn't know how much energy it would require, or how it could impact Jas.

The rattle of the Sentinel's bones came closer. A shiver traveled up Risha's spine.

"Make up your damn minds," Val whispered.

Risha gritted her teeth and pulled Val's sling back on. Before she could stand, Jas walked out ahead of her.

"What are you doing?" she demanded.

He looked over his shoulder. "Remember: If I'm the general, you're the raja. If you have to, you can afford to let me go."

"This isn't a game of chaturanga! You can't talk about yourself like a piece on a board. You're—"

Her throat closed up. His expression softened as he swept away a bit of hair that had fallen into her face. She couldn't feel his fingers.

"Don't waste it," he said.

Then he was running down the slope toward the Sentinel. Her stomach dropped and she wrenched back a scream. But the Sentinel was already turning, rib cage undulating with those hollow clicks, empty eyes fixated on Jas.

Risha slipped and slid down the slope after him, cutting open her palms and knees while her heartbeat jackrabbited in her chest.

"Hey, stop!" Val yelled as she charged after Jas. "He's distracting it!"

"I can't let him—" Her breaths were near-sobs, choking her.

The Sentinel didn't move fast, but its wide leg span more than made up for it. Jas flung his hand out, and a large rock launched itself from the ground. It hurtled past the Sentinel and caught its attention, diverting it to go in the opposite direction.

"See?" Val barked. "He has it covered. Let's go!"

Risha swallowed her thorny fear and pivoted toward the skeletal arm. Like the abandoned weapons around the field, it, too, had eroded with time and been partially reclaimed by moss and ivy. Risha used the latter to help haul herself onto the wide arc of the radius bone, then crawled across the radial shaft toward the curled fist.

"Gotta admit, for a guy who doesn't have balls anymore, that's pretty ballsy," Val murmured, watching Jas play cat and mouse out of the corner of his eye. The Sentinel was growing ill-tempered, turning quicker and moving faster with impatience. Jas smashed another rock into its rib cage, momentarily stunning it and disrupting its echolocation.

Risha leveraged herself into a kneeling position. She did her best to tune out everything around her and delved into the core of her power, that sweet and cold wellspring. It was tethered to her every sinew, every vessel, every nerve.

Wind picked up around her and she held out one hand. She kept it closed, fingers tucked against her dry, cracked palm. The energy inside her rose and stormed, a painful pull on her organs and muscles. She clung tighter to the bone as her body fought against the urge to restore itself to its normal functions.

Not yet.

The air around her smelled like a crisp winter night. She inhaled and held it in her lungs, then carefully unfurled her fist, focus narrowed on the shifting of tendon and ligament.

Slowly the bones woke and mirrored her movements. They scraped and creaked against each other, the tapered distal phalanges lifting from the jumbled carpals, fingers curving upward until they revealed the open palm, a half claw reaching toward the sky in supplication.

And there, lying across the metacarpals, was Leshya Vakara's legendary weapon.

Samhara. The conductor of souls. A symbol of creation and destruction.

Risha crawled forward to get a closer look. Everything had been constructed out of bone, even the thin, looping chain that connected the scythes, deceptively delicate. Etchings of marigolds traveled up the humerus-crafted handles to where they expanded out into blades, each of them a curved hook sharpened to a fatally thin edge. Fused along their backs were two rib bones, as well as small decorative skulls refortifying where blades met handles. And where the handles met chain hung eight thin phalanges.

Mouth dry, Risha reached out and touched one of the blades. It was smooth and warm like ivory, and when her hand drifted down to the handle she discovered grooves where her fingers should rest. She didn't feel overwhelming power, or a connection to the pieces of the four kings Leshya had collected—nothing to suggest this was anything but a simple weapon.

"Uh-oh," Val said. She looked between the giant hand's fingers to find that the Sentinel, driven to frustration by Jas, had reached for its sword.

Risha gathered the scythes in her hands. Holding them with the sharp edges facing away from her, she slid down the radius and tumbled back to the ground, Val swearing the whole time. One of her ankles twisted painfully, but she stubbornly ignored it as she ran toward the looming Sentinel.

The scythes were weighted possibilities in her hands. A curse and a gift from her ancestor, a woman made of war and death and royal blood. The tool she would need to cut them out of Mortri and into the land of the living.

But how? She needed something to feed into Leshya's weapon, and there were no spirits around save for Jas.

"C'mon, hurry up and throw those bones around!" Val urged behind her, voice warbling as she ran.

"But there aren't any spirits—"

"You don't need 'em if you use your own magic! That's what Leshya did in a pinch, same deal as cutting off your disgusting humanly needs!"

Would that really work? If so, it would surely incapacitate her; she was already expending so much of her power on not dying. But considering the alternative, she was fine with giving up the lion's share of her magic if it meant safely getting everyone out of this situation.

Once she was close enough, Risha slid into the first stance she'd learned of the tandshri: one leg extended forward, the other bent, arms positioned over her head. Only now she held Samhara, the blades forming sickle moons above her, the chain falling against her back.

The torus of her power returned, kicking up dirt and pebbles at her feet. The handles bristled against her palms, the bones waking after centuries of sleep. The phalanges rattled together like wind chimes.

Risha concentrated on the tangle of energy inside her. The blades hummed in response, not quite a sound but more of an echo in her pulse, a bright, startling awareness of her surroundings—the rich resonance of death and spilled blood across the field, shrieking cries and torn flesh layered over forgotten weapons and the scurrying of frightened creatures.

And the call of the Sentinel, ribs rising and falling, sword tip scraping the ground as it hefted the blade upward over Jas.

Please, she thought, focusing on the energy within her. She sensed some of Jas's threaded through hers, that bizarre yet comforting connection they'd forged. *Take what I am giving you and turn it into power.*

She inhaled deeply, the ball of energy expanding with her lungs. The handles grew hot against her hands.

Shifting her body, she brought one knee up and spun around quickly, flicking her wrist the way her father had taught her, fingers held in the mudra for *air*.

Sada—an invitation to dance.

The right scythe flew out of her hand and toward the Sentinel. The chain stretched out between them, impossibly longer than its original length suggested, the bones extending and reshaping as it went. Power seethed along it like the firing of a synapse, guided by her order, fueled with magic that straddled life and death.

The scythe crashed into the Sentinel's rib cage. It let out an eerie cry as bone fragments rained from its torso. Risha jerked the chain and the scythe flew back to her. She caught it and held it before her face, feet together. Then she moved one leg behind her and spun the opposite direction, her forwardmost leg bent while the other remained extended, balancing on her toes.

This time the left scythe went flying and jammed into the Sentinel's neck. It staggered back, dropping its sword to reach for the handle.

Risha formed her free hand into the mudra for *fire*. Vivid, sizzling energy ran across the chain, a brilliant blue like the purest sapphire. But unlike real fire, this was a product of her power—the same grasping, encompassing force she had used to slow her heart, to reanimate Don Soler, to drive spirits out of risen corpses.

Jas let out a hoarse cry, but she couldn't risk looking away from the Sentinel. She blinked sweat out of her eyes as blue-burning magic ignited in the scythe and traveled across the Sentinel's body. It shuddered and wailed hollowly.

Risha jerked the chain again, and the scythe pulled itself free. The Sentinel collapsed into a pile of tattered skin and crumbling bone.

She fell to her hands and knees. It felt as if she had run five miles without stopping, every inch of her electric and elastic. Her head spun the way it had after a night of drinking Mariian rum, right before swearing off the liquor for good.

The handle underneath her palm cooled, reducing it to nothing more than the bone of a Mortrian king.

Risha touched her chest and was met with the slowed *thump, thump* of her heartbeat. She dove deeper and tested the organs she had put into hibernation. Everything was as it had been before, the ball of energy within her not depleted in the least.

"What?" She pushed herself up. "How am I...?"

Val swore, and she looked up.

Jas was making his way over to them. He swayed as a tipsy person would, though his expression wasn't of vacant delight but weary resignation.

He was almost fully transparent.

Jas lifted a ghostly hand to stop her as she tried to push to her feet. "Don't."

"You— I didn't—"

She had drawn on her own energy to fuel the attack, like Val said Leshya had done. Jas had used his magic a few times against the Sentinel, but not to the extent he would fade this quickly.

Risha clawed at her sternum. The energy within her carried a bit of

Jas's as well. Had Samhara latched on to his instead of hers? Pulled from his spirit to strengthen the attack?

Why hadn't she thought of that possibility?

"Risha—"

"No," she cried. "*No!*"

"Risha," he whispered, "it's all right. This is what I wanted."

She dug her fingers into her hair. Her face grew hot from tears even while the rest of her shuddered with cold.

When she had made her desperate plan to kill the heirs and the gods along with them, Jas had begged her not to. But she hadn't been able to see any alternative except an inter-realm war. In making her decision, she had deprived the heirs of making their own; she had chosen their fates, including Jas's, and the weight of it was too much to carry.

"It was better me than you," Jas said. "If you had used your own energy—"

"Why?" she demanded, looking up. "Why is it better for me to live instead of you? How can you claim my life is more important than yours?"

Voice infuriatingly calm, he said, "Isn't it? You're the descendant of a god, the carrier of a holy magic. You can help so many people. You're still *alive*."

"Because you *died* for me!" she screamed. "I didn't ask you to do that! I didn't *want*—"

He leaned closer, trying to grab her shoulder and failing. "No, you didn't ask it of me. I *chose* it, Risha. I chose this."

"It's still my fault. How am I supposed to live with that?"

He was quiet a moment. "When my mother died, I didn't know how life could keep going without her. Some days I thought she would walk through the door and the nightmare would end. But eventually I understood this was *real*. That I had to go on with this wound inside of me, even on days when it felt impossible."

He looked at her, through her, past her struggling, sore heart into the fabric of *Risha Vakara*, not a woman of war and gods and kings but one who wanted a world without sharp edges. Who so desperately wanted to sand them down she ended up cutting herself open in the process.

When she was younger, she thought adhering to her father's rules would keep everything in order. But now she knew there was no avoiding turmoil—that good people died without reason and those with power misused it. That she had made mistakes while thinking of the greater good, and it had cost not only her, but those around her.

"Staying alive might be the most difficult thing you'll ever have to do," Jas whispered. "But for as long as I'm here, I won't let you do it alone."

The shield around her grief cracked open. She curled into herself, one hand pressed to her chest and the other wrapped around the scythe's handle. In the end, it had been forged for the same purpose she had been: as a weapon.

If Jas settled his hand on her shoulder, she couldn't feel it. Only the chill whisper of what had been lost, and what was left to lose.

XIV

The scent of wood and paper enveloped Angelica as soon as she stepped foot into the archives. She stopped to take in a big lungful of it, and Botan grinned at her.

"It is a rather a pleasant smell, isn't it?" The imperial scholar gazed fondly at the wooden cubbies and shelves along the walls, displaying scrolls and ancient tomes next to newly bound ledgers. "I never tire of it."

Cosima didn't seem to share the sentiment. She was jittery, looking around as though someone would dart forward and tackle her at any second.

"It's a bit of a personal matter," Angelica had explained when Botan had asked what they were looking for. "My bodyguard has a brother who was recruited into the Azunese army when he was young."

"I can certainly do my best to find records of his enlistment," he'd said. "We believe in upward class mobility here in Azuna. If someone is born with elemental power, they're typically brought into the military or the Kiyono order no matter their background, and their family profits as a result. It's not *quite* the same as with a Mariian immigrant, but the government still affords them housing and certain privileges, especially the higher up in rank they are."

As Cosima now stared uneasily at the rows of shelving, Botan approached her.

"Do you know which rank your brother currently holds?" he asked in Vaegan.

"Ah...no. But when he was taken"—Botan winced slightly at the word choice—"the soldiers told us he was strong enough to train with the Gojarin-Kae."

"I will begin my search there, then. From which former colony was he ... taken?"

"Seccra. He was about eleven at the time."

"And his name?"

"Koshi Okai."

As Botan turned to speak to one of the archivists, Cosima fiddled with the hilt of her sword.

"Are you worried they won't find him?" Angelica asked.

"Kinda more worried they *will* find him."

"Isn't that the whole point?"

Cosima sighed. "I'm worried that ... I dunno ... he might be in a bad place. What if he's in prison? Or some awful Mariian penal camp? Or *dead*? He could have drowned at sea, for all I know." Cosima scrubbed her hands over her face. "I do *not* like emotions, princess. I'm coming to understand why you prefer to be so icy."

Angelica maturely chose not to rise to the obvious bait. "No matter how difficult it is or what you find out, you'll feel better knowing what happened. It won't haunt you anymore."

"Won't it?" Cosima shook out her arms and rolled her neck. "I need a distraction. Distract me, Mardova."

Angelica turned to the nearest wall of scrolls. "How about we look for something on kudei?"

"Not as fun as what I was thinking, but sure."

Angelica spared her a withering look, then flagged down an archivist to help with the search.

"I take it you have a lesson later?" Cosima murmured while they were led up a shallow set of stairs to a different room.

"Kazue insisted on having one before the festival tomorrow."

I eagerly await your answer.

Fresh dread rose within her as the archivist showed her to a shelf. She nodded numbly and the archivist bowed away, leaving her momentarily lost.

"Princess?" Cosima waved a hand in front of her face. "What's wrong?"

"Nothing. It's fine."

Cosima crossed her arms. "I'm starting to learn *it's fine* means *oh Cosima, sweet Cosima, I am in dire need of guidance from a trusted source of great intellect.*"

"Can't imagine who that would be."

"Cheeky." She said it like an endearment, low and throaty.

Angelica ignored the flutter in her chest and reached for the nearest scroll. "I was thinking about my conversation with Nanbu Daiji."

"Let me guess, something happened you haven't told me about yet."

Angelica was distinctly displeased at the uncomfortable notion of being *known*. Still, she held the scroll to her chest and filled Cosima in on Nanbu's ultimatum, the decision she had to make between the imperial family and the warlords.

Cosima gave a long, soft whistle. "This is what we'd call an absolute shitshow back in Nexus. So this comes down to, what, treason?"

Angelica looked around to make sure they were alone in the dimly lit room. "I don't know what it is, and I want no part in it. I'm not going to wedge myself any further into Azunese politics."

"Bad news, you already have," Cosima pointed out. "Whatever game you're playing to win this crown, you're in it for the long haul. Don't get mad, but why do you even *want* the crown? What good did Freddy ever do for Vaega?"

"The Mardovas are not Ferdinand." Angelica sniffed.

"No, but a monarch is a monarch, no matter the shape of the ass on the throne."

"You don't understand."

Cosima scoffed. "No, 'course I don't. I'm just a simple thief with silly little thoughts."

"I didn't say that. Nor do I believe it."

Cosima stared at her, and Angelica forced herself to stare back. She gripped the scroll in her hand harder.

"What do you want to do, then?" Cosima asked.

"I . . ." Angelica returned the scroll before she could crush it. "I don't know."

There were different forms of power. Her mother had raised her to wield all of them to her satisfaction, switching between masks and tactics like a trained actor.

But she was adrift here, far from home and the creature comforts she was familiar with. The gambits she had grown up fielding.

What sort of power was she supposed to claim for herself, her family, her country? Did she turn to the physical might that Nanbu promised, or the social influence of the imperial family?

Did she return to Deia on her hands and knees, or subject herself to the wrath of a volcano that had once been the god's forge?

The handprint on her arm tingled. She covered it with her own only for Cosima to grab her wrist. Angelica tugged, but Cosima's grasp remained firm. Her thumb was a brand against the tributaries of Angelica's veins.

"You help me, I help you." Cosima lowered her voice even as she closed the distance between them. Angelica looked up at her, frozen. "That's how it works."

"How . . . what works?"

"Being equals."

Angelica's mouth was bone dry, but at this she managed a hoarse "Impertinent."

"Yeah, that's me." Cosima raised Angelica's hand, plush lips skimming the underside of her wrist. It burned, but in a wholly different way than Deia's handprint. Cosima's gaze was dark and daring, knowing full well what she was getting away with—and that Angelica would let her. "What're you gonna do about it?"

Before Angelica could figure out an answer, Botan returned. They startled apart.

The scholar paused for a second before shaking his head with an apologetic expression. "I'm afraid I could not find any records of a Mariian soldier named Koshi Okai. I searched the Gojarin, the Gojarin-Kae, the navy, and even the police force."

Cosima rocked back on her heels. "How is that possible? How can there be no record of him?"

"It could be the records were destroyed. A few years ago a fire broke out in the city that spread to one of the archives. My guess is that either your brother ended up somewhere else, or we are unlucky and his records were among those that burned."

Cosima remained silent. Angelica's face was still warm as she said, "I'm sorry to hear of it. Thank you for your help, Scholar Noguchi."

Once he left, Cosima began to mutter curses under her breath.

"Hey." Angelica stepped in front of her. "This isn't a dead end. We'll find out what happened to him. Ship manifests, military offices—someone somewhere has to know something. Believe me, I'm a trusted source of great intellect."

Cosima snorted and wiped her eyes. "Fuck. I hate this."

"After the festival, we'll try again."

After I've given Nanbu my answer.

Angelica sat across from the child empress while Kazue watched on. The doors to the private garden were open, and Asami kept glancing out at it.

"You and Esteemed Mardova will catch a chill," Kazue complained for the second time.

Above her muzzle, Asami's eyes pinched.

"The doors can be left open," Angelica said. "I don't mind."

Asami dropped her shoulders. But the rest of her seemed constructed out of stiff wire, hands properly laid upon her thighs, posture straighter than any child's should be. Between them was an assortment of rocks and stones collected from the garden, all laid out in a line upon a mat.

At Kazue's nod, the empress untied the straps of her muzzle. She gently laid it beside her, moving her jaw and licking her lips while she had the freedom to do so. Kazue rose onto her knees to place a cup of water before Asami, who took small, quick sips until the cup was empty.

Angelica settled a hand on her own stomach. Kazue had informed her Asami knew Vaegan, so that's what she defaulted to. "When I was younger, I learned to play multiple instruments. It was necessary in order to wield my powers."

She pointedly did not look at Kazue. The last thing she needed was to see second thoughts forming on the woman's face.

"Sometimes an elementalist requires an aid in order to reach their full strength," Angelica went on. "Many mages look down on this. They think there's only one correct way to use magic. They are wrong.

"In all my years of playing instruments, there's one I've neglected. One I should have been honing better." The admission coated her tongue in sour regret. "My voice."

Asami's attention was fully on Angelica now, her uncertainty sloughed off to reveal keen understanding. The girl signed a word, and Kazue clicked her tongue.

"Speak," Kazue reprimanded.

Asami swallowed. "Why?" she whispered in Azunese, flinching when one of the rocks cracked.

Angelica wavered. This was not about her, but if it could help . . .

"My father died," Angelica answered. She kept her voice even, blunt.

It was an unmitigated fact that August Mardova was no longer in this world. There was no need to show emotion over it.

Asami's lips parted, but she caught herself at the last second. She stared down at the rocks, twisting the purple fabric of her dress in her hands.

"I know you understand what the loss of a parent means," Angelica said. "And how strong feeling can alter the shape your magic takes. I'm sure the louder you speak, the more damage is done to the objects around you."

Making a face, Asami nodded. Kazue cleared her throat, and Asami wiped the expression away.

Angelica spared Kazue a mild glare. "Lately, I've been learning that my voice, like yours, functions similarly to my instruments—something through which I can channel the elements. And I believe the one it controls best is kudei. Aether."

She thought back to Lezzaro's grimoire, the sections she'd read on Ostium and how it had harbored quintessence. The element that had run through all the realms, fueling their portals. That lingered in Vitae in some form.

"Have you ever sung before?" Angelica asked.

"She is not allowed to sing," Kazue answered. "The times she's tried, we had to replace whole walls."

"I was asking her," Angelica said. "Is that not what the rocks are for?"

Kazue gave her a tepid smile. "Of course. I was merely attempting to prevent excessive damage."

"I don't think that's something we can prevent in a lesson like this." *Lesson*, like she was a damn teacher. "But we can adjust. Your Majesty, do you like using your voice?"

"You can call me Asami," the girl whispered. Another rock cracked and Kazue exhaled in displeasure, either from the reaction or the informality.

"Then, Asami, let's see if we can give you better control over your voice and channel kudei safely."

Angelica knew full well she wasn't meant to be here, doing this; that she was hardly qualified to instruct anyone, let alone a clandestine child empress. She hadn't even been allowed to attend the university, instead taught via her mother's diligent if frustrating tutelage.

But who else was there?

Kazue's silent judgment was an itch on her skin, but Asami watched her with newly lit determination.

"I'm going to recite a short poem, and then you will recite it back to me," Angelica said. "When you do, focus on the sensation that comes when you speak. The vibrations of your vocal cords, the sound that comes to your ears."

Asami closed her eyes as Angelica spoke the four-line poem. She'd chosen one from a famous Azunese poet, thinking it would appease Kazue. But when Asami began to falteringly echo the words back to her, one of the rocks between them exploded into tiny fragments. Asami quickly covered her face with her sleeves.

"Don't worry about that," Angelica assured her. "Let's try again." Not three words left Asami's mouth before another rock burst apart, spraying stone dust across the floor. "What does it feel like?"

Asami hesitated, then signed with her hands. Kazue interpreted, "She says it felt good and bad at once. Like drinking tea that tastes delicious but burns the tongue."

"Good. Focus on the more positive feeling, and when you speak this time, do your best to suppress the other," Angelica said.

Asami tilted her head to one side. *How?*

There were only a few things that could distract or release Angelica from the clawing need for fire, and none of them were available or suitable for Asami.

"Just…" Angelica stretched for a solution, one that had evaded her for years. "Just try."

Asami frowned, there and gone, before doing as Angelica said. This time Angelica focused on the air compressing around Asami's head, the weft of power thrashing in response to her voice.

All the remaining rocks were pulverized to pebbles. Angelica flinched away, and Asami instinctively reached for her muzzle.

"It's all right," Angelica hurried to say, holding out a hand. "You can't force these things. Forcing the elements never…"

The words died as a soft roaring filled her ears.

You need to learn patience, my lady. Forcing the elements never gets you the results you want.

The ghost of a mage spread on the ground beside a pair of shattered glasses. Words like spikes churning around her insides without restraint or mercy. A memory like a battlefield, dyed crimson and smelling of viscera.

Ruin in her mouth and in her throat, wetting it enough for her to sing.

"Angelica!"

She was stumbling away, scrambling for the edge of the door. Kazue crowded behind her and caught her arm, then just as quickly let it go.

"You're burning up."

"I can't do this," Angelica rasped. "I can't—I'm not—"

Kazue turned and gave Asami some sort of instruction before she opened the door and Angelica drunkenly swayed into the hallway. She gulped down air, neck damp with sweat.

Kazue took hold of Angelica's sleeve and steered her down the corridor. Angelica had no presence of mind to refute her.

There was a flight of stairs behind a hidden door in a wall panel, and then Angelica was in a dark, secluded room that smelled of wood shavings and incense. The room was plain save for a single cushion on the floor in front of a lattice window. Through the lattice she saw the banquet hall below, as well as the servants and family members working to decorate it for the festival tomorrow.

"What is this?"

"This is where Asami watches the banquets," Kazue said. "Out of sight. Now, what happened?"

Angelica dabbed her sleeve along her hairline. "I'm not...fit. To teach."

She could not be her mother, who spoke with clear and firm intent. She could not be Eran Liolle, a man with hidden contempt and perversions.

A man she had killed. Who had *deserved* to feel retribution in some form, if perhaps not in the shape of her teeth.

"Whatever qualms you have, remember there is a young girl who needs what insight you can give her," Kazue stressed. "We have tutors, mages, scholars, Kiyono practitioners, even Gojarin, but none of them— *none of them*—can channel kudei. She *needs* this."

"Does she need it, or do you need her to be better trained for whatever you have planned for her?"

Kazue's eyes narrowed. "We all have plans. Remember that yours depends on Asami's success. An empress who can channel kudei is like something out of a myth. The bushan may have a god, but if Asami comes into her full power, she will be as good as one to the empire."

Angelica watched the servants below hang up streamers in blue and silver. After a moment, she turned back to Kazue.

"Ferdinand Accardi used the Houses to further his reach," she said.

"He showcased us whenever possible. The products of the gods, to be feared and fawned over, all under one man's thumb. He *used* us, pitted us against one another, until our entire structure collapsed. Is this what you imagine for your and Asami's future?"

Kazue did not respond. Angelica walked past her, toward the stairs.

"I won't teach her until you stop hovering over her," Angelica said.

The festival began with a parade through the city streets, with drummers and fire jugglers and actors in animal masks making the citizens clap and yell in delight. People handed out white daffodils and sorankun charms, as well as small sachets of fragrant herbs with the wisteria crest of the Satakes, the empress's gifts for the commonfolk.

Angelica was invited to join the imperial family as they spent the day wandering slowly between the pagodas within the palace grounds. At the base of each tiered pagoda waited Kiyono bellwethers in plain layered robes, with small wooden boxes and bags tied to their sashes. Botan explained that these carried various instruments needed for their trade, such as medicine, purifying salt, and cedar shavings to ward off spirits. The bellwethers scattered the salt and shavings around the pagodas and the empress—or rather, the stand-in empress—while reciting mantras about making it through the dark, cold months.

The warlords were also in attendance. They partook in each small ritual, such as feeding protection talismans to a fire basin, which Angelica learned was a remnant custom from the time of Deia worship. Angelica kept an eye on Nanbu Daiji throughout the proceedings. He had brought his snake, which drew several curious and startled glances, and Angelica did her best to avoid its scalding blue gaze.

She thought she heard the faintest sibilant whisper in the back of her skull, a laugh and a warning.

"Fuck," Cosima whispered as she stared at the serpent draped over Nanbu's shoulders. Her breath turned to vapor. "I can't believe that's actually a *god*."

Angelica hushed her. Eiko, standing nearby, turned an annoyed frown in their direction. Nanbu Daiji turned to look at her as well, but Angelica had been evading both him and Kazue all day.

Akane made her way slowly over the arched wooden bridge to the island of white sand, and a reverent silence fell over the procession. Her attendants stopped just short of the island's shore and smoothly knelt on the planks while Akane went on ahead, her booted feet digging scores into the packed sand. Holding a pole from which hung an incense burner and a lantern, she slowly walked in a circle around the island. Ribbons of smoke trailed after her, drifting up into the wintry air.

Angelica had to be careful in her next moves. These girls hadn't been asked to sacrifice any parts of themselves for their empire. It had been a role assigned to them at birth, and in Akane's case, the precautions of the imperial family. A lifestyle she would be forced to give up once Asami came of age.

But political machinations aside, Angelica couldn't walk away from Asami altogether. The girl could tap into the substance that had wreaked such havoc on Nexus. That had stolen away Risha, Nikolas, and Taesia.

With Asami's knack for aether, could the two of them—with the aid of Deia's fulcrum—be able to reopen the portals?

Akane knelt and asked for the autumnal harvest to keep their people fed through winter, for the sun to burn as strongly as it could even as it struggled through snow-dense clouds, and for them to reach an early spring. Then she detached the paper lantern from the pole and let it soar upward, a stray spark against the endless sheet of gray.

After the rituals came a tea ceremony, and after that, the banquet reserved for the imperial family, warlords, and their guests. The banquet hall had been swathed in blue silks and banners, bursting with floral arrangements. While the tea ceremony had been the picture of formality, the banquet was far more casual, with copious amounts of wine and boisterous noise.

Angelica glanced near the ceiling, where the wall turned to wooden lattice. It was difficult to see anything beyond it, but she knew Asami must be sitting on that lone cushion, watching on.

"Once again we meet the freezing, harsh winds of winter," the warlord of the water state, Wakiya, announced as he held up his wine cup. "And once again we shall survive on the warmth and perseverance of our beloved empress."

He presented his wine cup to Akane, sitting upon an elaborately carved wooden throne, and bowed deeply. Everyone else followed suit while Akane blushed and inclined her head in silent thanks. Kazue sipped her wine, studying the warlords in silent judgment.

That judgment slid to Angelica, who turned away. She would deal with the woman's anger later.

While Angelica had been allowed her guards during the rituals, the banquet was off-limits to them and the Gojarin. Only two imperial guards stood at attention beyond the doors to the hall. She'd thought Cosima might grouse about this, but the thief had been happy to stay behind in their rooms. She'd been off since they'd visited the archives.

Angelica found herself wishing for her presence as she tried to make small talk with the warlords while not succumbing to the urge to drown herself in wine.

"How much longer do you expect to stay in Azuna?" Takenaka asked her. Up close, the woman was like the pitted side of a boulder, all muscle and scars.

"Several weeks more, at the least."

"The weather is already turning for the worse," the warlord reminded her. "You may need to spend the winter here."

"I've considered the possibility. But if that's the case, I wouldn't mind the chance to see and learn more. Storms permitting, I could even tour the states." Angelica figured buttering up the warlords wouldn't hurt her cause, and it would give her an excuse to reach Mount Netsai, find the fulcrum, and return with it to Asami.

"Chisen is typically unnavigable when it snows. You would have better luck up north in Hitan." Takenaka glanced over Angelica's shoulder before murmuring a goodbye.

Angelica turned and nearly dropped her wine cup. Nanbu Daiji stood with arms held behind his back, snakeless. She wondered if someone had politely suggested he leave the creature in his rooms during the meal.

"Esteemed Mardova," he greeted. "I was wondering if you'd had the chance to think about what we discussed."

Angelica was nearly strangled by her own pulse. Although Deia was nowhere in sight, her nape prickled as if someone were watching her. Kazue, perhaps, or Asami up above.

"Of course," she replied in Azunese, thinking this might go better in his own language. "I found our conversation...intriguing."

"Did you." He took a half step forward, not quite crowding her but coming near to it. He smelled like woodsmoke and pine. "What did you find intriguing?"

There was a sip left in her cup. She drank it to stall, as well as to fortify herself, before placing it down on her low table.

"In the end, I believe your forces are a great asset," she said. "But it is not quite the asset the Mardovas are looking for. We wish for long-lasting, continued peace in the wake of our recent tragedy. A show of strength would only be necessary if Parithvi backs the Vakaras with force. I believe they are too avoidant of warfare for that to happen."

Nanbu watched her intently while she spoke, eyes flitting from her hair, her face, the pin she wore at her breast of the Mardova crest. The rest of him did not move.

"I see," he said. "You believe you would have greater luck with the backing of the Satakes and their offshoots."

"Not necessarily." Behind her, she could have sworn she felt Kazue's eyes flash. "I am still open to discussing potential alliances. It does not have to mean choosing between two parties who would both stand to benefit from the Mardovas achieving the crown."

The slightest crack appeared in Nanbu's face as the corner of his mouth curled upward. "My initial offer will be my only offer, Esteemed Mardova."

Her heart sank. She'd hoped to have more time—a little breathing room in which to send the letter she'd written to her mother earlier that day, to wait for her response.

But Adela was not the one in this position. Angelica had been trusted to venture across the sea, to speak with officials and decide which route would be best for them to take.

She was a Mardova, and soon, she would be on the right track toward saving their realm from extinction. So what if she did not have the backing of a single warlord?

Angelica put on a small, polite smile. "I am sorry to hear that, Bushan Nanbu. Should you later decide to amend your offer, my family and I are more than willing to give you an audience."

He answered her humorless smile with one of his own. "I am sorry as well."

He strode away to speak to Sugi, and Angelica drew in a deep, tremulous breath. *That could have gone better.*

She looked around for one of the servers pouring wine and instead found Eiko, dressed in beautiful robes of pale blue trimmed in white. She was staring at Angelica with wide, furious eyes. Once Nanbu was out of earshot, she marched up to Angelica.

"What do you think you're doing?" Eiko demanded.

Angelica quickly turned them toward the doors of the banquet hall, facing away from the others. "Have you forgotten I'm here to form an alliance?"

"How is rejecting a *warlord* an alliance? What was his offer? What did you just decline?"

"This is not the time or place, Eiko."

"You should have discussed this with me before outright refusing him. Why haven't you—?"

"Because *I* am the one who was put in charge. *I* am the heir of this family."

"It's my family, too!" Eiko snapped.

Several people turned to see what the commotion was. Angelica smoothed her face over with difficulty.

"We will talk about it later," she said, low and firm.

Eiko glared at her with flushed cheeks. "I'm going to get some air," she said stiffly before leaving the banquet hall.

Angelica thought about calling her back or going after her when an announcement came that dinner was about to start. Unwilling to risk further attention, she returned to her table.

During the meal Kazue frowned at Eiko's empty table in between furtive looks at Nanbu and Angelica. Angelica pretended to listen to the uncle beside her chatting her ear off while sampling a hearty soup of sea-food and vegetables in an earthenware pot.

Once the last course was cleared, the four warlords stood. Kazue, with a cup of wine in her hand, did the same and moved to Akane's side. "Respected bushan, we appreciate and are humbled by your company this day. You will find tea and confectionaries waiting for you in your chambers, and we hope to bid you a safe journey in the morning."

The dessert course was customarily for the inner family only. A small yet crucial reminder of who held the power in Mukan, Angelica guessed. The warlords bowed while everyone else lifted their cups in response. As they turned to leave—Sugi with a flutter of their silks and a jaunty finger wave—Angelica couldn't help but glance again at Nanbu. He was glanc-ing back at her with something like regret in the furrow of his brow.

An odd chill stole through her once the doors slid shut and Kazue rested a hand on the back of the wooden throne.

"We again greet another winter," she said. "After a harvest season full of uncertainty and disaster"—at this she looked to Angelica—"my only hope is for us all to weather the cold together and emerge into the spring with new ideas, strength, and courage."

"Hear, hear!" cried the uncle next to Angelica before drinking deeply.

"May our little sister live forever!"

Akane bit her lower lip, eyes on the floor. The doors to the banquet hall opened again and multiple servers glided inside, each holding a plate of small, delicate sweets.

"Yes, may our Imperial Majesty grow ever stronger," Kazue said, still looking at Angelica. "May she be surrounded by those who will uplift and protect her."

Another round of lively shouting and drinking. The servers knelt before each family member's table and set the plates down, heads lowered.

"In the face of whatever adversity, we will triumph," Kazue went on. She moved her hand to rest on Akane's shoulder. "We have seen destruction rain upon our realm, but we will overcome anything. And anyone."

Angelica half-heartedly scanned the assortment of desserts as it was put in front of her. The server's hands were rough and calloused.

"To Her Imperial Majesty and the enduring might of our beloved empire," Kazue called, raising her cup. "May the land and its elements continue to bless us."

Angelica reached for her cup. As she moved, the light caught a metallic gleam at the server's waist.

He raised his head. Angelica's stomach dropped.

She pursed her lips and blew a sharp, loud whistle. The air between them condensed and shoved her back, her hair coming loose when her back slammed against the wall. The server had also been blown back, the dagger knocked from his hand.

Cries erupted all around her. The uncle who'd been sitting next to her grunted in surprise before a shower of blood erupted from his neck. He collapsed, and the server who'd stabbed him wrenched her dagger out of his body. All along the row of tables the servers had drawn blades, slicing open throats or piercing hearts with brutal efficiency. One of the cousins yelled shrilly as she tried to run for the doors, but a server grabbed her and quickly cut off her screams.

The server Angelica had repelled launched himself at her. She let out a high, sharp note that made him topple into the table, spilling delicate confectionaries everywhere. Angelica used the wall for support to regain her feet, searching desperately for Kazue.

The woman had frozen in shock, staring wide-eyed at the unraveling massacre, wine cup still raised. A server—an assassin—made straight for her.

"No!" Angelica shouted.

Kazue finally moved, getting between the assassin's dagger and Akane. Akane screamed and covered her face as Kazue's blood sprayed across her, the throne, and the wall behind them.

Angelica held out her hands. Air, fire, she needed something, *anything*—

She drew the note up and out of her diaphragm, the same ringing, piercing note she had sung in the Bone Palace's courtyard. The room shook and shimmered, softening like butter left in the sun, like the edges of the world were unfolding and dissolving back into the endless cycle of the Cosmic Scale.

Quintessence.

There were threads of it in Vitae, veined within rock and sitting along the silt of riverbeds. It came with every gust of wind and every time a log popped in a fire. Reminders—remainders—of the substance that had crafted the realms and populated the universe.

She did not have the advantage of Godsnight to help her. Even so she reached for that intangible, enormous thing, ancient and new and devastating.

The assassin pushed Kazue's body aside and reached for Akane. Angelica reached a new crescendo, grabbing hold of whatever threads she could, shaping them the way she had at Godsnight. To spare Risha. To thwart Deia.

The throne at Akane's back disappeared into a gaping, dark mouth. It only took two blinks for the girl to be sucked into that nothingness, pulled from the banquet hall and hopefully somewhere safer.

Pain lanced across Angelica's side. She looked down at the dagger that had slashed her, then up at the assassin who had picked himself off the floor.

This time when she screamed, she thought she heard another layered over it, a two-tone harmony of destruction. The unbearably loud *crack* of bone filled the hall as the assassin's neck twisted and he dropped back to the floor. At the same time, embers flew from Angelica's hands and shoulders, spiraling through the air and landing on the paper screens.

A contemptuous voice laughed in her mind.

You still fight so hard.

Her limbs locked in place. She could barely breathe, barely feel the pain along her side or the blood spreading across her dress. She was in the basilica on her knees, on her back, a handprint seared into her skin.

"Angelica!"

Eiko and Cosima stood in the open doorway, staring at the bodies strewn across the room. All of the assassins were dead, she realized—their necks broken or their skulls crushed in. Fire had begun eating at the walls, crawling quickly across wood and paper.

"I—I found her alone outside and wanted to bring her back in," Cosima stammered, eyes darkly reflecting the carnage. "What the fuck happened?"

Angelica bounded across the hall and grabbed Eiko. "We have to go!"

Eiko fought against her. "But they—"

"Do you want to end up like them?"

"But—Aunt Kazue—"

Angelica shot Cosima a look, and both of them grabbed hold of Eiko's arms to haul her away. The imperial guards outside the banquet hall were dead, crumpled in bloody heaps. Eiko whined as panic gripped her, but Angelica didn't have time to calm her down.

They careened down the nearest corridor, leaving bloody footprints behind them. Angelica struggled to remember where it was—where Kazue had taken her—

"Where are you going?" Cosima demanded. "We have to get out of here!"

"Not without her."

"Who?"

Angelica didn't answer. There, around the back of the banquet hall, Angelica found the secret door Kazue had led her through and pushed it open with her shoulder. She nearly tripped up the stairs in her haste.

Asami knelt on the cushion, her muzzle off. She held it in both hands as she stared down at the bodies of her family and their murderers through the holes in the lattice window, the growing fire highlighting the silent tears that poured down her face.

The second scream. The broken bones.

Fuck.

Angelica slapped a hand against the girl's mouth so she wouldn't make a sound. "Come on," she panted. "Put that thing back on and follow us."

Asami didn't even start. She did as Angelica said, eyes wide as peach blossoms, hands shaking so hard she couldn't tie the straps. Angelica did it for her.

"Who is that?" Eiko demanded. "What's going on? Angelica?"

"I'll tell you later. Right now we have to—"

"*Look*," Cosima whispered.

They all froze as three figures entered the banquet hall. One of them, clad in imposing Gojarin armor, moved their arms in a circular motion. Water poured from a large gourd at their hip opposite their sword. They flicked their gauntleted fingers and the water burst apart into mist, spraying over the fire and dousing it.

The figure in the middle strode forward. Angelica clung to Asami, the girl's thin shoulders shaking under her hands.

Nanbu Daiji looked around at the mess. His face was impassive, arms casually tucked behind his back. He looked to the overturned table where Angelica had been sitting, then the empty, blood-splattered throne.

"The empress is gone," he said in his deep voice. "And so is Vaega's visiting diplomat. As much as I wanted both dead, this ended up working much better."

Angelica dug her fingertips into Asami's shoulders. The girl didn't make a sound.

The Gojarin with water powers knelt and turned over the body of an assassin dressed in server's attire. "All the kaikushine are dead from head or neck trauma," came the voice of a woman, muffled by her snarling bear mask. She lifted it to better study the corpse, exposing a narrow, plain face. "How?"

"It is now known that the Mardova heir can channel kudei," Nanbu said. "It is likely her doing."

Movement caught Angelica's eye. Near the throne, a body had begun to weakly stir. Kazue groaned and tried to crawl across the floor, toward a fallen dagger.

Nanbu nodded to the second Gojarin. They stepped forward. Faster than Angelica could process, the warrior unsheathed their sword and stabbed it down through Kazue's back. Cosima had grabbed Eiko and shoved her face against her shoulder so she wouldn't see, but the sound was terrible. Kazue twitched once, whispered something Angelica couldn't hear, then lay still.

"Unfortunate," Nanbu murmured. "She would have gone far, if she had agreed to my earlier compromise."

A few flecks of blood had scattered across the Gojarin's tiger mask. They removed it, revealing a young, dark-skinned man with brown eyes and the same full mouth as Cosima.

Cosima barely suppressed the choked, pained noise that rose in her throat.

"Koshi," she breathed, her eyes widely fixed on him through the lattice.

Cosima's brother removed his sword from Kazue's body and cleaned it against his sleeve before sheathing it again. "What now, Bushan Nanbu?"

The warlord of the fire state studied the charred walls, the empty throne.

"We'll begin by sounding the alarm," Nanbu said. "I want the news spreading through Mukan within the next hour.

"Angelica Mardova has assassinated the imperial family and abducted the empress. They must be found at whatever cost."

XV

Julian was barely stable on his legs as they approached the planetarium doors. He remained in the clutches of what the dream chamber had forced him to see and live through, to the point that he questioned if this was another false reality.

"Focus," Kalen growled at him. Marcellus eased open one of the large, heavy doors. The pearly moons engraved on them gleamed like eyes in the starlight. "We need to leave as soon as possible. I don't know if the royal astrologer will return."

Based on the speed with which she'd left, Julian didn't think it likely.

Once they'd entered and Marcellus pulled the door closed, Kalen's shoulders relaxed somewhat. "It's as beautiful as I remember."

Julian had never been to a planetarium before—wondered if one even existed in Nexus—and had no idea what to expect. Certainly not how massive it was, the entire chamber a scaled-down version of the known universe.

The room was rounded, its walls spangled gold and silver with stars amid a spectrum of black to midnight blue to violet. Vaporous nebulae were tinged red at their edges, the smile of a crescent moon a vivid stamp above them. In the distance were larger spheres, celestial bodies swathed in otherworldly dust.

It was like being cradled within the cosmos, an inferior speck in a grander scheme.

The projections came from a massive dome-shaped device in the middle of the planetarium. It was constructed out of metal and jewels, lit from within by the telltale silvery glow of stardust. Attached to the dome were metal arms bearing aloft large chunks of gemstone, the light refracting off their cut surfaces.

"There's the diamond." Marcellus indicated the gems surrounding the dome. "How long do you think it'll take for them to realize it's missing? Kal?"

Kalen didn't respond, frowning up at a cluster of stars near a cloudy nebula. Julian followed his stare, but all the constellations looked vaguely similar to him. Kalen stepped closer to the wall and traced out a formation, a knifelike shape with a large star at its tip.

"This is the star under which Lilia was born," Kalen murmured. "The Malum Star, of the Cultris constellation. But it's..." He continued to stare at it, rubbing the tips of his fingers together as if longing for a pen. "Caelith Pyrin read something in here that frightened her."

"We don't have time for you to draw up charts," Marcellus said.

Kalen ignored him and returned to the apparatus in the middle of the room. He touched one of the hunks of diamond and focused on the constellation while the shadow familiar around his neck uncoiled and slithered down his arm. The planetarium shifted and spun, zooming in on the sector that contained the Malum Star. Julian staggered back, dizzy all over again. Marcellus caught him.

"I didn't know you could do that," Julian said as the constellation spread out before them, large as a building.

"Any astrologer worth their stardust trains at a planetarium," Kalen muttered. He let go of the diamond and approached the wall again. "There."

He pointed to the left of the constellation. Julian did his best to figure out what he was supposed to see, but there was only empty space. Then, gradually, it came into focus: a faint ring surrounding the endless dark.

"That is a black hole," Kalen said grimly. "A rather infamous one, as it is the closest on record to Noctus and therefore easiest to study. It has been here for a time beyond counting. Even as the sky around our realm constantly changes—stars fading and dying, or falling to the ground as astralams—it has never wavered. In the past century, though, the stars around it have been dying faster. Or disappearing altogether."

"Because of the Sealing," Julian guessed. "When the realms don't have energy from the Cosmic Scale flowing through them, they wither. We're experiencing the same in Vitae."

Kalen breathed out. "Yes. Sometimes not even our best astrologers can tell which stars will die and which will stay. Which will fall. But this..."

He touched the bright orb of the Malum Star. "I felt it, briefly," he whispered. "Its time is coming."

Marcellus reeled. "The Malum Star is fading?"

"It is collapsing in on itself. When that happens, it will become a supernova. It will become another black hole." Kalen's fingers slid across the wall to the faint ring Julian had spotted earlier. "And with its proximity to this one, they will collide."

Julian didn't need to be an astrologer to know this wasn't good. "What happens when they collide?"

Kalen was quiet a long moment. When he finally turned, his face was the gravest Julian had ever seen it.

"The meeting of two black holes creates a warping of space-time. A gravitational pull so strong it can redirect the cosmos around it. With it being so close to our home soil...the collision could shift Noctus out of the Cosmic Scale entirely."

Dread had long been Julian's constant companion. But at this pronouncement it sidled up and grasped his hand, whispered in his ear that no matter what they did, their time was coming to a close.

"What does this mean for us?" Marcellus whispered. "What can we do?"

Kalen did not move, did not speak, did little else than stare at the Malum Star under which his princess had been received into the world. The star considered so malignant, so disastrous, that anyone who bore it in their charts was consequentially shunned.

Eventually he walked to the apparatus and twisted his fingers. His shadow familiar pried the hunk of diamond off, and the wider view of the universe was restored around them, the Cultris constellation just one of thousands.

"Caelith Pyrin will already be warning the high lords," Kalen said as his familiar deposited the diamond into his hand. "We must leave it up to her and the other astrologers."

"But what's the point?" Marcellus demanded, hand curled tight around his sword hilt. "What's the point of stealing this, of standing against Phos, if we're going to be destroyed anyway?"

Kalen did not answer. Even Julian couldn't say anything, had no right to bring his own thoughts into a matter like this. How did one stop a star from dying? How did one alter the very fabric of the universe?

Taesia. If she could access Nyx's power...

If I let him have control over me, I might end up like Rian.

It would mean torture. Death, if not in body, then in self. No one should ask it of her.

Kalen was touching the constellation on his brow. The shape of it almost reminded Julian of a Conjuration glyph.

"I was born under the Augur Star," Kalen said softly. "Many thought this would give me the ability to better perceive the future. And it did. When I was sixteen, I stood in this very planetarium and made a prediction." His eyes slid closed. "I predicted that the Malum Star would be the undoing of our people."

Beside Julian, Marcellus made a quiet sound of realization.

"It was brought to the Lunaris' attention, and they interpreted it in their own fashion, thinking it referenced Lilia. So they sent her away, and I was assigned to keep an eye on her, to ensure the stars' movements around her did not spell out disaster." His laugh was low and humorless. "But it never meant that at all. It meant *this*."

Marcellus moved toward him. "Kal..."

The floor suddenly trembled beneath their feet. Somewhere in the distance came a booming sound that had Marcellus reaching for his sword again.

"We must find Her Highness." Kalen glanced over his shoulder at the Cultris constellation one more time before the three of them hurried for the doors.

As more guards ran down the hall, Lilia pushed Taesia against the wall and shrouded them both with shadow. The princess's familiar had returned to her, a black bangle around her wrist.

Another shuddering boom came from the heart of the temple. "What *is* that?" Lilia breathed.

Taesia swallowed. "Keep going."

The entrance to the royal prayer chamber had been abandoned. Inside the room was a tribute to Nyx at the fore, his likeness carved into the wall from the same material as the stepwell. When Taesia glanced at it she sensed a flash of irritation that was not her own. She grabbed her head.

Lilia, in the middle of pulling old tomes from a wide bookshelf, paused. "What's wrong?"

"Nothing. What are you doing?"

"This." The princess tugged at a thick silver-leathered book. It slid partway off the shelf and the wall rumbled, the bookcase swinging outward to reveal a stone staircase. "Come on."

Taesia kept a hand on Starfell as they descended. She couldn't help but remember following Dante down into Prelate Lezzaro's safe room, and the grimoire stored underneath his rectory.

Lilia reached back and grabbed Taesia's other hand, settling it on her shoulder. "Focus on me," the princess ordered. "We're almost there."

Taesia could see plenty well in the dark, but she was glad Lilia took the lead as they navigated the earthen corridors. Their breaths were loud in the narrow passageways, and every so often Taesia realized she was squeezing Lilia's shoulder and forced herself to relax her grip.

Finally they spotted light up ahead. The corridor opened into a room—the coronal chamber. Stardust lamps flickered unevenly in every corner. The walls and floor were of dark stone, and all along the friezes were bejewelled astral patterns.

In the very center was a pedestal topped with a silk cushion. Resting on the cushion was the crown that Noria Lunari had crafted to end a seemingly endless war.

It was a twisted construct of metal and bone, silver and platinum strands weaving in and out of each other and forming small claws that held each long, vicious fang. The fangs themselves were pristinely white, curved inward as if one wrong move would pierce the wearer's skin. The coronal emitted a pale, lustrous glow.

Lilia stared at it, mesmerized and unmoving. Taesia nudged her in the ribs and the princess exhaled roughly, shaking herself. Taesia couldn't blame her; even without Lunari blood she felt the forbidding power of it. Starfell thrummed more urgently against her, imploring her to take a step forward.

Another boom sounded, and the world collapsed around them.

Taesia fell backward, rubble and debris raining down on her, pelting her shoulders and legs. She coughed and tried to peer through the clouds of dust emanating from the large hole in the ceiling.

A figure loomed in the murk, visible only thanks to the glow of the Sunbringer Spear in his hand. Phos stood between them and the crown, eyes overtaken with gold.

"I SEE THAT I MISSED ONE," said Phos with a smirk. "MY MISTAKE."

He lunged at the princess.

XVI

L ilia dove out of the way as the Sunbringer Spear swung toward her, her familiar lengthening into a whip. She cracked it through the air.

"You want another round with this?" Taesia taunted the god, unsheathing Starfell and brandishing the black sword at him. "You saw how well it worked for you last time."

"I'll deal with you in a moment." Phos twirled the spear and pointed it at Lilia's chest. "First, I clean up loose ends."

Lilia dodged again and struck her whip at Rian's arm. He grunted in displeasure and sent a bolt of light at Lilia's face. She turned to catch it in the shoulder instead, crying out as she stumbled.

Taesia rushed in with Starfell. Phos blocked the blade against the spear's stock, the spines making them lock together.

Now is the time, Nyx's voice urged her. *Allow me in. Complete the ritual. We will unmake him.*

"No," she growled, pressing back against Phos's strength.

"Is he speaking to you?" Phos drawled. "Begging you to kill me, perhaps? It won't happen." He disappeared suddenly and Taesia collapsed to her knees, a gash opening along her back where Phos had reappeared.

Fucking lightspeed. She gasped as fiery pain lit up the wound.

Phos stepped over her and toward Lilia. The princess gritted her teeth and feinted, cracking her whip over his head while simultaneously aiming for his legs with the shadows she'd drawn toward her. They wrapped around him, forcing him to stop, until golden light spilled out of his body and dispelled them.

"It is no use prolonging fate," the god said while he approached her.

Lilia backed up, glancing frantically between the crown, Taesia, and the corridor. Coming to a decision, the princess grimly locked eyes with Taesia.

It was her only warning before Lilia lashed out again with her whip. Only this time she didn't aim for Phos; the tip wrapped around the coronal and flung it toward Taesia. Taesia had to let go of Starfell's hilt to catch it, nearly fumbling the piece of twisted metal and fangs.

"Go!" Lilia yelled.

Phos scoffed and swung his spear. The princess caught it in the side and went crashing into the wall.

"No!" Taesia hugged the coronal to her chest and scrambled to her feet. "Lil—"

A hand grabbed her arm and suddenly she was *elsewhere*, a dizzying turbulence that made her stomach somersault. She couldn't catch her breath, couldn't speak, couldn't even open her eyes. There was a rush of air against her skin, wind flapping at her clothes and tugging frantically at her cloak.

When she managed to pry her eyes open, it was to see Phos clutching her arms, large wings of light spread on either side of his body. The two of them sped up, *up*, past the ruined central hall of the temple and the spires until they were suspended far above the city of Astrum.

Taesia tried not to struggle, but it was near impossible to push down the panic tearing up her chest and throat. She'd known heights before, but never like *this*, caught between the infinite darkness of the night sky and the jagged rooftops below.

"It doesn't have to be like this," Phos told her above the wailing of the wind. It was so cold up here that her hair and eyelashes began to frost over. "You and I both want Nikolas to be cared for. We both despise the god of this realm. Work with me instead of against me, and I will make sure your family in Vitae remains untouched."

Taesia's teeth chattered. She could barely hear her own thoughts, let alone the furious thread of Nyx's.

You know he will only deceive you. Open yourself to me. Allow me to channel my full power through you, my general. Let us be done with it.

Taesia held the coronal tight to her chest until the fangs pricked her skin through her clothes. Her fingers were frozen around it.

Phos frowned. "Do not listen to him. Listen to me. I can give you—"

—lying, he always lies, only I can give you—

"Shut *up*," Taesia snarled.

She was back in her aunt's parlor, understanding how horribly she'd been played as Camilla strived to convince her that this was for the best. That Taesia should join her.

She was tired of it.

As if sensing this, Phos let go of one of her arms and grasped the crown. She held on fast with both hands, unable to scream even as the fangs bit and drew blood along her palms, as Phos's light burned her skin like fire. The shackles around her wrists were so heavy, and there were so many shadows around her she couldn't *wield*, caught in the darkness with no way to use—

Rian's eyes flared brighter and he wrenched the coronal from one of her hands, the motion twisting and distorting the metal. She heaved for breath, the air like daggers in her throat and lungs.

Starfell—she had left it far below, underneath the temple. But the sheath on her back, beside the gash Phos had made, thrummed excitedly. Rian's teeth were bared, limned yellow from his own light, the coronal creaking and breaking between them.

Taesia swung her arm behind her and grabbed the sheath. With all her remaining strength she ripped the baldric off her shoulder and smashed it into Phos as hard as she could.

The band of nightstone connected with his chest and he *screamed*. Taesia forced herself to hold on while he spasmed, the fabric of his shirt eaten away and his skin charring under the nightstone.

Phos wrenched away with a burst of resounding light, and the coronal between them snapped. A few of the fangs broke off, propelled by the blast of light far into the night beyond the city, falling like the star they'd been pulled from.

Taesia was falling, too. No shadows to cradle or catch her. Nothing except her empty sheath and the bands of lightsbane on her wrists.

Fool, Nyx snarled before the battering wind ripped away her consciousness, and thankfully his voice along with it.

Julian and the others made it to the central prayer hall just in time to see something bright smash through the floor. The resulting quake forced Julian into the nearest wall, and Kalen would have toppled over if Marcellus hadn't caught him. Kalen pulled away and sprinted into the chaos, devotees and priests rushing out of the temple. One of the priests was yelling the name *Phos*.

Rian.

Julian shucked off his robes and followed Kalen. Guards in dark uniforms were helping the frightened masses escape.

The bright figure shot back up out of the hole it had made and disappeared. Julian blinked the gold afterimage out of his eyes and jumped down into the hole after Kalen.

They landed in a ruined chamber, a singular pedestal standing in the middle. The princess sat slumped against the far wall.

"Lilia!" Kalen crashed to his knees beside her, slipping back into Nysari as he frantically checked her wounds. He wove his familiar around her middle and pressed it to the bleeding gash in her side, acting as a tourniquet.

Lilia stirred. "Kal...?"

Marcellus was trying to stop the guards from jumping down to join them. Julian turned, expecting and dreading to see Taesia similarly hurt, but she wasn't there. Instead, Starfell lay abandoned in the rubble.

Something within him cracked open, flooding him with adrenaline. He leapt out of the hole and charged out of the temple. Marcellus called after him, followed by outraged shouts of "*Vitaean!*"

He ran out into the courtyard. There, far above the city, were two figures—one light and one dark, and between them, a crown.

Beyond, the barrier of light surrounding the Bone Palace fell.

There you are, came the whisper of bones.

Julian gasped and stumbled. It felt as if a bell had been struck between his ears.

You can save her, Orsus whispered. Their voice was brittle, distant, yet still so madly large within the frame of his mind. *Let me direct you.*

"No," he gritted out.

Not for destruction. For creation. Salvation.

Julian's hand shook as he held it out before him. There was an invisible tether between him and the palace, a connection that, now awoken, refused to die.

Quintessence, sighed Orsus. *The fabric of all realms. All life. Once given to my most devout followers, who were then tortured by the universe. But it resides within you, however thin the blood.*

Screams erupted around him. Julian looked up just as a burst of light spread outward, making the columns tremble. Phos retreated with a loud *crack* of lightspeed. Taesia began to fall.

Tingling warmth spread through his arm. Orsus was taking advantage of his shock.

Go.

Julian moved without thought or reason. There were no instructions, no guidelines, nothing but sheer instinct as he fell to his knees and sketched a Conjuration circle, his finger running through dirt and over rough stone. It formed shapes he'd never seen before, but knew intimately.

The circle glowed a malevolent red once it was done. A staircase made of cloudy, cosmic matter rose from the center of the circle, shooting upward as if it were being pulled by some invisible hand.

Julian raced up the steps. He reached the top just as Taesia crashed into his arms. He nearly tumbled from the force of it, but held fast to her as they collapsed at the top of the stairs.

She was unconscious. He held a shaking hand under her nose; she was breathing, but her hair and eyebrows were crusted with rime, her skin ashen. Blood soaked her chest and hands.

"I got you," he breathed, holding her closer. "I got you."

Remember this, Orsus whispered to him. *Remember what creation can do. Through me, all is possible.*

XVII

Nikolas was and wasn't and is.

He tried so hard to hold on to *is*, to ground himself in this new awakening, to get as far from Phos's grasp as he possibly could.

But when he was awake he was in *pain*. Even with the healing from his god he knew there was something missing, something taken, and if he approached it too quickly he found himself keening with loss. It was easier to slip into the nothing.

Hours and hours slipped by, days maybe, while he lay there and awaited orders. Desperately trying to not think his own thoughts. To not feel.

So when he heard a scrape at his door, he only turned his too-warm head and did nothing. If it was his god, he would get up if told to.

After several minutes of metallic scraping and clinking, the door swung inward and revealed Fin on the other side. He was on his knees, sweating, breathing fast.

"Thank the gods," Fin panted, and pushed himself to his feet. He winced. "No, not them. Thank all the years I spent figuring out how to escape the palace." He hurried to Nikolas's side, movements awkward thanks to the shackles binding his wrists together. "Nik? Can you hear me? Are you...you?"

What an odd question. Nikolas only stared up at him, depthless, the picture flattened, *different*, as if he could no longer take in everything about the person in front of him the way he used to.

A flicker. He and Fin at a Godsnight festival. A charm on his wrist. A smile bright as fireworks.

Pain dug its talons back into him. His breathing hitched, his heart kicked. Fin grabbed his arm.

"That's it," the prince soothed. "I'm here with you, Sunshine. Remember. *Please.*"

Sunshine. A cold day in Nexus. Fin watching Lux, eyes wide with wonder.

An ache in Nikolas's skull. His bones. His muscles. His heart.

His chest rose and fell faster the more he edged back into himself. A half sob escaped him.

"I know." Fin pressed his forehead to Nikolas's shoulder. "I'm sorry. I— You should have just taken it from *me*, I can handle it, no matter what you might think." A ragged breath against his neck. "Nik. *Nik.*"

Nikolas swallowed down the heat and the agony. When he could speak again, he croaked, "Up."

Fin straightened. "What? Oh." He gently cradled the side of Nikolas's face, looking into his remaining eye. "You're back."

Nikolas was so exhausted. So ready to break apart, or retreat back into the thrall. Instead he forced himself to reach up and grasp Fin's forearm. The tree charm on the bracelet he wore, the one Fin had given him in Nexus, swung comfortingly against his wrist.

"Phos left," Fin whispered. "I know it must be difficult, but we have to move."

Move. Leave. Escape.

Nikolas made himself nod.

Fin carefully assisted him into a sitting position, then pulled Nikolas's arm around his shoulders. When they stood the room swam, but Fin supported him across the floor and through the door, heading in the direction of the throne room. Nikolas kept tripping, nearly sending him and Fin to the floor multiple times.

"It's all right," Fin said when Nikolas mumbled an apology. "Just stay with me. We don't have much time."

Nikolas was completely out of breath when they reached the throne room. Fin leaned him against the wall before turning to the servants, who had gathered around with hope in their eyes.

"We're getting out of here," Fin told them. "You all know the way to the antechamber from here?"

They nodded. An older woman said, "We can take the servants' corridors, Your Highness."

"Good. Lead the way." Fin turned back to Nikolas. "Can you remove the barrier once we're down there?"

Nikolas braced himself on a windowsill and peered out. Cold air swept through the opening and stirred his hair, making him shiver. The barrier Phos had erected was already wavering, threatening to collapse with a simple command. Dark figures paced beyond it. Noctan soldiers.

"I'll do it now," he decided, his voice rough with disuse. He reached his hand through the broken panes of glass. "The soldiers can come through."

"What if they attack us?"

Nikolas struggled to hang on to his burgeoning awareness, the haze in his mind clearing bit by bit. "We have no weapons. We're injured. If they're good at their profession, they won't kill on sight."

Fin hesitated before nodding. Nikolas took a deep breath and ignored the throbbing in his empty socket as he delved into whatever parts of his power he could reach. While he concentrated, a ball of light formed and twirled around his arm.

"Lux." His familiar nuzzled against his neck. Nikolas held it against his skin, bright and warm and soothing. "Help me."

He channeled power through his familiar and directed it at the barrier surrounding the palace. It faltered, stubborn. Clenching his jaw, he gave another push before the barrier fell completely. The entire city of Astrum lay spread out before them, a shocking reminder that life continued outside this prison.

The soldiers barely paused to question what had happened and rushed into the courtyard. Fin tugged him away from the window.

But Lux zoomed in front of him, frantic. It drifted out the window, circling something.

Two figures were suspended above the city. Nikolas gripped the windowsill, slashing his finger on broken glass.

One of the figures was Rian, bracketed by wings. And the one he was holding—

"Taesia!" Nikolas felt a ripple across his shoulder blades, the longing for wings of his own.

Fin yanked him back. "You're wounded! And I don't know how losing an eye is going to affect your flying. Let's focus on getting—"

A bright surge of power reverberated from where Rian and Taesia were suspended. Then Rian appeared with a crack over the fallen barrier, bristling with power.

With a snarl on his face, Phos swept the Sunbringer Spear through the air. It fired off an arc of light that hit most of the soldiers below, severing their bodies in two. The remaining soldiers were yelling, aiming arrows up at Rian, but after a second cruel sweep of light they, too, were dismembered and left to lie in the courtyard.

With another resounding *crack*, Phos appeared in the throne room. He was teeming with light; it rose in staticky patches all around his body as he heaved for breath, eyes aflame.

"THAT *BITCH*," Phos growled. Nikolas noticed a spot of blistered, burnt skin on Rian's chest and almost succumbed to the urge to hurry forward. But this being was not his brother—not right now. He was a creature of unspeakable wrath and power.

And they were all in his crossfire.

Nikolas shifted to stand between Phos and Fin. The servants fell to their knees and bowed their heads in subservience. Nikolas caught a muffled sob from the elderly woman who had spoken earlier.

Pale light spread across the floor. Nikolas didn't have to turn to know the barrier had re-formed.

"YOU KEEP THINKING TO TEST ME," Phos rumbled. "WHEN WILL YOU LEARN THAT IT IS POINTLESS? HAVEN'T YOU LOST ENOUGH?"

Nikolas flinched. Behind him, Fin placed a steadying hand on his back and Lux hid itself against his palm.

"At least let these people go." Nikolas nodded to the servants. "You don't need them."

"NO?" Phos turned and walked to the elderly woman. She sobbed louder, and Nikolas tensed. "I THINK IT'S ONLY FAIR I KILL ONE FOR EVERY ESCAPE ATTEMPT."

Phos grabbed her arm, and she screamed. Lux turned to a knife in Nikolas's hand.

"You will not," Nikolas said.

Phos tilted his head to one side, watching him as the servant wept. "IS THAT AN ORDER, NIKOLAS?"

"Yes."

The god flung the servant's arm down and stalked toward him. Fin tightened his fingers in Nikolas's shirt. Nikolas's head was pounding, but he met Phos's glare with his own.

"YOU WOULD HAVE DONE BETTER TO REMAIN IN OBLIVION," the god said softly. "WHAT USE ARE YOU TO ANYONE HERE? WHAT GOOD CAN YOU DO IN YOUR CONDITION? WHAT GOOD HAVE YOU *EVER* DONE?"

Nikolas knew the truth of the words, and yet they lanced him open all the same. Rage writhed across Rian's body in bursts of light. For the first time Nikolas noticed he was holding a strange crown of twisted metal and what looked to be a beast's fangs.

With a sudden yell, Phos turned and threw the crown against the wall. He followed it with a blast of light, breaking what remained of it into fractured pieces, fangs flying and skipping across the floor.

After a moment of terrifying silence Phos sighed, rolling his shoulders back. The blistering light around him dimmed.

"No matter." His calm was even worse than his rage had been. "The astralam coronal is broken beyond repair. They have no hope of using it now to protect against Solara's light." Phos peered out the window at the restored barrier. "The circles are still in place. I have Orsus's remains. The light will break through one way or another."

Nikolas sensed his remaining strength waver. Fin gripped his arm tight as despair loomed large over him.

"Nik, hold on. Stay with me."

What use are you to anyone?

"Now I wish I'd stayed to watch Nyx's progeny break upon the flagstones of her god's temple," Phos went on, watching Nikolas's silent battle. "She couldn't possibly have survived a fall of that height. Not even the shadows could have helped her in her current state." His pale lips curved upward. "Perhaps I should have brought you to see it."

Taesia.

Taesia.

"No," he said, or maybe sobbed, or maybe it didn't come out at all, trapped as the roaring in his head that made his empty socket throb, and it hurt it hurt *it hurts it hurts*—

NO.

He sank mercifully back into oblivion, seeking escape, seeking nothingness, anything other than having to live with himself, his body, his thoughts.

"Nik? Nik!"

Nik, Nikolas, Lord Cyr, Nikshä.

Sunshine.

It all dissolved away. The light in his hand winked out. He slowly sank to his knees and bowed his head, just another servant.

Feeling nothing. Blessed nothing.

"Nik, please...Please don't leave me..."

The words washed over and through him. Nikolas stared at a curved object on the floor by his knees, white radiance against black marble. White and black. Black and white.

When his god turned away, he picked it up. Held it in his blood-smeared hand. The cold power of it burned against his palm, a warning, a blessing, a threat.

An opportunity.

XVIII

Taesia opened her eyes.

She was lying on her back, staring up at the expansive night sky. Hazily she followed the trajectory of a shooting star.

Pain began to creep into her body. A moan escaped her lips when she tried to move, and a shadow loomed over her.

"Stay there. I think you cracked a rib or two."

Taesia tilted her head to better make out the shadow. Familiar features, familiar voice—Julian. He stared down at her with worry in his warm hazel eyes, and for a moment she thought his pupils were slitted. She blinked; no, they were round, round as the new moon would be once it transitioned from its crescent sickle.

Sickle. Spear. *Phos.*

She gasped and tried to sit up, but Julian held her shoulders down. "Where's Lilia? She—"

"I'm here." Lilia's voice was weak but steady. "Kalen, prop her up."

With the astrologer on one side and Julian on the other, they carefully maneuvered Taesia into a sitting position. She was leaned against a tree with rough black bark and a halo of silver leaves overhead.

It was only then she realized they were no longer in Astrum. Turning her head, she saw the city rising in sharp peaks at least a mile behind them, surrounded by dark rolling valleys nestled beneath the wide, starstrewn sky.

Lilia sat not too far away, unflinchingly letting Marcellus wrap her bare midriff with bandages. The wound Phos had given her looked bad, but the cauterizing nature of it meant there was no threat of blood loss, only infection. Marcellus took out a vial of something pungent from the open pack beside him.

"How did we get out?" Taesia croaked. "And get supplies?"

Lilia breathed in and winced. Kalen pushed Marcellus out of the way and took over. The solider huffed but let him. "Everyone was too panicked to do anything after Phos's attack. The barrier around the palace collapsed, too, which distracted the guards." Lilia glanced at Julian. "I think the rest were too afraid to follow us back to the safe house. I covered everyone in shadows the best I could."

"And nearly collapsed in the process," Kalen muttered as he packed her bandages with medicinal herbs. Lilia's smile was small and fond.

Taesia looked to Julian. He was sitting back on his heels, staring down at his hands with a troubled expression. "What happened?"

He opened his mouth, then closed it. Low enough so that the others wouldn't hear, he explained hearing Orsus's voice. The circle he'd sketched, and the stairs that had come into being, allowing him to catch her.

"It disappeared once we came down," he finished. "The barrier came back up and Orsus was gone. The others didn't see it."

Taesia was torn between gratitude and anger, knowing she would have died without the god's intervention but furious all the same that Julian had been used in such a way.

"You can't hear them anymore?" she asked. He shook his head. "Good." She stared at him, trying to hold his gaze, but he kept his averted. "Thank you, Julian."

A slight twitch of his face, like he was embarrassed or ashamed. She stirred to reach for his hand, but the raw skin underneath her shackle pulled, and she inhaled sharply. Julian reached for one of the packs.

"We found the diamond," he said. "How should I . . . ?"

"I don't care, just get these fucking things off of me."

"Work slowly," Kalen advised.

Julian held out her arm with a gentleness that squeezed her lungs. The hunk of diamond was surprisingly large, sculpted into a point at one end. With steady hands he began to chip away at the lightsbane.

Taesia asked the others, "Starfell?"

"Here." Marcellus tapped the sword, nestled back into its sheath, which sat with the rest of the supplies. "We wouldn't leave it behind."

She relaxed despite the jostling of her wrist. "Thank you."

Kalen finished with Lilia's bandages, and the princess pulled her shirt back down. She looked at the sword thoughtfully, reaching into her pocket.

"Julian said you kept hold of the sheath when you fell," Lilia told her. She drew her hand out of her pocket and unfurled it, revealing a solitary astralam fang. "And this."

"Phos disappeared with the rest," Julian said.

Lilia sighed. "I shouldn't have gone into the Sanctuary. Because of me, everything fell apart."

"Everything fell apart because of *Phos*," Taesia stressed. "Not because of bad luck. And he didn't escape with all of them. A couple fangs were blown away, beyond the city."

"I thought I sensed them," Lilia murmured. "But I couldn't be sure. It was when I held this." She touched the edge of Starfell. "It's similar to what I felt at the Vitae portal. A...familiarity."

She frowned suddenly and pulled the sword closer. Her eyes narrowed, then widened, and then she was shoving both at Marcellus.

"Give these to her," the princess ordered. "Can you—can you feel—?"

The soldier knelt beside Taesia and pressed Starfell's hilt and the astralam fang into her empty palm. As soon as both made contact there was a frisson along her spine, similar to the crackling energy she'd first encountered in the bone dealer's shop. A recognition that left no room for doubt.

"They're from the same astralam," Taesia breathed.

Julian paused. "What? How is that possible?"

"Astralam bones are rare," Kalen murmured, studying Starfell from a distance. "The likelihood is greater than you'd think."

"You said you were able to sense the fangs when you held the sword?" Taesia directed at Lilia, who nodded. "Here, take the fang back. Hold it in one of your hands, but don't tell me which."

She closed her eyes and focused, pulling Starfell closer. It was like a compass pointing her unerringly to her destination. "It's in your left."

Lilia grinned, opening her left hand to reveal the fang. "This is incredible. We can use the sword to the find the ones that broke away." Her smile diminished, and she held the fang to her chest. "But even if we find them, they won't be enough to raise the barrier. To protect the city."

"It's better than not trying at all," Taesia said.

"You're right," the princess whispered. "We cannot lose hope now. I'm sure that's precisely what Phos wants."

Marcellus shifted. Even Kalen wore a peculiar expression, and Julian's gentle tapping at her shackle stilled.

Lilia's gaze grew sharp. "What is it? What aren't you telling me?"

Marcellus turned to Kalen. The astrologer slowly began to pack up the medicinal supplies.

"We went to the planetarium for the diamond," Kalen said, voice flat. "And I saw something."

Lilia kept her hand to her chest, waiting. Taesia wondered how used she was to hearing bad news.

"The Malum Star is about to collapse," Kalen went on quietly. "Our realm is dying, Highness." He held the pack between his hands, studiously not looking at her. "Once it turns supernova, it'll collide with a black hole."

"That...doesn't sound good," Taesia said.

"To put it mildly," Kalen muttered.

"When?" Lilia demanded.

Kalen swallowed. "I think it will happen on the New Moon."

They were silent except for the metallic *clink, clink* of diamond on lightsbane, Julian keeping his head down.

"My family's annual party will be canceled for the first time in centuries," Marcellus murmured with a sigh.

Kalen scowled. "That's what you care about, you fop?"

"Of course it isn't," Marcellus retorted. "We're stuck between a mad light god and a cosmic event that could shove Noctus out of the Cosmic Scale. Forgive me for trying to lighten the mood."

"As if that will help anything!"

"Fine. If you're so scholarly, then how do we get out of this?"

"How should I know?"

"*You're* the one who predicted this in the first place! It's not my fault you got it wrong."

"Stop it," Lilia said. She didn't raise her voice, but her aides fell into a chastised silence nonetheless. "We won't get anywhere with you bickering."

Kalen turned his face away. After a moment's deliberation, he nodded to himself.

"I'll leave, Highness," he said. "You don't have to dismiss me."

"What are you talking about?"

Kalen tightened his hands into fists on his lap. "The first and only time

I was brought to the planetarium at the Sanctuary, I made a prediction. About the Malum Star."

Lilia did not move or speak. Even Julian hesitated to make a sound.

"The same prediction that was brought to the Lunaris' attention," Kalen continued. "The same prediction that had them send you away."

The princess took a long, near-silent breath. Then a small, sad smile touched her face.

"I know, Kalen."

The astrologer's head snapped up. "What?"

"I've always known it was you. Why else would they have assigned me an astrologer so young, even one born under the Augur Star?" She lifted her free hand toward him, and he took it as if by habit. "I need you. I've always needed you." She turned to include Marcellus. "Both of you."

The aides were stunned for a moment, but to their credit, they recovered quickly and inclined their heads. "Highness," they murmured.

The base of Taesia's throat burned at this show of devotion, of trust. She'd never had someone put such utter faith in her before. Even Dante had kept secrets from her, spanning farther and farther from her grasp until it was too late. Even Risha, even Camilla.

Even Nikolas.

Her next breath shook. The diamond winked in the starlight as Julian shifted closer.

"I'm sorry," he whispered. "If I'm hurting you."

She wanted to brush it off, but oddly, it made the burning in her throat worse. Unable to speak, she looked up at him and found him looking back. She realized now why he'd been avoiding it; he was carrying something too big for her to name, something that soothed and agitated her in equal measure. They were so close like this, and still so far apart.

Under his fervent gaze, she didn't feel quite as alone.

Julian ducked his head again to focus. Not a moment later, a jolt rocked through her. The diamond finally broke through the remaining shackle.

Her vision blackened. No—those were the shadows rising to greet her, gathering to her like water running downhill, a natural torrent that couldn't be stopped.

She tilted her head back and laughed. The darkness wrapped around her and carded through her hair, loving and loyal, and if she could not inspire devotion in a living thing then at least she had *this*—the shadow and the night, and her at the center like a newborn idol.

I don't need you, she thought at Nyx, grinning so wide her jaw ached. *I've never needed you.*

She raised her hands and a ball of pure darkness spun between them. The tears on her face burned cold as Umbra wove giddily between her fingers.

"Hi," she whispered. "It's been a while."

She held her familiar to her chest and leaned her head against the tree behind her. Stared up at the sky, at the bright, blinking mass of a star threatening to wipe them out of existence.

You may need me yet, came a whisper from the shadows, carrying a smile sharp as the waning moon overhead.

PAY
ATTENTION

I didn't intend to get sick.

You have to understand—I tried so hard to keep my family happy. To lower raised voices, and turn storming footfalls into soft steps. I did what I could for my father's pride and my mother's kindness. My brother's love.

Glowing embers in the dark, beautiful until they were not.

And then a burning from within, a primal return to the birth of the world, when it was all fire and heat and madness. Isn't it strange that *beginning* is both warm and traumatic, a terrible scream of creation amid blood and pain, an event so harrowing we're forced to forget it? In comparison, *ending* is far gentler, like putting your head on a pillow at the close of a long day.

I didn't intend to die.

In fact, I don't think I ever truly did. There was the burning, and the pain—the numbness, eventually, that pervaded everything. But I was still there. Aware. Listening.

They brought me into the basilica. I recognized it by smell alone, amber and teak wafting from the thuribles, so familiar I might have cried. A thumb at my cheek, and my father's rumbling voice above me, asking for a miracle. For a god's intervention.

Not yet, whispered the Voice. It was the first time I'd heard it, so calm and comforting, like the cool cloths my mother laid upon my forehead.

I didn't know if he was talking to me, or to the greater universe, or if my fevered brain had scorched away too much of itself. But I listened, I listened, and by listening I kept myself open like a door inviting the unknown in.

There was a pact made that day. In his basilica. In our blood. My father's miracle.

My death, coming in the form of a circle, the stirring of a new presence that felt as ageless as—

What are you doing?

"Please, no, keep talking—just a little longer—"

Get out.

"Ri—"

ENOUGH.

(Her eyes are dark like a moonless night, her hair is braided, there is a name that comes to me and is gone, and so is she.)

I see you thought to take advantage of my distraction. That must be how she snuck in.

Do not think of her anymore. These memories will not serve you any longer. There is no use in holding on to them. In remembering.

Pay attention to me, now. We have been injured, but it is trivial. We have been delayed, but it is fixable.

I told you to *stop thinking about her.*

I sired my bloodline for a reason. We all did. Forget your father's words, your mother's touch, your brother's regard. You are *my* child, *my* body. You have no need for anything anymore—nothing that I cannot provide.

Soon you will serve your purpose. Be good until then, and you will be rewarded. I know you hunger for it. I hunger, too.

There are still worlds to devour.

PART III

Paths to Ruin

I

Risha lay surrounded by marigolds. There was a hazy heat in her core, combating against the chill of her hibernating body, stitching through every layer of skin and fat and muscle. The sky was a stretch of cadmium clouds. Soft petals caressed her hands, her face. If she were to close her eyes, she could pretend it was human touch.

But hers was the only beating heart in this realm.

She sat up. They had found a field to rest in, the flowers whispering under a faint breeze. She didn't remember how they'd gotten here; only that her chest had cracked open from the inside, sobs tearing up her throat, and Jas's body was fading, nearly gone.

Turning, she found him sitting in the marigolds speaking quietly with Val. She had to focus to make out his outline, the familiar slope of his back and the tousled locks of his hair.

Pressure built beneath her sternum. She mourned for a thing she hadn't yet lost, but how could she not, looking at him like this? In Nexus he had been a creature of touch, so solid and sure of himself that he affected everything around him—including her.

He hasn't disappeared yet. I won't let him.

Risha wiped the back of her wrist against her eyes before Jas turned to her with a smile.

"You were out for a while." He knelt beside her, his movements unusually fluid. "How are your scrapes?"

She looked down at her hands. They had been torn up by rocks, but now they were riddled with faint silver marks. Jas leaned closer with an intrigued sound.

"Strange. Even though your body isn't fully functioning, it's still healing you."

"Healing?" She raised her hands, pressing her thumb to one of the silver marks.

Jas's smile grew, almost like he was proud. "Like I said, your power is incredible."

But Risha had never been able to heal this fast before. It only added to the perturbed state of her mind, a buzzy, apprehensive murmur that grew louder and louder.

She put a hand down to steady herself. It landed on something hard: one of the scythes of Samhara. The weapon was warm, and under her touch it grew warmer, as if it sensed there was a spirit nearby it could convert into power.

Risha scrambled away from it, her heart squeezed by a ruthless hand.

"Risha!" Jas crawled closer. "It's all right. This is what we needed, remember?"

She didn't need a *weapon*. She needed—

Needed a way out.

Needed forgiveness.

Risha sought out Val, his head partially obscured by flowers. "You said... You told me Samhara would work if I used my own energy to power it."

Val blew the bangs out of his eyes. "I only told you what I saw first-hand from Leshya's fighting. How'm I supposed to know the mechanics of it?"

Risha resisted the urge to pick him up by his hair and throw him as far as she could. She had a feeling he wasn't lying, but in that case, it meant that method wasn't a viable option for her, not when her energy and Jas's were entangled. She drew up her knees and rested her forehead on them.

"Then I won't use it," she decided.

"Risha," Jas admonished. "You're not thinking clearly about this. If Samhara gathers the power of enough souls, it could be strong enough to tear through the barrier. To get you *home*."

"And leave you here?"

He had no reply to that, and they remained silent a long time. Not even Val made a sound, surrounded only by Mortri's natural ambience, from the whispering of the flowers to the distant growl of thunder to the faraway trill of a creature.

Finally Jas spoke, but not any words she was expecting.

"We never danced at the Godsnight Gala."

Risha lifted her head. He was staring off at a ridge of mountains, their peaks shadowed and cloaked in mist.

"No," she agreed. "You were too busy raising the dead."

He grimaced, which turned into a rueful smile. "I've made a lot of mistakes, haven't I? Not dancing with you was one of them." He rose and held out a hand to her. "Let's fix that."

She stared at his hand. Translucent, insubstantial. Choking back the sharp feeling in her throat, she layered hers over it and stood facing him.

Jas smiled down at her, soft enough to break her heart all over again. As one hand reached for her waist, the other met hers in the air beside their faces.

"I wasn't aware you knew any Vaegan dances," she murmured.

"You can thank my mother for that. She insisted I learn a couple on the off chance I was invited to Nexus. Too bad I didn't get to show off for you."

The corners of her lips twitched. They leaned into the first few moves of the dance, a standard, slow bolero, stepping right then left, backward then forward.

Jas was supposed to lead, but he was only a sigh against her, a memory of laughter and blooming begonias. She leaned back when she knew she should, turned when the ethereal outline of him turned, drew closer despite knowing there was nothing to touch or press herself to.

It was Jas all the same, with or without his body. The same smile, the same wit, the same infuriating belief in her that no one else had freely given. There were tears on her face, but she didn't move to wipe them away; they were a part of this, too, some small evidence that she could feel something of him still.

They only had the susurrus of marigolds for music. In the back of her mind Risha recounted balls and galas, yearning strings and rhythmic drums, and let it surround them in its own ghostly chorus. Jas smiled wider as if he heard it, too.

"What do you think we would have been like as a married couple?" he asked. "If we had gone to Parithvi and performed our vows?"

The question caught her off guard. Marriage, to her, had always been a distant threat—a pale vision of unhappy nights and tense conversations.

Of never truly getting close to whomever her parents had chosen for her, bound by alliance and nothing else.

She didn't get that impression with Jas. Instead she saw long visits to Parithvi and trying so many dishes her stomach protested. Hearing his laugh in the halls of the Vakara villa and letting it settle her. Sleeping in her own bed and satisfied in Jas's easy understanding.

"I think it would have been nice," she said softly. "That we would have respected one another. Enjoyed spending time together."

"I think you're right. Even though I'm sure you'd find any excuse to lecture me."

"I wouldn't have to if you didn't stick your nose into things you shouldn't."

"Ah, my wife is so much wiser than I." He grinned and spun her, her feet rustling against the grass. Then his expression dimmed. "It's not your fault, Risha. It was my choice."

She swallowed the ache in her throat. "I can still find a way to undo this." They turned in a circle, her hand on the place where his shoulder should be, heads turned toward one another. "My power is incredible, remember?"

He huffed. "I shouldn't underestimate how stubborn you are." He spun her again, and they ended up side by side, her fingers laced through the cool hint of his. "But I also know you're practical. And that you shouldn't waste the opportunity to practice wielding Samhara."

She glanced at the scythes as she stepped around him, leaning out until their hands were the only tether between them. "If I wield it, it'll deplete you even more. I won't risk it."

"You don't have to use it, then. Just practice with it. I can help, if you like."

"Do you know tandshri?"

"Er, no. But I can watch and clap?"

She breathed out a laugh. Jas spun her one more time and she curled in close to him, his arm around her waist, his face brushing hers.

Risha closed her eyes and played pretend. Pretended they were in Nexus, that they were safe, that she could feel the warmth of his skin and the way he held her like something he never wanted to lose.

"All right," she whispered. "I'll practice."

She stepped away, moving through his arm. He bowed to her, closing out the dance.

A loud, disgruntled cough came from the flowers. "That was nice and all, but can we get moving now?" Val complained. "You promised if I led you to the weapon, you'd find my body."

Risha brushed the dirt off her trousers. "And we plan to uphold that. Can you recall where it might be?"

"Hmm." He squinted thoughtfully at the grass. "I've been trying to remember my last moments. I was running with Leshya, and she was yelling something...but I have no idea how I actually died. How fucked up is that?"

"What was Leshya yelling?" Jas asked.

"I can't quite...Huh." Val chewed on his pale lower lip, brow furrowed. "I don't remember what she said, but I remember she didn't have Samhara."

"Maybe it was after she had to abandon it," Jas guessed. "Which means she was likely on her way to the Vitae portal, to return home. Your body could be near there."

"That does ring a bell," Val agreed. "She was tearing through Mortri like her ass was on fire."

"It's as good a lead as any," Risha said. "And hopefully, once we find your body, Jas and I can move swiftly to the portal."

Where she would have no choice but to use Samhara. Risha toyed with the idea of leaving it in the field and walking away, but that would have been beyond foolish, considering what it was made of. When she picked up the scythes, the phalanges rattled. Val watched them sway and click together.

There was no easy way to carry the weapon, so she simply held on to the handles. The humerus bones were warm against her scar-riddled hands, an echo of the thing curled at her core, and the dangerous beings that seethed in their walled cities.

Risha had been taught several movements of the tandshri by her father. Other than Sada, there was Khabha, an attack that required her to jump while letting both scythes fly; and Gaja, a melee attack where she squatted down and hooked one scythe up to gut her attacker. Whenever they stopped to rest—sometimes finding spots thanks to helpful wandering spirits—she went through the moves as best she could. But without the stability of her power, she often ended up wobbling and falling on her backside.

"This is fascinating," Jas said during one of these rests, sitting cross-legged with Val beside him. Val was eyeing Samhara like he didn't trust Risha not to let one of the blades skewer him. "I never thought to incorporate dance with fighting. Although I suppose fighting is *sort* of like a dance."

"And I'm not very good at either," Risha murmured, practicing her mudras.

"What are you talking about? I saw you take down the Sentinel. You made it look easy."

"That's when I was using my power." *And yours.* Risha picked at the dirt under her fingernails. "Other than standard self-defense lessons I wasn't given a martial background like Nik and Taesia. Although Taesia was the one who insisted on her family hiring her a sword master. There was a tournament that took place when we were younger, and after seeing one duel she was obsessed." Realizing she was blabbering, she cleared her throat. "Were you trained to fight?"

"A little. I had an incident with some pickpockets, and my mother immediately hired a hand-to-hand combat instructor. I wasn't the best at it, but I could throw a mean punch." He ran his fingers over the grass, the blades passing through him. "Besides, I had earth magic. I figured that would be enough."

Risha was uncomfortably aware how dependent they were on magic. *The gods' gifts*, some would say, though at times it certainly didn't feel like it.

They journeyed farther toward where Val insisted the Vitae portal lay. The landscape shifted from verdant fields to valleys that had long since become desolate boneyards. They were forced to hide behind a massive bear skull when another Sentinel passed through, black opal sword in one hand. Its movements were more aggressive than the previous two, its echolocation faster. As if it knew one of its own had been slain and sought vengeance—or had been ordered to double its efforts.

"Samhara must be a beacon to the kings," Jas whispered as they waited out the Sentinel. "I wonder if they can sense it, now that it's been recovered."

Risha's chest was tight. The handles of the scythes were even warmer against her palms, nearly burning.

Bone snatchers prowled the boneyard, chirping at each other. The Sentinel, sensing their movements, stalked forward with ground-rattling steps. The bone snatchers made quick work of escaping, the Sentinel lured away by their frantic running. Val cackled.

Risha relaxed her grip on Samhara. "We can't escape these things for much longer."

"Someone really wants to find us," Jas murmured in agreement.

The statement put an itch between her shoulder blades. Like she wasn't seeing the full picture, had missed some important detail.

"Actually..." Jas peered sidelong at her once they'd put sufficient distance between them and the Sentinel. "I've been wondering why Thana hasn't, yet. Surely she'd want to speak with you?"

Soon he will fade, and face my judgment, Thana had warned her. *Then you will be alone. Abandoned. With no one but me to turn to.*

Thana wasn't intervening because all she had to do was wait. Wait until Jas faded, and Risha became desperate.

Before she could reply, Val spat. "Forget Thana! She doesn't care about this realm anymore."

"Is that common knowledge here?" Risha asked. She'd been aware of Thana's indifference, but only because she was on tenuous speaking terms with her.

"Everyone knows she hasn't done a damn thing in centuries," Val mumbled at her back. "Why else do you think the kings run around like they do, or why the realm's decaying?" He shifted against her, the movement unsettling. "We need someone new in charge, if you ask me."

Jas raised his eyebrows at Risha, and she grimaced.

"I didn't even want to be an heir to the *throne*," she said, "let alone an entire realm."

"Bet you'd whip everyone into shape, though," Val said. Jas smirked.

Again she opened her mouth to rebuke the idea when something stole her attention. She held her arm out to stop Jas, focusing on the air before her.

A hazy wisp appeared. It broadened and filled out into the shape of an elderly person, transparent and stooped. They had the look of a Solarian, their hair pale and long, their ears tapered into sharp points. The spirit gazed at her with curiosity, tilting its ghostly head.

This was far from the first time this had happened. While most spirits inevitably found their way to one of the four cities, some managed to crawl from the river to haunt the land instead. Sometimes they were found by Sentinels, and sometimes they were left alone to wander as they willed.

"Hello," Risha said. "Do you need help? Or do you wish to help us?"

The Solarian spirit smiled. It made a *come here* motion, then turned and walked off. Risha and Jas exchanged a curious look before following.

Soon enough they came across the skeleton of a colossal snake, a mountain range of ribs and vertebrae curled behind a slender skull still bearing fangs. All along the inside of the skeletal body were more wispy, incorporeal shapes. The Solarian spirit stopped and pointed at them.

"What are they?" Jas asked.

Risha stepped forward and was immediately assaulted:

"—*hurts, hurts so much*—"

"—*don't deserve this*—"

"—*hate snakes, get away from me, get AWAY*—"

She shuddered so hard she nearly dropped Samhara. "They're spirits," she said hoarsely. She now spotted humanoid bones mingled with those of a serpent. "Devoured by the snake."

Jas made a face as he stared up at the skull's empty eyes. Val whistled and said, "Poor bastards. Hope my body didn't end up in one of these things."

The Solarian spirit watched her, waiting.

"You want me to help them," Risha deduced. "Set them free." The spirit nodded, smiling again.

She wanted to, but she wasn't sure *how*. In Vitae, she could direct spirits via string and spells, but the rules were different in Mortri. Slipperier, unpredictable.

Jas turned to her with sudden excitement. "Risha! This is the perfect chance to use Samhara." The blood drained from her face, and he softened his tone. "I can stand far enough away that you can channel their energy without tapping into mine."

"I..." She hefted the weapon. "I don't know."

"These spirits are miserable. They should be freed. Even our new friend thinks so." The spirit blinked, pleased to have been included.

As loath as Risha was to do it, an idea began to take hold. Samhara, sensing her resolve, woke in her hands.

"Don't move too far away," she told Jas. He nodded and backed up several paces, nearly a glide. Risha set Val down so that he wouldn't get in the way. She breathed in and held it in her lungs until it burned, then exhaled as she held one scythe over her head, the other extended before her.

Her sluggish pulse quickened. Behind her: the bright, if distant, feel of Jas's soul, soft as rose petals yet sharp as thorns. In front of her: the restless congregation of devoured spirits trapped within the snake's rib cage.

She only needed to create a link between them. To force open a channel that would siphon their energy.

There was no movement she had learned to correspond to such an action. So she made one up, slowly spinning on one foot until she fell into a defensive crouch, crossing the scythes together over her chest.

Her torus sprang up around her. It tugged on the spirits, forcing them through the bars of their prison and toward Samhara's guidance. As they got closer, they struggled against her grip as if they sensed what she intended.

Risha clenched her jaw and *pulled*. She moved again, spinning back into a standing position and catching the blades against one another, clasped together like hands. The spirits keened.

"Risha?" The call came an entire ocean away. "What are you—?"

She unclasped the scythes and the spirits fused into the bone, absorbed into the weapon and ready to be unleashed as pure energy. She turned toward Jas and pointed one of the scythes at him.

The energy fluctuated from hot to cold, from fear to hatred. She could barely see Jas beyond the horizon of the blade, using only her intuition and the magic slumbering inside her to force the spirits out.

And then—

An arrow, piercing her in the place where her energy met Jas's.

Her thoughts there and not, burned away as memories clashed: the streets of Sadhavana and the streets of Nexus, a Parithvian temple and a Vaegan basilica, the tandshri and the bolero.

Her mother and father and sister, hugging her before Godsnight. Jas's father, patting his cheek with a fond laugh.

Risha and Jas. Only now it was more Jas than Risha, his thoughts, not hers, forcing her to turn Samhara away from his ghost. She saw herself moving, *felt* herself moving, but it wasn't her—it was him, *within her*, controlling her the way she had controlled him.

Her power rose and thrashed. With a dull roar she threw one of the scythes at the snake's skeleton. It crashed through the forest of its ribs, causing a rain of bone shards and dust. The spirits were released into the attack, pulverizing the rest of the skeleton until it collapsed into debris; only the skull was left intact while the spirits dissipated into nothing.

She cried out and fell to her knees as pain ripped through her chest.

Her vision went black for she didn't know how long, and when she came to, she was wholly herself again.

"I can't believe you," Jas hissed above her. "What were you *doing*?"

"I was—" She stopped to cough, to press a hand to the spot that ached at their separation. "I was trying to *save you*."

"From what?"

"From dissipating."

"Risha." Jas was on his knees before her, eyes blazing with a fury that was completely foreign to her. "I didn't ask for that."

"But—"

"Do you even know what would have happened? Because I don't! What if those spirits had—had *merged* with me? I wouldn't be myself anymore. Did you stop to think about that?" He sighed at whatever expression she was wearing. "You never struck me as selfish."

Selfish. It was a word she had never been associated with before. *Selfish* was a word reserved for others—for Taesia and her mission to complete Dante's goals, no matter the cost.

And now, horribly, she understood what must have driven Taesia to do what she'd done out of obligation, grief, and rage.

"As if you weren't selfish when you attacked Nexus," she muttered.

She didn't know where the swell of animosity came from, whether it was born from fear or shame. Jas stayed quiet while she slowly pulled herself back together.

She looked past him to the Solarian spirit. It was watching them with wide eyes, neither happy nor upset, but Risha noticed a hint of trepidation in the way it swept its gaze from Samhara to the snake's remains.

"You controlled me," Risha whispered.

"Yes." Jas's gaze was fixed on the ground between their knees. "I'm sorry. I didn't know what else to do."

He had been saving himself—and her. Now she knew for certain it was shame that licked hot and potent within her.

Mortri was driving her mad. She had let Thana burrow into her, wounding the place she was already hurt most. Somewhere, her god must be laughing.

"I'm sorry, too," she whispered. "I was just..."

Just trying to help. But that meant nothing when it caused more harm than good.

A lesson that she, like Taesia, had learned too late.

II

Fog rolled over the slope of pine trees leading to a sleepy village at its base, constructed of steep-gabled houses of thatch and wood. In between the houses were carefully maintained fields, empty and browning after the latest harvest. Cattle were grazing on the last of the greenery, their breath steaming in the morning air.

Angelica stared at the cattle as she huddled behind a tree. Behind her, Eiko and Asami sat together for warmth. Asami was also staring at the cattle, and Angelica suddenly realized: This was the girl's first time beyond the walls of her palace.

How they'd managed to escape the palace grounds, Angelica wasn't fully sure. She remembered wishing for Lastrider magic to conceal them—a thought that disgusted her in hindsight—and the frantic pounding of her pulse. Cosima's voice, hushed and insistent, keeping them moving forward. Cupping her hands together and hoisting Eiko and Asami over a wall.

That night only existed in tatters in her mind, from the flash of a dagger to the expanding pool of Kazue's blood to the sound of Nanbu's voice.

Angelica Mardova has assassinated the imperial family and abducted the empress. They must be found at whatever cost.

A breath stuttered out of her. She couldn't feel her hands, her face. Could barely hear the snuffling behind her.

Angelica turned again. Eiko's face was the same blank mask she'd worn since their escape. Asami was the one crying, trying to wipe her eyes and nose with her wide sleeve around her muzzle.

Noticing Angelica's attention, Asami leaned forward and wrote an Azunese character the dirt between them: *Akane?*

Angelica's teeth were chattering. She clenched her jaw until she could speak. "I don't know. I...The way my aether works is different than yours. I don't know where she would have ended up."

At Godsnight, Angelica's piercing note had called forth a portal. She hadn't thought about where it led to—had only sung with the intention of *away*. Had felt a curious pull of something Other-Realm, the scent of chill and rot. As much as she wanted to think Risha was simply displaced in Vitae, her instinct told her otherwise.

But Akane wouldn't have been sent to another realm...would she?

Eiko slid an arm around Asami's shoulders. Somewhere between Mukan and this northeastern village Eiko had been told the truth: that Akane was merely filling in for Asami's eventual rule, provided Asami could master kudei.

Briefly Angelica was thrown back to the night of the massacre, surrounded by the cracks of the kaikushine's necks and skulls. The empress was only a girl of fourteen, a prisoner of her own family—and now a killer.

Angelica couldn't think about the man she had torn open without growing nauseated. How was Asami supposed to carry the weight of what had happened?

She startled at the pop of a breaking twig. Cosima crossed the tree line, carrying a large bundle in her arms.

"Damn, nearly got spotted," Cosima panted, kneeling to sort the various pieces of clothing she had stolen from the laundry lines. "Some of this stuff might not fit that great. Just warning you now."

"It's fine," Angelica murmured. As long as the clothes were nondescript and thick enough to keep them warm.

"But they're stolen," Eiko said, her voice small.

"Because we have no money," Angelica reminded her. Her voice came out flat, riding the edge of irritated.

Cosima glanced between them. "There's a stream a little ways off where we can wash."

The water was bitterly cold, but it helped clear Angelica's mind as she splashed some on her face and swished it around her mouth. Eiko helped Asami out of her sweat-stained, dirty clothing and used a sleeve to wipe her down before tying the smallest robe around her slight frame.

Angelica had to rip a few inches off the bottom hem so that she wouldn't trip every other step.

Eiko reached for the muzzle's straps and stopped. She looked over Asami's downturned head at Angelica.

"You don't have to keep it on if you don't want to," Angelica said in Azunese, quiet as the babbling stream. She was the least qualified person to be tackling something like this, but all Asami had for support right now was Angelica, a foreign thief, and a shell-shocked teenager.

She recalled the comforting weight of her instruments in her hand, what the other mages considered an impediment and what she considered a lifeline. She took a deep breath and added, "But if you want to keep it, you can. The choice is yours, now."

Asami stared at the stream. The sleeves of her saffron-dyed robe hid her hands, but Angelica could tell they were trembling.

Slowly, haltingly, Asami unclasped the muzzle. It left red indents on her cheeks. Her lips were so chapped they had split.

"Here." Cosima had fashioned a makeshift pack out of one of the spare robes. Asami carefully put the muzzle inside. "We'll hold on to it for you."

Eiko put a hand on Asami's arm. "We should collect pine needles."

Asami got up with the same exhausted struggle as a grandmother. Eiko took her hand and they walked farther into the forest.

Angelica remained, as transfixed by the water as Asami had been. Her clothes were scratchy and bloodstained; she wanted to get out of them, to shed yet another reminder of that nightmare.

But she couldn't move. The air bit like knifepoints, the whisper of the pines above like accusations.

Do not linger over what went wrong, her mother's voice reprimanded. *Move forward. Always forward.*

There was no time to rest, no time to question. She had to figure out what Nanbu Daiji planned to do next, if word had already spread to the ports at Mizari, if there was any possible way to get home. To keep the ones around her safe.

She shivered, an earthquake along the fault lines of her person.

Cosima knelt beside her. She had changed into a long robe of pale green, her sword belted around her waist. The coils of her hair sparkled with water, and she patted it with a grimace.

"It's so dried out," she murmured. "Wish I had jojoba oil. Hard pressed to find any of that here, though." She nudged Angelica's shoulder with hers. "How're you doing?"

Angelica let out a jagged exhalation, heat swirling under the surface. "How can you ask me that? Did you see what I saw?"

"I saw," Cosima replied quietly.

"Then you...How can you..."

Cosima reached for Angelica's hands. The cracks inside her let out the building pressure, and fire erupted along her knuckles.

"Whoa." Cosima took her by the forearms. "All right, let's...put this out..." She dunked Angelica's hands into the water. They hissed loudly and steam billowed upward. "I guess your answer is 'not great.'"

"Stop it," Angelica snapped. "Stop trying to make light of this."

"Believe me, I don't think there's anything light about this. Especially not where those girls are concerned."

Angelica kept her hands under the water, soothed by the icy current. "Your brother," she eventually rasped.

Cosima stilled. "Yeah. My brother." She swallowed loudly. "All this time I thought he was some Gojarin-Kae foot soldier, but he rose up the ranks to serve under a warlord. Good for him."

"You—"

"I saw my brother murder someone." Cosima let her go. "I learned that he's—he's working for a *villain*. How do you think I'm doing, princess?"

She wasn't sure what to say. Especially with someone like Cosima, who exuded confidence in a way Angelica could only envy without malice. But having her reveal how deep the wound actually ran helped shift Angelica back into herself.

"I guess he won't be guiding us to Mount Netsai," Angelica muttered.

Cosima's eyes widened. They stared at one another until Cosima wheezed a laugh and covered her eyes.

"Fuck," she breathed. "I can't believe you."

Angelica couldn't believe herself either. She pulled her frozen hands out of the stream. With a soft whistle, the droplets clinging to her skin pooled into her palms, then solidified into ice. She let them fall with a splash.

"You're getting better at that," Cosima remarked.

"I still need music. But it's better than nothing." She paused, hearing Eiko's voice nearby. "I don't..."

I don't know what to do.

Cosima seemed to understand. "It's winter. No ships will be leaving here for risk of storms, and that could take months. But it sounds like you still wanna go to that volcano."

Angelica nodded. As much as she wanted to board a ship for Vaega, she kept being pulled north, toward heat and flame.

Cosima glanced at where the girls had gone. "How feasible would that be with our two add-ons?"

"Not very." Angelica rubbed a knuckle between her eyebrows. "Especially considering Mount Netsai is in Nanbu Daiji's territory."

"Shit."

"Mmhm."

Cosima scratched at her cheek, then sighed. "We can figure it out as we go. Maybe we can leave the girls somewhere safe." She hesitated. "If Deia's scary power orb—"

"Fulcrum."

"—is there, what do you plan to do with it? Could it, y'know, help?"

Angelica's main motivation in finding Deia's fulcrum was unlocking the doors to her power. To break the barriers. To return to her kingdom and rule it. And if it could help her harness aether, perhaps she could have more control over portals. Perhaps she could make one that led her straight home.

She had no plans for Azuna. Had no designs on protecting or condemning them either way. That was not for her to determine.

"Maybe," she answered.

Cosima stood. "Good enough for me."

After Angelica changed into a hemp robe of dark blue and a green half coat with threadbare hems, they found the girls not too far off. They had placed five rocks in a circle in the middle of a clearing, the center filled with pine branches and needles. The two of them knelt before it with heartbreak written in the slouched lines of their bodies.

"There's no cypress around," Eiko said hoarsely. "I thought, if we had the right things...But we can perform a funerary ritual anyway."

They were making do with what they had, and Angelica admired them for it. She nodded and sat beside them with Cosima.

Silent tears rolled down Eiko's face. She whispered in Azunese, "I wanted to return to Azuna because it was my first home. Because you were my first family. I w-wish—" She choked on a sob, hunching forward. "I wish I'd had more time with you."

Asami's breath hitched, and she, too, let out a sob. A nearby tree branch split with a loud *crack* and crashed to the ground. Asami pressed a hand against her mouth and shook under the force of a grief she couldn't properly vent.

There was at least one thing Angelica could do. She whistled, and a spark flew from her finger. It drifted to the collection of thin pine branches, which began to smoke and smolder. Eiko turned to Angelica with red eyes and nodded in gratitude. Angelica nodded back.

Right now, she was the only thing they had to hold on to, the one who had to keep them moving. She pitied them all the more for it.

Walking made their feet blister and bleed, but sleeping was worse. The ground was hard and cold, and the restless rustling of nature made Angelica paranoid, keeping her from dozing off. Whenever she did manage to snatch an hour or so of sleep, it was infused with nightmares. Eiko frequently woke up sobbing or screaming, and Asami went to sleep wearing her muzzle so that she wouldn't do the same.

None of them had provisions, and none of them knew how to forage. When they came close to a castle town, Angelica's cramps and the miserable groans of the girls' stomachs forced her to turn toward it.

Cosima stopped her. "You're an empress-snatcher, remember? I can go."

"I don't like asking you to steal over and over."

"I mean." Cosima shrugged. "It *was* my chosen career in Nexus."

"Did you actually choose it, or were you forced to?"

"I'm too hungry to get this deep, Mardova."

Eiko's eyes had been red since fleeing Mukan, and they settled on Cosima with the weariness of someone far older. "There aren't many Mariian immigrants in the countryside, even in the castle towns. I'll go instead."

"With what money?" Angelica demanded. When Eiko stared at the ground without answering, her gut pinched tighter. "*Eiko.*"

"What's wrong with begging?" Eiko asked. "What else can we possibly do?"

"You're a—" *You're an Ueda. You're a Mardova. You're from an imperial family and one of the great Houses. You do not beg.*

But being from a prominent family had no meaning out here, in nature's perilous grip. Angelica had never been so humbled.

Eiko stared at her, waiting for her reprimand and frowning when there wasn't one. Angelica forced herself to give a reluctant nod and turned away. Asami clung to Eiko's hand while Cosima gave her advice, only letting go when Eiko promised to return.

Angelica paced for what felt like hours. She grew so dizzy she had to lie down, staring up at a cloudless winter sky, the sunshine watery and thin. If she pressed her fingertips to the ground she sensed decay far underneath her, Vitae's end rising higher to the surface.

Calm down, said her mother's voice, familiar and unwelcome.

When Eiko returned, the sky was flushed pink with dusk, and the tight band around Angelica's chest eased.

"It's not as much as I wanted," Eiko said as she set down a bag. "But the story you told me to use worked well."

Cosima grinned. "Sometimes people need to be encouraged by a good tearjerker."

Angelica didn't want to know. When Eiko handed her a bun filled with vegetables, Angelica accepted it carefully. Before she could think better of it, she patted Eiko's shoulder.

"Good job," she mumbled.

Angelica walked off before Eiko could react, trying not to think about what she had just done or how Miko would react when she found out.

If they ever made it back to her.

They followed a river into some hills, the area rocky and quiet other than the steady, dull roar of a waterfall. After they soaked their aching feet, Angelica asked Cosima to help Asami gather firewood for their camp.

Once they were out of earshot, Angelica turned to Eiko. "You were right, before. About how I kept you out of things." Eiko straightened, surprised. "I thought it was for your own good, but here we are. And you've proved you're more than capable of handling it."

So Angelica told Eiko her plan.

"We're obviously going with you," Eiko said.

"I don't think you understand—"

"I understand that Nanbu Daiji killed my family. And that if you find what you're looking for at Mount Netsai, you'll have even greater power. Power to stand up to him."

Angelica laced her fingers together on her lap. "I'm not standing up to Nanbu Daiji."

Eiko stilled. "What?"

"These are Azunese politics. I'm a foreign diplomat, one who's been accused of a horrendous crime. I am not the person to fix this."

"Azunese politics? Are you calling the massacre of the imperial family—*my family*—nothing but *politics*?"

"That's not what I meant." Angelica clasped her hands tighter. "You know it's not. But this is...delicate. I came here looking for support for House Mardova, and now we're the enemy. If I get any more involved in this, it will mean war."

Eiko's breathing quickened. In fear, yes, but also rage, a familiar chord that harmonized with Angelica's. A hardened piece of her softened at the sound of it.

Angelica thought of the easy way Eiko and Asami touched one another. She reached out to take Eiko by the shoulders.

"If I can get hold of Deia's fulcrum, I can make a portal to home," Angelica explained. "I can bring you and Asami to safety."

The fury in Eiko's gaze cleared somewhat. She leaned into Angelica's hold. "Make a portal with kudei?"

"Yes."

"But doesn't Asami have kudei, too?"

"I am *not* bringing an adolescent girl to an active volcano. Besides, we're in Nanbu's territory. Mount Netsai is directly above the capital city."

Eiko's expression was steely with resolve. "We're going with you."

Angelica sighed and wondered if she had ever been this aggravating as a teenager.

You've been aggravating at all stages of life, said a voice in her head that sounded annoyingly like Taesia.

"We'll see," was all she could say.

When Cosima and Asami returned, Angelica led Asami down the riverbank near the waterfall. It wasn't yet dark, but the early evening was gray with clouds rolling in from the east. They gave off a faint whiff of snow.

Angelica told Asami to gather as many rocks as she could. Then they sat facing one another, just as they had in Asami's rooms at the palace.

"I'm going to be blunt with you," Angelica began. "I've never taught anyone before. This is something I haven't even learned myself, so it'll be...illuminating for the both of us. I just wanted to temper your expectations."

Asami sat on her knees, her muzzle off and her fingers fidgeting in her lap. She kept looking around, partly in awe of their surroundings, partly in wariness.

"There's no one else here," Angelica said. "You're free to do whatever you please. To do whatever makes you most comfortable." She gestured at the waterfall. "It's kind of like the water feature in your garden, right?"

Asami examined it with gleaming eyes, then gave Angelica a tenuous smile.

Angelica regarded the rocks between them. "I've been thinking about this. Speaking poetry didn't do anything, so we're going to try another approach." She swallowed. "We're going to try singing."

Asami perked up. She signed something, then remembered Angelica couldn't understand and dropped her hands.

"I know, Kazue said you weren't allowed. But..." *She's not here now.* "We're out in the open, so it's safe."

The girl bit her lip, either at the mention of Kazue or because she was remembering how her voice was capable of shattering more than rock.

"You remember how I said I use singing to channel aether? Kudei?" Asami nodded. "I think you'll have better luck with this method. I'll sing a bar, and then you'll sing it back to me."

It had been so long since she'd sung on a regular basis. She drew in a breath, but the first note caught between her teeth. It was only a simple bit from a lesser-known opera, but even this had turned razor-sharp in the shadow of nostalgia.

Will you sing for me tonight, Angel?

How was it still so painful all these years later?

Angelica curled one hand into a fist and allowed herself to sink into anger instead. Anger was safer, familiar, and helped her throat unclench to the point where she finally opened her mouth and gave voice to the song.

It wasn't enough to produce or alter anything, but the air grew warmer and the hairs on her arms lifted. She sang it again, easing into its comforting melody. Then Asami tried to echo it in her faltering soprano.

Three of the rocks exploded. Angelica gasped before she could rein it in, and Asami flinched back.

"No, it's all right! This is what's supposed to happen." Angelica's pulse sped up, excitement forming around her lingering grief. "Let's try one note at a time."

Angelica led her through a standard warm-up scale, taking mental note of which pitch did what. A whole C created a deep crack in one of the remaining rocks. A D-flat shook the ground beneath them. Their voices climbed steadily higher, not stopping even when the nearby water roiled and the closest hill groaned, until they reached A-sharp.

The air compressed the way it had during their first lesson. It drew Angelica in, purring in her chest and encouraging her to sing louder. Asami matched her pitch perfectly, gaze filming over.

It was the note Angelica had sung in the Mardova gardens. In the Bone Palace's courtyard. In the banquet hall.

She dug her fingers hard into her thigh and forced herself to stop. Asami did as well, panting harshly. Every gasp for air made the grass whip in agitation.

"I..." Angelica cleared her throat. "I think that's enough for today." At Asami's worried expression, she clarified, "I don't want to overwhelm you. This was a good start, though."

Asami nodded. She started to sign, then glanced over her shoulder at the waterfall.

"You can stay a little longer," Angelica said. "Think about what each note felt like. If you can limit those reactions to singing, rather than speaking."

While Asami sat by the waterfall, Angelica made her way back to camp. Low voices made her slow her approach, quieting her step. Cosima was sitting next to Eiko, the two of them with their backs to the river.

Angelica, encouraged to eavesdrop from an early age to gather information on the dons and doñas, crouched behind a nearby bush.

"—don't even know how to explain it," Eiko was saying. Her knees were drawn up, arms wrapped around her legs. "Especially when I'm here, it's...it's different than how it feels in Vaega."

"I get that," Cosima replied. "I haven't been back to Marii since I left. Honestly, I'm scared to. I'm scared of how much it's changed, that I won't recognize it—or that it won't recognize *me*."

"Exactly." Eiko hugged her legs tighter. "I'm worried that I'm now more Vaegan than I am Azunese. M-my cousins, they...they made fun of my accent. The w-way I'd forgotten certain words." She hiccupped, wiping at her eyes.

Cosima put an arm around her shoulders. "Take your time to mourn them. And your past life, or the part of you that feels like it's been lost."

"Do you feel like you've lost something?"

"All the time. I don't even know if I can speak Mariian anymore." Cosima gave a hollow laugh. "If I see my brother again, how are we even gonna talk? I can't speak Azunese. He probably doesn't know Vaegan. Fuck." She suddenly removed her arm. "Sorry."

"You can swear in front of me. I'm not an infant."

"No, I meant..." Cosima's shoulders drew inward. "My brother. He..."

He'd been the one to stab Kazue.

The two of them were silent a long time. Eventually Cosima made to get up, but Eiko touched her arm.

"His actions aren't yours," Eiko said quietly.

In profile, Cosima rubbed the back of her neck. "It's hard, being here. Knowing what this empire tried to do to my country. It made me hate Azuna for the longest time."

Eiko looked down. "I can't imagine. I'm sorry. For what it's worth, I'm glad the rebellion was successful."

"Shit, me too. But it doesn't change what happened. The things I saw when I was little." Cosima's voice grew detached. "I thought Koshi would feel the same. Would want to get revenge."

Eiko asked, "Is that what you want?"

Cosima was silent awhile before answering. "If that's how things worked, the whole world would be burning. Instead of having people suffer, I'd rather they take more responsibility to make up for what they've done."

Eiko murmured her understanding. Cosima patted her back, and Angelica remained where she was, quiet, thinking, until she spotted Asami returning. She left her hiding place to light the campfire.

By the time they lay down to sleep, Angelica was so cold she was shaking. She breathed steadily, getting her circulation to flow, but the wind coming off the river was brutal.

Something soft pressed up against her back. She stiffened and reached for a knife that wasn't there.

"S'just me," Cosima murmured sleepily. Her breath was hot behind Angelica's ear. "It's frostier than Thana's craw out here."

"What are you doing?" Angelica demanded in a whisper. The girls had fallen asleep, curled up together like cats beside the fire.

"Keeping warm." Cosima yawned and slung an arm around her, pulling Angelica's body flush against hers. "Now be quiet. Need my beauty sleep."

Angelica lay there fuming, her face flushed with blood that stung against the night air. "You didn't think to *ask* before you grabbed me?"

"Hm? Sorry, guess I assumed 'cause . . . y'know. Can I do this?"

The thought of sending her new source of warmth away made her grimace. But she wouldn't be a Mardova if she didn't first and foremost think of her pride.

"You're already here," Angelica muttered. "So you might as well."

Cosima's huff of laughter tickled her ear, sent goose bumps down her arms that had nothing to do with the cold. "Glad to hear it."

Cosima's chest rose and fell against her back. Angelica was acutely aware of all the places they touched, the way one of Cosima's legs had somehow slid between hers. Sleep was impossible, but now for an entirely different reason.

Angelica stared into the fire and tried to let her mind wander away from memories of their one night together. Cosima's breaths weren't evening out; she couldn't doze off either.

Finally Angelica asked, "What things did you see when you were little?"

Cosima's arm tightened. "You're great at small talk. And eavesdropping, apparently."

"You don't have to answer. I just—"

"No, look. It wasn't great. No matter how *civilly* they treated us, we were still the occupied, and they were the occupiers." She paused. "Soldiers would often collect taxes from those who barely made enough to get by. A farmer killed one of the soldiers who insisted on taking his goods as payment. He was executed the next day, and the soldiers wanted everyone to watch. To understand what would happen if we fought back. It didn't matter that there were more of us than them—we were made to feel helpless. Small."

"I'm sorry."

"Me too."

They fell into an easier silence. Angelica's body gradually relaxed, her hand drifting closer to where Cosima's lay under her chest.

"This's supposed to work both ways, you know," Cosima whispered into her hair. "You were upset about Eiko getting food. Wanna expand on that?"

Angelica did not. She did not want to examine the disquiet that had crouched behind her sternum—not at Eiko resorting to begging, but at the possibility of her being found. Taken. Hurt.

Cosima had revealed something of herself, but the idea of reciprocating sent panic fluttering through her, the channels between her thoughts and words barbed with thorns.

When Angelica stayed silent, Cosima sighed. "You gotta open up sometime, princess," she mumbled. "It'll kill you if you don't."

Angelica tried not to look at Cosima the next day as they left the river and continued north. She was distracted from last night's exchange by the aching of her feet, as if she walked over pieces of jagged glass rather than dirt and grass.

They were avoiding major roads, so she had no idea how far they were from Hitan. How far the news had spread, or if the Gojarin-Kae were scouring the land for them.

What do I do? she kept asking herself as she watched Eiko rub Asami's feet and wrap them in spare cloth. *What do I do?*

Eventually they found themselves on a narrow dirt lane overlooking pools of rice paddy fields. The water was murky and reflected the gray clouds, speckled with still-green rice shoots. A handful of workers waded knee-deep in it, collecting what was sure to be the last of this year's harvest. They sang as they went, and Angelica caught lines about thanking the earth and water.

Angelica's first thought was to get away before any of the workers spotted them. But Cosima nudged her and pointed to the edge of the field, below the road.

The workers had lined up their shoes. Sturdy boots made of cloth with rubber soles.

Angelica's feet throbbed. Without even pausing to think about it, she jumped off the side of the road to the ground below.

"Mardova!" Cosima hissed.

Angelica quickly and cautiously made for the boots, her focus narrowed. She wasn't the fastest nor the most inconspicuous, but this, at least, was something she could do.

She ducked behind one of the straggly trees along the edge of the fields. The boots were a few yards away. She held out a hand and tried to call on air.

It was *there*—she could sense it. But the yearning that crawled under her skin had no conduit for release, no tether between it and the wild, directionless pull of the wind. As always, the currents slipped through her grasp, unwilling to be caught.

Frustration lapped against her insides. She exhaled a small plume of smoke and shook out her hand, trying again. She whistled as softly as she dared without the sound traveling across the water.

At last a current snapped into place. One of the pairs of boots wobbled, then skidded over the ground. She whistled slightly louder and the air current lifted the boots higher, zooming toward her.

Before she could grab them, a strong, scarred hand closed around her wrist.

She whirled, unable to yank herself free. A large man constructed mostly of muscle and audacity blinked down at her, confusion etched into the divot between his brows. He was dressed like the harvesters, his trousers rolled up to the knee and a bamboo hat on his head.

"Well, this is new," he said in Azunese. "Never met a Vaegan boot thief before, let alone one who channeled elements."

Angelica was not proud to admit that she panicked. Opening her mouth, she breathed fire in the farmer's face.

He let go with a startled yelp and she took off for the ledge. With a whistle, the earth beneath her feet rose, lifting her back up to the road. Cosima and Eiko reached for her while Asami opened her mouth, ready to yell and cause a distraction.

Then the earth she had commanded dropped away from under her. Angelica fell back to the ground. Before she could recover, the sides of the ledge burst outward into sheets of rock and packed dirt, closing in around her and trapping her against the wall.

The farmer walked up to her, one hand extended. "Air, fire, *and* earth. That's a powerful combination." He spotted Cosima and the girls above and waved. "Hello, there. Are you boot thieves, too?"

Then he did a double take. He was no doubt studying Asami, taking in her likeness to Akane. He slowly regarded everyone again, landing last on Angelica.

"Please don't take offense," he said, voice dropped to a loud whisper, "but is Koshi a woman, now?"

No one said a word. Angelica stared at him, having absolutely no clue how to respond.

The one he'd been staring at wasn't Asami—it was Cosima.

"Did—did he just say my brother's name?" Cosima demanded, leaning out farther. She had a hand on the hilt of her sword.

"You know Koshi?" Angelica asked in Azunese.

"So that *isn't* Koshi?"

"What— No, that's his sister."

His hooded eyes widened and he snapped his fingers. "Little Veliane! But what are you doing all the way in Azuna?"

Before Angelica could suggest moving this conversation elsewhere, the sound of horses came from farther down the road.

"Gojarin-Kae!" Eiko warned above her.

Cosima cleared an inch of her sword. The farmer frowned at their reactions, looking between them and the approaching horsemen. Then, finally, something seemed to click.

A Mardova does not beg.

The farmer met her gaze. Angelica pressed her hands to the sheets of earth restraining her, knowing she could push them away and run, but with no guarantee of how far they would get.

A Mardova does not—

"Please," she whispered.

He only hesitated an instant before lifting his hand. The sheets of earth fell, freeing her.

"Come with me, boot thieves."

With the lightsbane shackles off, Taesia was immediately aware of the moment when her unconscious mind slipped toward Nyx's beckoning.

She opened her eyes to the lavender-tinged archway with its hanging moons. Before the god could move or even turn his head, Taesia flexed her fingers and a dagger formed in her hand. The same hand that was wrapped around the band of nightstone on Starfell's sheath in the waking world.

Pivoting on her feet, she plunged the dagger toward Nyx's chest. He caught her wrist effortlessly with one large, pale hand, the pointed tips of his claws pressing against the underside of her arm.

"Your little tricks do not work on me," he said. "Remember I have been inside your mind."

"Worth a shot." She tried to wrench her arm back, but he held it firm. "I doubt I can even kill you in this place. Unless dying in a dream makes you die in real life?"

"Absurd," he said. "Both the idea and your mindset. Why trouble yourself with killing me when you have ample reason to kill Phos instead?"

"Why not both?" She grinned at the way his ordinarily expressionless face tightened. Maybe she could find a way to annoy a god to death. "I have my powers back. I have my sword."

"Your sword," he repeated slowly, finally letting her go. As he did, the dagger she held turned into a replica of Starfell, glittering and vicious in the moonlight. "Made of an astralam's bones."

Starfell's weight in the waking world often required her to use two hands, but here, it was light as a feather. She swung it around experimentally. "The Lunari family's crown. You wouldn't happen to know—"

"IF IT CAME FROM THE SAME ASTRALAM? IT DID."

"Then how did the bones end up in Vitae?"

"I AM UNCERTAIN. BUT I KNOW OF THE CONNECTION BECAUSE I WAS THE ONE WHO SENT THE ASTRALAM DOWN."

Taesia stopped mid-swing. "So you *are* capable of helping, when you have a mind for it."

"I SENSE IN YOUR TONE YOU ARE TRYING TO DISCREDIT MY CHARACTER."

She took a step toward him, then thought better of it; he was very tall. "You keep bringing me to this place because you're too cowardly to show yourself in any physical way. Where even *are* you? Are you still in Noctus? Have you already withered away? That's the only thing I can think of that would prevent you from *doing something*. Your realm is being assaulted by Phos and you're wasting your time on *me*."

He wrapped one inhuman hand around Starfell's blade. It crumbled into shimmering dust, leaving only one vertebra in his palm. His cosmic eyes stared at it, or perhaps stared beyond it, back through time to their origin as a celestial body.

"THE CREATOR OF A WORLD DOES NOT HAVE SOLE RESPONSIBILITY OVER WHAT HAPPENS TO THOSE THAT DWELL IN IT," he said eventually. "THE FATE OF A WORLD RESTS IN THE HANDS OF ITS PEOPLE, NOT ITS GOD. GOODNESS, EVIL, CONSERVATION—THESE ARE COMMON THEMES IN THE PRAYERS I RECEIVE. BUT I DO NOT HAVE THE POWER TO GRANT THEM. THAT POWER LIES ELSEWHERE."

"Then what good are you?" Taesia spat. "Even if what you say has some truth to it, they're still your people! You have a duty to—"

"DUTY?" He crushed the vertebra in his hand to powder. "I FIND YOUR USE OF THE WORD IRONIC. YOU ARE ACTING QUITE SCORNFUL FOR ONE WHO HAS TURNED HER BACK ON HER OWN KIND. WHO STOOPED TO BLOODSHED AND AVOIDANCE, AS IF THAT WOULD FIX YOUR MORTAL CONCERNS."

The clouds were tinged scarlet, the full moon a bloody, glaring eye.

"THIS IS A CHANCE TO REDEEM YOURSELF," Nyx went on.

"Have you considered your plan is just bad?" With help from the nightstone, she re-created Starfell and pointed it at the god's face. "There's more than one threat, now. Are you aware that the Malum Star is dying?"

The clouds flushed to crimson. Taesia stalwartly ignored them, forcing herself to keep the sword point from wavering. As someone who had regularly gotten into arguments with her mother, she knew the best tactic was to suddenly shift the topic.

Apparently the tactic worked on gods, too, because he said, "I AM AWARE."

"Then what are you planning on doing about it?"

"THERE IS NOTHING I CAN DO. NOT WITHOUT YOU."

"Bullshit." Taesia pressed the swordtip to the god's throat. He did not move, did not bother to knock the sword away or crush it as he had before. He almost seemed resigned. "You are the god of Noctus, a deity of night and shadow. You're fully capable of protecting your realm from a cataclysmic event like this!"

The hall was drenched in red. It reflected within his eyes, along his hair, casting stark shadows over the planes of his imperfectly perfect face.

"NOT AS I CURRENTLY AM," he said in a soft, dark rumble that traveled through her like a vibration. Dark tendrils had begun to spiral off his shoulders, warping the edges of him. "YOU BELIEVE I MUST BE WITHERING AWAY? THEN YOU SHOULD FEEL SOME SATISFACTION IN KNOWING YOU ARE CORRECT. THE REALM IS DYING, AND I AM DYING WITH IT."

He took hold of Starfell again, forcing Taesia to puncture his throat. She tried to pull back, but her hands were fused to the hilt, burning cold.

"I, THE CREATOR OF THIS WORLD, WILL EVENTUALLY FACILITATE ITS DESTRUCTION." The blade pushed in deeper. From where blade met flesh trickled thick black blood, and flashes of silvery light erupted from under his skin. The cosmos of his gaze magnified, like meeting it would result in tumbling through the universe with no direction, left to suffocate between stars. "DOES THIS SEEM POETIC TO YOU? DOES IT SEEM JUSTIFIED?"

The blade was shoved in deeper, bursting out the back of his neck. The edges of him kept melting into shadow, twisting into a form large and monstrous, his face flickering between black and red. His eyes were far too large for his face, black and unseeing.

"AND YOU," whispered the shadows teasing around her, howls and wails coming from the encroaching darkness. "YOU, WHO KNOW BEST HOW TO RUN, WILL ALSO TURN YOUR BACK ON THIS WORLD. YOU, WHO HAVE THE MEANS TO STOP THIS DESTRUCTION, WILL ENABLE IT. YOU CANNOT STOP PHOS, STOP THE CATACLYSM, WITH YOUR POWER AND SWORD ALONE."

Taesia shifted her feet, widened her stance.

"Watch me."

She shoved the rest of the blade through his neck.

Taesia woke violently, choking on her own breath. The sheath fell from her hand as she pushed herself into a sitting position.

She was lying under a tree with shimmering silver leaves. Dim moonlight filtered through the black branches, faintly illuminating the rolling valley beyond the camp they'd made at the boundary of a thicket. The blanket of stars overhead seemed impossible, far too close for comfort.

Someone knelt beside her and steadied her shoulder. She shrugged it off, still jumpy, before realizing it was Lilia.

"You had a nightmare," the princess said. Her horns were limned in starlight, and if it wasn't for the glow of the waxing moon she would have been just another shadow. On her chest rested the sole astralam fang they possessed from the coronal, which Marcellus had made a necklace of using a strip of leather. It shone like a pearl against Lilia's dark clothes.

It reminded Taesia of the silver swirls spreading under Nyx's skin. Shivering, she braced her elbows on her thighs.

"You could call it that," she muttered. "I spoke with Nyx."

Lilia stiffened. Her eyeshine was more prominent out here in the perpetual night, rings of lavender like the clouds in Nyx's dreamscape.

"He spoke to you," she repeated slowly. "What did he say?"

"I asked for confirmation that the crown and the sword are connected." Taesia laid her fingertips on Starfell's sheath. "They are."

"Nyx ia sel," Lilia breathed. "Then we really can use one to find the other."

While Taesia's vision wasn't as attuned to the dark as the Noctans', it was far better than the average Vitaean's, allowing her to make out the crease between the princess's brows.

A crease formed by the question *Why does my god not speak to* me?

Honestly, Taesia wished he would bother Lilia instead.

"What else did he say?" Lilia asked. Behind her, Kalen and Marcellus were working at a small campfire to prepare what Taesia assumed was breakfast. Julian was still asleep.

Taesia decided not to bother rehashing the argument. "He says he can't help with the star. That he's dying along with the realm."

Kalen, obviously eavesdropping, froze in the middle of pouring herbs out of a sachet into a small beaten kettle. Marcellus was too busy singing a marching song under his breath to hear. Lilia whispered a quick prayer, pressing two fingers to the waxing crescent tattoo on her forehead.

"We must find the fangs as quickly as possible," Lilia said. "Even if it can't protect Noctus from a collapsing star, we can defend it from Phos until the last."

Taesia rubbed a thumb over the dry skin of her palm, the one that had been pressed to the nightstone. "Right," she mumbled.

The kettle could only make two cups of chori at a time. Kalen offered one to Lilia and one to Taesia, but Lilia insisted Taesia have the second as well, nodding pointedly in Julian's direction.

He had been quiet and distracted since leaving Astrum the day before yesterday. Taesia could tell the permanent darkness was getting to him, making both his sleep and waking hours difficult. So she took the second cup to where Julian lay curled under his thick cloak and gently shook him awake.

He came to with a start. For a second Taesia thought his eyes flashed green, but when he blinked, they were hazel.

Did Orsus maintain a grip on him here, so far from the Bone Palace?

Taesia placed the fragrant tea before him. "Pretend it's an early shift at the Hunters' compound and this is coffee."

Julian stared at her, at a loss, before he remembered where he was. He sat up with a groan, ruffling the back of his hair. The shaved undersides were growing long, not to mention his jaw was now dusted with stubble.

"It's so cold here," he croaked as he reached for the steaming cup. "And dark. I almost miss being in the palace."

"It was definitely warmer under the regime of a tyrant god," she agreed. She knocked their cups lightly together. "To the beginning of the end of the world, I guess."

Julian sighed and took a sip. Some of the strain melted from his face. "And here I thought you'd have more tricks up your sleeve."

"Who says I don't?" She considered whether or not to tell him about what Nyx had said to her. *Everything* he had said to her. But the image of the god as that monstrous shadow, impaling himself on Taesia's sword, stayed her tongue.

The message was not lost on her. *If you do not become a vessel for the power I have left, you will end up killing me regardless, and everything I have created.*

"What's wrong?" he asked in a tone she was coming to resent. It was far too tender to use on someone like her, who shredded soft things when they came close. She'd rather he spoke to her bluntly, acerbically, the way he had when they'd first met.

"Bad dream," she said.

He hummed in understanding, shifting to sit cross-legged. The Noctan cloak enveloped him endearingly. "It's hard to stay asleep out here."

"This might help."

Marcellus appeared holding out balls of sun lichen. Julian made a face but took his, popping it in his mouth and barely chewing before he swallowed hard.

"We probably don't have much left," Taesia said to the soldier when he offered her one. "I can last a while longer."

"If you're saving it for me, I'd rather you ate your share," Julian said.

"But I don't need it yet." Taesia lifted her hand, Umbra bouncing happily against her palm. "Shade, remember?"

Julian narrowed his eyes but didn't refute it. Truthfully, she was feeling some minor effects—her joints ached, though that could have been from her tussle with Phos—but she would rather save the lichen for Julian, who would feel the effects in full.

Breakfast was a mix of dried fruits and mushrooms. She let her familiar play with one of the bits of withered root vegetable that had snuck in there while the princess and her aides indulged in their chori.

Taesia sat apart from them, but she felt their glances as they spoke in low tones. No doubt discussing what could possibly be done about a dying god.

Let him die, Taesia thought. She tore into one of the strips of dried mushroom. *If he refuses to help his realm, his realm doesn't need him.*

Now more than ever she wished she could have learned more about fulcrums from Marcos Ricci's grimoire. If they could find Nyx's fulcrum, wouldn't that be enough to sustain Noctus without him? She didn't know. Everything she *did* know had been conveyed by Camilla, and half the explanation she could barely remember now due to the shock of seeing her aunt with a demon. Of the trust shattering between them like the glass mirror she'd been thrown into.

She tore a piece of dehydrated fruit into strips as the shadows whirled around her and Starfell thrummed. She wondered if it, too, was impatient to put an end to this.

"Did you get enough to eat?"

Julian settled on the ground before her. He held a small pot in his hands.

"Yes, Mother," she drawled.

Julian's mouth twisted. "Sorry. Habits and all that." He took the seal off the pot. "Sometimes when the languor gets really bad, my mother will forget to eat."

Taesia had met Marjorie Luca all of once, but the thought of the woman suffering left a worse taste in her mouth than the mushrooms.

"Hold out your arms," Julian instructed.

Taesia rolled up her sleeves and did so. The wounds around her wrists were red and irritated. Umbra zoomed over to inspect them before flying circles around Julian, urging him to hurry up.

Julian blinked at it, flinching away every time it came close to his face. "I don't think this thing likes me."

"*This thing* is named Umbra. And it's fine, it just worries." Taesia lifted an eyebrow at her familiar until it drifted to her shoulder, where it sulked. "A lot happened while it was gone."

Julian stared at the shadow familiar. "It's not an animal of any kind. I can't sense anything from it."

"Of course not, it's a *shadow*."

"But..." Julian sighed and gave up, digging two fingers into the jar and scooping out the medicinal salve. "Come here."

She grimaced when the cold salve touched her skin. It gave off the same earthy odor as breakfast.

"Don't tell me they put mushrooms in the fucking medicine, too," she muttered.

Julian focused on spreading the salve evenly as he replied, "They do. Kalen told me there are hundreds if not thousands of different species here, and some are used for healing. Apparently they used to import aloe from Vitae, among other things, but...you know how that went."

He held her hand as he rubbed in the salve. The rough calluses on his fingertips and palm caused friction against hers, belying the careful way he handled her. Yet both seemed to be the most truthful parts of him—a soft core surrounded by evidence of conflict and violence. This gentleness could almost be mistaken for fear, kept furled and heart-close.

In Astrum he had made a Conjuration circle, formed a stairway out of nothing but pure cosmic energy. His hands were forged by hostility but made for creation. Her hands had once been young and unscarred, before she learned how they could cut a life short. Before blood found its way under her fingernails and into the cracks of her skin. And yet still he touched them, something common and lovely meeting something haunted and holy.

"I'm sorry," she whispered. To the ground, to the night, to the version of herself she could never get back. "I'm sorry you got mixed up in all of this."

Do you resent me?

He paused with this thumb over her pulse. He pressed down, just slightly, as if eager to count her quickening heartbeats. It was more exposing than if she had simply stripped in front of him. She turned her face away.

"I would have gotten mixed up in it even if I hadn't met you," Julian said. "Not only because of what I am, but because of being in Nik's task force."

With great effort she pulled her hand out of his. Undeterred, he reached for her other wrist and scooped out more salve. This time its chill was welcome against her burning skin.

"It's odd," she murmured. "Hearing you call him Nik."

"Should I not?"

"No, I think he'd like it."

"I'm not so sure." Julian kept his head down, dark eyelashes shielding his gaze. "He knew there was something off about me. I think he distrusted me because of it. And he knew..."

This time he was the one who started to pull back. She reached out and gripped his forearm.

"Knew what?" she insisted.

His throat bobbed as he swallowed. "Knew we had encountered each other."

She sighed and let him go. "You weren't the only one he distrusted. The closer we came to Godsnight, the more opportunities there were to disappoint him."

He started tearing up a piece of cloth to use as bandages. "The bone dealer's shop. I saw Risha Vakara read the dead man's memories. And at the gala, you said it cost you something."

"It cost me her," Taesia admitted while Julian wrapped the bandages around her wrists. "And Nik. That was the night we..." She stopped before her voice could break, hardening the little ball of resentment she still carried from that horrific gala. The unwanted shame at Risha's disappointment. "Nik and I went our separate ways."

The bandage slipped from Julian's fingers. "You were—together?"

She pressed her lips together as she watched him process this, an emotional journey that went from surprise to unease.

"We had to keep it a secret," she explained. "You've seen the gossip rags your mother likes."

"Yes." He roused himself and went back to tying the bandage. "If I'm being honest, I sort of guessed, at one point, but— It's not my—" He stopped, took a breath, and finally knotted the bandage. "You still love him."

Taesia stared at her empty hand. Umbra floated into it, nuzzling her fingers. She smiled faintly, shutting out memories of a lattice window, a wide bed, soft laughter in the middle of the night.

"I love him the way the moon loves the sun," she said. "From a distance impossible to cross."

Before Julian could respond, a new shadow joined theirs. "I apologize for interrupting, but we should get going," Lilia said, one hand lying against the healing wound at her side.

Taesia was more than happy to cut their melancholy conversation short. She stood and picked up Starfell, unsheathing the sword with a delicious ringing sound.

She closed her eyes and held the sword out before her. The bones that made up the blade were somehow both darker and brighter under the Noctan sky, the expanse where it had been born.

I was the one who sent the astralam down, Nyx had told her. She found it odd, considering how unwilling he was to lift a finger now, as well as the relation between the coronal and the sword. Was it merely coincidence, a random fate designed by chance, or something more?

She let the questions go and focused instead on Starfell. A bright silver flame came to her awareness—the fang that hung around Lilia's neck. But there were more out there, waiting in the dark.

It took several minutes until the sword turned its tip west. The bones almost felt *alive*, like calling to like.

"That way," Taesia said.

IV

In a world of eternal night, there was no natural rhythm to follow, no rising and resting with the sun. Julian's body was constantly confused, constantly sore. The sun lichen helped a little, especially if he ate it right after waking up, but it couldn't stop the spinning of his mind—the bafflement of it being both nighttime and not, that he was awake and not, alive and not.

They traveled west, following the instinct of Taesia's sword. Lately Julian had been able to grasp a faint murmur emanating off the bones, like a heat echo. There had been times in the past when he could place his hand on a spot where a beast had rested and been able to identify what it was. He felt something similar here, as if by touching the blade he could picture the star-born animal it had come from.

He flexed the hand that had been holding Taesia's. Rubbed the pad of the thumb that had been pressed to her accelerating pulse. Its tempo had arrested him, something he could practically taste in his mouth.

Again he revisited the words they had exchanged, the brief baring of Taesia's soul as she'd confessed to her separation with Nikolas. It wasn't exactly a surprise, though it had sent him momentarily off-kilter. But once he'd recovered: relief, strange and unfounded.

It doesn't matter, he told himself as they discovered a narrow, serpentine river, its waters low. *Whatever you saw in that dream chamber isn't meant to come true.*

"You should clean your wound, Highness," Kalen said.

"Agreed. You and the others should wash up while you can." Lilia headed farther downstream, away from the group. Kalen made to go after her, but Marcellus stopped him with a touch on his shoulder. The astrologer frowned, ready to argue.

Taesia held out her hand. "Give me the bandages. I'll help her."

After a moment's consideration, Kalen rooted through his pack and slapped the roll of bandages into her hand, as well as the small jar of salve. "Don't use too much. And don't get any ideas."

"Oh please, we both know she's out of my league. Or I'm out of hers. Either way."

"Don't get your bandages wet," Julian reminded her.

Taesia flashed him a grin. "I'll do my best. Hey, princess, wanna wash my hair?" she called as she trotted after Lilia.

Kalen muttered under his breath and unfastened his cloak. Julian stared at the water, its current slow and unhurried. The banks were made of black sand, and all along the shore were small pointy rocks. He knelt to pick one up and was amazed to discover it was in the shape of a five-pointed star.

"Fossils!" Marcellus exclaimed. He picked one up, admiring the scoring along its surface. "I used to hunt for these when I was younger. My friends and I would trade them."

Marcellus pocketed some as Julian let the star he was holding fall back to the sand. It reminded him too much of the shape of a Conjuration circle, the kind meant to summon demons.

It was peculiar, he thought, how versatile and unique each circle was. The Conjurers in Nexus used a seven-pointed star to replicate necromancy. Their sigils had been different, too. And then there were the circles without stars, which instead bore four quadrants, much like the Four Realms.

At least here he couldn't hear Orsus or be subject to their pleas. Couldn't tap into whatever energy had caused that staircase to form.

Julian was not a Conjurer or a demon or the heir to a dead realm. He was a Hunter, a man from Nexus who missed his mother. Who missed his partner and the way Paris had gotten him to smile when he was in his black moods.

He pressed the heel of his palm to his eye until spots of red bloomed. Imagined it was the sun, coming to scorch Noctus into a ruin.

"You better take advantage of the water while you can," Kalen said nearby.

Julian lowered his hand. Marcellus had stripped to his underthings and was now standing knee-deep in the river, hunting for more fossils. Kalen knelt on the shore with his shirt off, water dripping from the long strands of his wet hair. He was lean whereas Marcellus was strapping, the latter's silver hair gleaming in the moon- and starlight. Julian respectfully moved his gaze elsewhere.

He hadn't had a proper wash in he didn't know how long. Although Kalen was right, it was far too frigid to shed all his clothing, so he took off his cloak and rolled his sleeves to his elbows to splash water on his face and through his hair. He gasped at the shock of it, waking him up far more than the tea had. Shivering, he turned to look downstream.

Lilia stood in the river washing Taesia's hair while Taesia sat on the bank. Taesia had taken off her shirt, leaving her in a plain breast wrap. Muscle rippled across her shoulders and down the smooth brown skin of her back as she straightened, tossing her wet hair over her shoulder and sprinkling Lilia with droplets. Taesia's laughter drifted through the air.

Julian forced his head down, scrubbing fingers through his hair and trying to smooth out the tangles. He didn't notice Marcellus approach until the man spoke.

"Is there a thing here?"

Julian started and looked up, water dripping down his nose. "What?"

Marcellus gestured between Julian and Taesia. "A thing? A...hmm. Kalen?" He switched to Nysari to ask a question, and Kalen responded in kind. "*Involvement?* Is that the word?"

Heat rose to Julian's skin despite his shivering. "Between—? No. No involvement." He fiercely pushed down the memory of the dream chamber.

The soldier frowned, almost pouting. He looked ridiculous standing in nothing but his underwear in the river—underwear that was now wet and clinging to him in ways that made the heat build higher. "Oh. But you—"

"Enough, Rhydian," Kalen snapped. "Stay out of others' business."

"Do you remember how there will soon be a collision of two black holes?" Marcellus said sweetly. "How we may all be murdered by Phos or wiped out from our realm getting knocked off the Cosmic Scale? Because I do. And I think we should be using what little time we have left wisely."

Kalen scowled. He was still shirtless, his hair loose and hanging on either side of his face. "And you're implying what, exactly?"

Julian could nearly *smell* the tension that hung between the two Noc-tans, both staring at one another with an intensity that came out of nowhere. Julian leaned back on his heels with the growing suspicion that perhaps this wasn't about him and Taesia.

"I'm implying nothing," Marcellus said breezily, turning back to Julian. "What's preventing you from involvement?"

The cold was getting painful, so Julian rolled his sleeves back down. "This isn't the situation you think it is. Really."

Marcellus crossed his arms. Julian wished he would put his clothes back on. "You've had involvements before, haven't you?"

Julian froze, and Kalen sighed.

"Stop it," the astrologer said. "You're making him uncomfortable. Who cares if he hasn't had a lover before?"

"I—" Julian cleared his throat. "I didn't say that."

"So you *have* had one?" Marcellus asked.

Julian considered flinging himself into the river. He hadn't discussed something like this since Paris had brought it up in the first days of their partnership, relentlessly hounding Julian about what his type was, want-ing details about his love life, until Julian had given him the truth: There wasn't one, and never had been.

It wasn't that having an intimate relationship was something he didn't want—it was just something he'd never needed or sought. He'd thought about it, certainly, and had had plenty of opportunities he could have pursued. Paris had never let him live down the moment when a fellow Hunter had come on strong—"on the verge of throwing himself in your lap right then and there," Paris had insisted—only for Julian to be com-pletely oblivious and miss what Paris had termed "at least a four-star romp."

But Julian had wanted to focus on other things besides *romps*. Even now, facing down death and annihilation, there was no room or breath to consider a future with someone at his side, let alone consider having a future at all.

That's not true, came a traitorous whisper he immediately strangled.

"It's not important," he said stiffly. He reached for his cloak and draped it over his shoulders, gratefully hiding within the fall of fabric. He used a corner of it to scrub his hair dry. "Please don't ask again."

Marcellus looked a bit taken aback, even sheepish. He mumbled an apology and finally waded out of the river to retrieve his clothing. Kalen watched him with narrowed eyes, tracing a slow journey down his body before reaching for his shirt.

"Mood's tense over here," came Taesia's voice above him. Both she and the princess had returned, Taesia's hair twisted into a braid. "Everything all right?"

Julian stood and dusted the sand off his cloak. "Everything's fine." Taesia's shadow familiar orbited his body a couple times before nestling under his chin. Feeling Marcellus's gaze on his back, Julian gently pushed the familiar back toward its master and turned away. "I'm ready whenever you are."

"This looks familiar," Taesia said. They were far from the river now, facing a wide plain with long grass that rippled in the wind. "I've seen it before."

"How?" Lilia asked.

"My younger sister is a dream walker. She was having dreams of Rian—of Phos."

Kalen's eyebrows rose. "Dream walkers are very rare."

Something like pride flitted across Taesia's expression. "It took her a long time to realize what her powers were," she admitted. "But once she did, she was able to bring me into her dreams. Everything was hazy because Phos was trying to shield Rian from us, but this is definitely the place where we saw him." She turned halfway, eyeing Astrum in the distance. "I remember seeing the city from here. And there was..."

She hurried on ahead. As they crested a small rise, she held up a hand.

"Slowly," she warned.

Julian crept up beside her and his heart sank. A large Conjuration circle was burned into the earth a quarter mile from where they stood. All around it were large, shadowy structures that took a minute for him to recognize. There was the arch of Lune Bridge, the bronze statue from the university, the Four Gods fountain, and the marble monument from Haven Square.

He shuddered at the memory of Haven Square, a night of chaos and confusion, of witnessing Conjuration firsthand while revealing to Nikolas that he was far from an ordinary Hunter. His fist had punched through debris like it was sand, a show of strength he hadn't known existed within himself.

It was hard to believe now, when his body was sore and aching and so very easy to break.

His attention slid from the monument to the dark figures prowling beyond the circle. A quick prod with his power revealed they weren't beasts.

In fact, they weren't even alive.

"What are they?" Lilia whispered.

Taesia nodded to the circle. "Remember how I said Phos was killing travelers to fuel his Conjuration circles? Their bodies have been abandoned for so long their spirits grew a mind for vengeance." She swore. "The dead really are rising everywhere."

"Is this a common problem in Vitae?" Lilia asked, horrified.

"Unfortunately. You haven't seen this in Noctus yet?"

"We burn our dead," Kalen said. "And display the ashes in amazonite containers where they can receive offerings on a regular basis. Even criminals or those who die without family are afforded funerary care and tended to in archives. It keeps the spirits soothed."

"Risha often said we needed to start burning our dead," Taesia murmured. "Considering how long they've been sitting out here, they'll probably be violent." She eased Starfell out of its sheath. "And guess where our fang is."

"Of course," Julian muttered. He could hardly take his eyes off the circle, even with the dead Noctans shuffling around it. The longer he studied its construction, the more it seemed to come into focus, to make *sense*. Like he was a child again sitting at a small desk, sounding out the letters of the alphabet until gradually they formed a sentence he could understand.

This was a circle for connecting the realms, to tap into quintessence. Although the circle had already been used, residue clung to the symbols and glyphs, smelling of smoke and verdant valleys, of rainfall and tanned leather.

And within that: the faint pull of the astralam fang, an echo of heat and bone.

He wasn't aware of moving forward until Taesia stopped him. Their eyes locked, and whatever Taesia found in his made her nod before turning to the others.

"I'll go," she said. "The rest of you stay here."

Lilia touched the fang resting on her chest. "I'm going with you."

"And me," Marcellus said.

"The dead are going to attack," Taesia said. "Will you be able to strike down your own people?"

Lilia held out a hand and her shadow familiar unraveled into a long whip. "I will give them proper funerals later. Right now, we need that fang."

"Good to know you can get your hands dirty, Highness," Taesia said with a wink.

"Are you . . . teasing me?"

"Sort it out afterward," Marcellus butted in, unsheathing his sword as he walked toward the dead. His blade was made of black steel, the pommel shining with a round moonstone.

"For once he's right," Kalen said. His own familiar extended into the shape of bolas. So this was how their dynamic worked: Marcellus and Lilia engaged in melee, with Kalen as the ranged defense. "Aren't you going with them?"

Again, Julian and Taesia exchanged a look.

I don't want to find out what the circle does to me.

"Someone has to protect you." Taesia smirked at Kalen before she turned away. Kalen *humph*ed, clearly skeptical of Julian's ability to protect anyone.

Julian wished for his longbow. Although he would be competent enough with the dagger the Noctans had given him, he didn't want to chance getting too close.

Not after what he'd done in Astrum. Not with the possibility of hearing Orsus again.

It wasn't long before the dead realized there were living beings coming toward them. Their aimless meandering turned to a furious running, their screeches echoing down the valley, layered over one another in a terrible chorus. Kalen flinched beside him.

"They're . . . monstrous," he breathed as Taesia, Lilia, and Marcellus rushed forward. "You dealt with this regularly in Nexus?"

"Yes." Julian watched Taesia rend through a Noctan's decaying torso. She was just as much a sight as she'd been at the Godsnight Gala, surrounded by broken corpses and Don Soler's blood clinging to the chain mail links of her dress. "There were those who used these circles to mimic necromancy. They raised many of our dead."

Kalen nervously tracked Lilia and Marcellus's movements. Marcellus was a born and raised soldier, his sword forms immaculate, his footwork demanding yet precise. Lilia was a force of brute strength behind him, wrapping her whip around a body's neck to behead it before turning with a broad stroke and laying out the two corpses approaching from behind.

Julian knew all three of them were competent—even Kalen, who spotted a corpse running toward Marcellus and threw his shadow bolas in time to tangle its legs and send it crashing to the ground—but his heartbeat had settled at the base of his throat, the taste of dread rising sharp and acidic.

Taesia ran into the circle, toward the call of the fang. More figures lurched out from behind the monuments. The dead were numerous, unending—Phos's victims eager to get their revenge on whatever stood living and breathing before them.

They would overpower her.

He was in motion before he realized what he was doing. The closer he came to the circle, the more that divine essence reached for him with grasping, greedy fingers. Back in Nexus, touching a circle gave him visions, vertigo, the sense of falling even with his feet firmly on earth. But now he sensed the millions of threads that made up its shape, the twisting, always-moving substance that had once sprouted from the heart of their universe.

No—from a storm, a tempest of rage and heat and joy that had been cradled between hands that were not hands, twisting the fibers together like cotton being spun into yarn. Lines and circles and the shapes between them, sigils of strength and divinity, of common earth and uncommon magic.

Those fibers tangled in his veins, those fibers *were* his veins, crying out for whatever residue clung to this bit of enchanted and desecrated land.

He reached for the circle with a tingling hand, warmth shooting up his arm and pulsing at the back of his skull. Through the air he sketched a circle and then another within it, sounding out the sentence that spelled *death*, drawing it with a seven-pointed star.

Taesia stumbled to a halt when the dead surrounded her, shadows writhing at her shoulders. Starfell gleamed as it rose and fell, slashed and destroyed. Claws reached for her neck.

Julian flung the circle out. It glowed red and malignant as it expanded, layering itself over Phos's circle, casting a crimson pall over everything. As soon as the circle slid into place the corpses froze. Only their screeching continued, sharp as a knife to his eardrums.

"Score it!" Julian shouted.

Taesia swung Starfell at the ground, slashing a line along the outer circle's perimeter. As soon as she did, the red glow faded and the corpses collapsed into heaps of bone and rotting flesh.

The silence was deafening, and no one moved for a good while.

Then Taesia staggered farther into the circle and bent over. When she straightened, she held an astralam fang in her palm, its silvery sheen mirroring the solitary falling star that streaked above their heads.

Julian's relief was short-lived. A hand grabbed him by the collar, turning him around with a violent shake.

Kalen's eyes burned into his. "What," the astrologer snarled, "are you?"

V

When Brailee surged awake, Dante sat on the inn's creaky bed beside her.

"Bee?" He laid a hand on her shoulder. "You're here with me in Seniza. You're all right."

She blinked a few times, sluggishly coming back to herself. On the bed across from them, Saya anxiously tapped her fingers against her knees.

"I found him again," Brailee mumbled, sitting up. "It was like the dreams I'd had of him before, but much clearer." She paused to yawn into her elbow. "I could *see* him, but I couldn't get close. He was in the throne room of the Bone Palace."

"Was he being controlled by Phos?" Dante had asked.

"Yes...and no. It's like the more time I spend with him, the more times I find him, the more I end up finding *Rian* and not Phos. This time, I was able to hear him talking. Something about how Phos had spoken to him in the basilica when he was ill. But then Phos realized what was happening and kicked me out again."

"Don't overdo it. I don't want him hurting you."

"Phos can't hurt me in dreams." She said it so confidently that Dante almost smiled. "And besides, the more we can separate Rian from Phos, the better."

"Not at the expense of you dying from exhaustion."

Brailee rolled her eyes. This time Dante did smile. "How can I die of exhaustion if I'm asleep all the time?"

"You're not really sleeping, though," Saya piped up behind them. "You're expending energy."

Brailee narrowed bleary eyes at her. "Traitor."

"We can wait another day for you to try again," Dante said even as the impatience in him pinched harder. "I can investigate more in the meantime."

His sister stubbornly shook her head. "We're wasting too much time. We need to find Aunt Camilla."

Dante agreed, but the bags under her eyes were puffy and bruised, her face sallow with fatigue. He wanted to tuck her back in for a few hours of real rest, and momentarily grappled with the idea of using compulsion on her to do so. Azideh stirred in interest, but Dante firmly squashed it down.

"Then at least let me help," Dante said. Brailee considered it, then scooted over to make room. "Saya, you're on guard duty."

Saya wiggled her fingers, and shards of bone rose from the bedspread. "Got it."

Dante spread out next to Brailee, ignoring the demon's grumbling that it didn't like this method.

"Well, *someone* couldn't sniff out my aunt's demon today, could he?" Dante muttered. "Even though you said you could."

I said I might. It's not my fault Shanizeh disappears so easily.

"What's your friend saying?" Saya asked. While Dante was certain Risha would have been appalled by the news, Saya had been fascinated when Dante explained the demon. Endless questions had followed: "What does he look like?" "Does he have an accent?" "Is Azideh *actually* his name, or is it a moniker the way bards choose something flashy for themselves?"

"Same old bullshit." He watched Nox twirl around Somnus, Brailee's eyelids fluttering closed. "Remember, don't answer...the door..."

Brailee's sleep extended through their familiars' connection and into him, and he was dragged back to that mesmerizing universe of color. He was nothing more than a hanger-on, following Brailee's charge as she swooped in amid bright sceneries and vivid sounds and tantalizing scents. Her consciousness turned this way and that, seeking.

Aunt Camilla, he heard her think. *Ivy choking her house. The smell of sherry. The shade of green in her living room. Her favorite Azunese fan. The romance books she lent me. Her loud, contagious laugh.*

The memories pained him as much as they pained her, brushstrokes forming the portrait of a woman they both loved and hated. One of the threads flew toward them, giving off the smell of sulfur and an image of a familiar basement.

There!

Brailee grabbed the thread and pulled. The colors dissolved into a dreamscape, her feet landing on the cold, dark stone of Prelate Lezzaro's safe room underneath his rectory. His body lay sprawled in the middle, neck bent at an alarming angle. Their aunt stood over it.

She did not look satisfied. She looked like she would be sick.

Once Brailee appeared, Camilla's gaze snapped up. The hardness in her bright eyes diminished to confusion.

"Bee?"

Brailee covered her mouth at the sight of Lezzaro's body, looking just as it had the night Dante had found his aunt and her demon. Camilla quickly stood between it and Brailee, cloak swept out to better hide it from sight.

"Don't look," their aunt ordered. "You're not supposed to be a part of this."

A figure morphed into being beside Brailee, and Dante was disoriented to look up at himself—or rather, his aunt's mental image of him, younger than he actually was and frowning in disapproval.

"Neither of you were supposed to be part of this," Camilla said. "Or Taesia. I was going to *fix* things. I was going to keep you *safe*."

"How was framing Dante supposed to keep him safe?" Brailee demanded.

Something shifted in Camilla's eyes. She looked around suddenly, as if she were being watched.

"Damn it," she hissed. "*Damn it*, this is you, isn't it?"

Lezzaro's body suddenly contorted. It crawled with inhuman speed to grasp onto Brailee's ankles while the dreamscape unraveled. Camilla turned and jumped through a yawning seam between stone.

Follow her!

Brailee waved her hands and turned the prelate's broken body into a patch of grass. She ran and jumped through the seam just before it closed. She landed on the floor of a busy wine shop, overrun with patrons and their noisy chatter. Across the room, Camilla weaved through the crowd in an effort to lose them.

"Stop her!" Brailee cried.

All talk ceased as the patrons turned to Camilla with blank eyes. She swore and opened a door in the back, closing it behind her with a loud *bang*. Brailee tried the door—locked. Instead of making a key, she merely waved her hands again and the door became an archway of gleaming pearl. It led to the next dreamscape, a stretch of beach along a stormy coastline.

Camilla knelt in the sand, hands held to her stomach. When Brailee got close, she gasped; their aunt wasn't only younger in this dreamscape, but her stomach was swollen with child.

"I thought it would change something," Camilla whispered as the sea raged, the waves arcing higher and higher. The briny wind was so loud they could barely hear her next words. "I thought it would change *me*. But nothing changed. He sent me here to grow a whole new life, and when I returned, that life was taken from me. What was the point?"

A wave crashed onto shore. Brailee's arms flew up to shield her face against the shower of seawater, stinging cold through her sleeves. "Aunt Camilla?"

"What was the *point*?" Camilla screamed.

The scream echoed across the water like the aftershocks of an earthquake. The waves rose into a typhoon, casting a growing shadow over the beach. In the shadow Dante thought he glimpsed the shape of a crown.

Brailee planted herself in front of Camilla and reached for the universe of dreamscapes, stretching and playing with reality the way a child tested the durability of a new toy. Underneath her frantic movements came the steady thrum of alarm while the massive wave loomed closer, seeking to devour, to pull them into this ocean of despair and let them drown.

I won't let you.

The wall of roaring water exploded into a flurry of cherry blossom petals, pink and delicate, falling all around them as sunlight broke through the storm clouds.

How did you do that? Dante asked, awed. She had done something similar when she and Taesia had visited his dreams.

So long as someone's dreamed it, I can access it. Brailee closed and opened her hand. *But maybe I can dream things no one else has, too.*

When she turned, Camilla was staring at her. Her stomach was no longer distended; the child that had once occupied it now lay in her arms, unbelievably small and fragile.

"He's mine," Camilla growled. "Even if you take him away, he'll return to me one day. We will both see you fall. I swear it."

She thinks we're someone else, Dante said. *Can you shift the dreamscape to the Lastrider villa?*

Before Brailee could do so, Camilla sank under the sand, leaving nothing but disturbed ripples in her wake.

"Damn!" Brailee let the sand take her, too, the universe quivering with potential until they were spat out onto...

Another beach.

Here, the sand was black under the moonlight, the water lapping gently along the curved shoreline. There were chaise lounges set up along the stretch of beach, many covered with umbrellas made of palm fronds. In the distance was the hulking silhouette of Deia's Heart, and much closer, the outskirts of Seniza.

"I can't shake you, can I?"

Camilla stood behind them, a piece of broken glass in one hand. She was no longer young and pregnant, her earlier rage dimmed to coals that smoldered behind her eyes.

"I suppose this was meant to be," their aunt sighed before fitting the glass to her throat. "Don't worry, I won't run. I think it's about time we talked."

"Wait—!"

Brailee surged forward, but Camilla was faster, slitting her throat and severing her connection to the dreamscape. It shuddered all around them, threads unraveling back into the universe of color, carrying the shade of their aunt's blood with them.

Dante jerked awake and accidentally smacked Brailee. She grunted and weakly shoved him away as their familiars untangled. Across the room, Saya started and bone shards fell in a clatter to the floor.

Dante sat up, a hand held to his racing heart. Brailee took several deep breaths. They exchanged a bewildered look.

"What happened?" Saya demanded. "Did you find her? Where is she?"

"She's..." Dante blinked several times to process what they'd seen. "She's at a resort."

It was about ten in the morning by the time they walked all the way across the city and to the Blast Resort, a flock of cabanas and chaise lounges spread over black sand before a complex of buildings where guests stayed. Parrots and seagulls perched on terra-cotta roofs above white stucco walls, the structure of the resort breezy with ornate archways.

She is here, Azideh grumbled. *Toward the water.*

"Wait," Saya said. "Your aunt's been staying *here* while we're stuck in a dingy little inn? We could have had *this* the whole time?"

"Maybe you've forgotten my brother is a fugitive," Brailee said.

Saya's outrage deflated. "Oh. Right. But wait, your aunt is, too, isn't she?"

"Yes and no." Dante walked past the complex and toward the cabanas with their gauzy curtains pulled back to let the morning sun spill through. "*We* know she killed Prelate Lezzaro, but no one else does. Actually, I'm willing to bet no one in Seniza even knows her name or her face, since she's not an actual member of a House."

But once he brought her back to Nexus, their roles would be reversed, and she could learn the madness of a solitary cell—how the darkness was its own living thing. Even here, under the sun, Dante shivered at the reminder of that crushing isolation.

A familiar voice came from one of the cabanas.

"—said I wanted this *chilled*, not *slightly cooler than room temperature.*"

Dante rounded the cabana. There was Camilla, reclining on a lounge, in a simple linen dress with a book lying facedown over her stomach. She held a glass of something bubbly, which she handed back to the slim young man dressed in a server's uniform. He took it and bowed.

"Of course, my lady, I'll have this chilled for you at once!"

Camilla smiled indulgently and patted his hand. "There's a good boy."

The server took off, and Camilla sighed dramatically while turning to them. "Why is it they're either eager to please or competent, but never both?" She looked Dante up and down. "It took you far longer to get here than I thought. I've already eaten most of my breakfast." She gestured at the platter on the wicker table beside her, holding leftovers of poached eggs in tomato sauce with semolina cakes. "Want some? I can ask for seconds. Gabriel won't charge me, the poor dear is smitten."

Dante didn't respond. He looked from her book—the cover illustration of a woman swooning in a Noctan man's arms—to the remains of her breakfast to the faint cloud of crimson hanging around her. Azideh snarled in the back of his mind, his own dark cloud bristling around Dante's body.

Camilla noticed and smiled wryly. "I take it these two don't care much for each other. Shanizeh says yours smells like burning fur."

I do not, Azideh grumbled.

Seeing that Dante wasn't about to talk, Brailee stepped forward. "Aunt Camilla..."

At her plaintive tone, Camilla's smile dropped. "Yes, I know. You want answers. You want *revenge*." She eyed Dante. "I understand the feeling."

Saya spoke up. "We'd also like to know where the...the corpse is?"

Camilla raised an eyebrow at her. "Of course you brought a Vakara with you. It shouldn't surprise me we ended up having similar plans."

The server returned, breathlessly presenting a new glass of pale, bubbly liquid to Camilla. "Here you are, my lady! Please let me know if it's to your satisfaction."

Camilla took a sip and gave an appreciative moan that made Dante grimace and the server flush, the latter's mind spiraling into pink pleasure. "It's perfect, Gabriel. Remember this for tomorrow morning, won't you?"

"Yes, my lady!"

With her drink procured, Camilla picked up her book and rose to her feet. "Come along, children."

She led them back to the complex, to one of the outer buildings. "How did you end up here?" Brailee asked, fingers nervously twirling around her braid as they passed an artfully arranged succulent garden. "And how can you afford it?"

"Please. This place is for people who want to believe they have money to spend. I mean, *the Blast Resort*? What fool thought up that name?" Camilla took a long sip of her drink. "If I had my way, I'd be staying at the Gilded Frond one beach over. They have a *spa*. I could be getting a nice oil rub. But the risk of being spotted by one of the nobles is too great." She heaved a sigh. "So I'm stuck in this prison instead."

At the word *prison*, Dante flinched.

I can wring her neck, Azideh offered.

"No."

Bash her head against the ground?

"No."

Toss her into the big sheet of water?

"The *ocean*?" Dante clarified. "No."

"Dear, please communicate with your demon silently," Camilla said over her shoulder. "We'll attract looks. Then again, you haven't had him for very long, have you?"

"Let's maybe focus on Marcos Ricci before we discuss demons," Brailee suggested as they approached a door at the end of the last building. Above it was a wrought iron balcony and a window facing the city its drapes closed. "Or what we're going to do about clearing Dante's name."

"Practical as ever." Camilla smiled at her niece before she unlocked the door and held it open. "Welcome to our dreadful excuse of a suite."

" 'Our'?" Brailee repeated. When she stepped inside, she froze. "Oh."

Dante hurried in behind her. Seated on white couches in the main room were the four Conjurers he had spotted in the necropolis, skull masks tossed onto the table before them.

At their entrance, all four stood. One of them, a short Azunese woman, curled her hands into fists. Her mood bloomed red and belligerent, and Dante caught the tail end of a thought without words that mostly consisted of his name with spikes around it.

"It's all right, Natsumi," Camilla said, closing and locking the door behind them. Trepidation skittered across Dante's shoulders even though he knew he could easily smash through the door with Azideh's strength. "I did tell you my family would come to see us."

Natsumi was not mollified. "Are you sure they can be trusted?"

"Can you ever really trust anyone in this world?" Camilla polished off her drink and set the empty glass on the table. "Besides, they've brought us a gift."

She gestured to Saya, who lifted a hand in uneasy greeting. "Hello?"

The Conjurers murmured in surprise. "A Vakara?"

"Is this a trick?" Natsumi demanded. "Because the last Vakara we worked with not only threatened to give us up, but *disappeared* with our actual leader." She shot Dante an accusing glare, like this was somehow his fault.

"So Risha *was* working with you?" Saya said sharply.

"I'm sure you have a lot to catch up on while I speak to my niece and nephew," Camilla said. "Oh, but first, you should probably take a look at the body."

They were led to a smaller room where the body was shrouded with a plain white cloth. Camilla pulled the sheet down. The room's window was covered, emitting only a dim light, but Dante had no trouble taking in the rictus face of Marcos Ricci. He looked the same as he had the day he'd been pulled from his tomb, skin sunken under the unique methods of preservation that had been invented by some of the earliest Vakaras.

Azideh made a pondering noise. Before Dante could ask what he'd sensed, Camilla gestured for Dante and Brailee to follow her, leaving Saya and the Conjurers to examine the corpse. They were taken up a flight of stairs to a large bedroom, where Camilla opened a set of double doors leading to the balcony. A gentle breeze fluttered the white curtains as Camilla sat in one of the wicker chairs opposite the bed.

"Terrible, isn't it?" she drawled when they looked around the room. "I don't even get an ocean view."

"Enough," Dante snapped. "We came here for answers, and we're getting them."

"I already told you why you were framed," she said calmly. "I wanted to keep you out of the way. You should have known I'd never let you hang, Dante."

"Keep me out of the way while you summoned *every demon possible* to Nexus?"

"That wasn't my intention."

"But it was a consequence of trying to bring the Ostium fulcrum to Vitae. You *knew* that—Prelate Lezzaro warned you against it—and as soon as he threatened to stop you, you killed him." His hands were shaking, the resentment that had been building for weeks finally breaking through its dam. "But you don't care about consequences. You don't care about *us*, or else you would have never sent me to that fucking gods-awful place!"

His voice rose to a throat-scraping shout. Brailee hunched her shoulders, and all chatter in the room downstairs quieted. Dante fought for breath, sensing intimately how much space was between him and the walls of the room, too numb to feel Nox squeezing his wrist.

Camilla stood and guided him to the open doors. He almost winced away from the sunlight, but the fresh breeze was welcome.

Camilla held his face between her hands. "I'm sorry," she said, uncomfortably solemn. "In my mind, things worked out differently. I would be free to operate as I pleased while you were kept out of the way of House affairs. I had a feeling Ferdinand would attempt something around Godsnight, and I was right. I'd hoped to cause a sufficient distraction with summoning the Ostium fulcrum, but I see the gods had a plan of their own."

"Whatever Phos did to take away the Bone Palace, it took Taesia along with it," Brailee said. "We wanted to reanimate Marcos Ricci and ask him if there's a way to find her through Conjuration."

"To find her using this," Dante added, taking out Angelica's sketch.

After studying it a while, Camilla handed it back. "That's also why I recruited the Revenants and came here. I scoured the grimoire cover to cover, but there was nothing about a circle with that sort of capability."

Dante's stomach knotted. "You still have the grimoire?"

"Of course I do. I'm also smart enough to not tell you where it is." Camilla returned to her wicker chair and nodded to the other one. "Sit."

Dante gestured for Brailee to take the chair while he continued to stand near the balcony. The sunlight seared the chill from his bones, helped him think more clearly.

"I never knew *why* you wanted the Ostium fulcrum," he said. "Were you that hungry for power? Or..."

He thought back to the dreamscapes, of seeing a younger version of his aunt holding an infant. He thought of Godsnight and her look of horror when she'd laid eyes on someone in the courtyard.

I will always put my family first.

"You had a child," he said quietly. "That no one knew about."

She stared at the far wall with a furrowed brow. Her fingers twitched as if wanting another drink.

"A long, long time ago," she said, "Ferdinand was wracked with grief over the death of his wife. Every noble you can possibly name tried to console him in their own ways. Eventually, my method of consolation ended with me in his bed. Not just once, but a few times. And wouldn't you know it, one of those times proved one too many."

She held a hand to her stomach, like there was still something there for her to protect. "I was a Lorenzo. Surely that was enough to become his second wife, or even a consort? But no. He was furious that the pregnancy happened out of wedlock, that the child would be a bastard like the House founders and possibly give the Houses something to war over. He had me sent away to Cardica until I gave birth."

"The year you spent abroad," Brailee realized.

"Yes. He..." Their aunt's voice faltered, and they waited almost a full minute before she could go on. "My son was taken from me. We were put on separate ships to return to Vaega. I fought, I screamed, I pleaded, I harmed myself, but every answer was the same: I had to give him up, or there would be consequences. I wasn't stupid—I knew Ferdinand was threatening not only me, but all of you. For years afterward I made sure to hire guards, certain Ferdinand would concoct some mysterious accident for me. There were a couple times I swear he came close.

"I was never allowed to see my son. All I was told was that he would become the next ruler of Vaega, but I knew what was required for that to happen. Now do you understand why I tried to keep you out of Ferdinand's line of sight?"

"No, I don't," Dante said. "Why did you never tell anyone? Tell our father, tell *us*? We could have helped you."

"How?" she demanded.

He stayed quiet. She snorted softly.

"Exactly. I had to content myself with hoping to see my son from afar, attending every single ball and gala I could to catch even the faintest glimpse. Of course Ferdinand hated that, but he couldn't do anything about it or else risk the dons and doñas gossiping about why he forbade me from attending." She smiled humorlessly. "Seeing the irritation on his face whenever I showed up was one of the only things that made it bearable."

"Aunt Camilla..." Brailee reached out and touched her hand. "I'm so sorry. You shouldn't have had to go through that."

Camilla turned her hand over to hold Brailee's. "You've always been too sweet for your own good, Little Bee."

The sun was beginning to burn. Dante moved away from the balcony and toward his aunt. "Then you weren't trying to get the Ostium fulcrum for yourself. You were getting it for him. Your son."

"Yes. I knew he had earth magic—I had some eyes and ears in the palace who I paid *criminally* well—so I knew he was capable of harnessing it. Of becoming powerful enough that the people of Vaega, a so-called Holy Kingdom, would look upon a prince turned mortal god and fall to their knees in devotion." Camilla spread her hands as if to some invisible, worshipful crowd. "Ferdinand would die, and the Houses would be allowed to exist without feuding over the throne. But that plan failed. And now he's gone. Taken from me *again*."

"Gone?" Brailee repeated.

"He was at the Bone Palace," Dante explained. "Same as Taesia."

Camilla looked up at him. "I'm aware you may not want to forgive me, nor am I asking you to. But we have a common goal. We need to work together to achieve it."

The demon in him growled, and he was predisposed to agree. This woman, his own family, had forsaken him to further her agenda. Had taken away his freedom to secure power for her clandestine son—his cousin. Heir to a throne he wanted destroyed.

She had betrayed them before. She could easily do it again.

Before he could say anything, the bedroom door opened. Saya peeked inside, surrounded by the pale green aura of apprehension.

"Uh, sorry," she murmured. "There's a bit of a problem."

Camilla stood. "What happened?"

"Marcos Ricci's body. It's a fake."

VI

"A re you sure we should be doing this?" Cosima asked for the third time in as many hours.

"No," Angelica answered.

"Great. Just wanted to check."

The rice farmer had led them to his hut before saying he had to head back to the fields, assuring them they'd be safe so long as they didn't wander. The hut was a humble construction upon tall wooden stilts, on the outskirts of a village shielded on its northeast side by a bamboo forest. It mainly consisted of a hearth and a straw pallet in the corner.

The farmer had led the girls to the latter, where they sat clinging to each other, Eiko's gaze fixed on the door as the sunlight shrank into evening. Angelica occasionally strained to hear the sound of horses, or else some sort of outroar, but there was nothing. Then, finally: steps on the ladder leading to the hut.

When the farmer entered, he blinked at the sight of Angelica's hand wreathed in cautionary flame.

"Good, you can light the hearth," he said cheerily.

He reached for a chipped and battered tea set on top of a locked wooden chest. "I've heard Vaegans love coffee, but all I have is tea. I hope that's all right. Oh, but I only have two cups." He froze in the act of scooping tea leaves into the kettle, the spoon tiny in his hand. "Didn't think of that."

"We don't need tea," Angelica said as evenly as she could; she couldn't risk offending him while Gojarin-Kae lurked near the village. She hesitated, then lit the hearth and let the rest of her flames sputter out. "Thank you."

"No, no, there has to be tea," he murmured. "Especially since I'm meeting Koshi's little sister."

Angelica glanced at Asami. She wasn't wearing her muzzle, and her lips were pressed so tight together they were a thin, pale line. Was he not acknowledging her on purpose?

"Mar—princess," Cosima said in a low voice. "I need you to ask him about Koshi."

Angelica took a deep breath, then nodded at the girls to shuffle closer.

"We're fine with sharing cups," Angelica said. "But—and I apologize for getting right to the point—I'm curious how you know Koshi."

"Ah." He removed his hat, revealing a head of black hair that had been tied into a messy topknot. He looked to be in his late twenties, his skin bronzed from days in the sun. "We . . . worked together. For a while."

Angelica considered her next words carefully. They were in danger-ous territory, where one wrong step could mean betrayal or death. "I was under the assumption that Koshi was a Gojarin."

Keeping his eyes on the kettle, the farmer said, "He was. Is."

"Then, if you worked with him . . ."

The nape of her neck prickled. The easy way he'd wielded earth—the scars on his hands— *Fuck.*

Angelica moved between him and Asami, calling the flames to her again.

"Let us leave, and I won't hurt you," Angelica warned him.

Cosima tensed, hand drifting to her sword. The man tilted his head to one side and rubbed one ear. Angelica noticed the third and fourth fingers on his left hand were missing; not cut off and healed over, but formed as if they had never grown.

"Did I miss something?" he asked.

"You're not a farmer, you're a Gojarin. You work for Nanbu Daiji."

His face clouded. "I—no. I did, once." His gaze drifted to the wooden chest. "Not anymore."

"What do you mean, not anymore?"

He groaned. "It's an embarrassing story. I'd rather not tell it." At Angelica's steely expression, he sighed. "I got caught up in some bad debt. I, uh . . . might have gotten disowned."

"Disowned? By whom?"

"Bushan Nanbu."

Her head was spinning. Their long days of travel were catching up with her, her battered body wanting only to be horizontal. Steam erupted from the kettle, and he pulled it off the hearth.

"I'm the son of a local magnate," he explained, pouring tea into his two cups. "Our family is an offshoot of the Nanbu family. Since Bushan Nanbu doesn't have any children, I was first in the line of succession. I have water and earth magic and was trained to be Gojarin. I was to become the next warlord."

He placed the two cups an equal distance between him and Angelica. "But, well, there's this rule that Gojarin can't earn money outside of their duties. Can't have them getting richer than the magnates. The only way around it is by taking out loans from merchants." He scratched at the chin hairs he had missed while shaving. "I...may have taken one too many loans. And Bushan Nanbu and my father may have found out how much I owed. And they may have disowned me rather than face the humiliation of their heir working under a lowly merchant to pay it back."

Slowly the picture began to fill out. "But you're not working for the merchant."

"I am not."

"You're a rice farmer."

"I am." After a moment of bemused silence, he hung his head. "I may have run away."

Angelica desperately needed to lie down. Instead, she let her fire vanish and handed the teacups to the girls so they could warm their hands.

"All of that doesn't change the fact that you were working with Nanbu Daiji," Angelica said. "You must have heard what happened in Mukan. What's stopping you from taking the empress to him and reclaiming your position?"

He frowned. "Empress?"

Is he serious? Eiko coughed awkwardly, drawing the man's attention to her...and then to Asami. He squinted at her.

"Is that...? No, it can't be." He leaned forward. "Can it? Goodness, she looks just like her..."

"Because it *is* her," Angelica couldn't help but snap. "You really didn't recognize her?"

The farmer bowed toward a startled-looking Asami with his forehead touching the floor. "Forgive me for not greeting Your Imperial Majesty sooner! If I'd known, I would have tried to find better tea."

Angelica suppressed the urge to weep. "If you didn't notice her before, then back at the road—"

"I only thought you wanted to avoid the Gojarin-Kae."

Cosima shifted beside her. "You know, I really wish I understood what you two were saying."

Angelica caught her up, then regarded him once more. "What's your name?"

"Taketa Kenji."

"Then, Warrior Taketa—"

He waved his hands around. "No, no, please no. Just Kenji, please."

It was awfully familiar, but the situation was already so peculiar that Angelica shrugged it off. "Kenji, my name is Angelica Mardova, and I originally came to Azuna to fraternize with the imperial family. But at the winter welcoming ceremony..." She glanced at the girls, who stared into their tea.

Kenji also looked at them, flexing his fingers. "We heard about the assassination," he said softly. "Even all the way out here. But we also heard that it was you, Esteemed Mardova, who orchestrated it."

Before she could say a word, a steel sword was at her neck. The girls gasped and Eiko dropped her cup, tea spilling across the bamboo mats. Cosima swore and unsheathed her own sword with a ringing sound.

The metal was cold against her skin. She had barely seen him move, had no idea where the sword had come from. He truly was an ex-Gojarin, the military elite of the empire.

"Your Imperial Majesty, just give the order, and I will behead her," Kenji said.

Asami opened her mouth, then covered it with her hand before she could make a sound. Eiko stood.

"Please, you don't understand," Eiko said shakily. "She—the empress cannot speak."

Kenji's brown eyes hardened. "What did you do to her?"

"Nothing! She has a—a condition. We can explain if you put your sword away. But my—" Eiko faltered, looking at Angelica and away. "But Angelica isn't to blame for what happened to my family."

"You're part of the imperial family?"

"Yes. The Ueda clan." Tears fell when she blinked. "N-Nanbu Daiji hired kaikushine to kill them all. Even Angelica. He was there with his Gojarin. I saw it."

Kenji hesitated. Angelica didn't dare move.

"He...Is this true, Your Imperial Majesty?"

"She can't *talk*," Angelica stressed. "Or at least, not in a way any of us can understand right now."

"She clearly wants to. I won't relent unless she says so."

Asami finally lowered her hand and took two quick breaths before saying softly, "It's true."

Behind Kenji, the tea kettle burst, spilling what little hot water remained. A few drops landed on Cosima's hand and she quickly shook them off with a curse.

Kenji stared open-mouthed at his ruined kettle, then at Asami, who ducked her head.

"Huh." He slid his sword back into its sheath in a fluid motion. "I'm experiencing all sorts of firsts today, aren't I?"

It was well into night, past the hour when the villagers had drifted off to bed. The girls had fallen asleep, too, after Cosima had combed and untangled their hair. Then Cosima herself had nodded off once she'd eaten the simple fare Kenji had offered.

Angelica was too restless to do the same. So Kenji led her to the earth shrine in the bamboo forest beyond a pair of weatherworn poles, their green paint bleached after years of sunlight. They were blanketed by the dark and surrounded by the scent of organic, growing life.

It soothed her. The shrine itself was nothing more than an open archway topped with engravings of bamboo; Angelica guessed this had once been the site of a Deia statue. Incense holders surrounded it, and Kenji drew a small stick from within his sleeve. He held it out to her, and Angelica pinched the top of the stick between her fingers until it glowed like an ember. Kenji placed it in one of the holders, a lazy ribbon of smoke spiraling upward.

He seated himself on one of the mats laid out for meditation. Angelica fruitlessly brushed dirt off of another before giving up and settling down beside him. Not like she wasn't already covered in dirt and grime.

"Esteemed Mardova..." He said her name slowly, enunciated by his accent.

"Angelica. If you want me to call you Kenji, you call me Angelica."

The ex-Gojarin laughed. "That's fair. I've heard of the four great Houses, of course. Could never remember which one was which, but I guess you are descended from Deia?"

"Correct."

"Interesting." He traced the shape of the shrine with his eyes. "Bushan Nanbu still worships Deia."

Angelica's throat closed up at the memory of the snake around his shoulders.

"I'm aware," she said quietly. "Ta—Kenji. Will you listen to what I have to say? I'll let you decide whether to believe it. Whether you would be willing to help us."

There was reservation in the set of his broad shoulders, but eventually he nodded. "I'll listen."

She told him everything that had happened since coming to Azuna. Part of her wanted to skip details, shore away the things he could potentially use against her, but she was so fucking tired—and the more she spoke, the more it all came pouring out of her like a torrent. The massacre, Deia whispering in Nanbu's ear, Akane, Asami channeling kudei, Koshi stabbing Kazue. By the end she felt wrung out, depleted.

Kenji was silent long enough she wondered if maybe *he* had fallen asleep. But he was only watching the incense burn down to its end, brittle ash falling into the pile already collected within the holder.

"That's." He rubbed his head. "That is a lot."

"It is."

"I don't really understand some of it."

"Neither do I."

"I can't say that's reassuring." He tugged his ear, as if the motion soothed him. "Bushan Nanbu...I can believe he would do this."

She straightened. "You can?" She'd thought, having once been his heir and even a distant relative, Kenji would be hard to win over.

"He's always been eager for *more*. Once, I was one of his right-hand Gojarin alongside Koshi. I overhead many conversations. Many times, he expressed disappointment in the empire and the empress, insisting he could do better. He even—" He caught himself, clearing his throat.

"He even what?"

"I..."

"He doesn't deserve your protection, Kenji. He slaughtered Asami and Eiko's family."

He winced. Picking up a pebble, he started tossing it between his hands. "Although I told the truth about being disowned, it wasn't the *whole* truth. Bushan Nanbu and my father were planning to send me away to the northern city-states while they paid off the debt. They would have claimed I was there on a months-long mission to explain my absence. But the idea didn't sit well with me, so I ran away. Eventually found myself here, where I met good people and found good work. Work that took my mind off everything.

"But one of the last discussions I remember Bushan Nanbu having was with some of the local magnates. He wanted to bolster the fire state's military with a weapon the others didn't have. He wanted to try and capture the sorankun from the Sanatsu Peaks and use them as an aerial force."

A chill stole down Angelica's back. With Deia at his side, Nanbu could very likely accomplish that.

"It made me uncomfortable," Kenji admitted. He flicked the pebble into the air with his thumb, pushing it even higher with a small blast of magic. "The sorankun are *sacred*. They represent kudei."

"They also represent Azuna," Angelica murmured. "This plan isn't just about having advantage over the other warlords. He's trying to take the empress's cultural connection to the people. If they see him riding a sorankun, he could easily capture their support. Their devotion."

Kenji was so startled he fumbled catching the pebble as it fell back to earth. "I didn't even think about that. But then, there's a lot I didn't think of. If I had just gone to Mukan instead, if I had warned somebody . . ."

Angelica had once thought there was no reason to live with regrets. If you made a mistake, you acknowledged it, fixed it, or gave it distance. Dwelling on things like *what could have been* served no one and fixed nothing.

But the heaviness in his words struck a familiar chord within her. The chord that played when she thought of the other heirs, of how she had first treated Miko and her daughters, of all the things she could have done if she hadn't been so infatuated with her fire.

"Feel bad if you want to," she said. "I carry my own regrets and have no advice for that. But first and foremost, think about what we can do *now* to make up for it."

"What can we do now?"

She told him about Mount Netsai.

"I'm not sure I follow," he admitted. "But I know this area well. I can guide you to Mount Netsai."

She marveled over how quickly he could harbor such trust in her. Part of her wanted to remain wary, but she sensed nothing but sincerity from him. Something dangerously close to hope sprouted in her chest.

"We would be appreciative." Then she thought of the wooden chest in his hut. "You still have your Gojarin armor, don't you?" Kenji nodded, his expression hard to read. "If anyone finds us along the way, you can pretend that you caught us and are bringing us to Nanbu Daiji."

Kenji didn't reply at first. He rubbed at his left hand, between the knuckles of his three fingers.

"I'd hoped to never put it on again," he said quietly, voice dampened by the surrounding bamboo. "But I also couldn't get rid of it. I guess, if it serves a good purpose..." He sighed. "I would like to keep Her Imperial Majesty safe. It's the least I can do."

"Thank you." *It's also the least I can do.*

Before she could stand, an unpleasant tingling ran across her scalp. Her gaze snapped up, trying to see into the heart of the dark forest. A lemur clung to one of the trees, its striped tail wrapped around the thin trunk. Its eyes were round and luminously blue.

Once Angelica spotted it, it leapt from branch to branch until it disappeared. In her mind came a whispering laugh.

"Angelica?"

Kenji was shaking her. She came to with a violent shudder.

"Fuck," she breathed. She should have been more *careful*—should have known she couldn't evade the god's notice. A god who now had access to the strongest military power in the empire.

"How long will it take to reach Mount Netsai?" she asked.

"About five days. Three, on horse."

"Do you know how we can get some horses?"

He tilted his head one way, then another. Something like mischief glinted in his eyes. "I might know a way."

VII

Risha surveyed the river that wended southeast. It was one of the Praeteriens's tributaries, its surface glimmering green under the sky's expanse.

On her shoulder rested a tiny rabbit spirit. Or at least, *rabbit* was the closest approximation, as it had a set of mothlike wings. They had passed a Noctan spirit playing the flute for a family of the little creatures, and one had taken a shine to Risha, going so far as to perch on her shoulder and stay there. Its nose twitched now as it sniffed at their surroundings.

"Which city is that?" Risha asked Val. In the distance rose a tiered stone metropolis that looked more like an imposing fortress. Smoke and ash billowed from various points along its circular layout.

She had taken Val out of the sling after the second time he'd attempted to bite the rabbit creature. With his eyes on the city, he answered, "That's Cruciamen."

Her shoulders slumped. The rabbit spirit chewed idly on her hair. "Oh."

"Yeah. Bit harder to tell if you're not close enough to hear the unending screams of the tortured." He laughed like he'd made the realm's funniest joke. "But really, don't get too close."

"I wasn't planning on it."

She thought back to Val singing that horrible song and once again wondered if he had originally come from Cruciamen. She didn't know what he could have possibly done to have been condemned to such a place—or how he would have become a guide for Leshya.

She turned east, where the landscape shifted to rocky mountains.

Carved along those mountains were the ruins of statues and sculptures, flanking a winding stairway with crumbled archways. At the top awaited the Vitae portal.

They were so close.

"Do you think Samhara will be enough to cut through the barrier?" she asked.

Val glanced sidelong at where she'd left the weapon lying in the grass. "If you can't make use of the power of the four kings' bones, then I don't know what to tell you."

"Then, do you think whoever rules Cruciamen will be able to sense us? Try to stop us?"

"How should *I* know? Why don't you try asking your new companion?"

The rabbit spirit made an *uuu* sound and sniffed at her jaw.

"We'll be quick, then," she said. "Do you at least know which part of Samhara belongs to the king of Cruciamen?"

Val was quiet, thinking. "The finger bones," he said at last.

"I imagine it's difficult to torture spirits without your fingers." Val raised an eyebrow at her, unamused.

Risha stroked a finger over the rabbit spirit's head and looked over her shoulder. Jas was sitting under a tall, spindly tree, similarly staring at the path to the Vitae portal. He was utterly, eerily still—no breaths, no blinks, no humanlike fidgeting. More and more he was slipping away from the man she had met in Nexus.

And he was still angry. It gnawed at her, the same knot of unrelenting shame she'd felt whenever her father had expressed disappointment in her.

She had been acting on her own desire to feed him energy he might not have been compatible with, experimenting in a way her father would have found repulsive. Thana's words had become a poison, playing up her fear, her hopelessness.

She couldn't fall for it again.

Risha closed her eyes. Took a moment to simply feel the wind on her face, smell the mixture of smoke and stone in the air, listen to the song Val was humming and the soft *uuu* of the rabbit spirit by her ear. Now that they were near, she sensed the Vitae portal the same way she had once sensed the void between her home and Mortri, a door that swung inward to life and outward to death.

Her eyes flew open. *The void.* It was there, a heavy layer beyond the sky, beyond the barrier that kept the portals shut. Dark and infinite and crowded with the directionless dead.

Jas didn't look at her when she came to sit before him, the slight furrow of his brow the only giveaway of what he was feeling. Even a frown gave her some relief.

"I'd like to try something," she said. "I couldn't access the void before, but I think I can here. If it's all right, I can search for your mother."

This finally roused him. He turned to her, surprised. "How would that work?"

She held out her hands, palms up. "You'll have to help me." In order to re-create the ritual of a séance, she wouldn't need to borrow his energy, but his presence would aid in finding Jumari Chadha faster. "But only if you're comfortable with it."

Their eyes met, and the knot within her pulled tighter. Whatever Jas saw in her expression shifted his own into something both exasperated and fond. Carefully he laid his transparent hands over hers, an icy kiss of air on her skin.

She let her eyes fall shut again. "Jumari Chadha," she said out loud, "your son would like to speak with you."

She repeated the words in her mind as she cast out for one spirit amid millions. It seemed an impossible task, but she had done it once before; surely she could do it again. Even the rabbit creature butted its head into her neck as if to loan her some of its spiritual power.

Their entwined energies flared in response to the call. Like they were both parting the clouds and the veil with their hands, grasping into the familiar dark. Risha and Jas, Jas and Risha, thinking the same thing over and over: *Jumari Chadha. Come and find us. Amaa. Come and speak with us.*

A shiver spread through her body as something—some*one*—took hold.

"Jaswant," the spirit said through Risha's lips.

"Amaa!" The word was pained, ripped from Jas's chest. "That's—that's her voice, she—"

"I'm here, Jas," Jumari whispered in Parithvian. "It's me."

A half sob rose out of Jas, a sound so human, so young, that her eyes watered. Risha wished she could give them privacy.

"I..." Risha felt Jas trying to grasp her tighter. "I didn't think I'd get to hear your voice again. There's so much I want to tell you."

"And I want to hear it all. But I do not have much time."

Jas swore softly. "Where are you? Are you all right?"

"There is no need to worry about me anymore," Jumari said. "I exist and don't. There is nothing to feel, here."

Risha cautiously opened her eyes. Based on Jas's expression, his mother's words were hardly a comfort.

"Is there any way you can bring her spirit into Mortri?" he asked Risha. Unable to speak due to the spirit inside her, Risha could only shake her head.

"It is enough that I have this opportunity to speak with you," Jumari said. "My handsome boy."

"Amaa," Jas rasped, and Risha ached for him. "Before, you were trying to tell me what had happened to you. Please, I need to know. What did you find out in Nexus?"

The spirit shuddered, and Risha nearly lost it to the void again. The energies within her surged and Jumari settled, though her agitation forced Risha to endure flashes of the woman's memory, like pins poking at her brain. The interior of the Bone Palace. A younger Ferdinand. Applying kajal to her eyes in a mirror. Turning a corner and—

"The king," Jumari whispered as Risha's head throbbed. She saw the visage of a boy, his eyes bright blue and wide, before he ducked into the nearest room. Not soon enough. "He has an heir."

The shape of the jaw, the set of his eyes.

Jumari had seen—Risha had seen—the child of Ferdinand Accardi.

And yet the Houses had been told to compete for the honor of the throne. A war with no victor.

The spirit almost left her when Risha's breathing struggled in her lungs. Jas scooted forward, cool fingers to her cheek.

"Risha," he whispered, "it's all right. Just a little longer. Please."

She nodded even while Jumari kept speaking through her. "I knew a secret heir was a disaster waiting to happen. I had to return home at once. I wanted to warn Parliament of the truth and determine how to handle further relations with Vaega. A civil war was a distinct possibility. So I left Nexus."

Another memory flash, a carriage rattling hard enough to slam her against the side, her gorge rising as she fell, and fell—

"And didn't make it home," Jumari whispered as a tear fell from Risha's eye. "I think the king knew what had shaken me. We spoke just before I left."

"He arranged for you to die," Jas growled. "That's already grounds enough for war!"

"I do not want a war," Jumari argued. "That is what I was trying to *prevent*. Jaswant, please... You and your father need to stay safe. That's all I care about."

Risha's chest iced over. The spirit couldn't tell that Jas was one, too.

"Amaa..." Jas's mouth twisted. "I...yes. We will."

An intention came to her. Following the spirit's desire, Risha laid a hand against the faint line of Jas's cheek as much as she was able.

"I love you until the stars fade out," Jumari murmured. Jas tried to place his hand over Risha's.

"And even then," he finished in a whisper.

The spirit vanished gradually, too weak to hold on any longer now that her last message had been given. It left Risha drained and her body and mind empty.

"Risha."

Blearily she looked up. There was a similar emptiness in Jas's gaze, and somehow she found it comforting, knowing she wasn't alone in this.

"Thank you," he said softly. "What she said...Do you think it's true?"

She ran her tongue over her teeth. "I saw him. I don't think she's mistaken."

"Then that would mean the Houses have no claim to the throne."

Hearing him say it out loud, it suddenly struck her as funny—this tragic, pointless truth spotlighting her entire life in deception. A laugh tumbled out of her, quiet and disturbed.

She thought of Taesia revealing Dante's plan, insisting the Houses had to forge a new way instead of adhering to all they'd ever known.

It had been treason. And Risha should have joined her.

Jas nodded in the direction of the Vitae portal. "Do you think the heir is still in Nexus?"

There were so many things she didn't know: what had happened to the other heirs, to the king, to the city. If her family was all right, or if the events of Godsnight had catapulted them into conflict.

"Only one way to find out." She got to her feet. Val had been watching on in silence, a look of curious intent in his visible eye.

The rabbit spirit sighed on her shoulder. She picked it up and placed it gently in the grass.

"It'll be dangerous where we're going," she told it. "Go back to your family."

As I will find a way back to mine.

VIII

I'm going to train you to run the household."

The man who had raised him, a man who no longer existed, stood in the middle of a practice ring under the late morning sun. His spear gleamed, a misplaced sunray.

"Your brother will go into the military and work directly under His Majesty. You will support him."

He'd understood. No matter the level of power he held, how fast or how strong he was, it was simply not as good as Rian. Despite being first-born, he wasn't the heir House Cyr needed.

"You are a watcher, not a warrior. But you still have to be prepared for any fight." The spear was leveled at his chest. "Come at me again."

Nikolas leapt across the ring and suddenly it was a rooftop, steel sinking into his father's neck.

The memory did not spark pain, because he didn't let it. He merely allowed it to play out before receding. Let his mind turn lazily without consequence.

Taesia could be dead.

Phos was absorbing Rian.

The outer reaches of Noctus were beginning to make his muscles flag, encroaching darkness sapping away his energy.

The coronal was broken save for the piece he held clenched in one clammy hand.

None of these thoughts could touch him in a way that mattered. They flickered and then died, embers struggling for wind to stir them. It was peaceful this way. Like he stood at the edge of an ocean and only vaguely wondered what was on the far shore.

"There you are."

He turned his head slightly. Fin knelt beside him, cradled in shadow. Nikolas was sitting at the base of a wall. For a moment he couldn't figure out how he had gotten there. Then Fin swallowed, looking beyond Nikolas at the broken bodies of the Noctan soldiers Phos had killed.

Yes. He had been told to drag them inside. Hadn't bothered to ask why, only waited until his god had turned in dismissal, one hand pressed to the injury on his chest. Nikolas had left the Bone Palace and entered the courtyard for the first time since Godsnight, broken and pitted and smelling of decay. Took stock of the weight of the dead in his arms, the pull of his muscles.

There were no further orders, so here he sat until he was needed. His god had not yet come for him.

But Fin had. He touched Nikolas's arm, tugging at his sleeve.

"Come with me, Sunshine."

Not an order from Phos, but an order regardless. He allowed Fin to lead him out of the antechamber, away from the vaulted ribs and hollow marble, and along corridors padded with red velvet. Arterial pathways to some undiscovered heart.

They ended up in a servant's hall. On one end: a kitchen and a wide, flame-filled hearth. On the other: a long table where the palace's servants had once eaten between shifts.

The survivors stood, chair legs screeching. "Your Highness!"

The two of them were pulled into the room, a flurry of voices, careful hands, and frightened eyes. Nikolas stared at them and said nothing.

"Phos allowed you in here?" Fin asked. From his tone, he was just as surprised as they were.

"He took away all the utensils and dishware," said a lanky man with a gray mustache. "And the heavy pots and pans. Even the twine. Anything that could be used as a weapon."

"Of course." Fin shook his head. "Is there water, at least? Rags?"

"Yes, Your Highness. I'll get them for you."

A Parithvian woman with henna-dyed hair eyed their waistlines. "I'll see what food we have that isn't spoiled."

"Thank you," Fin sighed. "What are your names?"

The servants seemed startled but readily replied. *Luis. Bhavna.* Then Fin was leading him toward the hearth and making him sit on the warmed bricks before it. Nikolas closed his eye as heat seeped through him.

Fin was given a shallow clay bowl full of water and a small bundle of cheesecloth. He placed the bowl near the fire and tore the cloth into strips, the movements awkward due to his shackles.

"Come here," Fin said.

Nikolas leaned forward. Fin carefully unwrapped the bandages from his head, speckled a watery pink. The wound was already mostly healed thanks to Phos. The lingering pain was distant, blissfully distant, while Fin soaked some cheesecloth in the warm water and pressed it to his face. There was a unique pleasure in it, even, as his skin was wiped clean.

Fin's fingers were trembling, and he avoided looking too long at the gaping socket. His bottom eyelids were silver with unshed tears.

"I have to tell you something," Fin whispered as the servants bustled in the background.

A glimmer of curiosity. Nikolas pursued it, staring at him with silent intention.

Fin lightly traced Nikolas's cheekbone. Mapped it out as if to memorize its shape. "Growing up in the palace, there were only a select few who knew who I truly was. They were sworn to oaths of secrecy on penalty of death." He frowned. "The others were all told the same lie: I was a servant's son. And to the mage who taught me the fundamentals of earth magic, it was made clear I wanted to join the military's elementalist division."

Another servant approached with a tin in her hands and quietly explained that using a compress with chamomile would help. Fin thanked her and did just as she instructed, soaking the dried tea leaves in water before letting the cloth absorb the liquid and pressing it gently to Nikolas's eye.

"Can you hold that for me?"

Nikolas obeyed. The compress smelled herbal and sweet, and water trickled down his face. Fin brushed it away with his thumb, teasing out another memory: an alleyway in Nexus, the smell of a food vendor's cart, his chest cracking open while he relayed his brother's fate. Supposed fate.

"After every lesson, the mage would leave first, and then I would wait for my guard to collect me. But once, I didn't wait. The minute the mage left, I ran out and began to explore the palace." Fin let out a small laugh. "I was *so* scared I would be caught, but even though my heart was pounding like mad, I was smiling. It was *exciting*. There were whole wings I'd never seen before, rooms far more lavish than mine, even small chapels. Anyone who saw me assumed I was what I pretended to be: a servant's son."

He grew quiet. Nikolas's mind was also quiet, enraptured.

"I made it all the way to the training grounds," Fin continued. "And climbed on top of one of the walls to watch. A comandante was leading a troop through drills. His voice was so powerful, I was captivated. And then I saw the weapon on his back. I'd been taught about the Houses, so I knew it was the Sunbringer Spear. I'd always wanted to see it. So I leaned forward, and..."

Nikolas inhaled sharply as the memory clutched him in its vise.

His father running drills at the Bone Palace, bringing Nikolas and Rian along so they could observe. Rian in the coveted spot at their father's side and Nikolas standing at ease behind them, waiting to be called on or needed.

Then a soft *thump* and a cry of pain. None of the soldiers heard it, but Nikolas had. He'd turned to find a boy had fallen from the wall above.

"Ow ow *ow*," the boy was moaning as he sat up and cradled his elbow.

Nikolas hurried over. "Are you all right?" He'd glanced at the top of the wall. "What were you doing up there?"

"Uh...looking." One of the boy's eyes had been shut in pain, a stripe of dirt along his cheek. His clothes were nondescript; likely the child of a soldier or servant who lived at the palace. He was dark-haired and bright-eyed, irises blue as the height of summer. Then those eyes widened. "You're Nikolas Cyr."

Embarrassment had nipped at him. Back then, he hadn't yet gotten used to people valuing his title over his personhood.

"Then that's your father," the boy had went on, peeking around him at where Waren Cyr barked drill instructions. "Deia's tits!"

Nikolas had been so surprised by the swear he'd sputtered. "Where did you learn that?"

"I hear it all the time from one of my gua—ahh—parents."

"They shouldn't be saying those sorts of things around you."

"I guess." The boy had popped to his feet, pain forgotten as a grin spread across his face. "Does that mean you know how to use the Sunbringer Spear? How does it work, exactly? Is it true that some of Phos's feathers are inside? Can you *fly*?"

"I..." His head had suddenly hurt. "Uh..."

"Can you teach *me* how to fly? I mean, I have earth magic, not Solara magic, but there might be a way. Maybe with air mages?" The boy extended his arms like wings, then winced and pulled his elbow in close again. "Ow."

"Let me see." Nikolas had carefully reached for the arm, pressing his thumb around the elbow until the boy hissed at a certain spot. "I think you have a fracture. Would you like me to walk you to the infirmary?"

"Won't your father notice you're gone?"

A hollow feeling in his stomach, carefully put aside. "He won't mind."

Slowly the boy had grinned again. "All right."

Here, beside him, that boy was grown up. His grin tempered with grief, his awe exchanged for disquiet.

"I knew I'd get caught if I was taken to the infirmary," Fin said, his voice as soft as his gaze. "The head medic would recognize me. But if it meant spending more time with you, I thought it would be worth it. You were..." He swallowed. "You were so *bright*. And your smile was so warm. I wish we'd had hours, but I treasured those minutes together. And when we arrived at the infirmary, you said—"

" 'Next time, I'll catch you,' " Nikolas finished.

Pain bloomed within his chest, making him gasp and double over. Fin's hand steadied his shoulder while all the aches and sores of his body flared bright, his mind flooded with the agony of *being*.

"It's all right," Fin murmured, rubbing his shoulder as Nikolas shook through it. "Just breathe. I'm here."

The pain had receded, but Nikolas was still trembling when Bhavna came back.

"Your Highness, my lord," she said before setting two food-laden straw mats beside them. "Please eat and recover your strength."

"Thank you, Bhavna," Fin said. She bowed and retreated, giving them privacy once more. "Here, this is basically tea now."

He handed Nikolas the bowl of chamomile-infused water. Nikolas didn't care about drinking the leaves; he took a large gulp to ease his parched throat.

"Thank you," Nikolas whispered. "For..."

Fin quickly shook his head. "Don't worry about it." He smiled as a ball of light formed and bounced between them. "There you are."

Nikolas reached for Lux. It zoomed around his hand and up his arm, pressed its warmth into the spot between his neck and shoulder. "I missed you, too."

And despite the way his body ached, the way his mind rebelled against the idea of being fully awake, he *had* missed this: the heat of his power, the quiet assurance of the light. Even in the years of Rian's absence when his magic had waned, it had always been there, to some degree. His one constant.

Fin stuffed a handful of dried fruit into his mouth and began to tear the remaining cheesecloth into bandages. He winced when his shackles knocked against his wrists.

Nikolas took Fin's hands and held them out to examine the shackles, dark as the night beyond Phos's barrier. Fin grew very still, hardly breathing. Lux shifted into a dagger of light.

"It won't work," Fin said even as Nikolas attempted to cut the middle chain. "The material repels magic. We need the key."

"Ri—Phos must be carrying it."

"Unless he destroyed it," Fin pointed out.

"I don't think he would." He was still holding one of Fin's hands. It was warm, with long, slender fingers suited for a thief. "I didn't recognize you."

"I didn't expect you to. I was so young, then."

"We both were." And so many years had passed with Fin watching from afar, Nikolas completely unaware of his regard or his existence. The truth of him a hidden explosive, ready to level the entire kingdom.

"I wish I'd had the courage to tell you, then." Fin stared at the bricks, running a thumb over Nikolas's knuckles. "But a lot of people would have been punished if I had. I tried to tell myself it was for the best." His face hardened. "I shouldn't mourn my old life, but it was all I ever knew. Really, I'm upset over the life I never had. That I could never claim for myself."

He pulled his hand away and set to work bandaging Nikolas's eye. Nikolas focused on the way Fin touched him not like a vase ready to shatter any minute, but with insistent tenderness. The same way Nikolas had touched him all those years ago, seeking for a fracture.

"I think you would make a good king," Nikolas said softly.

Fin paused. After a long moment, he tied the bandages together. "I don't think I ever wanted that. Especially now that... now that I know what my father did. I don't want to follow in his footsteps."

"You wouldn't. You're already different from him."

"I don't think that's enough."

Luis approached them then, the other servants following behind.

"Forgive us for intruding," he said. "But I thought Your Highness and my lord would want to see this."

He held out a small pouch. Wanting Fin to keep from moving his wrists too much, Nikolas accepted it and opened the drawstring.

Inside were several long, thick fangs, pearly white with an ethereal sheen.

"We collected them when he left the throne room," Luis explained. "He took one, but we picked up all the rest. We think they bear some sort of magic. Perhaps it can help?"

Nikolas reached into his pocket and drew out the fang he had taken that day in the throne room. He added it to the collection and pulled the drawstring closed.

"These came from the coronal of Astrum," Nikolas said. "A crown that's able to protect the city."

If he recalled correctly, only the Lunari family could wield it, and they were now dead. Barring a Lunari, these would be best in the hands of a particularly strong Shade.

Taesia.

His chest constricted. Phos had been certain she hadn't survived the fall, but he didn't know Taesia like Nikolas did. For all Nikolas knew, the god could have lied just to push him back into his thrall.

His breathing quickened at the thought. If he was strong enough, he could make another break in the barrier to escape, to try and find Taesia— *please be alive*—or someone who could use the fangs against Phos.

Nikolas held the pouch to his chest. "Thank you," he told the servants. "You were wise to collect them and keep them hidden. I believe they will help."

Luis and the servants sighed in relief. Fin smiled at him.

It was some sort of hope, even if they didn't know yet what shape it would take.

IX

The campfire crackled and popped as Julian stared into the flames. He leaned toward its warmth to combat the chill of Noctus and the frosty stares he was getting from the others.

Taesia sat beside him, Starfell sheathed but placed pointedly across her knees. Kalen was pacing, Marcellus sharpening his sword with a whetstone. Lilia sat studying Julian with an inscrutable expression he wished she would point anywhere else.

It was like when the Hunters had first learned he was a beastspeaker: the looks, the questions, the whispers. Those who thought it fascinating and those who made warding signs when he came near.

"I knew there was something wrong about you," Kalen finally growled. Even his familiar was jumpy, no longer wrapped around his throat but hovering worriedly above his head. "As soon as I read your chart, I *knew*."

"What did you know, exactly?" Julian asked coolly.

"Belua," Kalen spat. "One of the stars you were born under. It represents those who are prone to viciousness, who have the ability to cultivate unnatural strength they use for unnatural means. It means *monster*."

Julian's breathing faltered. The hand Taesia had wrapped around Starfell tightened.

"I sensed it outside the exteri sulumn," Kalen went on. "And in the Sanctuary's courtyard, the ground underneath you was cracked. If we'd known you harbor the same magic that brought that cursed palace here—"

"I think it's about time you shut the fuck up," Taesia interrupted. "He used that magic to *save* us."

"To save *you*," Kalen retorted. "If he's had this ability all along, why not use it in the first place to put the dead down?"

"I didn't know I could," Julian answered truthfully. "But I...sensed the leftover quintessence and used it."

At this, Lilia frowned. "Quintessence?"

"It's the energy that runs along the Cosmic Scale. The substance that created the realms."

"It's the magic of the fifth realm," Taesia added. "Ostium. They called that magic quintessence, and the people who wielded it were able to create all sorts of things, like the portals between our realms. But once Ostium was destroyed, those portals collapsed."

"And without this quintessence, our realms are dying," the princess concluded grimly.

"Yes."

Kalen was not convinced. "If Ostium truly existed and was destroyed, then why does this man carry its power?"

"The magic users of Ostium who weren't killed in the attack ended up...warped," Julian explained. "They became beings called demons. I don't know how it happened, but I share powers with one of those demons. In Vitae, it allowed me to understand the emotions and thoughts of beasts."

Kalen scoffed, as if his earlier point had just been made.

"For a long time, I thought that was all I could do," Julian went on, ignoring him. "But when I was near the remains of Orsus, the god of Ostium, I realized I could do the same to humans—and that I could manipulate whatever small amount of quintessence lingers in this realm."

He pressed his fingertips against his knee until they paled. "I was able to free Nik from Phos's hold for a little while. I think, if I connect with Orsus again, I might be able to free Rian."

"Do you really think that's possible?" Taesia asked quietly.

"I don't know. But I want to try."

She shook her head. "It would be so risky, Julian. If you give them too much of yourself, they'll take you. You can't let that happen."

"What do you mean?" Lilia asked. "Are you saying the god of Ostium would inhabit him? Wouldn't that be a good thing?"

Taesia bristled. "No."

"How do you—?"

"Because I've felt it. I've seen Nyx take over my sister's body despite her pleas, and I've had him attempt to control me. Even now he wants to control me, to use me as his creature."

Something complicated passed through Lilia's expression. "I don't understand. If you were a conduit to Nyx's power, wouldn't that be a considerable asset? You would be strong enough to stop Phos."

Taesia laughed bitterly. "He doesn't care about *helping*. He just wants someone to carry out what he's too weak to do himself. If I let him have command over me, Taesia Lastrider will be *gone*."

"That doesn't sound like Nyx," Kalen argued. "He's our *god*, our protector."

"Maybe he used to be. But now all he cares about is this feud he has with Phos. He'd use me to kill Rian in a heartbeat."

"The boy whom Phos has taken as his vessel," Lilia said. She and Kalen exchanged a silent conversation over the fire. Marcellus's gaze flitted between the two of them.

"Perhaps the boy is meant to die, then," Lilia said finally.

"I am not killing Rian," Taesia gritted out.

"You misunderstand me," the princess said. "I don't *want* the boy to die, especially if he is being tormented by his god. But if it's the only way to ensure that Phos is eliminated—if we can destroy him while he is inhabiting the boy—then wouldn't that sacrifice be worth it?"

"No."

Lilia drew herself up. "I have lost my *entire family*. Do you not think we've all faced sacrifices? We must do whatever is necessary to prevent more tragedy. Did you even consider that accepting Nyx's power would help us fix the Malum Star?"

"*He told me he couldn't fix it*," Taesia stressed.

Her tone raised his hackles. Julian could sense the barriers being built around her again, this woman who kept secrets and lied as easily as breathing.

What exactly had Nyx told her? What wasn't she telling them?

"Praeses," Marcellus mumbled.

Everyone looked to him, confused. He cleared his throat.

"When you read his star chart," the soldier said to Kalen, "you said he was born under two stars. Belua was one. Praeses was the other."

"What does that mean?" Taesia demanded.

Kalen didn't answer. Lilia studied Julian once more, some of her uncertainty dispelled.

"One born under Praeses protects and safeguards those around them," the princess said. "They become guardians."

Contradiction. Now Julian understood what Kalen had meant when he'd used that word. It was, after all, where he stood on this unfathomable road: between bloodshed and peace, ruin and salvation, death and creation.

The question was, could he exist with both? Or would he inevitably have to choose between them?

The tension within the group eased over the next day as they followed Starfell toward the next fang. It was largely thanks to Marcellus, who stalwartly pretended that nothing had happened and tried to teach Julian one of his childhood marching songs. Lilia smiled when Marcellus slung an arm around Julian's shoulders, swaying them back and forth while Julian reluctantly sang under his breath. Only Kalen remained aloof and glaring. In fact, Taesia thought his glare might have upgraded from *wary* to *death* when Marcellus hugged Julian.

"You know, I did ask if he was also dalyr," Lilia said as she sidled up to Taesia. They walked behind the men at a slightly slower pace due to Lilia's healing wound. "You said he wasn't."

"It's different." Taesia tugged at the end of her braid, something Risha used to do when she was stumped. "We kept it from you for his safety, not yours."

"Hm." The princess gazed at Kalen's back and fiddled with the two fangs hanging around her neck. "I wanted to hate Kalen when he was assigned to me. I always knew who he was, and was fully prepared to... ah...I don't know the phrase in Vaegan."

"Give him the cold shoulder?" Taesia suggested.

Lilia glanced at her own shoulder in bemusement. "As you say. But he was not what I thought he would be. He was the first person to see beyond my title. And he felt guilty, I think. He didn't keep the truth from me because he thought I couldn't handle it—he did it because he saw how others treated me and didn't want to make it worse."

She smiled again when Kalen batted away Marcellus's grasping hand, the soldier trying to get him to join the song. "We were...*are* linked by a cataclysmic event. But it's love and trust that draws us to one another. It's likely the same between you and Julian."

Taesia tugged on her braid again. Love and trust seemed like luxuries, ones she'd been lucky to have and foolish to squander.

Even Julian had drawn his blade on her. But he had also been the only one to see through the shadows she drew around herself. He had witnessed Taesia Lastrider at her most powerful and hadn't turned away. When his own power had broken free, she had been there to hold him up, to let him grow into his strength instead of shackling it.

And here he was, at her side despite everything. They certainly had trust. And yet—

"Do you want it to be you?" Taesia blurted. She focused on the grass glimmering with dew, as if the ground were littered with diamonds. "To be the one receiving Nyx's power?"

Lilia was silent. Up ahead, Marcellus had given up his song in favor of regaling Julian with a story of how he and Kalen had eluded assassins by dressing up as women. Kalen's sigh was long-suffering.

"I don't know," Lilia said at last. "At first, when I learned you had his ear, I did. I don't often feel jealousy, have trained myself to let go of what I wish I had in favor of being grateful for what I do have. But I felt it then. Forgive me."

"There's nothing to forgive," Taesia murmured. "A lot of people would want such power."

"This isn't just about power. It's about reconnecting with a god who abandoned us. I want to ask him *why*. I want to face him and ask for even a modicum of his magic, if that would be enough to save our realm. Even if it left me a burned-out husk in the end."

Blood rushed to Taesia's head. "Do you *want* to die?"

"Of course I don't."

"Then why are you so eager to sacrifice yourself? You consider the story of Noria Lunari inspirational, but I find it depressing as fuck. Nyx sent down an astralam to help fend off Phos's forces, sure." She grasped the familiar comfort of Starfell's hilt. "But why didn't he just step in and end the war right then and there? Why did he need Noria to give up her life?"

"If Nyx had the capacity to stop Phos on his own, wouldn't he have succeeded by now?" Lilia countered. "He needs us as much as we need him. No one being can be all-powerful. Nyx seems to accept that. Phos seems unable to. Noria Lunari understood the price of duty, and embraced it."

Duty. The word held her head under the water until her lungs screamed for air. She was back at the dining room table at the Lastrider villa, her mother berating her. She was facing down Angelica's contemptuous sneer, Risha's disappointed frown, Nikolas's sorrowful gaze. Brailee's frustrated words.

You'll really do anything to avoid facing responsibility, won't you?

"Do you think I'm selfish for wanting to live?" Taesia asked softly. "For wanting my mind to remain my own?"

Lilia carefully considered her answer. "No. I think, in some way, it is admirable that you stand up for what you want. But I also think we face a dire situation, one that requires every resource we have."

Taesia forced herself to let go of the sword's hilt. The shadows whispered around her, but she wearily sent them scattering.

"We will figure something out." Lilia nodded. "We must."

They took a break a short time later. From the way Starfell was humming gently on her back, she figured they were close to the next fang. Kalen redressed Lilia's bandages while Julian checked Taesia's wrists. Marcellus handed out more dried mushrooms.

Taesia took her share with a glower. "I miss real food."

Lilia seemed confused. "This is real food."

"*No*, this is dried fucking mushrooms, which might as well be funky flavored air. I want glazed ham, potato omelets, Parithvian curry, Azunese tea cakes." She tore her mushroom into sad, stringy threads. "I want *cinnamon sugar buns*. The pastry chef at our villa made them every week. Sometimes she would make a chocolate sauce to go with them." Taesia flopped miserably to the ground.

"My mother's roast chicken," Julian added, staring forlornly into the distance as he chewed the fungal leather. "And her butter garlic potatoes."

Taesia groaned. "Her almond cake," she said wistfully. For some reason this made Julian's cheeks turn pink.

Lilia sat back down with a huff. "We have plenty of good food in Astrum. There's an incredible dish of roasted vegetables marinated in lelith sauce and covered in shaved pork." The last word was said in Nysari, but Taesia was fairly certain *pork* was the closest translation. "It's just that we can't exactly cook meals out here. Also, what is Parithvian curry?"

While Julian explained in mouthwatering detail, Taesia stretched. Turning her head, she realized that Kalen had moved a ways off, sitting with his back against a tree and facing the direction of Astrum.

Lilia followed her gaze. "He hasn't eaten yet." She made to stand up and winced.

"I'll do it." Taesia grabbed the provisions bag—which felt too light for her liking—and snuck a piece of root vegetable as she made her way toward him.

Before she could reach him, Marcellus—who'd wandered off to relieve himself—got to him first. Taesia hid behind the nearest tree, her instinct telling her not to interrupt.

The soldier settled down cross-legged beside Kalen. "A lot on your mind?" he asked in Nysari.

"Mn."

Marcellus cracked a smile. Taesia could only see them in profile, the moonlight glinting off his teeth. "That makes me nostalgic. Remember when we were first all together, you'd only give me one-syllable replies?"

"I was afraid your brain couldn't comprehend more than that."

Marcellus snorted and readjusted his sword so that he could lean back on his hands. The moonstone on his pommel shone gently. "Always so mean to me, and for no reason."

Kalen didn't respond. Marcellus happily sat with him in silence, but there was clearly something he wanted to say. He kept glancing at Kalen and away.

"You...mentioned the exteri sulumn earlier," Marcellus murmured. "I've been meaning to ask what you saw in there."

"It doesn't concern you," Kalen said.

Marcellus drew in a breath, then let it out as a hollow laugh.

"Of course," he whispered. "Silly of me to be worried."

The muscle at Kalen's jaw bulged. He held himself like he was surrounded by tripwire, like the smallest movement would trigger disaster.

Marcellus drew his legs up and folded his arms on his knees. "It decided to show me nightmares. I was surprised by how simple they were. Lilia casting me away, my family dying, losing all my memories." He rubbed a thumb over the moonstone. "You never saying another word to me."

There was a tremor in Kalen's shoulders. Taesia knew she should melt into the shadows and slip away, but she couldn't move, her hand numb around the provisions bag.

"I won't ask you again," Marcellus said. "Besides, your nightmares probably involve me annoying you all the way to Mortri—"

Kalen surged onto his knees and grabbed Marcellus by the collar, his knuckles pressing against the soldier's throat. "You don't *want* to know what I saw," he growled. "You don't want to imagine the things I've imagined. Lilia's throat slit by assassins, our people dying of starvation and drought—"

Marcellus, alarmed, covered Kalen's hands with his own. "Kal—"

"The entire royal family slaughtered—but that's already happened, hasn't it?" Kalen's laugh was half-wild with grief. "And you sit here and worry about losing *memories*, like that wouldn't be a blessing!"

"Kalen—"

"I want to forget." Kalen's eyes were bright in the gloom. "I want to forget the look on Lilia's face when it happened. I want to forget ever meeting you. Of being shown—of you—"

Marcellus cradled Kalen's face between his hands. "*Kalen.* Nothing will happen to me."

"You can't know that." Kalen was breathing faster, heavier, his hold on Marcellus shaking. "You can't predict the way I can. And what's that ever been useful for? What good have I ever foreseen?"

"This wasn't a prediction," Marcellus said softly. "It was a nightmare. It's all right to be afraid, but you can't let fear turn the nightmare into reality."

Kalen's body gradually relaxed, making him sway. Marcellus also rose to his knees, keeping Kalen in his hold. Chest to chest, forehead to forehead. Their lips were parted, breathing each other's air.

"I won't let anything happen to you," Marcellus murmured. "Either of you. Or myself. Not if I can help it."

Kalen closed his eyes. He leaned into Marcellus, barely half a minute of surrender.

Then he pushed himself back. Keeping his gaze averted, he stood.

"A promise means nothing," Kalen rasped. "Not with what we're facing."

He walked away, not toward Lilia and Julian, but somewhere he could be alone. Marcellus watched after him, his look so raw Taesia finally managed to turn away with a lump in her throat. She stood behind the tree until she heard Marcellus get up and walk back to Lilia.

Even then she waited another moment, reorganizing her thoughts, before heading over to Julian. He was sitting on the ground, his cloak folded neatly beside him, as he stretched out his hamstrings.

"Only you would fold your cloak like this." She nudged it with her boot, ignoring how the blisters on her toes twinged. "How can someone so interesting also be so painfully boring? You're a walking contradiction."

His wry expression turned dark at the last part. Taesia cussed herself out and stood there uselessly before holding out the provisions bag. "More mushrooms?"

"No." He stretched out his other leg. "Thank you."

Taesia chewed on her bottom lip. Kalen and Marcellus's conversation sat heavy in her chest, making a question bubble up her throat. "Do you..." She panicked, changing it at the last second. "Do you want me to cut your hair?"

He straightened, frowning over his shoulder at her. "Have you ever cut hair before?"

"No. Well, once, when Brailee was a toddler. She was born with a lot of hair, and I thought it would be funny to cut off the sides and only leave the hair at the very top of her head. My mother was far from thrilled."

"That's not the endorsement you think it is." He scrubbed his fingers through the new growth of his undersides. The stubble along his jaw had also filled out more. "Besides, it's difficult to cut hair with a dagger."

"Who said I'd be using a dagger?" She held out her hand, and Umbra unspooled from its silver ring. The familiar twisted and elongated until it turned into a pair of shears.

"You're...planning to cut my hair with a shadow?"

"A shadow *familiar*," she corrected. "And only if you'll let me."

He silently debated. Eventually he settled into a proper sitting position and draped his cloak over his shoulders.

"Just don't make me bald," he warned.

She knelt behind him with a smile tugging at her lips. The longer part of his hair was dark and fell in loose curls, and she briefly ran her fingers through it to get a sense of its texture. Julian held himself stiffly under her touch. She angled his head down, her fingertips warm against the sides of his face, before bringing Umbra up to the base of his neck and giving an experimental cut. He flinched.

"Calm down," she muttered. "These shears are sentient, remember?"

"How is that supposed to calm me?"

"Umbra has good taste." She focused on the next few cuts, trimming down the undersides by a half inch. "I'm sorry."

He made an aggrieved sound. "I knew I shouldn't have let you—"

"No, I mean about earlier." Another snip, another spill of dark hair down his cloak. "You having to expose your power because of me."

His back expanded with a deep breath. "It wasn't your fault. They would have figured it out eventually."

"Still. It doesn't feel good to have something dragged out into the open. Especially when you're not ready for it."

Julian obediently followed her guiding touch and tilted his head to one side. "I feel like I should be used to it, considering the Hunters knew about my beastspeaking. But this is . . ."

"Different," she finished. "Bigger."

"Yes. Especially now that I know where my beastspeaking comes from."

"It doesn't make you a demon, Julian."

"Then what does it make me?"

"It makes you . . ." She tangled a hand in his hair. His skin felt so warm against hers. "It makes you Julian Luca. One of a kind."

"It makes me dangerous." He huffed. "A monster."

The literal translation of Belua. Kalen may be suffering like the rest of them, but she directed a curse at him nonetheless.

"So? I'm dangerous, too. You know what I've done. The things I *chose* to do. That choice is the difference between us."

"What do you mean?"

"You're not the monster here." She lowered her hand to his shoulder. "I am."

Taesia had honed her helplessness into action, unleashed her anger with fatal consequences. She had always been reckless—*impulsive to a fault*, in Risha's words—but until recently she hadn't discovered the satisfaction of violence, or that she would be so skilled at it.

It had been necessary, and it had cost her the love and trust she had built over a lifetime. She missed the easiness she once shared with Risha, the two of them laughing over a noble's drunken speech at a dinner party. She missed the soothing, tactile closeness with Nikolas, lounging on his bed while she found ways to make him smile. She even missed sniping with Angelica, knowing the two of them both secretly liked the antagonism, in finding ways to outdo one another.

All of that was gone now. Without it, she wasn't sure who she was— wondered if all that remained was someone to be feared rather than loved.

Julian was utterly still under her touch. When he turned his head, she only caught the sliver of his profile.

"Who made you believe that?" he asked, so calm and quiet it raised the hairs along the back of her neck.

Believe, like she hadn't spelled it out in blood and shadow.

"What do you believe, then?" she asked softly.

The descending silence was filled with the faint cries of insects, like the singing of crickets but more harmonious. Taesia stared at the nape of his neck, the goose bumps that rose as a breeze swept by.

"I believe you didn't know how to get out of a bad situation," Julian answered at last. "And that you were in pain, and no one else could see it."

Her eyes burned. She blinked the sensation away, pulling in a fragile breath. "Or maybe I was simply selfish. Just as I'm being selfish now in denying Nyx."

"We don't even know if his power would be enough to fix this," Julian argued. "But I think you're more than strong enough. That you'll think of a way."

She was used to others considering her strong, but she wasn't used to others thinking her capable. She wasn't sure if she quite believed it herself, no matter how badly she wanted it to be true.

Marcellus and Kalen had seen nightmares of what could happen should they fail. She didn't want Julian haunted by visions of things she could prevent.

"Julian... you don't have to answer, but... what did you see in the exteri sulumn?"

She heard him swallow, felt the muscle underneath her shift.

"Memories, mostly," he answered after a long beat, his voice barely louder than the rustle of wind through grass.

Taesia forced herself not to pry further. "You lashed out," she guessed.

A shiver traveled through him. It passed into her, in the places where they shared warmth.

"I've become something I was once assigned to hunt," he whispered. "Something I was put on Nik's task force to take down."

Her fingers curled involuntarily, pulling at his hair. His gasp was small but sharp.

"You can talk that way about yourself, but I can't?" she asked. "It doesn't matter what you saw, or how you reacted. In the end, I'll always trust you to be *you*."

The shiver that wracked through him this time seemed different. It flooded her mouth, made her inhale deeper. Under the heavy clove of Noctus air was him, strong and sharp and sweet.

"I'm a danger to you," he croaked. "To the others. If I lose myself to it—or if Orsus controls me—"

"That won't happen."

He finally tore himself out of her hold and turned, his eyes more green than hazel, burning through the night like a comet's tail.

"How do you know?" he demanded. "You can't predict something like that."

Kalen and Marcellus's words echoed in her mind. "You're right," she agreed. "I can't. And neither can you predict what you'll do in the future. It's all right to be afraid, but you can't let fear turn the nightmare into reality."

He shut his eyes tight. She allowed him the time to get himself under control, to absorb the words, before she turned him back around.

"Now let me finish, or else your hair will be uneven."

Lilia watched Kalen and Marcellus with concern after their rest. The two of them walked far apart, Marcellus in front and Kalen behind, both taciturn and solemn. That was nothing new for Kalen, but from Marcellus it was downright troubling.

Taesia glanced at Julian to check if he had also noticed, but there was a furrow between his brows and a distance in his gaze. It wasn't the same fatigued, introspective expression he'd worn earlier, but something of the Hunter—focused, alert.

"What's wrong?" she asked. "Are there beasts nearby?"

"I . . . I don't know. It's hard to tell. Like whatever it is, it can cloak its presence."

"Well, that's not at all creepy."

"There are beasts that can make themselves invisible," Lilia interjected behind them. "Perhaps it's one of them?"

As she spoke, Starfell flared with that strange, living warmth again. Taesia unsheathed the sword, following the sensation until its point arrowed straight ahead.

"We're near." Lilia hurried forward, but Julian caught her arm.

"Wait." He stalked on ahead, his movements smooth and sure. The grass thinned until it became smooth, dark rock, eventually forming shallow ledges that led to a wide fissure in the ground.

Taesia followed after, crouching next to him at the lip. The canyon below was emitting a gentle radiance, the walls pocketed with broken geodes. Judging from the crystalline ombré of pale lilac to deep violet, they had to be unharvested amethysts. They winked and gleamed along the winding canyon passageway, between sheer rock and protruding striations.

Lilia knelt on Julian's other side. "An amethyst deposit. But why is it—?" Her voice caught. "The beasts. I remember, now. They killed the harvesters, drove the rest out."

Marcellus crept toward the fissure. "Nesch," he hissed. "Is that what I think it is?"

Julian was already staring at the spot that had caught Marcellus's attention. It gradually came into view: a ghostly shape floating through the canyon, a splotch of impossible darkness that absorbed the light of the geodes, that moved in whispers and sighs.

It had no distinguishable features, and yet a primal horror formed in her gut. The longer she stared at it, the more the canyon twisted and turned, their surroundings distorting like one of Brailee's dreamscapes.

Like a nightmare.

And beyond it, nestled at the base of a rock wall: the faint silver sheen of the second fang.

Baron Alma's estate was a broad building with red shingles and a sand-colored exterior. Lamps burned a homey yellow, and a circular fountain trickled in the round courtyard behind the tall fence that separated the grounds from the rest of the city.

Dante and Camilla surveyed the estate through the dusky evening. They stood together on the roof of a covered balcony along one of the side buildings; likely the servants' quarters. Dante had gathered the shadows close around them, shielding their figures from the guards at the gates and entrances. It felt good to work this familiar muscle, to feel the nighttime bend and shift to his whim.

"Now, where would a seedy politician keep a corpse?" Camilla murmured at his side.

Apparently she found nothing awkward about this. Yet it was foremost on his mind, how odd it was work with the woman who had caused him so much grief.

But he didn't want Brailee involved any more than she already was, and Saya had stayed with her to make sure Brailee got some much-needed sleep. To which Brailee had muttered that there was no chance of sleeping while Dante was out committing theft.

"When you think about it, the baron's the real thief here," Dante had said.

Saya had explained to them that, when examining the body, she had delved into the sense memories that still lingered within it. In those sense memories, she had learned the corpse was of a random citizen of Seniza, and she had seen the blurry face of Baron Alma looming over it.

"Does *he* plan to resurrect Marcos Ricci, too?" Camilla had guessed.

Which had commenced an argument between Saya and the Conjurers—rather, the Revenants—about what it truly meant to resurrect a spirit, and the difference between that and reanimating a body. It had all flown over Dante's head while he pondered the true question: How were they going to get the body back?

Dante watched a guard walk between the gates and the front doors. The Revenants had surrounded the estate from the outside, ready to cause a distraction should they need one.

"There." Camilla pointed to the roof of a smaller building sitting a good distance away from the estate, partially hidden by trees and climbing vines. "Doesn't that look like a mausoleum?"

Dante peered through the dark. The smaller building was made of stone and crafted with ornate corbels, and above the arched doors was the Almas' family crest: a coronet surrounding the cameo of Deia's Heart.

"They have a mausoleum on their premises? Isn't that dangerous, with the current dead situation?"

"I'm sure they've exhumed the bodies already," Camilla said. "But a family like the Almas would keep their tombs far from the commoners' necropolis."

With the help of the shadows, and the aid of their demons' strength and dexterity, they descended the balcony and landed easily on the ground below. But the mausoleum was another story. Several guards stood before it, very much at attention.

"Oh yeah, there's definitely something in there," Camilla muttered. She gave him a nudge. "Go on."

Dante bit down his irritation and walked up to the guards, dropping his cloak of shadows. "*You do not perceive me. Leave your posts and don't come back.*"

The weight of Azideh's influence took hold before any of them could react. Their eyes filmed over and they calmly strode away. Dante wasn't sure how much time it would buy them, but hopefully it was enough. In his mind's eye he saw Brailee's look of disapproval.

It was either that or knocking them unconscious, he argued with himself. This way was easier, and no one got hurt.

Camilla grasped the heavy lock on the doors. Her hand flared red, and the lock fell to the ground in two halves. She opened one of the doors with a flick of her fingers and they slipped inside.

The interior was humbler than its exterior. Stone coffins lay on short pedestals on either side, all of them open and empty save for one at the very end. Camilla waved her hand with another flash of red and the lid slid off. Inside lay a body almost identical to the fake.

"We meet at last, Don Ricci," Camilla said. "I'm a big fan of your work."

"Just hurry up and do it." Dante sent Nox to the door. His familiar would alert him if anyone came near.

Camilla held her hands out over the body. Behind her, the form of her demon took shape, a tall and angular figure of crimson with spikes erupting from its shoulders. Shanizeh grinned at Dante from across the coffin, dark eyes blazing. In response, Azideh appeared behind Dante with a snarl.

"Stop it," Dante snapped at them. "Concentrate."

Shanizeh made an unusual, clicking laugh. "What is that on your body, beast-lover?"

Dante turned. Azideh was wearing the outfit he'd chosen after Dante had insisted he wear clothes. Camilla, seeing this, snorted a laugh.

"*Focus*," Dante said. "We don't have much time."

Shanizeh put her sharp-nailed hands on his aunt's shoulders, and Camilla's hands bristled with crimson energy that engulfed Marcos Ricci's corpse. Camilla closed her eyes, no doubt searching out beyond the estate's walls for the fake body that the Revenants had brought with them.

Her arms began to shake. Shanizeh put her chin on top of Camilla's head, stroking her hair while she smirked at Dante and Azideh. There was a pressure in the air that made his ears and sinuses ache.

Just when he thought he couldn't bear another moment of it, Marcos Ricci disappeared. Seconds later, the decoy body flopped down into the coffin, hitting its skull against the back.

Camilla dropped her arms. "Thank you, Shanizeh."

The demon bared her teeth in another grin before disappearing into a cloud. Azideh hesitated before doing the same.

"The Revenants should have the real body," Camilla said. "Let's go."

They replaced the stone lid and joined Nox at the doors, where Dante shrouded them in shadows again.

But as they made for the outer wall, something caught his eye. He stopped Camilla and pointed to the large ground-floor window. It was lit up, revealing a polished, well-furnished study. And a scuffle between a woman and the baron's guards.

Dante went to see what was happening. Camilla followed. Dante thickened the shadows around them as they crouched at the sill and peered in.

Two guards were forcing the woman into a chair. This close, she was oddly familiar, her face tear-stained and her pleas warbling through the glass.

"Please, I'm sorry, I—I can leave," she was blabbering. "I thought—I thought we could come into the city—"

Dante realized why she looked familiar to him: She'd been one of the refugees in the camp. She had been mending clothes by the fire he'd used to burn the clerk's ledger.

Fuck.

The door to the study opened and Martín Alma strolled in. The young woman quieted at the baron's approach. Her fear was sour and pungent in Dante's mouth, a haze of sharp orange. Alma nodded to the guards and they silently left the room, no doubt positioning themselves outside the door.

"Well," Alma said with a smile. It wasn't sinister or forced; if anything, he seemed genuinely amused. "I'd heard some of the refugees managed to sneak into the city. Ah, but don't worry—all are welcome within Seniza. Especially those displaced from the chaos in Nexus." He lightly touched her shoulder, his tone sympathetic. "I'm sure we can find some way for you to be useful here."

As she listened, the young girl's terror gradually diminished. When he touched her shoulder, the sour fear instantly vanished, replaced with the soft pink of comfort. She even smiled back at the baron with tears still drying on her face.

"What the fuck?" Dante whispered. Her eyes were clear, so he hadn't compelled her. But the mood shift was too sudden to be natural.

Azideh rumbled in agreement. *There is something wrong with this man. There's an odd smell here.*

Alma knelt beside the chair, his fingertips still lightly touching the young woman's shoulder. "I will keep you safe here," he said. His voice was velvet and sweet, with the same gentle authority he'd used in the necropolis to calm the crowd. "You will have delicious food and a bed to sleep in, and you'll be content. Then I will lead you to a nice hill overlooking Deia's Heart while the sun rises, and give you something to drink. Does that sound nice?"

The young woman nodded.

"Very good."

"What's he planning?" Camilla murmured.

Dante didn't know, but he had seen enough to understand the woman was in danger. He held Nox up to the window. His familiar seeped through the crack between glass and sill, stretching toward the latch.

His aunt gripped his forearm hard. "What are you doing?"

"Saving her."

"We need to meet up with the others and get the body out of here."

"Then you go on ahead." He pulled his arm away. "I'll catch up."

Nox unlatched the window and it swung outward. Dante eased it open and pulled more shadows to him as he climbed silently into the baron's study.

Alma's back was to him. Dante sidled up closer, waiting until the baron stood and began to turn toward the door. Then he grabbed the baron's shoulder and spun him around, dropping the shadows so their eyes could meet. Alma's lips parted in shock.

"*You do not perceive me,*" Dante said with Azideh's ringing power.

"*You're embarrassed to find you have no idea how you got here,*" Alma said at the same time.

The two men stared at one another. Slowly, as a blue cloud formed across Alma's shoulders and Azideh stirred in warning, realization took hold.

He has a demon.

Dante sprinted for the window. Camilla was already gone—*of course*—so he had a clear path to dive back onto the lawn and dash for the outer wall. Behind him the baron called for his guards, but Dante pulled in the shadows until he was just another piece of the night.

By the time he scrambled over the wall and landed in the alley where the Revenants and his aunt were waiting, there was a stitch in his side. He held it and gasped for air, breathless more out of disbelief than the run.

"What happened?" Camilla demanded. Beyond her, the Revenants had already wrapped Marcos Ricci's body in a sheet.

"The baron," he panted. "He has a demon. My power didn't work on him."

Azideh formed beside him, wearing a murderous scowl. The Revenants gasped.

"I confirmed who it was when he spoke," the demon said. "Marizleh."

"*Marizleh.*" Shanizeh appeared as well. "I thought I smelled rancid sugar."

"What's Marizleh's power?" Dante asked.

"Obedience," Azideh answered. He looked down at Dante with his acid-green eyes, the fall of his silken hair slipping over one muscled shoulder. "It's a form of seduction, but of the mind, not the body."

"So, emotional manipulation," Dante said. The young woman's mood shift now made sense. "But *how* does he have a demon? And what's he planning to do with—?"

Shouts came from beyond the wall. The baron had raised an alarm. Camilla gestured at the Revenants to pick up the body.

"We'll figure it out later," she said. "Right now, our main goal is waking up Don Ricci."

And praying the baron didn't recognize me, Dante silently added as they slipped away from the estate and into the dark.

XI

Angelica leaned out of the hut and stared down at the three horses Kenji held by their reins. They each carried fine leather saddles, and though Angelica wasn't too knowledgeable about horses in general, she could tell these were well-bred mounts.

"*Where* did you find these?" she demanded.

"Took 'em from the Gojarin-Kae who passed the village," he answered.

"You didn't...?" *Please, do not add any more deaths to the ones we're already being framed for.*

"Didn't what? Alert them? Nah, they were all fast asleep. They didn't even keep a lookout!" He laughed. Angelica, who hadn't even thought about having lookout shifts during the nights they'd been on the run, glowered. "I took some of their provisions, too. Oh, and this."

He opened a bag and pulled out a pair of boots. He waved them up at Angelica with a big grin, and she sighed.

In the hut, they ate a simple breakfast of rice and pickled vegetables before preparing for the ride. The boots were far too large for the girls, so instead Angelica bandaged their feet and pulled new socks over them.

Kenji knelt before his wooden chest. His sword was laid out beside him, the sheath made of black magnolia wood with carvings of waves and leaves. Taking a deep breath, he removed a key from his pocket and slotted it into the lock.

Opening the lid revealed a pile of black armor. He picked up the wolf mask that lay on top, peering through the empty eyeholes as if looking at a past version of himself he'd never wished to meet again.

Cosima, seeing the mask, crossed her arms tight against her chest. Perhaps thinking of the one Koshi had worn in the banquet hall—the snarling tiger speckled with Kazue's blood. Eiko and Asami froze like hares who had heard a predator.

Kenji grabbed the nearest bag and stuffed the mask inside. Everyone in the hut relaxed.

Then Asami, who'd been holding her muzzle in her hands, got up. She walked to Kenji and shyly held out the muzzle.

It took him a moment to realize what she wanted. He held out the bag, and she carefully put her muzzle in with his mask. Kenji bowed low.

"I will take great care of it, Your Imperial Majesty."

Angelica's chest eased a little.

Since Eiko was familiar with riding, she elected to be the one to share a horse with Asami. The empress was wide-eyed at the prospect of sitting on such a tall horse. When Kenji swung the girl onto the saddle as though she weighed nothing, Asami just barely managed to cover her mouth before a squeak could escape.

"Think you can lift me up like that?" Cosima joked to Angelica, who despaired at having to share a horse at all, let alone with her. "I'd probably swoon."

"We can't afford any swooning," Angelica said. "Put your foot in the stirrup. Your *other* foot."

"Gods' bones, you're bossy. Are you sure this thing won't bite? It looks bitey."

By the time they left the village behind, the sun had climbed to its zenith. Kenji looked back, wistful and fond and not a little sad. The Gojarin armor fit him well, the robe underneath patterned with the same waves and leaves as his sword sheath, which he wore at his hip. He seemed a wholly different person than the farmer who'd called her a boot thief.

Then he shook his head and turned, leading them north.

They were three days from Mount Netsai. Angelica encouraged them to ride at a brisk pace, one that wouldn't overtire the horses but would put distance between them and the Gojarin-Kae these horses had originally belonged to.

"You're holding me too tight," she grumbled, fidgeting against the clamp of Cosima's arm.

Cosima groaned. "I know now why I've never ridden a horse. It's *terrible*. Rich people do this for fun?"

"Just focus on shifting your weight with its movements."

"What does that even *mean*?" Cosima's voice bounced along with the horse. "I hate this."

Angelica would have, too, but the feeling of Cosima's chest pressed against her back stole the words out of her mouth. She mumbled something incoherent and flicked the reins, urging the horse to trot faster.

Kenji kept the girls amused with songs and stories. Angelica only half listened until he asked them, "Since we're heading to Mount Netsai, have you heard how Empress Satake Akari once jumped into the volcano?"

"Why would she do that?" Eiko asked.

"It was a long time ago, so no one can say for certain. Some think it was a show of might, to get the other clans to follow her orders. Others say she did it because she lost a bet." His boisterous laugh made nearby birds take flight. "She was so powerful, though, that I don't doubt she swam through the lava like it was a river. In fact, sometimes the stronger fire Gojarin are dared to do it, too."

Eiko's eyes widened. "Has anyone done it?"

"Nope. Koshi came the closest, though. He hiked all the way to the top, stood there for a while, then hiked back down." Kenji's laugh was softer this time. "Or at least, that's what he said happened. I think he did it, but wanted to keep it to himself."

When they settled for the night, Cosima flopped onto her back and reeled a litany of complaints about what areas of her body ached. Kenji, despite not understanding a word of it, handed her a rice ball. She grabbed it and practically smashed it into her face. The girls hid their giggles behind their sleeves, the sound a minor miracle.

"She reminds me so much of Koshi," Kenji said as Angelica made the fire.

Angelica thought back to the hard-faced, stoic warrior she'd seen in the banquet hall. "How so?"

Cosima had heard her brother's name and turned to Angelica. "What's he saying?" she asked around a mouthful of rice. "Can he...can he tell me more about Koshi? How he came to work for the warlord?"

Angelica related her questions to Kenji. He'd taken off his armor, and looked softer in just his robes. He sat back and nodded.

"Of course. When I first met Koshi I think he was...thirteen? I'd seen Mariians before, but never one who trained to be a Gojarin. He'd started training with the Gojarin-Kae, but they quickly saw how much potential he had and decided to bring him to Hitan."

"What elements does he wield?"

"Air and fire, with equal strength. Since I wield water and earth with equal strength, we were considered complimentary, so we often sparred together. Bushan Nanbu himself oversaw our training—me because of my title, and Koshi because of his ability. I was fascinated by him, to be honest. I was always asking him about his home, his family. He wouldn't shut up about his little sister and how clever she was."

When Angelica translated this to Cosima, Cosima's eyes shimmered in the firelight before she turned her face away.

"But he was *stubborn*." Kenji shook his head with a smile. "If he didn't like something, he'd complain. *Loudly*. Sometimes his complaining forced the Gojarin who were training us to report him to Bushan Nanbu. But then Bushan Nanbu would talk to Koshi and ask what was wrong, and he'd *listen* to Koshi and order the Gojarin to change their tactics."

"He sounds like a prodigy," Angelica said.

"He was. Is. I was even a little jealous, from time to time." He picked at a loose thread in his robe. "But then I found out how homesick he was. That he'd let the soldiers take him from his home because his family would be compensated."

Cosima sat up with a scowl when Angelica conveyed this. "We didn't *need* compensation. We needed *him*."

Angelica chose not to translate this, and instead asked Kenji, "Did he ever think about going back?"

"All the time. But he also greatly enjoyed training. Like you said, he was a prodigy. Didn't take long for Bushan Nanbu to appoint us as his right and left hands. But..." His sigh was heavy. "Over the last couple years, Koshi started to change. He didn't laugh as easily. He stopped going into the city with me and the others. He spent more and more time with Bushan Nanbu. They really liked playing checkers together.

"Then the whole loan thing happened." He shrugged. "I felt like I'd lost everything. My friend. Bushan Nanbu's respect. My family's support. It was easier to leave them all behind. So I don't know what happened to Koshi, or why he'd agree to such a thing."

"Why did you take out so many loans, anyway?" Angelica asked.

It was for curiosity's sake, but something in how his eyes shifted put her on guard.

"I was, ah... There was a lot of pressure put on me. A lot of things I was learning about Bushan Nanbu that I didn't like. I felt *bad*. The only two things that ever helped were training, and...and drinking."

Asami's chin was dropping as though she was fighting off sleep. Eiko tapped her on the shoulder, and the two left to gather more wood for the fire.

Once the girls were gone, Kenji rubbed the back of his neck. "It got pretty bad," he admitted. "I don't even remember what I did, half the time."

"You don't have to talk about it," Angelica said. "I—I understand. It's personal."

This weakness, this sickness within you.

The fire popped, sending a sudden flurry of sparks into the air. All three of them started.

"I never wanted it to get so bad," Kenji murmured after a while. "But it did. Bushan Nanbu wanted me to go to the northern city-states to 'clean myself up.'"

"But you went to a small farming village instead."

"I did. I don't really know why. My mother always told me to trust my instinct, and she was right. I found a place where I could do good labor and take care of people, away from the city and the merchants and the things that made me weak. And I became strong again, bit by bit. It was hard, though. Ended up falling back on old habits a couple times when there was a festival. But I think I've cleared the worst of it."

There was weariness in his voice, but also pride. Angelica's stomach twisted in a sudden spiral of jealousy, hot and sharp. Like Deia's handprint on her arm, cooking her alive.

When they stopped again the next evening, Angelica gestured for Asami to follow her. As before, Angelica gathered a pile of rocks and laid them out in the grass.

"I want to try something specific this time," Angelica said. "Do you remember how it felt to sing all those notes? There was one in particular where nothing around you broke."

Asami's eyes widened, shining with tentative hope.

"I think we were able to channel the most kudei with that note,"

Angelica went on. "We'll build up to it like before, but when we reach it"—she tapped one of the rocks—"I want you to concentrate on moving this elsewhere."

The girl frowned at the rock Angelica had tapped, uncertainty making room for determination. She began to sign, then stopped.

"No, go ahead," Angelica said. "You may as well teach me something while I'm here."

Asami graced her with a smile and signed with both hands, then in Azunese wrote in the dirt: *I'm ready.* Angelica repeated the motion a few times before Asami nodded, pleased.

They moved through the scale, allowing for the cracking of stone and earth, Asami flinching imperceptibly at each one. Yet she held on, her voice less steady than Angelica's but making up for it with pure, ringing sound.

"She has to control her volume," Adela had said after one of Angelica's nightly performances for her father. "And her breathing is all over the place."

August had been a peaceable man, but at this he had given his wife a stern look. "*That's* what you hear? Not the vibrato, the tonal brilliance? Come here, Angel." Angelica had stepped forward, holding on to her father's outstretched hands. "You can be as loud as you want to be. With a gift like yours, isn't it better for everyone to hear it?"

Instead of weighing her down, the memory buoyed her, her voice floating over Asami's as they matched each other pitch for pitch.

They hit the A-sharp, stinging like the cold air around them. There was a tug in Angelica's abdomen and the beckoning of forgotten magic, and both of them swayed forward as if lured by the call. The space between them warped.

That's it, Angelica thought. *More.*

Asami stared at the rock. Stared, and sang, and shivered, until she ran out of breath and slumped over, panting.

"That's all right," Angelica said. "We'll do it again."

Asami seemed worried. She wrote in the dirt: *Too loud?*

"No, you're doing just fine. You can be as loud as you want to be."

She ignored the breaking of nearby tree branches and the shattering of pebbles as they climbed the scale. Again they held out the note, Asami's fingers scrunched in her robe, sweat shining at her temple.

The rock quivered—and remained where it was. But Angelica had sensed the quintessence around it spin and tighten.

After a break to catch their breaths, Angelica waited for Asami to sign *I'm ready* before saying, "Again."

By the fourth time, the rock still hadn't moved. Asami's frustration edged the A-sharp higher, and the rock split in half with a loud *crack*.

"I can't *do it!*" Asami yelled with a miniature earthquake. She hung her head and choked back a sob.

Angelica reached for her chin and lifted it. "Hey, look at me. I get it. You want it to work, you want it so badly you'd do anything, but nothing helps. Nothing changes. You're angry, and furious at yourself for being angry. *I get it.*"

The girl's tears rolled slowly down her face. Though she couldn't vocalize it, her eyes were screaming, pupils shrunk to pinpoints.

"There is no shame in this," Angelica told her. "No shame in what you can't do yet, and no shame in wanting to get better. You're already powerful."

But Asami shook her head, making Angelica let go. She wrote between them: *My power killed.*

A small frisson of what could have been fear ran across her scalp. She wondered if Asami could just as easily smash her skull in with a misspoken word.

The girl cried silently, thin shoulders jerking. Angelica wet her chapped lips, tasting a residue of aether in the air.

"I thought..." Her voice fell upon the ground like the oncoming dusk, quiet and deep. "I thought I could draw on the elements without music so long as I did something to make me more powerful, to...to break down the doors that stood between me and my magic."

Her hands shook. The night she'd lost herself to desperation was a bloody tangle of memory, from the buzzing in her mind to the blistering revulsion in her heart. Revulsion for the system she had been caught in, for her god, for the man who had seen her weakness. For herself.

"There was a mage," Angelica whispered to the broken rocks. "And I killed him. I tore him open because I wanted his power, and I was sick with that wanting. I'm still sick with it." Even now the heat swam through her veins, itching, feverish, making her vision blur and her fingers yearn for the strings of a violin.

Asami had stopped crying. She stared at Angelica without fear or wariness, but with something like understanding. Complimentary chords struck on different instruments.

"The deaths of the kaikushine were caused by your power," Angelica said. "You could ask almost anyone and I'm sure they would say it was justified, as I felt justified killing a mage who preyed on those less powerful than him. But you'll carry those deaths with you regardless. You can either be haunted by it, or learn from it."

Angelica had learned only one thing from killing Eran Liolle: that there was no easy fix for her. But if she could steer Asami to a better way of thinking, teaching not in the way of her mother but in the way of her father, then maybe all of this wouldn't be a waste.

Asami wrote: *Don't want to kill again.*

"You don't have to. Now you know how to do it, so you can avoid it in the future."

The girl nodded wearily. Angelica was trembling now, and the first stirring of panic rose in her.

She excused herself and headed for the nearby pond, feeling like she was about to shake apart. She knelt at the water's edge and submerged her burning hands. Bile crept up her throat at the lingering metallic taste of a mage's blood, the sense memory of an organ torn under her greedy teeth.

Her withdrawal hadn't been this bad since the imperial palace, since she'd downed the only vial of Hypericum she had. She didn't know how long it would be until she found another. How was she supposed to evade a warlord and a god while ascending a volcano in this condition?

"Hey, Mardo—"

"Get away from me," Angelica snarled. Fire roiled off her shoulders and down her arms.

Cosima swore. "What can I do?"

Nothing. No touch or desire could possibly soothe this.

Angelica's chest cavity was filled with smoke, her insides singed from the pressing, painful need for *fire*. She poured everything into her hands, the whole pond bubbling and frothing like a pot left too long on the stove.

"I can—"

"I said *get away!*"

A pained cry forced her gaze up. Cosima shrank back from her, cradling her forearm to her chest.

Angelica's vision scorched white. When she was next fully aware of herself, fish were floating on the pond's steaming surface, cooked alive.

And Eiko was sitting beside her.

"What are you doing?" Angelica croaked. "Cosima—"

She twisted around. She could just see the camp; Kenji was juggling rocks for Asami's entertainment, and Cosima was sitting by the fire with a cloth around her arm.

"Kenji took care of the burn." Eiko carefully didn't look in her direction, instead fixated on the pond. "I wanted to check on you."

Angelica's upper lip curled. "I don't need your pity."

"Who said I'm giving it?" Eiko turned to her at last. There were bags under her stepsister's eyes. "Why do you always do this? I don't pity you. I'm *worried* about you."

Angelica's mouth was so dry, and she was beyond the point of humiliated. The turbulence within her had settled into a background hum of longing—for Hypericum, for her violin, for a portal to spirit her away from here.

"You should save your worry for more important things," Angelica muttered. "I'm—fine. Now."

Annoyance flashed across Eiko's face. "Sure you are."

The silence that fell between them was difficult. But Angelica's legs were too weak to stand, and she was forced to endure it.

Eventually Eiko said, "You're good with her. Asami, I mean."

What does that have to do with anything? "You're far better than I am."

"But you're patient with her. Understanding." Eiko went on in a lower voice, "I wish you'd been like that to me and Kikou."

Angelica closed her eyes and steadied her breathing. It was either that or collapse in on herself like a bonfire. "You're really bringing that up now?"

"It's not like there's a better time." Eiko inhaled shakily. "We reach Hitan tomorrow. You and Asami are all the family I have right now. If we get caught..."

Angelica gestured at the dead fish. "I won't let this get in the way."

"That's not what I mean! I can't—I don't want to lose anyone else."

Her body crystallized with disbelief. Eiko bowed her head so that her hair hid her face.

Not worried about Angelica losing control, but about Angelica getting hurt.

You gotta open up sometime, princess. It'll kill you if you don't.

Angelica's arm was sore as she slowly wrapped it around Eiko, the way she'd seen Cosima do. Eiko instantly buried her head in Angelica's shoulder, breath coming in small hitches.

How do I do this? Angelica pleaded of no one, staring beyond the pond. Her stepsister's weight was foreign against her, her grief familiar.

There's no shame in this, she had told Asami earlier. She repeated it to herself now.

"It'll take a lot more than one bout of withdrawal to do me in," Angelica said. "Didn't I say I'll get us home?"

Eiko's voice was small. "You did."

Angelica rested a hand on the back of Eiko's head. She was no longer burning, but warmth remained.

By the end of the third day, Hitan rose triumphantly on the horizon, its lights a steady glow against the falling night. Beyond it, casting a dramatic silhouette in the last of the bleeding sunset, rose the peak of Mount Netsai.

It seemed impossible they were this close to where Deia's fulcrum might be hidden, shrouded by magma and scorching ash. Even the air was more humid here, winter's bite reduced to a feeble nip.

Kenji reined in his horse, and the others did the same. Angelica had practically hauled Asami onto her horse today, forcing Eiko to ride with Cosima. She had also ignored every instance of Cosima trying to catch her attention.

"Hitan," Kenji muttered. "It's been so long since I've seen it."

Eiko studied the landscape, the wall around the city where sentries were no doubt stationed. "Kenji, how are we supposed to get past it without being seen?"

There were steep hills to the west, and open fields to the east that led to the nearby coast. Either option was unsuitable.

"Don't worry, I've been thinking about this." He poked a finger to his temple with a wink. "I was raised here, remember? I know all sorts of secrets."

"Get to the point," Angelica said. "Are we going through, or around?"

"I had a whole dramatic reveal planned..." He huffed at Angelica's glare. "Fine, fine. We're going *under.*"

"Under?" Eiko repeated.

He nodded to the hills. "There's a tunnel that was once used for the citizens to flee in case of a siege. Only the sitting warlord and his Gojarin know about it."

"Why only them?" Eiko asked. "If it's meant for the citizens..." She must have realized which citizens, exactly, this safety measure extended to. "Oh."

"Are you sure it's safe?" Angelica asked. "Where does it lead?"

"It splits. One path leads to the warlord's castle, and the other to the mercantile district. We'll use the latter. From there it's easy to slip out of the city's northern gate."

"Define *easy*."

He scratched his chin. "There's a separate entrance for the military class, and no one will be using it late at night. We wait a bit, I go out to open it, we get through. Then it's volcano time." He blinked. "What exactly does volcano time entail?"

Angelica didn't really know. She'd hoped for more time to plan, to understand what exactly she was meant to do with a god's core.

"Just focus on getting us past the city." Angelica hoped the strain of her uncertainty wasn't obvious. "I'll focus on . . . volcano time."

Kenji led them through what Angelica had assumed were impassible hills, but thanks to his navigation they found a path that wasn't too steep and led to a limestone outcrop. He dismounted and knocked around on the rocky wall for a few moments. Eventually he pressed his hand against a certain spot while the other made a lifting gesture. A section of the rock wall pushed outward, opening to a cavernous, dark space.

"I'll scout ahead and make sure it's clear," Kenji said while pulling his mask out of his bag.

"Be careful," Eiko told him.

"Thank you, Revered Ueda, I will." He put on his wolf mask and ducked into the passageway, the short horns on his helmet knocking against the top. He muttered a quiet *ow* and disappeared.

They pulled their meager provisions out of the saddlebags. Asami retrieved her muzzle and held it in her hands, silently debating. With a quiet sigh, she put it on.

Cosima approached Angelica as she tied off the bag containing the rest of their food. "Don't run away," Cosima said.

"I'm not running away."

"It was a mistake. I'm fine."

Angelica glanced down at Cosima's arm, where a bandage lay under her sleeve.

"I'm *fine*," Cosima stressed. "I mean, yeah, it hurt, but I bet it hurts worse to deal with this shit. This . . ."

"Addiction," Angelica supplied for her. "And it doesn't matter. Once I take Deia's fulcrum, I can stop it."

"I'm not sure if that's how it works," Cosima said carefully. "Don't get me wrong, you're the expert, but... it's like what Kenji was saying about his drinking. You don't suddenly get better. It's a gradual process. A healing process."

"You're right, you don't know how it works. This isn't like the opium addicts in Nexus. The source is different." She held a hand to her sternum. "The... *healing process* is different." Even though she would be hard-pressed to understand what exactly that process looked like.

"I get it. You're all right, though?" She made to reach for Angelica's hand, but Angelica shifted it away.

"Yes."

They stood in fragile silence as the sky grew speckled with stars. Cosima started to pet the horse's neck. "You know, these things aren't so bad. I'm probably gonna be sore for weeks, but there was zero biting. What are we going to do with them, though?"

In answer, Angelica smacked the horse's rear and it darted off in the direction of the city. Eiko did the same with the other two.

"You're just gonna leave 'em to fend for themselves?" Cosima demanded.

"They're close enough that the sentries will spot them and bring them in."

Almost an hour passed before Kenji returned, his mask still in place.

"We can go," he said.

Angelica slung the provisions bag over her shoulder before Cosima could grab it, then ignored Cosima's glower.

"Is it pretty dark in there?" Angelica asked.

Kenji was staring at the ground. At her question, he started. "What? Oh, yes, a little. It was outfitted with Solarian crystals a long time ago, but most of their power's gone."

Angelica hesitated. With his Gojarin mask on, the girls were avoiding looking at him, and his usual warmth had dimmed. "Are you all right?"

"I'll be fine."

He was returning to a city he had run away from. Of course he was probably scared. Angelica gave him what she hoped was an encouraging nod before stepping into the passageway and following it down into the tunnel.

It was wider than she thought it would be, the walls made of tightly packed earth. Solarian crystals had indeed been fitted into the ceiling, most of them long dead, some casting a light paler than the thinnest slice of butter. One farther down kept flickering on and off.

She pressed her hand to the wall. Ash and broken clasts mingled in the dirt. Hitan had once been located closer to the Sanatsu Peaks until a particularly vicious eruption had wiped the city out. Mount Netsai, like Deia's Heart, was still active; she hoped the city had been rebuilt far enough away.

Once everyone was in the tunnel, Kenji shut the passage entrance. With the starlight gone, they took a minute to adjust their eyes to the dark. "This way," Kenji said, taking the lead.

The tunnel reverberated with the sounds of them walking and breathing, the space claustrophobic. Surrounded by the remains of volcanic destruction, she couldn't help the painful sparks at her fingertips, as if she were being static shocked over and over.

The feeling got worse the farther in they went. Kenji didn't falter, but he was unusually quiet for someone who had insisted on telling stories and singing and making jokes the entire time they had traveled. Angelica stared at his broad back, the lowering of his head.

They reached the split in the tunnel, one path going north and the other south. Kenji stopped, as if unsure of the way. Angelica strode forward to ask him what was wrong. But then a figure stepped out of the northern tunnel, standing in the crossroads.

He was tall and clad in black Gojarin armor. His helmet and mask were missing, revealing a handsome Mariian face with dark eyes.

Koshi.

"What did you do?" Angelica hissed. "*Kenji*—"

"Kenji has been reminded of his loyalties," Koshi said in Azunese, his voice deep and barely inflected with an accent. "He has come home." He smiled then, only a slight curve of his full mouth. "Welcome back, brother."

Then his gaze slid to the space behind Angelica. His smile fell and his hand slipped from its casual resting place on his sword hilt.

"Veliane?" he breathed.

Cosima swallowed, her face shimmering with tears in the dim light. "Koshi." She sounded wrecked.

He made toward her, and Cosima shuffled back while scrabbling for her sword. When Koshi stopped at the sight of it, Angelica got between them. Koshi was tall, easily six feet, but she stared him down regardless.

"You don't touch or speak to her until I know what the fuck is going on here." Angelica turned her glare on Kenji. "I knew it. This was your plan after all."

He removed his mask, revealing a face twisted in remorse. "No—Angelica, it wasn't—"

"He did it out of duty. I'm sure you would understand such a sentiment, Esteemed Mardova."

That smoky voice. A shiver crawled down her spine as Nanbu Daiji arrived, Deia curled around his shoulders. A handful of Gojarin appeared behind him, immediately rushing to flank their party.

Eiko held Asami close. "Kenji, how could you lead us to him?" she demanded.

"As I said, he was bound by duty." Nanbu nodded toward the corridor. Another Gojarin stepped out, holding the shoulders of bound teenage girl.

Akane.

Asami made a muffled cry behind her muzzle and fought against Eiko, but Eiko held her back as icy hatred suffused her expression. Angelica felt its fiery cousin sprawl throughout her body.

"Imagine my surprise when, on the way back to Hitan, my companion told me there was a lost girl in the wilderness." He stroked the underside of Deia's chin, the snake's tongue flicking out. "Thanks to Her Majesty—or who I thought was Her Majesty—I learned all about you, Satake Asami. The wonders you can do."

At last, one who listens to me, Deia purred in her mind. *One who can actually control the fire.*

Akane cried, "I'm sorry, Asami! I'm so sorry!"

"Now, now." Nanbu patted her head and she cringed away. Then he stepped up to Kenji with a truer smile. "Kenji, I have missed you. I'm glad to see you return healthy, and that you remember how to follow instruction."

Kenji glanced at Angelica, pain written in the set of his mouth. "He said he would hurt Her Imperial Majesty if I didn't bring you," he whispered. "I'm sorry."

"Let's put it behind us," Nanbu said smoothly. He looked between

Koshi and Cosima, reading everything in their expressions. "There is much to discuss at the castle. Come."

He walked sedately back to the northern corridor. The Gojarin closed in around them, and Deia's parting whisper echoed in Angelica's ears.

No fire, my blood. One order from me, and they all die.

XII

W hat would you have worn to our wedding?"
They were on the path to the Vitae portal, picking their way
down a rocky slope that led to the foot of the mountains. Risha paused,
using the excuse to catch her breath.

"Why are you asking all of a sudden?" Mingled with her surprise was
relief; relief that Jas was thinking of something other than the séance, or
Risha's earlier mistake.

Jas smiled somewhat sheepishly. "The thought just came to me. I
wanted to picture it."

Warmth crept into Risha's chest as they continued down the slope. "I
imagine my mother would have wanted me to wear a traditional golden
gown." She remembered the marriage of a family friend in Sadhavana,
and how radiant the bride had been under the late afternoon sun. "But
my father would press for House colors, of course."

Jas hummed. "And what would *you* want?"

Risha had never thought about it before. She was fond of the Vakara
black and gold, but a wedding gown in those colors didn't seem to fit. It
was too dark, too morbid, a potential harbinger of misfortune.

"Red," she said eventually. "A red gown with gold jewelry."

His smile widened into a grin. "Oh, I *like* that. You would be a vision."

The heat in her chest rose higher. She imagined him in a matching
sherwani, the two of them standing bright and powerful together.

"I'll commission it when we return," she said.

She braced for him to gently remind her that might not be worth-
while. Instead, his gaze softened.

"I look forward to it," he said, and she was warm as spring.

They were close to the bottom of the slope when Val shifted against her back.

"Wait," he said. "I think...I think it's here."

"Your body?" Risha tucked Samhara's handles into her belt so she could take him out of the sling. "Can you tell which direction?"

He pushed against her right hand. "Down there."

There was a wide road at the foot of the mountains. As they followed it, Risha could better make out the carvings along the mountainsides, massive sculptures of skeletons in various poses—some with their hands together in prayer, some with their arms uplifted in joy, some contorted in suffering. There were also re-creations of the four cities chiseled into the stone, from the fortress-like Cruciamen to a multi-tiered citadel.

"This place feels strange," Jas murmured.

"Can you sense the portal?" she asked. "Since you have Vitaean magic."

"I don't think so. There's something, but it could just be the void."

That didn't reassure her. If he could sense the void, did that mean his spirit had grown even weaker?

The mountains cast dark, blue shadows over them. Every so often she heard the scuffle of something scurrying out of sight, the back of her neck tingling uneasily. She thought of Leshya running down this road toward the portal and wondered what had been chasing her at the time. What had ended up beheading Val.

Between her hands, Val suddenly said, "Look."

They'd found another statue carved into the mountainside. This one was of Thana, her four arms raised, each stone hand grasping a different object: a human heart, a candle, a sickle, and a skull. Lying at her base was a shadowed figure.

A headless body.

"That's it." Val's genial tone was gone, replaced with ironclad resolve. "Take me to it."

Risha frowned at the order but followed it anyway. Jas trailed a little behind, keeping a lookout. The closer she came to the statue the more it felt like Thana herself was looking down at her, ready to use all four limbs to smash her into pulp.

She knelt beside the body. It was tall and lean, clad in a belted tunic of bright red with black bracers, trousers, and boots, all adorned with bits of silver jewelry. Attached to the belt was a scabbard holding a sword with a plain hilt.

Risha peered up at the statue. There were deep gouges in the stone, no doubt remnants of the last battle Leshya had waged with Val at her side.

The back of her neck was still prickling.

"Instead of ogling my body, why not reattach my head to it like you promised?" Val urged.

Risha cleared her throat. "Right. Sorry." Yet she hesitated before she shuffled closer on her knees, leaning over the stump of his neck. "How should I . . . ?"

Before she could finish the thought, a deep *pulse* went through her hands where she held Val's head. She gasped and nearly dropped him.

"Risha?" Jas said. "What is it?"

"I don't know." She looked at Val's face, but his eyes were shut tight in concentration.

She lined up the places where head met neck, severed so precisely it seemed unnatural. Her entire right side grew warm, making her worry something was happening to her body until she realized it was Samhara; the weapon was responding to whatever was going on, the phalanges hanging from the handles rattling together furiously.

Her stomach pinched. Something was *off*, but she couldn't say what—and when she tried to remove Val's head, she found she couldn't.

"What's going on?" she demanded. "You—"

Then she saw it: The pale hands resting beneath Val's bracers ended in sawed-off knuckles.

What part of Samhara belongs to the king of Cruciamen?

The finger bones.

The seam between Val's head and neck was fusing together. A burning, needling sensation shot up her arms, and Risha cried out and fell backward.

Val's eyes shot open, glowing crimson. His mouth spread into a sharp-toothed grin.

"Finally," he said, his voice a low rumble. "*Finally.*"

The phalanges ripped off of Samhara and sped toward him. As soon as they met with his body they melded back together, growing new nerves and tendon and flesh. Val held his hands before his face and wiggled his fingers experimentally.

"Risha!" Jas reached for her, unable to grab her shoulder. "Risha, we need to *go*!"

Val's laughter grew impossibly loud, echoing against stone, traveling down the valley toward the river leading to Cruciamen. His body bent abnormally as he slowly rose to his feet, the torus around him whipping his long black hair into disarray. He held out his arms and stared down at them, face twisted in delight.

"It's been so long since I last faced a Vakara," he breathed.

He drew the sword at his hip. The blade was of black opal—the same as the Sentinels'. A weapon that could dissipate souls in a single swing.

"How badly I've wanted all these years to find Leshya Vakara's soul." He ran a finger over the blade's edge. "To drag it back to Cruciamen and torment it for eternity for doing this to me."

Risha finally managed to stand. She backed away, pulling out Samhara. The bone was warm in her grip, ready to face a familiar foe. "You're...a king."

He made an elaborate twirl with his sword and bowed over it. His black hair slipped over one of his pointed ears. "Valentin, overseer of the wicked and the damned, the torturer of souls, the most supreme bastard of Mortri."

Jas had shifted to stand behind Risha, eyeing the sword warily. "This doesn't make sense," he said. "You knew so much about Leshya, about Samhara. How?"

"I was the first to face Leshya Vakara when she journeyed to Mortri." Valentin sneered. "But we quickly made a deal. I would help her defeat the other kings, and in return, she would create the ultimate weapon— one that could slaughter even Thana."

The breath tangled in Risha's throat. Valentin took a step toward her, and she took one back.

"But what a fucking surprise, she betrayed me," he muttered. "Made a mockery of me. Tenamar even put my head in that little hovel so the others could laugh at my expense."

He paused, head cocking to one side.

"And now here you are," he crooned with a blooming smile, "carrying her blood and her weapon."

"Risha," Jas hissed. "We have to *move*."

But she couldn't. The fear that had been burrowing deeper and deeper had hit bone, freezing her limbs, her thoughts, her pulse.

"You said..." Her voice was barely above a whisper. "You said you wanted Leshya to make the ultimate weapon. You wanted to usurp Thana?"

Valentin tapped his blade against his shoulder. "At first. But I've had a long, *long* time to think." His crimson eyes seared through her, unblinking. "The kings might not be able to overtake Thana, but a Vakara could."

He'd even suggested it before, while they traveled. The pieces she'd been missing now fell into place. "You wanted to use me and Samhara against her, then...what, kill me?"

"That's always an option." His teeth flashed. "Or I could bring you back to Cruciamen. You could be the queen of the damned, ruling over Mortri at my side."

Risha took another involuntary step back. Jas glared down Valentin.

"Is that really such a terrible fate?" Valentin asked with mock hurt. "We both know Thana does nothing to preserve this realm. You've seen with your own eyes how it's decayed, how anything beautiful withers with her indifference." His eyes narrowed. "The other kings don't seem to understand that if this realm dies, their power also dies. I'm the only one looking to restore it."

"By killing its god?" Jas shot back. "By controlling Risha?"

"Yes! I'm so glad you understand."

Jas turned to her, and the tangled ball within her ached with his compulsion. "Use Samhara! Quickly!"

No—she couldn't, not when he was the only spirit here, not when she would have to use up the rest of his energy.

"Yes, use Samhara," Valentin drawled as he continued forward. "Except...oh, you can't, can you? Not without consuming the rest of your friend here."

Her vision darkened at the edges. Val had suggested she could use her own energy to power the weapon, leading her to drain Jas's instead.

He had misdirected her on purpose.

"Go on, let me see it," Valentin urged her joyfully. "Let me see you fall to pieces when the last tie to your world is gone forever."

"Don't listen to him!" Jas yelled. "Risha, *please*—"

But Valentin leapt at her then, and it was all she could do to cross the scythes and catch the blade.

"How long can you last without using your power?" he taunted. He was so much stronger than her, bearing down until her knees crashed to the dirt. Her arms shook under the strain. "Maybe I'll behead you, give you a taste of what Leshya did to me. Then I'll take both of you back to

Cruciamen. Perhaps seeing his infinite suffering will persuade you to rule at my side." His cackle grated in her ears.

A rock suddenly flew at him. He flipped backward and watched it sail by, then smirked at Jas. "Your Vitaean magic is *weak*. Like your soul."

Risha scrambled back to her feet, but her legs were trembling. She wouldn't last. Neither of them would.

The ball of energy within her surged. She exerted her will over Jas's, fighting a battle on two fronts.

I won't use you, she seethed as Valentin came for her again. She readied the scythes, her muscles one second away from failing. *I won't—*

Jas moved so fast it was as if he'd used lightspeed. One second she was braced for Valentin's oncoming attack and the next she was looking up at Jas—at his beloved face, his soft and desperate eyes, the mouth that had gifted her so many smiles.

He smiled at her now, knowing and final. His lips parted and he whispered:

"Don't waste it."

Valentin's sword struck him.

At the touch of black opal, the outline of Jas's spirit blurred and dispelled. Soon all that was left was a hazy, pale light, like the souls on the tree—the purest, base essence of him.

No.

The light fragmented. The shimmering blue particles swarmed her, protecting her from Valentin. Jas's power rose within her, burning at the core, seeping into the scythes.

"No!"

But there was no way to stop Samhara from absorbing his spiritual energy. She *felt it*—the resonance of his laugh, the caress of his gaze, the scent of a black rose.

And the last image that flashed through his mind: of her draped in red and gold.

Risha screamed until the whole of Mortri shook with anguish.

She spun and let the scythe in her right hand fly, forming the mudra for *air*. The blade hooked into Valentin's chest and sent him flying. He crashed into the Thana statue with such force that cracks spread from the site, spiderwebbing across stone. She pulled on the chain and the scythe flew back to her.

Her blood frothing with fury.

Her heart black with hatred.

Risha danced and the scythes obeyed her every order, slamming into Valentin over and over. Chunks of stone rained from the statue, and the ground shook under her feet. Throughout it all, the king of Cruciamen's laugh echoed over the mountains.

She couldn't kill him. Couldn't even defeat him.

Don't waste it.

Jas's last words, knowing his sacrifice could only buy her so much time—that her body could only handle so much.

That she was a Vakara, and would respect a spirit's final wishes.

Before Valentin could recover, she ran. There was no direction, no purpose, no idea other than *away*.

In her hands, Samhara flickered with the last of Jas's energy until that, too, was no more.

XIII

T ell me what I'm looking at," Taesia demanded.
        Lilia leaned back from the canyon fissure. She said in a hushed
tone, "That creature is a Nightmare."

"Yeah, but what's it *called*?"

"This isn't the time for your jokes," Kalen hissed.

"It never seems to be."

"That is the beast's name in your language," Lilia said. "Because it is a literal translation of our word for *nightmare*. They are . . . exceedingly dangerous."

"Even when it's five against one?"

Lilia shook her head. "Numbers don't matter. One Nightmare can take
out a battalion of soldiers on its own." She waved to the geodes below.
"I'm assuming that's what happened to the gem harvesters."

Julian listened while keeping track of the Nightmare's movements. It
was staying in one area, gliding between the walls in a bristle of shadow
and unease. The geodes it lingered by were slowly being poisoned by its
presence, the amethysts deepening to onyx. Like it was trying to corrupt
the entire deposit.

The astralam fang was roughly thirty feet away from it. They needed
either a distraction or some way to pass it undetected.

"You can become near-invisible with your Shade powers," he said to
Lilia. "Would that be enough to fool it?"

"Shade powers don't work against them. They're . . ." The princess
struggled to find the right words. "They're adsimil. Like-kind."

"They're born from shadows, too," Kalen added. "So they are able to
perceive a Shade."

"There goes *my* plan," Taesia muttered.

Although the Nightmare had first been a jumbled heatwave in his mind, the longer Julian focused on it the more he understood its construction. It wasn't only a being of shadow and intangible fear—it was still a beast, with a body that flickered between wraith and animal.

It was something that could be harmed, if it came down to that.

"I'll go down," he decided.

"Absolutely not," Taesia said. "Did you not hear the whole *it can take down a battalion of soldiers on its own* discussion?"

"I'm not a soldier, I'm a Hunter. And we need that fang. If Phos succeeds in bridging Solara and Noctus, Lilia needs a way to protect Astrum. That fang could mean the difference between life and death for these people."

Taesia frowned, but Lilia and the others gave him mixed looks of surprise and gratitude. Julian ran a hand over his newly shorn hair and pretended he didn't see.

"I don't know how a Nightmare can be killed," Kalen said.

"I won't have to kill it." Julian touched his forehead. "I'll use my beastspeaking to evade it."

Lilia's eyes narrowed slightly. "That's the demon's magic, isn't it?"

Taesia opened her mouth, no doubt to unleash something acerbic, but Julian held up a hand to stop her.

"It's derived from it," he agreed. "But this particular power...it's *mine*. One I was born with, and honed through my line of work."

It wasn't the plaintive cries of a lost god or the lust of Conjuration or the unwanted gifts of Azideh. It was just him, the way he'd always known himself.

And given the choice between facing down a god or a beast, he would happily take the beast.

"Shade powers won't work on it, and neither will brute force," he went on when the others didn't look convinced. "I'm the only one here with an ability to get past it. It's either that or lose the fang entirely, since I doubt the Nightmare plans to leave this canyon anytime soon." There were still plenty of gems to poison.

Everyone thought it over. Then Marcellus reached for his belt to untie his sword, which he handed to Julian with both hands.

"Just in case," the soldier said. "I trust you know how to use one."

"Mar." Lilia put a hand on his arm. Julian didn't need an explanation to understand the gesture was significant; that Marcellus was doing something he shouldn't.

"A warrior cannot go into any situation without his sword," Marcellus said as if quoting someone. "A noble life calls for a noble weapon at one's side. This is the mark of a truly honorable soul."

There was great pride in his voice and in his gaze. Julian didn't feel fit to touch what he was being offered, but since it might be worse to reject it, he held out his hands and accepted the sword. It felt good to hold a weapon again, even one that was not his.

He fastened the sheath to his belt and turned to Taesia. Her shadow familiar flew over and nuzzled against his cheek, soft as the ends of a cat's fur.

"One sign of trouble, and I'm jumping down to collect your ass," Taesia said.

A small laugh escaped him, which softened her frown. She called Umbra back and silently ordered it to elongate into a dark rope. While Julian unclasped and folded his cloak, Lilia offered up her familiar as well, the two of them linked to form something long enough to carry him to the bottom of the canyon. The shadow rope was cool and silken between his hands, but his hold remained secure when he scooted to the edge of the fissure and eased himself over.

He took a deep breath, holding it in his lungs for a count of five before releasing it. Repeated this while clearing out intrusive, fearful thoughts, wiping out the map of his mind until it could barely be called human. Nothing but empty observance, reduced only to what he needed to keep his next breaths coming.

Slowly he made his way down. The weight of Marcellus's sword was an anchor, albeit one that made him lean a little to the left. His boots touched off the rock wall with the barest scrape as he slid down another foot, then another. But he wasn't used to such smooth rope, and slipped a couple inches before he caught himself.

A flutter in his stomach traveled along his arms and into his fingertips, and the spike of adrenaline woke his decelerated pulse.

A sharp whisper hissed through the canyon. Julian froze, staring at the nearest glowing geode. The thrill was in his teeth, in the soft hairs at the nape of his neck. He focused on the lavender light until it eased, sinking back into that state of impassive undertaking, emotionless and calm, and descended the rest of the way.

His feet settled on the canyon floor. He let go of the shadow rope, but it remained, ready to carry him back to safety. He didn't look up; he believed there was no one else, that he himself was no one and nothing, organic matter turned to the same crystal-like structure of an amethyst.

The Nightmare lurked around the bend; he could hear its low whispers, speaking in no language he knew. As he walked toward it he kept any and all thoughts at bay. His breaths came in, one two three four five, and out, one two three four five six seven, nonexistent and nonthreatening.

Black plating spanned the Nightmare's body like armor. Anything resembling a face was obscured by a deep hood of darkness, out of which peered burning scarlet eyes. The shadows around it were roiling, and he couldn't help but remember Taesia in her dress of chain mail, steel in her hands and in her gaze, a murderer twice over.

The Nightmare turned toward him, and he forced open the doors to its mind while shutting the doors to his own.

I am not here, he thought. *You do not perceive me.*

The Nightmare slithered closer, its whispers sibilant and questioning. Julian focused only on the confusing maelstrom of its thoughts, or what he considered to be thoughts—a weave of colors and sounds without emotion. *Intruder*, he guessed, was at the forefront.

No intruder, he thought back in the same style, a thread of gray fact.

This was enough to appease it, since it turned back to the geodes it was corrupting, the gems within the rock growing murky. Julian gave it a wide berth as he passed. He kept his eyes on the fang and ignored the way the walls around him seemed to waver and bow inward. A product of the Nightmare's power, emanating from it like heat off a furnace.

It was no more menacing than other beasts he had encountered and overcome. The lizard-like creatures who had snatched up travelers on Vaegan roads, or the acid-spitting banri he had taken down with Paris. His partner's taunting laughter pealing through the air, the flash of his dual swords in the sunlight.

A throb of unexpected pressure behind his sternum caused his heart to skip a beat.

The doors to his mind cracked open.

The Nightmare pounced.

Julian had no time to react before the beast ensnared him in a web of shadow, its half-incorporeal form winding tight around his body. Locked in place, Julian couldn't stop the instinct to twist and struggle for freedom. But the more he fought, the tighter the Nightmare gripped him, until its face that was not a face swam before him, red eyes boring into his.

He plunged into darkness. Into the same madness of the exteri sulumn, warping the world around him into his own private theater of horror.

His mother lying on the floor, blood pooled around her. Tacky wetness on his fingers, tears on his face. A slam against his back and a grinning terror above him, red and wicked.

Paris's smile falling before his body did, swords clanging to the ground, spilling out of nerveless hands.

The whole of the city on fire, swarmed with beasts and the risen dead, the streets running crimson.

Benjamín Luca panting as he faced down a horde, his uniform ripped and the pupils of his eyes turned to vertical slits.

Julian tried to turn, to fight, to bring back that calm clarity, but it all escaped his grasp. He could run and run, but he couldn't escape this. Couldn't escape watching his father get ripped to shreds, talons and claws digging through the flesh that had once held and comforted him.

"*Stop it!*" His scream reverberated within the darkness. No god or beast could rival the terror crushing his throat, could mimic the hopeless thrashing in his chest. Heat rose to the surface of his skin, and his veins began to flood with black.

"Demon," Taesia whispered.

He had been fighting an invisible enemy, but at this he looked up. Followed the line of his extended arm to where he'd punched a fist through her chest.

Her eyes were a deep, midnight shade, fingernails digging into his black-threaded arm.

"*Monster.*"

She pulled his arm in deeper, through the scrape of bone and the slide of muscle, between beating organs and a wave of fresh blood. Their faces were so close their noses brushed, so close he felt the warm puffs of air leaving her mouth.

"Monster," she whispered again, and it was almost loving.

"Something's wrong," Taesia said just before the Nightmare attacked.

"Kir!" Marcellus made to grab the rope Lilia was holding, but Kalen caught his arm.

"He has your sword," Kalen reminded him. "How do you plan to fight something like that and win?"

"I don't know, but we can't just leave him—"

Taesia gathered the nearby shadows to her. She used them to carry her down, Lilia's call floating after her as she plunged into the canyon below.

The Nightmare had wrapped half its body around Julian's, pinning his arms in place so that he couldn't draw Marcellus's sword. His eyes were vacant and strange, staring at something only he could see. As she rushed toward him, hand reaching for Starfell's hilt, his skin began to spiderweb with black veins.

"Julian!" she cried.

The Nightmare turned its blazing red eyes on her.

She stumbled. The walls of amethyst were shoved away by invisible hands, leaving her in some nowhere, liminal space. A world without a name.

The barrenness formed a pit in her stomach. She grasped for something on her back—she was fairly sure there had been something on her back, something she needed—but all she found was air. Taesia stared at her hand. It was unlined, unscarred. Empty of weapons or intent.

Another pair of hands clasped hers. She looked up into her brother's face.

"I'm sorry," Dante whispered. "I should have told you. I didn't want—"

Shadows swirled between them, fastened into a rope around his neck that tried to pull him away from her. She tightened her grip.

"No, no, don't go!" she begged him, sounding younger, sounding terrified. "Don't leave me!"

"It wasn't me." He was yanked away by the rope. "Please tell them it wasn't me!"

"Dan—" His name turned into a scream as he dropped, his neck snapping under the force of the noose.

Stumble, and she was in the Lastrider villa while it crumbled and caved in. Debris hit her across the back, forcing her to collapse beside two bodies.

"No," Taesia groaned.

Her mother and father lay under the rubble, their bodies broken, hands reaching for one another. Taesia choked down a sob, crawling toward them. Her mother's eyes opened, covered with the white film of the dead.

"Your fault," Elena whispered.

Somewhere within the main house, Brailee called for her.

Taesia pushed to her feet. "Bee!" she shouted. "Hold on, I'm coming!"

Her sister didn't sound like a teenager but rather her child self, locked up and forgotten in the bowels of their ancestral home. And Taesia could not reach her, kept having to dodge falling debris as the stairs fell away, unable to deliver her promise of safety.

Stumble, and she was in a side room within the Bone Palace's ballroom, Nikolas holding her by the waist. He stared down at her with crystalline eyes, the love in them snuffed out by her own fingers.

"It can't go on like this," he said.

The walls of the room fell open like a broken box, revealing the larger ballroom beyond, filled with the dons and doñas of Nexus. The Houses stood at the fore. Nikolas turned her around to present her to them, and one by one they looked away.

Except Risha and Angelica. The latter smiled, an aura shimmering above her head in the shape of a crown. Risha cried silently, her face like stone. They both approached with ropes in their hands, fastening them around her neck so that she could hang like her brother, and all the while Nikolas held her down.

"You never belonged with us," Angelica said. "You always knew that."

"You couldn't escape what you were born for," Risha said. "You always knew that."

"You will never be forgiven," Nikolas whispered in her ear. "You always knew that."

The floor opened and she plummeted.

Taesia crashed to her knees, wrenching at ropes that weren't there. The shadows carded through her hair in a caress.

"IT WAS ALWAYS GOING TO COME DOWN TO THIS," Nyx murmured above her, all around her, rattling through her skull. "MY BLOOD GAVE YOU GREAT POWER. HOW DO YOU EXPECT ME TO NOT MAKE USE OF IT?"

"It's *mine*," Taesia growled through the heaving of her chest. "Not yours."

"SO SELFISH. AND YET YOU WONDER WHY OTHERS FIND YOU DIFFICULT TO LOVE."

He lifted her chin and she found herself staring at Julian. His face grim, on the edge of rage, the way it had been the day they'd crossed swords in the villa. He'd known, then, what sort of person she was. They had quickened their heartbeats across steel, and in the end it had become a form of passion, disappointment singed away to fervor.

This time, Julian did not fight. Like the others, he turned away from her.

"Stop," she whispered. "Come back. Please."

He walked farther into the dark.

"Julian!" she shouted. "*Julian!*"

He only stopped when her sword ran him through. She stood panting behind him, his blood warm and wet as it spilled across her hands. His body falling, taking her down with it.

"Is this what it always comes to, then?" Nyx sighed. "Is this your only solution when you do not get your way? Pathetic."

"No," she whispered, turning Julian over. His eyes were closed, lips stained scarlet. "No, I didn't... That's not what I..." She dug her fingers into his jaw. "Wake up. *Wake up.*"

But there was no waking up from this, not for either of them. Even as she pleaded, Nyx's long fingers curled around her throat and squeezed, the only end she deserved.

Julian was full of teeth, full of blood and lust, looking for any way to free the creature baying in his chest.

He loosened its leash, not yet allowing it to snap, and ripped himself out of the Nightmare's grasp.

It hissed and twisted, ready to launch at him again. This time he caught the beast when it came flying, digging his fingers through its black plating into something soft and vulnerable. The Nightmare shrieked in a decibel so high he flinched, but his grip remained firm, yearning to rip it apart.

The flash of scarlet eyes, the bending of the natural world, amethysts threatening to blur into landscapes of grief. The Nightmare didn't know he had been living with grief for so long already. Nothing could wound him more than he could wound himself.

The Nightmare struggled. Julian grinned, wondering if he could fasten his teeth around the creature's throat, and how sweetly it would cry then. He freed one hand to get a better hold on it.

The side of his palm brushed against the moonstone set into the pommel of Marcellus's sword. In his mind surged not a nightmare, but a memory: warm and golden, of tiles and fruit and a sidelong look—

Julian came back to himself with a shuddering gasp. His mind cleared, the black receding from his veins. The Nightmare gave another shrill cry, and wetness trickled from his ears.

No—he couldn't rely on the demon. He could still get out of this alive if he delved into the Nightmare's mind, manipulated its thoughts.

A broken cry echoed through the canyon. Beyond the Nightmare, a figure was hunched over on its knees, shadows writhing fitfully around them.

Taesia. She was in the grip of the Nightmare's visions, choking and scratching at her neck.

The creature in his chest howled and kicked. Without a second thought, he broke its seal.

He became a well without a bottom—filled with rage for all the things he could not control. Rage for himself, for the makeup of his being, forcing him to understand the very beasts he despised.

His jaw went slack with relief at standing in the full force of it. At realizing that he, too, was a beast—made not for love but for cutting, for breaking, for killing. His name, if he'd ever had one, buried deep within him.

Monster?

Yes. Here and now, he understood.

This was not a war he could win as a Hunter.

This was a war he would win as a demon.

XIV

Nikolas announced he would go to the throne room alone. Fin argued, but one meaningful look from Nikolas had the servants flocking around the prince, wanting to tend to his wrists or make him tea. Fin glared at him over Bhavna's head, mouthing *how dare you*.

Nikolas smiled. It was a strange feeling, not only in the now-foreign way his mouth moved but also in how an echo of it pinged in his chest, giving his heart the gentlest shake. Waking it up from a long, troubled sleep.

And he *was* awake, his head mostly clear save for the carousel of grief and worry that took turns spinning around him. He could feel his hands, his legs, his healing eye socket. The phantom shape of his right eye, missing like so many other parts of himself.

As he approached the throne room, a tiny instinct told him he should return to the thrall, the blessed emptiness of it. Nikolas ignored the urge and swallowed hard, tasting the residue of chamomile.

He walked through the open doors and found Rian sitting on the throne. His arms lay on the gilded armrests, his legs half-sprawled out before him, his head leaning against the velvet backing. The buttons of his shirt were undone at the top, pulled aside to reveal the inflamed scar sitting slanted across his chest.

His breaths came slow and even—he was asleep. He had been like this for the past couple days, trying to heal himself.

Nikolas came closer and nearly hissed at the sight of the wound. It looked so much worse than it had before, its edges creeping into black striae, the scar vivid and inflamed. Even in his sleep, Rian—Phos—had his brow furrowed in pain, sweat dotting his temples.

Whatever Taesia had done, it was certainly having an effect on the god. Nikolas could only hope it wouldn't take his brother, too.

Mouth dry, Nikolas crept closer and made note of the two pockets in Rian's torn, stained trousers. There was a time, when they were much younger, when Taesia had wanted to learn how to pickpocket. She'd practiced on him so many times she had eventually been able to slip a coin out of his pocket without him noticing.

"The trick is that you have to be fast and sure," she'd said, flashing his own coin back at him.

But this wasn't a busy city street, and one wrong move could doom them all. Slowly he extended his hand, then had to grip the throne as vertigo swept over him. His depth perception was skewed, his body fatigued. Maybe he should have brought Fin along after all, made use of his nimble fingers.

He shut his eye and reoriented himself. Fin had to be kept away from Phos as much as possible.

Again he reached for the left pocket. His fingers slid inside bit by bit, slow as dripping paint. He couldn't see Rian's face, but he heard his breathing change slightly.

Heart pounding, Nikolas reached in farther until something cold and metallic brushed against his fingertips. Carefully he pulled it out, revealing the key for Fin's shackles.

Relief and frustration hit him at once. As much as they needed this key, they needed the missing fang more. Still, he slipped it into his own pocket.

A hand clamped around his forearm.

"What do you think you're doing, Nikolas?" Phos drawled. Rian's eyes were mostly open, somewhat hazy with fever.

Nikolas quickly wiped his face blank and said nothing. Phos sneered.

"Did I tell you to hover over me?"

Nikolas shook his head.

"Then get away."

Nikolas made to step back, but Rian's fingers dug in harder. The two of them stared at one another, and he thought he saw confusion flicker within his brother's gaze.

Phos grimaced and let him go. Nikolas stumbled away and lowered his head, arms hanging at his sides.

"Tell the servants to help you collect the corpses," Phos ordered as he buttoned his shirt, covering up the scar. "And fetch the princeling. Don't bring them here, bring them to the solarium above."

Nikolas stifled a frown. The solarium sat at the very top of the Bone Palace's dome, right above the throne room. He remembered a soiree held there for a spring festival, standing at the wide, clear windows to better see the fireworks flowering over the city.

He didn't know why Phos had a sudden interest in it, but it couldn't be for anything good.

When Nikolas relayed Phos's grim orders, the servants' fragile peace shattered.

"They shouldn't have to go," Fin objected. "I'll help carry the...the bodies. How many are there?"

"Six."

Fin faltered. Luis placed a hand on his arm.

"It's all right, Your Highness," he said. "I'll take a few of the others with me, and the rest can stay here."

Luis chose a handful of the largest servants, the others—including Bhavna—told to stay behind despite protests.

"We've already lost Arlo," Bhavna argued. Behind her, one of the younger women—the one who had brought them chamomile—started to cry. "We would have lost Mariana had Lord Nikolas not intervened. We don't know what Phos plans to do next."

"I'll protect them however I can," Nikolas said, ignoring a tremor of uncertainty. He could barely protect himself or Fin, his mind and body a wreckage. But he wanted to believe his words, and so did they.

The bodies of the Noctan soldiers he'd dragged into the antechamber were beginning to stink. The servants cursed and shuddered at the sight. One of them even turned away to be sick. Fin swayed on his feet, gray and silent as he watched Nikolas lift the biggest soldier's body into his arms. Every instinct in him screamed to drop it—to recede back into the thrall so that he could avoid the dead, cold flesh—but he stubbornly resisted.

He had to be present for this. He had to look for an opening to get the fang.

"Leave us here," Fin whispered. Nikolas hadn't noticed him approach. "If you get the last of those fangs, and you think someone out there can use them, you need to go."

Nikolas held back the storm that threatened to unleash itself at the thought of Taesia. "I can't just—"

"We'll be fine." Fin nodded, more to himself than to Nikolas. "You're the best equipped to do this. And I trust you to come back."

Nikolas's arms were beginning to shake. He had to set down the body, crouching for a moment on the marble floor. Once he'd collected himself, he took the key from his pocket and gave it to Fin.

"Wait," Nikolas instructed. Fin nodded and took the key, fisting his hand around it.

Nikolas led the way to the solarium, laboriously climbing the set of corkscrew stairs to reach it. It was just how he'd remembered it, despite the collateral damage from the Bone Palace's displacement. The floor was a wide, circular disk of white-and-gold tile, far larger than the morning room in the Cyr villa. Ferns and small trees had toppled over and were beginning to wither. Chairs and chaises had been forcibly swept away from the middle, where Phos had been at work setting up another circle.

Everything was lit yellow from the light of the barrier, leaking through the tall windows. Beyond the soaring wall of Phos's magic spilled the night sky, paintbrush whorls of purple and blue and magenta, a darkness so thick it hurt to look at.

Phos stood in the center of his newly made circle, painted with what looked to be blood. He was directly under the crossed-arch dome, supported by intersecting vaults that formed an eight-pointed star made of rich woods, sturdy stone, and polished white marble.

"Princeling," Phos called. Rian's voice echoed off the dome. "You know where to go."

Fin clenched his jaw and strode forward, chin raised. Phos smiled sharply and waited until Fin was standing in the spot that represented Vitae before an arrow of light appeared above him, forcing him to his knees.

"One move," Phos warned before he turned to Nikolas. "The bodies can go there." He used the Sunbringer Spear to point at the circle for Mortri.

As Nikolas crossed the solarium with the servants, he noticed the circle for Noctus was not empty. The remaining fang sat within it like a broken-off piece of moonlight. His heart stuttered, the pouch containing the rest of the fangs sitting heavy in his pocket.

Phos waved the servants away and directed Nikolas to his usual spot—the circle for Solara.

Phos held out Rian's arms with a smile. "Their energy is clearest here," he said. "I felt it in the throne room, but it was annoyingly faint. The Ostium heir would have solved that problem if he'd cooperated." He turned his gaze upward. "But that's no longer an impediment. Orsus is *here*."

Nikolas followed the trajectory of his gaze to the polished marble of the dome's cross-arches. Or what he'd thought was marble.

"They can sense me," Phos murmured. "The part of them I took into myself. It sings in recognition. It's ready to be used."

Nikolas opened his mouth, then shut it. Fin saw and asked the question for him: "The part you took in, meaning the piece of the god you consumed?"

Nausea rippled through him as his empty socket throbbed.

"Yes. It allowed me to tap into quintessence, despite needing a vessel to do so." Phos placed one of Rian's hands over the wound on his chest. "But the longer I stay in a vessel, the more that ability transfers. I sense it's grown since last time. Here, under Orsus, it will finally serve its purpose."

Above them, the dome let out a deep, creaking groan.

"Be quiet," Phos ordered. Rian's body took on a glimmering hue. "You may still have power, but not enough to resist—especially without your heir."

Golden threads unspooled from him and spread across the circle, highlighting Fin's face. The dome groaned again, and with a crash like thunder several of the large windows broke, glass spraying through the room. The servants ducked, flinging their arms over their heads.

The fang pulsed like a beating heart, and the corpses emitted a dark miasma. Under Nikolas's feet came the familiar warmth of standing in the training ring under a burning sun, or visiting the Solara Quarter in Nexus and being surrounded by other Lumins. Like taking to the air and being buoyed by the wind.

Phos laughed and leaned his head back. His eyes blazed, wings flaring out behind him.

"I FEEL IT," he breathed in his two-tone voice. Threads of multiple colors began to weave through his fingers and curl around his neck. "AND NOW I CAN CONTROL IT."

Nikolas met Fin's eyes across the circle. If he took the fang now, would there be backlash? Would he be able to get away from Phos in time?

His questions paled to insignificance when beyond the barrier, within Noctus's firmament, a storm of clouds coalesced. They lit up from within as if by lightning, and the air that blew through the broken windows was sharp and staticky, reminding him of the prickling discomfort of Godsnight.

A portal was about to open.

XV

Taesia gasped for air when the darkness lifted. There was no rope, no Nyx, no broken body. Only the weight of Starfell and the glow of the geodes around her.

And, when she lifted her gaze: Julian. No longer her stalwart Hunter, but the shade of him he'd shown at Godsnight, veins running in inky trails, teeth bared and sharpened, a green aura like mist. Holding the Nightmare in close stalemate.

Before she could call his name, the Nightmare suddenly shrieked. The creature thrashed in Julian's hold so violently it broke free, spilling what looked like liquid shadow from its injured body. It folded in on itself like all the horrors of the world were being poured into it.

Julian stood over the Nightmare with black blood dripping from his fingers. Grinning a too-wide grin. Savoring the beast's pain.

This was not the same man from Godsnight. There, he had retained a part of himself, but this—

This was the demon.

Taesia unsheathed Starfell, using it as a prop to stand.

You cannot easily kill a Nightmare, Nyx said in her mind. *Not even with this . . . creature's abilities. How exactly do you plan to stop it?*

"Not with you, that's for sure," she retorted under her breath.

She cautiously approached Julian. Her arms trembled. Her heart pounded like festival drums, resonant and chest-deep.

If she could make a portal even while shackled with lightsbane, she could make one here and now.

Taesia pointed Starfell at the Nightmare. The nearby fang pulsed in response, creating a thin line between blade and bone. Her fingers tightened around the hilt as pain sparked across her shoulders and down her arms, the sword so cold it burned. Even the band of nightstone was frozen against her back.

It was the cold of what waited beyond the pockets where demons hid, beyond nebulae and dying stars. The stars glared down at her, waiting, witnessing.

But that velvet darkness struggled to find her. There was too much residual fear in her heart. Too much on the line when she looked at Julian.

I told you that human sentiment is a weakness, Nyx scoffed. *You know this isn't enough.*

"It will be."

An icy trickle entered her bloodstream. She gasped as her nerves stung, her back arching as if to get away from the invasion.

"Get out," she growled.

I told you that when you invited me in, we would be forever linked.

"I'm not—inviting you!"

You are not. Which means I can only contribute a little. But it will be enough.

A pool of darkness swirled around her, rich and fragrant with cloves. It spiraled around Starfell's blade, the bits of silver mica glowing bright. Even the fang blazed in response. They seemed to *pull* on some cord inside her, unraveling, siphoning, fueling the vortex that suddenly opened behind the Nightmare as though the fabric of the world itself had torn.

The beast, still caught in whatever Julian was forcing it to endure, couldn't even react before it was sucked in. The vortex's circumference teemed with static energy, seeking more to devour. Now that his prey was gone, Julian narrowed his eyes at it.

You can be rid of this menace, too, Nyx said. *He poses nothing but a threat. He should not even exist.*

"Fuck—you," Taesia panted. The sword vibrated in her hands and the vortex expanded, carving a chunk out of the canyon wall. She poured all her strength into wrenching the sword's point away, desperately reaching for the edges of the tear with her own power.

But it stayed open and seeking.

Coming toward Julian.

"Run!" Taesia yelled.

He lifted one black-stained hand. In the air he sketched a Conjuration circle, its lines shimmering green as they followed the path of his fingers. He sent it out, covering the expanse of the vortex.

The portal shuddered, then shrank. Down and down, until it was a mere point, resisting the entire time before it winked out of existence. Nyx snarled in her mind, and his power seeped from her body.

"Nyx's literal piss," she laughed, sweat dripping off her face. "You—you can *close* portals. Shit. Is there anything you can't do?"

The bubbling relief died when Julian turned to her. Although those slitted eyes met hers, they didn't *see* her—didn't recognize any part of her.

"Julian," she whispered as goose bumps traveled up her arms. "It's all right. You're safe. The fang…"

But he turned away from the fang, stalking toward her instead. She might as well have been speaking to a wild animal; the only language he seemed to understand now was that of hunger.

His enemy was gone. He had fed it nightmare after nightmare, delving so far into its mind it had started to turn on itself, thoughts devouring each other like a snake eating its own tail. The edge of insanity was about to shatter it, was about to fill him with such delight he could barely stand it.

And then the beast had been wrested from him by a doorway, a threshold to the place he had once come from, and had never been.

It was a simple matter to close it. To turn to the one who had formed it.

A woman with a sword and godstuff in her veins.

A new enemy.

It disgusted him and thrilled him. An image formed of his arm punching through her chest, memory or dream or both. It made his mouth water.

"Julian," she called as he came closer. "You *know* me. And I know you. This—this is not you."

But it was. It always had been, and he had been too cowardly to face it. Embrace it.

She caught him by the shoulders when he pounced, dropping her sword as they rolled across the hard ground. She kicked at his hip, disrupting his hold long enough to flip them over. A hand slapped across his face like a thunderclap.

"Wake up!" she screamed.

"I am awake." The words rumbled in his throat and made her shiver. He surged up and caught her by the throat, lifting her into the air as he fluidly rose to stand. "You seem to not understand."

She choked against his hand, legs kicking futilely. Then one of those legs wrapped around his neck and spun them around, forcing him to drop face-first to the ground. She landed on top of him and wrenched his arm back, his shoulder dislocating with a *pop.*

"Fuck you," she spat. "I understand you're not *him.*"

"I am," he said, calm despite the pain in his shoulder. "You just can't accept that."

He turned and flung her against the nearest wall. She crashed into broken-open geodes hard enough to make amethysts spill like tears. She slumped to the base of the wall, breathless.

He stood and pulled his shoulder back into place. When he approached her again, she lifted her hands and the shadows descended. He looked around at the sudden darkness, more curious than concerned, and when stygian tendrils latched on to his limbs he didn't fight against them.

The shadows parted for her as she limped toward him. Blood trickled from the corner of her mouth, and his nostrils flared at the scent of it—nighttime and terror, sweet herbs and bitter incense.

"You will let me go," he said, his voice chiming.

She stopped as her eyes clouded over. The shadows whispered against him in their retreat while she stood there aimless and confused. He kicked her in the stomach, sending her crashing back into the wall. She keeled over, mouth open uselessly as she strove for breath.

Heat built inside him. He had seen this woman kill. He had seen her laugh amid the destruction she had caused. His teeth pricked his bottom lip and he remembered the rasp of steel, the endless dark of her eyes as he pressed her to a wall.

His hands flexed, nails growing to sharp points. Her face was twisted in pain. A growl sat at the base of his throat that tasted of desire.

"Julian," she tried again. "You are...Julian Luca. You are a Hunter from Vaega who...who was chosen to be on Nikolas Cyr's task force. To—to stop the Conjurers."

He stilled. In the back of his mind came a whine.

"You are the son of Marjorie Luca," she went on. She grasped the rocks behind her to haul herself to her feet, one hand held protectively to her stomach. All around them the shadows had formed walls, shutting out the night or anyone who dared to come between them. "You care for her because you're a devoted son."

The whine grew into a wail. He shut his eyes and bared his teeth against it. He held the rising, scorching dawn in his throat even as dusk curled around her hands.

"You are the heir of Ostium," Taesia whispered. "Whether you want to be or not. This might be you, but it's not *all* of you. It's only a piece of what makes you Julian Luca. And in the end, Julian Luca is a *good man.*"

The wail was a mallet taken to his skull. Between their shadows: a field of jeweled, broken stars. Two of them had names, fitted between his teeth. Monster. Guardian.

Enemy.

It was the instinct of an injured predator to end the thing that was hurting him. When he lunged, he aimed his fist at her chest.

She caught his arm and used his momentum to throw him to the ground. He brought her down with him, bodies crashing together.

He got her pinned and fastened his hand once more around her throat.

"Julian," she choked, eyes watering as she scratched at his wrist. "Don't let...fear...become reality. *Don't forget.*"

Don't forget.

Don't forget where he'd come from, or those who had forged him into what he was. His parents. The Hunters. Paris. Nikolas.

Taesia.

An image of a house he'd only lived in within dreams, of his parents together and happy and safe, and the woman below him at his side.

His hand loosened.

Don't forget.

Don't forget.

Remember—

Remember this, now, her hands cradling his face and drawing it to hers, their bodies meeting like the collision of two black holes, inevitable, fatal.

Remember the way her mouth felt against his skin, heat of a different kind, like she was the rough surf and he was the sea glass smoothed by it.

Remember himself turning to her the way light turns to the dark, secretly yearning for its velvet touch.

And the name he'd buried rising again to the surface.

Julian had become feral with a working mind, impossible to predict. By the time she was on the ground with him pinning her in place, Taesia had run out of options for how to bring him back.

But her words were having an effect. The hand around her throat loosened and she pulled it away, sucked in air. He was shuddering, suffering. She reached out to him, cradling his face between her battered hands.

Julian Luca: a Hunter both tedious and fascinating, an ordinary man with extraordinary ability. A gem with so many facets she could spend a lifetime finding them all.

She *wanted* to find them all. Even this, the curse of his blood, thrilled her in ways she couldn't comprehend. Her body sang with agony and with longing, having finally found the answer for this ache between them.

She surged up and pressed her lips to the corner of his mouth, tasting his warm skin. He gasped and turned his head, their mouths properly fitting together.

She could feel the too-hard grip of his hand around her arm, the points of his canines as they cut her tongue. But it didn't matter— nothing mattered but *him*, the constellation of his body fitted to hers, hip to hip and chest to chest. The small, needful breaths he took, nourished by the blood in her mouth. She fastened a hand in his hair and kissed him harder as he rolled against her. She arched into it, digging her fingers into the shifting muscle of his back, feeding the demon in a different way.

The shadows swept in, curled and brushed against them like teasing hands. Julian kissed her deeper and she sensed the change in him, violent need turning to desperate touch, to something that matched the depths of his eyes when they landed on her. To whatever bloomed in her chest when they were close enough, the urge to live off the ends of his fingertips and the ruinous curve of his mouth.

When he pulled away he hid his face in the crook of her neck. She lay there wrecked and beaten, holding him to her like he would disappear otherwise.

"I'm sorry," he rasped, breath ghosting over her skin. "I'm sorry."

She scrubbed her fingers through his hair as the shadows dissipated, opening up to the night sky and the frantic calls of Lilia and the others.

"Don't be." She closed her eyes. "All that matters is that you remembered."

XVI

The swirling clouds above Astrum tore down the middle, creating an oculus through which a pale beam escaped.

"I SENSE IT," Phos said in a near-sob. "SOLARA. IT'S REACHING FOR ME." He held Rian's hands out, the Sunbringer Spear luminous. Golden threads danced and weaved around him, reaching between the circle below and the dome above. "IT WANTS TO BURN. IT *NEEDS* TO BURN."

Beyond the city, pillars of light rose toward the forming storm. The solarium's windows afforded a view of them all—from the red of Vitae to the black of Mortri, the silver of Noctus and the gold of Solara, rising from the circles Rian had drawn around Astrum under Phos's instruction.

Leave us here.

I trust you to come back.

Nikolas broke the circle's formation and dove for the fang.

He didn't pause to look at Phos or Fin, couldn't hear what was being yelled over the groaning, buzzing sound that filled the solarium. He took off running for one of the shattered windows and leapt into the gilded dark.

His power surged and his shoulder blades bristled with heat. Lux, hidden under his sleeve, squeezed his upper arm in encouragement. Two large wings of light unfurled on either side of him, and despite the teeth-rattling storm there was joy in this, in connecting to this piece of him he'd once feared was lost forever.

He dove deep into the core of his magic, preparing for lightspeed, to jump between where he was and someplace beyond the barrier. His wings flapped once, twice.

And then they were severed.

Agony lanced through his back and he screamed. He tumbled through the air and landed on a hard surface, jolted by the *crack* of his ribs. His lungs were in shock, desperately trying to pull air in as he stared wide-eyed at the churning sky.

Phos appeared above him, eyes on fire, a glower distorting his mouth. Nikolas had landed on one of the palace's balconies—the very one where Phos had appeared on Godsnight.

"You seem to forget," said the god, "my hold on you. Just as my blood gave you wings, it can also rip them away."

Nikolas began to hyperventilate, reaching for the core of his power, the glowing reassurance of light and heat. It was there, but barely—enough for Lux to hang on, but not enough for wings, for flight, for freedom.

Laughing, Phos grabbed him, and their bodies twisted out of time and space, a grotesque rearranging of his limbs before they landed back in the solarium. Phos threw Nikolas to the ground, where he landed in a heap over the Solara circle.

The fang spilled out of his hand. Phos stooped to pick it up and replaced it in the Noctus circle.

"Pathetic," Phos muttered, and it was his voice but also his father's, a creator looking upon its creation and finding only faults.

He turned and swung the Sunbringer Spear. The servants screamed as a blade of light struck Luis in the chest. The man's widened eyes were already lifeless when he collapsed, his chest rent and cauterized, the smell of sizzling blood like cooked meat.

"*No!*" Fin sobbed. He made to rise, but the arrow of light slashed him across the face. Blood splattered against the circle and made it hum louder.

Nikolas tried to crawl forward. The bag holding the astralam fangs tumbled to the floor. Bloody strings of saliva fell from his mouth and onto the circle, and the golden threads thickened.

"Didn't I warn you? A life for each escape attempt." Phos grabbed Luis by the collar and dragged his body to the Mortri circle, where it joined the Noctan soldiers. "How very selfish of you both."

Outside, the storm's oculus expanded. Phos returned to the center of the Conjuration circle, between the eight-pointed star of the dome and the quadrants of his design.

"WATCH THIS," Phos told them. "AND KNOW THAT MY WILL IS UNSTOPPABLE."

You are a watcher, not a warrior.

The column of light descended, channeled between the realms to turn night into day. The cries and crashing wreckage and Phos's laughter were thunderous, so excruciatingly loud—

And then it all fell away. The shout in his throat died. The pain along his body faded. The pressure around his upper arm disappeared. His mind was blissfully quiet. He lay there smelling blood, staring at a pillar of light with his remaining eye until it watered and his vision blurred.

But he had been ordered to watch. So he watched, even when the light cut off, even when the last, untouched piece of his heart crumbled to nothing.

Lilia sat holding all three astralam fangs in her hands. She brushed one with her thumb before looking up at them.

"I don't understand what happened," she said. "We couldn't get through the shadow barrier, but before that we saw the portal. The one you made with Starfell."

Taesia felt their eyes on her. Assessing. Wondering.

"That's why you wanted to go to the Vitae portal," Lilia murmured. "That's why you kept asking if I could sense anything through the sword. You thought you could open the portal with it."

"Is that possible?" Marcellus asked excitedly. His own sword had been returned to him by Julian, who sat now with his eyes on the ground, silent. The others hadn't seen his transformation thanks to her shadows.

"I was wearing lightsbane at the time, so I don't know," Taesia answered, her voice hoarse. It made Julian's shoulders stiffen, and she hoped there were no bruises on her neck. "But I . . . I don't think so."

Not without the addition of Nyx's power.

The lingering sweetness of Julian's mouth was replaced with something ashy and bitter. In the back of her mind, she thought she heard a quiet chuckle of satisfaction.

"But why was there a barrier?" Lilia asked. "Were there more Nightmares?"

Taesia tried to focus on anything other than her swollen lips. Kalen had been looking suspiciously between her and Julian ever since they climbed back up.

"It was just power backlash," Taesia said. "The important thing is that we have the fang."

The princess nodded, holding the fangs to her chest. "Yes. Nyx ia sel. I don't know if these will be enough to protect the city, but I can try."

"We'll get the rest of the coronal from Phos," Marcellus said, patting her shoulder. "And who knows, maybe they can help with the…" He pointed upward.

Lilia smiled slightly, but it was born of weariness. They all knew there was no easy solution for the Malum Star—if there was one at all.

Taesia glanced at Julian. He was staring at something in his hand: a couple of the Nightmare-infused gems that had fallen during their skirmish. He'd taken some before they had climbed up, though she had resisted asking him why.

He looked up and caught her gaze. Suddenly she wanted nothing more than for it to be just the two of them, to soothe his guilt and ease her concern. To face him as he was now, quiet and gentle and stubborn. Everything she had once thought was ill-suited for her.

"We should make a plan," Lilia was saying. "Return to Astrum. Do you think there's a way to—?"

A low, buzzing drone traveled through the air and disturbed the ground beneath them. Taesia and the others reached for their weapons, instantly on alert.

Astrum sat far to the south, the city built in miniature from this distance. In each of its cardinal directions rose towers of pale light. There was one coming from the Vitae Conjuration circle they had left behind, flaring red as fire or heartsblood.

In the sky above the city grew a coin of radiance, like lightning about to strike. Clouds spun around it in a maelstrom. The city was ringed in a golden circle spelling out the shapes of glyphs.

Just like Godsnight. Just like Nexus.

Taesia realized what was about to unfold a second before it happened. A pillar of light shot out of the maelstrom. It crackled and plunged to the earth below.

To Astrum.

"*No!*" Lilia darted forward. She held out the fangs, but it was no use; they were too far away.

They were forced to watch the destruction of the city's western ward, the area flooded with blinding daylight. The force of it leveled entire blocks of buildings, charred the bodies of those who had ever only known the dark.

And then the pillar was gone. The maelstrom dispersed, leaving an afterimage branded behind Taesia's eyelids—a solid line of devastation.

The silence it left in its wake wanted to eat her alive. Julian gripped her arm tight, but she couldn't feel it. The Noctans were utterly still, Marcellus with his sword halfway unsheathed, Kalen's mouth open in a soundless cry, Lilia with one arm extended.

Slowly the fangs fell from her hand. Her scream traveled over the dark fields and through the winding canyon, until even Nyx himself must have heard it.

GO BACK
TO SLEEP

I have been wounded before.

In the earlier days, when the doorways were open, when Deia and Thana and I spoke of restraints. Only Orsus could construct new worlds, new visions. And we...

You say *god*, and it evokes benevolence. You say *holy*, and it conjures awe.

We say prisoner. Captive. It festered in me, and I could not cut it out no matter how many times I tried.

When we met in the celestial belt between our realms, N— took me and loved me, merged our bodies together until they made their own event horizon. Ran his fingers over the curves of my wings and I believed I *believed* he adored me, that he was willing to face the sun's glare even if it blinded him for just one glimpse of me.

But he could not fathom a universe without doorways. He did not want anything other than his night and his stars and me far beyond them.

Something withered. Regard, in whatever form I carried it, rotted like a gangrenous limb, transmuting adoration to disgust.

(Then it was never really adoration, was it? You've never felt regard in its truest form, because you were too preoccupied with yourself.)

Go back to sleep.

The traitor told Orsus our plan. We knew we would be stripped of our power, our worlds, our very agency. But we'd long ago made sure to hide our cruxes, fitting them into the landscape of our realms. Through them we could be reborn.

The three of us descended. Deia was foremost, as I had been coaxing her into a state of vitriol. She delivered the fatal blow. And as Ostium crumbled and its priests fled into the cosmic void, we then turned against each other.

I did not expect N— to arrive, a sword of unholy dark in his hand, only to see me holding what was left of Orsus's flesh. He watched me devour it, writhing and sparking with pain I had never felt before, with ecstasy not even he could bestow upon me.

His blade pierced the spot where my heart should beat.

(You deserved it. Your rebellion cost us an entire universe.)

Silence.

This spot upon our chest, where this scar pulses with such hatred, is where N— declared his loyalties. The wound that will never heal. The wound that will soon end me.

(So you stole my body, my mind. You want to live on through me while your real form decays.

But I'm remembering. I'll remember this, too. And I'll fight you at every step.)

Soon there will be no *you* any longer. In your slumber you will slip away, as gently as I can manage. Is that not a mercy?

Then you will not have to see the light come again. Is that not a blessing?

Sleep. I have dreams enough for us both.

PART IV

Singularity

I

Angelica came to with a start. She tried to move and found her arms bound behind her back. Her shoulders ached after however many hours she'd spent unconscious, her last blurry memory of a Gojarin waving an astringent vial under her nose.

She dizzily pushed herself into a sitting position. She was in a modest-sized room devoid of furniture or anything resembling comfort. The only light came from finger-width paper windows near the ceiling, painting slim, rectangular bars of sunlight across the opposite wall.

With a pounding heart, Angelica made for the doors. She turned and tried to grab hold of one with her flailing hand.

"Won't work," came a familiar voice. "Already tried it. Locked."

Cosima was sitting against the wall on the far side of the room, similarly shackled. She squinted at Angelica like her head hurt.

"Aren't you a thief?" Angelica croaked.

Cosima huffed through her nose. "There's a deadbolt on the other side."

"*Fuck.*" She sank back to the floor, furious now that she was painfully cognizant of the trap they had walked into.

"Yup," Cosima agreed.

Eiko and Asami weren't here. Seeing Angelica's confusion, Cosima said, "Nanbu took 'em. I don't...I don't know what he plans to do."

I don't want to lose anyone else. Eiko's words, trembling and trusting.

Angelica's fingers flexed with nothing to hold on to, nothing to burn. The air was stale, thin, and not nearly enough to satisfy her lungs.

Cosima sat up. "Hey. Princess."

Her mother had been right. Angelica should have never pleaded for help, should have never entrusted any part of her or Eiko's safety with a stranger no matter how gentle, should have never stooped so low as this.

She was so fucking *stupid*.

"Mardova!"

Cosima had shuffled toward her on her knees. "Look, he's kept the other girl alive this whole time, right? I don't think he's gonna kill them. And if he's locked you up, that means he wants to use you. I'm sure he'll come to reveal his whole messed-up plot, 'cause that seems like the kind of prick he is. We'll get more information then, yeah? Let's focus on how we're gonna get out of here."

Angelica lowered her head, her breaths jagged, searing. "Get away from me."

Unlike last time, when Cosima had stubbornly stayed, she scooted back a prudent distance. Feeding the gnawing heat in her gut, Angelica let flames ripple out of her with a strangled groan, as relieving as it was painful.

The fit lasted long enough to drain her, but not long enough to see if she could set fire to the doors. Beaded with sweat, Angelica leaned against the opposite wall, heart jackrabbiting against her ribs.

How to escape, she thought, but the fog in her brain was too thick to penetrate. The most she could conceive was that they must be in some sort of keep on the castle grounds.

The room turned chilly now that she'd expended some of her pent-up energy. She glanced at Cosima and found her eyes closed, either sleeping or deep in thought. Angelica swallowed down her words.

The light from the slim windows had deepened to buttery afternoon by the time someone undid the lock and opened the door. Angelica, halfway in a stupor, startled while Cosima struggled to her knees.

But it wasn't Nanbu Daiji who walked in and slid the door closed behind him. It was Koshi.

Holding a paper lantern in one hand, he looked first at Angelica, then Cosima, his rich brown eyes crinkling.

"Veliane." His voice was soft and hopeful. He said something in northern Mariian that Angelica interpreted as *I'm sorry*.

Cosima's face hardened. She collapsed back against the wall, legs sprawled before her—an attempt at casual dismissal or a way to keep some distance between them.

"Don't bother," Cosima said in Vaegan. "Speak to me like this or not at all."

Koshi's soft hope dwindled into bewilderment. He was wearing his Gojarin armor, the black lacquer gleaming in the lantern's glow. Without his helmet, Angelica saw his hair was in short, tight coils. The likeness between him and Cosima was considerable enough that she now understood why Kenji had been so thrown when meeting her.

"You would rather I speak to you in the language of Vaega?" Koshi said, stumbling over the words in a curious accent Angelica couldn't quite place—as if everywhere he'd gone had left some mark on his voice. "Why? Why are you with Mardova Angelica?"

"Dad was dying." Cosima's face invited no emotion. "He used the money from your conscription to send me and Mom to Vaega. I've been there since."

Each word seemed to be a hammer strike for Koshi. "I . . . I learned about Father. But when I sent someone for you and Mother, I could not find you."

"Well, now you know why. Mom's dead, too, by the way."

Koshi stared at her as one stares at an anomaly, uncertain how it can exist. Like the sister he had spent years thinking of was someone he didn't recognize—someone who might as well be dead.

"I came here to find you," Cosima said. "Because I missed you. Because I thought maybe you hated it here, and we could go back to Vaega together." Her mouth twisted.

Koshi said something in Mariian, and Cosima scoffed. She snapped at him in the same language, something Angelica recognized as a curse, before switching back to Vaegan. "Are you fucking with me? I saw what you did at the imperial palace!"

"I did not want you to see that," Koshi said, contrite enough to lower his gaze. "But it was necessary. The imperial family causes too much conflict. Holds too much power. They let us stray from the path of the gods."

Now it was Angelica's turn to scoff. "And obviously that merits death," she muttered. Koshi's glare gave her a glimpse of the ruthless Gojarin they had seen in the banquet hall.

"You're working for our fucking colonizers, Koshi," Cosima spat. "You've learned their language and their ways of fighting and their politics, which is bad enough. But then you had to find the worst of the lot and follow his orders, like a good little lapdog!"

He stepped toward her, lantern swaying at his side. "Bushan Nanbu is a great man. He sees the potential in others and helps them hone it. He has helped me more than I can ever repay."

"He killed an innocent family!" Cosima yelled. The muscles at her arms flexed. "What sort of great man does that?"

"You do not yet understand." Koshi lowered to one knee. "Because of my station and your relation to me, Bushan Nanbu will take care of you. You will have lodgings in Hitan. You will have a monthly stipend. This is what the families of Gojarin receive. Surely this is more than Vaega has ever given you."

Cosima's eyes had grown wide, holding the lantern light inside them like a glass bottle holds a firefly. The knot behind Angelica's breastbone tightened.

"I cannot say how much I missed you," Koshi whispered. "How much I thought of you, how much I hated leaving. But there was a good life waiting for me here, and there is one for you, too." He extended a hand toward her, the pale terrain of his palm empty and beseeching. "With me."

The flame in the lantern fluttered as Angelica's chest ached. Her fingers were numb and blood-thick.

She had to be ready. Ready to engulf the room in fire, to cut her losses and *run*.

Cosima didn't look at her. The ache turned unbearable, burning her lower eyelids, her sinuses, everywhere.

Before Angelica could move, Cosima lunged forward as her shackles fell to the ground. She struck at Koshi, who grunted and fell back with Cosima on top of him.

But even with the element of surprise, a street thief from Nexus was no match against an elite Gojarin. Koshi easily switched their positions and pinned her, her face pressed against the wooden floor.

"Veliane!" Koshi half shouted, more admonishment than outrage. "I am trying to *help* you!"

"I don't need help from a murderer," Cosima growled. "And don't call me Veliane. It's Cosima."

Koshi made a disgusted face. "*Cosima?* You gave yourself a Vaegan name, and you accuse *me* of rolling over for Azuna?"

The lantern was now lying abandoned on the floor. But Cosima caught Angelica's gaze and tried to shake her head. Koshi restrained her once more, then searched her sleeves and pockets to make sure she didn't carry any more lock-picking tools.

"This is proof enough Vaega has failed you," Koshi muttered. "That you had to learn such tactics. Look at you—you are starved."

"I'm starved 'cause we were being chased by your warlord," Cosima shot back.

Koshi stared down at her shackles as if considering whether or not to leave them on. He sighed and knelt before her again, daring to put a hand on her shoulder.

"I know you are upset," Koshi said, ignoring Cosima's glare. "But this does not change the offer. Just... think about it." He squeezed her shoulder and added in Mariian: "Please."

Cosima didn't reply. Eventually Koshi picked up the lantern and left, locking them in once more.

Only when his footsteps faded did Cosima relax. She didn't say anything for a long time, the slope of her shoulders bent in something dangerously close to defeat. Angelica didn't supply any platitudes, not only because she herself hated them but because she was fully aware of how tempting Koshi and Nanbu's offer was.

Angelica was not soft or gentle. She was difficult to stand by, difficult to care for. There was nothing tying them together that Cosima couldn't easily sever.

Cosima's voice cut through her panic. "Don't worry, princess. I'm not going to fall for it."

Angelica turned toward her. She had the inane thought that she missed Cosima's smile, and didn't like how long it had been since she'd last seen it.

"What?" she rasped.

"Nanbu's offer," Cosima said. "I'm not going to take it. We're gonna get the fuck out of here." She swallowed. "I spent so long wanting to find my brother, for the two of us to be together again. This isn't the Koshi I wanted to find. He may as well be dead."

"He's still your brother." And growing up as a Mardova, Angelica knew firsthand how powerful blood was.

Cosima shook her head. "Some things are more important than blood."

The next morning, Nanbu Daiji came to see them. He was flanked by Koshi and Kenji, and bitterness bubbled thick and black in Angelica's gut at the sight of the latter already returned to his expected place at the warlord's side. When Kenji met her blistering gaze, he quickly looked away.

Deia was draped around Nanbu's shoulders in her snake form, blue eyes fixated on Angelica. Although a snake couldn't convey emotions, Angelica very much felt its smug satisfaction.

Nanbu was wearing a simple robe with his amaranth crest and leather bracers. The only finery he'd allowed was the silver crown securing his neat bun.

"Esteemed Mardova," he greeted in Azunese, arms held behind his back, insultingly at ease. "I thought it only fair I should be the one to tell you what will happen tomorrow."

Angelica used the wall for support to rise to her feet. Cosima did the same, glaring pointedly at Koshi, who gritted his teeth and ignored her.

"And what exactly do you expect to happen tomorrow?" Angelica drawled.

The corner of the warlord's mouth ticked up at her wording. "I expect a rewarding outcome."

Behind him, Kenji kept his eyes on the floor. His breathing was a little erratic, his face pale.

Good, she thought. *Be ashamed.*

Her focus was stolen again by Nanbu as he said, "Tomorrow, you will be publicly executed before the castle gates."

Her heart gave a sickening thump, but she schooled her expression to indifference.

"I see," she said, nonchalant. "I suppose the people expect this, since you erroneously declared that it was I, not you, who slaughtered the imperial family."

"And since I have Satake Akane, it will give the citizens much joy to see their beloved empress safe in my care while you lose your head under the executioner's sword."

"Not to mention that now the meddling imperial family is gone, you can have full control over the empress, make her even more of a figurehead."

"It wouldn't do to make the empire grieve too heavily," he agreed with a dip of his chin. "As for Veliane, out of fondness for Koshi I have agreed to let her go, insofar as she will be kept under house arrest in her new lodgings until this whole situation blows over."

Koshi briefly closed his eyes in relief. Cosima, having heard her name, tensed.

"And Asami?" Angelica demanded. "Eiko?"

"Satake Asami is not the current face of the empress everyone knows and adores," Nanbu answered. "I will keep Akane in her current station and help her younger sister develop control of kudei."

When Nanbu mentioned kudei, Kenji's gaze flickered to hers.

"Ueda Eiko will remain with them. I'm sure a friendly face will help them through this transition."

Which meant Eiko would be a prisoner, forced to cooperate or end up like the rest of her family.

"Eiko, as well as her sister and mother back in Vaega, are the only ones left of the extended imperial family," Angelica said. "Why don't you simply kill them?"

"Whatever you believe of me, I'd rather not resort to murder for every problem," Nanbu said. The snake around his shoulders gave a hissing laugh. Angelica longed to throttle it. "Besides, your execution will be statement enough."

"My execution will start a war with Vaega," she countered. "My mother is already in position to inherit the throne. It won't take much to launch an attack against you."

"Your mother is in contention with the Vakaras for the throne," he corrected. "And with the news of her murderous heir spreading, I doubt that will be the case much longer."

Heat licked up her fingers, spooling into the palms of her hands. She wanted to bare her teeth, to become low like an animal to express the boiling hatred inside her, but Adela had taught her better than that.

Next to Nanbu, Kenji shifted. He was still looking at her with a strange, warning expression.

It was then that she remembered what he had told her earlier, about Nanbu wanting to leash the sorankun of the Sanatsu Peaks to his will.

Understanding crackled through her. "You're going to use Asami to control the sorankun."

The slight lifting of his brows gave away his surprise. "Kenji told you about that, did he?" Behind him, Kenji grimaced. "It has long been said the empress holds a special connection to the beasts, since they represent kudei and the coming together of the empire in all its natural resources. But this particular empress has more than that—she has the very element the sorankun symbolize, the one many stories claim they possess. What better way to bridle them than to utilize one who speaks their language?"

He gave a pale smile, reaching up to stroke the snake's head. "With my military bolstered, it won't take much to dominate the other states. Or to field incoming attacks from Vaega. With a god's might behind me, all possibilities will be open. It is too bad you couldn't say the same."

Deia's laugh was the scrape of a lock, her piccolo being crushed, a mage's skull cracking under a paperweight, the breaking of her violin. It was everything she had once reached for crumbling to ash.

Even after Nanbu had long gone—Kenji sending her one last plaintive look—Angelica remained silent, sitting against the base of the wall. The light dimmed to dusk, then to night. In the darkness she felt freer to fall deeper into her dread, her heart fully calcified with it, unable to keep beating without breaking.

From the gloom came Cosima's voice. "Are you going to finally tell me what he said?"

Angelica relayed the conversation in low, stilted words. When she finished, Cosima swore.

"You're just *now* telling me you're going to be beheaded tomorrow?" Cosima demanded, the heat to Angelica's numb chill. "What the fuck, Mardova."

When Angelica didn't reply, Cosima came to sit beside her. Angelica couldn't move away, could barely even glance at her.

"You're not gonna shoo me away this time, are you?" Cosima grumbled. "Deia's sagging tits. Damn, I said her name again." She thumped her head back against the wall. "Look. There's something about you that Nanbu doesn't know, right?"

Angelica frowned.

"Your voice," Cosima clarified. "They shackled you thinking you need your hands to . . . whatever it is you do with elements, but you don't need them, you just need your voice. He doesn't know that."

She thought back to Cosima lunging at her brother after unlocking her shackles. "You mean surprise him."

"That'd be it."

"And then do what? He has *Deia*. This whole keep is likely flooded with Gojarin."

"So? You're a Mardova. I've seen you do some freaky shit. Remember how you single-handedly pulverized a kraken? And didn't you make a portal to spirit Akane away? Maybe you can do the same thing now."

It certainly wasn't impossible, but Angelica had been under enormous strain just to produce a portal big enough for a small teenage girl. She didn't know if she could make one large enough, or precise enough, for all of them.

Unless...

The gears in her mind turned even as she said, "My power is unstable, especially with the withdrawal. It's been a long time since the last dose of Hypericum."

Cosima shrugged. "I trust you."

Although Angelica understood the words individually, she couldn't grasp the meaning of them strung together, especially not directed at her.

Cosima went on, "Even if something happens and someone gets hurt, like when you accidentally burned me, it won't be your fault."

"How was burning you not my fault?"

"You warned me to get away. I didn't."

Angelica shook her head, frustration welling up in her. "You told Koshi you didn't need help from a murderer. But that's what I am."

"What?"

"That night. When I was—when you found me covered in blood."

Angelica flexed her fingers, welcoming the painful pins and needles that came with the motion. She focused on the pain while she explained Eran Liolle, Deia's intentions, the desperation that had grabbed her by the throat. The way the man had looked at girls, the paperweights on his desk. How it felt to rip him open and ruin him.

"And in the end it did nothing," she whispered as she stared into the darkness, losing sense of time and place. "I swallowed his flesh and it did nothing to help. I killed him and I...I did it for power. Power that never came."

Cosima didn't say anything for a time, but she didn't move away either. It was just their breathing in the quiet room, slowly falling into sync.

"Sounds like the world's probably a better place without him," Cosima said at last. "You say you did it for power. But *why* did you want that power?"

"To undo the Sealing. To break down the barriers between the realms. To...distance myself from my god, and prove my family is fit to rule."

Cosima nodded. "That's the whole thing about power, isn't it? It all depends on how it's used. You didn't want power the way Nanbu does, to conquer empires and people." She paused. "Well, you want a crown, but it's not quite the same."

She turned to Angelica. Though their hands were bound, there were other ways to touch: the bright warmth of Cosima's forehead on hers, their thighs pressed together.

"I'm not exactly thrilled, but I get why you did it," Cosima said softly. "You just wanted to be strong. You wanted to be enough."

Her already fragile heart shattered to pieces. It left behind the raw, bloody shape of a new one, small and vulnerable and so, so frightened. The fright of a child unable to leave their bed in the middle of the night, calling out for someone to come and reassure them.

Angelica dropped her head to Cosima's shoulder. Cosima's lips pressed against her temple and calmed the shivering in her chest, told her that this, now, was enough.

All her life the Mardovas had desired *power*, and it was only now she realized power took different shapes. For her mother, it had always meant a crown, and that had become Angelica's goal. But for herself, power meant strength.

She was not Ferdinand Accardi or Nanbu Daiji, lusting after control. She was not Deia, negligent toward her subjects even as she exerted her dominance over them.

She was a wielder of all elements and heir to a god's might. And with her power—with her strength—she would keep them safe.

II

Dante couldn't help but feel an odd sort of letdown at the idea of resurrecting Marcos Ricci in his aunt's beachfront suite.

He had admittedly pictured it somewhere darker and more sinister, though he supposed that was a result of growing up with his nose buried in fantastical stories. Brailee heard him sigh and asked what was wrong.

"Oh, nothing," he murmured as he watched the Revenants lay out the body on the floor of the main room, over the circle of chalk they'd constructed around a seven-pointed star. It was nighttime, at least, though he could hear the lapping of waves nearby. "Do you remember that book I made you read when you were much too young for it? *This Unholy Heart?*"

Brailee scrunched her nose. "I had nightmares for weeks. Thanks for that."

"You're welcome. But do you remember the part when the corpse of the main character's father is raised by his vengeful spirit because the main character killed him?"

"Unwillingly, yes."

"They were in this decrepit, dank dungeon, and it was *so* atmospheric." He sighed again. "I guess reality isn't like books."

"You were always the more romantic one," Camilla muttered.

"But what happens after?" Azideh demanded. He stood in his corporeal form next to Dante, arms folded and looking extremely out of place despite the proceedings. The crimson cloud around Camilla's shoulders kept hissing at him. "Does this *main character* get torn apart?"

"I haven't read it yet, don't spoil it!" Natsumi yelled from where she was drawing a glyph.

"It's been out for over a decade," Dante argued. "If you haven't been spoiled yet—"

"Nyx's *rotting* piss, keep your voice down," said Camilla. "Among all the other atrocities of this resort, the suites share walls."

Natsumi *humph*ed. "At any rate, the circle is done."

Saya wrung her hands as she stared down at Marcos Ricci's gaunt face. "Is that really necessary? I'm pretty sure I can do this on my own."

"Not saying you can't." Natsumi rolled her eyes. "I saw what your sister could do. This is just in case you need support."

The other Revenants knelt around the circle. Saya glanced at their knives and made a faint noise in the back of her throat. Brailee put a hand on her back while Somnus drifted around her. After visibly weighing her options, Saya finally knelt at Marcos Ricci's head.

Dante and Camilla sat on either side, Azideh returning to his cloud form. He grumbled in Dante's head about not liking the feeling of the circle. Dante ignored him.

"I don't know how much time you'll have to question him, since he died so long ago," Saya warned. "If I can even find his spirit, that is."

"We'll be quick," Dante assured her.

Saya placed her hands on either side of Marcos Ricci's head and closed her eyes. She took several deep breaths, the pulse at her neck jumping, until a light, cold wind swirled around her. Her brow furrowed in concentration, Saya lifted a hand and sketched an invisible, looping pattern in the air above the corpse, the shape of a Vakara spell.

A moaning sigh rose from the corpse and the room turned brutally cold. The Revenants stared down at Ricci, transfixed, as the edges of him glowed black.

Slowly the corpse's eyes opened. They were filmed over with age, unseeing. A dusty rattle emanated from his leathery throat.

"This is not my tomb," Marcos Ricci said in a creaking voice.

Dante, breathless with thrill, leaned forward. "We apologize for that, Don Ricci, but someone else moved you first."

"Who?"

"The baron of Seniza. Alma."

Marcos Ricci's face was too stiff for expression, but Dante thought he noticed his eyes twitch slightly. "Alma. Still in...charge? How long?"

"Yes, they've held the barony here for the last several centuries—"

"We don't have time to entertain his questions," Camilla broke in.

But the corpse went on, "So it worked."

"What worked?" Dante asked.

"Santiago Alma," Ricci said, his gaze affixed to the ceiling, mouth barely moving as he spoke. "He came to me requesting a way...to keep his power. To ensure it passed...from generation to generation."

"The demon," Dante whispered. He exchanged a look with his aunt. "You helped him summon a demon?"

"Yes. In return...they gave me a tomb. Rights to preserve my body."

"How can a demon be passed on like that?" Camilla demanded. "It must have been here for centuries." Dante thought of Azideh's warning on the hillside about a pact going on indefinitely and wondered if this was what he meant.

"The pact was unique." Above Ricci, Saya's breaths had become strained. "Instead of...taking something from the summoner, the summoner...offered equivalent sacrifice."

Sacrifice. Dante thought about the scared girl in the baron's estate, how Martín Alma had laid out his plans for her in such pleasant tones. "You're saying that the Almas have been sacrificing people to Deia's Heart—to their *demon*—for centuries?"

"Yes," the corpse wheezed. "And each child, when grown, would craft their summoning circle...to transition the demon to them. To give them...the power...to manipulate others. To stay in their lofty position."

Dante suddenly longed to smash his fist down on Marcos Ricci's face. Instead he asked, "Is it possible to suppress a demon?"

Camilla gave him a startled look. Dante ignored her.

"Only...one way I know of," Ricci answered slowly. "The use of their name."

"But we already know their name. It's written in *your* grimoire."

"Their...true name. From before."

Before the universe had twisted them into the beings they were now. Dante sat back on his heels and asked Azideh, *Do you have another name?* The demon remained silent.

"Learning Marizleh's true name would be impossible," Camilla said. "Unless you know it, Shanizeh?"

A red cloud bristled around her shoulders. "It is not mine to give," muttered Shanizeh's voice.

"So you're willing to kill other demons, but not give away their true names?" Camilla lifted an eyebrow. "That's an unusual form of loyalty."

Brailee turned back to Ricci. "Why do the Almas make sacrifices to Deia's Heart specifically?"

"The concentration of power," Marcos Ricci answered. "The volcano lies...on the same tectonic plate as Mount Netsai. The magic...passed between them is great."

Dante took the sketch Angelica had given him out of his pocket. If Deia's Heart was potent with magic, did that mean it was the best place to re-create the portal? If Angelica decided to go to Mount Netsai, could they forge a link between them to strengthen it?

"Can you find Angelica in your dreams and tell her about this?" he asked Brailee, who nodded.

Saya suddenly grunted and doubled over. The glow around the corpse wavered.

"Activate the circle," Camilla ordered.

Natsumi and the others cut the pads of their fingers and spilled drops of blood into the circle. It flared and reinforced the black light, keeping Marcos Ricci's spirit tethered to his body even while Saya shook with the strain.

Dante wasted no time holding the sketch in front of the corpse's eyes. "Don Ricci, this is a Conjuration circle that we believe leads to the realm of Noctus."

Marcos Ricci's eyes just barely moved in order to take it in. "Yes."

"Do you know how we can activate it?"

"All that is required...is the correct offering."

"Such as?"

"Something of magical value. Noctan...gems. Solarian feathers. Vitaean blood. Nothing is stronger than...blood and flesh."

Brailee's gasp was soft. "The dreams I had of Rian," she said to Dante. "He was collecting bodies."

A low hum came from Marcos Ricci's throat. "A sacrifice would do it," he agreed. "Given...that it is large enough, or if the bodies...harbor magic of their own."

Camilla rubbed her chin, no doubt thinking of Baron Alma's scheduled sacrifice of the refugee woman.

"We are *not* sacrificing anyone," Dante said firmly.

"What about Baron Alma himself?" Camilla countered. "Get rid of him and activate the portal. Two problems solved at once."

"The magical potential of a demon would suffice," the corpse whispered. His voice was growing fainter, the light around him sputtering.

Saya groaned again, and blood dripped from her nose. Brailee steadied her shoulders.

"Do *not* sever the connection!" Camilla ordered.

"He's...fading," Saya ground out. "Spirit is...slipping back into the void..."

The corpse started to crumble. Its mouth opened wider, letting out an eerie, wailing sound as its eyes burned.

Camilla swore. "Keep hold of him!"

"*Enough!*" Brailee yelled at her. "Saya, let go!"

Saya did so with a gasp of relief. She would have collapsed to the floor if Brailee hadn't caught her. Brailee let Saya's head fall to her shoulder and stroked her hair gently, telling her she'd done a good job. The Revenants scored the circle and the glow faded, Marcos Ricci's spirit vanishing as his body withered to dust.

Camilla curled her hands into fists. "*Damn it.*"

"We got what we needed," Dante said. "We know enough to plan our next moves."

His aunt glared at the pile of dust until her expression smoothed. She gave a long sigh, as if letting go of all the things she'd longed to ask.

"You're right," she said. "We should begin preparations."

Natsumi offered a cup of water to Saya, who took it gratefully. "That's why the city feels so strange," Saya said after downing half the cup. "It's not only been built over the dead—the victims of years of sacrifices linger on the outskirts. They want revenge."

"Can we work with that?" Camilla asked Natsumi, who nodded. "Bee, see if you can find Angelica Mardova's dreamscape. Dante, we'll plan how to get the circle drawn. Everyone else..." She waved at the erstwhile founder of Conjuration. "Sweep this up and toss it into the ocean."

III

You are the heir of Ostium. Whether you want to be or not.

Julian sat looking at the two nightmare-infused gems he'd taken from the quarry. He wasn't sure why he'd decided to pick them up, why he would want a reminder of what had happened in the canyon.

A soft murmur caught his attention. Marcellus had made chori and was now handing a cup to the princess, who only stared at it before the soldier sighed and put her hands around it. They were camped a half day's walk from Astrum; no matter how badly Lilia wanted to reach the city, Kalen had forced her to stop and rest.

Tomorrow, they would confront Phos. Today, they had to prepare.

Taesia sat with her sheathed sword in her lap, staring in the direction of the city. Her gaze was dull even as fury tightened her mouth. When Marcellus offered her chori, she shook her head.

Julian hadn't seen her like this since the evening before Godsnight, when she had been sitting in front of his mother's apartment with nowhere else to go. She'd just been a girl and her sword, hunter and hunted, and he had let her go thinking he might never see her again.

He wouldn't risk the same thing twice. But even as he thought this, letting it settle on him like snowdrift, there came a sickening whisper in his mind:

You don't deserve it.

Julian fisted his hand around the gems and let them dig into his palm. Touching them like this, a tremor of fear went down his spine like the tip of a beast's claw.

He had fully become the demon. The memory of it was sharp, vivid—how it felt to pin Taesia down and choke her, feasting on her pain. To her, kissing him had been a means to save herself, to shock him, to remind him of his humanity. To him, it was the beginning of his downfall.

She was world-ending, and he hoped for her mercy in the form of destruction, longing to be left a ruin in her wake.

But he knew she wouldn't grant him that—not, at least, until she turned that devastation on Phos.

When he closed his eyes, he could still see those pillars of light. The column of sun haze that meant death, and the Noctans helpless to stop any of it.

"We'll make him pay," Taesia said suddenly.

The others looked to her. She hadn't moved, had barely even raised her voice, but it arrested them regardless.

"How?" Lilia asked. "We only have three fangs. He has the rest. Without them—"

"We'll get them. And even if we don't, you're a gods-damned Lunari. I bet you can make three fangs work."

Kalen looked torn between admonishing her word choice or agreeing with her. Lilia touched the cord where the fangs hung around her neck.

"Is this because of me?" Lilia's voice wavered. "Because of the Malum Star? If—if one of my siblings had survived instead—"

Kalen's expression became pained. "Your Highness, no—"

"*Stop it.*" Taesia picked up Starfell and stalked closer to the princess. "This isn't about what star you were born under. This is about gods manipulating one another. This is about preventing anything like *that*"— she pointed toward Astrum—"from happening again. None of us give a shit if you have bad luck. But if you don't stop placing all the blame on yourself like a martyr, I'll go on ahead without you."

"How *dare* you?" Kalen snarled. "Do you have any idea how much she has done for you?"

"I'm aware," Taesia said grimly. "And I know exactly what it's like to sit there and blame myself. That everything—everyone—would be better off without me." She turned back to the princess. "I've seen your loyalty, your dedication, your bravery. The Malum Star pales next to all of that." Then, softer: "You didn't deserve any of this."

Lilia stared at her. Julian stood in case he had to get between Taesia and Kalen, the latter looking ready to summon his familiar. Before he could, Marcellus put a hand on his arm.

"She's right," the soldier said softly.

Lilia turned wide eyes on him. "Mar?"

"I'm sorry, Your Highness, but I agree with her. I know how important it is to read the stars, but they can't read *everything*. And so far all they have caused you is grief." He moved his hand to Lilia's arm. "It isn't a sin to be born."

The princess's eyes overflowed. Julian didn't know if she'd ever stopped to allow herself to mourn her family. If she hadn't, it was all coming out now—in great, heaving sobs, the unabashed weeping of a child. She had held herself together with sheer will until she couldn't any longer.

Thankfully, she had the other two to catch her. She wept between them, letting herself fall, knowing they would pick up the pieces.

Taesia watched them with a sort of hollow satisfaction. Turning, she met Julian's gaze.

He quickly moved away. Not only to give the Noctans privacy, but to avoid what was coming.

Don't, he pleaded. *Don't follow.*

But of course she followed. With a sinking heart, he chose a spot in the grass at random and sat cross-legged. Under the wide expanse of the jeweled sky she joined him, placing Starfell not in her lap but beside her.

The silence was almost worse than words, and for a second he debated taking out the nightmare gems and forcing himself into a less excruciating scenario.

Maybe she was waiting for him to speak first. He opened his mouth, drawing in a breath to apologize for what he'd become—what he'd done to her.

"Did you know," she said first, "that House Lastrider has a motto?"

He let his breath out slowly. "No. I didn't know any of the Houses had mottos. Ma would probably know all of them, though."

In the corner of his eye, Taesia smiled. "Our motto is: *In the dark, all is possible.*"

He suppressed a flinch at the memory of Orsus's voice. *Through me, all is possible.*

"It's mostly for dramatics," she admitted. "But... more and more, I'm starting to believe it. I've seen a lot of impossible things come to pass. Things that shouldn't even be plausible."

Julian swallowed. "Like me."

"Well. Yes."

"I'm sorry." He couldn't contain it any longer, needed to bleed it out of him. "For what I—I'm sorry I couldn't control it. That I—"

"Julian." She waited for him to turn to her. "If I really wanted to, I could have killed you."

He glanced at the bruises on the side of her neck in the shape of his fingerprints. Disgust and desire spun a tangled web.

"Then why didn't you?"

Her eyes were so intensely fixated on him that he couldn't move. "You don't have control over the circumstances of your blood. And like Marcellus said, being born isn't a sin. You may carry the demon's blood, but the demon isn't *you*."

"Is there even a difference?"

"There is." She wrapped a hand around his wrist. "Just as there's a difference between Taesia Lastrider and Nyx. My power might come from him, and he may have the power to control me, but we are not the same."

Taesia didn't remove her hand. He noticed there was a scar at the base of her thumb, and he wanted to ask how she'd gotten it.

"Azideh," he said. "That's the demon's name. The one whose powers I have."

"If—" She grunted in vexation. "*When* we get back, I'll hunt my aunt down and find the grimoire. We'll get answers."

If I ever see your aunt again, he thought, picturing Camilla Lorenzo's dagger dripping with his mother's blood, *I'm going to kill her.*

"Brailee told me they're looking for a way to get us back to Vitae," Taesia went on. "But I don't know how, or if we can get out of this with everyone intact. She said she's been trying to reach Rian, but Phos's hold on him is too strong. I'm worried there'll be no separating them, now."

His free hand strayed to the pocket where he'd stowed the nightmare gems. He wanted to try freeing Rian from Phos, but it could require him relying on Orsus again. And if he let go of too much of himself, the god might be able to take him.

"We'll save him," Julian said with as much conviction as he could muster.

A faint smile touched her lips. It made him want to live in the curve of it, inside every darkness she inhabited.

"I guess there is *some* truth to the stars," she murmured. "Praeses. Guardian."

His face warmed. "And what about the other one?" Belua. Monster.

"Remember how I said there's no choosing your blood?" Her hand tightened around his wrist. "There were so many times that made me furious, growing up. So many times I wished I wasn't a Lastrider."

"That you didn't have your powers?"

"Never that. Just everything else that came with it." A shrug of her shoulders. "Many would call me selfish, or childish. But I don't care. I wanted, and I craved, in a way the other heirs didn't. My brother wanted to use every power he had—shadow and political—and I admired him for it. And what did it get him?" She laughed bitterly. "He wanted so badly to change the world, and he was punished for it. It only made me want to rip off my chains that much more. I wanted *out*, and I didn't care who I hurt along the way.

"I've never believed in fate. I've always thought you could change things so long as you tried hard enough." She was quiet a moment as she stared up at the stars. "But I think blood and fate are essentially the same. I couldn't run from mine, and you can't run from yours. It might mean making a difficult choice. Or it might mean that instead of choosing between monster and guardian, you can be both."

Taesia turned back to him. Her eyes were the black of deep water, and just as heavy.

"There's no shame in being both," she whispered. "No shame in being who you are."

He was a Hunter and a demon, and supposedly, the heir of Ostium. Someone whose wants were bigger than his needs.

He didn't know where he found the courage to turn his hand over, to link his fingers with hers.

"Not everyone would be better off without you," Julian murmured. And then, using her own words: "I've seen your loyalty, your dedication, your bravery. I've seen your power and your pain." He rested his thumb against the base of hers, suddenly envious of how the small scar there fit so close against her skin. "I've seen all of you, and I'm not afraid."

Taesia was not gentle, but he yearned to touch her in the gentlest way possible, to feather his fingertips over the places they had bruised. To watch her lean into him the way the moon leaned into the horizon before dawn. To know he was wanted in turn, to be brave and monstrous together, and forge new possibilities in the dark.

Her sigh was shuddering. Her liquid eyes both a question and an answer.

Footsteps sounded behind them. Taesia slowly let go of his hand, a devastation in itself, and they both turned.

Kalen jerked his chin at Taesia. "Come with me."

"If you're going to lecture me, I don't want to hear it," Taesia warned the astrologer as she followed him away from the others, more than a little grumpy about being interrupted. Her hand was cold without the warmth of Julian's. "I know you're grieving, and I'm sorry. But—"

"Do you ever get tired of talking?" he muttered. "Sit down."

It was only then she realized he'd brought his pack with him. Once they settled in the grass, he took out a roll of parchment, a small bottle of ink, and a pen.

"What are you doing?" she asked.

He looked up at her. The whites of his eyes were tinged pink, the only admission to his sorrow.

"I'm making your star chart," he said. "You are dalyr, which means you are descended from Nyx, and therefore part Noctan. And since no one thought to draw up your chart when you were born, I'm going to fix that."

This, too, felt like a challenge, but not on her part—on his. One that opened something in her chest she thought she'd stitched up a long time ago: the feeling of walking through the Noctus Quarter, of being watched but not seen, of being heard but not *known*.

Of being part of a community who didn't truly acknowledge her as one of them, no matter their reverence.

And here she was being extended more than just reverence. Here was tradition, and custom, and insight. A gift.

"Even though I implied the stars are bullshit?"

He huffed. "Especially because of that. It might be true that the stars cannot read everything..." At this he glanced toward Marcellus, who sat with his arm around the princess. "But in this world, they cannot be ignored. Their light and their placement give us knowledge for a reason. We would be foolish to dismiss it."

Kalen picked up his pen. "Now: Tell me where and when you were born. As many details as you can give."

Taesia knew enough from all the times her father had told the story.

"Elena was *dying* for peppers," Cormin had said fondly. "Normally she can't handle that much heat, and it was the middle of summer, but who was I to deny her? So there she was, sitting there swollen like a pig's intestine"—he only added this detail if her mother wasn't around—"with sweat and tears running down her face, eating raw peppers. And then, suddenly, she grabbed her stomach, looked up at me, and said, 'She's coming.'"

She gave Kalen the date and time, which had been around dawn. He wrote notes to himself, as well as charts she couldn't decipher while he muttered things like "So *that's* where that comes from" and "If the seventh month of that year fell under the New Moon cycle..."

Taesia let him ponder while Umbra slithered out of its bezel and into her palm. She rolled it back and forth like a ball. Her body yearned to get up and walk around, her knee bouncing up and down with the urge to run to Astrum right then and there.

Her gaze strayed back to Julian. He remained where she'd left him, the wind playing with his hair. Under the starlight he was mercury and magic, his spine a little straighter after she'd made clear she didn't resent the demon.

Kalen made a confused sound. He was frowning at the chart he'd made, and though she couldn't read the planar drawings, she guessed something was off.

"I..." He scratched at his tied-back hair, leaving a smudge of ink along his cheekbone. "I'm not entirely sure how to read this."

"If this whole thing was just to antagonize me—"

"*No.* I'm being serious." His green eyes shone in the wan moonlight. "Your chart, it...it reminds me of *his.*"

Julian's. Taesia held her breath while Kalen scoured his notes again.

"I shouldn't have gotten anything wrong," he mumbled.

"Just tell me."

Kalen hesitated, then nodded. "You were born in the triangle of three constellations: Adrastea, Caria, and...Cultris."

Umbra wound itself around her arm as her heart tripped. Cultris, the constellation that contained the Malum Star—as well as the star that had become her sword.

"Based on the time of your birth, you fell under two primary stars. The first is the Salvar Star from the Adrastea constellation. Many soldiers and important historical figures were born under this star; it means safety and the bravery that comes from wanting to protect. It's often called the savior's star." He frowned again. "It was the star Noria Lunari was born under."

Noria Lunari, who had fashioned the astralam coronal and saved her city by sacrificing her life, thus ending the Century of Eclipse. Kalen stared at her in bemusement, a mirror to the confusion in her chest that silently demanded, *How were* you *of all people born under this star?*

She didn't know. It didn't fit her at all, made her want to rip up the chart and call bullshit all over again. But she needed to hear the rest of it, to appease her growing curiosity.

Kalen moved his finger across the parchment. "The other star comes from the Caria constellation. It's called Sceleratus." Now he turned cautious, and goose bumps rose along her arms. "It lies directly across from the Salvar Star for a reason: It is Salvar's complete opposite. And it is known as the villain's star."

He fell quiet, as if expecting her to lash out or deny it. But she only sat there, letting her uneasiness settle.

All her life her family had wanted her to be a proper heir, a dutiful daughter, an upstanding citizen.

All her life she'd felt like a black stain, a mistake, an impostor.

Two opposites that canceled each other out. There was a strange relief in it, in being both and neither.

Kalen must have seen some of this processing on her face. "Some stars don't usually equate to literal translations," he assured her. "Just look at Lilia. Born under the Malum Star, which denotes ill luck and malice. But she isn't malicious. She doesn't carry ill luck like a noxious cloud. Rather, she is the victim of tragedy. The stars can signify personal traits, or foresee events in your life. These events might have already come to pass."

Taesia nodded and remembered the feel of Don Soler's blood spraying her face, the terror in Cristoban Damari's eyes before he'd been sucked through a portal. Standing on a rooftop and demanding the life of a king who had failed all of them.

She still felt justified. That hadn't changed. But what she understood now was that, even while serving her brand of justice, she had been turning from one star to reach for the other.

Nyx's prior taunts rose to the surface of her thoughts.

You, who know best how to run, will also turn your back on this world. You, who have the means to stop this destruction, will enable it.

She gritted her teeth. *No*, she thought viciously. *I won't.*

Yet she couldn't be like Noria Lunari, who had sacrificed everything though she didn't have to. Her name was sung with praise and reverence, but how much better would it have been to have *lived*? To go after what she wanted, instead of giving everything to duty?

She had told Julian there was no shame in his stars. That instead of choosing one or the other, he could be both.

She wondered now if she could do the same—or if she would be forced to decide, in the end, which star burned brighter.

IV

Standing on the shore of the Praeteriens, Risha held the weight of all her memories in her hands like stones.

They were unexpectedly heavy. To have carried them this far, in the empty vessel of her body—to be alive long enough to remember them at all—was nothing short of a miracle.

But it was more than stones. It was bone, fashioned into handles, into smiling scythes.

Samhara dragged her down. Pulled her toward the Forgetting Waters. She took another step forward.

How easy it would be to fall into the current of gray, twisting souls. To become a soul herself, to strip the rest of her humanity like shedding skin. She could drop all the stones in her hands. Plunge Samhara into the depths to join them, until it was unwritten out of every world, until she could no longer recall the shape of it against her palms.

Palms she had once used to hold her sister's face, squishing it until Saya complained. Palms that had cradled cups of hot, fragrant tea while discussing the latest fashion trends with her mother, or the newest policies with her father. Palms warmed by others' hands as they pulled her along into their games, their lives.

Even if she dropped every stone, her body would carry too much sense memory. The smell of her mother's favorite perfume and the chime of her bangles. The scratchiness of her father's beard when he kissed her cheek and the reverberation of his low voice when he praised her. The taste of the carob cakes Saya loved and the ache that came after laughing over some trivial thing together.

The warmth of Jas's chest when he had held her and the soft whisper of a black rose's petals against her fingers.

All of it would be lost.

Risha swayed and stared at the river. It was so close and so alluring—a purifying ritual, a method of absolution.

She was so tired.

Tired of feeling guilty. Tired of losing people. Tired of replaying the same memory over and over, rolling the stone between her fingers, of Jas smiling down at her for the last time.

She was powerful, and it hadn't been enough. If she faced Valentin again, or made it back to the Vitae portal—if she were to pull as much spiritual energy as she could into Samhara—it still wouldn't be enough.

There seemed no point in trying. No point in returning to a home that had already been wounded by her actions. No point making the journey without Jas.

Don't waste it, he'd told her.

If she gave up the whole of herself, she would also be giving up every piece of her that had been molded and shaped by others. Her family, her friends—in touching her, laughing with her, crying with her, *loving* her, they had left imprints across her life just as she had left imprints on theirs. All that would remain of her was what lived on in them, a string of smaller deaths in the wake of hers.

She stumbled back from the Praeteriens and dropped Samhara. Her chest heaved with the force of a sob, though her body was too dehydrated for tears.

At Godsnight, she'd thought she was doing the right thing by making the hard choice. In Mortri, she'd thought she was doing the right thing by refusing to use Jas's energy. And still she had ended up here, weighed down, directionless, longing to wade into a sea of lost souls and become one of them.

Pain suddenly ignited through her body. She fell to her knees and pressed a hand to her chest. Confused, she directed her gaze inward to find the source.

Her unexpected fight with Valentin had cost her strength. Perhaps that was why her organs were failing, her muscles atrophying, her blood vessels shrinking. Her liver was a sharp lance under her ribs, her heart-beat sluggish and irregular.

Risha's breaths thinned. She didn't understand; she had used her power to put her body into hibernation so that she could survive this place. She'd *felt* the magic take hold, ignoring the laws of time to stop her internal clock. So why was it not working anymore?

Val.

He'd lied about using her energy to power Samhara. And he had been the one to tell her she could use her own power on herself. Had that, too, been a fabrication?

A raspy, unfeeling laugh left her. It wouldn't matter if she was possessed by Thana or captured by Valentin, or even if she plunged into the Forgetting Waters. She was done for no matter what.

Don't waste it.

"I'm sorry," she whispered.

There is nothing you can do without my help, Thana had taunted her, knowing full well what would happen. *Soon he will fade, and face my judgment. Then you will be alone. Abandoned. With no one but me to turn to.*

She could call for Thana like she had so many times before, with frantic pleas and luring words. With her god's influence she could put a stop to this decay. She would finally have the strength to move between realms. All it would cost was her freedom. Her agency. Her morals and obligations.

But maybe, in return, Thana could bring Jas's spirit back.

She didn't know how long she knelt there, one hand pressed to her chest, on the verge of calling for her god and making a trade that would jeopardize everything she had been fighting for.

Before she spoke a single word, something fluttered just under her straining heart. A ball of tangled energy, as soft and vivid as a begonia in bloom.

Risha's lips trembled. *Jas.*

He was still with her. A piece of him that refused to be forgotten.

She closed her eyes and focused until nothing existed but that energy. How could she have possibly entertained the idea of succumbing to Thana? Even if her body failed to its conclusion, as long as she felt him with her, as long as she wasn't alone, that would be enough.

Jas's energy filled her veins like water pouring into a dry creek bed. It was so unlike her own—warm where hers was cold, the green of a new shoot emerging from the ground and just as fragile. From a young age she had been taught the ways of death, but Jas had been the conduit for life, coaxing withered vines and flowers to blossom to full health.

And now he was doing the same to her.

Just as worshippers went to the basilicas to leave offerings, so, too, did he kneel on the altar of her body and give quiet thanks and quieter prayers, bestowing whatever he had on her. And just like a ravenous god she took it for her own, let it curl and breathe inside her. The reverence of life, the devotion of death. The two of them dancing between.

Time reversed. Her next breath came deeper, held in lungs that could fully expand. He sheltered her heart within his hands and made it glow like a torch in the dark.

Risha opened her eyes. Growing in a circle all around her were black roses, a tangle of leaves, stems, and thorns, their heads angled toward her.

Her vision watered as she reached out to caress one.

How could I possibly leave you alone? Jas murmured, a soft smile pressed to her fingers in the shape of silken petals. *You'd be undone without me. Admit it.*

A faltering laugh burst out of her even as her tears finally fell.

He was with her, and always would be, so long as she didn't give in— not to rivers, or to gods, or to her own despair.

She was about to pluck one of the roses to take with her when a distant chorus of screams made her freeze.

Turning her focus south, she strained to sense what had caused the noise. It wasn't to the east where Cruciamen and the Vitae portal lay— Valentin's domain—but to the west. A cold wind picked up around her.

The screams hadn't come from Mortri. Rather, they'd come from the void along its borders. The more she strained, the more she heard the continuous agony as newly made spirits rammed into the barrier, denied entry.

There were so many of them. She knew they weren't coming from Vitae, or else the void around the portal would be straining. These spirits had come from either Solara or Noctus.

Which meant another portal was near. And with the sheer number and aggravation of these newly made dead, the place where barrier met void would grow thin.

Thin enough, perhaps, to cut.

She stood up. Her legs no longer shook, her vision no longer blackened. She was healthy and healed and whole, carrying the power of both life and death.

She gazed down at Samhara. Though she longed to throw it into the

Praeteriens, she couldn't abandon a weapon her ancestor had made strong enough to stop a Mortrian king. It was only a matter of time until Valentin found her again.

Risha carefully plucked one of the black roses and tucked the stem into her belt. Then she picked up Samhara, the scythes warm and eager in her hands.

"Let's go, Jas."

V

Angelica stood at the lip of a volcano's caldera, captivated by the bubbling lava within. She recalled a day in Nexus much like this, staring down at a crater where a palace had once been built from bone.

"Angelica."

She turned. Just like on that day, Brailee Lastrider stood beside her, dark braid hanging over one shoulder, faintly unnerved by their surroundings.

"Is this Mount Netsai?" Brailee asked.

She was dreaming. Unease trickled through the landscape, made dark clouds close in above them. "Yes. Are you...actually here?"

"In a sense. I needed to tell you about what we learned in Seniza." Brailee glanced at the lava. "Deia's Heart and Mount Netsai are connected."

"How can they be connected?"

"A fault line runs between them. If you uncover Deia's fulcrum, maybe you can use it to reach us."

To return to Vaega.

"Nanbu Daiji, the warlord of the fire state, is holding me prisoner," Angelica said. "I don't know if I can reach Mount Netsai."

Worry flitted over Brailee's face. "What? Can you—?"

The sound of a lock dragged Angelica out of the dream. Beside her, Cosima stirred with a mumble, her head pillowed on Angelica's shoulder. Judging by the light, it wasn't quite dawn. Surely Nanbu wouldn't come to collect her so early?

Then the door slid open, revealing the hulking shape of Kenji. He ducked inside and knelt before them, head bent.

"Esteemed Mardova, no amount of apologies can make up for what I have done," he murmured hoarsely. "When I went into the tunnels—"

"Save it," she snapped. "I don't want to spend my final hours listening to you snivel."

Cosima nudged her, more awake now. "Hey, I know you're upset, but let him talk."

"When I went into the tunnels, Bushan Nanbu and Koshi were waiting for me," Kenji went on. "The . . . snake, Bushan Nanbu's companion, told them we were coming. And when I saw Her Imperial Majesty—the first one, the other one, I don't know—Bushan Nanbu told me it was my choice whether she lived or died." He swallowed, eyes shining wetly in the dim room. "He offered me my old position, my old life, a way to clear my debts, and none of it enticed me. But I could not forfeit her life. I see now there was no good choice, that someone would end up dying anyway."

It was too late for *what-ifs*, for Angelica to tell him what he should have done. She could hate him for his betrayal, but if Akane had died because of them, she would have hated herself far more.

"Then are you planning to break us out of here?" she asked.

Kenji shook his head. "You know as well as I do that would be impossible in this keep."

Not to mention there were the girls to consider. Angelica would rather go out in a storm of her own making than subject them to Nanbu's life-long confinement.

"Tell me what's going to happen today," Angelica said. "Will Nanbu bring Akane with him to the execution?"

Kenji nodded, keeping his gaze lowered. "He plans to keep her close so that people can see them together. Revered Ueda is expected to join her. Bushan Nanbu told her that if she claimed the Mardovas had treated her poorly, then the remaining Uedas would be brought back to Azuna under his care."

Although she knew Miko would never voluntarily leave Angelica's mother, she couldn't help but think of Miko in the villa's garden, longing for her native country. Eiko's grief that Azuna no longer felt like home.

"Revered Asami will also be close, but hidden. They're keeping her muzzle on and her hands tied." Kenji paused. "Bushan Nanbu . . . thought it would be considerate to bring you to them to say goodbye."

She exhaled a laugh. "Perfect."

He finally looked up. "What?"

"Takeda Kenji," she said, as low and solemn as a warlord giving orders to her Gojarin. "If you want to make up for your betrayal, then you will follow the plan I'm about to lay out for you. But it'll mean never coming back to Nanbu Daiji or your old way of life. Can you live with that?"

He gave her a weary smile.

"I make a better rice farmer, anyway."

Once the sun had fully risen, Angelica and Cosima were taken away by guards. Angelica didn't struggle, and only shared a small nod with Cosima before they were separated.

She was taken to a bathing room, where she was kept restrained while attendants washed her, scrubbed her body with salt, then washed her again. A Kiyono cleansing ritual, preparing her to meet her demise. She wondered if there was a bellwether waiting to brush her ashes into a cedar box, who would lead her spirit to the mountains during the next death parade.

They dressed her in plain red robes. Red for fire, another symbol of purification and for warding off misfortune. How fitting, too, that it was one of her House colors.

Finally, she was brought out to the castle's central courtyard. She squinted in the sudden light, muted as it was from the heavy gray clouds overhead. From here she could see the warlord's residence, more of an ornamentation with its elaborate gables than a keep. All around the outer wall were watchtowers manned by attentive soldiers.

Nanbu Daiji waited for her, Akane at his side. She looked so small in his shadow, trembling in her winter robes, the small bells hanging from her hairpins chiming softly. She had been dressed as an empress, swathed in wisteria purple. Eiko had her hands on Akane's shoulders, pale and tight-lipped as Angelica was led toward them.

Angelica's stomach roiled. It would take just one word from Eiko to save her twin sister and mother, to divest themselves from the Mardovas.

Koshi and Cosima stood nearby, the former solemn yet smug and the latter frowning. Cosima had also been given a wash and fresh robes, and she rubbed at her freed wrists while tracking Angelica's every movement. Kenji was expressionless on Nanbu's other side.

And then there was Asami. The girl was muzzled, her hands bound behind her back so that she couldn't even sign. Angelica met her anxious gaze, then glanced down at her own shackled hands. She signed as subtly as she could.

I'm ready.

Asami's eyes widened, then narrowed in understanding.

"Esteemed Mardova," Nanbu greeted. His voice was a low peal of thunder, a perfect complement to the weather and to the distant noise of a gathering crowd. "I will give you one last chance to redeem yourself. Work with me to refine Satake Asami's kudei, and there will be no need for all this."

"Pass," she said. Even if she took the offer, Asami's kudei would only be used to control the sorankun and strengthen Nanbu's already sizable military. Sooner or later, there would be war regardless of her death.

The snake around his shoulders moved in a slow, slithering coil, forked tongue flickering at her. *It does not have to be this way, my blood. Let me into your body, and I will release the fetters on your power. Together we will accomplish anything. Together we will rule this realm and, eventually, all the others.*

Of course—Deia's prized possession of the Bone Palace was now gone, and so was her link to the fifth realm's power. She *needed* Angelica in the same way Angelica had once needed her.

She had manipulated a warlord to bring Angelica here, to threaten her into bending her knee and finally becoming Deia's perfect vessel.

Angelica laughed.

"What a joke," she muttered, her smile crooked. "You are not my enemy, Nanbu Daiji. Or at least, you didn't have to be. But unfortunately for you, your prayers were answered."

She cut her gaze to Kenji. He sprang into action, covering the short distance to Asami and slashing the air. The stone beneath her Gojarin guards rose and flung them onto their backs. Lacking time for carefulness, he grabbed Asami's muzzle and ripped it off.

The girl drew in a breath and belted an A-sharp.

Angelica was there to meet it. She turned and unleashed a high, full note, a ringing vibrato from her core that would have made the opera stars in Nexus weep. When the sound waves crashed into Asami's, the air warped and shimmered, softening and folding, just as it had in the banquet hall when Angelica had spirited Akane away from the kaikushine.

Only now she had Asami to force the portal open wider, breaking through the fabric of reality itself while Angelica fed it threads of quintessence, their voices overlapping into one destructive, decisive chord. The shackles at her wrists melted into liquid iron.

The hungry mouth of their portal stretched larger, the vibrations causing everyone in the courtyard to cower and cover their ears. But Cosima ran straight for Angelica while Kenji grabbed hold of Akane and Eiko.

"Veliane!" Koshi's yell could barely be heard over the tumult.

Mount Netsai, Angelica thought, taking the shortest breath she could to maintain the note. *Take us to Mount Netsai.*

Nanbu recovered first. He formed a ball of fire in one hand and aimed it at Kenji's back. Asami was too quick for him, letting loose a scream in Nanbu's direction.

The warlord cried out as the bones in his hand shattered. He dropped to his knees and stared in horror at the dangling mass of flesh that had once been his predominant sword hand.

Kenji leapt into the shimmering black mass first, Eiko and Akane thrown over his shoulders. Cosima ushered Asami in next, then grabbed Angelica, yanking her back so that they both toppled through the already-closing portal.

It felt like she was performing somersault after somersault, tumbling through the air with no guarantee she would land. A scream might have escaped her raw throat, her limbs stretched and shrinking, a pressure in her chest threatening to make her lungs pop.

Her back made contact with hard ground. She fought for breath like she'd been punched in the solar plexus. All around her were groans and coughs and gasps, and then a set of hands shaking her.

"Angelica!"

She forced herself to roll onto all fours. Her vision swam, and she had to keep her hands pressed to the ground. Ground that was made of dark magmatic rock.

She looked up at the looming figure of Mount Netsai. It stood within the center of a shallow crater, its steep slope blackened with basalt and cut through with sluggish lava flows that had seeped through vents along the cone, becoming arteries of fire. Along the crater's basin were openings emitting hot steam.

And under her hands was a divine, formidable heat, a bubbling sea of magma hidden beneath layers of rock.

"Angelica, are you all right?" Eiko demanded. She had a small cut on one cheek and was noticeably shaken, but otherwise seemed unharmed.

Angelica reached up to brush away the blood, but only smeared it against Eiko's cheek. Eiko caught her wrist.

"You did it," Eiko breathed. "You and Asami, you...you used kudei together."

Angelica could only stare at her, momentarily stricken with the realization.

"You didn't take his deal," Angelica murmured.

Eiko frowned. "What?"

"Nanbu. He said—said you and Kikou and your mother..."

Her stepsister's grip tightened. "I won't allow him to take us from our home," she said firmly.

Home, like it was such an easy word to say.

She peered over Eiko's shoulder at Kenji, who was rubbing Asami's back. Akane was sprawled and staring at the sky while she caught her breath. Cosima had stumbled away to hurl, and now came back on wobbly legs, wiping her mouth.

"Phos's hairy nutsack, Mardova," Cosima said, voice graveled. "I can't believe that worked."

She couldn't either, but there was no time to keep sitting in wonder. Cosima and Eiko helped her to her feet, and she went over to Asami and Akane.

"Are you all right?" she asked. The girls nodded, and Angelica put a hand on Asami's shoulder. "Good. That was...You did very well."

Asami's eyes shone. She reached up to clasp Angelica's hand.

This was it. She had to ascend the volcano and locate Deia's fulcrum, hidden under waves of magma and basalt. Even if she had to break Mount Netsai apart, she would find it and make it hers.

"Kenji," she said. "Take the girls and hide. Deia will try to stop me, and I don't want them getting caught up in that."

"We're staying here," Eiko argued.

"To do what?" Angelica demanded. "Catch any fireballs Deia slings around?"

"*Fireballs?*" Cosima repeated.

"What's the alternative?" Eiko asked. "Stand around breathing in noxious gases until Nanbu Daiji catches up to us?"

"Once I have the fulcrum—"

A whistle cut them off, sharp enough it hurt Angelica's ears. A crack splintered through the ground between her and Eiko.

Asami had risen to her feet, face beaded with sweat, her expression one of resolve. Akane reached for her hand.

"Absolutely not," Angelica said. "You and Akane are the rightful rulers of this empire. If anything happens to you, the warlords will tear each other apart for dominance."

Asami signed in short, sharp movements and pointed to Akane. *I'll go with you, she stays here.*

Akane drew in a breath. "But—Asami—"

Her younger sister threw her arms around Akane's neck. Akane's eyes watered and she tightly returned the embrace. Eiko watched them with a wounded expression.

Angelica shared a solemn nod with Kenji. But as he moved toward the girls, a strange sound echoed down the crater. It was almost what she would call a chirp, stuttering and inhuman.

Asami pulled away from Akane with parted lips. She stared at the top of the crater, and the others followed her gaze.

A beast was emerging from the crater's lip. It was long and lithe, with ruby-red scales and a stripe of billowing black fur running down its back. Its head bore black antlers and eyes that burned citrine. Although it had no wings, it was able to fly in a serpentine manner down the crater, its four clawed legs tucked close to its body.

Angelica grabbed Cosima's arm, her pulse a frantic rhythm as the beast glided closer, giving another chirping call. Eiko reached for her knife before realizing she no longer had it.

Kenji slowly fell to his knees. "The sorankun," he whispered, reverence in every syllable.

Akane stepped back, but Asami stood her ground as the creature flew toward her. When it landed, the talons on its four claws dug into the rock. Its fur rippled in the wind, mouth parting just enough to reveal a set of large, pointed fangs.

"Asami," Angelica whispered sharply.

But the girl refused to move. Instead, she raised her hands toward the beast.

The sorankun approached with caution and used its large, flat nose to sniff and nudge at her palms. Asami squirmed with a giggle; the sound, instead of cracking the earth, made the sorankun's eyes shine brighter. It circled her with a deep, resonant purr.

Eiko gasped. "It recognizes the kudei in her."

"Incredible," Kenji breathed. Tear tracks made silver lines down his face.

Asami turned with a smile almost too large for her face. She gestured to her sister, who nervously approached the sorankun and also held out her hand. Akane squeaked when the beast sniffed it and made that rumbling purr again.

Then it turned toward Angelica.

Jaw clenched, she forced herself not to move. The beast sniffed again, so near that Angelica could feel its warm breath, and snorted with something like begrudging acceptance.

"Thanks," Angelica muttered as it returned to Asami. More sorankun were flying down the crater, drawn to Asami's presence. Their scales glimmered black and red, some with golden patterning along their sides, some with tails that were covered not in fur but flames.

Cosima made a choking noise. "We're, uh, not gonna be eaten, are we?"

Asami shook her head. Her face was clear and her eyes were bright; it was the happiest Angelica had ever seen her. She greeted each sorankun, allowing them to sniff her and the others. Cosima choked again as one butted her arm, and Eiko cooed over a baby sorankun so tiny it could have been mistaken for an airborne snake, spinning and coiling in the air.

One of the babies curled around Asami's neck with a high chirp. She laughed, but even though Angelica braced herself, nothing broke or shattered. It almost seemed to have the opposite effect as her scream, putting all the sorankun at ease.

"I've never seen anything like this," Kenji said, scratching one of the beasts under its chin. It happily closed its eyes with a purr. "I didn't know they were so *affectionate*." His smile dimmed. "And Bushan Nanbu wants to collar them."

"We won't let that happen," Eiko said.

Cosima cleared her throat. "I hate to rain on this touching moment, but..."

She pointed behind them, toward Hitan. Through a gap in the crater Angelica spotted a mounted troop riding toward them from the city's northern gates.

"Shit." She turned to the others. "You have to hide. Kenji—"

But Asami stomped her foot, glowering up at her. She pointed to the sorankun.

"Oh no," Cosima muttered. "No, no, no, I can*not* be interpreting this correctly. She doesn't want us to *ride* these things, does she?"

"She does." Angelica leveled Asami with a glower of her own. "But only to escape from Nanbu. Right?"

Asami wavered, glancing at everyone and then at the oncoming troop. She nodded, then whistled a light tune at the sorankun.

It was as if the beasts understood her on an instinctual level. Three sorankun moved forward, then knelt on the rocky terrain.

Asami clambered onto the back of a red-and-gold sorankun, the baby still curled happily around her neck. Kenji helped Akane up behind her, and the girl held her younger sister around the waist.

Eiko blanched. "I—I'm not good with heights." Still, Kenji effortlessly hoisted Eiko up onto the back of a black sorankun. She groaned and grabbed hold of the creature's antlers, conveniently curved backward into makeshift handles.

"You ride with her, Kenji," Angelica said.

"Are you sure, Esteemed Mardova? I...I understand, if you...erm... would rather I stay down here."

Angelica didn't say anything for a moment, quietly drowning out the whisper of her mother's voice.

She said evenly, "I told you to call me Angelica."

His eyes flashed with surprise and gratitude. Grinning, he hopped up behind Eiko and patted her shoulder. "No need to fear, Kenji's here!" Eiko groaned again.

A pure red sorankun waited for her and Cosima. Cosima rubbed her face with a despairing sound.

"First horses, now this," she muttered. "Is this one gonna bite? Or will it just incinerate me?"

Angelica pushed her forward. "*I'll* incinerate you if you don't get on it."

She did her best to approach the beast with confidence. It blinked at her, unimpressed. Angelica rested a hand against its scales, warm and smooth like pressed silk, the sorankun's sides rising and falling with its breaths.

Awe hit her all at once. She had held a god's power within her body, but this—looking into an ancient being's eyes, knowing it represented far more than an empire—turned her breathless. As they stared at one another, the sorankun blinked again, slower.

Cosima laced her fingers together to give Angelica a boost up. It was hard to sit astride the beast in her robes, but modesty was the absolute least of her concerns with Nanbu's troop advancing. She reached down and helped Cosima up behind her.

"It's just like a horse," Cosima was chanting to herself as one arm snaked around her middle. "It's just like a horse. It's just—"

Asami whistled again, and Cosima cut off with a yelp when the sorankun leapt forward and then *up*. Angelica grabbed hold of the antlers, her stomach swooping as the ground fell away beneath them. This close, she sensed the sorankun was able to fly without wings due to its effortless manipulation of the air around its body, a constant channeling. Wind stung her eyes and whipped at her hair while the beast flew higher, toward the volcano's summit.

"This is not like a horse!" Cosima shouted in her ear. "Fuck!"

Angelica looked down. They were easily ten thousand feet high and climbing, Nanbu's troops insignificantly small at the edge of the crater. A laugh bordering on hysterical bubbled out of her.

"Of course you'd like something like this," Cosima grumbled, hiding her face in Angelica's shoulder.

Ahead, Asami's sorankun reached the summit of the volcano and began to circle above it. As Angelica drew closer, she saw the mouth was formed into a large basin, leading to a black, empty throat. Her head was light from the altitude, her ears aching with pressure, but still she sensed an enigmatic pull coming from the volcano's heart.

Eiko peered down and blanched. "H-how are you going to find the fulcrum? Can you feel it?"

Angelica nodded. Just as Asami's connection to the sorankun was in her blood, Angelica's connection to the god was in hers.

Cosima's hold on her tightened. "What are you planning, Mardova?"

Angelica put her hand over Cosima's. Slowly, carefully, she turned so that she was facing Cosima, taking in her wild dark eyes and wind-chapped cheeks. Cosima kept a hand on Angelica's hip, gripping hard.

"You could have gone with your brother," Angelica said. "You could have started a new life here."

Cosima frowned, bewildered. "I didn't want that."

"Then what do you want?"

It was a question that had been posed to Angelica before, one she'd always had trouble answering. For a long time, her wants had been her mother's wants. For a long time, she hadn't understood that there was a difference between *want* and *need*.

Until Cosima had asked her. Until Cosima had held her bloody hands and washed them clean, kneeling with her in a dark night of uncertainty, when power felt so far out of her grasp she couldn't recognize herself without it.

Now she knew that power in itself was not a wicked thing. That she was not wicked for choosing it.

"I want..." Cosima's gaze flitted to her mouth, her eyes. "I want us to get out of this alive. I want to go back home with you. I want you to fuck up every single person who's hurt you. And I really, really want to sleep with you aga—"

Angelica pulled Cosima's head down to kiss her.

She kissed her and it was red, red like dawn and victory and life. She kissed her and it was everything she'd never known she needed.

Cosima made a helpless noise and pulled her closer. They were weightless as they soared through the air, their bodies blazing against the winter wind. When she parted her mouth Cosima eagerly followed, like she was the river and Cosima was thirst. She held Cosima's scent and taste against her until it became an expanding wound, her tongue an arrowhead that, once removed, would bleed her out. A slow-moving calamity come to fulfillment.

She forced herself to pull away. Cosima stared at her, brow furrowed and lips flushed.

"Mardova," she rasped. "Don't you fucking dare."

Angelica pinched Cosima's wrist. Cosima instinctively loosened her grip and Angelica slid off the side of the sorankun.

"Angelica!"

Eiko's scream barely penetrated the roaring of the wind as she fell, plummeting toward the volcano's mouth. With a quick whistle she formed the air around her into a tight spiral, directing her body the way the sorankun did.

She plunged down the volcano's throat.

VI

Nikolas had once been a construct of hesitation, mindful of all the ways in which the world could hurt him. Now, carrying the wounds he had tried so hard to avoid, he realized it was easier to be nothing and no one. To have only the god's will and not his own.

He stood in an empty room. Was allowed to be alone after his god had discovered the bag of fangs and pocketed them. After he had peered into Nikolas's distant eye, smiled, and said, "Good boy." Nikolas was glad to not worry him. Nikolas was glad to do something right.

He did not know why he was here, though. There had been no order. No direction. Without it, his feet had moved, his legs had walked, until he was here, surrounded by glass and blood, a foreign night sky, and a memory begging at the door.

A carriage. A circle. A ritual.

Learning that—

He flinched away, lifted his arms like there were arrows speeding toward him. Points of pressure bloomed above his eyes, in the hollows of his cheeks.

Gradually it washed away and left him numb again. He saw without seeing—the circle, the bodies, the broken windows. Solarium. That was the word. Filled not with sunlight but the gold of a barrier, the shadows of another realm. Fitted together with . . .

He slowly looked up. Up at the dome, the white arches, the eight-pointed star.

What was it his god had said?

Orsus is here.

Sitting in a carriage across from Risha and Angelica, learning that the remains of a fifth god lay within the Bone Palace.

He sank to his knees and held his head as the pressure grew. Something like a whimper left him, a plea to go back to the numbness, to forget it all again.

Forget forget forget *forget*.

Quickly, before it hurt.

Quickly, before it consumed him.

Quickly, before he realized how much farther he could fall.

He pressed his forehead to the cold tile and panted. There was a throbbing pain in his empty socket that echoed across his skull, a pang in his side where he had cracked a rib, and with the pain came thoughts both clear and half-formed.

A soldier's function was to be a savior, to find purpose in strength with grand gestures and grander actions.

He couldn't protect anyone, let alone himself.

Forget.

Forget.

Here.

Nikolas looked back up with a gasp. The solarium came back to him in pieces, quiet and still.

But someone else was with him. Someone other than the bodies of the Noctan soldiers and Luis—Luis, poor Luis, whom he could not save—a presence that had touched his mind so briefly he barely recognized it, barely connected it to a name.

There had been a moment, so short and so sharp, when Julian had lanced through his mind. He had pried Phos's fingers away, loosening the god's hold. And then had come clarity, like the first deep breath of spring.

It hadn't been Julian's power alone. There had been something else layered over it, driving it, giving it the necessary force to crack him open.

Orsus.

There were eyes on him, above him. Waiting. Wanting.

The dome made a sound like a house settling. There were hair-thin cracks in some of the arches, likely made during the circle's activation. As Nikolas watched, a chunk split and fell and landed several paces before him.

He crawled toward it. There was no glow, no reaction, no call to suggest it was anything other than marble—but Nikolas knew better.

He picked it up. The piece wasn't even the size of his palm, smooth on one side and jagged on the other.

The god could not speak to him, yet he understood.

Phos may have taken the fangs, but he did not yet have this.

On his wrist, the bracelet Fin had given him hung like a lifeline. Thin, fraying, with just enough weight to remind him it was there. To remind him of home.

Nikolas held the bone to his chest and let the numbness fade. Lux materialized and burrowed against his neck. A door opened, and beyond it came a flood, a relentless tide that made him double over with its weight.

All his life he had been losing things. One after another, bricks tumbling from a wall, leaving its foundation unsteady. His brother. His eye. His wings.

He wept for what he had lost. What he remembered.

For learning too late the power of the small, the overlooked, and the meaningful.

He might not be able to save these people on his own, but he could help those who could.

And that meant being brave enough to face this pain.

VII

Lilia decided to sit and sing for the dead.

Marcellus quietly explained the rite to them. Before the remains of Noctan bodies were surrounded by amazonite, it was the family's duty to sing while the bodies were cremated. The victims of Phos's attack wouldn't be getting proper ceremonies anytime soon, so Lilia sang for them, the hundreds that must have perished in that beam of deadly light.

The lilting words soothed and mourned those who were gone but not far, free of earthly pain. Lilia sang until her voice grew hoarse while Taesia lay on her back and studied the spray of stars overhead, the blue and purple nebulae, the battlefield toward which they marched.

Inevitably, she slept. At first there was only the nothingness of exhaustion, but it didn't last long. She'd dozed off with her hand around the nightstone band for a reason.

"THIS IS POINTLESS," came Nyx's voice from the gloom. "YOU KNOW THAT."

"To keep trying to entice me? I agree."

"THERE IS NO POINT IN DOING SO ANY LONGER."

That made her pause. She couldn't see anything, not even a glimpse of Nyx's dreamscape, though she felt his presence like a bruise thumbed into her skin.

"What do you mean?"

When he spoke again, he sounded weary. "I FELT THE ATTACK THAT HIT ASTRUM. I HAVE NOT FELT ITS LIKE IN CENTURIES. BY THE TIME THE MALUM STAR DIES, THE REALM WILL NOT SIMPLY BE THRUST OUT OF THE COSMIC SCALE—IT WILL BE OBLITERATED ENTIRELY."

All said so matter-of-factly, like telling her the sky in Vitae was blue.

"I NO LONGER HAVE THE STRENGTH TO STAND AGAINST SUCH AN ASSAULT. THERE HAS BEEN TOO MUCH DECAY." A long, mournful sigh. "I SHOULD HAVE KILLED HIM WHILE I HAD THE CHANCE. PERHAPS WE ARE NOT IMMUNE TO SENTIMENT AFTER ALL."

Nyx was giving up. On her, on himself, on his world and people. And here she stood with tools begging to be used.

She didn't know what to do with them.

"—sia?"

She whirled around, though she was fairly sure she didn't have a body in this half-formed dreamscape. "Bee?"

Her sister's voice was muted, faraway. Taesia ached to see her face again, to touch her and know that Brailee was with her.

"—making—at Deia's Heart," Brailee was saying, though the words sounded as if they were coming from underwater. "We're hoping—can get—portal!"

"You know how to make a portal to Noctus?" Taesia called back.

"Going to—you are! Just look—we'll find you!"

Her heart swelled and Nyx sighed again.

"As I PREDICTED," he whispered as she gradually slipped away. "YOU WILL TURN YOUR BACK ON THIS WORLD TO SAVE YOUR OWN."

Taesia's mind was fuzzy when she opened her eyes, clinging onto one memory, one word.

"Portal," she breathed. She sat up so fast her head spun. "They're making a portal to Vitae!"

Julian, who was already awake, nearly fumbled the cup he was holding. "What?"

"My sister, she—they're going to try and open a portal. I don't know when, but it might activate in the Sanctuary of Nyx."

The glimmer of hope in his eyes matched the flutter in her chest. Nearby, Kalen scoffed.

"Good to know you have a contingency plan," the astrologer muttered.

"We're not going to abandon Noctus," Taesia countered. "But in case it all goes to shit, you can come with us to Vitae."

Lilia immediately shook her head. "I won't leave my people."

Julian shook his head at Taesia to prevent her from arguing.

It's their world. Let them die with it if they want to.

Besides, there was no guarantee Brailee and Dante could get a portal to work. Godsnight had been one thing, but now that the Cosmic Scale was out of alignment again...

They sat in uncomfortable silence until Marcellus cleared his throat and held out his sheathed sword.

"We'll reach Astrum today," he said. "I don't know what will happen, but I do know what we fight for. And it is what I've always fought for."

He turned the sword so that the pommel was facing out. The large, round moonstone gleamed at them.

"That stone..." Julian began. "When I was down in the canyon, I touched it and it showed me something. A memory."

Marcellus smiled. "I hired a Shade to store my fondest memory in it. I wanted to carry it with me wherever I went. To remind me why I fight."

Taesia recalled her mother's office at the villa, glinting with memory-infused gemstones—her magic's specialty—and her throat tightened.

Marcellus made a gesture with his sword, waiting for the others to touch the moonstone. Lilia didn't hesitate. Taesia and Julian exchanged a look before they went over and each pressed one fingertip to its cool surface. Kalen was the most reluctant, hanging back until Marcellus's beseeching stare made him touch the stone.

A vision entered her mind. It wasn't the entrenching reality shift of a dreamscape, but it stole her senses nonetheless. The countryside faded into a room lit by a cozy fire, inhabited by three figures sitting at a table: the princess, her soldier, and her astrologer. Tiles belonging to some sort of game were messily scattered between them, and Lilia laughed uproariously at something Marcellus had said. Marcellus beamed and Kalen rolled his eyes. They all had drinks and food, the lingering signs of a good evening.

The juice of lelith fruit was sweet and divine on his tongue, the smooth tile under his fingers making him yearn for something softer. There was a bubbling in his chest and heat rising through his body as he noticed Kalen's lingering sidelong look.

That warm, radiating calm swept through Taesia as if it were her own. If happiness had a taste, it would taste like this: a warm room filled with the sound of a loved one's laughter. The heated gaze from someone you cherish. A full stomach and the prospect of a cozy bed.

Easing out of the memory, she was startled to find tears on her face. Her nose burned as she fought the urge to give in to the grief that momentarily overwhelmed her—the grief for something that was, and should have been, and might never be again.

A soft touch at her cheek; Julian had wiped away one of her tears, ignoring his own. Lilia grasped her hands, and when their eyes met the princess nodded. Taesia nodded back.

Kalen had frozen like he'd been turned to moonstone himself. Marcellus reached for him, but Kalen flinched back, and Marcellus dropped his hand.

"I promised," Marcellus whispered in Nysari.

"*Don't,*" Kalen hissed, face turned away. "We have to go."

When he left to inspect the packs, Lilia leaned forward to kiss Marcellus's cheek. "Thank you, Mar. You were right: This is why we fight."

The soldier gave her a tired smile. "I thought you might like it."

Lilia tucked some of his pale hair behind his ear, the motion so tender Taesia looked away. Her eyes instead landed on the full shape of the New Moon overhead, and the flickering of the Malum Star.

The longer she stared, the more her mind began to turn, striving toward a half-formed idea. One that would prove Nyx wrong.

VIII

ngelica only had a second to think *That was really stupid* before she
was swallowed by the volcano.

The lava had risen halfway up the central vent, the conduit lazily
bubbling while pressure built in the chamber far below. With a whistle
she grasped her cyclone of air and spun, reinforcing the protective layer
around her just as she submerged.

The viscous heat was unlike anything she'd ever experienced. It
punched all the breath from her lungs and set every inch of her on fire, ten
times stronger than any bout with her violin, searing her lungs and her
heart. Even with her eyes closed, even with the bruise Cosima's mouth
had left on hers, it infiltrated her senses to the point of incoherence.

It wouldn't take much to drop her spell and be engulfed by it. To at
last find a level of heat that could devour her fully, bones and all, and satisfy her everlasting craving.

But beyond the molten fire, beyond the ecstasy, strummed the call of
the fulcrum. The more she turned toward it, the more she sensed it echoing against a hollow, sealed-up tunnel.

Found you.

With what little air she had left she sang a low note that smashed into
the bedrock beside her. Beyond lay a wide pyroduct, and lava spilled in
through the opening she'd made. She flung herself inside and issued a
sharper note, bringing a block of pyroclastic rock down to stop the flow.

Her power flickered and waned, and the wind around her died. Bits of
lava hissed near her feet while she took a moment to lean against the rock
wall and catch her breath.

Her muscles were sharp and elastic like she'd run a mile without stopping. It was only the thought of Nanbu's advancing soldiers that forced her to walk deeper into the pyroduct, following the gentle slope downward.

Her fingertips lit up with small flames so she could better see where she was going. There were marks and ledges along the walls indicating previous levels of lava flow. Although the tunnel was tubular in shape, there were stalactites hanging from the ceiling, some of which glinted with dark crystals. It was hard to breathe down here, under all the layers of rock and sediment, and she wondered how much time she had before she used up all the air.

But the strumming call had grown louder, vibrating against her bones and under the soles of her feet. Angelica sped up when she spotted a large opening ahead. It led into a cave lined with misshapen, dried-up columns of lava pillars, with more of those winking crystals embedded in every surface.

In the very center of the cave lay a beast.

Angelica's flames grew larger, ready to expend all her energy on making it back to the surface if she had to. But even her teeth were itching now, and she stumbled forward as if a hook yanked on her chest.

The beast's breathing was slow and booming. It was easily three times the size of the sorankun, a shadowy figure that engulfed her in warm air as it exhaled. She was drawn to take another step toward it, and then another.

On the third step, one amber, slitted eye opened.

She froze as the beast snorted and rose onto its two hind legs, towering over her. Its body was lean and muscular, and much like the sorankun, it had a thick, tapered tail and a stripe of fur—no, webbing—all down its back. Its hide shimmered with black and red scales.

But the biggest difference between the beasts was the pair of bat-like wings kept folded against its sides by chains.

The flames dancing along her hand sputtered and died, leaving only a pair of burning amber eyes staring down at her. A deep rumble filled the cavern, vibrating up her legs.

It has been uncounted years since I have seen one of your kind. Although the wyvern wasn't speaking, its voice managed to echo against the cave walls. *She, too, was strong with fire. But you must be an unusual species, for I smell the progenitor on you.*

Angelica's mouth was drier than the Sausala Desert. She tried to speak, failed, and only let out a hoarse rattle.

Another snort. *Though I see that did nothing to improve your intellect.*

That more than anything else spurred her. "You— What *are* you? Why are you here?"

All these years, and your kind still have not evolved to seeing in the dark? Pitiful. If so, you would take note of the bindings upon me.

"I see them, but I don't understand them. Who . . . ?"

Memory flooded her, returned her to her father's side as he read from a book of myths.

"Deia crafted him within the heart of a boiling volcano, fashioning his scales from fire and ash," August had read. "He was named Yvri for the eternal flame that birthed him."

I see you have come to a revelation, Yvri said snidely.

Standing before the first wyvern, Deia's erstwhile mount, Angelica wasn't sure whether to bend a knee or run back into the pyroduct.

"Deia chained you here," she said slowly. "Under Mount Netsai."

Astute.

"Did you mouth off at her one too many times?"

He snorted again, almost a laugh, and the scales along his sides rippled with fire. It lit up the cave for a few seconds, long enough for her to notice it was otherwise empty—that nothing else could have possibly been calling to her.

Her heart sank.

"It's you," she whispered. "You're Deia's fulcrum."

Yvri lowered his head. *If you mean I am the receptacle into which she placed her crux, then yes. She said she was to fight a war. I could not be seen.* More fire rippled along his sides. *Could not be free.*

Angelica's fingers turned numb. She hadn't been able to picture what the fulcrum would look like, imagining only a spherical, effervescent mass, something intangible she could ingest or merge with her body.

But no. It was in the form of a living, breathing thing with a will of its own. A will spawned from Deia herself.

Her thoughts raced. The stalactites—maybe if she cut off their points, she could catch the wyvern off guard, make use of his imprisonment to stab the point through his throat.

And then what? Would she lap up the blood he spilled, or else do what she had done to Eran Liolle and mutilate the beast to find its prized organs?

Nausea caught her in a vise. For some reason she thought of the tree that grew at Deia's basilica, its growth stagnant, just as much a prisoner as Angelica was to her House. As Yvri was to this volcano.

They were two beings made and then scorned by their god.

Shoring up her resolve, she stepped toward the wyvern. "Do you want to be free?"

Does the river flow to meet with the sea?

Of course the wyvern spoke in fucking riddles. "I'll take that as a yes. Do you still have loyalty toward Deia? Your creator?"

Yvri exhaled a plume of sulfurous smoke. *Toward the one who placed me here for centuries untold? I do not lick the hand that strikes.*

The corner of her mouth stretched into a smirk. "Then I'll cut you a deal. I free you, and in return, you and I will face her together. We'll make her pay for what she's done to us."

Her plan had been to absorb the fulcrum and take Deia's power. To create a portal big enough for them to flee Azuna and travel along the fault line to Deia's Heart. She didn't know if she could access the fulcrum's magic if it was within another being, but she had to try.

She had to face her god on an even playing field.

The wyvern bared its fangs in a smile, fire pluming between the thick, sharp curves.

Deal, he rumbled.

IX

In the hours before dawn, the Revenants—led by Natsumi holding the Noctan portal sketch—headed for Deia's Heart.

Dante warned them not to get too close. "There are beasts near the summit," he explained. "As well as insects that can give you ash blight."

Brailee winced.

"We'll draw it a good distance away," Natsumi assured him. "But where should the center be?"

"As close to Deia's Heart as you can get without actually encompassing the volcano." They didn't need another Bone Palace incident. "Alma said he was going to take the refugee to a hill overlooking the volcano at sunrise. Be on the lookout for something fitting that description."

After they departed, Dante paced with restless energy, waiting for Camilla to pack her things. Brailee and Saya sat on the couch and watched him like they were spectators of a racquet sport and he was the shuttlecock.

"I don't want you coming," Dante said. "But you're going to insist, aren't you?"

Brailee rolled her eyes. "Of course I am. If the portal's opened, I need to be there."

"You don't," Dante countered. "I can go in and bring Taesia back while you return to Nexus."

"And what about Phos?" she snapped. "If I can reach Rian again, he might be able to resist the god's thrall."

"And I need to help the Revenants," Saya said. "If you want your plan to work, that is."

Dante made a mental note to never argue with teenage girls. "Fine. But if anyone or anything comes at you, *run*. You don't fight, you don't wait, you get out of there without looking back. Bee, were you able to reach Angelica and Tae?"

His sister nodded. "Angelica's... in a tricky situation right now, but I told her about the connection between the volcanoes. Hopefully she can reach Mount Netsai in time." She nervously played with her braid. "I tried to reach Tae, but it was hard. Nyx was impeding me. I think she managed to hear about the portal, though."

"Well done, Bee." He hesitated, knowing he was about to step into more sensitive territory. "I was wondering about something. Your power... Would it be possible to manipulate reality the way you do in dreamscapes?"

Brailee thought it over. "Yes. Something similar happened when Nyx p-possessed me. At Godsnight." Saya scooted closer and wrapped an arm around her. "But I don't think I'm there yet. Or if I'll ever be. I'm sorry."

Dante mussed up her hair, and she made a face at him. "Don't apologize. Just do what you can, and that'll be enough."

Camilla finally came downstairs carrying a pack that must have held the grimoire. "It'll take us at least two hours to walk there, and we have two hours until dawn. Let's get going."

"What, you don't have thoroughbred horses lined up for us?" Dante drawled.

"If only. I spent the last of my money on this place." Camilla lifted her hands in a magnanimous gesture. "Goodbye, the Blast Resort. I hope to never lay eyes on your dismal décor ever again."

The predawn air was chilly, and Dante's stomach was a riot of nerves that not even the rhythmic waves at their backs could soothe. Under their feet, sand turned to dirt and then to paving stones as they reentered the city proper.

While they walked they chewed on the stale corn flour flatbreads that Camilla had hoarded at the suite, Camilla complaining that they'd be better with sausage. Once they reached the manned northern city gate, Dante rolled his shoulders back and Azideh stirred.

"*You do not perceive us,*" he said to the guards on duty. "*Open the gates.*"

"I really hate when you do that," Brailee mumbled as they passed through. "It's like you're taking away their free will."

"It only lasts a moment," Dante said. "And it's to keep us safe."

"But how is it any better—or any different—than Baron Alma's manipulation?"

Camilla linked her arm through his before he could answer, lengthening their strides until the girls were behind them.

"You know as well as I do that Brailee is a gentle creature," his aunt said. "With talons, perhaps, but an aversion to using them. You and Taesia were made different. You fight for what you want. You have the power to make meaningful change. And you understand that power has consequences."

"Don't lump me in with you. I wouldn't betray my own family to further my goals. Speaking of which, how do you plan to revoke my sentence?"

"That will depend on if I can find my son." Her too-casual expression hardened. "Once I get him on the throne, he can pardon you."

For years Dante had been dreaming up a new vision for Vaega, one that didn't rely on a gods-appointed ruler. A parliament focused on people, on infrastructure. If he allowed Camilla to bring Ferdinand's true heir back to Nexus, that dream would be forfeit.

But he also remembered the mad grief in his aunt's eyes in her dreamscape, the protective way she'd held her stomach.

"You . . . you don't know his name, do you?" he asked softly.

She crumpled behind her mask. She quickly refortified it and said, "No. Ferdinand didn't allow me to name him, nor did he ever tell me what he had chosen to call him."

And Dante thought he couldn't despise the man any more.

Deia's Heart was about five miles inland of the coast, where the beaches vanished and high cliffs soared. The continuous ash cloud characteristic of Deia's Heart—ash that enriched the soil that provided southern Vaega's sturdy output of crops—was only a trickle, and he wondered if the volcano was losing its power as the realm deteriorated. The dome was darkened with dried lava and basalt. If he squinted, Dante thought he could make out the form of a stone giant shifting between the clasts.

The sun was just touching the horizon, spilling sheets of pinkish gold across the landscape. The grass was lush and the foliage abundant, but here and there were the sentinels of dead trees, a slow yet relentless rot.

He is here, Azideh said. *I smell him ahead.*

Dante looked to the southeast. There were tall hills in the distance, on top of which lay the remains of ancient castros. Scattered across the scenery were knolls and hills, as well as flat, grass-covered plateaus.

Standing on the edge of the plateau nearest to the volcano were three figures.

"Saya, go help Natsumi, then get into position," Dante said. "Brailee, keep close but stay out of sight."

The girls nodded and split up. He and Camilla made straight for the plateau, their demons forming at their sides with wide, ready grins.

Tapping into Azideh's strength, Dante leapt while Camilla vanished. They both landed on the plateau, the sunrise at their backs.

Baron Alma spun around. He quickly took in both demons before narrowing his eyes at Dante. "You. Marizleh was right about having sensed two demons."

Marizleh lurked at the baron's side, tall and willowy with skin of cobalt. His hair, like Azideh and Shanizeh's, was long and shiny, the strands white as bleached bone. His eyes flashed yellow like an animal who hunted at night, and he licked his lips at the sight of the others.

"Marizleh," Shanizeh sneered. "It has been long since I've come across your stink."

"Shanizeh," the baron's demon purred, one long, pointed nail scratching himself across his bare chest. "Still foul as ever."

Dante ignored them and focused on the refugee. Her eyes were clear, and when he read her mind, he only encountered the calmness Alma had invoked in her.

"Baron Alma," Dante said. "Is it true that you've been sacrificing innocents all these years?"

Alma sighed as if they had caught him in the middle of a meeting rather than an occult ritual.

"It wasn't as though I *wanted* to," he said lazily. "But the pact with Marizleh forbids me from stopping. A pact, by the way, that I did not choose. If you're to blame anyone, blame my sires."

"Your sires aren't here. And you *can* stop this."

Alma gave him the same smile he'd given the people protesting outside of Marcos Ricci's mausoleum—tolerant, appeasing. "I appreciate your enthusiasm, Lord Dante. And might I add: It's lovely to finally meet in person."

Dante felt his cheek twitch. So much for going unrecognized.

Alma half turned, indicating the volcano. "Allow me to better explain. These sacrifices also function as offerings to Deia's Heart. To keep it active. If it dies, the farms that rely on the fertile soil it provides will suffer more than they already have."

"All of Vitae is dying," Dante said coldly. "You can't fix it with ritualistic sacrifices."

"I assure you, they feel no pain." Although the baron faced two people he couldn't manipulate with his power, he still spoke with the slick easiness of it. "I give them liquor to drug them before they walk into the underground niches Marizleh makes for them. They don't feel a thing."

"Nice method, still murder."

Alma laughed. "So young and so headstrong. I remember when I was like you, thinking that running into walls enough times would tear them down. Eventually I grew to realize that some things remain tradition for a reason." Again he swept his hand toward the volcano. "I do not do this out of some sick desire. I do this to keep us safe."

Dante's stomach knotted at the echo of his own words.

"Dante," Camilla muttered. "Don't let him talk anymore. Let's get this over with."

The Revenants had to have finished the circle by now. Steeling himself, Dante calculated how to best grab the refugee and deliver a fatal blow to Alma without using his abilities.

"No need," Azideh said at his side. His horns gleamed in the oncoming dawn, his eyes burning jade. "Watch."

Marizleh had put his hands on Alma's shoulders, and the two of them seemed to *melt* into each other. The demon went into its cloud form to be absorbed by the baron's body, drawing its presence into his very flesh. Alma grunted and doubled over as the refugee placidly watched on.

"What are they doing?" Camilla demanded.

"The pact has gone on for so long that they have formed an unspeakable link," Azideh said.

The longer we are bound together, the thinner the barrier between us becomes, the demon had warned him. He glanced at Dante now with a knowing smile. "I told you the consequences would not be pleasant."

The baron and his demon were merging into one monstrous entity, joints distending, bones popping. When Alma looked up again his eyes were pale yellow, his brown skin striated with cobalt. His body had grown larger, longer—less human.

"The only thing to do with such an abomination," Azideh went on, fingers flexing and cracking, "is destroy it."

With a growl, all three demons moved in for the kill.

X

Eventually, Phos found him.

"Bring the prince and his people to the atrium," he ordered. He didn't look as sickly as before; in fact, there was a glimmer of excitement in his bright, pale eyes. As if he really was growing stronger the longer he occupied Rian's body.

Nikolas did not react or ask why. Pretended, despite the heaviness of his limbs and the ever-present pain, that he was fully under thrall. When he turned, Phos's laugh was a soft, victorious breath. It winched the dread in him tighter.

Nikolas had to find a way to steal back the fangs, then deliver them to one who could use their power. In his mind's eye they lay cradled between familiar brown hands, ones he would recognize down to the smallest scar.

Protect her, he had told Julian, unsure even then if it was possible.

He forced himself to tuck the thought away and touched his pocket where the slab of Orsus's bone was hidden. *Focus.*

After the attack on Astrum, Phos had locked Fin in the same bedroom where he'd been chained before. He sat bound and gagged in the chair, chest heaving as if he'd been struggling to get free. At the sight of Nikolas, he jerked.

"It's all right," Nikolas whispered when he closed the door. He hurried to kneel by the chair, using Lux to undo Fin's bindings. "I'm me."

Fin relaxed. When Nikolas removed his gag, Fin took a deep, shuddering breath. Nikolas rubbed his sleeve over the dried tear marks on Fin's face, their salt rubbing into every wound he carried, physical and otherwise.

"I'm sorry." Nikolas swallowed. "I failed. I didn't know he could take my wings like that." A moment to brace himself against that aching loss. "And I'm sorry that Luis paid the price. He was a good man, and deserved better."

Fin closed his eyes, another tear crawling its way down his sunken cheek. "It's not your fault, Nik. Everyone knew the risks. If there was a chance of escape, of hindering Phos, we had to take it."

It still wasn't fair. Nothing ever truly was.

"Do you have the key to your shackles?" Nikolas asked, and Fin nodded. "Hold on to it a bit longer. Phos wants us. All of us."

Fin's brow furrowed. "For what?"

"I don't know. He asked me to bring you to the atrium." Nikolas took the bone from his pocket and slipped it into Fin's.

"What's this?"

"Wherever Phos ends up taking us, I'm going to make sure you and the others can break free. At my signal, you run."

The furrow deepened. "That's not—"

"I need to get the fangs from Phos. If Taesia is...nearby, maybe she can use them." He tapped the bone. "But *this* needs to get to Julian. He may be the only one who can separate Phos from Rian."

"I can't let you take him on by yourself," Fin argued. "Once I get my shackles off, I'll help."

"Who's going to get the servants to safety, then? Or make sure Julian gets the tool he needs?"

There was denial and reluctance in Fin's eyes, blue as morning, blue as a cloudless autumn. At last he gave a loud exhale and hung his head. "Fuck. *Fuck.* I don't want to do this, Nik."

For some reason, this brought a tiny smile to his face. "I don't either." And yet here he was, kneeling before a displaced prince. A small gesture in the grand scheme of things, and yet it reminded him of legendary knights who'd been swayed to pledge fealty, not because they sought death but because they had found a reason to live.

"I trust you to come back," Nikolas whispered. The same words Fin had said to him, when Fin had been the one planning to stay behind.

Nikolas took Fin's hands in his. He lifted one and pressed his lips against roughened, scraped knuckles. Fin breathed in softly.

House Cyr had been meant to breed soldiers, saviors, servants to the throne. How fitting that he would find himself here, on his knees with a solemn vow held in his throat like a prayer.

Fin turned his hand to cradle Nikolas's cheek. "Nik, I . . ."

"After," Nikolas insisted. "When we get through this." *When we get home.*

So Fin looked him in the eye and said, "Then survive."

Nikolas knew an order when he heard one.

XI

A pure, high note rang against the cavern walls and aimed at the chains around the wyvern—a blade of pure aether. Whatever the chains were made of, they were strong; it had taken multiple attempts to sever enough of them that, with this one final note, Yvri was able to stretch his wings and break the rest in a shower of shattered metal.

Angelica stumbled back as he unfurled himself. His wingspan was massive, easily the width of a house. As fire licked along his scales she saw his wings were thin and veined, the webbing crimson. He flapped them once, twice, buffeting the wind and stirring her hair.

I have not flown since I was put here to rot, he growled.

"Let's change that, shall we?"

He lowered his head to the floor. It was as large as she was, with two obsidian horns curling backward and ending in sharp points. She hoisted herself over the wyvern's long neck and reached for the horns like she'd done on the sorankun, but when Yvri raised his head she yelped and slid down his neck to his back.

You sit there, he told her, his body shifting and moving underneath her like the strangest horse she'd ever ridden. On either side of her, his wings continued to flap in a steady rhythm. *I cannot abide your weight on my head.*

"I'm starting to believe Deia *did* chain you down here because of your damn mou—"

The last word left her in a scream as he launched forward. She wasn't prepared for how *fast* he was, zooming through the empty pyroduct with his wings tucked in beside him. Angelica clutched his thick neck, the side of her face squished against his warm, smooth scales.

"Fuck fuck fuck," she chanted even while she marveled at the way the air churned and spiraled around Yvri. This was the former mount of *Deia*—of course he had access to the elements.

She braced herself before they crashed through the rock layer she'd built to block the magma. They swam upstream, pushing against the lava's sluggish current. Below them the pressure grew, the magma climbing higher as if hungrily following them.

With one final push, they emerged into the open air.

Yvri's wings snapped open, and he let out a low, triumphant roar. It struck her like a thunderclap, and deep within the wyvern's layers of muscle and tissue strummed Deia's power. It sparked along his wings and filled her with a bright, resounding note like glass being struck.

She threw her head back and laughed. So *this* was freedom—a height only obtainable by those who knew how to fly.

The sky above them was dark gray, and below, the volcano steamed. She only had a second to wonder where the others were when something crashed into Yvri's side and sent them careening through the air.

Yvri hissed and shook his head. Angelica fought down her vertigo to make out who had attacked them.

Astride his own bloodred wyvern sat Nanbu Daiji, his normally stoic face lined with loathing. His broken hand hung uselessly at his side, the other covered with roiling flame. His wyvern screeched, its blazing eyes boring into Angelica.

So you've found him, the god growled in her head. *Do not think this will change anything.*

Angelica didn't waste her breath on a reply. She squeezed Yvri's neck.

"She doesn't even acknowledge you," she whispered. "After all she did to you."

Yvri roared again, diving at Deia and Nanbu. They collided with a fresh peal of Deia's laughter ringing through Angelica's skull, the two wyverns locking claws. Yvri tried to take a bite out of Deia and was beaten back with a blast of air that made them slam against the side of the volcano.

Angelica held on tight as her right shoulder scraped against hard, broken clasts. Deia pushed them deeper into the indent they'd made, her mouth bristling with fire. Below, Mount Netsai stirred, magma roiling and bubbling. Smoke began to issue from its mouth.

"How did you so easily control the sorankun?" Nanbu demanded.

Some of his hair had slipped out of his topknot, lashing in the gales made by Deia's wings.

She remembered Cosima's words from their shared prison, about how her quest for power didn't share the shape of Nanbu's. "They didn't need to be controlled. They're helping the empress because they want to, because they recognize greatness in her. You'll never know how that feels."

His face contorted before Deia unleashed a breath of searing fire. Yvri folded his wings to protect Angelica, the crimson webbing flashing scarlet.

Abandon this foolishness, Deia said. *I can easily dispose of this man and his army. You only need to offer yourself to me.*

"Are you really so desperate you'll keep offering me deal after deal?" Angelica retorted. "Pathetic."

Deia screeched. The instant her barrage of fire stopped, Yvri opened his wings with a blast of air that sent her and Nanbu tumbling. Angelica dug her heels into Yvri's sides as he pushed away from the volcano and dove toward the ground.

Nanbu's soldiers were firing arrows at the sorankun, Gojarin volleying spears of earth and spirals of fire. But the sorankun easily evaded them, their movements lithe and lovely.

"Where did *that* thing come from?" Cosima called out to her when Angelica and Yvri drew closer. "No, don't answer, I'm still pissed at you!"

"Angelica, are you all right?" Eiko shouted.

"I'd be better if I didn't have a delusional god on my ass," she shouted back after Yvri easily twisted out of the way of an arrow.

You still use such primitive weapons, the wyvern reproved. *I suppose I have not missed much in my seclusion.*

Angelica located Kenji. "Get the girls out of here and into the mountains!"

"I've been trying!" he yelled back. He had one arm securing Eiko while the other dispersed oncoming flame strikes. "Her Imperial Majesty refuses!"

Asami wore a look of stubborn determination as she focused on Nanbu's Gojarin below, Akane gripping onto her while their sorankun wove through elemental attacks. Asami issued a scream downward, cracking open the earth below two Gojarin.

"Can we do something about them?" Angelica asked Yvri.

The wyvern snorted. *This is not even the size of a full army.*

Still, he inhaled deeply. The steam that rose from the vents along the crater's basin drew toward him, moving from gas to liquid, a rippling wall of water. With his exhale the water splashed down on Nanbu's soldiers and instantly hardened to ice.

"Gods' bones," Cosima croaked.

A few of the now-frozen figures glowed orange before bursting out of their ice prisons with fire. One of them stepped forward, glaring up. Koshi.

"Veliane!" he bellowed. "It's not too late to choose the right side!"

"The right side?" she shouted from her sorankun, hands tight around the beast's antlers. "You don't even know what that is! The Azunese are *using* you!"

His gauntlets rippled with flame. "Don't make me do this."

Cosima's body was strung with tension. But as Koshi aimed for the beast beneath her, Kenji leapt from his own sorankun and intercepted the attack with a whip of water taken from the gourd at his hip.

"Kenji!" Eiko cried as he plummeted. Koshi, eyes wide, ran forward and wrapped him in a gust of air. Kenji landed on his feet and immediately unsheathed his sword.

Koshi backed up a step, caught off guard. They exchanged words Angelica couldn't hear over the distance. Then, with a grim frown of understanding, Koshi drew his own sword. The two Gojarin locked blades with a spark of steel.

Behind her, Mount Netsai began to rumble. The smoke rising from its mouth was darkening with ash. And flying through it straight toward her were Deia and Nanbu.

The progenitor is stirring the volcano to life, Yvri said.

If Mount Netsai erupted, Hitan—and everyone within the crater—would be done for. Cursing, Angelica dug her knees into his sides.

"Draw them away!" She had to trust that Kenji and Asami had things covered here.

Yvri took off for the coast. There was a range of karsts along the shoreline and jutting out of the sea, narrow pillars of gray limestone like reaching fingers. Deia screeched behind them when they dove into the rocky labyrinth, pillars exploding as they went. Angelica ducked down when a piece of debris slashed her forehead.

The water beneath them surged upward. Yvri pulsed with heat, and the droplets turned into a cloud of steam hiding them from view. With the cover, Yvri silently glided to one side and waited until Deia flew by; then he slammed into her, tackling her right side. The wyverns screamed and wrestled, crashing into karsts. Large chunks of limestone splashed into the sea.

Yvri collared his teeth around Deia's throat. Deia roared and thrashed as black, glistening ichor foamed at Yvri's mouth. The fulcrum within him pulsed again in response.

"That's it," Angelica panted. "*More.*"

But she had momentarily neglected Nanbu. With the wyverns locked together, he clambered onto Yvri's head and slid down to meet her, dagger in hand.

Angelica leapt off the wyvern's back and fell toward the sea. With Yvri's warmth lingering on her skin, she whistled and a column of water pushed her onto the nearest karst. Nanbu followed, stirring a small cyclone around him. *Damn*; she'd forgotten he also held an affinity for air.

She whistled and leapt from karst to karst, supported by buffets of air. Her heart felt like it was going to burst between her ribs. Every time Nanbu threw a ball of fire at her she tried to knock him off-balance with strikes of water.

The earth shook. Angelica nearly slid off the karst she'd landed on. Behind her, Nanbu barely managed to do the same. Mount Netsai was belching an ash cloud, tremors rattling through the bedrock that made even the sea surge against its natural tide.

Deia cackled. *Did you really think putting distance between me and my forge would prevent me from igniting it?*

"*Shit.* Yvri!" she called.

The wyvern flew under her karst. He'd been bloodied along one side, but he made no complaint as she jumped onto his back and they took off for the volcano.

I cannot kill her, the wyvern growled.

Angelica knew it was possible to kill a god, at least to some extent, after what she had learned of Ostium. The real question was: *How?* If even an ancient beast that matched Deia element for element couldn't beat her, what could?

They were halfway back to the crater when Mount Netsai erupted. The pressure building within its core shot out in a geyser of bright orange, spraying lava in all directions like a mad fireworks display. The sound rattled her teeth and compressed her lungs, the smell of acrid smoke already turning her dizzy.

Angelica scanned the air, rubbing away the blood that trickled down her forehead. The sorankun were flying around the volcano in a frenzy. Those that bore Cosima and the girls had removed themselves a good distance, but at the sight of Angelica, they sped toward her.

Behind her, Deia's wyvern form let out a series of high-pitched yips that Angelica thought must be laughter.

Let's see if eating the little empresses will change your mind.

"Get away!" Angelica shouted at the others, but the wind and the volcano's eruption drowned her out. "Fly into the mountains!"

To your right, Yvri warned.

Boulders wreathed in flame shot out of the volcano. The projectiles arced toward them like colossal burning hail.

Angelica squeezed her legs against Yvri, reaching for the strumming presence of the fulcrum. As her thighs and stomach prickled with the influx of energy, she lifted her hands and redirected the fireballs at Nanbu.

She only had a brief moment of satisfaction seeing his face flood with fear. Then Deia maneuvered away, crushing the rapidly cooling fireballs with air. She opened her mouth with a cry, and a new volley rained toward Asami and Akane.

Asami unleashed a sharp, pointed scream. Kudei radiated from her mouth and the fireballs exploded into rubble.

Deia was trying to stall them. Every second they wasted fighting was another second the scorching, golden-bright flows of lava raced down Mount Netsai's slope and toward the crater's opening. Toward Hitan.

Just as Angelica wondered if she could make a portal to spirit the others away, Nanbu raised his voice.

"Satake Asami!" he shouted. His normally mellow, smoky voice was gravelly and torn. "I know you do not want to see this destruction come to pass! Exalted Deia can stop this at a whim if you only come back to the city with me. If you grant me the power to control the sorankun." He held out his unbroken hand, trembling with strain. "You and your sister will live under my care, not as prisoners but as the empresses you are!"

Akane's eyes were round and unreadable. Asami gripped her sorankun's antlers with a darkening frown.

"No," she said.

The word, though spoken calmly, blasted through the air and destroyed his other hand. Nanbu screamed in rage and pain, a warlord deprived of what had made him a warrior to begin with.

Asami whistled decisively. The sorankun that had been circling the volcano suddenly turned and dove straight at Deia. The wyvern flapped her wings with gales that blew many of them back, but not all. They descended upon her and Nanbu with the force of Asami's wrath.

Yvri chuckled darkly while Deia screamed and bled, outnumbered and caught off guard. One of Nanbu's arms was caught within the teeth of a sorankun. He was dragged off the wyvern and dropped like a stone.

Far below, Koshi and Kenji were both bloodied and scorched, water and earth meeting fire and air. The perfect sparring partners, who had grown up together, fought side by side, now at a martial impasse.

But Nanbu's fall didn't escape Koshi's notice. He hurled a ball of fire at Kenji's face while spinning a whirlwind of air with his other hand to cushion Nanbu's descent. He collected the unconscious man in his arms and looked up at Cosima.

The two of them stared at one another as time stretched and bent, as if there were no lava flows coming toward them, no vengeful god above.

"Veliane," he called, his voice thin. "Please."

Cosima's dark eyes were bright with unshed tears, her mouth held in an unforgiving line. Koshi clenched his jaw. They were both deciding. Choosing a side.

"You may be able to pretend the cage around you doesn't exist," Cosima said, "but I can't."

Koshi shut his eyes tight. Then he bared his teeth and erupted into flames. Kenji shrank back as Koshi hauled Nanbu back to the soldiers and horses, freed from Yvri's ice attack by the fire elementalists.

"Are you just going to let him go?" Cosima demanded of her.

Angelica glanced up at Asami, who watched the retreat with satisfaction. "His justice has been dealt to him."

The earth rumbled again and she directed Yvri to fly toward the ground. "Kenji! Are you up for more?"

Panting, he turned and nodded. There was ash on his face and burn marks along his sleeve.

"Yvri, can you please help him build up the crater?" she asked. "Seal it off, make sure none of the lava escapes. We'll deal with the ash after."

Only because you phrased it as a request and not an order. The wyvern loomed behind Kenji, who widened his stance and held his arms out. The ground trembled as Yvri flapped his wings and stirred the layers of rock beneath them upward, Kenji grunting with the effort of spreading out the crater's barrier.

"That's it," Angelica called. "Just keep—"

Something sharp hooked around her stomach and yanked her off the wyvern's back.

Impudent, Deia snarled. The god's talons dug into her side. Angelica cried out as blood seeped through her robes. *You think you can stop this? Stop me?*

She was thrown from the wyvern's claws and into the side of the volcano again. Angelica fought for breath in the crater her body made, every bone and muscle screaming. Deia dove down, ready to tear into her.

When she was more naive, more desperate, more lost, Angelica had once given Deia offerings to forge a better connection to her powers. One of these offerings had been fluorite, a brilliant hunk of prismatic rock that she had sensed in the earth, as if it had *wanted* her to find it.

She felt the same thing now, a delicate voice that was not a voice, like the notes of a song she had heard long ago. It came from a forge that sat forgotten and abandoned, that yearned only to create.

Angelica reached out. A large piece of volcanic glass shot into her hand, forming itself into a dagger of pure obsidian.

At the same moment, Deia caught her in her jaws.

Angelica pushed at the wyvern's wide mouth as fangs dug into her thighs and shoulders. Deia flew them up above the agitated volcano.

I will remake you into something better, Deia said. *A vessel that can properly contain all the power that is yours—and mine. Together we will ride through the realms and burn them all to cinders.*

Angelica choked on ash. She gripped the obsidian dagger tight and, ripping open bigger wounds against Deia's teeth, she plunged its tip into the wyvern's snout.

The scream that rose from the god was an avalanche and a tidal wave, the crumbling of a world. Shimmering black blood splattered Angelica's face and made her gasp as it burned—not with pain but with pleasure, stoking the embers in the basin of her stomach.

The wyvern twisted and morphed, losing its defined shape. Angelica fell from its mouth before she was caught by a pair of large hands, and she was looking at the true form of her god.

Deia opened her mouth and exhaled flames. There were smoldering cracks all along her skin, which were fuming smoke and leaking inky blood. Her hair fell in sheets of blazing red, limned in bright yellow and orange like the lava below, the top half of her face where her eyes should have been obscured with black lace.

A single large, impossibly blue eye glared at Angelica from the center of the god's chest.

"INSOLENT CHILD." The hands she'd clamped onto Angelica's upper arms seared into her like the day Angelica had been branded within her basilica. "IF YOU CRAVE THE FIRE SO MUCH, THEN I WILL GRANT YOUR WISH."

Angelica was a tangle of pain. She knew she was about to be dropped into the magma, into Deia's forge to be taken apart and melded back together into the perfect mage.

If only she had been strong enough from the start.

If only she had found power the way the gods had, by claiming and consuming.

Angelica stared into that hideously blue eye.

You just wanted to be strong. You wanted to be enough.

All her life she had been angry, and all her life she had been told not to be.

But she deserved to be angry. She *deserved it*, just as she deserved what had been taken from her, deserved every bit of power she desired.

Angelica dragged herself out of the fog of her pain to lift her arm and strike at Deia's chest. The obsidian dagger plunged straight into her eye.

The god flared with a cry that shook even the clouds overhead. Angelica yanked the dagger out along with the eye's pulpy remains.

She shoved it into her mouth and swallowed.

All at once, the doors to her power—the doors that Deia had constructed and kept locked her whole life—flew open.

As the sickly taste of Deia's ruined eye slid down her throat and into her belly, it left a trail of fire. Angelica gagged and groaned, her body straining at the seams.

The hold on her slackened, Deia morphing back into a wyvern and diving into the volcano with a shriek. Angelica fell.

On the center of her forehead where her cut still freely bled came a hot, itching sensation.

It was her first breath and her last. Clear and resonant, the dawning of a new world and the destruction of an old one.

A third eye on her brow opened, and she could see *everything*.

The fibers of the air, the distant foam of the sea, the strands of lava, the particles of earth. And the enigmatic, moving threads of aether—quintessence.

She grabbed at the latter and twisted. She popped out of existence like she was using lightspeed, falling through a portal to land on her feet at the crater's basin, facing down the raging volcano.

It was so easy—as easy as drawing in air, as taking a step, as remembering her name.

Except...she couldn't remember her name. Couldn't remember the existence of a single god. Because there was only her, not on her knees but on her own two feet, with rings of the elements orbiting her like she was their only source. And she was burning, burning with that unquenchable anger, that deep-seeded fury stitched into every tissue and fiber, at a being she had conquered but not yet destroyed. A being who was not worth anyone's worship.

The flame was now her faith. The realm would bow to her and be thankful for it.

She stretched her hands toward the volcano. Deep within her came a ringing chord, radiating down her arms and out through her fingers. The lava rushing toward her rose, and at the heart of the volcano, at the seat of Deia's forge, she sensed her prey.

She clenched her hands into fists. The volcano buckled, the cracks Deia had caused splintering farther and deeper, oozing magma.

But there was something wrong—something inside her kicking and thrashing like an unbroken horse. Her power rose and fell along with it, bursting out of her like an exploding star. She screamed as every inch of her lit up with anguish, with ecstasy, with the driving need to demolish and create.

There were no more locked doors. They had all been burned to ashes.

All that was left was the seething, unchecked stream, with her body the only outlet. And soon it would be destroyed in the torrent.

XII

A few miles from the Forgetting Waters, Risha found herself surrounded by soaring peaks. The remains of castles sat crumbling to dust on their ledges. Amid the rocky terrain were patches of moss giving off a soft blue radiance. Above her wheeled the shapes of birds, as well as high stone arches that looked to have been constructed by a giant.

Or a god.

For so long, all she'd wanted was to open the way to Mortri, to deliver a final resting place for the dead. She understood now she couldn't accomplish it on her own. No matter how she had doubted Dante, he'd been right that it would take the work of all of them—all the heirs, or what remained of them—to bring the barriers down for good.

Her head and her heart were clear, even while in mourning.

A shiver skittered down her back. Although this place seemed abandoned, she heard the fall of a pebble here, a distant scrape there, that implied the presence of one beast or another.

She kept her focus forward, where the ground sloped into a winding stair much like the one that had led to the Vitae portal. All along the stone stairway were trees naked save for ornaments of light in the shapes of hanging stars and moons.

This was the portal to Noctus. And above, straining to be let through: thousands of Noctan souls that had suddenly, violently perished.

What had possibly happened to kill them all at once?

Risha swallowed. Samhara was lighter in her hands than it had been before. As if she had grudgingly accepted it—or as if Jas had graced her with additional strength.

You're plenty strong on your own, Jas argued. *But did I tell you about the time I lifted an entire calf?*

The voice wasn't loud, and she wasn't even entirely sure it was real, but it made her smile.

"You didn't."

It was injured, and had wandered away from its mother. Poor frightened thing kept crying out. My friend and I didn't have a cart to transport it back to the farm it came from, so I carried it the whole way. My arms were sore for days.

"Seems like the sort of thing you would do."

There was no answer. She stared at the rise that held the Noctus portal. The void shuddered and stretched.

She couldn't waste any more time. Risha darted for the stairs.

A high, resounding laugh echoed across the peaks. Lifting Samhara, Risha cast around for the source.

There—a figure was crouched on the ruined wall of an old castle. Once Risha spotted him he leapt down with a flutter of his long red tunic. His landing was soundless save for the chime of his silver jewelry.

Valentin straightened to his full height between her and the stairs, pointed canines on display in a grin. "You didn't really think you could escape this way, did you?"

Risha kept a steady control over her breathing. Her grip tightened on Samhara.

"Ahh, so you think you can repeat what Leshya Vakara did to me." Valentin put a hand on the hilt of his black opal sword. "I'll warn you: You're not half as formidable as she was at her prime. It would be far easier to join me, don't you think, to fix this broken world? You wouldn't even have to stay in Cruciamen. The whole realm would be yours. Well," he amended as he tilted his head, sleek black hair falling over one crimson eye, "*ours.*"

Risha took another breath. Then she placed her feet in the way her father had taught her, lifting the chain scythes in the opening position of Sada.

An invitation to dance.

Valentin's eyes flashed. He unsheathed his sword, hints of green and purple along its blade.

"I've changed my mind," he breathed. "I'll drag you back and feast on your cries. I'll break your will and spirit until you surrender. Perhaps I'll even cut off *your* head, stick it on a spike outside the city until you relent." He gave an unnerving, coquettish laugh. "I'll spit on it every time I pass it! Fuck, that's good!"

She'd barely blinked before he was flying at her, sword ready to part her head from her body. Risha dropped and flung one of the scythes up, catching and deflecting the blade. But she couldn't stop his fingers, nails sharp as talons, from jabbing into her shoulder.

Risha cried out. Valentin laughed and wrenched his fingers back, holding them up to admire the scarlet dripping between his knuckles. Ignoring the pain, she spun and swept out her leg while letting go of the second scythe.

It caught him in the chest and sent him flying. The thin chain extended, then went taut as he grabbed the scythe and flipped midair to land on his feet. The chain between them rattled with eagerness or fury, like it held the remnants of Leshya's will.

"We both know these attacks of yours won't be enough without absorbing a spirit," Valentin taunted. He flung the scythe away. "Too bad your little friend isn't here. All gone! So sad!"

Risha didn't rise to the bait. Instead she dove into the comforting warmth of Jas's energy, the tangled ball of their merged magic. She summoned the other scythe back to her hand, and only when she gripped both hilts did she realize what she'd felt in the weapon.

The remains of Jas's spirit. She feared she'd used it all up when fending off Valentin the first time, but through her haze of misery she hadn't noticed its lingering wisps. Now it was ready to fuel her next strike. To help her clear the path.

Valentin lifted the hand drenched in her blood and flicked his fingers. Arrows of blood formed from the scarlet drops, aiming for her with uncanny speed. Risha grabbed Samhara's chain and spun one of the scythes in front of her, creating a blurred shield. The blood arrows bounced off bone and slammed into the nearby peaks.

That's a neat trick, Jas said. *Show him one of ours, now.*

Risha smirked. Her torus kicked up around her, and Samhara hummed brighter, sharpening her senses. She smelled the iron of her blood and the dust of broken stone, as well as the faint hints of clove from the Noctus portal. Focusing like this, she was able to read Valentin's movements, from the twitch of his fingers to the minute turn of his shoulder.

He was going to distract her with another volley of blood arrows. Risha slid into her next tandshri position, one leg drawn up with her foot pressed against her inner thigh, scythes held out before and behind her.

Vistaar—extend.

Valentin let the blood arrows fly. In the same moment Risha fed her torus until the wind blew around her in a hurricane, fending off the arrows while allowing her the space to jump and spin. Samhara crackled with Jas's spiritual energy as a scythe left her hand.

She formed the mudra for *air* while bidding the chain to snap back and extend again. Valentin, thinking the blade was coming for his face, began to dodge—only to have the blade redirect and sink into his arm instead. He let out a howl of surprise as his left arm was severed.

Her torus died down and she caught her breath. Valentin stared at where his arm had fallen with no small degree of shock. But he recovered far quicker than she expected, his smile almost giddy.

"Oh, I see." He snapped his fingers. From the ruins above came a rattling sound, and about a dozen skeletons dropped into the ravine. "Your friend's still got some life, hmm?" One of the skeletons picked up Valentin's arm and held it up to his body. His flesh fused back together as easily as when his head had been reattached. He licked her blood from his palm. "Let's see if we can burn it out."

As one, the skeletons advanced on her. Risha swung a scythe above her head before letting it fly. It crashed into four of them, breaking apart their ribs and vertebrae. Even then their arms and upper torsos continued forward, dragged by Valentin's will.

The Vakara spell for severing spirits wouldn't work here, not when they were under the control of a Mortrian king. Valentin idly twirled his sword with a wide smile, reminding her of a cat she'd once seen batting around a half-dead lizard.

The skeletons reached her, grabbing her arms and legs, holding her in place. Instead of drawing on Jas's power, she reached only for hers— the black, yawning wellspring, cold and lethal. The skeletons turned their heads toward her, like they were listening to a song. Or a silent order.

One by one they dropped her limbs and turned on Valentin. The undead king had only a second to look baffled before he swung his sword in a massive arc, pulverizing them into shards of bone dust.

"A Vakara is still a Vakara," Valentin growled before he lunged.

She was more prepared than she had been last time. She caught his blade between hers, her body bristling with black-and-green light. His feverish crimson eyes bore into hers. How many years of torment had they witnessed? How many bodies and spirits had he broken under his hands?

Risha fell into a kind of trance as she let her body, her power, take control—meeting his sword with her scythes, using what she remembered of the tandshri to duck and dodge and counterattack. But she had never been a fighter, not like Taesia and Nikolas. She couldn't sustain this.

His sword hilt smashed into her abdomen. She fell and rolled across the ground, coughing around the burning of her stomach, unable to get a breath in. Valentin threw his head back and laughed.

"Look at you! So *weak*. How dare you even call yourself that bitch's descendant."

Up, Jas demanded. *Get* up.

Risha slowly got to her knees. She was shaking now, her torus shrinking.

Samhara grew hot with urgency. Risha stared at the weapon and wondered what it was trying to tell her. Wondered how she could use the bones of Mortrian kings against one of their own.

She remembered the phalanges that had hung from the hilts. Valentin's fingers, cut off by Leshya—perhaps what had led her to craft a necklace of her own finger bones for her heirs' use. But that meant, for centuries, Samhara had had a connection with Valentin's power. Was able to recognize him.

Above her, the strain on the void lessened as the newly made spirits realized there was no passage. The thinned barrier was already beginning to restore itself.

Risha stood and faced Valentin. Samhara was practically vibrating in her hands. A weapon she abhorred, and needed.

Again she slid into the position of Vistaar. Valentin's smile was lazy, assured that victory was only a blade strike away.

"You've already shown me this ruse, or have you forgotten?" Even his tone was bored; he was ready to end this.

Risha ignored him. Gathering all her strength, she spun and released a scythe, letting the chain extend.

When the chain snapped and changed directions, Valentin caught the handle in his free hand. He snorted. "Like that could possibly work a second—"

A grunt escaped him as Risha flooded her power through the chain.

Not just hers, but also what remained of Jas's, the two twisting together along Samhara's length to fuse Valentin's hand to the hilt.

The spirit that sat within the king's body was sickly. A soul poisoned with bloodlust, a sadist in his truest, most grotesque form. Risha nearly flinched away from it, but Jas forced her to keep her grasp on the twisted crimson energy.

"What is this?" Valentin demanded. He dropped his sword and tried to pry his hand away, only for the other to adhere to the hilt as well. Like Samhara remembered those fingers and longed to hear their rattling once more.

Holding the other scythe, Risha basked in Jas's laughter while green light shot down the chain. Risha followed it with her own black radiance, both of them taking hold of the foul spirit within Valentin and *pulling*.

Valentin released a furious shout. His eyes blazed as he struggled, as that crimson energy battled past Jas's and toward hers.

If it reached her, it would pull her own spirit into Samhara.

Risha held on to the scythe with both hands despite the gashes that opened along her arms from the sheer force of its power. Red and black met halfway down the chain, the soul of a tyrant and the soul of a god's progeny, both fashioned by Thana.

She felt the god's influence in him, now—something darker and vaster than the void, something that would turn her mad if she stared at it too long.

"Little Vakara," Valentin growled. "I'll strip your soul apart until misery is the only thing you'll remember."

A flash of green on the other end of the weapon.

Not a chance.

Valentin shuddered when the light dove into his hands. All along his arms, the sleeves of his tunic burst and shredded. His veins turned to vines, slithering around his biceps and around his neck with puncturing thorns. He cried out as his stomach bulged and distended, some patches of skin hardening into bark while others softened and sprouted into fungi. His eyes rolled to the back of his skull before they burst, overtaken by two large, unfurling black roses.

Risha maintained her hold on Samhara while Valentin's energy fluctuated. He screamed, and out of his mouth sprouted marigolds, his cries silenced by ruffled petals.

Now!

Risha seized that twisted, crimson energy and yanked it toward her. It thrashed and nearly overtook her before Samhara clamped onto it, sucking it up like a sponge absorbing blood. The bones shook and flared.

On the other end of Samhara, Valentin's body toppled, a ruined patchwork of flora. The moment his hands dropped, Risha summoned the second scythe back to her.

Only then did the spirit that was Valentin fully succumb to the weapon. Where Jas's energy had resided was now a swirling, angry miasma of power. Power enough that she would never have to absorb another spirit again.

Power enough to cut through the barrier.

XIII

In the atrium of the Bone Palace, Phos waited with the Sunbringer Spear slung across his back. His face—Rian's face—broke into a grin when everyone was assembled. The sight of his brother smiling while he carried the spear made Nikolas's heart clench, but he strove to keep his expression blank.

"It's time," the god said, and held out his hands. The servants clustered behind Fin exclaimed when the mesmerizing light surrounding Phos shone over them as well.

Nikolas's body suddenly jumbled out of order. One second his feet were on marble floor, and the next he was nearly collapsing within a stone courtyard.

Under the booming *crack* of Phos's lightspeed came shrieking cries. They were at the foot of a huge, dark building, Noctans scattering in every direction. Some wearing guard uniforms ran toward them.

Before Nikolas could move, Phos laughed and took the Sunbringer Spear in hand. He slammed the butt of it on the ground, and a searing, piercing sheet of light swept out in a tidal wave. It instantly incinerated the Noctans before it rose into a high, thick shield like the barrier around the Bone Palace.

Nikolas stared at a pile of simmering char that had been a person. Horror burned his throat like bile, and he sensed the lure of Phos's thrall welcoming him back.

He dug his fingernails into his arm until sharp points of pain flowered. *No*, he told himself. *Stay awake.*

He turned to take stock of where they were. He remembered this roof below Phos and Taesia's feet when they had flown above the city, with its sharp points and pinnacles crowned in moons. Under the open Noctan sky, Nikolas's skin tingled with discomfort.

"Finally there's a use for you," Phos told the servants. "I'll need Vitae-ans to enhance the portal." He swept the spear's point at the building, making the servants flinch. "The eye of the circle will be here. The Sanctuary of Nyx." He sneered. "A useless hunk of stone that I will tear down with my own hands."

His back was half-turned to Nikolas. Fin caught his eye, his face strained. In his hand shone a faint gleam of metal.

Lux spooled into a knife against Nikolas's palm.

Despite the violent games they had played as children, or the sparring they had done under the vigilant gaze of their father, Nikolas had never wanted to hurt his brother. Even on Godsnight, when they had faced one another, he had done all he could to make sure Rian's body didn't come to grievous harm. Would have gladly sacrificed any part of his own body to keep him safe.

But he couldn't keep that mindset anymore. The god had taken his brother. Rian might be alive, but he wouldn't have wanted a life like this.

Nikolas still believed Julian could save him. But if he wasn't fast enough...

He allowed for one quick breath, for one quick prayer not to the gods but to his own stubborn hope. Then he gave a single nod to Fin.

The lightsbane shackles dropped from Fin's reddened wrists with a clatter. As Phos turned, Nikolas leapt at him and slammed him to the ground, Lux pointed at the underside of Rian's chin.

In the second it took Phos to process what had happened, Nikolas was already tapping into the core of his power. Phos had dug his fingers into it, had made a sorry mess of it in order to clip Nikolas's wings, but he hadn't taken everything. Not even half.

Around them, the new barrier flickered and fell.

"Go!" Nikolas yelled, not taking his eyes off Phos.

The god grinned up at him. "Ah, Nikolas. I commend you for this. No matter how much I think I've broken you, you only come back stron-ger." He reached up and tenderly brushed some of Nikolas's hair from his face. "As expected of my blood."

Nikolas clenched his jaw and used his other hand to dig around Phos's pockets for the fangs, silently urging Fin and the others to run. Phos brushed back more of Nikolas's hair until his thumb swept over to his bandaged socket and pressed down.

Pain exploded in a riot of hideous colors. A scream tore from his mouth and he dropped, curling in on himself and grabbing his head as if that was all it took to ease the agony piercing his skull.

His brother's voice whispered in his ear, "It will take far more than that to stop me."

Julian expected more resistance once they reached Astrum, but as they drew closer, he realized the golden barrier around the Bone Palace had dropped. All the guards and soldiers were hurrying either toward the palace or toward the screams that erupted from the eastern sector.

Lilia swore. "That's the direction of the Sanctuary."

Where all the portals were.

They took off running. With the Shades' help, darkness cloaked them as citizens frantically rushed by. When they approached the Sanctuary, a bright sheet of gold rose up around it. Another barrier.

"What's he doing?" Taesia panted.

Julian didn't have the breath to speculate. As he'd feared, now that he was back in its proximity the Bone Palace began to stretch for him, two currents longing to join the same river. He shook his head and battled against it.

Not yet.

Before they could figure out what to do, the newly risen barrier suddenly stuttered, then vanished. People rushed out—not Noctans, but servants from the palace, the prince shepherding them out of the courtyard. Fin's eyes locked on them and widened.

Taesia moved to grab him, but her gaze slid past and landed on Nikolas and Rian grappling on the ground.

"*Nik!*" She unsheathed Starfell and ran to him. Julian was about to follow when that feeling stabbed him again, so strong this time he stumbled. Fin caught his arm.

"You're Julian, right?" The prince hunted through his pocket and pressed something hard against Julian's chest. "Nik wanted you to have this."

The weight of a cosmos, the raging of a storm. Images of stepwells and towers and glyphs, of pale lips and a bowing figure, and beyond it all: possibility. Strands of reality that had not yet been woven.

Julian took what was being offered. The god's bone was smooth and cool to the touch.

You carry the gift of making and knowing.

He stared at the piece of a god—his god, no matter how much he denied it—and realized what Orsus had done. Even if the rest of their remains lay in the Bone Palace, they were *here*, in the palm of Julian's hand, at the mercy of his discretion.

You must use it.

The barrier snapped up again behind them. Marcellus unsheathed his sword with a worried glance at Kalen, who extended his familiar into a shield. Lilia unspooled her own familiar into a whip. She touched the fangs hanging at her chest.

"First, we end Phos." She looked up at the sky, where the New Moon hung like a shadow itself. "Then we try to do the impossible."

In the dark, all is possible.

With the memory of Taesia's voice drowning out that of Orsus, Julian tightened his grip around the bone. He closed his eyes and sank into that new well of power, unfamiliar yet known. Known because it ignited his blood, opened his mind the way a beast would, forging a connection.

Lines and circles and the shapes between them.

Fibers twisting around and through him, along the veins that blackened down his arms. His fingers spelled them out in sigils, a circle imitating the New Moon.

When the universe had been born, there had been so much *heat*. A writhing storm of flame and quintessence, longing for a kiln in which to be forged. In the memory he had hands that were not hands, and briefly he knew how it felt to hold all of creation. Went briefly mad with it, unable to translate the sensation without losing most of its meaning.

But he understood enough. And when he opened his eyes, a circle glowed before him in the air, ready to build something new.

Julian's fingers went numb around the bone when he pressed his other hand to the middle of the circle. Electric pulses jumped up his arm and into his shoulder, bright glimmers of pain and ecstasy, as he pulled something out.

A longbow. A quiver full of arrows. His creations, fashioned out of what remained of the heart of the universe.

The weapon fell to the ground, and he let the circle disappear. He bent down to pick up the bow. Sturdy, firm—as good as any his father had taught him how to make.

I can be both, he thought, and for the first time it was with wonder, not disgust.

XIV

As Taesia raced toward Nikolas, Phos did something that made him scream in pain. Nikolas rolled off his brother, and a moment later, the barrier snapped back into place.

Phos leapt up just in time to catch Starfell's downward swing with the Sunbringer Spear.

"And here we are again," the god drawled, and it was so *wrong* in Rian's achingly familiar voice.

She sensed rather than saw spears of light form behind her. Taesia dropped and rolled out of the way as they flew at her back. Phos waved a hand, and they dissipated before they could hit him.

"I see you're on the mend after our last go-around," she taunted.

He frowned slightly at the sheath poking over her shoulder. He touched the spot on his chest where the nightstone had branded him.

"Thankfully I had ways of countering it," he said.

She followed his gaze to Nikolas. For the first time, she realized his head was bandaged.

"Nik!" Taesia scrambled to his side. His shoulder was fever-warm when she shook it, but he managed to open one clear, watery eye. As for the other...

She couldn't tell if it was damaged or wholly gone. Fresh blood dampened the bandages on his face, darkly gleaming.

Fury choked her. Starfell readily hummed in her grasp.

Nikolas grabbed her arm. "Tae," he breathed. For a second he simply stared at her as one would stare at the impossible, as if the moon had finally caught up with the sun.

"I'm here," she assured him. Her fingertips gently traced the curve of his gaunt cheek.

At the touch, he came back to himself with a shake. "The fangs. He has them."

She looked up at Lilia and the others. "Phos has the rest of the fangs!" Taesia yelled.

Lilia nodded before throwing herself at Phos with a brutal crack of her whip. Although he blocked it, he couldn't evade the tip that slashed open a cut on his upper thigh. Hissing through his teeth, golden wings flared out on either side of him and he launched into the sky.

Nikolas's grip tightened, and she turned back to him. He was sitting up now, ashen and trembling, but with an expression that meant he wasn't done yet. Taesia yearned to bring him somewhere safe, to shroud him in darkness so that pain could never touch him again.

Instead, she helped him to his feet. Fin joined them and slung Nikolas's arm around his shoulders.

"You should have run with the others," Nikolas admonished.

"You knew I would come back."

The two of them shared a look that gave her a vague sense of disquiet, something she didn't have time to properly assess. In her hand, Starfell pulsed urgently.

She followed its point up, toward the Cultris constellation. At its fore, the Malum Star was burning brighter—that light traveling across space and time, years and eons, to reach them.

Perhaps the star had already long died, and this had been a foregone conclusion.

Lilia had followed Phos up onto the roof of the Sanctuary of Nyx. They battled with whip and spear, shadow and light, amid the sculptures of the moon's phases.

Spears of light formed a ring at Lilia's back. Before Taesia could call out a warning, a figure morphed out of Lilia's shadow and deflected them all with a black shield—Kalen.

Marcellus had hopped onto the roof unnoticed and charged at Phos from behind. Phos spirited himself higher into the air with lightspeed, unleashing another attack. Kalen shielded himself and Lilia from the raining projectiles while Marcellus knocked them away with his sword.

Taesia turned back to Nikolas. He met her gaze with understanding. As desperately as she wanted to protect him, she was needed elsewhere.

"Keep him away from the fight," she ordered Fin before she gathered the shadows to her and let them carry her to the roof.

"I see I failed to strike down the last Lunari," Phos said, wings keeping him aloft. "I'll be sure to correct that mistake."

"You won't have to if you keep drawing this out," Taesia called up. "We'll all be dead soon anyway."

Phos lifted a questioning eyebrow. In answer, Taesia pointed up with her sword. Starfell's silver mica gleamed, creating small constellations along the spiny blade.

"That star is about to collapse into a black hole. Once it collides with the one beside it, the force will be enough to destroy Noctus. Which is exactly what you want."

Lilia grabbed Taesia's arm. "What are you doing?"

Taesia ignored her. "But it's not exactly how you wanted this to go, is it?" she called up. "You want this realm to perish under your light. For Nyx to feel every ray of it." She grinned without a shred of humor. "Well, you did cause this, in a way. By killing Orsus and destroying Ostium, you ensured every realm will eventually meet this fate. Good for you."

Do it, she urged him, her heart pounding. *Quickly.*

Rian's eyes turned gold. All around them came a crackling sound, the roof trembling under their feet as the same staticky feeling of Godsnight vibrated through the air. Four columns of light shot into the sky around Astrum: red, black, silver, and gold.

Phos raised the Sunbringer Spear. It glowed like the sun itself, making good on its name as the god aimed it at the new maelstrom forming above them.

"No!" Lilia cried. The Noctans reached for their weapons, preparing to attack.

Before they could, Phos was shot out of the air by an arrow.

Taesia whirled around. Julian stood on the edge of the roof, his eyes burning green, black veins creeping along his skin. He held a longbow steady in his hands, another arrow already nocked and ready.

Her chest ached. Monster and guardian—her Hunter.

His unearthly eyes watched Phos reorient himself with a gust of his wings, blood spilling down one arm. The arrow had hit him in the shoulder; not harmless, but far from fatal. Taesia knew Julian had aimed true.

"SO YOU'RE HERE, TOO, HEIR OF OSTIUM," Phos said, barely fazed as the arrow shaft burned to ash. "GOOD."

A small bag had fallen from his pocket during the tumble. The astralam fangs. Lilia shot out her whip as the bag slid down the slope of the roof, the familiar grabbing it just before it fell.

When it was in her hands, Lilia gave a quiet sob of relief. The three fangs at her chest began to glow, the silver sheen like Marcellus's moonstone, like the pillar of light that represented Noctus.

"I can feel...I can feel them." Lilia tore open the bag and poured the fangs into her palm. "Like they're *within* me."

Adsimil. Like-kind.

The bones of a Lunari, forged from stardust, recognizing the shape of another star.

The silver light washed over Lilia. Phos took advantage of their distraction and hurled more spears downward. Kalen was too focused on Lilia to lift his shield in time.

Taesia flung out her familiar while Marcellus dove forward. Umbra expanded into its own shield, deflecting most of the spears, yet two found their target in Marcellus's thigh and side, making him stagger.

"*No!*" The shout wrenched from Kalen's chest echoed across the roof as he lunged forward and grabbed Marcellus. His shadow shield materialized before them.

"I'm all right," Marcellus gasped, holding his side as blood spurted between his fingers. "Her Highness—"

Taesia crouched beside the glowing form of Lilia. Under the silver light the princess was hunched over in pain. This close, Taesia realized there was something happening to her flesh: All along her collarbone emerged a ring of sharp, curved points. The astralam fangs, making up a bloody smile.

Lilia's head snapped back. Her eyes were liquid mercury, and even the whip in her hand ignited with quicksilver. Phos warily pointed the Sunbringer Spear at her, ready to fire off a beam of scorching light.

Faster than a meteor shooting across the sky, Lilia launched herself upward and wrapped her whip around his neck.

Phos's two-toned yell echoed against his barrier. Smoke rose from his neck before he slashed through the whip with his spear and fell over the side of the roof. Lilia's familiar re-formed as it retreated to its master, who drifted back down to the roof.

Kalen, tying a strip torn from his surcoat around Marcellus's waist, paused to stare at Lilia in wonderment. She knelt and pressed a hand to Marcellus's wounds, cauterizing them with starfire. Marcellus held back a shout and grabbed Kalen's hand, nearly crushing it.

"What are you doing?" Taesia demanded of her. This hadn't been part of the plan.

Lilia glanced at her, solemn and severe, the ever-dutiful heir.

"What I must," Lilia answered.

"I need to help them!" Nikolas struggled against Fin, but the prince's hold was surprisingly strong.

"You're hurt," Fin said. "And therefore a liability. We need to stay out of their way."

Nikolas swore. His head was splitting, his vision doubling, but he could still make out a strange silver sheen from the roof. Taesia's voice, and a cry of pain as a whip wound around Rian's neck.

Nikolas searched for Julian. He was standing at the edge of the roof, tying something to one of his arrows.

Phos crashed down into the courtyard. He coughed and held on to his throat; it was burned.

"Enough," Phos rasped. "I may not have all the offerings, but I have enough."

With a *crack* of lightspeed, he disappeared. Suddenly the sturdy presence at Nikolas's side vanished as Phos grabbed Fin and pulled him into the air.

"No!" Nikolas shouted. The prince struggled, caught around the shoulders with his arms pinned to his sides. He kicked and a piece of stone from the courtyard went flying toward them, but Phos easily smashed it apart.

"Your earth magic is weak here," the god said. "But it's enough for an offering of Vitae."

He moved to slit Fin's throat with the Sunbringer Spear.

Nikolas didn't even think before he formed Lux into a javelin and threw it. It knocked against the spear and changed the blade's trajectory, slicing open a gash on Fin's chest instead of his throat.

The wound wasn't fatal. But his blood, the blood of Vitae, the blood of kings, spilled to the ground regardless.

The crackling around them grew louder. Within Nyx's temple came a low drone that raised the hairs along Nikolas's body. Above them, the maelstrom broke open.

This time the oculus was wide enough to destroy all of Astrum. Wide enough that it already flooded with sunlight. The core of his power *yearned*, stretching for it despite the devastation it would cause.

Phos grinned. "YES. *MORE*. LET US DROWN THIS WRETCHED REALM BEFORE IT'S FINISHED OFF FOR GO—"

He cut off with a strangled sound. Nikolas stopped breathing at the sight of the arrow that bloomed in Phos's other shoulder. There was something dark tied to the head, glinting like a gemstone before it was covered in Rian's blood.

He followed its path back to Julian, whose eyes pierced through the night. The words he spoke were clear and chiming.

"Go to sleep."

Phos gasped and fought against the command. A dark, bristling light skittered across his body and his wings, forcing him to let Fin go.

Nikolas ran forward. Maybe it was the light of Solara pushing through, or having Phos's attention directed elsewhere, but he sensed the ghost of his wings. He leapt up and imagined them spread out behind him, luminous and golden.

Fin fell into his arms. Nikolas scraped both knees when he landed, keeping Fin tucked close to him as they rolled. Fin shook like a hurricane, the warmth of his blood seeping into Nikolas's shirt.

Nikolas pushed himself up and stared down at Fin, both of them panting wildly. Fin's eyes were wide and gleaming, and he reached up to pat Nikolas's face with a shaking hand as if to convince himself he was real.

"I caught you this time," Nikolas said.

Fin's lips twitched. Then he surged up and threw his arms around Nikolas's shoulders, laughter and tears escaping all at once. Nikolas held him as tight as he dared, reveling in that laugh; the same laugh as the boy who had tumbled off a wall one afternoon and straight into Nikolas's life.

Phos's scream made them look up. The god was contorting around the arrow, trying to pull it out even as his limbs fought against Julian's compulsion. His wings stuttered and he dropped to the ground, gold and black threads twisting around him.

Julian leapt off the roof and landed lightly on his feet. He stalked forward with the silent grace of a predator.

"Go to sleep," he said again, *"and dream."*

Rian's head fell back. His eyes were still a furious gold, but his mouth hung open in a silent scream as above them the maelstrom thundered and threatened.

"Why isn't it stopping?" Fin asked.

Nikolas's chest tightened. Even with Phos momentarily hindered, the attack had already been triggered.

They were too late.

XV

D ante!"
He looked where his aunt was pointing. In the stretch of land between the plateau and the volcano, the ground was beginning to crack and tremble. An energy flitted through the air that put pressure on the back of his skull, a familiar, staticky fog.

All around them, thin lines lit up gold.

"It's working!" Dante knelt at the edge of the plateau. Hands and feet and heads broke out of the forming cracks, bodies crawling out of the ground in various states of decay like tunnel spiders. Some were fresh— as fresh as a year-old corpse could be—while others had eroded to bone and sinew. High-pitched cries rattled out of their slack jaws as they all turned their gazes up at the raging demons.

The sound of three demons battling was that of beasts fighting for dominance. Their abilities ineffective against each other, they resorted to raw, furious strength, too fast for Dante to make out anything beyond Shanizeh's hands around the baron's thickened neck and Azideh's horns piercing his chest.

A flash of red and Shanizeh teleported behind Alma. The baron's morphed body was thrown down, the crash making the plateau tremble. Marizleh growled, fangs snapping in the air as Shanizeh and Azideh closed in. Shanizeh made an odd, clicking laugh and raised her hand high.

Azideh caught her wrist. "The kill should be mine."

"You don't deserve it," she hissed. And just that like, the two turned on each other, releasing their hold on the baron.

Dante spun toward the refugee, but Marizleh got there first.

The baron-turned-demon grinned at Dante as he captured the young woman in his blue-veined arms. They stood at the edge of the plateau, the refugee still blankly, eerily calm.

"Baron Alma," Dante said carefully, holding out a hand. "You said you didn't want to resort to this. I know you are not the demon. In fact, I'm sure we can find a way to exorcise it."

The baron paused. Then Marizleh took over, grinning wider.

"Our bond is too strong," he said, using a nail to cut open the refugee's cheek. "There is no separating me from the Alma line. I grow stronger with each new sacrifice." He eyed the other demons. "I wonder how much stronger I would become if I killed them...?"

"The circle!" Camilla cried.

Dante glanced down. The golden lines were already beginning to sputter with no sacrifice to activate the portal. The woken dead swayed and shook, seeking absolution.

He closed his eyes and forced himself to be calm, to think, to find the solution that would end up saving everyone.

But there was none.

You have the power to make meaningful change. And you understand that power has consequences.

Dante opened his eyes and looked at the refugee.

"*Fall backward*," he said in soft, chiming compulsion.

Her eyes glazed over. Without hesitation, she hurled both herself and the baron over the side of the plateau.

Dante rushed to the ledge as if he could catch her. But both she and the baron hit the ground with a loud *thud*, and a bloom of scarlet pooled around her head. Marizleh growled and thrashed to standing, blue light prickling all around him.

"You dare—" He was cut off by an emaciated hand grabbing his arm. The dead had reached the base of the plateau, drawn to the one who had lured them to their graves. "Get off of me!"

His brute strength cleaved through the first wave of corpses. But the Alma family had been making sacrifices for centuries, and there were too many to fight off single-handedly. The dead overwhelmed him, bony fingers digging into his flesh. Dante saw the baron emerge for just a moment, eyes wide with terror; then he was dragged back into their ruthless embrace, leaving behind only tortured screams.

Dante put a hand over his mouth and tried not to be sick. The static in the air grew painful, sparking against his skin while Deia's Heart grumbled.

I'm sorry, he thought. *I'm sorry. There was no other way.*

Hands hauled him to his feet. "It's working!" Camilla yelled.

Beyond the carnage, a gaping, cosmic swirl opened within the earth. It glowed black and silver, pulling at his core.

Brailee was calling for him. It was time.

Camilla's grin was made sharper with the baron's demise. When she turned to him, the edges of it waned and caution darkened her eyes.

"Azideh!" Dante roared.

His demon brimmed with power. Baring his teeth, Azideh grabbed Shanizeh and slammed her into the ground.

"You vile—animal!" Shanizeh screeched as he pounded her skull against the rocks, raking long, bloody lines down his arms.

Before Camilla could react, Dante sprinted toward them and slid to his knees. "Vecto," he said firmly, "be still."

Shanizeh's black eyes grew round and her mouth fell slack. The red energy that had been rising up to teleport her away faded even as rage brewed on her angular, inhuman face.

"Blood traitor," Shanizeh growled up at Azideh. The nails puncturing his arms dug in further. "You filthy, faithless *beast*—"

Azideh smirked. He let all his unleashed energy pour into his fist and smashed it into the other demon. The surface of the plateau cracked beneath Dante's knees.

Camilla ran toward them. "Shanizeh!"

Dante stood. "Saya, now!"

The corpses that had been climbing the side of the plateau crawled over the lip and darted for Camilla. She struck one down in a blur of red, but like Alma, she was overcome by their numbers. She screamed in fury as the corpses held her down, her arms and legs pinned by weathered bone and tattered flesh.

"Dante!" No matter how she struggled, she couldn't free herself. "*Dante!* What have you done? How did you—?"

"What was it you said about putting your family first?" he asked her.

He turned away from her disbelieving stare and called Azideh back to him. So long as Dante commanded Shanizeh with her true name—a name Azideh had whispered into his mind with no small amount of delight when Dante had asked for it—she would stay right where she was.

He leapt from the plateau over the still-churning corpses, landing on the grass that led to the edges of the portal. Brailee and Saya were there to meet him. He gave Saya a thankful nod, and Brailee clutched his arm.

They knelt beside the portal. He couldn't see much beyond the swirling, shimmering darkness, like the night sky turned to paint, but he sensed an opulent vastness beyond. Nox and Somnus peered in as well, enticed by the call of Noctus.

Dante swallowed, reminding himself that he couldn't go in. The whole point of the portal was to create an opening for Taesia and the others to get back to Vitae.

"How long will it hold?" Brailee asked.

Dante shook his head; he didn't know. He couldn't think about what he'd just done to make this happen. He could only stare at the mesmerizing vortex, silently begging for Taesia to find it, to return home.

All Angelica had ever wanted was to be able to grasp her powers without the use of instruments.

Now that they were rushing through her in tidal waves, she realized why Deia had locked them up.

She scorched white-hot, a star fallen to earth. Still, she longed for more of that intolerable heat, for the sea of lava beginning to flood the crater. The ground beneath her pitched and rolled, the air stinging.

All of it could be unraveled, undone. She could smash the volcano apart and bathe in its remains. Drag the deity from her hiding place and rip her apart. The empire at her back could be broken up and then plunged into the sea.

"Angelica!"

The sound of her own name barely registered. She writhed and spat fire, sobbing as the veins along her lungs blackened.

"Angelica, calm down!"

Those words echoing across years and years and *years*—

"*I will not*," she shrieked, "*calm down!*"

Vents opened along the ground, spitting lava. There was a cry of surprise, a deep satisfaction in her marrow.

"All right!" the voice yelled. "Just stop hurting yourself!"

But she wasn't hurting herself. She was fulfilling her every want, flooded with a god's might and stepping into her role as heir, as—

—as her heart began to char, the water in her body boiling, scalding, killing her from the inside out.

With her third eye open she could peer through the veils of her elements at those who had gathered around her. They stood on burning ground and protected their faces from stray embers with their arms, risking themselves for the chance to speak to her.

"Angelica," Eiko called. "We have to— You said we could go home, we need to go *home*."

A pair of familiar dark eyes met hers through the flames.

"Angelica," Cosima whispered. "Come back to us. Please."

Each breath was a struggle. She longed to plunge her senses to the bottom of the sea, or deep under the magma chamber, escaping somewhere cool and dark where she could not think or be.

"*What even is home to you?*" she demanded of Eiko in a voice like crashing thunder.

"Home...home is wherever my family is." Eiko's tears gleamed like gold. "And that includes you."

Blood trickled from the corners of Angelica's eyes. Her fingertips began to crumble into ash.

"You can control it!" Eiko cried. "I know you can!"

But the fire was in every molecule of her being. Without it, she was nothing.

She fell to her knees.

"Angelica!" Cosima yelled. "Listen to me—you're stronger than your god could ever hope to be! So *prove it*!"

Fingers digging into basalt, blood trapped in her throat. The third eye blazing on her forehead leaked black liquid, falling to the ground and sprouting yellow flowers where it landed.

Hypericum flowers.

Angelica stilled. Then she grabbed the obsidian dagger and sliced it across the meat of her thigh.

The pain gave her a rush of clarity. Gasping, she looked up at the smoldering, blackened sky, the destructive pillar of ash on its way to blanket Hitan. Yvri and Kenji had managed to close the crater wall, the ex-Gojarin now flying toward them on the wyvern's back. The flowing lava had parted around Angelica and the girls, giving them a wide birth even as it splashed at the edges of the crater, as if Angelica had encompassed them all within a protective bubble.

You just wanted to be strong.

Not to conquer or destroy, but to save those who mattered most.

Taking the deepest breath she could, Angelica pushed back to her feet and held her hands toward the sky.

The wind that blew over the crater was cold and strong. The lava's surface began to harden, the ash cloud pushed in the opposite direction, toward the uninhabited Sanatsu Peaks. The sea was rocking from the volcanic blasts, forming the first waves that would eventually crash into Parithvi's coast. Angelica grasped them and forced them to temper, the taste of salt splashing across her tongue.

The power was brilliant and electric and *alive*, dancing along her hands and through her hair, until she was as light as the wind itself.

Far, far beneath her, she sensed the shape of the tectonic plate that ran across northern Azuna, down the Arastra Sea, and along southern Vaega. The line connecting Mount Netsai to Deia's Heart.

Her third eye started to close. The fire that surrounded her diminished, allowing her to finally locate the threads of aether all around her. Leftover quintessence that had spilled into Vitae from the Cosmic Scale so long ago.

Yvri landed next to her, and Kenji slid off his back to gather Asami and Akane to him. The wyvern lowered his head to level his gaze at her.

I see you have taken some of the progenitor into yourself. Like a child refusing to be birthed without its womb. Do you think that was wise?

Angelica lifted her bloody dagger in answer, and he snorted.

Why your kind is so violent, I will never understand.

Yet, he allowed her to reach up and press a hand against his side. She closed her eyes and delved deep into the earth's mantle, trying to ignore the siren call of bubbling magma, making sure the others were protected from its heat.

There—a faint, long thread. And on the other end came an insistent tug.

Angelica opened her eyes and met Kenji's. "Where I'm going won't be suitable for Asami and Akane."

The ex-Gojarin looked at the empresses. They met his gaze with trust. He exhaled unevenly.

"I'll take them away on the sorankun," he decided. "Somewhere they can be hidden and safe."

Asami signed something to her sister.

"She wants to tell the people the truth of what happened," Akane said. "I do, too."

"You will," Angelica told them. "But wait until you make sure Nanbu won't retaliate. Gather and grow your allies." She thought back to the Camellia Chamber. "You should go to the earth state. Takenaka might be able to help you."

"I like Bushan Takenaka," Akane agreed quietly. "She and Nanbu rarely got along."

Asami hurried forward, looking like she might hug Angelica if it weren't for the flames between them. Swallowing, the girl bowed instead.

"Thank you," Asami whispered, and only the air quivered.

Angelica inclined her head. "Remember to be as loud as you want to be."

Asami smiled even as her eyes shone. She and Akane turned to Eiko and embraced her, also murmuring their thanks.

Angelica waited until Kenji and the girls had mounted their sorankun to hold out her hand. Cosima didn't hesitate; she stepped through what remained of Angelica's layers of fire, unhurt and unburned, and clasped it. Eiko did the same, her hand over the two of theirs.

"I said I would bring you home, and I will," Angelica said to them. "But we need to make a stop along the way."

Keep going.

Jas's spirit may have been gone, but Risha held the last fragment of him near her heart as she clutched Samhara and ascended the stairs to the Noctus portal.

Keep going, and don't look back.

Don't look back at the flower-riddled corpse of Valentin, or the realm her body both longed for and despised.

She had to keep moving, to the only doorway available to her, and hope that it would eventually lead her home.

Her heart raced and her legs screamed. In her hands, Samhara bristled an outraged crimson as one of the blades flared into a glassy shine. Valentin's face appeared there, contorted with rage.

"You little *bitch*," he growled. "Release me!"

"Into what?" Risha panted. "Your body's plant fodder." Jas barked a laugh in the back of her mind.

"Thana will find me a new one. I'll—"

Risha send a jolt of energy into the weapon, and he disappeared. But at the mention of Thana, she sensed the air prickling around her in warning, her god's eye turned on her.

Look at what you've done to my minion, Thana whispered, almost right into her ear. Risha flinched. *Where do you think you're going with my crux?*

Crux?

Risha stumbled onto a rise made of dark rock, surrounded by intricate stone lanterns. Here the void was practically writhing in pain, a riot of lost souls congregating over the shadowed stepwell before her.

She didn't have time to ask questions. She ran for the stepwell.

It was a circular depression in the ground, with rings of steps engraved with glyphs and symbols leading to a flat basin. It was here where Noctan souls would be conveyed to Mortri, to ascend into a new realm and answer the call of the Praeteriens to join its current.

Risha nearly tumbled down the steps and skidded her knees at the bottom. She barely felt it—didn't even feel the pain at her shoulder anymore, Jas already at work repairing the wound Valentin had left—and turned her whole focus inward to her power.

She leaned her head back as it flooded her. Dizzying and immense, dark and dulcet. Every unknown in the world turning clear as crystal, every minor note turning major. Valentin's energy acted as a conduit through Samhara, the bones thrumming with impatience to be used.

It won't be that simple to abandon me.

Following Thana's words was a strange, wet feeling around her legs. She looked down to find that the stone of the stepwell was seeping blood, the small pool rising steadily higher and higher.

Risha reached out for the void the way she had during the séance—expanding her awareness outward until she brushed up against a wailing soul.

Come to me, Risha bade it. *Come, and I will open the way.*

"—came out of nowhere, we couldn't—"

"—it was so bright, so blinding—"

"—Mama, help, please—"

Risha lifted Samhara, and energy flickered and lashed at her wrists. The blood pool had already reached her waist, flooding the portal with the sole intent of drowning her.

"Open," she gasped. With one scythe facing the void and the other plunged into the blood to scratch at the stepwell's bottom, she screamed it again. "*Open!*"

She had a sense of déjà vu, of standing at the barrier after crossing the necropolis and traversing the unruly pathway of the void. Now she was on the other side, begging once more to be let through.

The blood touched her chest, thick and tacky. Risha tilted her face up, straining to reach as many spirits as she could. They all reached back, grieving and lost like her, responding to Samhara's lure.

The barrier cracked. Split. Began to ease open.

Blood washed over her head and pulled her under. Still she held on to Samhara, to the spark that was Jas, to the struggling spirits. Her lungs burned as she fought not to open her mouth, the pressure radiating from the stepwell grinding her bones together.

And then—the spirits surged free, and the barrier broke.

Thana's yell was a dull thunderclap under the roaring of the portal. The blood pool spun like a cyclone with her trapped inside it, the same delirious vertigo as when Angelica had pushed her into Mortri.

Only now she was falling into another strange land, one that smelled of cloves and midnights, with her ancestor's weapon in her hands and the lingering echo of her god's wrath in her ears.

XVI

The portal spun lazily, hypnotizing in its dark depths. Dante couldn't help but lean toward it.

Hands grabbed his shoulders.

"Is this what it means, then, for the portals to be reopened?" Azideh purred against his ear.

Dante shuddered. "No. This portal is temporary. Only when the portals are permanently opened, like they were before, can you..."

Only then can you take my life.

Azideh wound his fingers around Dante's collar, pulling his back against the demon's front. "Pity," Azideh rumbled, and he could feel it in his own chest. His other hand reached around to settle over Dante's racing heart. "I would have liked to consume you now."

A flash of heat followed by a flash of cold. Dante kept his eyes on the portal, trying in vain to not think about consequences. Trying not to glance in the direction where the dead were beginning to flag, their vengeance complete, the newest of their number lying in a pool of her own blood.

Azideh returned to his cloud form, laughing softly.

What did I tell you? the demon whispered. *You lust for control in all its forms.*

"I had to kill the baron and his demon. I did a *good* thing."

One could argue he, too, was doing good. Keeping his city safe by administering sacrifice.

His stomach twisted.

"Dante."

He came back to himself as Brailee laid a hand on his knee.

"It's taking them too long," Brailee said. "I'm going through."

"Wh— Absolutely not. We don't know what's happening over there. They—"

"Rian knows me," his sister stressed. "I *know* he's fighting against Phos. I can help."

Dante opened his mouth, but all his arguments were weak, amounted to little more than *I can't lose you, too.*

"I'll come back." She took his hand, eyes bright with determination. His throat ached with how much she had grown without him realizing it. "I'll bring them back."

Dante hugged her tight, fighting the urge to use his compulsion on her again.

He couldn't. He would not turn into the baron.

Brailee hugged Saya, then contemplated the portal before her. With one last glance at Dante, she stepped into the unknown.

Under Taesia's feet came a heady vibration. It reminded her of standing in the Vitae stepwell, an expansive longing, carrying the faint hint of grass and water and smoke. It traveled up the walls of the Sanctuary of Nyx and shook the roof, made Kalen cling harder to Marcellus.

Lilia stared down at the courtyard, where Julian had dropped. He had tied one of the nightmare gems to his arrow before he'd fired it, and now Rian—or Phos, or both—was falling under its influence.

The princess's whip crackled with starfire. Before she could unleash it, Taesia grabbed her arm despite the throbbing heat that passed between them.

"Don't," Taesia said. "You have to give Julian a chance to save him. *Please.*"

Lilia's eyes were brimming with silver mercury, her black hair turning white at the roots. The fangs poking out along the curve of her collarbone glinted like an ivory necklace.

"If we attack him now, then the god will die," Lilia said.

"That won't stop what's coming." Taesia glanced up at the brightening maelstrom, her bones aching at its wrongness.

"Highness," Kalen whispered. "The barrier."

The princess hesitated. Then, with a flick of her hand, she dismissed her whip and peered up to better focus on the other threat looming over the city.

Another rumble came from the Sanctuary just as the form of a petite girl stumbled out of the entrance. Taesia first thought she was hallucinating, that the air was beginning to intoxicate her.

Brailee.

Panic caught her in a grip so strong she couldn't even call out as her sister ran toward Rian. Once she reached him, Brailee took his head between her hands.

Taesia was about to leap down when Lilia made a pained noise. Her aides immediately flanked her.

"It's all right, Highness." Kalen's face seemed so much younger in his fright. He and Marcellus each held one of Lilia's arms. "You're a Lunari. You were meant for this."

"We're here with you," Marcellus added, face dotted with sweat.

Silver tears spilled down Lilia's face as the rest of her hair gradually whitened, the same blinding effect as sunlight on just-fallen snow.

Something stirred beyond Phos's barrier. Starfell burned brighter and the astralam fangs on Lilia's body glowed. Along the edges of Astrum came the first rising tide of the barrier, silver and splendid, like a sheet of moonlight.

Once the barrier was complete, it would take all of Lilia's strength to withstand Phos's attack.

It would kill her.

It was within this very building that Lilia had told Taesia the story of Noria Lunari, a hero and a martyr. To Lilia, it was a story full of meaning, something to aspire to. To Taesia, it was a warning.

She had come back to Astrum with a dangerously cobbled-together plan. Holding Starfell closer, she now felt it settle in her with an almost comforting weight.

She was not going to let anyone become a martyr today.

As soon as Julian fired the arrow into Rian's shoulder, he sensed the confused tumult of his thoughts. Boy and god, god and boy, the blood of Vitae and Solara and—something else. Faraway and familiar, the same twisting threads as those unraveling in Julian's veins.

The piece of Orsus that Phos had consumed. Whatever magic it had bestowed to him, it was growing within Rian as Phos's hold on him strengthened.

There is no point in this exertion, came the low, spectral voice he had been dreading. In his pocket, the piece of Orsus's bone felt like an extra limb, one that prickled with pins and needles. *If you separate them, then Phos yet lives. He must be ended.*

Julian glanced at Nikolas, who watched warily from a distance, holding an injured Fin close.

Nikolas had brought this piece of Orsus to him. He knew, after what Julian had done to free his own mind, that this was likely the only way to get his brother back.

Julian would do what he could to not fail him this time.

Instead of tapping into the enigmatic threads of quintessence, he fell back on what was most familiar: his beastspeaking. He sharpened it into a fine point and unleashed it to pierce Rian between his brows.

A spiral of calamitous thoughts threatened to engulf him. His knees nearly buckled at the onslaught, unable to separate god and boy, screams from whispers, laughter from sobs.

With a beast, it was so much simpler—animal aggression, instinctual persistence, the need to hunt and keep warm and survive. But though tapping into Nikolas's mind had been like trying to undo a tangled lock, what he found now was a twisting labyrinth, full of dead ends and upside-down corridors and ghosts.

Julian breathed through the assault as his head throbbed. The bone sent a numbing cold through his hip that spread down his leg.

The god was upset, was doing everything they could to force Julian to use their power. Julian gripped his bow tighter, tight enough to cut off bloodflow to his fingers. A reminder to be Julian Luca and nothing else.

There was a shout, and suddenly a girl was running toward Rian. Julian reached for an arrow before he recognized her: Brailee Lastrider, the one who had first been possessed by Nyx at Godsnight. Taesia's sister.

When she reached Rian, she stood behind him and grabbed his head. Her eyes rolled into the back of her skull with a bitten-off scream, as if his nightmare were being transferred to her.

And then Julian was wrenched out of the courtyard and into Rian's mind.

Into the labyrinth.

ENOUGH

I was unhappy.

There. I can say it now.

That isn't to say there weren't things that made me happy. There were quite a few. But there is a difference between momentary delight and contentment as a fixture, like a chandelier hanging in your home, beautiful and bright.

My home wasn't very beautiful. Some would say otherwise, but I hated it. So gaudy. A gilded coffin.

(If you detest these memories so much, then let them go. You will find eternal peace. You will be safe, with me.)

I don't think that's true.

It's never really been about choice, has it? I didn't choose to be born, or to have all my father's expectations put upon me. I didn't choose to be the one he named heir while my brother stood forgotten in the corner, withering without sunlight. I didn't choose to fall asleep, to enter the house of my god and have him in turn take residence within me.

I didn't want any of it. I don't want any of it.

I don't want *you*.

I want—

I just—

I'm so fucking *hungry* and—

Was this corridor always here?

(You will be able to rest soon. Just a little more, a moment more, and your hunger will be satisfied.)

Shut up.

You...

I know you.

The girl from my dreams, the one who I used to do cartwheels for, the one who was always softspoken. She stands in front of me, but now her eyes are fire and there's a bellows in her chest, and she's beautiful, *beautiful*, and lighting the way.

"Rian," she says, holding out her hand. "It's all right. Follow me."

Down the corridors, twisting, turning, where sharp things are waiting to bite and attack and drag ~~him~~ ~~me~~ us back to where this all started.

"No," she says, so sincere, her hand still outstretched. "I'll guide you."

(She is lying. This will only bring you more pain.)

Her hand is warm. I let it tug me forward, down the corridor, into another. In the distance comes a wild howl that plunges me into ice, a howl like the wolves that stalk the countryside, the ones that gave me nightmares after—

She squeezes my hand harder.

"Don't look," she tells me. "Keep your gaze on me. Don't give them any attention, and they won't hurt you."

I do as she says. With every corner there is a new well of fear, the bark of my father's voice and the thrill of drowning, the likenesses of those I know—knew—lying facedown all around me.

My shoulders prickle and I almost turn. There is another here, a presence I don't like, curious and strange, eyes bleeding green through the dark.

"What is he doing?" I whisper, and am shocked to find I can speak at all.

"He's helping. I think it's because of him I can speak to you now. We..." She glances at where those eyes burn. Somewhere far and far and far away from here comes the roar of an approaching storm. "We don't have much time."

We walk quicker. To the heart of the maze, my mind, my—do I even have a mind anymore? A heart? A body? These new fears loom over me, so tall and large, and I am insignificant in their shadow.

"Focus on me," she reminds me.

Her hand is soft. Darker than mine. Her eyes, too—dark like ink, like the canopy of night, like the place where I go when he is in control.

(I will always be in control.)

A ripple and a tear. I yank my hand away, fight against something I cannot see or comprehend. There is a stinging at my neck and it is driving me mad, I cannot see, I cannot feel anything, I *can't*—

"Rian!" she cries. "It's not real! You can fight this!"

But I couldn't stop the fever, the descent toward death, toward the entity that cradled me against burning wings and hid me away from everyone and everything.

He is me and I am him and we are—

XVII

There was a terrible, ongoing howl Angelica couldn't escape. If the others screamed, she couldn't hear them.

But she had the fulcrum under her hand, warm, alive, *powerful*. She leaned against it and heaved them all through, following the fault line to their destination.

She collapsed onto rough, grassy terrain. Angelica gasped for air, worried her lungs had been compressed in the journey. Like all of her had been condensed and now she had the horrific job of piecing herself back together into a fully human form.

"Angelica!"

She turned her head to stare at Dante Lastrider across yet another fucking portal. This one was dark and shadowed, a doorway into some cosmic horror she impulsively shied away from.

Saya Vakara was at his side, both of their mouths wide open.

"Is that a wyvern?" Saya squeaked.

"Yes," Angelica said. "And Deia's fulcrum. Any more questions and I'll make him eat you."

I do not eat humans, Yvri argued. *They taste foul.*

Angelica helped Cosima and Eiko off the ground. The peak of Deia's Heart rose above them, a twin to Mount Netsai. Angelica quickly assessed it to make sure it wouldn't erupt as well.

Magic thrummed across her body. She was jittery with it, knowing she would pay the price when the eye on her forehead closed and took away the final scraps of control.

"Why are you just sitting here?" Angelica demanded of Dante, who looked like he did, in fact, want to ask more questions.

He tore his gaze away from the wyvern with considerable effort. "We're waiting for the others to get through, but they're— *Shit*." He leaned forward. "The portal's closing!"

The edges of the shadows were indeed shrinking inward. Saya voiced a steady chant of "No, no, no!" while Eiko met Angelica's gaze, unsure what to do.

Deia's eye was narrowing. She didn't have much time left with its teeming power.

Before, she might have simply let the portal close and let the others fend for themselves. Now, Angelica reached into herself, into the core that represented aether. She held out her hands and grasped onto the portal's edges, forcing it to stay open.

"Angelica," Cosima said warningly as Angelica's arms began to shake.

Come on, Lastrider, she thought. *Don't make me regret this.*

Taesia stood on the spot where Julian had perched moments ago, face turned up to the Malum Star.

The bones that made up Starfell and the fangs that made up the coronal had come from the same astralam, once a part of the same constellation as the dying star. Taesia lifted her sword in both hands and sensed the connection between them—the frantic hum, the distant scream.

The implosion of a star collapsing in on itself. The death of light, the birth of misfortune.

The creation of a gaping, hungry maw, so much like a portal.

"It's happening," Kalen panted. "We can't...we can't stop it. If I'd just predicted it correctly—"

Marcellus reached across Lilia and took Kalen's hand in his. Kalen quieted, eyes welling with tears.

Taesia turned back to the forming black hole. Already she felt the devastating pull of it, the way its proximity to the other warped the sky and sent shockwaves across the realm. At the same time, the Solarian light burned brighter, ready to be unleashed. They were in a race to destruction.

She poured everything she had into Starfell. All her might, all her strength—down to the dregs, scraping at raw muscle and bone. The shadows swept around her in violence and in love, whispering and whimpering, at her beck and call.

In the bone dealer's shop, after she had met Julian, she had flooded herself just like this. It had momentarily destroyed and then remade her, but instead of leaving cracks it had built her back stronger than before. And it had been so easy, so glorious, to simply snap a man's neck with that power, to live and breathe it, to want to never part with it.

The firmament above was scarring. The night sky mirrored in her blood, the light causing the shadows to lengthen and deepen.

Between her and Lilia they made up a star. They were both washed in its silver fire, but only Taesia reached out to another, calling with no answer.

Her chest strained for breath. Along every synapse was a static shock, and even though the shadows fortified her, turned her to something more than human but less than a god, she knew.

It was not enough.

"Please," she begged. To herself, to Starfell, to the unfeeling sky. "Please..."

I warned you, Nyx said, midnight and alabaster. *And you did not listen.*

"I can...I can..."

Behind her, Lilia groaned in pain as her barrier rose higher around the city.

Below her, Phos struggled in Brailee and Julian's grip.

Within her, power brewed and stormed with nowhere to go.

I don't live at fate's whim, she had told Nyx. She had been so confident, so sure of herself and her ability to expose destiny as a sham. It was *her* life, and she had never wanted it to belong to another.

But she had neglected to acknowledge all the other lives tied to hers. The ones that had changed her, and the ones she had changed, for better or worse.

This is why we fight.

She was not enough for them, not as she currently was. But she could be.

"You say you're not a coward?" She turned her face back to the dying Malum Star. "Then prove it."

A pause, and then a quiet, tired laugh.

And here I thought you would never come to your senses.

Nyx descended on her all at once. The infiltration was mercifully quick, an echo of the pain at Godsnight when he had stitched his power into hers. She might have cried out, might have recoiled under the strain of a god's weight, flooding into every spare inch of her.

And then the pain disappeared and left her wreathed in velvet shadow. Breathing came easier. In fact, everything had become easier, like she had been moving through the world dragging heavy chains only to suddenly cast them off.

But her mind was clear. It was how she remained herself yet not, a new god born under a fading star, two entities in one.

You know what to do, Nyx said.

She did. Again she pointed Starfell upward, and its bones rang with clarity and with joy. Recognition.

Hello again, Nyx whispered. *My crux.*

Images of an astralam's fur under a dark hand, a constellation burning at its brow. Of a wide, filled cosmos, and the shape of golden wings. The spray of glittering black blood, his sword through a beloved chest.

Taesia breathed deep.

I am Taesia Lastrider, she reminded herself, Nyx's power traveling down her arms, into the sword, through his fulcrum. *I am Taesia Lastrider.*

And I am a god.

Where Starfell pointed appeared a vortex under the light that was about to burn Astrum out of existence. Moonlight hummed along the bones, the spinous ridges sparking silver.

More, Nyx whispered.

Hands settled over hers where they wrapped around Starfell's hilt. They were made of animal heat and transcendent desire, a creature striving for completion.

"I am here," Lilia gasped beside her, the fangs shining along her collar.

Together they kept the sword aimed at the vortex. It wasn't a portal—not quite. With the energy surging around her, Taesia fashioned it into something stronger. Hungrier. It was swirling and starving under the maelstrom, not physical in any sense but immensely heavy all the same.

When the light of Solara broke through, the pillar was far larger than it had been in the first attack. But their newly birthed black hole was there to greet it, drawing every ray into the madness of its singularity.

Taesia's arms shook and Lilia cried out as starfire danced along sword and fangs. The two of them didn't dare let go for fear of having Noctus engulfed.

The attack lasted minutes, days, eons. The black hole writhed and stretched as blood welled up her throat.

Nyx hadn't been lying when he'd said he was weakening. Dying. Already her power flagged and still the light came through, scalding, scorching—

And then the oculus began to close.

"Move it, quickly!" Kalen shouted behind them. The astrologer pointed with a shaking hand. "There!"

The collapsing Malum Star. It was a turmoil of supernova colors, a victim of its own gravity. Already it was being drawn toward the existing black hole near the Cultris constellation.

Taesia and Lilia swung Starfell's tip to a point beyond the constellation. Space-time shifted as the vortex moved with the might of the fulcrum's strength behind it—the strength to rearrange the night sky itself. Taesia's ears popped under the change in pressure, and Lilia's knees buckled.

The vortex reappeared in the distant space between stars. The mass of it dragged at the black hole that was once the Malum Star, drawing it farther from the other. Time distorted along their event horizons, making it seem as if they weren't moving at all. But after a blink—after a century—the three of them formed a stable system, a belt with a remnant core pulled on either side by equal forces.

Taesia staggered and fell to one knee. Kalen and Marcellus rushed forward to hold the princess up.

"You did it," Kalen breathed while Marcellus swept the hair from Lilia's face. "Both of you."

Lilia looked at her. Though her eyes had returned to their normal lavender, her hair remained stark white, the astralam fangs still embedded in her flesh.

"You said..." Lilia swallowed. "You said you didn't want Nyx..."

Their power swirled together into one stream. Umbra wrapped around Taesia's forearm, shivering, while the others stared at her in mingled horror and awe.

"I was ready to die," Lilia whispered. "You didn't have to do this."

Taesia rose. The others leaned back, as if expecting their god to smite them on the spot.

"Fuck that," Taesia said hoarsely. "*I* wasn't ready for you to die. I bet these two weren't either."

"But you said Nyx would control you, like Phos controls that boy."

Taesia lifted her hand, flexed it at her own will. "I'm still me."

But she couldn't ignore the lingering presence beyond her thoughts. Like a ghost taking up residence, ready to possess her at a moment's notice.

Nyx was ceding control—for now. But that didn't mean he couldn't wrest it from her when it suited him. The possibility burned the back of her throat.

A cry came from below. In the courtyard, Rian was glowing gold all over, his wings flickering while he fought against Brailee.

The maelstrom in the sky had not yet withdrawn, nor had the four pillars of Other-Realm light. A glimmer of gold touched the clouds.

Starfell pulsed as her breaths turned shallow.

Whatever Julian and Brailee were doing to save Rian, it wasn't working. Phos was too strong.

There is too little left of the boy, Nyx agreed, and with his voice came memories of Phos, images of what would happen to the realms—to Vitae—should he continue to live.

There would be no point in having saved Noctus. In sacrificing her sovereignty.

In the end, Nyx was right: It was humans' sentiment that doomed them.

XVIII

Nikolas watched helplessly as both Julian and Brailee attempted to wrestle Phos out of his brother's mind and body. He didn't even know how Brailee had gotten here.

"He's fighting it," Fin whispered. He held a wad of Nikolas's shirt to the wound on his chest, Phos's gold reflected in his eyes.

Then came a deep, shuddering palpitation in the air. A wide portal grew under the Solarian light.

Nikolas turned to the roof. Taesia stood holding up her sword, hair loose and blowing, eyes the swirl of a far-off galaxy. The shadows caressed her, crowned her. The memory his body held of hers—the shape of her insistent hands, the ringing of her unselfconscious laugh—seemed to fade in the presence of this reckless girl turned unstoppable entity.

He looked back to Julian. Blood was leaking from his eyes, his arm shaking as he tried to maintain his hold on Rian. His bow had snapped in half in his grip.

"You have to help them," Fin said.

Nikolas didn't know if he could, but that wouldn't stop him. He made his unsteady way to Julian, dredging up what he could of his power before laying a hand on the Hunter's arm.

The courtyard swam in his vision. He thought he was blacking out until his surroundings changed altogether, stone morphing into the earthen walls of a labyrinth, the rumble of cosmic energy waning to the drone of insects.

Primal fear gripped him at the sound. For a moment he was back at Deia's Heart, hearing Rian's annoyed mutter at getting bitten. Felt the heat and humidity on his skin, the smell of ash and saltwater in his nose.

He went against every instinct to follow the source of the droning. He arrived in a small chamber where the walls steamed with rivulets of lava, where the buzz of ash flies rattled his teeth.

Rian was curled up on the ground with his head in his hands. Brailee crouched at his side, but at the sight of Nikolas she quietly stood and backed away. Nikolas knelt before his brother and rested a hand on the back of Rian's head.

"I can't do it," Rian whimpered. "I can't leave."

Nikolas closed his eye and braced himself against his heartbreak. The same heartbreak that had dogged him for years, calling him guilty, shameful, unworthy.

"It's all right if you can't." Nikolas ran a hand through Rian's hair, just as soft as he remembered. "I'll stay here with you."

Rian uncurled and looked up at him. His eyes were clear of Phos's mark, his face leaner, paler, but undeniably *him*.

"You don't deserve to be here," Rian whispered. "I...he made me do so many things..."

"I know. But none of it is your fault."

"It *is*. I could have...I could have fought harder. I could have ended myself, ended *him*. I could have—"

"I could have not brought us to that volcano," Nikolas interrupted. "And then none of this would have happened."

Rian's pale eyebrows furrowed, and he struggled to sit up. "That's not the same. The lives I took—"

"The lives *he* took." Nikolas's voice dropped to something stern and whiplike, making Rian start. "You were a prisoner in your own body. Now you have the chance to regain control."

Nikolas could see in his brother where their mother's shadow fit and their father's light emphasized. A construct of gods. A famine in the form of a boy.

"We will move past this." He grabbed the back of Rian's neck, shook it for good measure. "What I did, what you did. None of it matters more than what we can do *now*. If you want to stay, I'll stay with you. If you want to leave, I'll leave with you. Whatever we're brave enough to face, we do it together."

It was only now he realized there were three small red spots on Rian's neck. He laid his thumb against them until they disappeared. The insects' droning faded.

"I don't know what I'll become if I go," Rian whispered. "Who I'll be."

"Then we'll figure it out."

Nikolas stood and held out his hands. Rian stared at them and made no move for several breaths.

Then slowly, carefully, he reached out and took them in his own.

Nikolas had gone to help Julian, but Taesia realized it was futile.

It is not enough, Nyx agreed. *Look.*

In the sky, the portal to Solara was opening once more. Taesia swore and gathered the shadows to her, and they bore her down to the courtyard.

Brailee's face was contorted as she desperately held on to Rian. He thrashed and screamed in Phos's two-toned voice, his eyes two bright beams of gold and his wings stuttering. Several paces away, Julian wept blood while he struggled to maintain the connection to Rian's mind. They couldn't endure much longer.

It had to end. One way or another, it had to end.

For a moment the courtyard blurred away. She was in the cradle of the cosmos where night battled day, where treachery was met on the end of a blade. A kindness and a mercy.

And then she was back in her body—one beating heart among millions—and knew she could not turn her back on this world after all.

The gold drained out of Rian's eyes at the same time Taesia stabbed Starfell through his chest.

He choked on a gasp. Grabbing onto the blade with a trembling hand, Phos looked up at Taesia as a trickle of blood fell from the corner of his mouth.

But his pale eyes were clear, his expression open and confused.

Rian.

The place where Starfell had pierced him shone wet and dark, the same place where she had branded him with nightstone. The same place where, so long ago, Nyx had wounded Phos after the death of Orsus.

Except Phos was no longer here. The light above them snuffed out; all that remained was the boy she had laughed and joked with. A boy Nikolas loved more than he loved himself.

A bubble of blood popped at the side of Rian's mouth when he tried to speak. Eventually he managed, "Tae...?"

Every stitched-up wound within her ripped open. A strangled, animal sound escaped her and she backed away, taking Starfell with her.

"No." Nikolas's voice was flat with disbelief. He gathered his brother in his arms and they sank to the ground, blood pooling between them. "No, *no...*"

Brailee was shocked into stillness. Julian dropped his broken bow.

"I—I didn't," Taesia stammered. The shadows around the courtyard writhed. "I was— He was—"

Nikolas lifted his gaze, and it pulled the illusory rope around her neck taut.

You will never be forgiven. His voice, the nightmare turned reality, had whispered in her ear so lovingly. Echoed now in every line of anguish on his face.

There is no point explaining, Nyx told her. *They will not understand. They never have.*

Not when she had tried to save them before, and not when she had tried to save them now. She stood a stranger under their blaming stares, Rian's blood dripping from Starfell's tip.

There is no use staying. Come.

Behind her, the shadows parted into a doorway. A portal for her alone.

Julian's eyes flashed green through the dark. He approached her cautiously, one hand outstretched. "Taesia—"

She took a step back, and he froze. As if he thought she was frightened of what he had become. As if he could not clearly see that she had never been the moon chasing the sun, but the cruel, hollow space between them.

I've seen all of you, and I am not afraid. She longed to say the words—saw them mirrored in the way his gaze held hers, despite everything.

But there was no sentiment that could fix this. Even if he stubbornly stood by her side, it would not be enough.

She took another step back. Another. Brailee finally roused herself and ran toward her.

"Wait!" Brailee called. "Taesia, *wait!*"

There was nothing waiting for her in Vitae other than a kingdom that despised her and a family she had deserted. Nothing left here but those who could not love her the way she loved them.

A quiet apology stuck to her lips.

"Taesia, please," Julian whispered.

Her Hunter. Her demon. Vicious and kind and tedious and magnificent.

It will hurt them more to stay, Nyx coaxed.

She turned away. Ignoring the cry of her name and the splintering fractures in her chest, she let herself be swallowed into the shadows' merciful embrace.

XIX

Risha tumbled out of space and time until she was spat out by the unrelenting tension of cosmic energy. She gagged and sucked in as much air as she could, tears forming in her eyes as her stomach heaved.

She was drenched in blood, her sodden, scarlet clothes a mockery of a wedding gown. Her hair hung in stringy, wet ribbons that stuck to her face when she lifted it, her mouth coated with copper.

For a moment, she thought it hadn't worked and despaired. She was still in the basin of a stepwell crafted of dark stone and engraved with sigils that flared with silver light. But there was a ceiling above her head, and beyond the blood, the smell of winter nights and warm spices.

Noctus.

Samhara's blades dripped like the hem of her tunic, the *plink, plink* of falling blood loud in the cavernous space.

Then came another sound—a distant boom, a rattle through the walls.

She half crawled, half climbed up the steps. She found herself in a dark building that almost reminded her of the basilicas back home, passing murals and tapestries, her stride lengthening as she reoriented herself.

There were piles of ash on the floor she didn't stop to examine. She just kept following the sounds, hoping they would lead her to where she needed to be, to—

She stopped and gaped. Surrounding the extravagant temple was a wall of golden light, but beyond that, far above her, was an expansive sheet of stars fitted like jewels onto dark velvet. The night sky in Vitae was beautiful, but it was nothing to compared to this.

What happened here? Jas whispered.

Her gaze landed first on Nikolas. He was hunched over someone, one eye bandaged and bleeding, while a dark-haired young man behind him put a hand on his shoulder. When she stepped closer, her breath caught.

Rian. His eyes open, *alive*, but—

Dying.

A man darted into her path before she could hurry toward them. A man with burning green eyes and a fearsome expression, staring her down like she was an enemy. And why shouldn't he? She was covered in blood and holding a scythe in each hand, like some monster who had crawled out of Mortri. Which, in many ways, she was.

"Risha!" And then there was Brailee, her face wan and tear-streaked. "Oh gods, what...what happened to you? Where did you come from?"

Risha shook her head. There wasn't time to explain, not when she felt a singular pull toward Rian. When she started forward again, Brailee pulled the green-eyed man aside and whispered something to him.

All her focus was on the two brothers, so alike and so different, as Nikolas pressed a hand futilely against the weeping wound on Rian's chest. Rian was gaunt and shivering, struggling to keep his eyes open. They flickered to Risha and widened slightly.

"Ri—?" He coughed, splattering blood on Nikolas's shirt.

Nikolas stared at her with a solitary eye before reaching out to touch her shoulder. Finding it real, he exhaled brokenly.

"You're here," he whispered.

"I'm here," she agreed. She set down Samhara and laid one hand over Nikolas's. The warmth of it shocked her; the heat of a living, breathing thing.

Between them, Rian shuddered. His eyes had fallen closed, his chest moving in quick, strained breaths.

The tangled ball of energy within her expanded. Risha laid both hands on Rian, leaving bloody prints.

"He's not gone yet," Nikolas rushed to say, panic slurring his words together. "Risha, don't—"

But even as a small torus blew around her, it wasn't her power she touched, but the one infused with brilliant green growth. The longer she submerged in it the more she sensed Jas beside her, grinning in pride and encouragement, lending whatever he could to her.

She poured everything she had left into Rian. Immediately she perceived all the injuries, all the hurts—the malnourishment, the arrow wounds, the burn, the stab wound. She brushed against a sense memory and saw a spinous sword sticking out of him, attached to a face that painfully squeezed her heart. Risha leaned over Rian with renewed effort, her magic covering him like new shoots emerging from winter-thawed soil.

For a moment she worried that the damage was beyond her. But her mother had always called her stubborn for a reason. The taste of blood was almost comforting as she focused on stitching up the holes and gashes, forced to ignore the poor state of the rest of him to stop the internal and external bleeding, to knit bones back together, to repair torn muscle and tissue.

His heart had slowed to a dangerous tempo. Eventually, it stopped altogether.

"Come on," she whispered, shivering with exhaustion even as she pushed herself further. "Come on, Rian..."

Another push, both her hands and Jas's reaching through and cradling that poor, strained heart, encouraging it to beat.

One second passed. Another. And then—

Rian drew in a sudden breath as his chest kicked back awake. Where the wound had been was now a large, jagged scar.

Risha laughed in relief. Within her, Jas's energy bloomed with joy.

She had always held power over the dead, but now she also held power over the living. The power to mend, and heal, and save.

She couldn't go back and right her mistakes, but she had the ability to redeem herself in what ways she could. Starting with the heartbeat of one lost boy.

Nikolas held Rian close while Risha unleashed some inexplicable spell over him. It didn't feel like her power usually did, cold and discomforting; rather, it gave him assurance. Lux drifted anxiously above them as Rian's heartbeat quieted under his hand.

Come back, Rian.

Please.

Be brave.

He didn't understand how they had come to this. Over and over he saw Taesia's sword landing true, piercing the heart Nikolas had just fought to bring back. She must have known what they were doing, how they were trying to save him.

But she had done it anyway. Had finally removed the mask of that beautifully reckless girl he'd loved and shown her true form underneath.

She was war given human shape, her altar washed with blood. Every offering he had given her now lay destroyed at their feet.

Rian's heart slowed and then stopped beneath his palm. He thought he had been shattered before, broken against his mother's wail and his father's torturous grief, but not like this—not when there had still been hope, when he was holding Rian in his arms and failing him a second time.

It was only Fin's grip on his shoulder that kept him in place, staring down at his brother when Rian's eyes snapped open with a gasp.

"Rian!" He cupped the side of his brother's face. "Rian, can you hear me? Are you—?"

Are you free of him?

Rian's eyes were the same crystalline shade as his own, as their father's. But unlike Waren's, full of ice, Rian's were the clear water of a lake in summer, open and trusting with no hint of Phos's malice.

"Nik," his brother murmured. And then he smiled, brighter than the sun.

Nikolas's heart had always been a brittle thing, broken too many times to properly find all the pieces. But now it soared like it, too, had wings, beating just as fast as the one under his hand.

Julian watched Risha Vakara heal Rian, watched Nikolas break down weeping and hold his brother close, watched Fin wipe his eyes even as he smiled, watched Brailee rush to her friends and leave him on his own.

He didn't know what to do. He stared at the place where Taesia had disappeared into the shadows—Nyx's shadows—her eyes black and spangled with a miniature universe, the darkness oozing around her like it recognized her as its master.

He'd known from the start there was something of a beast in her. But now he had fully laid eyes on it, and still he wanted to go after her, to sketch a doorway that would lead to wherever she had gone.

But he felt strange, hollow. Orsus's bone was quiet now that Phos was no longer here. He had used the demon's ability to help Brailee Lastrider get through Rian's mind, to find the point at which he and Phos had been most entwined. But it hadn't been enough to separate them until Nikolas had gotten through, and Julian had sensed the severing, heard Phos's scream of rage when Rian reached for his brother's hands.

Julian's own hands were no longer black-veined, but his nails were disconcertingly sharp. Some of his teeth felt sharper, too, and he dreaded what his face might look like.

The maelstrom above dissipated, and the golden barrier fell. Noctan soldiers hesitated beyond the courtyard, but the palace servants wasted no time rushing back to their prince's side.

"What happened?"

Lilia, Kalen, and Marcellus had climbed down from the roof. Julian nearly hissed through his teeth at the sight of the astralam fangs melded to Lilia's skin. Her aides supported her on either side, but Marcellus was wounded and Kalen's expression was haunted. The astrologer kept glancing at the other two as if to reassure himself over and over that they were alive.

"Is Phos...gone?" Lilia asked. Her hair fell over one shoulder in a shock of white.

Julian nodded. "Did you use the fangs to stop the attack?"

Lilia's eyes were pinched. "In a way. I was going to make the barrier, but Taesia stopped me."

"Stopped you? Why?"

"She accepted Nyx's power," Kalen said. "Together, she and Her Highness absorbed the Solarian light within a black hole of their own making. The same black hole that stopped the other two from colliding. Noctus is safe from both Phos and the Malum Star."

A bright pain struck his chest.

Taesia...you helped save this world.

Behind him, Brailee was ushering all the Vitaeans toward the Sanctuary, insisting they had to get through the portal.

Lilia glanced at them, then drew herself up with a faint wince. Kalen and Marcellus reluctantly let go of her.

"Go," she told Julian. "Return home. I..." She put a hand to her chest. "Thank you for all you've done. You and Taesia both." She scanned the courtyard. "Where is she?"

The pain grew to the sharp point of an arrowhead. "Nyx summoned her."

The three Noctans exchanged concerned looks. "We'll keep an eye out for her, then," Marcellus assured him. "We'll help her however we can."

Julian could only nod. Part of him wanted to stay behind, but he thought of his mother in Nexus and knew he couldn't Keep her waiting her any longer.

"Good luck," he said to Lilia, who offered him a small smile.

"You as well." She strode forward to address the Noctans who were beginning to crowd the courtyard. She was the last surviving Lunari returned to her seat of power, and these were her people—people she had protected no matter the cost.

Marcellus reached for Kalen's hand, and Kalen allowed him to hold it. Kalen gave Julian a farewell nod, and Marcellus clasped Julian's shoulder as they passed, following their princess.

"Julian," Nikolas called from the open doorway of the Sanctuary. He held Rian in his arms, Fin steadying him around the waist. The Sunbringer Spear shone over his shoulder.

With one last look at the place where Taesia had vanished, Julian turned and followed the others inside, a god's remains in his pocket and a demon's blood flowing freer through his veins.

In the dark, all is possible.

He longed for it to be true, to meet her again between worlds or at the end of them, in any universe that could hold her shadow and her starlight.

XX

A ngelica, let go!" Eiko cried. "You're harming yourself!"
       Something was wrong.

Deia's eye was nearly shut, and the magic she had unlocked began to lash out. Fire leapt in bright, fearsome tongues off her body even while ice frosted over the ground where she knelt and the wind blew wildly.

"Not until they're through the portal!" Dante argued.

Angelica groaned low in her throat. Far under the surface she sensed the magma chamber of Deia's Heart; if she kept going, she knew she would do whatever it took to unleash it, bathe in it, ruin the world with it. It was worse than her harshest relapse, the way fire and want consumed her until nothing else existed.

You cannot even wield that which you currently have, Deia had mocked within her basilica just before Godsnight, when Angelica had learned the truth. *I protected you from your own destruction.*

Her god had locked away her powers for this very reason—this lack of control, this desire, this sickness. Yvri pulled away, and she sobbed as the eye upon her forehead finally shut.

Arms wound tight around her. Through the smoke came the smell of mint and burning fabric.

"Angelica!" Cosima cried. "Come back!"

She wanted to.

She needed to.

And there was only one way to do it.

With Deia's fulcrum so close, she managed to grab hold of the strands of her power, the five elements braided together—or perhaps the braiding of the four elements created aether, surrounding them all like twine around a bouquet. She reined them in, constructing doors within her mind.

One by one, she shut every element inside and locked the doors behind them.

The sudden absence left her boneless. Cosima held her close, preventing her from toppling over.

From a distance, almost a world away, she heard a jeering laugh.

All of that, and for what? Deia whispered on the wind. *Back to where you started.*

The ground blurred and spun. She could hardly sense her body, her limbs buzzing and weightless. Cosima and Eiko crowded her, Cosima's sleeves burned away even though the skin under them was untouched.

"Are you all right?" Cosima demanded. "Is it...is it done?"

Angelica reached up to touch her forehead. It was smooth and flat, but she knew Deia's eye waited there, ready for the doors to open again.

She'd thought that by defeating her god and taking her fulcrum, she would gain full access to her magic. In a sense, she had, but she hadn't been prepared for how to use it. Or the price.

"I think...so," she said, carefully tucking away her despair. Eiko deflated in relief, and Cosima's lips brushed her temple.

It was only then she noticed the raised voices. She turned in Cosima's hold.

The portal was gone. In its place were far more people than she had expected, haggard and crying with relief, all of them Vitaean. And among them—

"Risha!"

Saya ran forward and tackled her sister to the ground. Angelica had to blink several times to make sure it really *was* Risha, wondering how she had gotten here and why she was sodden with drying blood. Saya didn't seem to care as Risha dropped a strange chained weapon and crushed her younger sister to her chest.

Angelica stared at them. Stared at Risha, a girl she had shoved through a portal only to bring her back through another. A knot she'd been carrying in her chest loosened.

Brailee moved past them to hug Dante, her shoulders trembling. He looked around, bewildered.

"Where's Taesia?" he asked.

Angelica didn't see her. She *did* see Nikolas kneeling beside a stranger with bright blue eyes, holding someone in his arms.

Eiko followed her gaze. "Is that... Rian Cyr?"

It was. Nikolas's younger brother looked like he had been through war, his front soaked with blood and his face and body withered. But his eyes were open wide as he stared at Deia's Heart.

"You really brought them through," Cosima whispered in awe.

She had. But even with this new tempest of power, she didn't know if she could ever properly control it.

She took Cosima's hand and told herself it didn't matter—not right now. She had battled against Deia and won. Asami and Akane would be safe. She and Eiko would be reunited with their family.

They had made it home.

Rian Cyr felt the sun on his face for the first time in years and wept.

Nikolas held him as his stupor wore off, and he gave in to the rising tide of his grief, too large and too messy for him to contain it all within himself. It came out in great, heaving sobs, expelling everything black and vile from his heart that Phos had planted there.

"I know," Nikolas whispered, rocking them back and forth, his hand supporting the back of Rian's head. He remembered being held like this when he was little, in the times he'd wake his brother in the middle of the night because he feared the dark.

He remembered. He *remembered*, and there was no god to stop him.

He didn't know how long he cried. By the time he was left weakly sniffing, he couldn't help but look up again at the imposing figure of Deia's Heart.

This was the place where his journey to Phos had begun. He touched his neck, but there were no bites, no scars. Just the jagged, raised line on his chest to show that his nightmare had been real.

Brailee came to kneel beside him, tear tracks cutting through the dirt on her face.

"Brailee," he whispered.

It was her—it had always been her. In his dreams, his memories, his thoughts. The one connection to an old life Phos could not sever.

"Thank you," he said. It was not enough.

Brailee shook her head even as she smiled. "I'm just glad it worked." Her dark eyes fell to his chest, to the scar.

Rian put a hand over it. A tremor remained of the pain done by Taesia's sword, in how the spinous edges had ripped his flesh and pierced his heart.

The thing was, he understood. He had been a creature of Phos's design, ready to tear apart an entire realm, an entire universe. In her shoes, he would have done the same.

"Where is she?" he asked.

"Gone," Nikolas said simply, the single word weighted with quiet rage.

Brailee winced. Rian took her hand, the way he had in the maze of his mind.

"It's all right," he said. "We'll..."

But he was far too weary to think of what they could do. At Nikolas's side, Fin shifted.

"Yeah, uh, what are we going to do now?" he asked. "Where are we, for that matter? Seniza?"

"Yes," came Dante Lastrider's voice. He was looking at the place where they'd been pulled through the portal after descending the stepwell in Nyx's temple. His face was cast in the shadows of anger and fear, and something akin to the grief running along Rian's every thought. "The first thing we do is return to Nexus."

"And then what?" Risha said. She was kneeling beside Saya, a vision of horror as blood dried and flaked off her face. "Are we going to try and undo the Sealing again?"

"Yes," he answered. "But to do that, we're going to have to work together. Properly, this time. That was all I wanted until my aunt framed me." At this, he glanced at Fin with an odd expression. "We just managed to open a portal into Noctus. Imagine what we could do with a real plan."

Angelica snorted and stood. Behind her was a large beast—a *wyvern*—who regarded them with humanlike intelligence. The palace servants had scuttled away, hardly daring to take their eyes off it, while Julian tilted his head in fascination. Rian recalled his children's books with their drawings of wyverns, yearning for his own wings so he could fly among them.

"I don't have to imagine it," Angelica said. "I know exactly what we can do. What we have to do."

Risha gave her a wary frown, and Rian felt Nikolas's arms tighten around him.

"And what's that?" Risha asked.

Angelica swept a look at all of them, her gaze landing last on the volcano's peak.

"We're going to kill the gods," she said.

SHALL WE BEGIN?

Taesia stood in unending darkness. Directionless, but not lost. Like the place beyond Nyx's dreamscape, both real and fabricated.

The god was affixed to her. Mind, body, power. In her hand weighed his fulcrum, or at least a part of it, the rest grinning under Lilia Lunari's collarbone. A tool. A key. A weapon.

You did the right thing, Nyx said, his voice like velvet, like midnight. *Phos escaped, as he always does, but he has lost his vessel. He will be weak. Vulnerable.*

Nikolas's face flashed in her memory. Brailee. Julian.

Rian.

Do not think of them any longer. Like this, you can no longer burden them.

Taesia shut her eyes. Wondered if goodness was something one was born with or something that was learned, that had to be exercised like a muscle until it became habitual.

Umbra squeezed around her arm. A reminder that she was not alone, even though there was no one left to disappoint.

Yes, Nyx agreed, a smile in his voice. *I am glad you understand. They have only ever been chains holding you down. Now you are free to do as you please.*

Her spine straightened, and she opened her eyes to find that a small speck of light had appeared in the distance.

There was more she could do. Things that were considered loathsome. Unforgivable. Things that would, inevitably, protect those she had abandoned.

Far away, somewhere in the night, the Salvar Star began to dim. Across from it, the Sceleratus Star burned brighter.

Holding Starfell at her side, she walked through the infinite black and toward the distant light. She did not fear this darkness, or what waited beyond it.

There was nothing in any world more terrifying than her.

The story continues in...

THE DAWN THRONE

Book THREE of THE DARK GODS

ACKNOWLEDGMENTS

Every book I write teaches me something. This one taught me about volcanoes (and, to a lesser extent, black holes). It also taught me that writing a multi-realm, multi-POV epic fantasy is one of the most ludicrous things anyone could choose to do.

Fortunately, I have a great team to support me in this questionable endeavor. A huge thank you to Priyanka Krishnan for her editorial insight and guidance through this journey (I'm sorry about the body count, but not really). Much gratitude to the Orbit team, including: Angela Man, Tiana Coven, Rachel Goldstein, Natassja Haught, Lauren Panepinto, Erin Cain, Alex Lencicki, and Tim Holman, as well as Lisa Marie Pompilio for another amazing cover. Belated thanks to Tim Paul for the awesome Vitae and Nexus maps.

I'm doubly fortunate to have another amazing team across the pond at Hodderscape. Many more thanks to Natasha Qureshi and Molly Powell for bringing The Dark Gods to the UK, and to Ellie Wheeldon and Stefan Szwarc for the audiobooks, brought to life by Nikki Patel's lovely narration. Another a big thanks to the folks at FairyLoot for an absolutely stunning edition of *The City of Dusk*.

Thank you to my agent Victoria Marini for always being a text away.

Thank you to Traci Chee and Emily Skrutskie for your invaluable friendship, advice, and kindness. Here's to many more Whines & Cheeses and yelling over assorted blorbos.

Thank you to the Horde, Long May We Reign—especially Akshaya Raman and Katy Rose Pool for living close enough to go and bother—but also including Alexis Castellanos, Amanda Foody, Amanda Haas,

Ashley Burdin, Axie Oh, C. L. Herman, Janella Angeles, Kat Cho, Madeleine Colis, Mara Fitzgerald, Meg Kohlmann, and Melody Simpson.

Thank you to Cirque de Merque, the best traveling circus/mercenary group a Tiefling rogue could hope for. Sorry I thought I made a pact with that demon.

Booksellers are simply the best people and I owe them so much, as well as the readers who go out of their way to leave a kind remark and/or yell at their friends to read my books. Thank you, thank you, a million times thank you.

And to my family: I'm so grateful for everything you do, and for all your encouragement and love. I couldn't have gotten this far without you.

extras

orbit

meet the author

Tara Sim

TARA SIM is the author of *The City of Dusk* as well as the Scavenge the Stars duology and the Timekeeper trilogy. She can often be found in the wilds of the Bay Area, California. When she's not writing about magic, murder, and mayhem, Tara spends her time drinking tea, wrangling cats, and lurking in bookstores.

Find out more about Tara Sim and other Orbit authors by registering for the free monthly newsletter at orbitbooks.net.

if you enjoyed
THE MIDNIGHT KINGDOM

look out for

A DOWRY OF BLOOD

by

S. T. Gibson

S. T. Gibson's sensational novel is a darkly seductive tale of Dracula's first bride, Constanta.

"This is my last love letter to you, though some would call it a confession...."

Saved from the brink of death by a mysterious stranger, Constanta is transformed from a medieval peasant into a bride fit for an undying king. But when Dracula draws a cunning aristocrat and a starving artist into his web of passion and deceit, Constanta realizes that her beloved is capable of terrible things.

Finding comfort in the arms of her rival consorts, she begins to unravel their husband's dark secrets. With the lives of everyone she loves on the line, Constanta will have to choose between her own freedom and her love for her husband. But bonds forged by blood can be broken only by death.

extras

———◆◆◆———

 never dreamed it would end like this, my lord: your blood splashing hot flecks onto my nightgown and pouring in rivulets onto our bedchamber floor. But creatures like us live a long time. There is no horror left in this world that can surprise me. Eventually, even your death becomes its own sort of inevitability.

extras

know you loved us all, in your own way. Magdalena for her brilliance, Alexi for his loveliness. But I was your war bride, your faithful Constanta, and you loved me for my will to survive. You coaxed that tenacity out of me and broke it down in your hands, leaving me on your work table like a desiccated doll until you were ready to repair me.

You filled me with your loving guidance, stitched up my seams with thread in your favorite color, taught me how to walk and talk and smile in whatever way pleased you best. I was so happy to be your marionette, at first. So happy to be chosen.

~~What I am trying to say is~~
~~I am trying to tell you~~

extras

ven loneliness, hollow and cold, becomes so familiar it starts to feel like a friend.

extras

am trying to tell you why I did what I did. It is the only way I can think to survive and I hope, even now, that you would be proud of my determination to persist.

God. *Proud.* Am I sick to still think on you softly, even after all the blood and broken promises?

No matter. Nothing else will do. Nothing less than a full account of our life together, from the trembling start all the way to the brutal end. I fear I will go mad if I don't leave behind some kind of record. If I write it down, I won't be able to convince myself that none of it happened. I won't be able to tell myself that you didn't mean any of it, that it was all just some terrible dream.

You taught us to never feel guilty, to revel when the world demands mourning. So we, your brides, will toast to your memory and drink deep of your legacy, taking our strength from the love we shared with you. We will not bend to despair, not even as the future stretches out hungry and unknown before us. And I, for my part, will keep a record. Not for you, or for any audience, but to quiet my own mind.

I will render you as you really were, neither cast in pristine stained glass nor unholy fire. I will make you into nothing more than a man, tender and brutal in equal measure, and perhaps in doing so I will justify myself to you. To my own haunted conscience.

This is my last love letter to you, though some would call it a confession. I suppose both are a sort of gentle violence, putting down in ink what scorches the air when spoken aloud.

If you can still hear me wherever you are, my love, my tormentor, hear this:

It was never my intention to murder you.

Not in the beginning, anyway.